Sidney
Midni[ght]

Angels, Master of the Game, If Tomorrow Comes, Windmills of the Gods, The Sands of Time, Memories of Midnight, The Stars Shine Down, Nothing Lasts Forever and Morning, Noon and Night, all Number One international bestsellers. His first book, *The Naked Face*, was acclaimed by the *New York Times* as 'the best first mystery novel of the year'. Mr Sheldon has won a Tony award for Broadway's *Redhead* and an Academy Award for *The Bachelor and the Bobby Soxer*. *Rage of Angels*, *Master of the Game*, *Windmills of the Gods* and *Memories of Midnight* have been made into highly successful television mini-series.

He has written the screenplays for twenty-three motion pictures, including *Easter Parade* (with Judy Garland) and *Annie Get Your Gun*. He also created four long-running television series, including *Hart to Hart* and *I Dream of Jeannie*, which he produced and directed. Sidney Sheldon lives in southern California.

By the same author

IF TOMORROW COMES
MASTER OF THE GAME
RAGE OF ANGELS
BLOODLINE
A STRANGER IN THE MIRROR
THE OTHER SIDE OF MIDNIGHT
THE NAMED FACE
WINDMILLS OF THE GODS
THE SANDS OF TIME
MEMORIES OF MIDNIGHT
NOTHING LASTS FOREVER
MORNING, NOON AND NIGHT
THE BEST LAID PLANS
TELL ME YOUR DREAMS
THE SKY IS FALLING

SIDNEY SHELDON

The Doomsday Conspiracy

The Stars Shine Down

Grafton

This omnibus edition published 1996 by
Diamond Books
An Imprint of HarperCollins*Publishers*
77-85 Fulham Palace Road,
Hammersmith, London W6 8JB

Reprinted in 2003

The Doomsday Conspiracy
Copyright Sheldon Literary Trust 1991

The Stars Shine Down
Copyright Sidney Sheldon 1992

The Author asserts the moral right to
be identified as the author of these works.

ISBN 0 00768 356 1

Printed and bound in Great Britain by
Mackays of Chatham Ltd, Chatham, Kent

All rights reserved. No part of this publication may be
reproduced, stored in a retrieval system, or transmitted,
in any form or by any means, electronic, mechanical,
photocopying, recording or otherwise, without the prior
permission of the publishers.

This book is sold subject to the condition that it shall not,
by way of trade or otherwise, be lent, re-sold, hired out or
otherwise circulated without the publisher's prior consent
in any form of binding or cover other than that in which it
is published and without a similar condition including this
condition being imposed on the subsequent purchaser.

The Doomsday Conspiracy

This is for Jerry Davis

ACKNOWLEDGEMENT

I wish to express my appreciation to
James J. Hurtak, Ph.D, and his wife Desirée,
for making available to me
their invaluable technical expertise.

MAY YOU LIVE IN INTERESTING TIMES
Ancient Chinese curse

Prologue

Uetendorf, Switzerland

SUNDAY, OCTOBER 14TH, 1550 HOURS

The witnesses standing at the edge of the field were staring in horrified silence, too stunned to speak. The scene that lay before them was grotesque, a primeval nightmare dredged up from some deep, dark depths of primitive man's collective unconscious. Each witness had a different reaction. One fainted. A second one vomited. A woman was shaking uncontrollably. Another one thought: *I'm going to have a heart attack!* The elderly priest clutched his beads and crossed himself. *Help me, Father. Help us all. Protect us against this evil incarnate. We have finally seen the face of Satan. It is the end of the world. Judgement Day has come.*

Armageddon is here ... Armageddon ... Armageddon ...

SUNDAY, OCTOBER 14TH, 2100 HOURS

**FLASH MESSAGE
TOP SECRET ULTRA
NSA TO DEPUTY DIRECTOR COMSEC
EYES ONLY
SUBJECT: OPERATION DOOMSDAY
MESSAGE: ACTIVATE
NOTIFY NORAD, CIRVIS, GEPAN, DIS,
GHG, VSAF, INS
END OF MESSAGE**

SUNDAY, OCTOBER 14TH, 2115 HOURS

**FLASH MESSAGE
TOP SECRET ULTRA
NSA TO DEPUTY DIRECTOR –
NAVAL INTELLIGENCE 17TH DISTRICT
EYES ONLY
SUBJECT: COMMANDER ROBERT BELLAMY
ARRANGE TEMPORARY TRANSFER THIS AGENCY,
EFFECTIVE IMMEDIATELY.
YOUR CONCURRENCE IN THE ABOVE IS ASSUMED
END OF MESSAGE**

BOOK ONE

The Hunter

Chapter One

DAY ONE
Monday, October 15th

He was back in the crowded hospital ward at Cu Chi Base in Vietnam, and Susan was leaning over his bed, lovely in her crisp, white nurse's uniform, whispering, 'Wake up, sailor. You don't want to die.'

And when he heard the magic of her voice, he could almost forget his pain. She was murmuring something else in his ear, but a loud bell was ringing and he could not hear her clearly. He reached up to pull her closer and his hands clutched empty air.

It was the sound of the telephone that brought Robert Bellamy fully awake. He opened his eyes reluctantly, not wanting to let go of the dream. The telephone at his bedside was insistent. He looked at the clock. Four a.m. He snatched up the telephone, angry at having his dream interrupted. 'Do you know what the hell time it is?'

'Commander Bellamy?' A deep, male voice.

'Yes . . .'

'I have a message for you, Commander. You are ordered to report to General Hilliard at National Security Agency Headquarters at Fort Meade at 0600 this morning. Is the message understood, Commander?'

'Yes.' *And no. Mostly no.*

Commander Robert Bellamy slowly replaced the receiver, puzzled. What the devil could NSA want with him? He was assigned to ONI, Office of Naval Intelligence. And what could be urgent enough to call for a meeting at six o'clock in the morning? He lay down again and closed his eyes, trying to recapture the dream. It had been so real. He knew, of course, what had triggered it. Susan had telephoned the evening before.

'Robert . . .'

The sound of her voice did to him what it always did. He took a shaky breath. 'Hello, Susan.'

'Are you all right, Robert?'

'Sure. Fantastic. How's Moneybags?'

'Please, don't.'

'All right. How's Monte Banks?'

He could not bring himself to say 'your husband'. *He* was her husband.

'He's fine. I just wanted to tell you that we're going to be away for a little while. I didn't want you to worry.'

That was so like her, so Susan. He fought to keep his voice steady. 'Where are you going this time?'

'We're flying to Brazil.'

On Moneybags' private 727.

'Monte has some business interests there.'

'Really? I thought he owned the country.'

'Stop it, Robert. Please.'

'Sorry.'

There was a pause. 'I wish you sounded better.'

'If you were here, I would.'

'I want you to find someone wonderful and be happy.'

'I did find someone wonderful, Susan.' The damned lump in his throat made it difficult for him to speak. 'And do you know what happened? I lost her.'

'If you're going to do this, I won't call you again.'

He was filled with sudden panic. 'Don't say that. Please.' She was his lifeline. He could not bear the thought of never speaking to her again. He tried to sound cheerful. 'I'm going to go out and find some luscious blonde and screw us both to death.'

'I want you to find someone.'

'I promise.'

'I'm concerned about you, darling.'

'No need. I'm really fine.' He almost gagged on his lie. If she only knew the truth. But it was nothing he could bring himself to discuss with anyone. Especially Susan. He could not bear the thought of her pity.

'I'll telephone you from Brazil,' Susan said.

There was a long silence. They could not let go of each other, because there was too much to say, too many things that were better left unsaid, that had to be left unsaid.

'I have to go now, Robert.'

'Susan?'

'Yes?'

'I love you, baby. I always will.'

'I know. I love you too, Robert.'

And that was the bittersweet irony of it. They still loved each other so much.

You two have the perfect marriage, all their friends used to say. What had gone wrong?

Commander Robert Bellamy got out of bed, and walked through the silent living room in his bare feet. The room screamed out Susan's absence. There were dozens of photographs of Susan and himself scattered around, frozen moments in time. The two of them fishing in the Highlands of Scotland, standing in front of a Buddha near a Thai klong, riding a carriage in the rain through the Borghese gardens in Rome. And in each picture they were smiling and hugging, two people wildly in love.

He went into the kitchen and put on a pot of coffee. The kitchen clock read 4:15. He hesitated a moment, then dialled a number. There were six rings, and finally he heard Admiral Whittaker's voice at the other end of the line. 'Hello.'

'Admiral . . .'

'Yes?'

'It's Robert. I'm terribly sorry to wake you, sir. I just had a rather strange phone call from the National Security Agency.'

'NSA? What did they want?'

'I don't know. I've been ordered to report to General Hilliard at 0600.'

There was a thoughtful silence. 'Perhaps you're being transferred there.'

'I can't be. It doesn't make sense. Why would they . . . ?'

'It's obviously something urgent, Robert. Why don't you give me a call after the meeting?'

'I will. Thank you.'

The connection was broken. *I shouldn't have bothered the old man*, Robert thought. The Admiral had retired as head of Naval Intelligence two years earlier. *Forced* to retire, was more like it. The rumour was that, as a sop, the Navy had given him a little office somewhere and put him to work counting barnacles on the mothball fleet, or some such shit. The Admiral would have no idea about current intelligence activities. But he was Robert's mentor. He was closer to Robert than anyone in the world, except, of course, Susan. And Robert had needed to talk to someone. With Susan gone, he felt as though he were living in a time warp. He fantasized that somewhere, in another dimension of time and space, he and Susan were still happily married, laughing and carefree and loving. *Or maybe not*, Robert thought, wearily. *Maybe I just don't know when to let go.*

The coffee was ready. It tasted bitter. He wondered whether the beans came from Brazil.

He carried the coffee cup into the bathroom and studied his image in the mirror. He was looking at a man in his early forties, tall and lean and physically fit, with a craggy face, a strong chin, black hair and intelligent, probing dark eyes. There was a long, deep scar on his chest, a souvenir from the plane crash. But that was yesterday. That was Susan. This was today. Without Susan. He shaved and showered and walked over to his clothes closet. *What do I wear*, he wondered, *Navy uniform or civilian clothes? And, on the other hand, who gives a damn?* He put on a charcoal-grey suit, a white shirt and a grey silk tie. He knew very little about the National Security

Agency, only that the 'puzzle palace', as it was nicknamed, superseded all other American intelligence agencies and was the most secretive of them all. *What do they want with me? I'll soon find out.*

Chapter Two

The National Security Agency is hidden discreetly away on eighty-two rambling acres at Fort Meade, Maryland, in two buildings that together are twice the size of the CIA complex in Langley, Virginia. The Agency, created to give technical support to protect United States communications and acquire worldwide intelligence data, employs thousands of people, and so much information is generated by its operations that it shreds more than forty tons of documents every day.

It was still dark when Commander Robert Bellamy arrived at the first gate. He drove up to an eight-foot-high cyclone fence with a topping of barbed wire. There was a sentry booth there, manned by two armed guards. One of them stayed in the booth, watching, as the other approached the car. 'Can I help you?'

'Commander Bellamy to see General Hilliard.'

'May I see your identification, Commander?'

Robert Bellamy pulled out his wallet and removed his 17th District Naval Intelligence ID card. The guard studied it carefully and returned it. 'Thank you, Commander.'

He nodded to the guard in the booth and the gate

swung open. The guard inside picked up a telephone. 'Commander Bellamy is on his way.'

A minute later Robert Bellamy drove up to a closed, electrified gate.

An armed guard approached the car. 'Commander Bellamy?'

'Yes.'

'May I see your identification, please?'

He started to protest and then he thought, *What the hell? It's their zoo*. He took out his wallet again and showed his identification to the guard.

'Thank you, Commander.' The guard gave some invisible sign and the gate opened.

As Robert Bellamy drove ahead, he saw a third cyclone fence ahead of him. *My God*, he thought, *I'm in the Land of Oz*.

Another uniformed guard walked up to the car. As Robert Bellamy reached for his wallet the guard looked at the licence plate and said, 'Please drive straight ahead to the administration building, Commander. There will be someone there to meet you.'

'Thank you.'

The gate swung open and Robert followed the driveway up to an enormous white building. A man in civilian clothes was standing outside, waiting, shivering in the chill October air. 'You can leave your car right there, Commander,' he called out. 'We'll take care of it.'

Robert Bellamy left the keys in his car and stepped out. The man greeting him appeared to be in his thirties, tall, thin and sallow. He looked as though he had not seen the sun in years.

'I'm Harrison Keller. I'll escort you to General Hilliard's office.'

They walked into a large high-ceilinged entrance hall. A man in civilian clothes was seated behind a desk. 'Commander Bellamy . . .'

Robert Bellamy swung around. He heard the click of a camera.

'Thank you, sir.'

Robert Bellamy turned to Keller. 'What . . . ?'

'This will take only a minute,' Harrison Keller assured him.

Sixty seconds later, Robert Bellamy was handed a blue and white identification badge with his photograph on it.

'Please wear this at all times while you're in the building, Commander.'

'Right.'

They started walking down a long, white corridor. Robert Bellamy noticed security cameras mounted at twenty-foot intervals on both sides of the hall.

'How big is this building?'

'Just over two million square feet, Commander.'

'*What?*'

'Yes. This corridor is the longest corridor in the world, nine hundred and eighty feet. We're completely self-contained here. We have a shopping centre, cafeteria, post exchange, eight snack bars, a hospital complete with operating room, a dentist's office, a branch of the State Bank of Laurel, a dry-cleaning shop, a shoe shop, a barber shop, and a few other odds and ends.'

It's a home away from home, Robert thought. He found it oddly depressing.

They passed an enormous open area filled with a vast sea of computers. Robert stopped in amazement.

'Impressive, isn't it? That's just one of our computer rooms. The complex contains three billion dollars' worth of decoding machines and computers.'

'How many people work in this place?'

'About sixteen thousand.'

So what the hell do they need me for? Robert Bellamy wondered.

He was led into a private elevator that Keller operated with a key. They went up one floor and started on another trek down a long corridor until they reached a suite of offices at the end of the hall.

'Right in here, Commander.' They entered a large reception office with four secretaries' desks. Two of the secretaries had already arrived for work. Harrison Keller nodded to one of them. She pressed a button and a door to the inner office clicked open.

'Go right in, please, gentlemen. The General is expecting you.'

Harrison Keller said, 'This way.'

Robert Bellamy followed him into the inner sanctum. He found himself in a spacious office, the ceilings and walls heavily soundproofed. The room was comfortably furnished, filled with photographs and personal artifacts. It was obvious that the man behind the desk spent a lot of time there.

General Mark Hilliard, Deputy Director of NSA, appeared to be in his middle fifties, very tall, with a face carved in flint, icy, steely eyes, and a ramrod-straight posture. The General was dressed in a grey suit, white shirt and grey tie. *I guessed right*, Robert thought.

Harrison Keller said, 'General Hilliard, this is Commander Bellamy.'

'Thank you for dropping by, Commander.'

As though it had been an invitation to some tea party.

The two men shook hands.

'Sit down. I'll bet you could do with a cup of coffee.'

The man was a mind-reader. 'Yes, sir.'

'Harrison?'

'No, thank you.' He took a chair in the corner.

A buzzer was pressed, the door opened and an oriental in a mess jacket entered with a tray of coffee and Danish pastry. Robert noted that he was not wearing an identification badge. *Shame*. The coffee was poured. It smelled wonderful.

'How do you take yours?' General Hilliard asked.

'Black, please.' The coffee tasted great.

The two men were seated in soft leather chairs facing each other.

'The Director asked that I meet with you.'

The Director. Edward Sanderson. A legend in espionage circles. A brilliant, ruthless puppet-master, credited with masterminding dozens of daring coups all over the world. A man seldom seen in public and whispered about in private.

'How long have you been with the 17th District Naval Intelligence Group, Commander?' General Hilliard asked.

Robert played it straight. 'Fifteen years.' He would have bet a month's pay that the General could have told him the time of day when he had joined ONI.

'Before that, I believe you commanded a naval air squadron in Vietnam.'

'Yes, sir.'

'You were shot down. They didn't expect you to pull through.'

The doctor was saying, 'Forget about him. He won't make it.' He had wanted to die. The pain was unbearable. And then Susan was leaning over him. *Open your eyes, sailor, you don't want to die.* He had forced his eyes open and through the haze of pain was staring at the most beautiful woman he had ever seen. She had a soft oval face and thick black hair, sparkling brown eyes and a smile like a blessing. He had tried to speak, but it was too much of an effort.

General Hilliard was saying something.

Robert Bellamy brought his mind back to the present. 'I beg your pardon, General?'

'We have a problem, Commander. We need your help.'

'Yes, sir?'

The General stood up and began to pace. 'What I'm about to tell you is extremely sensitive. It's above Top Secret.'

'Yes, sir.'

'Yesterday, in the Swiss Alps, a NATO weather balloon crashed. There were some experimental military objects aboard the balloon that are highly secret.'

Robert found himself wondering where all this was leading.

'The Swiss government has removed those objects from the balloon, but, unfortunately, it seems that there were some witnesses to the crash. It is of vital importance that none of them talk to anyone about what they saw. It could provide valuable information to certain other countries. Do you follow me?'

'I think so, sir. You want me to speak to the witnesses and warn them not to discuss what they saw.'

'Not exactly, Commander.'

'Then I don't under . . .'

'What I want you to do is simply track down those witnesses. Others will talk to them about the necessity for silence.'

'I see. Are the witnesses all in Switzerland?'

General Hilliard stopped in front of Robert. 'That's our problem, Commander. You see, we have no idea where they are. Or who they are.'

Robert thought he had missed something. 'I beg your pardon?'

'The only information we have is that the witnesses were on a tour bus. They happened to be passing the scene when the weather balloon crashed near a little village called . . .' He turned to Harrison Keller.

'Uetendorf.'

The General turned back to Robert. 'The passengers got off the bus for a few minutes to look at the crash and then continued on. When the tour ended, the passengers dispersed.'

Robert said slowly, 'General Hilliard, are you saying that there is *no* record of who these people are or where they went?'

'That is correct.'

'And you want me to go over and find them?'

'Exactly. You've been very highly recommended. I'm told that you speak half a dozen languages fluently and you have an excellent field record. The Director arranged to have you temporarily transferred to NSA.'

Terrific. 'I assume I'll be working with the Swiss government on this?'

'No, you'll be working alone.'

'Alone? But . . .'

'We must not involve anyone else in this mission. I can't stress enough the importance of what was in that balloon, Commander. Time is of the essence. I want you to report your progress to me every day.'

The General wrote a number on a card and handed it to Robert. 'I can be reached through this number day or night. There's a plane waiting to fly you to Zürich. You'll be escorted to your apartment, so you can pack what you need, and then you'll be taken to the airport.'

So much for 'Thank you for dropping by'. Robert was tempted to say, 'Will someone feed my goldfish while I'm gone?' but he had a feeling the answer would be, 'You have no goldfish.'

'In your work with ONI, Commander, I assume you've acquired intelligence contacts abroad?'

'Yes, sir. I have quite a few friends who could be use . . .'

'You're not to get in touch with any of them. You are not authorized to make any contacts at all. The witnesses you're looking for are undoubtedly nationals of various countries.' The General turned to Keller. 'Harrison...'

Keller walked over to a filing cabinet in the corner and unlocked it. He removed a large manila envelope and passed it to Robert.

'There's fifty thousand dollars in here in different European currencies, and another twenty thousand in US dollars. You will also find several sets of false identifications that may come in handy.'

General Hilliard held out a thick, shiny black plastic card with a white stripe on it. 'Here's a credit card that...'

'I doubt if I'll need that, General. The cash will be enough, and I have an ONI credit card.'

'Take it.'

'Very well.' Robert examined the card. It was drawn on a bank he had never heard of. At the bottom of the card was a telephone number. 'There's no name on the card,' Robert said.

'It's the equivalent of a blank cheque. It requires no identification. Just have them call the telephone number on the card. It's very important that you keep it with you at all times.'

'Right.'

'And Commander?'

'Sir?'

'You must find those witnesses. Every one of them. I'll inform the Director that you have started the assignment.'

The meeting was over.

Harrison Keller walked Robert to the outer office.

A uniformed marine was seated there. He rose as the two men came in.

'This is Captain Dougherty. He'll take you to the airport. Good luck.'

'Thanks.'

The two men shook hands. Keller turned and walked back into General Hilliard's office.

'Are you ready, Commander?' Captain Dougherty asked.

'Yes.' *But ready for what?* He had handled difficult intelligence assignments in the past, but never anything as crazy as this. He was expected to track down an unknown number of unknown witnesses from unknown countries. *What are the odds against that?* Robert wondered. *I feel like the White Queen in* Through the Looking-glass. *'Why sometimes I've believed as many as six impossible things before breakfast.' Well, this was all six of them.*

'I have orders to take you directly to your apartment and then to Andrews Air Force Base,' Captain Dougherty said. 'There's a plane waiting to ...'

Robert shook his head. 'I have to make a stop at my office first.'

Dougherty hesitated. 'Very well. I'll go there with you and wait for you.'

It was as though they didn't trust him out of their sight. Because he knew that a weather balloon had crashed? It made no sense. He surrendered his badge at the reception desk, and walked outside, into the chill breaking dawn. His car was gone. In its place was a stretch limousine.

'Your car will be taken care of, Commander,' Captain Dougherty informed him. 'We'll ride in this.'

There was a high-handedness about all this that Robert found vaguely disturbing.

'Fine,' he said.

And they were on their way to the offices of Naval Intelligence. The pale morning sun was disappearing behind rain clouds. It was going to be a miserable day. *In more ways than one*, Robert thought.

Chapter Three

Ottawa, Canada, 2400 Hours

His code name was Janus. He was addressing the twelve men in the heavily guarded room of a military compound.

'As you have all been informed, Operation Doomsday has been activated. There are a number of witnesses who must be found as quickly and as quietly as possible. We are not able to attempt to track them down through regular security channels because of the danger of a leak.'

'Who are we using?' The Russian. *Huge. Short-tempered.*

'His name is Commander Robert Bellamy.'

'How was he selected?' The German. *Aristocratic. Ruthless.*

'The Commander was chosen after a thorough computer search of the files of the CIA, FBI, and a half dozen other security agencies.'

'Please, may I inquire what are his qualifications?' The Japanese. *Polite. Sly.*

'Commander Bellamy is an experienced field officer who speaks six languages fluently and has an exemplary record. Again and again he has proved himself to be very resourceful. He has no living relatives.'

'Is he aware of the urgency of this?' The Englishman. *Snobbish. Dangerous.*

'He is. We have every expectation that he will be able to locate all the witnesses very quickly.'

'Does he understand the purpose of his mission?' The Frenchman. *Argumentative. Stubborn.*

'No.'

'And when he has found the witnesses?' The Chinese. *Clever. Patient.*

'He will be suitably rewarded.'

Chapter Four

The headquarters of the Office of Naval Intelligence occupies the entire fifth floor of the sprawling Pentagon, an enclave in the middle of the largest office building in the world, with seventeen miles of corridors, and twenty-nine thousand military and civilian employees.

The interior of the Office of Naval Intelligence reflects its sea-going inheritance. The desks and file cabinets are either olive green, from the World War II era, or battleship grey, from the Vietnam era. The walls and ceilings are painted a buff or cream colour. In the beginning, Robert had been put off by the spartan decor, but he had long since grown accustomed to it.

Now, as he walked into the building and approached the reception desk, the familiar guard at the desk said, 'Good morning, Commander. May I see your pass?'

Robert had been working here for seven years, but the ritual never changed. He dutifully displayed his pass.

'Thank you, Commander.'

On his way to his office, Robert thought about Captain Dougherty, waiting for him in the parking lot at the River Entrance. Waiting to escort him to the plane that would fly him to Switzerland to begin an impossible hunt.

When Robert reached his office, his secretary, Barbara, was already there.

'Good morning, Commander. The Acting Director would like to see you in his office.'

'He can wait. Get me Admiral Whittaker, please.'

'Yes, sir.'

A minute later Robert was speaking with the Admiral.

'I presume you have finished your meeting, Robert?'

'A few minutes ago.'

'How did it go?'

'It was . . . interesting. Are you free to join me for breakfast, Admiral?' He tried to keep his voice casual.

There was no hesitation. 'Yes. Shall we meet there?'

'Fine. I'll leave a visitor's pass for you.'

'Very well. I'll see you in an hour.'

Robert replaced the receiver and thought, *It's ironic that I have to leave a visitor's pass for the Admiral. A few years ago he was the fair-haired boy here, in charge of Naval Intelligence. How must he feel?*

Robert buzzed his secretary on the intercom.

'Yes, Commander?'

'I'm expecting Admiral Whittaker. Arrange a pass for him.'

'I'll take care of it right away.'

It was time to report to the Acting Director. Dustin fucking Thornton.

Chapter Five

Dustin (Dusty) Thornton, Acting Director of the Office of Naval Intelligence, had won his fame as one of the greatest athletes ever to come out of Annapolis. Thornton owed his present exalted position to a football game. An Army-Navy game, to be precise. Thornton, a towering monolith of a man, had played fullback as a senior at Annapolis, in the Navy's most important game of the year. At the beginning of the fourth quarter, with Army leading 13–0, two touchdowns and a conversion ahead, destiny stepped in and changed Dustin Thornton's life. Thornton intercepted an Army pass, pivoted around and charged through the Army phalanx for a touchdown. Navy missed on the extra point but soon scored a field goal. After the ensuing kick-off Army failed to make a first down and punted into Navy territory. The score stood at Army 13, Navy 9, and the clock was running.

When play resumed, the ball was passed to Thornton, and he went down under a heap of Army uniforms. It took him a long time to get to his feet. A doctor came running out onto the field. Thornton angrily waved him away.

With seconds left to play, signals were called for a lateral pass. Thornton caught it on his own ten-yard line, and took off. He was unstoppable. He charged through the opposition like a tank, knocking down everyone unlucky enough to get in his way. With two seconds to go, Thornton crossed the goal line for the winning touchdown and Navy scored its first victory against Army in four years. That, in itself, would have had little effect on Thornton's life. What made the event significant was that seated in a box reserved for VIPs were Willard Stone and his daughter, Eleanor. As the crowd rose to their feet, wildly cheering the Navy hero, Eleanor turned to her father and said quietly, 'I want to meet him.'

Eleanor Stone was a woman of large appetites. Plain-faced, she had a voluptuous body and an insatiable libido. Watching Dustin Thornton savagely plough his way down the football field, she fantasized what he would be like in bed. If his manhood was as big as the rest of his body ... She was not disappointed.

Six months later, Eleanor and Dustin Thornton were married. That was the beginning. Dustin Thornton went to work for his father-in-law and was inducted into an arcane world he had not dreamed existed.

Willard Stone, Thornton's new father-in-law, was a man of mystery. A billionaire with powerful political connections, and a past shrouded in secrecy, he was a shadowy figure who pulled strings in a dozen capitals of the world. He was in his late sixties, a meticulous man whose every movement was precise and methodical. He had razor-sharp features, with hooded eyes that revealed nothing. Willard Stone believed in wasting neither words nor emotions, and he was ruthless in obtaining what he wanted.

The rumours about him were fascinating. He was reported to have murdered a competitor in Malaysia, and to have had a torrid affair with the favourite wife of an emir. He was said to have backed a successful revolution in Nigeria. The government had brought half a dozen indictments against him, but they were always mysteriously dropped. There were tales of bribes, and senators suborned, business secrets stolen, and witnesses who disappeared. Stone was an advisor to presidents and kings. He was raw, naked power. Among Stone's many properties was a large, isolated estate in the Colorado mountains, where every year scientists, captains of industry and world leaders gathered for seminars. Armed guards kept out unwanted visitors.

Willard Stone had not only approved his daughter's marriage, he had encouraged it. His new son-in-law was brilliant, ambitious, and most important, malleable.

Twelve years after the marriage, Stone arranged for Dustin to be appointed Ambassador to South Korea. Several years later, the President appointed him Ambassador to the United Nations. When Admiral Ralph Whittaker was suddenly ousted as Acting Director of ONI, Thornton took his place.

That day, Willard Stone sent for his son-in-law.

'This is merely the beginning,' Stone promised. 'I have bigger plans for you, Dustin. Great plans.' And he had proceeded to outline them.

Two years earlier, Robert had had his first meeting with the new Acting Director of ONI.

'Sit down, Commander.' There was no cordiality in Dustin Thornton's voice. 'I see by your record that you're something of a maverick.'

What the hell does he mean? Robert wondered. He decided to keep his mouth shut.

Thornton looked up. 'I don't know how Admiral Whittaker ran this office when he was in charge, but from now on we're doing everything by the book. I expect my orders to be carried out to the letter. Do I make myself clear?'

Jesus, Robert thought, *what the hell are we in for here?*

'Do I make myself clear, Commander?'

'Yes. You expect your orders to be carried out to the letter.' He wondered whether he was expected to salute.

'That's all.'

But it was not all.

A month later, Robert was sent to East Germany to bring in a scientist who wanted to defect. It was a dangerous assignment because the Stasi, East Germany's Central Security Secret Police, had learned about the proposed defection and was watching the scientist closely. In spite of that, Robert had managed to smuggle the man across the border, to a safe house. He was making arrangements to bring him to Washington, when he received a call from Dustin Thornton, telling him that the situation had changed, and that he was to drop the assignment.

'We can't just dump him here,' Robert had protested. 'They'll kill him.'

'That's his problem,' Thornton had replied. 'Your orders are to come back home.'

Screw you, Robert thought. *I'm not going to abandon him.* He had called a friend of his in MI6, British Intelligence, and explained the situation.

'If he goes back to East Germany,' Robert said, 'they'll chop him. Will you take him?'

'I'll see what can be done, old chap. Bring him along.'

And the scientist had been given haven in England.

Dustin Thornton never forgave Robert for disobeying his instructions. From that point on, there was open animosity between the two men. Thornton had discussed the incident with his father-in-law.

'Loose cannons like Bellamy are dangerous,' Willard Stone warned. 'They're a security hazard. Men like that are expendable. Remember that.'

And Thornton had remembered.

Now, walking down the corridor toward Dustin Thornton's office, Robert could not help thinking about the difference between Thornton and Whittaker. In a job like this, trust was the *sine qua non*. He did not trust Dustin Thornton.

Thornton was seated behind his desk when Robert walked into his office.

'You wanted to see me?'

'Yes. Sit down, Commander.' Their relationship had never reached the 'Robert' phase.

'I've been told you've been temporarily transferred to the National Security Agency. When you come back, I have a . . .'

'I'm not coming back. This is my last assignment.'

'What?'

'I'm quitting.'

Thinking about it later, Robert was not sure exactly what reaction he had expected. Some kind of scene. Dustin Thornton could have shown surprise, or he could have argued, or been angry, or relieved. Instead, he had merely looked at Robert and nodded. 'That's it then, isn't it?'

When Robert returned to his own office, he said to his secretary, 'Barbara, I'm going to be away for a while. I'll be leaving in about an hour.'

'Is there some place where you can be reached?'

Robert remembered General Hilliard's orders. 'No.'

'There are some meetings you . . .'

'Cancel them.' He looked at his watch. It was time to meet Admiral Whittaker.

They had breakfast in the centre yard of the Pentagon at the Ground Zero Café, so named because it was once thought that the Pentagon was where the first nuclear bomb attack against the United States would take place. Robert had arranged for a corner table where they would have a degree of privacy. Admiral Whittaker was punctual, and as Robert watched him approach the table, it seemed to him that the Admiral looked older and smaller, as though semi-retirement had somehow aged and shrunk him. He was still a striking-looking man with strong features, a Roman nose, good cheekbones, and a crown of silvered hair. Robert had served under the Admiral in Vietnam and later in the Office of Naval Intelligence, and he had a high regard for him. *More than a high regard*, Robert admitted to himself. Admiral Whittaker was his surrogate father.

The Admiral sat down. 'Good morning, Robert. Well, did they transfer you to NSA?'

Robert nodded. 'Temporarily.'

The waitress arrived and the two men studied the menu.

'I had forgotten how bad the food here was.' Admiral Whittaker smiled. He looked around the room, his face filled with an unspoken nostalgia.

He wishes he were back here, Robert thought. *Amen*.

They ordered. When the waitress was out of earshot, Robert said, 'Admiral, General Hilliard is sending me on an urgent three-thousand-mile trip to locate some witnesses who saw a weather balloon crash. I find that strange. And there's something else that's even stranger. "Time is of the essence," to quote the General, but I've been ordered not to use any of my intelligence contacts abroad to help me.'

Admiral Whittaker looked puzzled. 'I suppose the General must have his reasons.'

Robert said, 'I can't imagine what they are.'

Admiral Whittaker studied Robert. Commander Bellamy had served under him in Vietnam and had been the best pilot in the squadron. The Admiral's son, Edward, had been Robert's bombardier, and on the terrible day their plane had been shot down, Edward had been killed. Robert had barely survived. The Admiral had gone to the hospital to visit him.

'He's not going to make it,' the doctors had told him. Robert, lying there in agonizing pain, had whispered, 'I'm sorry about Edward . . . I'm so sorry.'

Admiral Whittaker had squeezed Robert's hand. 'I know you did everything you could. You've got to get well, now. You're going to be fine.' He wanted desperately for Robert to live. In the Admiral's mind, Robert was his son now, the son who would take Edward's place.

And Robert had pulled through.

'Robert . . .'

'Yes, Admiral?'

'I hope your mission is successful.'

'So do I. It's my last one.'

'You're still determined to quit?'

The Admiral was the only one Robert had confided in. 'I've had enough.'

'Thornton?'

'It's not just him. It's me. I'm tired of interfering with other people's lives.' *I'm tired of the lies and the cheating, and the broken promises that were never meant to be kept. I'm tired of manipulating people, and of being manipulated. I'm tired of the games and the danger and the betrayals. It's cost me everything I ever gave a damn about.*

'Do you have any idea what you're going to do?'

'I'll try to find something useful to do with my life, something positive.'

'What if they won't let you go?'

Robert said, 'They have no choice, have they?'

Chapter Six

The limousine was waiting at the River Entrance parking lot.

'Are you ready, Commander?' Captain Dougherty asked.

As ready as I'll ever be, Robert thought. 'Yes.'

Captain Dougherty accompanied Robert to his apartment so he could pack. Robert had no idea how many days he would be gone. *How long does an impossible assignment take?* He packed enough clothes for a week and, at the last minute, put in a framed photograph of Susan. He stared at it for a long time and wondered if she was enjoying herself in Brazil. He thought, *I hope not. I hope she's having a lousy time*. And was immediately ashamed of himself.

When the limousine arrived at Andrews Air Force Base, the plane was waiting. It was a C20A, an Air Force jet.

Captain Dougherty held out his hand. 'Good luck, Commander.'

'Thanks.' *I'll need it*. Robert walked up the steps to the cabin. The crew was inside, finishing the pre-flight check. There was a pilot, a co-pilot, a navigator and a steward, all in Air Force uniforms. Robert was familiar with the plane. It was loaded with electronic equipment. On the outside, near the tail, was a high-frequency antenna that looked like an enormous fishing pole. Inside the cabin were twelve red telephones on the walls and a white, unsecured, phone. Radio transmissions were in code, and the plane's radar was on a military frequency. The primary colour inside was Air Force blue, and the cabin was furnished with comfortable club chairs.

Robert found that he was the only passenger. The pilot greeted him. 'Welcome aboard, Commander. If you'll put on your seat belt, we have clearance to take off.'

Robert strapped himself in and leaned back in his seat as the plane taxied down the runway. A minute later, he felt the familiar pull of gravity as the jet screamed into the air. He had not piloted a plane since his crash, when he had been told he would never be able to fly again. *Fly again, hell,* Robert thought, *they said I wouldn't live. It was a miracle . . . No, it was Susan . . .*

Vietnam. He had been sent there with the rank of Lieutenant Commander, stationed on the aircraft carrier *Ranger* as a tactics officer, responsible for training fighter pilots and planning attack strategy. He had led a bomber squadron of A-6A Intruders, and there was very little time away from the pressures of battle. One of the few leaves he had was in Bangkok for a week of R and R, and during that time he never bothered to sleep. The city was a Disneyland designed for the pleasure of the male animal. He had met an exquisite Thai girl his first hour in town, and she had stayed at his side the whole time and taught him a few Thai phrases. He had found the language soft and mellifluous.

Good morning: *Arun sawasdi*

Where are you from?: *Khun ma chak nai?*

Where are you going now?: *Khun kamrant chain pai?*

She taught him other phrases too, but she would not tell him what they meant, and when he said them, she giggled.

When Robert returned to the *Ranger*, Bangkok seemed like a faraway dream. The war was the reality, and it was a horror. Someone showed him one of the leaflets the marines dropped over Vietnam. It read:

'DEAR CITIZENS:

'The US Marines are fighting alongside the Government of Vietnam forces in Duc Pho in order to give the Vietnamese people a chance to live a free, happy life, without fear of hunger and suffering. But many Vietnamese have paid with their lives, and their homes have been destroyed because they helped the Vietcong.

'The hamlets of Hai Mon, Hai Tan, Sa Binh, Ta Binh, and many others have been destroyed because of this. We will not hesitate to destroy every hamlet that helps the Vietcong, who are powerless to stop the combined might of GVN and its allies. The choice is yours. If you refuse to let the Vietcong use your villages and hamlets as their battlefield, your homes and your lives will be saved.'

We're saving the poor bastards, all right, Robert thought grimly. *And all we're destroying is their country*.

The aircraft carrier *Ranger* was equipped with all the state-of-the-art technology that could be crammed into it. The ship was home base for sixteen aircraft, forty officers and three hundred and fifty enlisted men. Flight schedules were handed out three or four hours before the first launch of the day.

In the Mission Planning section of the ship's Intelligence Centre, the latest information and reconnaissance photos were given to the bombardiers, who then planned their flight patterns.

'Jesus, they gave us a beauty this morning,' Edward Whittaker, Robert's bombardier, said.

Edward Whittaker looked like a younger version of his father, but he had a completely different personality. Where the Admiral was a formidable figure, dignified and austere, his son was down-to-earth, warm and friendly. He had earned his place as 'just one of the boys'. The other airmen forgave him for being the son of their commander. He was the best bombardier in the squadron, and he and Robert had become fast friends.

'Where are we heading?' Robert asked.

'For our sins, we've drawn Package Six.'

It was the most dangerous mission of all. It meant flying north to Hanoi, Haiphong, and up the Red River delta, where the flak was heaviest. There was a catch-22: they were not permitted to bomb any strategic targets if there were civilians nearby, and the North Vietnamese, not being stupid, immediately placed civilians around all their military installations. There was a lot of grumbling in the allied military, but President Lyndon Johnson, safely back in Washington, was giving the orders.

The twelve years that United States troops fought in Vietnam was the longest period it has ever been at war. Robert Bellamy had come into it late in 1972, when the Navy were having major problems. Their F-4 squadrons were being destroyed. In spite of the fact that their planes were superior to the Russian MiGs, the American Navy were losing one F-4 for every two MiGs shot down. It was an unacceptable ratio.

Robert was summoned to the headquarters of Admiral Ralph Whittaker.

'You sent for me, Admiral?'

'You have the reputation of being a hotshot pilot, Commander. I need your help.'

'Yes, sir?'

'We're getting murdered by the goddamned enemy. I have had a thorough analysis made. There's nothing wrong with our planes – it's the training of the men who are flying them. Do you understand?'

'Yes, sir.'

'I want you to pick a group and retrain it in manoeuvres and weapons employment . . .'

The new group was called Top Gun, and before they were through, the ratio changed from two to one to twelve to one. For every two F-4s lost, twenty-four MiGs were shot down. The assignment had taken eight weeks of intensive training, and Commander Bellamy had finally returned to his ship. Admiral Whittaker was there to greet him. 'That was a damned fine job, Commander.'

'Thank you, Admiral.'

'Now, let's get back to work.'

'I'm ready, sir.'

Robert had flown thirty-four bombing missions from the *Ranger* without incident.

His thirty-fifth mission was Package Six.

They had passed Hanoi and were heading northwest toward Phu Tho and Yen Bay, and the flak was getting increasingly heavy. Edward Whittaker was seated on Robert's right, staring at the radar screen, listening to the ominous bass tones of enemy search radars sweeping the sky.

The sky directly ahead of them looked like the Fourth of July, streaked with white smoke from the light guns below, dark grey bursts from the fifty-five-millimetre shells, black clouds from the hundred-millimetre shells, and coloured tracer bullets from heavy machine-gun fire.

'We're approaching target,' Edward said. His voice through the headphones sounded eerily faraway.

'Roger.'

The A-6A Intruder was flying at 450 knots, and at that speed, even with the drag and weight of the bomb load, it handled remarkably well, moving too fast for enemies to track it.

Robert reached out and turned on the master armament switch. The dozen 500-pound bombs were now ready to be released. He was headed straight for the target.

A voice on his radio said, 'Romeo . . . you have a bogey at four o'clock high.'

Robert turned to look. A MiG was hurtling toward him, coming out of the sun. Robert banked and sent the plane into a steep dive. The MiG was on his tail. It loosed a missile. Robert checked his instrument panel. The missile was closing in rapidly. A thousand feet away . . . Six hundred . . . Four hundred . . .

'Holy shit!' Edward yelled. 'What are we waiting for?'

Robert waited until the last second, then released a stream of metal chaff, and went into a steep climbing turn, leaving the missile to follow the chaff and crash harmlessly into the ground below.

'Thank you, God,' Edward said. 'And you, pal.'

Robert continued the climb and swung behind the MiG. The pilot started to take evasive action, but it was too late. Robert loosed a Sidewinder missile and watched it crawl up the tail pipe of the MiG and explode. An instant later the sky was showered with pieces of metal.

A voice came over the intercom. 'Nice work, Romeo.'

The plane was over the target now. 'Here we go,' Edward said. He pressed the red button that released the bombs and watched them tumble down toward their target. Mission accomplished. Robert headed the plane back toward the carrier.

At that instant, they felt a heavy thud. The swift and graceful bomber suddenly became sluggish.

'We've been hit!' Edward called.

Both fire warning lights were flashing red. The plane was moving erratically, out of control.

A voice came over the radio. 'Romeo, this is Tiger. Do you want us to cover you?'

Robert made a split-second decision. 'No, go on to your targets. I'm going to try to make it back to base.'

The plane had slowed down, and was becoming more difficult to handle.

'Faster,' Edward said nervously, 'or we're going to be late for lunch.'

Robert looked at the altimeter. The needle was dropping rapidly. He activated his radio mike. 'Romeo to home base. We've taken a hit.'

'Home base to Romeo. How bad is it?'

'I'm not sure. I think I can bring it home.'

'Hold on.' A moment later the voice returned. 'Your signal is "Charlie on arrival".'

That meant they were cleared to land on the carrier immediately.

'Roger.'

'Good luck.'

The plane was starting to roll. Robert fought to correct it, trying to gain altitude. 'Come on, baby, you can make it.' Robert's face was tight. They were losing too much altitude. 'What's our ETA?'

Edward looked at his chart. 'Seven minutes.'

'I'm going to get you that hot lunch.' Robert was

nursing the plane along with all the skill at his command, using the throttle and rudder to try to keep it on a straight course. The altitude was still dropping alarmingly. Finally, ahead of him, Robert saw the sparkling blue waters of the Tonkin Gulf.

'We're home free, buddy,' Robert said. 'Just a few more miles.'

'Terrific. I never doubted . . .'

And out of nowhere, two MiGs descended on the plane with a thunderous roar. Bullets began thudding against the fuselage.

'Eddie! Bail out!' He turned to look. Edward was slumped against his seat belt, his right side torn open, blood spattering the cockpit.

'No!' It was a scream.

A second later, Robert felt a sudden, agonizing blow to his chest. His flight suit was instantly soaked in blood. The plane started to spiral downward. He felt himself losing consciousness. With his last ounce of strength, he unfastened his seat belt. He turned to take a final look at Edward. 'I'm sorry,' he whispered. He blacked out and later had no recollection of how he ejected out of the plane and parachuted into the water below. A May Day call had been sent out, and a Sikorsky SH-3A Sea King helicopter from the USS *Yorktown* was circling, waiting to pick him up. In the distance, the crew could see Chinese junks rapidly closing in for the kill, but they were too late.

When they loaded Robert into the helicopter, a medical corpsman took one look at his torn body and said, 'Jesus Christ, he'll never even make it to the hospital.'

They gave Robert a shot of morphine, wrapped pressure bandages tightly around his chest, and flew him to the 12th Evacuation Hospital at Cu Chi Base.

The '12th Evac' that served Cu Chi, Tay Ninh, and Dau Tieng bases had four hundred beds in a dozen wards, housed in Quonset huts arranged around a U-shaped compound connected by covered walkways. The hospital had two intensive care units, one for surgery cases, the other for burns, and each unit was seriously overcrowded. When Robert was brought in, he left a bright red trail of blood across the hospital floor.

A harried surgeon cut the bandages from Robert's chest, took one look and said wearily, 'He's not going to make it. Take him in back to cold storage.'

And the doctor moved on.

Robert, fading in and out of consciousness, heard the doctor's voice from a far distance. *So, this is it*, he thought. *What a lousy way to die*.

'You don't want to die, do you, sailor? Open your eyes. Come on.'

He opened his eyes and saw a blurred image of a white uniform and a woman's face. She was saying something more, but he could not make out the words. The ward was too noisy, filled with a cacophony of screams and moans of patients, and doctors yelling out orders, and nurses frantically running around ministering to the savaged bodies that lay there.

Robert's memory of the next forty-eight hours was a haze of pain and delirium. It was only later that he learned that the nurse, Susan Ward, had persuaded a doctor to operate on him and had donated her own blood for a transfusion. They had put three IVs into Robert's ravaged body, and pumped blood through them simultaneously, fighting to keep him alive.

When the operation was over, the surgeon in charge sighed. 'We've wasted our time. He's got no more than a ten per cent chance of pulling through.'

But the doctor did not know Robert Bellamy. And he did not know Susan Ward. It seemed to Robert that whenever he opened his eyes, Susan was there, holding his hand, stroking his forehead, ministering to him, willing him to live. He was delirious most of the time. Susan sat quietly next to him in the dark ward in the middle of the lonely nights, and listened to his ravings.

'. . . the DOD is wrong, you can't head in perpendicular to the target or you'll hit the river . . . tell them to angle the dives a few degrees off target-heading . . . tell them . . .' he mumbled.

Susan said soothingly, 'I will.'

Robert's body was soaked in perspiration. She sponged him off. '. . . you have to remove all five of the safety pins or the seat won't eject. Check them . . .'

'All right. Go back to sleep now.'

'. . . the shackles on the multiple ejector racks malfunctioned. God only knows where the bombs landed . . .'

Half the time Susan could not understand what her patient was talking about.

*

Susan Ward was the head emergency operating-room nurse and the best. She had come from a small town in Idaho, and had grown up with the boy next door, Frank Prescott, the son of the Mayor. Everyone in town assumed they would be married one day.

Susan had a younger brother, Michael, whom she adored. On his eighteenth birthday he was sent to Vietnam, and Susan wrote to him every day. Three months after he had enlisted, Susan's family received a telegram, and she knew what it contained before they opened it.

When Frank Prescott heard the news, he rushed over. 'I'm really sorry, Susan. I liked Michael a lot.' And then he made the mistake of saying, 'Let's get married right away.'

And Susan had looked at him and made a decision. 'No. I have to do something important with my life.'

'For God's sake! What's more important than marrying me?'

The answer was Vietnam.

Susan Ward went to nursing school.

She had been in Vietnam for eleven months, working tirelessly, when Commander Robert Bellamy was wheeled in and sentenced to die. Triage was a common practice in emergency evacuation hospitals. The doctors would examine two or three patients and make summary judgements as to which one they would try to save. For reasons which were never truly clear to her, Susan had taken one look at the torn body of Robert Bellamy and had known that she could not let him die. Was it her brother she was trying to save? Or was it something else? She was exhausted and overworked, but instead of taking her time off, she spent every spare moment tending to him.

Susan had looked up her patient's record. An ace Navy pilot and instructor, he had earned the Naval Cross. His birthplace was Harvey, Illinois, a small industrial city south of Chicago. He had enlisted in the Navy from college, and had trained at Pensacola. He was unmarried.

Each day, as Robert Bellamy was recuperating, walking the thin line between death and life, Susan whispered to him, 'Come on, sailor. I'm waiting for you.'

One night, six days after he had been brought into the hospital, Robert was rambling on in his delirium, when suddenly he sat straight up in bed, looked at Susan, and said clearly, 'It's not a dream. You're real.'

Susan felt her heart give a little jump. 'Yes,' she said softly, 'I'm real.'

'I thought I was dreaming. I thought I had gone to heaven and God assigned you to me.'

She looked into Robert's eyes and said seriously, 'I would have killed you if you had died.'

His eyes swept the crowded ward. 'Where ... where am I?'

'The 12th Evacuation Hospital at Cu Chi.'

'How long have I been here?'

'Six days.'

'Eddie ... he ...'

'I'm sorry.'

'I have to tell the Admiral.'

She took Robert's hand and said, gently, 'He knows. He's been here to visit you.'

Robert's eyes filled with tears. 'I hate this goddamn war. I can't tell you how much I hate it.'

From that moment on, Robert's progress astonished the doctors. All his vital signs stabilized.

'We'll be shipping him out of here soon,' they told Susan. And she felt a sharp pang.

Robert was not sure exactly when he fell in love with Susan Ward. Perhaps it was the moment when she was dressing his wounds, and nearby they heard the sounds of bombs dropping and she murmured, 'They're playing our song.'

Or perhaps it was when they told Robert he was well enough to be transferred to Walter Reed Hospital in Washington to finish his convalescence, and Susan said, 'Do you think I'm going to stay here and let some other nurse have that great body? Oh, no. I'm going to pull every string I can to go with you.'

They were married two weeks later. It took Robert a year to heal completely, and Susan tended to his every need, night and day. He had never met anyone like her, nor had he dreamed that he could ever love anyone so much. He loved her compassion and sensitivity, her passion and vitality. He loved her beauty and her sense of humour.

On their first anniversary he said to her, 'You're the most beautiful, the most wonderful, the most caring human being in the world. There is no one on this earth with your warmth and wit and intelligence.'

And Susan had held him tightly and whispered in a nasal, chorus-girl voice, 'Likewise, I'm sure.'

They shared more than love. They genuinely liked and respected each other. All their friends envied them, and with good reason. Whenever they talked about a perfect marriage, it was always Robert and Susan they held up as an example. They were compatible in every way, complete soulmates. Susan was the most sensual woman Robert had ever known, and they were able to set each other on fire with a touch, a word. One evening, when they were scheduled to go to a formal dinner party, Robert was running late. He was in the shower when Susan came into the bathroom, carefully made up and dressed in a lovely strapless evening gown.

'My God, you look sexy,' Robert said. 'It's too bad we don't have more time.'

'Oh, don't worry about that,' Susan murmured. And a moment later she had stripped off her clothes and joined Robert in the shower.

They never got to the party.

Susan sensed Robert's needs almost before he knew them, and she saw to it that they were attended to. And Robert was equally attentive to her. Susan would find love notes on her dressing-room table, or in her shoes when she started to get dressed. Flowers and little gifts would be delivered to her on Ground Hog Day and President Polk's birthday and in celebration of the Lewis and Clark Expedition.

And the laughter that they shared. The wonderful laughter . . .

The pilot's voice crackled over the intercom. 'We'll be landing in Zürich in ten minutes, Commander.'

Robert Bellamy's thoughts snapped back to the present, to his assignment. In his fifteen years with Naval Intelligence, he had been involved in dozens of challenging cases, but this one promised to be the most bizarre of them all. He was on his way to Switzerland to find a busload of anonymous witnesses who had disappeared into thin air. *Talk about looking for a needle in a haystack. I don't even know where the haystack is. Where is Sherlock Holmes when I need him?*

'Will you fasten your seat belt, please?'

The C20A was flying over dark forests, and a moment later, skimming over the runway etched by the landing lights of the Zürich International Airport. The plane taxied to the east side of the airport, and headed for the small General Aviation Building, away from the main terminal. There were still puddles on the tarmac from the earlier rainstorms, but the night sky was clear.

'Crazy weather,' the pilot commented. 'Sunny here Sunday, rainy all day today, and clearing tonight. You don't need a watch here, what you really need is a barometer. Can I arrange a car for you, Commander?'

'No, thanks.' From this moment on, he was completely on his own. Robert waited until the plane taxied away, then he boarded a minibus to the airport hotel where he collapsed into a dreamless sleep.

Chapter Seven

DAY TWO
0800 Hours

The next morning Robert approached a clerk behind the Europcar desk.

'*Guten Tag.*'

It was a reminder that he was in the German-speaking part of Switzerland. '*Guten Tag.* Do you have a car available?'

'Yes, sir, we do. How long will you be needing it?'

Good question. An hour? A month? Maybe a year or two? 'I'm not sure.'

'Do you plan to return the car to this airport?'

'Possibly.'

The clerk looked at him strangely. 'Very well. Will you fill out these papers, please?'

Robert paid for the car with the special black credit card General Hilliard had given him. The clerk examined it, perplexed, then said, 'Excuse me.' He disappeared into an office and when he returned, Robert said, 'Any problem?'

'No, sir. None at all.'

The car was a grey Opel Omega. Robert got onto the Airport Highway and headed for downtown Zürich. He enjoyed Switzerland. It was one of the most beautiful countries in the world. Years earlier, he had skied there. In more recent times, he had carried out assignments there, liaising with Espionage Abteilung, the Swiss intelligence agency. During World War II, the agency had been organized into three bureaux; D, P and I, covering Germany, France and Italy, respectively. Now its main purpose was related to espionage operations conducted under cover of United Nations diplomacy, from the various UN organizations in Geneva. Robert had friends in Espionage Abteilung, but he remembered General Hilliard's words: *You're not to get in touch with any of them.*

The drive into the city took twenty-five minutes. Robert reached the Dübendorf downtown off-ramp and headed for the Dolder Grand Hotel. It was exactly as he remembered it: an overgrown Swiss château with turrets, stately and imposing, surrounded by greenery and overlooking Lake Zürich. He parked the car and walked into the lobby. On the left was the reception desk.

'*Guten Tag.*'

'*Guten Tag. Haben sie ein Zimmer für eine Nacht?*'

'*Ja. Wie möchten Sie bezahlen?*'

'*Mit Kreditkarte.*' The black and white credit card that General Hilliard had given him. Robert asked for a map of Switzerland, and was escorted to a comfortable room in the new wing of the hotel. It had a small balcony that overlooked the lake. Robert stood there, breathing in the crisp, autumn air, thinking about the task that lay ahead of him.

He had nothing to go on. Not one damned thing. All the factors in the equation of his assignment were completely unknown. The name of the tour bus company. The number of passengers. Their names and whereabouts. *Are the witnesses all in Switzerland? That's our problem. We have no idea where they are or who they are.* And it wasn't enough to find some of the witnesses. *You must find every one of them.* The only information he had was the date: Sunday, October 14th, and the place: Uetendorf.

He needed a handle, something to grab onto.

If he remembered correctly, all-day tour buses left from only two major cities. Zürich and Geneva. Robert opened a desk drawer and took out the bulky *Telefonbuch*. *I should look under M, for miracle*, Robert thought. There were more than half a dozen tour companies listed. SUNSHINE TOURS, SWISSTOUR, TOUR SERVICE, TOURALPINO, TOURISMA REISEN ... He would have to check each of them. He copied down the addresses of all the companies and drove to the offices of the nearest one listed: Tour Service.

There were two clerks behind the counter, taking care of tourists. When one of them was free, Robert said, 'Excuse me. My wife was on one of your tours last Sunday and she left her purse on the bus. I think she got excited because of seeing that weather balloon that crashed near Uetendorf.'

The clerk frowned, '*Es tut mir sehr leid*. You must be mistaken. Our tours do not go near Uetendorf.'

'Oh. Sorry.' *Strike one.*

The next stop promised to be more fruitful.

'Do your tours go to Uetendorf?'

'Oh, *ja*.' The clerk smiled. 'Our tours go everywhere in Switzerland. They are the most scenic. We have a tour to Zermatt, the Tell Special. There is also the Glacier Express and the Palm Express. The Great Circle Tour leaves in fifteen...'

'Did you have a tour Sunday that stopped to watch that weather balloon that crashed? I know my wife was late getting back to the hotel and...'

The clerk behind the counter said, indignantly, 'We take great pride in the fact that our tours are *never* late. We make no unscheduled stops.'

'Then one of your buses didn't stop to look at that weather balloon?'

'Absolutely not.'

'Thank you.' *Strike two*.

The third office Robert visited was located at Bahnhofplatz, and the sign outside said SUNSHINE TOURS. Robert walked up to the counter. 'Good afternoon. I wanted to ask you about one of your tour buses. I heard that a weather balloon crashed near Uetendorf and that your driver stopped for half an hour so the passengers could look at it.'

'No, no. He only stopped for fifteen minutes. We have very strict schedules.

Home run!

'What was your interest in this, did you say?'

Robert pulled out one of the identification cards that had been given him. 'I'm a reporter,' Robert said earnestly, 'and I'm doing a story for *Travel & Leisure* magazine on how efficient the buses in Switzerland are, compared with other countries. I wonder if I might interview your driver?'

'That would make a very interesting article. Very interesting, indeed. We Swiss pride ourselves on our efficiency.'

'And that pride is well deserved,' Robert assured him.

'Would the name of our company be mentioned?'

'Prominently.'

The clerk smiled. 'Well, then I see no harm.'

'Could I speak with him now?'

'This is his day off.' He wrote a name on a piece of paper.

Robert Bellamy read it upside down. *Hans Beckerman.*

The clerk added an address. 'He lives in Kappel. That's a small village about forty kilometres from Zürich. You should be able to find him at home now.'

Robert Bellamy took the paper. 'Thank you very much. By the way,' Robert said, 'just so we have all the facts for the story, do you have a record of how many tickets you sold for that particular tour?'

'Of course. We keep records of all our tours. Just a moment.' He picked up a ledger underneath the counter and flipped a page. 'Ah, here we are. Sunday. Hans Beckerman. There were seven passengers. He drove the Iveco that day, the small bus.'

Seven unknown passengers and the driver. Robert took a stab in the dark. 'Would you happen to have the names of those passengers?'

'Sir, people come in off the street, buy their ticket and take the tour. We don't ask for identification.'

Wonderful. 'Thank you again.' Robert started toward the door.

The clerk called out, 'I hope you will send us a copy of the article.'

'Absolutely,' Robert said.

The first piece of the puzzle lay in the tour bus, and Robert drove to Talstrasse where the buses departed, as though it might reveal some hidden clue. The Iveco bus was brown and silver, small enough to traverse the steep Alpine roads, with seats for fourteen passengers. *Who were the seven, and where had they disappeared to?* Robert got back in his car. He consulted his map and marked it. He took Lavessneralle out of the city, into the Albis, the start of the Alps, toward the village of Kappel. He headed south, driving past the small hills that surround Zürich, and began the climb into the magnificent mountain chain of the Alps. He drove through Adliswil and Langnau and Hausen, and nameless hamlets with chalets and colourful picture-postcard scenery, until almost an hour later, he came to Kappel. The little village consisted of a restaurant, a church, a post office, and a dozen houses scattered around the hills. Robert parked the car and walked into the restaurant. A waitress was clearing a table near the door.

'*Entschuldigen Sie bitte, Fraulein. Welche Richtung ist das Haus von Herrn Beckerman?*'

'*Ja.*' She pointed down the road. '*An der Kirche rechts.*'

'*Danke.*'

Robert turned right at the church and drove up to a modest two-storey stone house with a ceramic tiled roof. He got out of the car and walked up to the door. He could see no bell, and knocked.

A heavyset woman with a faint moustache answered the door. '*Ja?*'

'I'm sorry to bother you. Is Mr Beckerman in?'

She eyed him suspiciously. 'What do you want with him?'

Robert gave her a winning smile. 'You must be Mrs Beckerman.' He pulled out his reporter's identification card. 'I'm doing a magazine article on Swiss bus drivers, and your husband was recommended to my magazine as having one of the finest safety records in the country.'

She brightened and said proudly, 'My Hans is an excellent driver.'

'That's what everyone tells me, Mrs Beckerman. I would like to do an interview with him.'

'An interview with my Hans for a magazine?' She was flustered. 'That is very exciting. Come in, please.'

She led Robert into a small, meticulously neat living room. 'Wait here, *bitte*. I will get Hans.'

The house had a low, beamed ceiling, dark wooden floors and plain wooden furniture. There was a small stone fireplace and lace curtains at the windows.

Robert stood there, thinking. This was not only his best lead, it was his *only* lead. *People come in off the street, buy their ticket and take the tour. We don't ask for identification . . . There's no place to go from here*, Robert thought grimly. *If this doesn't work out, I can always place an ad: Will the seven bus passen-*

gers who saw a weather balloon crash Sunday please assemble in my hotel room at 1200 tomorrow morning? Breakfast will be served.

A thin, bald man appeared. His complexion was pale, and he wore a thick, black moustache that was startlingly out of keeping with the rest of his appearance. 'Good afternoon, *Herr* . . . ?'

'Smith. Good afternoon.' Robert's voice was hearty. 'I've certainly been looking forward to meeting you, Mr Beckerman.'

'My wife tells me you are writing a story about bus drivers.' He spoke with a heavy German accent.

Robert smiled ingratiatingly. 'That's right. My magazine is interested in your wonderful safety record and . . .'

'*Scheissdreck!*' Beckerman said rudely. 'You are interested in the thing that crashed Sunday afternoon, no?'

Robert managed to look abashed. 'As a matter of fact, yes, I am interested in discussing that, too.'

'Then why do you not come out and say so? Sit down.'

'Thank you.' Robert took a seat on the couch.

Beckerman said, 'I am sorry I cannot offer you a drink, but we do not keep *schnapps* in the house anymore.' He tapped his stomach. 'Ulcers. The doctors cannot even give me drugs to relieve the pain. I am allergic to all of them.' He sat down opposite Robert. 'But you did not come here to talk about my health, eh? What is it you wish to know?'

'I want to talk to you about the passengers who

were on your bus Sunday when you stopped near Uetendorf where the weather balloon crashed.'

Hans Beckerman was staring at him. 'Weather balloon? What weather balloon? What are you talking about?'

'The balloon that . . .'

'You mean the spaceship.'

It was Robert's turn to stare. 'The . . . *spaceship?*'

'*Ja*, the flying saucer.'

It took a moment for the words to sink in. Robert felt a sudden chill. 'Are you telling me that you saw a flying saucer?'

'*Ja*. With dead bodies in it.'

Yesterday, in the Swiss Alps, a NATO weather balloon crashed. There were some experimental military objects aboard the balloon that are highly secret.

Robert tried hard to sound calm. 'Mr Beckerman, are you certain that what you saw was a flying saucer?'

'Of course. What they call a UFO.'

'And there were dead people inside?'

'Not people, no. *Creatures*. It is hard to describe them.' He gave a little shiver. 'They were very small with big, strange eyes. They were dressed in suits of a silver metallic colour. It was very frightening.'

Robert listened, his mind in a turmoil. 'Did your passengers see this?'

'Oh, *ja*. We all saw it. I stopped there for maybe fifteen minutes. They wanted me to stay longer, but the company is very strict about schedules.'

Robert knew the question was futile before he even

asked it. 'Mr Beckerman, would you happen to know the names of any of your passengers?'

'Mister, I drive a bus. The passengers buy a ticket in Zürich and we take a tour southwest to Interlaken and then northwest to Bern. They can either get off at Bern or return to Zürich. Nobody gives their names.'

Robert said, desperately, 'There's *no* way you can identify any of them?'

The bus driver thought for a moment. 'Well, I can tell you there were no children on that trip. Just men.'

'Only men?'

Beckerman thought for a moment. 'No. That's not right. There was one woman, too.'

Terrific. That really narrows it down, Robert thought. *Next question: Why the hell did I ever agree to this assignment?* 'What you're saying, Mr Beckerman, is that a group of tourists boarded your bus at Zürich, and then when the tour was over, they simply scattered?'

'That's right, Mr Smith.'

So there was not even a haystack. 'Do you remember *anything* at all about the passengers? Anything they said or did?'

Beckerman shook his head. 'Mister, you get so you don't pay no attention to them. Unless they cause some trouble. Like that German.'

Robert sat very still. He asked softly, 'What German?'

'*Affenarsch!* All the other passengers were excited about seeing the UFO and those dead creatures in it, but this old man kept complaining about how we had to hurry up to get to Bern because he had to prepare some lecture for the University in the morning...'

A beginning. 'Do you remember anything else about him?'

'No.'

'Nothing at all?'

'He was wearing a black overcoat.'

Great. 'Mr Beckerman, I want to ask you for a favour. Would you mind driving out with me to Uetendorf?'

'It's my day off. I am busy with...'

'I'll be glad to pay you.'

'*Ja?*'

'Two hundred marks.'

'I don't...'

'I'll make it four hundred marks.'

Beckerman thought for a moment. 'Why not? It's a nice day for a drive, *nicht?*'

They headed south, past the picturesque villages of Immensee and Meggen and through Luzern. The scenery was breathtakingly beautiful, but Robert had other things on his mind.

They passed through Sarnen, and Brünig, the pass leading to Interlaken. They sped past Leissigen and Faulensee with its lovely blue lake dotted with white sailboats.

'How much further is it?' Robert asked.

'Soon,' Hans Beckerman promised.

They had been driving for almost an hour when they came to Spiez. Hans Beckerman said, 'It is not far now. Just past the next town, Thun.'

Robert felt his heart beginning to beat faster. He was about to witness something that was far beyond imagination, alien visitors from the stars. They drove through Thun, and a few minutes later, as they neared a grove of trees across the highway, Hans Beckerman pointed and said, 'There!'

Robert braked to a stop and pulled over to the side of the road.

'Across the highway. Behind those trees.'

Robert felt a growing sense of excitement. 'Right. Let's have a look.'

A truck was speeding by. When it had passed, Robert and Hans Beckerman crossed the road. Robert followed the bus driver up a small incline, into the stand of trees.

The highway was completely hidden from sight. As they stepped into a clearing, Beckerman announced, 'It is right there.'

Lying on the ground in front of them were the torn remains of a weather balloon.

Chapter Eight

I'm getting too old for this, Robert thought, wearily. *I was really beginning to fall for his flying saucer fairy tale.*

Hans Beckerman was staring at the metallic object on the ground, a confused expression on his face. '*Verfälschung!* That is not it.'

Robert sighed. 'No, it isn't, is it?'

Beckerman shook his head. 'It was here yesterday.'

'Your little green men probably flew it away.'

Beckerman was stubborn. 'No, no. They were both *tot* – dead.'

Tot – dead. That sums up my mission pretty well. My only lead is a crazy old man who sees spaceships.

Robert walked over to the balloon to examine it more closely. It was a large aluminium envelope, fourteen feet in diameter, with serrated edges where it had ripped open when it crashed to earth. All the instruments had been removed, just as General Hilliard had told him. *I can't stress enough the importance of what was in that balloon.*

Robert circled the deflated balloon, his shoes squishing in the wet grass, looking for anything that might give him the slightest clue. Nothing. It was identical to a dozen other weather balloons he had seen over the years.

The old man still would not give up, filled with Germanic stubbornness. 'Those alien things . . . They made it look like this. They can do anything, you know.'

There's nothing more to be done here, Robert decided. His socks had got wet walking through the tall grass. He started to turn away, then hesitated, struck by a thought. He walked back to the balloon. 'Lift up a corner of this, will you?'

Beckerman looked at him a moment, surprised. 'You wish me to raise it up?'

'*Bitte.*'

Beckerman shrugged. He picked up a corner of the lightweight material and lifted it, while Robert raised another corner. Robert held the piece of aluminium over his head while he walked underneath the balloon toward the centre. His feet sank into the grass. 'It's wet under here,' Robert called out.

'Of course.' The *Dummkopf* was left unsaid. 'It rained all yesterday. The whole ground is wet.'

Robert crawled out from under the balloon. 'It should be dry.' *Crazy weather, the pilot said. Sunny here Sunday. The day the balloon crashed. Rainy all day today, and clearing tonight. You don't need a watch here, what you really need is a barometer.*

'What?'

'What was the weather like when you saw the UFO?'

Beckerman thought for a moment. 'It was a nice afternoon.'

'Sunny?'

'*Ja.* Sunny.'

'But it rained all day yesterday?'

Beckerman was looking at him, puzzled. 'So?'

'So if the balloon was here all night, the ground under it should be dry – or damp, at the most, through osmosis. But it's soaking wet, like the rest of this area.'

Beckerman was staring. 'I don't understand. What does that mean?'

'It could mean,' Robert said carefully, 'that someone placed this balloon here yesterday, after the rain started, and took away what you saw.' Or was there some saner explanation he had not thought of?

'Who would do such a crazy thing?'

Not so crazy, Robert thought. *The Swiss government could have planted this to deceive any curious visitors. The first stratagem of a cover-up is disinformation.* Robert walked through the wet grass, scanning the ground, cursing himself for being a gullible idiot.

Hans Beckerman was watching Robert suspiciously. 'What magazine did you say you write for, mister?'

'*Travel & Leisure.*'

Hans Beckerman brightened. 'Oh. Then I suppose you will want to take a picture of me, like the other fellow did.'

'What?'

'That photographer who took pictures of us.'

Robert froze. 'Who are you talking about?'

'That photographer fellow. The one who took pictures of us at the wreck. He said he would send us each a print. Some of the passengers had cameras, too.'

Robert said slowly, 'Just a moment. Are you saying that someone took a picture of the passengers here in front of the UFO?'

'That's what I am trying to tell you.'

'And he promised to send you each a print?'

'That's right.'

'Then he must have taken your names and addresses.'

'Well, sure. Otherwise, how would he know where to send them?'

Robert stood still, a feeling of euphoria sweeping over him. *Serendipity, Robert, you lucky sonofabitch!* An impossible mission had suddenly become a piece of cake. He was no longer looking for seven unknown passengers. All he had to do was find one photographer. 'Why didn't you mention him before, Mr Beckerman?'

'You asked me about passengers.'

'You mean, he wasn't a passenger?'

Hans Beckerman shook his head. '*Nein.*' He pointed. 'His car was stalled across the highway. A tow truck was starting to haul it away, and then there was this loud crash, and he ran across the road to see what was happening. When he saw what it was, the fellow ran back to his car, grabbed his cameras and came back. Then he asked us all to pose in front of the saucer thing.'

'Did this photographer give you his name?'

'No.'

'Do you remember anything about him?'

Hans Beckerman concentrated. 'Well, he was a foreigner. American or English.'

'You said a tow truck was getting ready to haul his car away?'

'That's right.'

'Do you remember which way the truck was headed?'

'North. I figured he was towing it into Bern. Thun is closer, but on Sunday all the garages in Thun are closed.'

Robert grinned. 'Thank you. You've been very helpful.'

'You won't forget to send me your article when it's finished?'

'No. Here's your money and an extra hundred marks for your great help. I'll drive you home.' They walked over to the car. As Beckerman opened the door, he stopped and turned toward Robert. 'That was very generous of you.' He took from his pocket a small rectangular piece of metal, the size of a cigarette lighter, containing a tiny white crystal.

'What's this?'

'I found it on the ground Sunday before we got back on the bus.'

Robert examined the strange object. It was as light as paper and was the colour of sand. A rough edge at one end indicated that it might be part of another piece. *Part of the equipment that had been in the weather balloon? Or part of a UFO?*

'Maybe it will bring you luck,' said Beckerman, as he placed the bills Robert had given him in his wallet.

'It certainly worked for me.' He smiled broadly and got into the car.

It was time to ask himself the hard question: *Do I really believe in UFOs?* He had read dozens of wild newspaper stories about people who said they had been beamed up into UFOs and had had all kinds of weird experiences, and he had always attributed those reports to people who were either looking for publicity or who should have thrown themselves on the mercy of a good psychiatrist. But in the past few years there had been reports that were less easy to dismiss. Reports of UFO sightings by astronauts, Air Force pilots and police officials, people with credibility, who shunned publicity. In addition, there had been the disturbing report of the UFO crash at Roswell, New Mexico, where the bodies of aliens had purportedly been discovered. The government was supposed to have hushed that up and removed all the evidence. In World War II, pilots had reported strange sightings of what they called 'Foo fighters', unidentified objects that buzzed them and then disappeared. There were stories of whole towns that had been visited by unexplainable objects speeding through the sky. *What if there really were aliens in UFOs from another galaxy?* Robert wondered. *How would it affect our world? Would it mean peace? War? The end of civilization as we know it?* He found himself half hoping that Hans Beckerman was a raving lunatic, and that what had crashed was really a weather balloon. He would have to find another witness either to verify Beckerman's story or refute it. On the surface, the story seemed incredible, and, yet, there was something nagging at Robert. *If it were only a weather balloon that had crashed, even if it did carry special equipment, why had he been called into a meeting at the National Security Agency at six o'clock in the morning and told that it was urgent that all the witnesses be found quickly? Was there a cover-up? And if so . . . why?*

Chapter Nine

Later that day a press conference was held in Geneva, in the austere offices of the Bundesgasse, the Swiss Ministry of Internal Affairs. There were more than fifty reporters in the room, and an overflow crowd outside in the corridor. There were representatives from television, radio and the press from more than a dozen countries, many loaded with microphones and television gear. They all seemed to be speaking at once.

'We've heard reports that it was not a weather balloon...'

'Is it true that it was a flying saucer?'

'There are rumours that there were alien bodies aboard the ship...'

'Was one of the aliens alive?'

'Is the government trying to hide the truth from the people...?'

The press officer raised his voice to regain control. 'Ladies and gentlemen, there has been a simple misunderstanding. We get calls all the time. People see satellites, shooting stars ... Isn't it interesting that reports of UFOs are always made anonymous? Perhaps this caller really believed it was a UFO, but in actuality, it was a weather balloon that fell to the ground. We have arranged transportation to take you to it. If you will follow me, please . . .'

Fifteen minutes later, two busloads of reporters and television cameras were on their way to Uetendorf to see the remains of a crashed weather balloon. When they arrived, they stood in the wet grass, surveying the torn metallic envelope. The press officer said, 'This is your mysterious flying saucer. It was sent aloft from our air base in Vevey. To the best of our knowledge, ladies and gentlemen, there are no unidentified flying objects that our government has not been satisfactorily able to explain, nor to our knowledge are there any extraterrestrials visiting us. It is our government's firm policy that if we should come across any such evidence, we would immediately make that information available to the public. If there are no further questions . . .'

Chapter Ten

Hangar 17 at Langley Air Force Base in Virginia was locked in complete and rigid security. Outside, four armed marines guarded the perimeters of the building, and inside, three high-ranking Army officers stayed on alternate watches of eight hours each, guarding a sealed room inside the hangar. None of the officers knew what he was guarding. Besides the scientists and doctors who were working inside, there had been only three visitors permitted in the sealed chamber.

The fourth visitor was just arriving. He was greeted by Brigadier General Paxton, the officer in charge of security. 'Welcome to our menagerie.'

'I've been looking forward to this.'

'You won't be disappointed. Come this way, please.'

Outside the door of the sealed room was a rack containing four white, sterile suits that completely covered the body.

'Would you please put one on?' the General asked.

'Certainly.' Janus slipped into the suit. Only his face was visible through the glass mask. He put large white slippers over his shoes, and the General led him to the entrance of the sealed room. The marine guard stepped aside, and the General opened the door. 'In here.'

Janus entered the chamber and looked around. In

the centre of the room was the spaceship. On white autopsy tables at the other side lay the bodies of the two aliens. A pathologist was performing an autopsy on one of them.

General Paxton directed the visitor's attention to the spaceship.

'We're dealing here with what we believe to be a scout ship,' General Paxton explained. 'We're sure it has some way of communicating directly with the mothership.'

The two men moved closer to examine the spacecraft. It was approximately thirty-five feet in diameter. The interior was shaped like a pearl, with an expandable ceiling, and contained three couches, resembling recliner chairs. The walls were covered with panels containing vibrating metal discs.

'There's a lot here we haven't been able to figure out yet,' General Paxton admitted. 'But what we've already learned is amazing.' He pointed to an array of equipment in small panels. 'There's an integrated wide-field-of-view optical system, what appears to be a life-scan system, a communication system with voice-synthesis capability, and a navigational system that, frankly, has us stumped. We think it works on some kind of electromagnetic pulse.'

'Any weapons aboard?' Janus asked.

General Paxton spread out his hands in a gesture of defeat. 'We're not sure. There's a lot of hardware here we don't begin to understand.'

'What is its source of energy?'

'Our best guess is that it uses monoatomic hydrogen in a closed loop so its waste product is water that can be continually recycled into hydrogen for power. With all that perpetual energy, it has a free ride in interplanetary space. It may be years before we solve all the secrets here. And there's something else that's puzzling. The bodies of the two aliens were strapped into their couches. But the indentations in the third couch indicate that it was occupied.'

'Are you saying,' Janus asked slowly, 'that one may be missing?'

'It certainly looks that way.'

Janus stood there a moment frowning. 'Let's have a look at our trespassers.'

The two men walked over to the tables where the two aliens lay. Janus stood there, staring at the strange figures. It was incredible that things so foreign to humanity could exist as sentient beings. The foreheads of the aliens were larger than he had expected. The creatures were completely bald, with no eyelids or eyebrows. The eyes resembled ping-pong balls.

The doctor performing the autopsy looked up as the men approached. 'It's fascinating,' he said. 'A hand has been severed from one of the aliens. There's no sign of blood, but there are what appear to be veins that contain a green liquid. Most of it has drained out.'

'A green liquid?' Janus asked.

'Yes.' The doctor hesitated. 'We believe these creatures are a form of vegetable life.'

'A thinking vegetable? Are you serious?'

'Watch this.' The doctor picked up a watering can and sprinkled water over the arm of the alien with a missing hand. For a moment, nothing happened. And then suddenly at the end of the arm, green matter oozed out and slowly began to form a hand.

The two men stared, shocked. 'Jesus! Are these things dead or not?'

'That's an interesting question. These two figures are not alive in the human sense, but neither do they fit our definition of death. I would say they're dormant.'

Janus was still staring at the newly formed hand.

'Many plants show various forms of intelligence.'

'Intelligence?'

'Oh, yes. There are plants that disguise themselves, protect themselves. At this moment, we're doing some amazing experiments on plant life.'

Janus said, 'I would like to see those experiments.'

'Certainly. I'll be happy to arrange it.'

The huge greenhouse laboratory was in a complex of government buildings thirty miles outside of Washington, DC. Hanging on the wall was an inscription that read:

> THE MAPLES AND FERNS ARE
> STILL UNCORRUPT,
> YET, NO DOUBT, WHEN THEY
> COME TO CONSCIOUSNESS,
> THEY, TOO, WILL CURSE AND
> SWEAR.
> RALPH WALDO EMERSON
> *Nature*, 1836

Professor Rachman, who was in charge of the complex, was an earnest gnome of a man, filled with enthusiasm for his profession. 'It was Charles Darwin who was the first to perceive the ability of plants to think. Luther Burbank followed up by communicating with them.'

'You really believe that is possible?'

'We know it is. George Washington Carver communed with plants and they gave him hundreds of new products. Carver said, "When I touch a flower, I am touching Infinity. Flowers existed long before there were human beings on this earth, and they will continue to exist for millions of years after. Through the flower, I talk to Infinity..."

Janus looked around the enormous greenhouse they were standing in. It was filled with plants and exotic flowers that rainbowed the room. The mixture of perfumes was overpowering.

'Everything in this room is alive,' Professor Rachman said. 'These plants can feel love, hate, pain, excitement ... just as animals do. Sir Jagadis Chandra Bose proved that they respond to a tone of voice.'

'How does one prove something like that?' Janus asked.

'I will be happy to demonstrate.' Rachman walked over to a table covered with plants. Beside the table was a polygraph machine. Rachman lifted one of the electrodes and attached it to a plant. The needle on the face of the polygraph was at rest. 'Watch,' he said.

He leaned closer to the plant and whispered, 'I

think you are very beautiful. You are more beautiful than all the other plants here . . .'

Janus watched the needle move ever so slightly.

Suddenly Professor Rachman screamed at the plant, 'You are ugly! You are going to die! Do you hear me? You are going to die!'

The needle began to quiver, then it moved sharply upward.

'My God,' Janus said. 'I can't believe it.'

'What you see,' Rachman said, 'is the equivalent of a human being screaming. National magazines have published articles about these experiments. One of the most interesting was a blind experiment conducted by six students. One of them, unknown to the others, was chosen to walk into a room with two plants, one of them wired to a polygraph. He completely destroyed the other plant. Later, one by one, the students were sent into the room to pass by the plants. When the innocent students walked in, the polygraph registered nothing. But the moment the guilty one appeared, the needle on the polygraph shot up.'

'That's incredible.'

'But true. We've also learned that plants respond to different kinds of music.'

'*Different* kinds?'

'Yes. They did an experiment at Temple Buell College in Denver where healthy flowers were put in three separate glass cases. Acid rock music was piped into one case, soft East Indian sitar music was piped into the second case, and the third had no music. A CBS camera crew recorded the experiment, using time-lapse photography. At the end of two weeks, the flowers exposed to the rock music were dead, the group with no music was growing normally, and the ones that heard the sitar music had turned into beautiful blooms, with stems and flowers reaching toward the source of the sound. Walter Cronkite ran the film on his news show. If you wish to check it, it was on October 26, 1970.'

'Are you saying plants have an intelligence?'

'They breathe, and eat, and reproduce. They can feel pain, and they can utilize defences against their enemies. For example, terpenes are used by certain plants to poison the soil around them and to discourage competitors. Other plants exude alkaloids to make them unpalatable to insects. We've proved that plants communicate with one another by pheromones.'

'Yes, I've heard of that,' Janus said.

'Some plants are meat eaters. The Venus flytrap, for example. Certain orchids look and smell like female bees, to decoy male bees. Others resemble female wasps to attract the males to visit them and pick up pollen. Another type of orchid has an aroma like rotting meat to coax carrion flies in the neighbourhood to come to them.'

Janus was listening to every word.

'The Pink Lady's-Slipper has a hinged upper lip that closes when a bee lands, and traps it. The only escape is through a narrow passageway out the rear, and as the bee fights its way to freedom, it picks up a cap of pollen. There are five thousand flowering plants that grow in the northeast, and each species has its own characteristics. There is no doubt about it. It's been proven over and over that living plants have an intelligence.'

Janus was thinking: *And the missing alien is at large somewhere.*

Chapter Eleven

DAY THREE
Bern, Wednesday, October 17th

Bern was one of Robert's favourite cities. It was an elegant town, filled with lovely monuments and beautiful old stone buildings dating back to the eighteenth century. It was the capital of Switzerland and one of its most prosperous cities, and Robert wondered whether the fact that the street cars were green had anything to do with the colour of money. He had found that the Berners were more easy-going than the citizens from other parts of Switzerland. They moved more deliberately, spoke more slowly, and were generally calmer. He had worked in Bern several times in the past with the Swiss Secret Service, operating out of their headquarters at Waisenhausplatz. He had friends there who could have been helpful, but his instructions were clear. Puzzling, but clear.

It took fifteen phone calls for Robert to locate the garage that towed the photographer's car. It was a small garage located on Fribourgstrasse, and the mechanic, Fritz Mandel, was also the owner. Mandel appeared to be in his late forties, with a gaunt, acne-pitted face, a thin body, and an enormous beer belly.

He was working down in the pit of the grease rack when Robert arrived.

'Good afternoon,' Robert called.

Mandel looked up. '*Guten Tag*. What can I do for you?'

'I'm interested in a car you towed in Sunday.'

'Just a minute till I finish this up.'

Ten minutes later, Mandel climbed out of the pit and wiped his oily hands on a filthy cloth.

'You're the one who called this morning. Was there some complaint about that tow job?' Mandel asked. 'I'm not responsible for . . .'

'No,' Robert reassured him. 'Not at all. I'm conducting a survey and I'm interested in the driver of the car.'

'Come into the office.'

The two men went into the small office and Mandel opened a file cabinet. 'Last Sunday, you said?'

'That's right.'

Mandel took out a card. '*Ja*. That was the *Arschficker* who took our picture in front of that UFO.'

Robert's palms felt suddenly moist. 'You saw the UFO?'

'*Ja. Ich bin* almost *umgekippt*.'

'Can you describe it?'

Mandel shuddered. 'It . . . it seemed alive.'

'I beg your pardon?'

'I mean . . . there was a kind of light around it. It kept changing colours. It looked blue . . . then green . . . I don't know. It's hard to describe. And there were these little creatures inside. Not human, but . . .' He broke off.

'How many?'

'Two.'

'Were they alive?'

'They looked dead to me.' He mopped his brow. 'I'm glad you believe me. I tried to tell my friends and they laughed at me. Even my wife thought I had been drinking. But I know what I saw.'

'About the car you towed . . .' Robert said.

'*Ja*. The Renault. It had an oil leak, and the bearings burned out. The tow job cost a hundred and twenty-five francs. I charge double on Sundays.'

'Did the driver pay by cheque or credit card?'

'I don't take cheques and I don't take no credit cards. He paid in cash.'

'Swiss francs?'

'Pounds.'

'Are you sure?'

'Yes. I remember I had to check the rate of exchange.'

'Mr Mandel, do you happen to have a record of the licence number of the car?'

'Of course,' Mandel said. He glanced down at the card. 'It was a rental. Avis. He rented it in Geneva.'

'Would you mind giving me that licence number?'

'Sure, why not?' He wrote the number down on a piece of paper and handed it to Robert. 'What is this all about, anyway? The UFO thing?'

'No,' Robert said, in his sincerest voice. He took out his wallet and pulled out an identification card. 'I'm with the IAC, the International Auto Club. My company is doing a survey on tow trucks.'

'Oh.'

Robert walked out of the garage, and thought dazedly, *It looks like we have a fucking UFO with two dead aliens on our hands*. Then why had General Hilliard lied to him when he knew Robert would discover that it was a flying saucer that had crashed?

There could only be one explanation, and Robert felt a sudden, cold chill.

Chapter Twelve

The huge mothership floated noiselessly through dark space, seemingly motionless, travelling at 22,000 miles an hour, in exact synchronization with the orbit of the earth. The six aliens aboard were studying the three-dimensional field-of-view optical screen that covered one wall of the spaceship. On the monitor, as the planet Earth rotated, they watched holographic pictures of what lay below, while an electronic spectrograph analysed the chemical components of the images that appeared. The atmosphere surrounding the land masses they passed over was heavily polluted. Huge factories befouled the air with thick, black, poisonous gases, while unbiodegradable refuse was dumped into landfills and into the seas.

The aliens looked down at the oceans, once pristine and blue, now black with oil and brown with scum. The coral of the Great Barrier Reef was turning bleach-white and fish were dying by the billions. The Amazon rain forest was a huge, barren crater, where the trees had been stripped. The instruments on the spaceship indicated that the earth's temperature had risen since their last exploration three years earlier. They could see wars being waged on the planet below, spewing new poisons into the atmosphere.

The aliens communicated by mental telepathy.

Nothing has changed with the Earthlings.
It is a pity. They have learned nothing.
We will teach them.
Have you tried to reach the others?
Yes. Something is wrong. There is no reply.
You must keep trying. We must find the ship.

On earth, thousands of feet below the spaceship's orbit, Robert placed a call from a secure phone to General Hilliard. He came on the line almost immediately.

'Good afternoon, Commander. Do you have anything to report?'

Yes. I would like to report that you are a lying sonofabitch. 'About that weather balloon, General . . . it seems to have turned out to be a UFO.' He waited.

'Yes, I know. There were important security reasons why I couldn't tell you everything earlier.'

Bureaucratic double-talk. There was a small silence.

General Hilliard said, 'I'm going to tell you something in the strictest confidence, Commander. Our government had an encounter with extraterrestrials three years ago. They landed at one of our NATO air bases. We were able to communicate with them.'

Robert felt his heart begin to beat faster. 'What . . . what did they say?'

'That they intend to destroy us.'

He felt a shock go through him. '*Destroy us?*'

'Exactly. They said they were coming back to take

over this planet and make slaves of us, and that there is nothing we can do to prevent them. Not yet. But we're working on ways to stop them. That's why it's imperative that we avoid a public panic so we can buy time. I think you can understand now why it's so important that the witnesses are warned not to discuss what they saw. If word of the idents, as we refer to them, leaked out, it would be a worldwide disaster.'

'You don't think it would be better to prepare people and . . . ?'

'Commander, in 1938, a young actor named Orson Welles staged a radio broadcast called *War of the Worlds*, about aliens invading the earth. Within minutes, there was panic in cities all over America. An hysterical population tried to flee from the imaginary invaders. The telephone lines were jammed, the highways were clogged. People were killed. There was total chaos. No, we have to be prepared for the aliens before we go public with this. We want you to find those witnesses for their own protection, so we can keep this under control.'

Robert found that he was perspiring. 'Yes. I . . . I understand.'

'Good. I gather you've talked to one of the witnesses?'

'I've found two of them.'

'Their names?'

'Hans Beckerman – he was the driver of the tour bus. He lives in Kappel . . .'

'And the second?'

'Fritz Mandel. He owns his own garage in Bern.

He was the mechanic who towed the car of a third witness.'

'The name of that witness?'

'I don't have it yet. I'm working on it. Would you like me to speak with them about not discussing this UFO business with anyone?'

'Negative. Your assignment is simply to locate the witnesses. After that, we'll let their respective governments deal with them. Have you learned how many witnesses there are?'

'Yes. Seven passengers plus the driver, the mechanic and a passing motorist.'

'You must locate them all. Each and every one of the ten witnesses who saw the crash. Understood?'

'Yes, General.'

Robert replaced the receiver, his mind in a whirl. UFOs were real. The aliens were enemies. It was a horrifying thought.

Suddenly the uneasy feeling Robert had had earlier returned in full force. General Hilliard had given him this assignment, but they had not told him everything. What else were they holding back?

The Avis rental car company is located at 44 Rue de Lausanne, in the heart of Geneva. Robert stormed into the office and approached a woman behind the desk.

'May I help you?'

Robert slammed down the piece of paper with the licence number of the Renault written on it. 'You rented this car out last week. I want the name of the person who rented it.' His voice was angry.

The clerk drew back. 'I'm sorry, we are not permitted to give out that information.'

'Well, that's just too bad,' Robert retorted, 'because in that case, I'm going to have to sue your company for a great deal of money.'

'I do not understand. What is the problem?'

'I'll tell you what the problem is, lady. Last Sunday, this car ran into mine on the highway and did a hell of a lot of damage. I managed to get his licence number but the man drove away before I could stop him.'

'I see.' The clerk studied Robert a moment. 'Excuse me, please.' She disappeared into a back room. In a few minutes when she returned, she was carrying a file. 'According to our records, there was a problem with the engine of the car, but there was no report of any accident.'

'Well, I'm reporting it now. And I'm holding your company responsible for this. You're going to have to pay to have my car repaired. It's a brand new Porsche, and it's going to cost you a fortune...'

'I'm very sorry, sir, but since the accident was not reported, we cannot take any responsibility for it.'

'Look,' Robert said in a more reasonable tone of voice, 'I want to be fair. I don't want to hold your company responsible. All I want to do is have that man pay for the damage he did to my car. It was a hit and run. I may even have to bring the police into this. If you give me the man's name and address, I can talk directly to him, and we can settle it between us and leave your company out of it. Is that fair enough?'

The clerk stood there, making up her mind. 'Yes. We would much prefer that.' She looked down at the file in her hand. 'The name of the person who rented the car is Leslie Mothershed.'

'And his address?'

'213A Grove Road, Whitechapel, London, East 3.' She looked up. 'You are certain our company will not be involved in any litigation?'

'You have my word on it,' Robert assured her. 'This is a private matter between Leslie Mothershed and me.'

Commander Robert Bellamy was on the next Swissair flight to London.

He sat in the dark alone, concentrating, meticulously going over every phase of the plan, making certain that there were no loopholes, that nothing could go wrong. His thoughts were interrupted by the soft buzz of the telephone.

'Janus here.'

'Janus. General Hilliard.'

'Proceed.'

'Commander Bellamy has located the first two witnesses.'

'Very good. Have it attended to immediately.'

'Yes, sir.'

'Where is the Commander now?'

'On his way to London. He should have number three confirmed shortly.'

'I will alert the committee as to his progress. Continue to keep me informed. The condition of this operation must remain Nova Red.'

'Understood, sir. I would suggest...'

The line was dead.

FLASH MESSAGE
TOP SECRET ULTRA
NSA TO DEPUTY DIRECTOR
BUNDESANWALTSCHAFT
EYES ONLY
COPY ONE OF (ONE) COPIES
SUBJECT: OPERATION
DOOMSDAY
1. HANS BECKERMAN – KAPPEL
2. FRITZ MANDEL – BERN
END OF MESSAGE

Chapter Thirteen

At midnight in a small farmhouse fifteen miles from Uetendorf, the Lagenfeld family was disturbed by a series of strange events. The older child was awakened by a shimmering yellow light shining through his bedroom window. When he got up to investigate, the light had disappeared.

In the yard, Tozzi, their German shepherd, began barking furiously, awakening old man Lagenfeld. Reluctantly, the farmer got out of bed to quiet the animal, and when he stepped outside he heard the sound of frightened sheep crashing against their pen, trying to escape. As Lagenfeld passed the trough, which had been filled to the brim by the recent rainfall, he noticed that it was bone dry.

Tozzi came running to his side, whimpering. Lagenfeld absently patted the animal on the head. 'It's all right, boy. It's all right.'

And at that moment, every light in the house went out. When the farmer returned to the house and picked up the telephone to call the power company, the phone was dead.

If the lights had remained on a moment longer, the farmer might have seen a strangely beautiful woman walk out of his barnyard and into the field beyond.

Chapter Fourteen

The Bundesanwaltschaft – Geneva, 1300 Hours

The government minister seated in the inner sanctum of the headquarters of the Swiss Intelligence Agency watched the Deputy Director finish reading the message. He put the message in a folder marked Top Secret, placed the folder in the desk drawer and locked the drawer.

'Hans Beckerman *und* Fritz Mandel.'

'*Ja.*'

'No problem, Herr Minister. It shall be taken care of.'

'*Gut.*'

'*Wann?*'

'*Sofort.* Immediately.'

The following morning on his way to work, Hans Beckerman's ulcers were bothering him. *I should have pushed that reporter fellow to pay me for that thing I found on the ground. These magazines are all rich. I probably could have got a few hundred marks. Then I could have gone to a decent doctor and had my ulcers treated.*

He was driving past Turler Lake, when ahead of

him, at the side of the highway, he saw a woman waving, trying to get a lift. Beckerman slowed down to get a better look at her. She was young and attractive. Hans pulled over to the side of the road. The woman approached the car.

'*Guten Tag*,' Beckerman said. 'Can I help you?' She was even prettier close up.

'*Danke*.' She had a Swiss accent. 'I had a fight with my boyfriend and he dropped me here in the middle of nowhere.'

'Tsk, tsk. That's terrible.'

'Would you mind giving me a lift into Zürich?'

'Not at all. Get in, get in.'

The hitchhiker opened the door and climbed in beside him. 'This is very kind of you,' she said. 'My name is Karen.'

'Hans.' He started driving.

'I don't know what I would have done if you hadn't come along, Hans.'

'Oh, I'm sure someone else would have picked up a pretty woman like you.'

She moved closer to him. 'But I'll bet he wouldn't have been as good-looking as you.'

He glanced over at her. '*Ja?*'

'I think you are very handsome.'

He smiled. 'You should tell that to my wife.'

'Oh, you're married.' She sounded disappointed. 'Why is it all the wonderful men are married? You look very intelligent, too.'

He sat up straighter.

'To tell you the truth, I'm sorry I ever got involved with my boyfriend.' She shifted around in her seat and her skirt climbed up her thigh. He tried not to look. 'I like older, mature men, Hans. I think they're much more sexy than young men.' She snuggled up against him. 'Do you like sex, Hans?'

He cleared his throat. 'Do I . . . ? Well, you know . . . I'm a man . . .'

'I can see that,' she said. She stroked his thigh. 'Can I tell you something? That fight with my boyfriend made me very horny. Would you like me to make love to you?'

He could not believe his luck. She was a beauty and from what he could see, she had a great body. He swallowed. 'I would, but I'm on my way to work and . . .'

'It will only take a few minutes,' she smiled. 'There is a side road up ahead that leads into the woods. Why don't we stop there?'

He could feel himself getting excited. *Sicher. Wait until I tell the boys at the office about this! They'll never believe it.*

'Sure. Why not?' Hans turned the car off the highway and took the little dirt road that led into a grove where they could not be seen by passing motorists.

She slowly ran her hand up his thigh. '*Mein Gott*, you have strong legs.'

'I was a runner when I was younger,' Beckerman boasted.

'Let's get your trousers off.' She undid his belt and helped him slide his pants down. He was already tumescent.

'*Ach! Ein grosser!*' She began to stroke him.

He moaned, '*Leck mich doch am Schwanz.*'

'You like to be kissed down there?'

'*Ja!*' His wife never did that for him.

'*Gut.* Now just relax.'

Beckerman sighed, and closed his eyes. Her soft hands were caressing his balls. He felt the sharp sting of a needle in his thigh and his eyes flew open. '*Wie...?*'

His body stiffened and his eyes bulged out. He was choking, unable to breathe. The woman watched as Beckerman slumped over the steering wheel. She got out of the car and slid his body into the passenger seat, then got behind the wheel of the car and drove back down the dirt road onto the highway. At the edge of the steep mountain road, she waited until the road was clear, then opened the door, stepped on the gas pedal and as the car started to move, she jumped. She stood there, watching the car tumble down the steep cliff. Five minutes later, a black limousine pulled up beside her.

'*Irgendwelche Probleme?*'

'*Keins.*'

Fritz Mandel was in his office ready to close the garage when two men approached.

'I'm sorry,' he said, 'I'm closing. I can't...'

One of the men interrupted. 'Our car is stuck down the highway. *Kaputt!* We need a tow.'

'My wife is waiting for me. We are having company tonight. I can give you the name of another...'

'It's worth two hundred dollars to us. We're in a hurry.'

'Two hundred dollars?'

'Yes. And our car is in pretty bad shape. We'd like you to do some work on it. That would probably come to another two, three hundred.'

Mandel was becoming interested. '*Ja?*'

'It's a Rolls,' one of the men said. 'Let's see the kind of equipment you have here.' They walked into the service area and stood at the edge of the pit. 'That's pretty good equipment.'

'Yes, sir,' Mandel said, proudly. 'The very best.'

The stranger took out a wallet. 'Here. I can give you some money in advance.' He removed some bills and handed them to Mandel. As he did so, the wallet slipped out of his hands and fell down into the pit. '*Verflucht!*'

'Don't worry,' Mandel said. 'I'll get it.'

He climbed down into the pit. As he did so, one of the men walked over to the control button that operated the raised hydraulic lift and pressed it. The lift started to descend.

Mandel looked up. '*Be careful! What are you doing?*'

He started to scramble up the side. As his fingers touched the ledge, the second man slammed his foot down on Mandel's hand, smashing it, and Mandel dropped back down into the pit, shrieking. The heavy hydraulic lift was inexorably descending on him.

'Let me out of here!' he cried. '*Hilfe!*'

The lift caught him on his shoulder and began pressing him down into the cement floor. A few minutes later, when the terrible screams had stopped, one of the men pressed the button that raised the lift.

His companion went down into the pit and retrieved his wallet, careful not to get blood on his clothes. The two men returned to their car and drove off into the quiet night.

FLASH MESSAGE
TOP SECRET ULTRA
ESPIONAGE ABTEILUNG TO
DEPUTY DIRECTOR NSA
EYES ONLY
COPY ONE OF (ONE) COPIES
SUBJECT:
OPERATION DOOMSDAY
1. HANS BECKERMAN –
TERMINATED
2. FRITZ MANDEL –
TERMINATED
END OF MESSAGE

*

Ottawa, Canada, 2400 Hours

Janus was addressing the group of twelve.

'Satisfactory progress is being made. Two of the witnesses have already been silenced. Commander Bellamy is on the trail of a third.'

'Has there been a breakthrough yet on SDI?' The Italian. *Impetuous. Volatile.*

'Not yet, but we're confident that the Star Wars technology will be up and functioning very soon.'

'We must do everything possible to hurry it. If it

is a question of money...' The Saudi. *Enigmatic. Withdrawn.*

'No. There's just a bit more testing to do.'

'When is the next test taking place?' The Australian. *Hearty. Clever.*

'In one week. We will meet here again in forty-eight hours.'

Chapter Fifteen

DAY FOUR
London, Thursday, October 18th

Leslie Mothershed's role model was Robin Leach. An avid viewer of *Lifestyles of the Rich and Famous*, Mothershed carefully studied the way Robin Leach's guests walked and talked and dressed, because he knew that one day he would appear on that programme. From the time he was a small boy, he had felt that he was destined to be *somebody*, to be rich and famous.

'You're very special,' his mother would tell him. 'My baby is going to be known all over the world.'

The young boy would go to sleep with that sentence ringing in his ears, until he truly believed it. As Mothershed grew older, he became aware that he had a problem: he had no idea exactly *how* he was going to become rich and famous. For a period of time he toyed with the notion of being a movie star, but he was inordinately shy. He briefly contemplated becoming a soccer star, but he was not athletic. He thought about being a famous scientist, or a great lawyer, commanding tremendous fees. His school grades, unfortunately, were mediocre, and he dropped out of school without being any closer to fame. Life was simply not fair. He was physically unprepossessing, thin, with a pale, sickly complexion, and he was short, exactly five foot five and a half inches. Mothershed always stressed the extra half inch. He consoled himself with the fact that many famous men were short: Dudley Moore, Dustin Hoffman, Peter Falk...

The only profession that really interested Leslie Mothershed was photography. Taking photographs was so ridiculously simple. Anyone could do it. One simply pressed a button. His mother had bought him a camera for his sixth birthday and had been wildly extravagant in her praise of the pictures he had taken. By the time he was in his teens, Mothershed had become convinced that he was a brilliant photographer. He told himself that he was every bit as good as Ansel Adams, Richard Avedon or Margaret Bourke-White. With a loan from his mother, Leslie Mothershed set up his own photography business in Whitechapel, in his flat.

'Start small,' his mother told him, 'but think big,' and that is exactly what Leslie Mothershed did. He started very small and thought very big, but unfortunately, he had no talent for photography. He photographed parades and animals and flowers, and confidently sent his pictures off to newspapers and magazines, and they were always returned. Mothershed consoled himself with the thought of all the geniuses who had been rejected before their ability was recognized. He considered himself a martyr to philistinism.

And then, out of the blue, his big opportunity had

come. A cousin of his mother's who worked for the British publishing firm of HarperCollins had confided to Mothershed that they were planning to commission a coffee-table book on Switzerland.

'They haven't selected the photographer yet, Leslie, so if you get yourself over to Switzerland right away, and bring back some great pictures, the book could be yours.'

Leslie Mothershed hurriedly packed up his cameras and headed for Switzerland. He knew – he really knew – that this was the break he had been looking for. At last the idiots were going to recognize his talents. He rented a car in Geneva and travelled around the country, taking pictures of Swiss chalets, waterfalls, and snow-capped peaks. He photographed sunrises and sunsets, and farmers working in the fields. And then, in the middle of all that, fate had stepped in and changed his life. He was on his way to Bern when his motor failed. He pulled over to the side of the highway, furious. *Why me?* Mothershed moaned. *Why do these things always happen to me?* He sat there, fuming, thinking about his precious time lost, the expense it would be to have his car towed. Fifteen kilometres behind him was the town of Thun. *I'll get a tow from there*, Mothershed thought. *That shouldn't cost too much.*

He flagged down a passing gasoline truck. 'I need a tow truck,' Mothershed explained. 'Could you stop at a garage in Thun and have them come and get me?'

The truck driver shook his head. 'It's Sunday, mister. The closest garage that's open will be in Bern.'

'Bern? That's fifty kilometres from here. It will cost me a fortune.'

The truck driver grinned. '*Ja*. There they get you by the Sundays.' He started to drive on.

'Wait.' It was difficult to get the words out. 'I'll . . . I'll pay for a tow truck from Bern.'

'*Gut*. I will have them send someone out.'

Leslie Mothershed sat in his disabled car, cursing. *All I needed was this*, he thought, bitterly. He had already spent much too much money on film and now he would have to pay some bloody thief to tow him to a garage. It took almost two interminable hours for the tow truck to arrive. As the mechanic started to attach the car to his truck, there was a flash of light from across the highway, followed by a loud explosion, and Mothershed looked up to see what appeared to be a bright object falling out of the sky. The only other traffic on the highway was a tour bus that had pulled to a stop behind his car. The passengers from the bus were hurrying toward the scene of the crash. Mothershed hesitated, torn between his curiosity and his desire to move on. He turned and followed the bus passengers across the highway. When he reached the scene of the accident, he stood there transfixed. *Holy God*, he thought. *It's unreal*. He was staring at a flying saucer. Leslie Mothershed had heard about flying saucers and had read about them, but he had never believed they existed. He gaped at it, awed by the eerie spectacle. The shell had ripped open and he could see two bodies inside, small, with large skulls, sunken eyes, no ears and almost no chins, and they seemed to be wearing some kind of silver metallic suits.

The group from the tour bus was standing around him, staring in horrified silence. The man next to him fainted. Another man turned away and vomited. There was an elderly priest there, clutching his beads and mumbling incoherently.

'My God,' someone said. 'It's a flying saucer!'

And that was when Mothershed had his epiphany. A miracle had fallen into his lap. *He – Leslie Mothershed – was on the spot with his cameras to photograph the story of the century! There was not a magazine or newspaper in the world that would reject the photographs he was about to take. A coffee-table book about Switzerland?* He almost laughed aloud at the idea. *He was about to astonish the whole world. All the television talk shows would be begging for him, but he would do Robin Leach's show first. He would sell his photographs to the London* Times, *the* Sun, *the* Mail, *the* Mirror *– all the English newspapers, the foreign papers and magazines.* Le Figaro *and* Paris Match, Oggi *and* Der Tag. Time *and* USA Today. *The press everywhere would be pleading with him for his photographs. Japan and South America, and Russia and China and – there was no end to it.* Mothershed's heart was fluttering with excitement. *I won't give anyone an exclusive. Each one will have to pay me individually. I'll start at a hundred thousand pounds a picture, maybe two hundred thousand. And I'll sell them over and over again.* He began feverishly adding up the money he was going to make.

Leslie Mothershed was so busy adding up his

fortune that he almost forgot to take the pictures. 'Oh, my God! Excuse me,' he said to no one in particular, and raced back across the highway to get his camera equipment.

The mechanic had finished hoisting the disabled vehicle in the air, ready to tow it away.

'What's going on over there?' he asked.

Mothershed was busy grabbing his camera equipment. 'Come and see for yourself.'

The two men moved across the highway to the wooded area, and Mothershed pushed his way through the circle of tourists.

'Excuse me,' he said. 'Excuse me.'

He adjusted the focus on his camera and started snapping pictures of the UFO and its eerie passengers. He took pictures in black and white and in colour. As the shutter clicked each time, Mothershed thought, *a million pounds ... another million pounds ... another million pounds.*

The priest was crossing himself and saying, 'It's the face of Satan.'

Satan, hell, Mothershed thought exultantly. *It's the face of money. These will be the first pictures that prove that flying saucers really exist.* And then suddenly a terrifying thought occurred to him. *What if the magazines think these pictures are fake? There have been a lot of faked photographs of UFOs.* His euphoria vanished. *What if they don't believe me?* And that was when Leslie Mothershed had his second inspiration.

There were nine witnesses gathered around him.

Without knowing it, they were about to lend authenticity to his discovery.

Mothershed turned to face the group. 'Ladies and gentlemen,' he called out. 'If you would all like to have your photographs taken here, just line up and I'll be happy to send each of you a print, free.'

There were excited exclamations. Within moments, the passengers from the tour bus were standing beside the remains of the UFO, except for the priest.

He was reluctant. 'I can't,' he said. 'It's evil!'

Mothershed needed the priest. He would make the most convincing witness of them all.

'That's just the point,' Mothershed said persuasively. 'Don't you see? This will be your testimony about the existence of evil spirits.'

And the priest was finally persuaded.

'Spread out a little,' Mothershed ordered, 'so we can see the flying saucer.'

The witnesses shifted their positions.

'That's it. Very good. Excellent. Hold still, now.'

He snapped half a dozen more pictures and took out a pencil and paper.

'If you'll write down your names and addresses, I'll see to it that each of you gets a print.'

He had no intention of sending any prints. All he wanted was corroborating witnesses. *Let the bloody newspapers and magazines try to get around that!*

And then, suddenly, he noticed that several people in the group had cameras. He couldn't allow any other photographs but his! Only photos that had the credit, 'Photograph by Leslie Mothershed', could exist.

'Excuse me,' he said to the group. 'Those of you who have cameras: if you'll pass them to me, I'll take a few pictures of you so that you'll have some taken with your own cameras.'

The cameras were quickly handed to Leslie Mothershed. As he knelt to frame the first shot, no one noticed that Mothershed clicked open the film compartment with his thumb and held it ajar. *There, a little bit of nice bright sunlight will help those photographs no end. Too bad, my friends, but only professionals are allowed to capture historic moments.*

Ten minutes later Mothershed had all their names and addresses. He took one last look at the flying saucer and thought, exultantly, *Mother was right. I am going to be rich and famous.*

He couldn't wait to return to England to develop his precious photographs.

'What the hell is going on?'

The police stations in the Uetendorf area had been inundated with telephone calls all evening.

'Someone is prowling around my house . . .'

'There are strange lights outside . . .'

'My livestock is going crazy. There must be wolves around . . .'

'Someone drained my watering trough.'

And the most inexplicable telephone call of all:

'Chief, you'd better send a lot of tow trucks out to the main highway right away. It's a nightmare. All traffic has stopped.'

'What? Why?'
'No one knows. The car engines just suddenly went dead.'
It was a night they would never forget.

Chapter Sixteen

How long is this assignment going to take? Robert wondered, as he strapped himself into his first-class seat on the Swissair flight. As the plane rushed down the runway, its huge Rolls-Royce engines hungrily swallowing the night air, Robert relaxed and closed his eyes. *Was it really just a few years ago that I took this same flight with Susan to London? No. It was more like a lifetime ago.*

The plane touched down at Heathrow at six twenty-nine p.m., on schedule. Robert made his way out of the maze, and took a taxi into the sprawling city. He passed a hundred familiar landmarks, and he could hear Susan's voice, excitedly commenting about them. In those golden days it had never mattered where they were. It was simply enough that they were together. They brought their own happiness with them, their own special excitement in each other. Theirs was the marriage that would have a happy ending.

Almost.

Their problems had started innocently enough with an overseas call from Admiral Whittaker while Robert and Susan were travelling in Thailand. It had been six months since Robert had been discharged from the Navy, and he had not talked to the Admiral in all that time. The call, reaching them at the Oriental Hotel in Bangkok, was a surprise.

'Robert? Admiral Whittaker.'

'Admiral! It's good to hear your voice.'

'It hasn't been easy tracking you down. What have you been up to?'

'Not very much. Just taking it easy. Having a long honeymoon.'

'How is Susan? It *is* Susan, isn't it?'

'Yes. She's fine, thank you.'

'How soon can you get back to Washington?'

'I beg your pardon?'

'It hasn't been announced yet, but I've been given a new assignment, Robert. They've made me Director of 17th District Naval Intelligence. I'd like you to come aboard.'

Robert was taken aback. 'Naval Intelligence? Admiral, I don't know anything about . . .'

'You can learn. You would be doing an important service for your country, Robert. Will you come and discuss it with me?'

'Well . . .'

'Good. I'll expect you in my office Monday morning at 0900. Say hello to Susan for me.'

Robert repeated the conversation to Susan.

'Naval Intelligence? That sounds so exciting.'

'Maybe,' Robert said doubtfully. 'I have no idea what's involved.'

'You must find out.'

He studied her for a moment. 'You want me to take it, don't you?'

She put her arms around him. 'I want you to do whatever you want to do. I think you're ready to go back to work. I've noticed in the last few weeks how restless you've become.'

'I think you're trying to get rid of me,' Robert teased. 'The honeymoon is over.'

Susan put her lips close to his. 'Never. Did I ever tell you how crazy I am about you, sailor? Let me show you . . .'

Thinking about it later – too late – Robert decided that that was the beginning of the end of their marriage. The offer had seemed wonderful at the time, and he had gone back to Washington to meet with Admiral Whittaker.

'This job requires brains, courage and initiative, Robert. You have all three. Our country has become a target for every little tin-horn dictatorship that can breed a terrorist group or build a chemical weapons factory. Half a dozen of those countries are working on atomic bombs at this moment, so that they can hold us at ransom. My job is to build an intelligence network to find out exactly what they're up to and to try to stop them. I want you to help me.'

In the end, Robert had accepted the job with Naval Intelligence, and to his surprise, he found that he enjoyed it and had a natural aptitude for it. Susan found an attractive apartment in Rosslyn, Virginia, not far from where Robert worked, and busied herself furnishing it. Robert was sent to the Farm, the CIA training ground for secret service agents.

Located in a heavily guarded compound in the Virginia countryside, the Farm occupies twenty square miles, most of it covered in tall pine forest, with the central buildings in a ten-acre cleared area two miles from the front gate. A network of dirt roads branches off through the woods, with locked swinging barricades, and 'No Entry' signs posted. At a small airfield, unmarked aircraft arrive and depart several times a day. The Farm has a deceptively bucolic setting, with leafy trees, deer running in the fields, and small buildings innocently scattered around the extensive grounds. Inside the compound, however, it is a different world.

Robert had expected to train with other Navy personnel, but to his surprise, the trainees were a mixture of CIA inductees and marines, and Army, Navy and Air Force personnel. Each student was assigned a number and housed in a dormitory-like room in one of several spartan two-storey brick buildings. At the Bachelor Officer Quarters, where Robert stayed, each man had his own room, and shared the bathroom with another. The Mess Hall was across the road from the BOQ cluster.

On the day Robert arrived, he was escorted to an auditorium with thirty other newcomers. A tall, powerfully built black Colonel in Air Force uniform addressed the group. He appeared to be in his middle fifties, and he gave the impression of quick, cold intelligence. He spoke clearly and crisply, with no wasted words.

'I'm Colonel Frank Johnson. I want to welcome you here. During your stay, you will use only your first names. From this moment on, your lives will be a closed book. You've all been sworn to secrecy. I would advise you to take that oath very, very seriously. You are *never* to discuss your work with anyone – your wives, your family, your friends. You've been selected to come here because you have special qualifications. There's a lot of hard work ahead of you to develop those qualifications, and not all of you are going to make it. You're going to be involved in things you have never even heard of before. I cannot stress enough the importance of the work you will be doing when you finish here. It has become fashionable in certain liberal circles to attack our intelligence services, whether it's the CIA, Army, Navy or the Air Force, but I can assure you, gentlemen, that without dedicated people like yourselves, this country would be in one hell of a lot of trouble. It's going to be your job to help prevent that. Those of you who do pass will become Case Officers. To put it bluntly, a Case Officer is a spy. He works under cover.

'While you're here, you're going to get the best training in the world. You'll be trained in surveillance and counter-surveillance. You'll have courses in radio communications, encoding, and weaponry and map reading.

'You'll attend a class in interpersonal relations. You'll be taught how to build a rapport, how to draw out an individual's motivations, how to make your target feel at ease.'

The class was hanging on every word.

'You'll learn how to meet and recruit an agent.

You'll be trained in how to make sure meeting places are secure.

'You'll learn about dead drops, how to covertly communicate with your contacts. If you're successful at what you do, you will carry out your assignments unnoticed and undetected.'

Robert could feel the excitement that charged the air.

'Some of you will work under official cover. It could be diplomatic or military. Others will work under non-official cover as private individuals – as a businessman, or archaeologist, or novelist – any profession that will give you access to the areas and types of people likely to have the information you're looking for. And now, I'm going to turn you over to your instructors. Good luck.'

Robert found the training fascinating. The instructors were men who had worked in the field and were experienced professionals. Robert absorbed the technical information easily. In addition to the courses Colonel Johnson had mentioned, there was a brush-up course on languages, and one on cryptic codes.

Colonel Johnson was an enigma to Robert. The rumour circulating about him was that he had strong connections at the White House, and was involved in high-level covert activities. He would disappear from the Farm for days at a time, and suddenly reappear.

An agent named Ron was conducting a class.

'There are six phases to the clandestine operational process. The first is spotting. When you know what information you need, your first challenge is to identify and target individuals who have access to that information. The second phase is assessment. Once you have spotted your target, you have to decide if he really has the information you need, and if he might be susceptible to recruitment. What motivates him? Is he happy in his job? Does he have a grudge against his boss? Is he over his head financially? If the prospect has accessibility and there's a motivation that can be exploited, you move along to phase three.

'Phase three is development. You build up a relationship with a prospect. You manage to run into him as often as possible, and built a rapport. The next phase is recruitment. When you think he is ready, you go to work on him psychologically. You use whatever psychological weapons you've got – revenge against his boss, money, the thrill of it. If a Case Officer has done his job well, the prospect usually says yes.

'So far so good. You have a spy working for you. The next step is handling him. You must protect not only yourself, but him. You will arrange surreptitious meetings, and train him in the use of microfilm and, where appropriate, clandestine radio. You will teach him how to detect surveillance, what to say if questioned, and so on.

'The last phase is disconnecting. After some period of time, perhaps your recruit will be transferred to a different job and no longer have access to the information, or maybe we will no longer need the information to which he does have access. In any case, the relationship is ended but it's important to end it in such a way that the recruit doesn't feel he has been used, and is looking for vengeance...'

Colonel Johnson had been right. Not everyone made it through the course. Familiar faces kept disappearing. Washed out. No one knew why. No one asked.

One day, as a group was preparing to go into Richmond for a surveillance exercise, Robert's instructor said, 'We're going to see how good you are, Robert. I'm going to send someone to tail you. I want you to lose him. Do you think you can do that?'

'Yes, sir.'

'Good luck.'

Robert took the bus into Richmond and began strolling the streets. Within five minutes he identified his trackers. There were two of them. One was on foot and one was in an automobile. Robert tried ducking into restaurants and shops and hurrying out back doors, but he was unable to shake them. They were too well trained. Finally, it was almost time to return to the Farm and Robert still had not been able to get away from them. They were watching him too closely. Robert walked into a department store and the two men took up positions where they could cover the entrances and exits. Robert went up the escalator to the men's department. Thirty minutes later, when he came down, he was wearing a different suit, a coat and hat, talking to a woman and carrying a baby in his arms. He walked past his pursuers without being recognized.

He was the only one that day who had successfully avoided surveillance.

The jargon taught at the Farm was a language unto itself.

'You probably won't use all these terms,' the instructor told the class, 'but you had better know them. There are two different kinds of agents; an "agent of influence" and an "agent provocateur". The agent of influence tries to change opinion in the country where he operates. An agent provocateur is sent to stir up trouble and create chaos. "Biographic leverage" is CIA code for blackmail. There are also "black bag jobs", which can range from bribes to burglary. Watergate was a black bag job.'

He looked around to make sure that the class was paying attention. They were spellbound.

'From time to time some of you may need a "cobbler" — that's a man who forges passports.'

Robert wondered whether he would ever use a cobbler.

'The phrase to "demote maximally" is a nasty one. It means to purge by killing. So does the word "terminate". If you hear someone talking about the "Firm", it's the nickname we use to refer to the British Secret Service. If you're asked to "fumigate" an office, you won't be looking for termites, you'll be looking for listening devices.'

The arcane expressions fascinated Robert.

'"Ladies" is a euphemism for females sent to compromise the opposition. A "legend" is the faked biography of a spy, to provide him with a cover. "Going private" means leaving the service.'

The instructor scanned the class. 'Any of you know what a "lion tamer" is?'

He waited for an answer. Silence.

'When an agent is sacked, he sometimes gets upset and may make threats to reveal what he knows. A muscleman, or lion tamer, is called in to soften him up. I'm sure none of you will ever have to deal with one.'

That drew nervous laughter.

'Then, there's the word "measles". If a target dies of measles, it means he was murdered so efficiently that death appeared to be accidental or due to natural causes. One method of inducing measles is tabun. That's a colourless or brownish liquid compound that causes nerve paralysis when absorbed through the skin. If someone offers you a "music box", they're offering you a wireless transmitter. The transmitter operator is called a "musician". In the future, some of you will be operating "naked". Don't rush to take off your clothes, it simply means that you're alone and without any assistance from outside.

'There's one more thing I want to discuss today. Coincidence. In our work, there is no such animal. It usually spells danger. If you keep running into the same person again and again, or you keep spotting the same automobile when you're on the move, cover your ass. You're probably in trouble.

'I think that's enough for today, gentlemen. We will take up where we left off tomorrow.'

From time to time, Colonel Johnson called Robert into his office, 'to have a chat,' as he put it. The conversations were deceptively casual, but Robert was aware of an underlying probing being carried on.

'I understand you're happily married, Robert.'

'That's right.'

They spent the next half hour talking about marriage, fidelity and trust.

Another time: 'Admiral Whittaker thinks of you as a son, Robert. Did you know that?'

'Yes.' The pain of Edward's death was something that would never go away.

They talked about loyalty and duty and death.

'You've faced death more than once, Robert. Are you afraid to die?'

'No.' *But to die for a good reason*, Robert thought. *Not senselessly.*

The meetings were frustrating to Robert, because they were like looking into a trick mirror. Colonel Johnson could see him clearly, but the Colonel remained invisible, an enigma cloaked in secrecy.

The course lasted sixteen weeks, and during that time none of the men was permitted to communicate with the outside world. Robert missed Susan desperately. It was the longest they had ever been apart.

When the four months were up, Colonel Johnson called Robert into his office.

'This is goodbye. You've done an excellent job, Commander. I think you're going to find your future very interesting.'

'Thank you, sir. I hope so.'

'Good luck.'

Colonel Johnson watched Robert leave. He sat there for five minutes without moving, then reached a decision. He walked over to the door and locked it. Then he picked up the telephone and made a call.

Susan was waiting for him. She opened the door of their apartment, wearing a sheer negligée that concealed nothing. She flew into his arms and held him close. 'Hi, sailor. Want to have a good time?'

'I'm having one,' Robert said happily, 'just holding you.'

'God, I missed you so much!' Susan drew back and said, fiercely, 'If anything ever happened to you, I think I would die.'

'Nothing is ever going to happen to me.'

'Promise?'

'Promise.'

She studied him a moment, concerned. 'You look so tired.'

'It was a pretty intensive course,' Robert admitted. He was understating it. With all the texts and manuals to study, in addition to the practical, hands-on lessons, none of the recruits had been able to sleep more than a few hours a night. There was little grumbling, for a very simple reason: they were well aware that what they were learning could one day save their lives.

'I know exactly what you need,' Susan decided.

Robert grinned. 'I'll say.' He reached for her.

'Wait. Give me five minutes. Get undressed.'

He watched her walk away and thought, *How damned lucky can a man get?* He began to get undressed.

Susan returned a few minutes later. She said softly, 'Umm. I like you naked.'

He heard his instructor's voice saying, *'Some of you will be operating naked. It means you're alone and without any assistance.' What have I gotten into? What have I gotten Susan into?*

She led him into the bathroom. The tub was filled with warm scented water, and the room was dark except for four candles flickering on the basin.

'Welcome home, darling.' She slipped out of her negligée, and stepped into the bathtub. He followed her.

'Susan . . .'

'Don't talk. Lean back against me.'

He felt her hands gently caressing his back and shoulders and he felt the soft curves of her body against him, and he forgot how tired he was. They made love in the warm water and when they had dried themselves, Susan said, 'So much for the foreplay. Now, let's get serious.'

They made love again, and later, as Robert fell asleep, holding Susan in his arms, he thought, *It will always be like this. Forever.*

Chapter Seventeen

The following Monday morning Robert reported for his first day of duty at the 17th District Office of Naval Intelligence at the Pentagon.

Admiral Whittaker said warmly, 'Welcome home, Robert. Apparently you impressed the hell out of Colonel Johnson.'

Robert smiled. 'He's quite impressive himself.'

Over coffee, the Admiral asked, 'Are you ready to go to work?'

'Eager.'

'Good. We have a situation in Rhodesia...'

Working in the Office of Naval Intelligence was even more exciting than Robert had anticipated. Each assignment was different, and Robert was given the ones classified 'extremely sensitive'. He brought in a defector who revealed Noriega's drug-smuggling operation in Panama, exposed a mole working for Marcos in the American Consulate in Manila, and helped set up a secret listening post in Morocco. He was sent on missions to South America and to the East Indies. The only thing that disturbed him was the long separations from Susan. He hated to be away from her, and he missed her terribly. He had the excitement of his job to occupy him, but Susan had nothing. Robert's caseload kept increasing. He spent less and less time at home, and that was when the problem with Susan became serious.

Whenever Robert came home, he and Susan would run hungrily into each other's arms and make passionate love. But those times began to be further and further apart. It seemed to Susan that no sooner did Robert return from one assignment, than he was sent away on another.

To make matters worse, Robert could not discuss his work with her. Susan had no idea where he went or what he was doing. She knew only that whatever he was involved in was dangerous, and she was terrified that one day he would leave and never return. She dared not ask him questions. She felt like a stranger, completely shut out of an important part of his life. Of *their* life. *I can't go on like this*, Susan decided.

When Robert returned from a four-week assignment in Central America, Susan said, 'Robert, I think we had better have a talk.'

'What's the problem?' Robert asked. He knew what the problem was.

'I'm frightened. We're slipping away from each other, and I don't want to lose us. I couldn't stand it.'

'Susan . . .'

'Wait. Let me finish. Do you know how much time we've spent together in the last four months? Less than two weeks. Whenever you come home I feel as though you're a visitor, instead of my husband.'

He took Susan in his arms and held her tightly. 'You know how much I love you.'

She laid her head on his shoulder. 'Please don't let anything happen to us.'

'I won't,' he promised. 'I'll have a talk with Admiral Whittaker.'

'When?'

'Immediately.'

'The Admiral will see you now, Commander.'

'Thank you.'

Admiral Whittaker was seated behind his desk, signing papers. He looked up as Robert entered and smiled. 'Welcome home, Robert, and congratulations. That was an excellent job in El Salvador.'

'Thank you, sir.'

'Sit down. Can I offer you some coffee?'

'No, thank you, Admiral.'

'You wanted to talk to me? My secretary said it was urgent. What can I do for you?'

It was difficult to begin. 'Well, sir, this is personal. I've been married less than two years, and . . .'

'You made a wonderful choice, Robert. Susan's a fine woman.'

'Yes, I agree. The problem is that I'm away most of the time, and she's unhappy about it.' He added quickly, 'And she has every right to be. It isn't a normal situation.'

Admiral Whittaker leaned back in his chair and said, thoughtfully, 'Of course, what you're doing isn't a normal situation. Sometimes sacrifices have to be made.'

'I know,' Robert said stubbornly, 'but I'm not prepared to sacrifice my marriage. It means too much to me.'

The Admiral studied him reflectively. 'I see. What is it you're asking?'

'I was hoping that you could find some assignments for me where I'm not away from home so much. This is such a large operation, there must be a hundred things I could do closer to home.'

'Closer to home.'

'Yes.'

The Admiral said slowly, 'You've certainly earned that. I don't see why something like that can't be arranged.'

Robert smiled in relief. 'That's very good of you, Admiral. I would certainly appreciate it.'

'Yes, I think we can definitely arrange that. Tell Susan for me that the problem is solved.'

Robert stood up, beaming. 'I don't know how to thank you.'

Admiral Whittaker waved a hand of dismissal. 'You're too valuable a piece of manpower for me to let anything happen to you. Now go home to your bride.'

When Robert told Susan the news, she was thrilled. She threw her arms around him. 'Oh, darling, that's wonderful.'

'I'm going to ask him for a couple of weeks off so

we can take a trip somewhere. It will be a second honeymoon.'

'I've forgotten what a honeymoon is like,' Susan murmured. 'Show me.'

Robert showed her.

Admiral Whittaker sent for Robert the following morning. 'I just wanted you to know I'm making some arrangements about the matter we discussed yesterday.'

'Thank you, Admiral.' Now was the time to mention taking a leave. 'Sir . . .'

Admiral Whittaker said, 'Something has come up, Robert.' The Admiral began to pace. When he spoke, there was a note of deep concern in his voice. 'I've just been informed that the CIA has been infiltrated. It seems that there has been a steady leak of Top Secret information. All they know about the spy is that his code name is "the Fox". He's in Argentina right now. They need someone outside the Agency to handle the operation. The Deputy Director of the CIA has asked for you. They would like you to track the man down and bring him back. I told them the decision is up to you. Do you want to undertake it?'

Robert hesitated. 'I'm afraid I'll have to pass on it, sir.'

'I respect your decision, Robert. You've been travelling constantly and have never turned down an assignment. I know it hasn't been easy on your marriage.'

'I'd like to take on this job, sir. It's just that . . .'

'You don't have to say it, Robert. My opinion of your work and dedication will always remain the same. I just have one favour to ask of you.'

'What's that, Admiral?'

'The Deputy Director of the CIA asked to meet with you, regardless of your decision. As a courtesy. You don't mind, do you?'

'Of course not, sir.'

Early the next morning Robert drove to Langley for his meeting.

'Sit down, Commander,' the Deputy Director said after Robert entered the large corner office. 'I've heard a lot about you. All good things, of course.'

'Thank you, sir.'

The Deputy Director was a man in his early sixties, reed thin with fine white hair and a small brush moustache that moved up and down as he drew on his pipe. A Yale graduate, he had joined the OSS during World War II and then moved into the CIA when it was formed after the conflict. He rose steadily up the ranks of the most powerful intelligence agency in the world.

'I want you to know, Commander, that I respect your decision.'

'I appreciate that.'

'There is one fact, however, that I feel I should bring to your attention.'

'What's that, sir?'

'The President is personally involved in the operation to unmask the Fox.'

'I didn't know that, sir.'

'He regards it – as I do, too – as one of the most important assignments this agency has had since its inception. I know of your situation at home, and I'm sure the President is sympathetic, too. He's a real family man. But your not taking on this assignment might throw – how should I say it – a *cloud* on ONI *and* Admiral Whittaker.'

'The Admiral had nothing to do with my decision, sir,' Robert said.

'I understand that, Commander, but will the President understand that?'

The honeymoon will have to be postponed, Robert thought.

When Robert broke the news to Susan, he said gently, 'This is my last overseas assignment. After this I'll be home so much you'll get sick of me.'

She smiled up at him. 'There isn't that much time in the world. We're going to be together forever.'

The chase after the Fox was the most frustrating thing Robert had ever experienced. He picked up his trail in Argentina, but missed his quarry by one day. The trail led to Tokyo and China and then Malaysia. Whoever the Fox was, he left just enough of a trail to lead to where he had been, but never to where he was.

The days turned into weeks and the weeks turned into months, and always Robert was just behind the

Fox. He called Susan almost every day. In the beginning, it was, 'I'll be home in a few days, darling.' And then, 'I might be home next week.' And then, finally, 'I'm not sure when I'll be back.' In the end, Robert had to give up. He had been on the Fox's trail for two and a half months, with no success.

When he returned to Susan, she seemed changed. A little cooler.

'I'm sorry, darling,' Robert apologized. 'I had no idea it would take so long. It was just ...'

'They'll never let you go, will they, Robert?'

'What? Of course they will.'

She shook her head. 'I don't think so. I've taken a job at Washington Memorial Hospital.'

He was taken aback. 'You've what?'

'I'm going to be a nurse again. I can't sit around waiting for you to come home to me, wondering where you are, and what you're doing, wondering whether you're dead or alive.'

'Susan, I ...'

'It's all right, my sweetheart. At least I'll be doing something useful while you're gone. It will make the waiting easier.'

And Robert had no answer to that.

He reported his failure to Admiral Whittaker. The Admiral was sympathetic.

'It's my fault for agreeing to let you do it. From now on, we'll let the CIA handle their own damned problems. I'm sorry, Robert.'

Robert told him about Susan taking a job as a nurse.

'That's probably a good idea,' the Admiral said thoughtfully. 'It will take the pressure off your marriage. If you took on some overseas caseloads now and then, I'm sure it won't matter as much.'

'Now and then' turned out to be almost constantly. That was when the marriage really began to disintegrate.

Susan worked at Washington Memorial Hospital as an operating-room nurse and whenever Robert was home she tried to take time off to be with him, but she was caught up more and more in her work.

'I'm really enjoying it, darling. I feel I'm doing something useful.'

She would talk to Robert about her patients, and he remembered how caring she had been with him, how she had nurtured him back to health, back to life. He was pleased that she was doing important work that she loved, but the fact was, they were seeing less and less of each other. The emotional distance between them was widening. There was an awkwardness now that had not existed before. They were like two strangers trying desperately hard to make conversation.

When Robert returned to Washington from a six-week assignment in Turkey, he took Susan out to dinner at Sans Souci.

Susan said, 'We have a new patient at the hospital. He was in a bad plane crash, and the doctors didn't think he was going to live, but I'm going to see to it that he does.' Her eyes were glowing.

She was like that with me, Robert thought. And he wondered if she had leaned over the new patient and said, 'Get well. I'm waiting for you.' He rejected the thought.

'He's so nice, Robert. All the nurses are crazy about him.'

All the nurses? he wondered.

There was a small, nagging doubt at the back of his mind, but he managed to get rid of it.

They ordered dinner.

The following Saturday, Robert left for Portugal, and when he returned three weeks later, Susan greeted him excitedly.

'Monte walked today for the first time!' Her kiss was perfunctory.

'Monte?'

'Monte Banks. That's his name. He's going to be fine. The doctors couldn't believe it, but we wouldn't give up.'

We. 'Tell me about him.'

'He's really darling. He's always giving us gifts. He's very wealthy. He flies his own plane and he was in a bad crash, and . . .'

'What kind of gifts?'

'Oh, you know, just little things . . . candies and flowers and books and records. He tried to give all of us expensive watches but, of course, we had to refuse.'

'Of course.'

'He has a yacht, polo ponies . . .'

That was the day Robert began calling him 'Moneybags'.

Susan talked about him every time she came home from the hospital.

'He's really dear, Robert.'

Dear was dangerous.

'And he's so thoughtful. Do you know what he did today? He had lunch sent from the Jockey Club for all the nurses on the floor.'

The man was sickening. Ridiculously, Robert found himself getting angry. 'Is this wonderful patient of yours married?'

'No, darling. Why?'

'I just wondered.'

She laughed. 'For heaven's sake, you're not jealous, are you?'

'Of some old man who's just learning to walk? Of course not.' *Like hell I'm not.* But he wouldn't give Susan the satisfaction of saying so.

When Robert was at home, Susan tried not to talk about her patient, but if she did not bring up the subject, Robert would.

'How is old Moneybags doing?'

'His name is not Moneybags,' she chided him. 'It's Monte Banks.'

'Whatever.' *It was too bad the sonofabitch couldn't have died in the plane crash.*

The following day was Susan's birthday.

'I'll tell you what,' Robert said, enthusiastically,

'we'll celebrate. We'll go out and have a wonderful dinner somewhere and . . .'

'I have to work at the hospital until eight.'

'All right. I'll pick you up there.'

'Fine. Monte is dying to meet you. I've told him all about you.'

'I look forward to meeting the old man,' Robert assured her.

When Robert arrived at the hospital, the receptionist said, 'Good evening, Commander. Susan is working in the orthopedic ward on the third floor. She's expecting you.' She picked up the telephone.

When Robert got off the elevator, Susan was waiting for him, wearing her white starched uniform, and his heart skipped a beat. She was, oh, so damned beautiful.

'Hello, gorgeous.'

Susan smiled, strangely ill at ease. 'Hello, Robert. I'll be off duty in a few minutes. Come on. I'll introduce you to Monte.'

I can't wait.

She led him into a large private room filled with books and flowers and baskets of fruit, and said, 'Monte, this is my husband, Robert.'

Robert stood there, staring at the man in the bed. He was three or four years older than Robert and resembled Paul Newman. Robert despised him on sight.

'I'm certainly pleased to meet you, Commander. Susan has been telling me all about you.'

Is that what they talked about when she was at his bedside in the middle of the night?

'She's very proud of you.'

That's it, buddy, throw me a few crumbs.

Susan was looking at Robert, willing him to be polite. He made an effort.

'I understand you'll be getting out of here soon.'

'Yes, thanks mostly to your wife. She's a miracle worker.'

Come on, sailor. Do you think I'm going to let some other nurse have that great body? 'Yes, that's her speciality.' Robert could not keep the bitterness out of his voice.

The birthday dinner was a fiasco. All Susan wanted to talk about was her patient.

'Did he remind you of anyone, darling?'

'Boris Karloff.'

'Why did you have to be so rude to him?'

He said coldly, 'I thought I was very civil. I don't happen to like the man.'

Susan stared at him. 'You don't even know him. What don't you like about him?'

I don't like the way he looks at you. I don't like the way you look at him. I don't like the way our marriage is going to hell. God, I don't want to lose you. 'Sorry. I guess I'm just tired.'

They finished their dinner in silence.

The next morning, as Robert was getting ready to go to the office, Susan said, 'Robert, I have something to say to you . . .'

And it was as though he had been struck in the pit

of his stomach. He could not bear to have her put what was happening into words.

'Susan...'

'You know I love you. I'll always love you. You're the dearest, most wonderful man I've ever known.'

'Please...'

'No, let me finish. This is very hard for me. In the last year we've only spent minutes together. We don't have a marriage anymore. We've drifted apart.'

Every word was a knife stabbing into him.

'You're right,' he said desperately. 'I'll change. I'll quit the Agency. Now. Today. We'll go away somewhere and...'

She shook her head. 'No, Robert. We both know that wouldn't work. You're doing what you want to do. If you stopped doing it because of me you would always resent me. This isn't anybody's fault. It just ... happened. I want a divorce.'

It was as though the world had caved in on him. He felt suddenly sick to his stomach.

'You don't mean that, Susan, we'll find a way to...'

'It's too late. I've been thinking about this for a long time. All the while you were away and I sat home alone and waited for you to come back I thought about it. We've been living separate lives. I need more than that. I need something you can't give me anymore.'

He stood there, fighting to control his emotions. 'Does this ... does this have anything to do with Moneybags?'

Susan hesitated. 'Monte has asked me to marry him.'

He could feel his bowels turning to water. 'And you're going to?'

'Yes.'

It was some kind of crazy nightmare. *This isn't happening*, he thought. *It can't be.* His eyes filled with tears.

Susan put her arms around him and held him close. 'I will never again feel about any man the way I felt about you. I loved you with all my heart and soul. I will always love you. You are my dearest friend.' She pulled back and looked into his eyes. 'But that isn't enough. Do you understand?'

All he understood was that she was tearing him apart. 'We could try again. We'll start over and . . .'

'I'm sorry, Robert.' Her voice was choked. 'I'm so sorry, but it's finished.'

Susan flew to Reno for a divorce, and Commander Robert Bellamy went on a two-week drunk.

Old habits die hard. Robert telephoned a friend at the FBI. Al Traynor had crossed Robert's path half a dozen times in the past, and Robert trusted him.

'Tray, I need a favour.'

'A favour? You need a psychiatrist. How the hell could you let Susan get away?'

The news was probably all over town.

'It's a long, sad story.'

'I'm really sorry, Robert. She was a great lady. I . . . never mind. What can I do for you?'

'I'd like you to run a computer check on someone.'

'You've got it. Give me a name.'

'Monte Banks. It's just a routine inquiry.'

'Right. What do you want to know?'

'He's probably not even in your files, Tray, but if he is ... did he ever get a parking ticket, beat his dog, run a red light? The usual.'

'Sure.'

'And I'm curious about where he got his money. I'd like a fix on his background.'

'So, just routine, huh?'

'And, Tray, let's keep this between us. It's personal. Okay?'

'No problem. I'll call you in the morning.'

'Thanks. I owe you a lunch.'

'Dinner.'

'You've got it.'

Robert replaced the receiver and thought, *Portrait of a man clutching at straws. What am I hoping for, that he's Jack the Ripper, and Susan will come flying back into my arms?*

Early the following morning, Dustin Thornton sent for Robert. 'What are you working on, Commander?'

He knows perfectly well what I'm working on, Robert thought. 'I'm winding up my file on the diplomat from Singapore, and . . .'

'It doesn't seem to be occupying enough of your time.'

'I beg your pardon?'

'In case you've forgotten, Commander, the Office

of Naval Intelligence is not mandated to investigate American citizens.'

Robert was watching him, puzzled. 'What are you . . . ?'

'I've been notified by the FBI that you have been trying to obtain information that is completely out of the jurisdiction of this agency.'

Robert felt a sudden rush of anger. That sonofabitch Traynor had betrayed him. So much for friendship. 'It was a personal matter,' Robert said. 'I . . .'

'The computers of the FBI are not there for your convenience, nor to help you harass private citizens. Do I make myself clear?'

'Very.'

'That's all.'

Robert raced back to his office. His fingers trembled as he dialled 202-324-3000. A voice answered, 'FBI.'

'Al Traynor.'

'Just a moment, please.'

A minute later, a man's voice came on the line. 'Hello. May I help you?'

'Yes. I'm calling Al Traynor.'

'I'm sorry, Agent Traynor is no longer with this office.'

Robert felt a shock go through him. 'What?'

'Agent Traynor has been transferred.'

'Transferred?'

'Yes.'

'To where?'

'Boise. But he won't be up there for a while. A long while, I'm afraid.'

'What do you mean?'

'He was struck by a hit-and-run driver last night while jogging in Rock Creek Park. Can you believe it? Some creep must have been drunk out of his mind. He ran his car right up on the jogging path. Traynor's body was thrown over forty feet. He may not make it.'

Robert replaced the receiver. His mind was spinning. What the hell was going on? Monte Banks, the blue-eyed all-American boy, was being protected. From what? By whom? *Jesus*, Robert thought, *what is Susan getting herself into?*

He went to visit her that afternoon.

She was in her new apartment, a beautiful duplex on 'M' Street. He wondered whether Moneybags had paid for it. It had been weeks since he had seen Susan, and the sight of her took his breath away.

'Forgive me for barging in like this, Susan. I know I promised not to.'

'You said it was something serious.'

'It is.' Now that he was here, he didn't know how to begin. *Susan, I came here to save you?* She would laugh in his face.

'What's happened?'

'It's about Monte.'

She frowned. 'What about him?'

This was the difficult part. How could he tell her what he himself didn't know? All he knew was that something was terribly wrong. Monte Banks was in the FBI computer all right, with a tickler: *No infor-*

mation to be given out without proper authorization. And the inquiry had been kicked right back to ONI. Why?

'I don't think he's . . . he's not what he seems to be.'

'I don't understand.'

'Susan – where does he get his money?'

She looked surprised at the question. 'Monte has a very successful import-export business.'

The oldest cover in the world.

He should have known better than to have come charging in with his half-baked theory. He felt like a fool. Susan was waiting for an answer and he had none.

'Why are you asking?'

'I was . . . I just wanted to make sure he's right for you,' Robert said lamely.

'Oh, Robert.' Her voice was filled with disappointment.

'I guess I shouldn't have come.' *You got that right, buddy.* 'I'm sorry.'

Susan walked up to him and gave him a hug. 'I understand,' she said softly.

But she didn't understand. She didn't understand that an innocent inquiry about Monte Banks had been stonewalled, referred to the Office of Naval Intelligence, and that the man who had tried to get that information had been transferred to the boondocks.

There were other ways of obtaining information, and Robert went about them circumspectly. He telephoned a friend who worked for *Forbes Magazine*.

'Robert! Long time no see. What can I do for you?'

Robert told him.

'Monte Banks? Interesting you should mention him. We think he should be on our Forbes Four Hundred wealthiest list, but we can't get any hard information on him. Do you have anything for us?'

A zero.

Robert went to the public library and looked up Monte Banks in *Who's Who*. He was not listed.

He turned to the microfiche, and looked up back issues of the *Washington Post* around the time that Monte Banks had had his plane accident. There was a brief item about the plane crash. It mentioned Banks as an entrepreneur.

It all sounded innocent enough. *Maybe I'm wrong*, Robert thought. *Maybe Monte Banks is a guy in a white hat. Our government wouldn't have protected him if he was a spy, a criminal, into drugs ... The truth is that I'm still trying to hold onto Susan.*

Being a bachelor again was a loneliness, an emptiness, a round of busy days and sleepless nights. A tide of despair would sweep over him without warning, and he would weep. He wept for himself and for Susan and for everything that they had lost. Susan's presence was everywhere. The apartment was alive with reminders of her. Robert was cursed with total recall, and each room tormented him with memories of Susan's voice, her laughter, her warmth. He remembered the soft hills and valleys of her body as she lay in bed naked, waiting for him, and the ache inside him was unbearable.

His friends were concerned.

'You shouldn't be alone, Robert.'

And their rallying cry became, 'Have I got a girl for you!'

They were tall and beautiful, and small and sexy. They were models and secretaries and advertising executives and divorcees and lawyers. But none of them was Susan. He had nothing in common with any of them, and trying to make small talk with strangers in whom he had no interest only made him feel more lonely. Robert had no desire to go to bed with any of them. He wanted to be alone. He wanted to rewind the film back to the beginning, to rewrite the script. With hindsight, it was so easy to see his mistakes, to see how the scene with Admiral Whittaker should have played.

The CIA has been infiltrated by a man called The Fox. The Deputy Director has asked for you to track him down.

No, Admiral. Sorry. I'm taking my wife on a second honeymoon.

He wanted to re-edit his life, to give it a happy ending. Too late. Life did not give second chances. He was alone.

He did his own shopping, cooked his meals for himself and went to the neighbourbood laundromat once a week when he was home.

It was a lonely, miserable time in Robert's life. But the worst was yet to come. A beautiful designer he had met in Washington telephoned him several times to invite him to dinner. Robert had been reluctant, but he had finally accepted. She prepared a delicious candlelight dinner for the two of them.

'You're a very good cook,' Robert said.

'I'm very good at everything.' And there was no mistaking her meaning. She moved closer to him. 'Let me prove it to you.' She put her hands on his thighs and ran her tongue around his lips.

It's been a long time, Robert thought. *Maybe too long*.

They went to bed, and to Robert's consternation, it was a disaster. For the first time in his life, Robert was impotent. He was humiliated.

'Don't worry, darling,' she said. 'It will be all right.'

She was wrong.

Robert went home feeling embarrassed, crippled. He knew that in some crazy, convoluted way, he had felt that making love to another woman was a betrayal of Susan. *How stupid can I get?*

He tried to make love again, several weeks later, with a bright secretary at ONI. She had been wildly passionate in bed, stroking his body and taking him inside her hot mouth. But it was no use. He wanted only Susan. After that, he stopped trying. He thought of consulting a doctor, but he was too ashamed. He knew the answer to his problem, and there was no solution. He poured all his energy into work.

Susan called him at least once a week. 'Don't forget to pick up your shirts at the laundry,' she would say. Or: 'I'm sending over a maid to clean up the apartment. I'll bet it's a mess.'

Each call made the loneliness more intolerable.

She had called him the night before her wedding.

'Robert, I want you to know I'm getting married tomorrow.'

It was difficult for him to breathe. He began to hyperventilate.

'Susan . . .'

'I love Monte,' she said, 'but I love you, too. I'll love you until the day I die. I don't want you ever to forget that.'

What was there to say to that?

'Robert, are you all right?'

Sure. I'm great. Except that I'm a fucking eunuch. Scratch the adjective.

'Robert?'

He could not bear to punish her with his problem. 'I'm fine. Just do me a favour, will you, baby?'

'Anything I can.'

'Don't . . . don't let him take you on your honeymoon to any of the places we went to.'

He hung up and went out and got drunk again.

That had been a year earlier. That was the past. He had been forced to face the reality that Susan now belonged to someone else. He had to live in the present. He had work to do. It was time to have a chat with Leslie Mothershed, the photographer who had the photographs and names of the witnesses Robert had been assigned to track down on what was going to be his last assignment.

Chapter Eighteen

Leslie Mothershed was in a state beyond euphoria. The moment he had returned to London, clutching his precious film, he had hurried into the small pantry he had converted into a darkroom and checked to make sure he had everything on hand: film-processing tank, thermometer, spring-type clothes pins, four large beakers, a timer, and developer, stop-bath solutions, and fixer. He turned out the light and switched on a small red overhead lamp. His hands were trembling as he opened the cartridges and removed the film. He took deep breaths to control himself. *Nothing must go wrong this time*, he thought. *Nothing. This is for you, Mother.*

Carefully, he rolled the film into reels. He placed the reels in the tank and filled it with developer, the first of the liquids he would use. It would require a constant temperature of 68°F and periodic agitation. After eleven minutes, he emptied the contents and poured the fixer over the reels.

He was getting nervous again, terrified of making a mistake. He poured off the fixer for the first wash and then let the film sit in a tankful of water for ten minutes. This was followed by two minutes of constant agitation in a hypocleansing agent and twelve more minutes in water. Thirty seconds in photo-flo solution ensured there would be no streaks or flaws in the negatives. Finally, very, very carefully, he removed the film, hung it up with clothes pins, and used a squeegee to remove the last drips from the film. He waited impatiently for the negatives to dry.

It was time to examine the negatives. Holding his breath, heart pounding, Mothershed picked up the first strip of negatives and held it up to the light. *Perfect. Absolutely perfect!*

Each one was a gem, a picture that any photographer in the world would be proud to have taken. Every detail of the strange spacecraft was outlined, including the bodies of the two alien forms lying inside.

Two things he had not noticed before caught Mothershed's eye, and he took a closer look. Where the spaceship had cracked open he could see three narrow couches inside the ship – and yet there were only two aliens. The other thing that was strange was that one of the alien's hands had been severed. It was nowhere to be seen in the photograph.

Maybe the creature had only one hand, Mothershed thought. *My God, these pictures are masterpieces! Mother was right. I'm a genius.* He looked around the tiny room and thought, *The next time I develop my films, it will be in a big, beautiful darkroom in my mansion in Eaton Square.*

He stood there fingering his treasures like a miser fingering his gold. There wasn't a magazine or newspaper in the world that wouldn't kill to get these pictures. All these years the bastards had rejected his photographs, with their insulting little notes. 'Thank you for submitting the photos which we are herewith returning. They do not fit our present needs.' And, 'Thank you for your submission. They are too similar to pictures we have already printed.' Or simply, 'We are returning the photographs you sent us.'

For years he had gone begging to the creeps for jobs, and now they were going to crawl to him, and he was going to make them pay through the nose.

He could not wait. He had to start immediately. Since bloody British Telecom had shut off his phone merely because he happened to be a few weeks late making his last quarterly payment, Mothershed had to go outside to find a phone. On an impulse, he decided to go to Langan's, the celebrity hangout, and treat himself to a much deserved lunch. Langan's was well beyond his means, but if there was ever a time to celebrate, this was it. Wasn't he on the verge of becoming rich and famous?

A maître d' seated Mothershed at a table in a corner of the restaurant, and there, at a booth not ten feet away, he saw two familiar faces. He suddenly realized who they were, and a little thrill ran through him. Michael Caine and Roger Moore, in person! He wished his mother were still alive so he could tell her about it. She had loved reading about movie stars. The two men were laughing and having a good time, not a care in the world, and Mothershed could not help staring. Their glances moved past him. *Smug bastards*, Leslie Mothershed thought angrily. *I suppose they expect me to come over and ask for their autographs. Well, in a few days they're going to be asking for mine. They'll be falling all over themselves to introduce me to their friends. 'Leslie, I want you to meet Charles and Di, and this is Fergie and Andrew. Leslie, you know, is the chap who took those famous photos of the UFOs.'*

When Mothershed finished his lunch, he walked past the two stars, and went upstairs to the phone booth. Directory Inquiries gave him the number of the *Sun*.

'I'd like to speak to your picture editor.'

A male voice came on the line. 'Chapman.'

'What would it be worth to you to have photographs of a UFO with the bodies of two aliens in it?'

The voice at the other end of the phone said, 'If the pictures are good enough, we might run them as an example of a clever hoax, and . . .'

Mothershed said waspishly, 'It so happens that this is no hoax. I have the names of nine reputable witnesses who will testify that it's real . . . including a priest.'

The man's tone changed. 'Oh? And where were these pictures taken?'

'Never mind,' Mothershed said cagily. He was not going to let them trick him into giving away any information. 'Are you interested?'

The voice said cautiously, 'If you can prove that the pictures are authentic, yes, we would be very interested.'

Damn right you would, Mothershed thought gleefully. 'I'll get back to you.' He hung up.

The other two phone calls were just as satisfactory.

Mothershed had to admit to himself that getting the names and addresses of the witnesses had been a stroke of pure genius. There was no way now that anyone could accuse him of trying to perpetrate a fraud. These pictures were going to appear on the front pages of every important newspaper and magazine in the world. *With my credit: Photographs by Leslie Mothershed.*

As Mothershed left the restaurant he could not resist walking up to the booth where the two stars were seated. 'Excuse me, I'm sorry to bother you, but would you give me your autographs?'

Roger Moore and Michael Caine smiled up at him pleasantly. They scribbled their names on pieces of paper and handed them to the photographer.

'Thank you.'

When Leslie Mothershed got outside, he savagely tore up the autographs and threw them away.

Screw them! he thought. *I'm more important than they are.*

Chapter Nineteen

Robert took a taxi to Whitechapel. They drove through the City, the business section of London, heading east until they reached the Whitechapel Road, the area made infamous a century earlier by Jack the Ripper. Along the Whitechapel Road were dozens of outside stalls selling everything from clothing to fresh vegetables, to carpets.

As the taxi neared Mothershed's address, the neighbourhood became more and more dilapidated. Graffiti was scrawled all over the peeling, brownstone buildings. They passed the Weaver's Arms pub. *That would be Mothershed's local*, Robert thought. Another sign read: 'Walker Bookmaker' . . . *Mothershed probably places his bets on horses there.*

They finally reached 213A Grove Road. Robert dismissed the taxi and studied the building in front of him. It was an ugly two-storey building that had been converted into small flats. Inside was the man who had a complete list of the witnesses Robert had been sent to find.

Leslie Mothershed was in the living room, poring over his windfall, when the doorbell rang. He looked up, startled, filled with a sudden inexplicable fear. The ring was repeated. Mothershed scooped up his precious photographs and hurried into the converted darkroom. He slipped the pictures into a pile of old prints, then walked back into the living room and opened the front door. He stared at the stranger who stood there.

'Yes?'

'Leslie Mothershed?'

'That's right. What can I do for you?'

'May I come in?'

'I don't know. What is this about?'

Robert pulled out a Defence Ministry identification card and flashed it. 'I'm here on official business, Mr Mothershed. We can either talk here or at the Ministry.' It was a bluff. But he could see the sudden fear on the photographer's face.

Leslie Mothershed swallowed. 'I don't know what you're talking about, but . . . come in.'

Robert entered the drab room. It was shabby-genteel, dreary, not a place where anyone would live by choice.

'Would you kindly explain what you're doing here?' Mothershed put the proper note of innocent exasperation in his voice.

'I'm here to question you about some photographs you took.'

He knew it! He had known it from the moment he heard the bell. *The bastards are going to try to take my fortune away from me. Well, I'm not going to let them do it.* 'What photographs are you talking about?'

Robert said patiently, 'The ones you took at the site of the UFO crash.'

Mothershed stared at Robert for a moment as though caught by surprise, and then forced a laugh. 'Oh, *those*! I wish I had them to give to you.'

'You *did* take those pictures?'

'I tried.'

'What do you mean . . . you tried?'

'The bloody things never came out.' Mothershed gave a nervous cough. 'My camera fogged. That's the second time that's happened to me.' He was babbling now. 'I even threw out the negatives. They were no good. It was a complete waste of film. And you know how expensive film is these days.'

He's a bad liar, Robert thought. *He's on the edge of panic*. Robert said sympathetically, 'Too bad. Those photographs would have been very helpful.' He said nothing about the list of passengers. If Mothershed lied about the photographs, he would lie about the list. Robert glanced around. The photographs and the list had to be hidden here somewhere. *They shouldn't be difficult to find*. The flat consisted of the small living room, a bedroom, a bathroom and what looked like a door to a utility closet. There was no way he could force the man to hand over the material. He had no real authority. But he wanted those photographs and the list of witnesses before the SIS came and took them away. He needed that list for himself.

'Yes,' Mothershed sighed. 'Those pictures would have been worth a fortune.'

'Tell me about the spaceship,' Robert said.

Mothershed gave an involuntary shudder. The eerie

scene was fixed in his mind forever. 'I'll never forget it,' he said. 'The ship seemed to . . . to pulsate, like it was alive. There was something evil about it. And then there were these two dead aliens inside.'

'Can you tell me anything about the passengers on the bus?'

Sure I can, Mothershed gloated to himself. *I have all their names and addresses.* 'No, I'm afraid I can't.' Mothershed went on, talking to conceal his nervousness. 'The reason I can't help you about the passengers is that I wasn't on that bus. They were all strangers.'

'I see. Well, thank you for your cooperation, Mr Mothershed. I appreciate it. Sorry about your pictures.'

'So am I,' Mothershed said. He watched the door close behind the stranger and thought, happily, *I've done it! I've outsmarted the sonsofbitches.*

Outside in the hall, Robert was examining the lock on the door. A Chubb. And an old model. It would take him seconds to open it. He would start surveillance in the middle of the night and wait for the photographer to leave the flat in the morning. *Once I have the list of passengers in my possession, the rest of the assignment will be simple.*

Robert checked into a small hotel near Mothershed's flat, and telephoned General Hilliard.

'I have the name of the English witness, General.'

'Just a moment. All right. Go ahead, Commander.'

'Leslie Mothershed. He lives in Whitechapel. 213A Grove Road.'

'Excellent. I'll arrange for the British authorities to speak to him.'

Robert did not mention the passenger list or the photographs. Those were his aces in the hole.

Reggie's Fish and Chip Shop was located in a little cul de sac off the Brompton Road. It was a small establishment with a clientele made up mainly of clerks and secretaries who worked in the neighbourhood. Its walls were covered with football posters and the parts that were exposed had not seen fresh paint since the Suez conflict.

The phone behind the counter rang twice before it was answered by a large man dressed in a greasy wool sweater. The man looked like a typical East Ender except for a gold-rimmed monocle fixed tightly in his left eye. The reason for the monocle was apparent to anyone who looked closely at the man – his other eye was made of glass and of a colour blue that was generally seen on travel posters.

'Reggie here.'

'This is the Bishop.'

'Yes, sir,' said Reggie, his voice dropping to a whisper.

'Our client's name is Mothershed. Christian tag Leslie. Resides at 213A Grove Road, E3. We need this order filled quickly. Understood?'

'Consider it done, sir.'

Chapter Twenty

Leslie Mothershed was lost in a golden daydream. He was being interviewed by the world press. They were asking him about the huge castle he had just bought in Scotland, his château in the South of France, his enormous yacht. *'And is it true that the Queen has invited you to become the official Royal photographer?' 'Yes. I said I would let her know. And now, ladies and gentlemen, if you will all excuse me, I'm late for my show at the BBC...'*

His reverie was interrupted by the sound of the doorbell. He looked at his watch. Eleven o'clock. *Has that man returned?* He walked over to the door and cautiously opened it. In the doorway stood a man shorter than Mothershed (that was the first thing he noticed about him) with thick glasses and a thin, sallow face.

'Excuse me,' the man said diffidently. 'I apologize for disturbing you at this hour. I live just down the block. The sign outside says you're a photographer.'

'So?'

'Do you do passport photos?'

Leslie Mothershed do passport photos? The man who was about to own the world? That would be like asking Michelangelo to paint the bathroom.

'No,' he said, rudely. He started to close the door.

'I really hate to bother you, but I'm in a terrible jam. My plane leaves for Tokyo at eight o'clock in the morning and a little while ago when I took out my passport, I saw that somehow my photograph had been torn loose. It's missing. I've looked everywhere. They won't let me on the plane without a passport photo.' The little man was near tears.

'I'm sorry,' Mothershed said. 'I can't help you.'

'I'd be willing to pay you a hundred pounds.'

A hundred pounds? To a man with a castle and a château and a yacht? It was an insult.

The pathetic little man was going on. 'I could go even higher. Two hundred or three hundred. You see, I really must be on that plane or I'll lose my job.'

Three hundred pounds to take a passport picture? Forgetting the developing, it would take about ten seconds. Mothershed began to calculate. That came to eighteen hundred pounds a minute. Eighteen hundred pounds a minute was one hundred and eight thousand pounds an hour. If he worked an eight-hour day, that would be eight hundred and sixty-four thousand pounds a day. In one week that would come to . . .

'Will you do it?'

Mothershed's ego jockeyed with his greed, and greed won out. *I can use a bit of pocket money.*

'Come in,' Mothershed said. 'Stand against that wall.'

'Thank you. I really appreciate this.'

Mothershed wished he had a Polaroid camera. That would have made it so simple. He picked up his Vivitar and said, 'Hold still.'

Ten seconds later it was done.

'It will take a while to develop it,' Mothershed said. 'If you come back in . . .'

'If you don't mind, I'll wait.'

'Suit yourself.'

Mothershed took the camera into the darkroom, put it into the black bag, turned out the overhead light, switched on the red light and removed the film. He would do this in a hurry. Passport pictures always looked terrible, anyway. Fifteen minutes later, as Mothershed was timing the film in the developer tanks, he began to smell smoke. He paused. Was it his imagination? No. The smell was getting stronger. He turned to open the door. It seemed to be stuck. Mothershed pushed against it. It held fast.

'Hello,' he called out. 'What's happening out there?'

There was no response.

'Hello?' He pressed his shoulder against the door, but there seemed to be something heavy on the other side of it, keeping it closed. 'Mister?'

There was no answer. The only sound he could hear was a loud crackling noise. The smell of smoke was becoming overpowering. The flat was on fire. *That was probably why the man had left. He must have gone to get help.* Leslie Mothershed slammed his shoulder against the door, but it would not budge. 'Help!' he screamed. 'Get me out of here!'

Smoke was starting to pour under the door, and Mothershed could feel the heat of the flames beginning to lick at it. It was getting difficult to breathe. He was starting to choke. He tore at his collar, gasping for air. His lungs were burning. He was beginning to lose consciousness. He sank down on his knees. 'Oh, God, please don't let me die now. Not now that I'm going to be rich and famous...'

'Reggie here.'
'Was the order filled?'
'Yes, sir. A bit overcooked but delivered on time.'
'Excellent.'

When Robert arrived at Grove Road at two o'clock in the morning, to begin his surveillance, he was confronted with an enormous traffic jam. The street was filled with official vehicles, a fire engine, ambulances and three police cars. Robert pushed his way through the crowd of bystanders and hurried over to the centre of activity. The whole building had been engulfed by the fire. From the outside he could see that the first-floor flat occupied by the photographer had been completely gutted.

'How did it happen?' Robert asked a fireman.
'We don't know yet. Stand back, please.'
'My cousin lives in that flat. Is he all right?'
'I'm afraid not.' His tone became sympathetic. 'They're just taking him out of the building now.'

Robert watched as two ambulance attendants pushed a stretcher carrying a body into the ambulance.

'I was staying with him,' Robert said. 'All my clothes are in there. I'd like to go in and...'

The fireman shook his head. 'It wouldn't do you any good, sir. There's nothing left of the flat but ashes.'

Nothing left but ashes. Including the photographs

and the precious list of passengers with their names and addresses.

So much for fucking serendipity, Robert thought bitterly.

In Washington, Dustin Thornton was having lunch with his father-in-law, in Willard Stone's offices, in his lavish private dining room. Dustin Thornton was nervous. He was always nervous in the presence of his powerful father-in-law.

Willard Stone was in a good mood. 'I had dinner with the President last evening. He told me that he's very pleased with your work, Dustin.'

'I'm very gratified.'

'You're doing a fine job. You're helping to protect us against the hordes.'

'The hordes?'

'Those who would try to bring this great country to its knees. But it is not just the enemy outside the walls we have to beware of. It is those who pretend to be serving our country, who fail to do their duty. Those who do not carry out their orders.'

'The mavericks.'

'That's right, Dustin. The mavericks. They must be punished. If . . .'

A man walked into the room. 'Excuse me, Mr Stone. The gentlemen have arrived. They're waiting for you.'

'Yes.' Stone turned to his son-in-law. 'Finish your lunch, Dustin. I have something important to take care of. One day, I may be able to tell you about it.'

Chapter Twenty-One

The streets of Zürich were filled with weird-looking creatures with odd shapes, misshapen giants with large, grotesque bodies and tiny eyes, with skin the colour of boiled fish. They were meat eaters, and she hated the fetid smells they exuded from their bodies. Some of the females wore animal skins, the remains of the creatures they had murdered. She was still stunned by the terrible accident that had taken away the life essence of her companions.

She had been on earth for four cycles of what these beings called *luna*, and she had not eaten in all that time. She was faint from thirst. The only water she had been able to drink was the fresh rain water in the farmer's trough, and it had not rained since the night she arrived. The other water on earth was undrinkable. She had gone into an alien feeding place, but she had been unable to stand the stench. She had tried to eat their raw vegetables and fruit, but they were tasteless, not like the succulent food at home.

She was called the Graceful One, and she was tall and stately and beautiful, with luminous green eyes. She had adopted the appearance of an Earthling after she left the site of the crash, and she walked through the crowds unnoticed.

She was seated at a table in a hard, uncomfortable

chair that had been built for the human body, and she read the minds of the creatures around her.

Two of the beings were seated at a table near her. One was speaking aloud. 'It's the chance of a lifetime, Franz! For fifty thousand francs you can get in at the start. You've got fifty thousand francs, haven't you?' She read the loud thoughts in his head. *Come on, you swine. I need the commission.*

'Sure, but I don't know . . .' *I'll have to borrow it from my wife.*

'Have I ever given you bad investment advice?' *Make up your mind.*

'It's a lot of money.' *She'll never give it to me.*

'What about the potential? There's a chance to make millions.' *Say yes.*

'All right. I'm in.' *Maybe I can sell some of her jewellery.*

I have him! 'You'll never regret it, Franz.' *He can always take a tax loss.*

The Graceful One had no idea what the conversation meant.

At the far end of the restaurant, a man and woman were seated at a table. They were talking in low voices. She stretched her mind to hear them.

'Jesus Christ!' the man said. 'How the hell could you get pregnant?' *You stupid bitch!*

'How do you think I got pregnant?' *Your cock did it!*

Pregnant was how these beings gestated, procreating clumsily with their genitals, like their animals in the fields.

174

'What are you going to do about it, Tina?' *You've got to get an abortion.*

'What do you expect me to do? You said you were going to tell your wife about me.' *You lying bastard.*

'Look, honey, I am, but this is a bad time.' *I was crazy to ever get involved with you. I should have known you were trouble.*

'It's a bad time for me, too, Paul. I don't even think you love me.' *Please tell me you do.*

'Of course I love you. It's just that my wife is going through a rough period right now.' *I don't intend to lose her.*

'I'm going through a rough period right now, too. Don't you understand? I'm having your baby.' *And you're damn well going to marry me.* Water was coming from her eyes.

'Calm down, honey. I tell you, everything is going to be fine. I want the baby as much as you do.' *I'll have to talk her into an abortion.*

At a table next to them, a male creature was seated alone.

They promised me. They said the race was fixed, that I couldn't lose, and like a fool, I turned all my money over to them. I've got to find a way to put it back before the auditors come. I couldn't stand it if they put me in jail. I'll kill myself first. I swear to God, I'll kill myself.

At another table, a male and female were in the middle of a discussion.

'... it's nothing like that. It's just that I've got this beautiful chalet in the mountains and I thought it would be good for you to get away for a weekend and relax.' *We'll spend a lot of time relaxing in my bed, chérie.*

'I don't know, Claude. I've never gone away with a man before.' *I wonder if he believes that.*

'*Oui*, but this is not a sex thing. I just thought of the chalet because you said you needed a rest. You can think of me as your brother.' *And we will try some good, old-fashioned incest.*

The Graceful One was unaware that the various people were speaking in different languages, for she was able to filter them all through her consciousness and understand what they were saying.

I must find a way to get in touch with the mothership, she thought. She took out the small, hand-held silver coloured transmitter. It was a divided neuro-net system, half of it consisting of living organic material and the other half a metallic compound from another galaxy. The organic material contained thousands of single cells, so that as they died off, others would multiply, keeping the connections constant. Unfortunately, the dilitheum crystal that activated the transmitter had broken off, and was lost. She had tried to communicate with her ship, but the transmitter was useless without it.

She tried to eat another leaf of lettuce but she could no longer stand the stench. She rose and started toward the door. The cashier called out after her, 'Just a minute, miss. You haven't paid for your meal.'

'I'm sorry. I do not have your medium of exchange.'

'You can tell that to the police authorities.'

The Graceful One stared into the cashier's eyes,

and watched her go limp. She turned and walked out of the feeding place.

I must find the crystal. They are waiting to hear from me. She had to concentrate to focus her senses. But everything seemed blurred and distorted. Without water, she knew she was going to die soon.

Chapter Twenty-Two

DAY FIVE
Bern, Switzerland

Robert had come to a dead end. He had not realized how much he had counted on obtaining Mothershed's list of names. *Up in smoke*, Robert thought. *Literally*. The trail was cold now. *I should have gotten the list when I was in Mothershed's flat. That will teach me to . . . teach*. Of course! A thought that had been in the back of his mind suddenly came into focus. Hans Beckerman had said, *Affenarsch! All the other passengers were excited about seeing the UFO and those dead creatures in it, but this old man kept complaining about how we had to hurry up to get to Bern because he had to prepare some lecture for the University*. It was a long shot, but it was all Robert had.

He rented a car at the Bern airport and headed for the University. He turned off Rathausgasse, the main street of Bern, and drove to Länggass-Strasse, where the University of Bern was located. The University is composed of several buildings, the main one a large four-storey stone building with two wings, and large stone gargoyles adorning the roof. At each end of the courtyard in front of the building are glass skylights over classrooms, and at the rear of the University is a large park overlooking the Aare River.

Robert walked up the front steps of the Administration Building and entered the reception hall. The only information Beckerman had given him was that the passenger was German, and that he was preparing his lecture for Monday.

A student directed him to the Office of the Administration. The woman seated behind the desk was a formidable figure. She had on a severely tailored suit, black-framed spectacles, and she wore her hair in a bun. She looked up as Robert entered her office.

'*Bitte?*'

Robert pulled out an identification card. 'Interpol. I'm conducting an investigation, and I would appreciate your cooperation, Miss . . .'

'Frau. Frau Schreiber. What kind of investigation?'

'I'm looking for a professor.'

She frowned. 'His name?'

'I don't know.'

'You do not know his name?'

'No. He's a visiting professor. He gave a lecture here a few days ago. *Montag.*'

'Many visiting professors come here every day to give lectures. What is his discipline?'

'I beg your pardon?'

'What does he teach?' Her tone was growing impatient. 'What subject did he lecture on?'

'I don't know.'

She let her exasperation show. '*Tut mir leid*. I can't help you. And I am too busy for frivolous questions like this . . .' She started to turn away.

'Oh, it's not frivolous,' Robert assured her. '*Es ist sehr dringend.*' He leaned forward and said, in a low voice, 'I'm going to have to take you into my confidence. The professor we're looking for is involved in a prostitution ring.'

Frau Schreiber's mouth made a small 'o' of surprise.

'Interpol has been on his trail for months. The current information we have on him is that he is German and that he gave a lecture here on the fifteenth of this month.' He straightened up. 'If you don't want to help, we can conduct an official investigation of the University. Of course, the publicity . . .'

'*Nein, nein!*' she said. 'The University must not be involved in anything like this.' She looked worried. 'You say he lectured here on – what day?'

'The fifteenth. Monday.'

Frau Schreiber rose and walked over to a filing cabinet. She pulled it open and scanned some papers. She extracted several sheets from a folder. 'Here we are. There were three guest professors who gave lectures here on the fifteenth.'

'The man I want is German.'

'These are all German,' Frau Schreiber said stiffly. She shuffled the papers in her hand. 'One of the lectures was on economics, one on chemistry and one on psychology.'

'May I see those?'

Reluctantly, she handed the reports to Robert.

He studied the sheets. Each one had a name written down with a home address and a telephone number.

'I can make a copy of these for you, if you wish.'

'No, thank you.' He had already memorized the names and numbers. 'None of these is the man I'm looking for.'

Frau Schreiber gave a sigh of relief. 'Well, thank God for that. Prostitution! We would never be involved in such a thing.'

'I'm sorry I troubled you for nothing.' Robert left and headed for a telephone booth in town.

The first telephone call was to Berlin. 'Professor Streubel?'

'*Ja.*'

'This is the Sunshine Tours Bus Company. You left a pair of glasses on our bus last Sunday when you were touring with us in Switzerland and . . .'

'I do not know what you are speaking about.' He sounded annoyed.

'You were in Switzerland on the fourteenth, were you not, Professor?'

'No. On the fifteenth. To give a lecture at the University of Bern.'

'And you did not take our bus tour?'

'I have no time for such foolishness. I'm a busy man.' And the professor hung up.

The second call was to Hamburg. 'Professor Heinrich?'

'This is Professor Heinrich.'

'This is the Sunshine Tours Bus Company. You were in Switzerland on the fourteenth of this month?'

'Why do you wish to know?'

'Because we found a briefcase of yours on one of our buses, Professor, and . . .'

'You have the wrong person. I have been on no tour buses.'

'You did not take a tour of ours to the Jungfrau?'

'I just told you, no.'

'I'm sorry to have bothered you.'

The third call was to Munich. 'Professor Otto Schmidt?'

'Yes.'

'Professor Schmidt, this is the Sunshine Tours Bus Company. We have a pair of your glasses that you left on our bus a few days ago, and . . .'

'There must be some mistake.'

Robert's heart sank. He had struck out. There was nowhere left to go.

The voice went on. 'I have my glasses here. I have not lost them.'

Robert's spirits soared. 'Are you sure, Professor? You *were* on the Jungfrau trip on the fourteenth, were you not?'

'Yes, yes, but I told you, I have not lost anything.'

'Thank you very much, Professor.' Robert replaced the receiver. *Jackpot!*

Robert dialled another number and within two minutes he was speaking with General Hilliard.

'I have two things to report,' Robert said. 'The witness in London I told you about?'

'Yes?'

'He died in a fire last night.'

'Really? Too bad.'

'Yes, sir. But I believe I've located another witness. I'll let you know as soon as I check him out.'

'I'll wait to hear from you, Commander.'

General Hilliard was reporting to Janus.

'Commander Bellamy has located another witness.'

'Good. The group is getting restless. Everyone is worried that this story will surface before SDI is operational.'

'I'll have more information for you soon.'

'I don't want information, I want results.'

'Yes, Janus.'

Plattenstrasse, in Munich, is a quiet residential street with drab brownstone buildings huddled together as though for protection. Number five was identical to its neighbours. Inside the vestibule was a row of mailboxes. A small card below one of them read 'Professor Otto Schmidt'. Robert rang the bell.

The apartment door was opened by a tall, thin man with an untidy mop of white hair. He was wearing a tattered sweater and smoking a pipe. Robert wondered whether he had created the image of an archetypical college professor, or whether the image had created him.

'Professor Schmidt?'

'Yes?'

'I wonder if I might talk to you a moment. I'm with . . .'

'We have already talked,' Professor Schmidt said.

'You are the man who telephoned me this morning. I am an expert at recognizing voices. Come in.'

'Thank you.' Robert entered the living room. The walls were crowded from floor to ceiling with bookcases filled with hundreds of volumes. Books were stacked everywhere; on tables, on the floor, on chairs. The sparse furniture in the room seemed to be an afterthought.

'You're not with any Swiss tour bus company, are you?'

'Well, I . . .'

'You are American.'

'Yes.'

'And this visit has nothing to do with my lost glasses that were not lost.'

'Well . . . no, sir.'

'You are interested in the UFO I saw. It was a very upsetting experience. I always believed they might exist, but I never thought I would see one.'

'It must have been a terrible shock.'

'It was.'

'Can you tell me anything about it?'

'It was . . . it was almost alive. There was a kind of shimmering light around it. Blue. No, maybe more of a grey. I . . . I'm not sure.'

He remembered Mandel's description: *It kept changing colours. It looked blue . . . then green.*

'It had broken open, and I could see two bodies inside. Small . . . big eyes. They were wearing some kind of silver suit.'

'Is there anything you can tell me about your fellow passengers?'

'My fellow passengers on the bus?'

'Yes.'

The professor shrugged. 'I know nothing of them. They were all strangers. I was concentrating on a lecture I was going to give the next morning, and I paid very little attention to the other passengers.'

Robert watched his face, waiting.

'If it will help you any,' the professor said, 'I can tell you what countries some of them came from. I teach chemistry, but the study of phonetics is my hobby.'

'Anything you can remember would be appreciated.'

'There was an Italian priest, a Hungarian, an American with a Texan accent, an Englishman, a Russian girl . . .'

'Russian?'

'Yes. But she was not from Moscow. From her accent, I would say Kiev, or very near there.'

Robert waited, but there was only silence. 'You didn't hear any of them mention their names or talk about their professions?'

'I'm sorry. I told you, I was thinking about my lecture: it was difficult to concentrate. The Texan and the priest sat together. The Texan never stopped talking. It was very distracting. I don't know how much the priest even understood.'

'The priest . . .'

'He had a Roman accent.'

'Can you tell me anything more about any of them?'

The professor shrugged. 'I'm afraid not.' He took

another puff of his pipe. 'I'm sorry I can't be of any help to you.'

A sudden thought came to Robert. 'You said you're a chemist?'

'Yes.'

'I wonder if you would mind taking a look at something, Professor.' Robert reached in his pocket and pulled out the piece of metal Beckerman had given him. 'Can you tell me what this is?'

Professor Schmidt took the object in his hand, and as he examined it, his expression changed. 'Where . . . where did you get this?'

'I'm afraid I can't say. Do you know what it is?'

'It appears to be part of a transmitting device.'

'Are you sure?'

He turned it over in his hand. 'The crystal is dilitheum. It's very rare. See these notches here? They suggest that this fits into a larger unit. The metal itself is . . . My God, I've never seen anything like it!' His voice was charged with excitement. 'Can you let me have this for a few days? I would like to do some spectrographic studies on it.'

'I'm afraid that's impossible,' Robert said.

'But . . .'

'Sorry.' Robert took back the piece of metal.

The professor tried to conceal his disappointment. 'Perhaps you can bring it back. Why don't you give me your card? If I think of anything more, I'll call you.'

Robert fumbled in his pockets for a moment. 'I don't seem to have any of my cards with me.'

Professor Schmidt said slowly, 'Yes, I thought not.'

'Commander Bellamy is on the line.'

General Hilliard picked up the telephone. 'Yes, Commander?'

'The latest witness's name is Professor Schmidt. He lives at Plattenstrasse 5 in Munich.'

'Thank you, Commander. I'll notify the German authorities immediately.'

Robert was on the verge of saying, 'I'm afraid that's the last witness I'll be able to find,' but something held him back. He hated to admit failure. And yet, the trail had become cold. A Texan and a priest. The priest was from Rome. Period. Along with a million other priests. And there was no way to identify him. *I have a choice*, Robert thought. *I can give up and go back to Washington, or I can go to Rome and give it one last try . . .*

Bundesverfassungsschutzamt, the headquarters of the Office for the Protection of the Constitution, is located in central Berlin on Neumarkterstrasse. It is a large, grey, nondescript building, indistinguishable from the buildings around it. Inside, on the second floor, in the conference room, the chief of the department, Inspector Otto Joachim, was studying a message. He read it twice, then reached for the red telephone on his desk.

DAY SIX
Munich, Germany

The following morning, as Otto Schmidt headed for his chemistry lab, he was thinking about the conversation he had had with the American the evening before. Where could that piece of metal have come from? It was astonishing, beyond anything in his experience. And the American puzzled him. *He said he was interested in the passengers on the bus. Why? Because they had all been witnesses to the flying saucer? Were they going to be warned not to talk? If so, why had not the American warned him? There was something strange going on,* the professor decided. He entered the laboratory and took off his jacket and hung it up. He put on an apron to keep his clothes from getting soiled and walked over to the table where he had been working for many weeks on a chemical experiment. *If this works,* he thought, *it could mean a Nobel prize.* He lifted the beaker of sterile water and started to pour it into a container filled with a yellow liquid. *That's strange. I don't remember it being such a bright yellow.*

The roar of the explosion was tremendous. The laboratory erupted in a gigantic blast, and pieces of glass and human flesh spattered the walls.

**FLASH MESSAGE
TOP SECRET ULTRA
BFV TO DEPUTY DIRECTOR NSA
EYES ONLY
COPY ONE OF (ONE) COPY
SUBJECT: OPERATION
DOOMSDAY
4. OTTO SCHMIDT – TERMINATED
END OF MESSAGE**

Robert missed the news of the professor's death. He was aboard an Alitalia plane, on his way to Rome.

Chapter Twenty-Three

Dustin Thornton was getting restless. He had power now, and it was like a drug. He wanted more. His father-in-law, Willard Stone, kept promising to bring him into some mysterious inner circle, but so far, he had failed to fulfil that promise.

It was by pure chance that Thornton learned that his father-in-law disappeared every Friday. Thornton had called to have lunch with him.

'I'm sorry,' Willard Stone's personal secretary said, 'but Mr Stone is away for the day.'

'Oh, too bad. What about lunch next Friday?'

'I'm sorry, Mr Thornton. Mr Stone will be away next Friday, also.'

Strange. And it became even stranger, because when Thornton called two weeks later, he received the same reply. *Where did the old man disappear to every Friday?* He was not a golfer, or a man to indulge in any hobbies.

The obvious answer was a woman. Willard Stone's wife was very social and very rich. She was an imperious woman, almost as strong in her way as her husband. She was not the sort of woman who would tolerate her husband having an affair. *If he is having an affair,* Thornton thought, *I've got him by the balls.* He knew he had to find out.

With all the facilities at his command, Dustin Thornton could have found out very quickly what his father-in-law was up to, but Thornton was no fool. He was well aware that if he made one misstep, he would be in big trouble. Willard Stone was not the kind of man to brook any interference in his life. Thornton decided to investigate the matter himself.

At five a.m., on the following Friday, Dustin Thornton was slumped behind the wheel of an inconspicuous Ford Taurus, half a block from Willard Stone's imposing mansion. It was a cold, miserable dawn, and Thornton kept asking himself what he was doing there. There was probably some perfectly reasonable explanation for Stone's odd behaviour. *I'm wasting my time*, Thornton thought. But something kept him there.

At seven o'clock, the driveway gates opened and a car appeared. Willard Stone was at the wheel. Instead of his usual limousine, he was in a small, black van used by the household staff. A feeling of exultation spread through Thornton. He knew he was on to something. People lived according to their pattern, and Stone was breaking the pattern. It *had* to be another woman.

Driving carefully, and staying well behind the van, Thornton followed his father-in-law through the streets of Washington to the road that led to Arlington.

I'll have to handle this very delicately, Thornton thought. *I don't want to push him too hard. I'll get all the information I can about his mistress, and then I'll confront him with it. I'll tell him my only interest is in protecting him. He'll get the message. The last thing he wants is a public scandal.*

Dustin Thornton was so wrapped up in his own thoughts that he almost missed the turn that Willard Stone had taken. They were in an exclusive residential district. The black van abruptly disappeared up a long, tree-shaded driveway.

Dustin Thornton stopped the car, deciding the best way to proceed. Should he face Willard Stone with his infidelity now? Or should he wait until Stone left and then talk to the woman first? Or should he quietly gather all the information he needed, and then have a talk with his father-in-law? He decided to reconnoitre.

Thornton parked his car on a side street and walked around to the alley at the back of the two-storey house. A wooden fence blocked off the back of the yard, but that was no problem. Thornton opened the gate, and stepped inside. He was facing huge, beautiful, manicured grounds with the house at the rear.

He moved quietly in the shadow of the trees that lined the lawn, and stood at the back door, deciding what his next move should be. He needed proof of what was going on. Without it, the old man would laugh at him. Whatever was happening inside at this moment could be the key to his future. He had to find out.

Very gently, Thornton tried the back door. It was unlocked. He slipped inside, and found himself in a large, old-fashioned kitchen. There was no one around. Thornton moved toward the service door, and pushed it open slightly. He was facing a large reception hall. At the far end was a closed door that could have led to a library. Thornton walked toward it, moving quietly. He stood there, listening. There was no sign of life in the house. *The old man was probably upstairs in the bedroom.*

Thornton walked toward the closed door and opened it. He stood in the doorway, staring. There were a dozen men seated in the room around a large table.

'Come in, Dustin,' Willard Stone said. 'We've been expecting you.'

Chapter Twenty-Four

Rome proved to be difficult for Robert, an emotional ordeal that drained him. He had honeymooned there with Susan, and the memories were overpowering. Rome was Roberto, who managed the Hassler Hotel for his mother, and who was partially deaf but could lip-read in five languages. Rome was the gardens of Villa d'Este in Tivoli, and the Ristorante Sibilla and Susan's delight at the one hundred fountains created by the son of Lucrezia Borgia. Rome was Otello at the bottom of the Spanish Steps, and the Vatican, and the Colosseum and the Forum and Michelangelo's Moses. Rome was sharing *tartufi* at Tre Scalini and the sound of Susan's laughter, and her voice saying, 'Please promise me we'll always be this happy, Robert.'

What the hell am I doing here? Robert wondered. *I don't have any idea who the priest is, or whether he's even in Rome. It's time to retire, to go home and forget all this.*

But something inside him, some stubborn streak inherited from a long-dead ancestor, would not let him. *I'll give it one day*, Robert decided. *Just one more day.*

*

The Leonardo da Vinci airport was crowded, and it seemed to Robert that every other person was a priest. He was looking for one priest in a city of — what? Fifty thousand priests? A hundred thousand? In the taxi on the way to the Hassler Hotel, he noticed crowds of robed priests on the streets. *This is impossible*, Robert thought. *I must be out of my mind.*

He was greeted in the lobby of the Hassler Hotel by the assistant manager.

'Commander Bellamy! What a pleasure to see you again.'

'Thank you, Pietro. Do you have a room for me for one night?'

'For you — of course. Always!'

Robert was escorted to a room he had occupied before.

'If there's anything you need, Commander, please...'

I need a bloody miracle, Robert thought. He sat down on the bed and lay back, trying to clear his mind.

Why would a priest from Rome travel to Switzerland? There were several possibilities. He might have gone on vacation, or there might have been a convocation of priests. He was the only priest on the tour bus. What did that signify? Nothing. Except, perhaps, that he was not travelling with a group. So it could have been a trip to visit his friends or family. Or maybe he *was* with a group, and they had other plans that day. Robert's thoughts were going around in a futile circle.

Back to the beginning. How did the priest get to

Switzerland? The chances are pretty good that he doesn't own a car. Someone could have given him a lift, but more probably he travelled by plane or train or took a bus. If he were on vacation, he wouldn't have a lot of time. So let's assume he took a plane. That line of reasoning led nowhere. Airlines did not list the occupations of their passengers. The priest would be yet another name on the passenger manifest. But if he were part of a group . . .

The Vatican, the official residence of the Pope, rises majestically on Vatican Hill, on the west bank of the Tiber, in the northwest end of Rome. The dome of St Peter's Basilica, designed by Michelangelo, towers over the huge piazza, filled day and night with avid sightseers of all faiths.

The piazza is surrounded by two semicircular colonnades completed in 1667 by Bernini, with 284 columns of travertine marble placed in four rows and surmounted by a balustrade on which stand 140 statues. Robert had visited there a dozen times, but each time the sight took his breath away.

The interior of the Vatican, of course, was even more spectacular. The Sistine Chapel and the museum and the Sala Rotonda were indescribably beautiful.

But on this day, Robert had not come here to sightsee.

He found the Office of Public Relations for the Vatican in the wing of the building devoted to secular affairs. The young man behind the desk was polite.

'May I help you?'

Robert flashed an identification card. 'I'm with *Time* magazine. I'm doing an article on some priests who attended a convocation in Switzerland in the past week or two. I'm looking for background information.'

The man studied him for a moment, then frowned. 'We had some priests attend a convocation in Venice last month. None of our priests was in Switzerland recently. I'm sorry, I'm afraid I can't help you.'

'It's really very important,' Robert said earnestly. 'How would I go about getting that information?'

'The group you are looking for . . . what branch of the Church do they represent?'

'I beg your pardon?'

'There are many Roman Catholic Orders. There are Franciscans, Marists, Benedictines, Trappists, Jesuits, Dominicans, and several others. I suggest you go to the Order they belong to and inquire there.'

Where the hell is 'there'? Robert wondered. 'Do you have any other suggestions?'

'I'm afraid not.'

Neither have I, Robert thought. *I found the haystack. I can't find the needle.*

He left the Vatican and wandered through the streets of Rome, heedless of the people around him, concentrating on his problem. At the Piazza del Popolo, he sat down at an outdoor café and ordered a Cinzano. It sat in front of him, untouched.

For all he knew, the priest could still be in Switzerland. *What Order does he belong to? I don't know. And I have only the professor's word that he was Roman.*

He took a sip of his drink.

There was a late afternoon plane to Washington. *I'm going to be on it*, Robert decided. *I give up*. The thought galled him. *Out, not with a bang, but with a whimper*. It was time to leave.

'Il conto, per favore.'

'Si, signore.'

Robert's eyes swept idly around the piazza. Across from the café, a bus was loading passengers. In the line were two priests. Robert watched as the passengers paid their fares and moved toward the back of the bus. When the priests reached the conductor, they smiled at him and took their seats without paying.

'Your check, *signore*,' the waiter said.

Robert didn't even hear him. His mind was racing. Here, in the heart of the Catholic Church, priests had certain privileges. It was possible, just possible . . .

The offices of Swissair are located at 10 Via Po, five minutes from the Via Veneto. Robert was greeted by a man behind the counter.

'May I see the manager, please?'

'I am the manager. Can I help you?'

Robert flashed an identification card. 'Michael Hudson. Interpol.'

'What can I do for you, Mr Hudson?'

'Some international carriers are complaining about illegal price discounting in Europe – in Rome, particularly. According to international convention . . .'

'Excuse me, Mr Hudson, but Swissair does not give discounts. Everyone pays the posted fares.'

'Everyone?'

'With the exception of employees of the airline, of course.'

'Don't you have a discount for priests?'

'No. On this airline, they pay full fare.'

On this airline. 'Thank you for your time.' And Robert was gone.

His next stop – and his last hope – was Alitalia. 'Illegal discounts?' The manager was staring at Robert, puzzled. 'We give discounts only to our employees.'

'Don't you give discounts to priests?'

The manager's face brightened. 'Ah, that, yes. But that is not illegal. We have arrangements with the Catholic Church.'

Robert's heart soared. 'So, if a priest wanted to fly from Rome, say – to Switzerland, he would use this airline?'

'Well, it would be cheaper for him. Yes.'

Robert said, 'In order to bring our computers up-to-date, it would be helpful if you could tell me how many priests have flown to Switzerland in the past two weeks. You would have a record of that, wouldn't you?'

'Yes, of course. For tax purposes.'

'I would really appreciate that information.'

'You wish to know how many priests have flown to Switzerland in the past two weeks?'

'Yes. Zürich or Geneva.'

'Just a moment. I will talk to our computers.'

Five minutes later, the manager returned with a computer printout. 'There was only one priest who flew Alitalia to Switzerland in the past two weeks.'

He consulted the printout. 'He left Rome on the seventh, and flew to Zürich. His return flight was booked for two days ago.'

Robert took a deep breath. 'His name?'

'Father Romero Patrini.'

'His address?'

He looked down at the paper again. 'He lives in Orvieto. If you need any further . . .' He looked up. Robert was gone.

Chapter Twenty-Five

DAY SEVEN
Orvieto, Italy

He stopped the car on a hairpin bend on Route S-71, and there across the valley, high on a rise of volcanic rock, was a breathtaking view of the city. It was an ancient Etruscan centre, with a world-famous cathedral, and half a dozen churches, and a priest who had witnessed the crash of a UFO.

The town was untouched by time, with cobblestone streets and lovely old buildings, and an open-air market where farmers came to sell their fresh vegetables and chickens.

Robert found a parking place in the Piazza del Duomo, across from the cathedral, and went inside. The enormous interior was deserted except for an elderly priest who was just leaving the altar.

'Excuse me, Father,' Robert said. 'I'm looking for a priest from this town who was in Switzerland last week. Perhaps you . . .'

The priest drew back, his face hostile. 'I cannot discuss this.'

Robert looked at him in surprise. 'I don't understand. I just want to find . . .'

'He is not of this church. He is from the church of

San Giovenale.' And the priest hurried past Robert. *Why was he so unfriendly?*

The church of San Giovenale was in the Quartiere Vecchio, a colourful area with medieval towers and churches. A young priest was tending the garden next to it. He looked up as Robert approached.

'*Buon giorno, signore.*'

'Good morning. I'm looking for a priest who was in Switzerland last week. He . . .'

'Yes, yes. Poor Father Patrini. It was a terrible, terrible thing that happened to him.'

'I don't understand. What terrible thing?'

'Seeing the devil's chariot. It was more than he could stand. The poor man had a nervous breakdown.'

'I'm sorry to hear that,' Robert said. 'Where is he now? I would like to talk to him.'

'He's in the hospital near the Piazza di San Patrizin, but I doubt if the doctors will allow anyone to see him.'

Robert stood there, troubled. A man suffering a nervous breakdown was not going to be much help. 'I see. Thank you very much.'

The hospital was an unpretentious one-storey building, near the outskirts of the city. He parked the car and walked into the small lobby. There was a nurse behind the reception desk.

'Good morning,' Robert said. 'I would like to see Father Patrini.'

'*Mi scusi, ma* ... that is impossible. He cannot speak with anyone.'

Robert was determined not to be stopped now. He had to follow up the lead Professor Schmidt had given him. 'You don't understand,' Robert said smoothly. 'Father Patrini *asked* to see me. I've come to Orvieto at his request.'

'He *asked* to see you?'

'Yes. He wrote to me in America. I've come all this way just to see him.'

The nurse hesitated. 'I do not know what to say. He is very ill. *Molto.*'

'I'm sure it would cheer him up to see me.'

'The doctor is not here ...' She made a decision. 'Very well. You may go into his room, *signore*, but you may only stay a few minutes.'

'That's all I'll need,' Robert said.

'This way, *per piacere.*'

They walked down a short corridor with small, neat rooms on either side. The nurse led Robert to one of the doors.

'Only a few minutes, *signore*.'

'*Grazie.*'

Robert entered the little room. The man in the bed looked like a pale shadow lying on the white sheets. Robert approached him and said softly, 'Father ...'

The priest turned to look up at him and Robert had never seen such agony in a man's eyes.

'Father, my name is ...'

He grabbed Robert's arm. 'Help me,' the priest mumbled. 'You must help me. My faith is gone. All my life I have preached of God and the Holy Spirit and now I know that there is no God. There is only the devil and he has come for us . . .'

'Father, if you . . .'

'I saw it with my own eyes. There were two of them in the devil's chariot, but, oh, there will be more! Others will come! Wait and see. We are all doomed to hell.'

'Father – listen to me. What you saw was not the devil. It was a space vehicle that . . .'

The priest let go of Robert and looked at him with sudden clarity. 'Who are you? What do you want?'

Robert said, 'I'm a friend. I came here to ask you about the bus trip you took in Switzerland.'

'The bus. I wish I had never gone near it.' The priest was becoming agitated again.

Robert hated to press him, but he had no choice.

'You sat next to a man on that bus. A Texan. You had a long conversation with him, remember?'

'A conversation. The Texan. Yes, I remember.'

'Did he mention where he lived in Texas?'

'Yes, I remember him. He was from America.'

'Yes. From Texas. Did he tell you where his home was?'

'Yes, yes. He told me.'

'Where, Father? Where is his home?'

'Texas. He talked of Texas.'

Robert nodded encouragingly. 'That's right.'

'I saw them with my own eyes. I wish God had blinded me. I . . .'

'Father – the man from Texas. Did he say where he was from? Did he mention a name?'

'Texas, yes. The Ponderosa.'

Robert tried again. 'That's on television. This was a real man. He sat next to you on...'

The priest was becoming delirious again. 'They're coming! Armageddon is here. The Bible lies! It is the devil who will invade the earth.' He was shouting loudly now. 'Look out! Look out! I can see them!'

The nurse came hurrying in. She looked at Robert reprovingly. 'You will have to leave, *signore*.'

'I need just one more minute...'

'*No, signore. Adesso!*'

Robert took one last look at the priest. He was raving incoherently. Robert turned to go. There was nothing further he could do. He had gambled on the priest giving him a lead to the Texan, and he had lost.

Robert returned to his car and headed back toward Rome. It was finally over. The only clues he had left – if they could be called clues – were the mention of a Russian woman, a Texan, and a Hungarian. But there was no way to pursue them any further. *Check and checkmate*. It was frustrating to have come this far and then to be stopped. If only the priest had remained coherent long enough to give him the information he needed! He had been so close. What was it the priest had said? *The Ponderosa*. The old priest had been watching too much television, and in his delirium, he had obviously associated Texas with the once popular TV show, *Bonanza*. The Ponderosa, where the mythical Cartwright family lived. *The Ponderosa*. Robert slowed the car, and pulled over to the side of the road, his mind racing. He made a U-turn and sped back toward Orvieto.

Half an hour later, Robert was talking to the bartender in a small trattoria in the Piazza della Republica. 'You have a beautiful town here,' Robert said. 'It's very peaceful.'

'Oh, *si, signore*, we are quite content here. Have you visited Italy before?'

'I spent part of my honeymoon in Rome.' *You make all my dreams come true, Robert. I've wanted to see Rome ever since I was a little girl.*

'Ah, Rome. Too big. Too noisy.'

'I agree.'

'We live simple lives here, but we are happy.'

Robert said casually, 'I noticed television antennas on many of the roofs here.'

'Oh, yes, indeed. We are quite up-to-date in that respect.'

'One can see that. How many television channels does the town receive?'

'Only one.'

'I suppose you get a good many American shows?'

'*No, no.* This is a government channel. Here we receive only shows made in Italy.'

Bingo! 'Thank you.'

Robert placed a call to Admiral Whittaker. A secretary answered the phone. 'Admiral Whittaker's office.'

Robert could visualize the office. It would be the kind of anonymous cubbyhole they kept for non-persons the government no longer had any use for.

'Could I speak to the Admiral, please? Commander Robert Bellamy calling.'

'Just a moment, Commander.'

Robert wondered whether anybody bothered to keep in touch with the Admiral now that the once powerful figure was part of the mothball fleet. Probably not.

'Robert, it's very good to hear from you.' The old man's voice sounded tired. 'Where are you?'

'I can't say, sir.'

There was a pause. 'I understand. Is there something I can do for you?'

'Yes, sir. This is rather awkward because I've been ordered not to communicate with anyone. But I need some outside help. I wonder if you could check on something for me?'

'I can certainly try. What would you like to know?'

'I need to know whether there's a ranch anywhere in Texas called The Ponderosa.'

'As in *Bonanza*?'

'Yes, sir.'

'I can find out. How will I reach you?'

'I think it would be better if I called you, Admiral.'

'Right. Give me an hour or two. I'll keep this just between ourselves.'

'Thank you.'

It seemed to Robert that the tiredness had gone out of the old man's voice. He had, at last, been asked to do something, even if it was as trivial as locating a ranch.

Two hours later, Robert telephoned Admiral Whittaker again.

'I've been waiting for your call,' the Admiral said. There was a satisfied note in his voice. 'I have the information you wanted.'

'And?' Robert held his breath.

'There *is* a Ponderosa ranch in Texas. It's located just outside of Waco. It's owned by a Dan Wayne.'

Robert heaved a deep sigh of relief. 'Thank you very much, Admiral,' he said. 'I owe you a dinner when I get back.'

'I'll be looking forward to that, Robert.'

Robert's next call was to General Hilliard. 'I located another witness in Italy. Father Patrini.'

'A priest?'

'Yes. In Orvieto. He's in the hospital, very ill. I'm afraid the Italian authorities won't be able to communicate with him.'

'I'll pass that on. Thank you, Commander.'

Two minutes later, General Hilliard was on the line to Janus.

'I've heard from Commander Bellamy again. The latest witness is a priest. A Father Patrini in Orvieto.'

'Take care of it.'

FLASH MESSAGE
TOP SECRET ULTRA
NSA TO DEPUTY DIRECTORY
SIFAR
EYES ONLY
COPY ONE OF (ONE) COPIES
SUBJECT: OPERATION DOOMSDAY
5. FATHER PATRINI – ORVIETO
END OF MESSAGE

The headquarters of SIFAR is on Via della Pineta, on the southernmost outskirts of Rome, in an area surrounded by farm-houses. The only thing that would cause a passer-by to give a second glance at the innocent, industrial-looking stone buildings occupying two square blocks would be the high wall surrounding the complex, topped by barbed wire, with security posts at each corner. Hidden in a military compound, it is one of the most secretive security agencies in the world, and one of the least known. There are signs outside the compound reading: *Vietare passare oltre i limiti.*

Inside a spartan office on the first floor of the main building, Colonel Francesco Cesar was studying the flash message he had just received. The Colonel was a man in his early fifties with a muscular body, topped by a pitted, bulldog face. He read the message for the third time.

So, Operation Doomsday is finally happening. È una bella fregatura. It is good that we have prepared for this, Cesar thought. He looked down at the cable again. A priest.

It was after midnight when the nun walked past the desk of the night duty nurses at the little hospital in Orvieto.

'I guess she's going to see Signora Fillipi,' said Nurse Tomasino.

'Either her or old man Rigano. They're both on their last legs.' The nun glided silently round the corner and walked directly into the priest's room. He was sleeping peacefully, his hands gathered almost as if in prayer, on his chest. A wedge of moonlight sliced through the blinds, casting a golden band across the priest's face.

The nun removed a small box from beneath her habit. Carefully, she took out a beautiful cut-glass rosary, and placed it in the old priest's hands. As she adjusted the beads, she drew one of them quickly across his thumb. A thin line of blood appeared. The nun took a tiny bottle from the box, and with an eye dropper, delicately squeezed three drops into the open cut.

It only took a few minutes for the deadly, fast-acting poison to work. The nun sighed as she made the sign of the cross over the dead man. She left as silently as she had come in.

**FLASH MESSAGE
TOP SECRET ULTRA
SIFAR TO DEPUTY DIRECTOR
NSA
EYES ONLY
COPY ONE OF (ONE) COPIES
SUBJECT: OPERATION
DOOMSDAY
5. FATHER PATRINI – ORVIETO –
TERMINATED
END OF MESSAGE**

Chapter Twenty-Six

Frank Johnson was recruited because he had been a Green Beret in Vietnam and was known among his comrades as 'the killing machine'. He loved to kill. He was motivated, and highly intelligent.

'He's perfect for us,' Janus said. 'Approach him carefully. I don't want to lose him.'

The first meeting took place in an Army barracks. A Captain was talking to Frank Johnson.

'Don't you worry about our government?' the Captain asked. 'It's being run by a bunch of bleeding hearts who are giving the store away. This country needs nuclear power, but the damned politicians are stopping us from building new plants. We depend on the damn Arabs for oil, but will the government let us do our own off-shore drilling? Oh, no. They're more worried about the fish than they are about us. Does that make sense to you?'

'I see your point,' Frank Johnson said.

'I knew you would, because you're intelligent.' He was watching Johnson's face as he spoke. 'If Congress won't do anything to save our country, then it's up to some of us to do something.'

Frank Johnson looked puzzled. 'Some of *us*?'

'Yeah.' *Enough for now*, the Captain thought. 'We'll talk about it later.'

The next conversation was more specific. 'There's a group of patriots, Frank, who are interested in protecting our world. They're pretty high-powered gentlemen. They've formed a committee. The committee may have to bend a few laws to get its work done, but in the end, it will be worth it. Are you interested?'

Frank Johnson grinned. 'I'm very interested.'

That was the beginning. The next meeting took place in Ottawa, Canada, and Frank Johnson met some of the members of the committee. They represented powerful interests from a dozen countries.

'We're well organized,' a member explained to Frank Johnson. 'We have a strict chain of command. There's a Propaganda Division, Recruiting, Tactics, Liaison . . . and a Death Squad.' He went on: 'Almost every intelligence organization in the world is part of this.'

'You mean the heads of . . . ?'

'No, not the heads. The deputies. The hands-on people who know what's going on, who know what danger our countries are in.'

The meetings took place all over the world – Switzerland, Morocco, China – and Johnson attended all of them.

It was six months before Colonel Johnson met Janus. Janus had sent for him.

'I've been given excellent reports about you, Colonel.'

Frank Johnson grinned. 'I enjoy my work.'

'So I've heard. You're in an advantageous position to help us.'

Frank Johnson sat up straighter. 'I'll do anything I can.'

'Good. At the Farm, you're in charge of supervising the training of secret agents in the various services.'

'That's right.'

'And you get to know them and their capabilities.'

'Intimately.'

'What I would like you to do,' Janus said, 'is to recruit those who you feel would be most helpful to our organization. We're interested only in the best.'

'That's easy,' Colonel Johnson said. 'No problem.' He hesitated a moment. 'I wonder . . .'

'Yes?'

'I can do that with my left hand. I'd really like to do something more, something bigger.' He leaned forward. 'I've heard about Operation Doomsday. Doomsday is right up my alley. I'd like to be a part of that, sir.'

Janus sat there, studying him a moment. Then he nodded. 'Very well, you're in.'

Johnson smiled. 'Thank you. You won't be sorry.' Colonel Frank Johnson left the meeting a very happy man. Now he would have a chance to show them what he could do.

Chapter Twenty-Seven

DAY EIGHT
Waco, Texas

Dan Wayne was not having a good day. As a matter of fact, he was having a dreadful day. He had just returned from the Waco county courthouse where he was facing bankruptcy proceedings. His wife, who had been having an affair with her young doctor, was divorcing him, intent on getting half of everything he had (which could be half of nothing, he had assured her lawyer). And one of his prize bulls had to be destroyed. Dan Wayne felt that fate was kicking him in the balls. He had done nothing to deserve all this. He had been a good husband and a good rancher. He sat in his study contemplating the gloomy future.

Dan Wayne was a proud man. He was well aware of all the jokes about Texans being loud-mouthed, larger-than-life braggarts, but he honestly felt he had something to brag about. He had been born in Waco, in the rich agricultural region of the Brazos River Valley. Waco was modern, but it still retained a flavour of the past, when the five Cs had been its support: cattle, cotton, corn, collegians and culture. Wayne loved Waco with all his heart and soul, and when he had met the Italian priest on the Swiss tour bus, he had spent almost five hours going on about his home town. The priest had told him he wanted to practise his English, but actually, as he thought back on it, Dan had done almost all the talking.

'Waco has everything,' he had confided to the priest. 'Our climate's great. We don't allow it to get too hot or too cold. We have twenty-three schools in the school district, and Baylor University. We have four newspapers, ten radio stations and five television stations. We have a Texas Ranger Hall of Fame that will knock you out. I mean, we're talking *history*. If you like fishing, Father, Brazos River is an experience you'll never forget. Then, we have a safari ranch and a big art centre. I tell you, Waco is one of the unique cities of the world. You must come and pay us a visit.'

And the little old priest had smiled and nodded, and Wayne wondered how much English he really understood.

Dan Wayne's father had left him a thousand acres of ranch land, and the son had built up his cattle herd from two thousand to ten thousand. There was also a prize stallion that was going to be worth a fortune. And now, the bastards were trying to take it all away from him. It wasn't his fault that the cattle market had gone to hell, or that he had gotten behind with his mortgage payments. The banks were closing in for the kill, and his only chance to save himself was to find someone who would buy the ranch, pay off his creditors, and leave him with a little profit.

Wayne had heard about a rich Swiss who was looking for a ranch in Texas, and he had flown over to Zürich to meet him. In the end, it had turned out to be a wild goose chase. The dude's idea of a ranch was an acre or two with a nice little vegetable garden. *She-eet!*

That was how Dan Wayne had happened to be on the tour bus when that extraordinary thing occurred. He had read about flying saucers, but he had never believed in them. Now, by God, he certainly did. As soon as he returned home, he had called the editor of the local newspaper.

'Johnny, I just saw an honest-to-God flying saucer with some dead, funny-looking people in it.'

'Yeah? Did you get any pictures, Dan?'

'No. I took some, but they didn't come out.'

'Never mind. We'll send a photographer out there. Is it on your ranch?'

'Well, no. As a matter of fact, it was in Switzerland.'

There was a silence.

'Oh. Well, if you happen to come across one on your ranch, Dan, give me another call.'

'Wait! I'm being sent a picture by some fellow who saw the thing.' But Johnny had already hung up.

And that was that.

Wayne almost wished that there *would* be an invasion of aliens. Maybe they would kill off his damned creditors. He heard the sound of a car coming up the drive and rose and walked over to the window. Looked like an easterner.

Probably another creditor. These days they were coming out of the woodwork.

Dan Wayne opened the front door.

'Howdy.'

'Daniel Wayne?'

'My friends call me Dan. What can I do for you?'

Dan Wayne was not at all what Robert had expected. He had envisioned a stereotype of a burly Texan. Dan Wayne was slight and aristocratic-looking, with an almost shy manner. The only thing that gave away his heritage was his accent.

'I wonder if I might have a few minutes of your time?'

'That's about all I've got left,' Wayne said. 'By the way, you're not a creditor, are you?'

'A creditor? No.'

'Good. Come on in.'

The two men walked into the living room. It was large and comfortably furnished with western-style furniture.

'This is a nice place you have here,' Robert said.

'Yeah. I was born in this house. Can I offer you anything? A cold drink, maybe?'

'No, thanks. I'm fine.'

'Have a seat.'

Robert sat down on a soft leather couch.

'What did you want to see me about?'

'I believe you took a bus tour in Switzerland last week?'

'That's right. Is my ex-wife having me followed? You don't work for her, do you?'

'No, sir.'

'Oh.' He suddenly understood. 'You're interested in that UFO thing. Damnedest thing I ever saw. It kept changing colours. And those dead aliens!' He shuddered. 'I keep dreaming about it.'

'Mr Wayne, can you tell me anything about the other passengers who were on that bus?'

'Sorry, I can't help you out there. I was travelling alone.'

'I know, but you spoke to some of the other passengers, didn't you?'

'To tell you the truth, I had a lot on my mind. I wasn't paying much attention to anyone else.'

'Do you remember anything about any of them?'

Dan Wayne was silent for a moment. 'Well, there was an Italian priest. I talked to him quite a bit. He seemed like a nice fellow. I want to tell you something, that flying saucer thing really shook him up. He kept talking about the devil.'

'Did you speak to anyone else?'

Dan Wayne shrugged. 'Not really ... wait a minute. I talked a little bit to some fellow who owns a bank in Canada.' He ran his tongue across his lips. 'To tell you the truth, I'm having a little financial problem here with the ranch. It looks as though I might lose it. I hate goddamn bankers. They're all blood-suckers. Anyway, I thought this fellow might be different. When I found out he was a banker, I talked to him about trying to work out some kind of loan arrangement here. But he was just like all the rest of them. He couldn't have been less interested.'

'You said he was from Canada.'

'Yeah, Fort Smith, up in the Northwest Territories. I'm afraid that's about all I can tell you.'

Robert tried to conceal his excitement. 'Thank you, Mr Wayne, you've been very helpful.' Robert rose.

'That's it?'

'That's it.'

'Would you like to stay for supper?'

'No, thanks. I have to be on my way. Good luck with the ranch.'

'Thanks.'

Fort Smith, Canada, Northwest Territories.

Robert waited until General Hilliard came on the line.

'Yes, Commander?'

'I found another witness. Dan Wayne. He owns The Ponderosa, a ranch outside of Waco, Texas.'

'Very good. I'll have our office in Dallas speak to him.'

FLASH MESSAGE
TOP SECRET ULTRA
NSA TO DEPUTY DIRECTOR DCI
EYES ONLY
COPY ONE OF (ONE) COPIES
SUBJECT: OPERATION
DOOMSDAY
6. DANIEL WAYNE – WACO
END OF MESSAGE

In Langley, Virginia, the Deputy Director of the Central Intelligence Agency studied the transmission thoughtfully. *Number six.* Things were going well. Commander Bellamy was doing an extraordinary job. The decision to select him had been a wise one. Janus had been right. The man was always right. And he had the power to have his wishes carried out. So much power ... The Director looked at the message again. *Make it look like an accident,* he thought. *That shouldn't be difficult.* He pressed a buzzer.

The two men arrived at the ranch in a dark blue van. They parked in the courtyard and got out of the car, carefully looking around. Dan Wayne's first thought was that they had come to take possession of the ranch. He opened the door for them.

'Dan Wayne?'

'Yes. What can I ... ?'

That was as far as he got.

The second man had stepped behind him and hit him hard across the skull with a blackjack.

The larger of the two men slung the unconscious rancher over his shoulder and carried him outside to the barn. There were eight horses in the barn. The men ignored them and walked to the last stall at the back. Inside was a beautiful black stallion.

The large man said, 'This is the one.' He put Wayne's body down.

The second man picked up a cattle prod from the ground, stepped up to the stall door, and hit the stallion with the electric prod. The stallion whinnied and reared up. The man hit him again hard across the nose. The stallion was bucking wildly now, confined in the small space, smashing against the walls of the stall, his teeth bared and the whites of his eyes flashing.

'Now,' the smaller man said. His companion lifted the body of Dan Wayne and tossed it over the half door into the stall. They watched the bloody scene for several moments, then, satisfied, turned and left.

**FLASH MESSAGE
TOP SECRET ULTRA
DCI TO DEPUTY DIRECTOR NSA
EYES ONLY
COPY ONE OF (ONE) COPIES
SUBJECT: OPERATION
DOOMSDAY
6. DANIEL WAYNE – WACO –
TERMINATED
END OF MESSAGE**

Chapter Twenty-Eight

DAY NINE
Fort Smith, Canada

Fort Smith, in the Northwest Territories, is a prosperous town of two thousand people, most of them farmers and cattle ranchers, with a sprinkling of merchants. The climate itself is demanding, with long and rigorous winters, and the town is living proof of Darwin's theory of the survival of the fittest.

William Mann was one of the fit ones, a survivor. He had been born in Michigan, but in his early thirties he had passed through Fort Smith on a fishing trip and had decided that the community needed another good bank. He had seized the opportunity. There was only one other bank there, and it took William Mann less than two years to put his competitor out of business. Mann ran his bank the way a bank should be run. His god was mathematics, and he saw to it that the numbers always came out to his benefit. His favourite story was the joke about the man who went to a banker pleading for a loan so that his young son could have an immediate operation to save his life. When the applicant said he had no security, the banker told him to get out of his office.

'I'll go,' the man said, 'but I want to tell you that

in all my years, I've never met anyone as coldhearted as you are.'

'Wait a minute,' the banker replied. 'I'll make you a sporting proposition. One of my eyes is a glass eye. If you can tell me which one it is, I'll give you the loan.'

Instantly, the man said, 'Your left one.'

The banker was amazed. 'No one knows that. How could you tell?'

The man said, 'That's easy. For a moment, I thought I detected a gleam of sympathy in your left eye, so I knew it must be your glass eye.'

That, to William Mann, was a good businessman's story. One did not conduct business based on sympathy. You had to look at the bottom line. While other banks in Canada and the United States were toppling like tenpins, William Mann's bank was stronger than ever. His philosophy was simple: no loans to start up businesses; no investments in junk bonds; no loans to neighbours whose children might desperately need an operation.

Mann had a respect that bordered on awe for the Swiss banking system. The gnomes of Zürich were bankers' bankers. So, one day, William Mann decided to go to Switzerland to speak to some of the bankers there to learn if there was anything he was missing, any way he could squeeze more cents out of the Canadian dollar. He had been received graciously, but in the end he had learned nothing new. His own banking methods were admirable, and the Swiss bankers had not hesitated to tell him so.

On the day he was to leave for home, Mann decided

to treat himself to a tour of the Alps. He had found the tour boring. The scenery was interesting, but no prettier than the scenery around Fort Smith. One of the passengers, a Texan, had dared try to persuade him to make a loan on a ranch that was going into bankruptcy. He had laughed in the man's face. The only thing about the tour that was of any interest was the crash of the so-called flying saucer. Mann had not believed in the reality of that for an instant. He was sure it had been staged by the Swiss government to impress tourists. He had been to Disney World and he had seen similar things that looked real, but were faked. *It's Switzerland's glass eye*, he thought sardonically.

William Mann was happy to return home.

Every minute of the banker's day was meticulously scheduled, and when his secretary came in and said that a stranger wished to see him, Mann's first instinct was to dismiss him. 'What is it he wants?'

'He says he wants to do an interview with you. He's writing an article about bankers.'

That was a different matter entirely. Publicity of the right kind was good for business. William Mann straightened his jacket, smoothed down his hair, and said, 'Send him in.'

His visitor was an American. He was well dressed, which indicated that he worked for one of the better magazines or newspapers.

'Mr Mann?'

'Yes.'

'Robert Bellamy.'

'My secretary tells me you want to do an article about me.'

'Well, not entirely about you,' Robert said. 'But you'll certainly be prominent in it. My newspaper...'

'Which newspaper is that?'

'The *Wall Street Journal*.'

Ah, yes. This was going to be excellent.

'The *Journal* feels that most bankers are too isolated from what's going on in the rest of the world. They seldom travel, they don't go to other countries. You, on the other hand, Mr Mann, have the reputation of being very well travelled.'

'I suppose I am,' Mann said modestly. 'As a matter of fact, I came back from a trip to Switzerland just last week.'

'Really? Did you enjoy it?'

'Yes. I met with several other bankers there. We discussed world economics.'

Robert had pulled out a notebook and was making notes. 'Did you have any time for pleasure?'

'Not really. Oh, I took a little tour on one of those buses. I had never seen the Alps before.'

Robert made another note. 'A tour. Now that's exactly the kind of thing we're looking for,' Robert said, encouragingly. 'I imagine you met a lot of interesting people on the bus.'

'Interesting?' He thought about the Texan who had tried to borrow money. 'Not really.'

'Oh?'

Mann looked at him. The reporter obviously

expected him to say more. *You'll certainly be prominent in the article.* 'There was this Russian girl.'

Robert made a note. 'Really? Tell me about her.'

'Well, we got to talking, and I explained to her how backward Russia was and what terrible trouble they were heading for unless they changed.'

'She must have been very impressed,' Robert said.

'Oh, she was. Seemed like a bright girl. For a Russian, that is. They're all pretty insulated, you know.'

'Did she mention her name?'

'No. Wait. It was Olga something.'

'Did she happen to say where she was from?'

'Yes. She works as a librarian at the main branch in Kiev. It was her first trip abroad, I guess because of *glasnost*. If you want my opinion . . .' he stopped to make sure Robert was writing it down, 'Gorbachev sent Russia to hell in a hand basket. East Germany was handed to Bonn on a plate. On the political front Gorbachev moved too fast, and on the economic front he moved too slowly.'

'That's fascinating,' Robert murmured. He spent another half hour with the banker, listening to his opinionated comments on everything from the Common Market to arms control. He was able to get no further information about other passengers.

When Robert returned to his hotel, he telephoned General Hilliard's office.

'Just a moment, Commander Bellamy.'

He heard a series of clicks, and then General Hilliard was on the line.

'Yes, Commander?'

'I've traced another passenger, General.'

'The name?'

'William Mann. He owns a bank in Fort Smith, Canada.'

'Thank you. I'll have the Canadian authorities speak to him right away.'

'By the way, he gave me another lead. I'll be flying to Russia this evening. I'll need a visa from Intourist.'

'Where are you calling from?'

'Fort Smith.'

'Stop at the Visigoth Hotel in Stockholm. There will be an envelope for you at the desk.'

'Thank you.'

**FLASH MESSAGE
TOP SECRET ULTRA
NSA TO DEPUTY DIRECTOR
CGHQ
EYES ONLY
COPY ONE OF (ONE) COPIES
SUBJECT: OPERATION
DOOMSDAY
7. WILLIAM MANN – FORT SMITH
END OF MESSAGE**

At eleven o'clock that evening William Mann's doorbell rang. He was not expecting anyone, and he disliked unannounced callers. His housekeeper had retired, and his wife was in her room upstairs, asleep.

Annoyed, Mann opened the front door. Two men dressed in black suits stood in the doorway.

'William Mann?'

'Yes.'

One of the men pulled out an identification card. 'We're from the Bank of Canada. May we come in?'

Mann frowned. 'What's this about?'

'We would prefer to discuss that inside if you don't mind.'

'Very well.' He led the men into the living room.

'You were recently in Switzerland, were you not?'

The question threw him off guard. 'What? Yes, but what on earth . . . ?'

'While you were gone we had your books audited, Mr Mann. Are you aware that there is a shortage in your bank of one million dollars?'

William Mann looked at the two men, aghast. 'What are you talking about? I check those books every week myself. There has never been one penny missing!'

'One million dollars, Mr Mann. We think you're responsible for embezzling it.'

His face was turning red. He found himself sputtering. 'How . . . how dare you! Get out of here before I call the police.'

'That won't do you any good. What we want you to do is repent.'

He was staring at them now, confused. 'Repent? Repent *what*? You're crazy!'

'No, sir.'

One of the men pulled out a gun. 'Sit down, Mr Mann.'

Oh, my God! I'm being robbed. 'Look,' Mann said, 'take whatever you want. There's no need for violence and . . .'

'Sit down, please.'

The second man walked over to the liquor cabinet. It was locked. He smashed the glass and pulled the cabinet open. He picked up a large water glass, filled it with scotch, and carried it over to where Mann was seated.

'Drink this. It will relax you.'

'I . . . I never drink after dinner. My doctor . . .'

The other man put the gun to William Mann's temple. 'Drink it or the glass is going to be full of your brains.'

Mann understood now that he was in the hands of two maniacs. He took the glass in his shaking hand and took a sip.

'Drink it down.'

He took a larger swallow. 'What . . . what is it you want?' He raised his voice, hoping that his wife might hear and come downstairs, but it was a vain hope. He knew what a sound sleeper she was. The men were obviously here to rob the house. *Why don't they just get on with it?*

'Take anything,' he said. 'I won't stop you.'

'Finish up what's in the glass.'

'This isn't necessary. I . . .'

The man punched him hard above his ear. Mann gasped with pain. 'Finish it.'

He swallowed the rest of the whisky in one gulp,

and felt it burning as it went down. He was beginning to feel giddy. 'My safe is upstairs in the bedroom,' he said. His words were beginning to slur. 'I'll open it for you.' Maybe that would wake his wife and she could call the police.

'There's no hurry,' the man with the gun said. 'You have plenty of time for another drink.'

The second man went back to the liquor cabinet and filled the glass to the brim again. 'Here.'

'No, really,' William Mann protested. 'I don't want it.'

The glass was shoved into his hand. 'Drink it down.'

'I really don't . . .'

A fist slammed into the same spot above his ear. Mann almost fainted from the pain.

'Drink it.'

Well, if that's what they want, why not? The quicker this nightmare is over with, the better. He took a big swallow and gagged.

'If I drink any more, I'm gonna be sick.'

The man said quietly, 'If you get sick, I'll kill you.'

Mann looked up at him and then at his partner. There seemed to be two of everybody.

'What do all of you want?' he mumbled.

'We told you, Mr Mann. We want you to repent.'

William Mann nodded drunkenly. 'Okay, I repent.'

The man smiled. 'You see, that's all we ask. Now . . .' He put a piece of paper in Mann's hand. 'All you have to do is write, "I'm sorry. Forgive me."'

William Mann looked up blearily. 'Tha's all?'

'That's all. And then we'll leave.'

He felt a sudden sense of elation. *So that was what this was all about. They were religious fanatics.* As soon as they left he would call the police and have them arrested. *I'll see to it that the bastards are hanged.*

'Write, Mr Mann.'

It was difficult for him to focus. 'What did you say you want me to write?'

'Just write, "I'm sorry. Forgive me."'

'Right.' He had difficulty holding the pen. He concentrated very hard and began to write. *I'm sorry. Forgive me.*

The man took the paper from Mann's hand, holding it by the edges. 'That's very good, Mr Mann. See how easy that was?'

The room was beginning to spin around. 'Yeah. Thank you. I've repented. Now would you leave?'

'I see that you're left-handed.'

'What?'

'You're left-handed.'

'Yes.'

'There's been a lot of crime around here lately, Mr Mann. We're going to give you this gun to keep.'

He felt a gun being placed in his left hand.

'Do you know how to use a gun?'

'No.'

'It's very simple. You use it like this . . .' The man lifted the gun to William Mann's temple and squeezed Mann's finger on the trigger. There was a muffled roar. The bloodstained note dropped to the floor.

'That's all there is to it,' one of the men said. 'Good night, Mr Mann.'

FLASH MESSAGE
TOP SECRET ULTRA
CGHQ TO DEPUTY DIRECTOR
NSA
EYES ONLY
COPY ONE OF (ONE) COPIES
SUBJECT: OPERATION DOOMSDAY
7. WILLIAM MANN – FORT SMITH – TERMINATED
END OF MESSAGE

DAY TEN
Fort Smith, Canada

The following morning, the bank examiners reported a million dollars missing from Mann's bank. The police listed Mann's death as a suicide.

The missing money was never found.

Chapter Twenty-Nine

DAY ELEVEN
Brussels, 0300 Hours

General Shipley, the Commandant at NATO Headquarters, was awakened by his adjutant.

'I'm sorry to wake you up, General, but we seem to have a situation on our hands.'

General Shipley sat up, rubbing the sleep from his eyes. He had had a late night entertaining a group of visiting senators from the United States. 'What's the problem, Billy?'

'I just received a call from the radar tower, sir. Either all our equipment has gone crazy or we're having some strange visitors.'

General Shipley pushed himself out of bed. 'I'll be there in five minutes.'

The darkened radar room was filled with enlisted men and officers gathered around the lighted radar screens in the centre of the room. They turned and sprang to attention as the General entered.

'At ease.' He walked over to the officer in charge, Captain Muller. 'What's going on here, Lewis?'

Captain Muller scratched his head. 'It beats me.

Do you know any plane that can travel 22,000 miles per hour, stop on a dime, and go into reverse?'

General Shipley was staring at him. 'What are you talking about?'

'According to our radar screens, that's what's been going on for the last half hour. At first, we thought it might be some kind of electronic device that's being tested, but we checked with the Russians, the British and the French, and they're picking up the same thing on their radar screens.'

'So, it couldn't be something in the equipment,' General Shipley said heavily.

'No, sir. Not unless you want to assume that all the radar in the world has suddenly gone crazy.'

'How many of these have appeared on the screen?'

'Over a dozen. They move so fast that it's hard to even keep track of them. We pick them up and they disappear again. We've eliminated atmospheric conditions, meteors, fireballs, weather balloons, and any kind of flying machine known to man. I was going to scramble some planes, but these objects – whatever they are – are flying so damned high that we'd never be able to get near them.'

General Shipley walked over to one of the radar screens. 'Is anything coming in on your screens now?'

'No, sir. They're gone.' He hesitated a moment. 'But, General, I have a terrible feeling they'll be coming back.'

Chapter Thirty

Ottawa, 0500 Hours

When Janus finished reading General Shipley's report aloud, the Italian stood up and said, excitedly, 'They are getting ready to invade us!'

'They have already invaded us.' The Frenchman.

'We are too late. It is a catastrophe.' The Russian. 'There is no way ...'

Janus interrupted. 'Gentlemen, it is a catastrophe we can prevent.'

'How? You know their demands.' The Englishman.

'Their demands are out of the question.' The Brazilian. 'It's no business of theirs what we do with our trees. The so-called greenhouse effect is scientific garbage, totally unproven.'

'And what about us?' The German. 'If they force us to clean up the air over our cities, we would have to shut down our factories. We would have no industries left.'

'And we would have to stop manufacturing cars,' the Japanese said. 'And then where would the civilized world be?'

'We are all in the same position.' The Russian. 'If we have to stop all pollution, as they insist, it would destroy the world's economies. We must buy more time until Star Wars is ready to take them on.'

Janus said crisply, 'We are agreed on that. Our immediate problem is to keep our people calm, and avoid the spread of panic.'

'How is Commander Bellamy progressing?' The Canadian.

'He's making excellent progress. He should be finished in the next day or two.'

Chapter Thirty-One

Kiev, The Soviet Union

Like most of her countrywomen, Olga Romanchanko had become disenchanted with *perestroika*. In the beginning, all the promised changes that were going to happen in Mother Russia sounded so exciting. The winds of freedom were blowing through the streets, and the air was filled with hope. There were promises of fresh meat and vegetables in the shops, pretty dresses and real leather shoes and a hundred other wonderful things. But now, six years after it had all begun, bitter disillusion had set in. Goods were scarcer than ever. It was impossible to survive without the black market. There was a shortage of virtually everything, and prices had soared. The main streets were still filled with *rytvina* – huge potholes. There were protest marches in the streets, and crime was on the increase. Restrictions were more severe than ever. *Perestroika* and *glasnost* had begun to seem as empty as the promises of the politicians who promoted them.

Olga had worked at the library in Lenkomsomol Square, in the centre of Kiev, for seven years. She was thirty-two years old, and had never been outside the Soviet Union. Olga was reasonably attractive, a bit overweight, but in Russia that was not considered a disadvantage. She had been engaged twice to men who had moved away and deserted her; Dmitri, who had left for Leningrad, and Ivan, who had moved to Moscow. Olga had tried to move to Moscow to be with Ivan, but without a *propiska*, a Moscow residence permit, it was not possible.

As her thirty-third birthday approached, Olga was determined that she was going to see something of the world before the Iron Curtain closed around her once again. She went to the head librarian, who happened to be her aunt.

'I would like to take my vacation, now,' Olga said.

'When do you want to leave?'

'Next week.'

'Enjoy yourself.'

It was as simple as that. In the days before *perestroika*, taking a vacation would have meant going to the Black Sea or Samarkand or Tbilisi, or any one of a dozen other places inside the Soviet Union. But now, if she were quick about it, the whole world was open to her. Olga took an atlas from the library shelf and pored over it. There was such a big world out there! There was Africa and Asia, and North and South America . . . she was afraid to venture that far. Olga turned to the map of Europe. *Switzerland*, she thought. *That's where I'll go.*

She would never have admitted it to anyone in the world, but the main reason Switzerland appealed to her was because she had once tasted Swiss chocolate, and she had never forgotten it. She loved sweets. The candy in Russia – when one could get it – was sugarless and tasted terrible.

Her taste for chocolate was to cost Olga her life.

The journey on Aeroflot to Zürich was an exciting beginning. She had never flown before. She landed at the international airport in Zürich, filled with anticipation. There was something in the air that was different. *Maybe it is the smell of real freedom*, Olga thought. Her finances were strictly limited, and she had made reservations at a small, inexpensive hotel, the Leonhare, at Limmatquai 136.

Olga checked in at the reception desk. 'This is my first time in Switzerland,' she confided to the clerk, in halting English. 'Could you suggest some things for me to do?'

'Certainly. There is much to do here,' he told her. 'Perhaps you should start with a tour of the city – I will arrange it.'

'Thank you.'

Olga found Zürich extraordinary. She was awed by the sights and sounds of the city. The people on the street were dressed in such fine clothes, and drove such expensive automobiles. It seemed to Olga that everyone in Zürich must be a millionaire. And the stores! She window-shopped along Bahnhofstrasse, the main shopping street of Zürich, and she marvelled at the incredible cornucopia of goods in the windows: there were dresses and coats and shoes and lingerie and jewellery and dishes and furniture and automobiles and books and television sets and radios and toys and pianos. There seemed to be no end to the goods for sale. And then Olga stumbled across Sprüngli's, famous for their confections and chocolates. And what chocolates! Four large store-front windows were filled with a dazzling array of them. There were huge boxes of mixed chocolates, chocolate bunnies, chocolate loaves, chocolate-covered nuts. There were chocolate-covered bananas and chocolate beans filled with liqueurs. It was a feast just to look at the display in the windows. Olga wanted to buy everything, but when she learned the prices, she settled for a small box of assorted chocolates and a large candy bar.

Over the next week, Olga visited the Zürichhorn Park and the Rietberg Museum and the Gross Münster, the church erected in the eleventh century, and a dozen other wonderful tourist attractions. Finally, her time was running out.

The hotel clerk at the Leonhare said to her, 'The Sunshine Tours Bus Company has a fine tour of the Alps. I think you might enjoy that before you leave.'

'Thank you,' Olga said. 'I will try it.'

When Olga left the hotel, her first stop was to visit Sprüngli's again, and the next stop was at the office of the Sunshine Tours Bus Company, where she arranged to go on a tour. It had proved to be most exciting. The scenery was breathtaking, and in the middle of the tour they had seen the explosion of what she thought was a flying saucer, but the Canadian banker she was seated next to explained that it was merely a spectacle arranged by the Swiss government for tourists, that there were no such things as flying saucers. Olga was not completely convinced. When she returned home to Kiev she discussed it with her aunt.

'Of course there are flying saucers,' her aunt said. 'They fly over Russia all the time. You should sell your story to a news paper.'

Olga had considered doing it, but she was afraid that she would be laughed at. The Party did not like its members to get publicity, especially the kind that might subject them to ridicule. All in all, Olga decided that, Dmitri and Ivan aside, her vacation had been the highlight of her life. It was going to be difficult to settle down to work again.

The ride from the airport into the centre of Kiev took the Intourist bus one hour, driving along the newly built highway. It was Robert's first time in Kiev, and he was impressed by the ubiquitous construction along the highway, and the large apartment buildings that seemed to be springing up everywhere. The bus pulled up in front of the Dnieper Hotel and disgorged its two dozen passengers. Robert looked at his watch. Eight p.m. The library would be closed. His business would have to wait until morning. He checked into the huge hotel, where a reservation had been made for him, had a drink at the bar and went into the austere whitewashed dining room for a dinner of caviar, cucumbers and tomatoes, followed by a potato casserole flavoured with tiny bits of meat and covered with heavy dough, all accompanied by vodka and mineral water.

His visa had been waiting for him at the hotel in Stockholm, as General Hilliard had promised. *That was a quick bit of international cooperation*, Robert thought. *But no cooperation for me. 'Naked' is the operational word.*

After dinner, Robert made a few inquiries at the desk, and meandered over to Lenkomsomol Square. Kiev was a surprise to him. One of the oldest cities in Ukraine, it was an attractive, European-looking city situated on the Dnieper River, with green parks and tree-lined streets. Churches were everywhere and they were spectacular examples of religious architecture: there were the Churches of St Vladimir's and St Andrew's and St Sophia's, the last completed in 1037, pure white with its soaring blue bell tower, and the Pechersk Monastery, the tallest structure in the city. *Susan would have loved all this*, Robert thought. She had never been to Russia. He wondered if she had returned from Brazil yet. On an impulse, when he returned to his hotel room, he telephoned her, and to his surprise the call was put through almost immediately.

'Hello?' *That throaty, sexy voice.*

'Hi. How was Brazil?'

'Robert! I tried to telephone you several times. There was no answer.'

'I'm not home.'

'Oh.' She had been trained too well to ask where he was. 'Are you feeling well?'

For a eunuch, I'm in wonderful shape. 'Sure. Great. How's Money . . . Monte?'

'He's fine. Robert, we're leaving for Gibraltar tomorrow.' *On Moneybags' fucking yacht, of course. What was the name of it? Ah, yes. The* Halcyon. 'The yacht?'

'Yes. You can call me on it. Do you remember the call letters?'

He remembered. *WS 337. What did the WS stand for? Wonderful Susan . . . Why separate . . . Wife stealer?*

'Robert?'

'Yes, I remember. Whiskey Sugar 337.'

'Will you call? Just to let me know you're all right.'

'Sure. I miss you, baby.'

A long, painful silence. He waited. What did he expect her to say? *Come rescue me from this charming man who looks like Paul Newman and forces me to go on his 250-foot yacht and live in our squalid little palaces in Monte Carlo, and Morocco, and Paris, and London, and God alone knew where else.* Like an idiot, he found himself half hoping she would say it.

'I miss you, too, Robert. Take care of yourself.' And the connection was broken. He was in Russia, alone.

DAY TWELVE

Early the following morning, ten minutes after the library opened, Robert walked into the huge, gloomy building and approached the reception desk.

'Good morning,' Robert said.

The woman behind the desk looked up. 'Good morning. Can I help you?'

'Yes. I'm looking for a woman who I believe works here, Olga . . .'

'Olga? Yes, yes.' She pointed to another room. 'She will be in there.'

'Thank you.'

It had been as easy as that. Robert walked into the other room, past groups of students solemnly studying at long tables, *preparing for what kind of future?* Robert wondered. He reached a smaller reading room and walked inside. A woman was busily stacking books.

'Excuse me,' Robert said.

She turned. 'Yes?'

'Olga?'

'I am Olga. What do you wish with me?'

Robert smiled disarmingly. 'I'm writing a newspaper article on *perestroika* and how it affects the average Russian. Has it made much difference in your life?'

The woman shrugged. 'Before Gorbachev, we were afraid to open our mouths. Now we can open our mouths, but we have nothing to put in them.'

Robert tried another tactic. 'Surely, there are some

changes for the better. For instance, you are able to travel now.'

'You must be joking. With a husband and six children, who can afford to travel?'

Robert ploughed on. 'Still, you went to Switzerland, and . . .'

'Switzerland? I have never been to Switzerland in my life.'

Robert said slowly, 'You've never been to Switzerland?'

'I just told you.' She nodded toward a dark-haired woman who was collecting books from the table. 'She's the lucky one who got to go to Switzerland.'

Robert took a quick look. 'What's her name?'

'Olga. The same as mine.'

He sighed. 'Thank you.'

A minute later, Robert was in conversation with the second Olga.

'Excuse me,' Robert said. 'I'm writing a newspaper article on *perestroika* and the effect that it's had on Russian lives.'

She looked at him warily. 'Yes?'

'What's your name?'

'Olga. Olga Romanchanko.'

'Tell me, Olga, has *perestroika* made any difference to you?'

Six years earlier, Olga Romanchanko would have been afraid to speak to a foreigner, but now it was allowed. 'Not really,' she said carefully. 'Everything is much the same.'

The stranger was persistent. 'Nothing at all has changed in your life?'

She shook her head. 'No.' And then added patriotically, 'Of course we can travel outside the country now.'

He seemed interested. 'And have you travelled outside the country?'

'Oh, yes,' she said proudly. 'I have just returned from Switzerland. Is a very beautiful country.'

'I agree,' he said. 'Did you get a chance to meet anyone on the trip?'

'I met many people. I took a bus and we went through high mountains. The Alps.' Suddenly Olga realized she shouldn't have said that because the stranger might ask her about the spaceship, and she did not want to talk about that. It could only get her into trouble.

'Really?' asked Robert. 'Tell me about the people on the bus.'

Relieved, Olga responded. 'Very friendly. They were dressed so . . .' She gestured. 'Very rich. I even met man from your capital city, Washington, DC.'

'You did?'

'Yes. Very nice. He gave me card.'

Robert's heart skipped a beat. 'Do you still have it?'

'No. I threw it away.' She looked around. 'Is better not keep things like that.'

Damn!

And then she added, 'I remember his name. Parker, like your American pen. Kevin Parker. Very important in politics. He tells senators how vote.'

Robert was taken aback. 'Is that what he told you?'

'Yes. He takes them on trips and gives gifts, and

then they vote for things his clients need. That is the way democracy works in America.'

A lobbyist. Robert let Olga talk for the next fifteen minutes, but he got no further useful information about the other passengers.

Robert telephoned General Hilliard from his hotel room.

'I found the Russian witness. Her name is Olga Romanchanko. She works in the main library in Kiev.'

'I'll have a Russian official speak to her.'

**FLASH MESSAGE
TOP SECRET ULTRA
NSA TO DEPUTY DIRECTOR GRU
EYES ONLY
COPY ONE OF (ONE) COPIES
SUBJECT: OPERATION
DOOMSDAY
8. OLGA ROMANCHANKO – KIEV
END OF MESSAGE**

That afternoon Robert was on an Aeroflot Tupolev Tu – 154 jet to Paris. When he arrived three hours and twenty-five minutes later, he transferred to an Air France flight to Washington, DC.

At two a.m. Olga Romanchanko heard the squeal of brakes as a car pulled up in front of the apartment building where she lived, on Vertryk Street. The walls of the apartment were so thin that she could hear voices outside on the street. She got out of bed and looked out of the window. Two men in civilian clothes were getting out of a black Chaika, the model used by government officials. They were approaching the entrance to her apartment building. The sight of them sent a shiver through her. Over the years, some of her neighbours had disappeared, never to be seen again. Some of them had been sent to the Gulag in Siberia. Olga wondered who the secret police were after this time, and even as she was thinking it, there was a knock on her door, startling her. *What do they want with me?* she wondered. *It must be some mistake.*

When she opened the door, the two men were standing there.

'Comrade Olga Romanchanko?'

'Yes.'

'Glavnoye Razvedyvatelnoye Upravleniye.'

The dreaded GRU.

They pushed their way past her into the room.

'What . . . what is it you want?'

'We will ask the questions. I am Sergeant Yuri Gromkov. This is Sergeant Vladimir Zemsky.'

She felt a sudden sense of terror. 'What's . . . what's wrong? What have I done?'

Zemsky pounced on it. 'Oh, so you know you have done something wrong!'

'No, of course not,' Olga said, flustered. 'I do not know why you are here.'

'Sit down,' Gromkov shouted. Olga sat.

'You have just returned from a trip to Switzerland, *nyet?*'

'Y ... yes,' she stuttered, 'but it ... it was ... I got permission from ...'

'Espionage is not legal, Olga Romanchanko.'

'Espionage?' She was horrified. 'I don't know what you are talking about.'

The larger man was staring at her body, and Olga suddenly realized she was wearing only a thin nightgown.

'Let's go. You are coming with us.'

'But there is some terrible mistake. I'm a librarian. Ask anybody here who ...'

He pulled her to her feet. 'Come.'

'Where are you taking me?'

'To headquarters. They want to question you.'

They allowed her to put on a coat over her nightgown. She was shoved down the stairs and into the Chaika. Olga thought of all the people who had ridden in cars like this before and had never returned, and she was numb with fear.

The larger man, Gromkov, was driving. Olga was seated in the back with Zemsky. He somehow seemed less frightening to her, but she was petrified by who they were and what was going to happen to her.

'Please believe me,' Olga said earnestly. 'I would never betray my ...'

'Shut up,' Gromkov barked.

Vladimir Zemsky said, 'Look, there's no reason to be rough with her. As a matter of fact, I believe her.'

Olga felt her heart leap with hope.

'Times have changed,' Comrade Zemsky went on.

'Comrade Gorbachev doesn't like us to go around bothering innocent people. Those days are past.'

'Who said she's innocent?' Gromkov growled. 'Maybe she is, maybe she isn't. They'll find out soon enough at headquarters.'

Olga sat there listening to the two men discussing her as though she were not there.

Zemsky said, 'Come now, Yuri, you know that at headquarters she will confess, whether she's guilty or not. I don't like this.'

'That's too bad. There's nothing we can do about it.'

'Yes, there is.'

'What?'

The man next to Olga was silent for a moment. 'Listen,' he said. 'Why don't we just let her go? We could tell them she was not at home. We'll put them off for a day or two, and they will forget all about her because they have so many people to question.'

Olga tried to say something, but her throat was too dry. She desperately wanted the man beside her to win the argument.

Gromkov grumbled. 'Why should we risk our necks for her? What do we get out of it? What is she going to do for us?'

Zemsky turned to look at Olga questioningly. Olga found her voice. 'I have no money,' she said.

'Who needs your money? We have plenty of money.'

Gromkov said, 'She has something else.'

Before Olga could reply, Zemsky said, 'Wait a

minute, Yuri Ivanovich, you can't expect her to do that.'

'That's up to her. She can either be nice to us or go down to headquarters and get beaten up for a week or two. Maybe they'll keep her in a nice *shizo*.'

Olga had heard about *shizos*. Unheated four-by-eight-foot cells with wooden plank beds and no blankets. *Be nice to us*. What did that mean?

'It's up to her.'

Zemsky turned to Olga, 'What do you want to do?'

'I . . . I don't understand.'

'What my partner is saying is that if you're nice to us we could just drop this whole thing. In a little while they'll probably forget about you.'

'What . . . what would I have to do?'

Gromkov grinned at her in the rear-view mirror. 'Just give us a few minutes of your time.' He remembered something he had once read, *Just lie there and think of the Czar*. He giggled.

Olga suddenly understood what they were getting at. She shook her head. 'No, I could not do that.'

'Right.' Gromkov started speeding up. 'They'll have a good time with you at headquarters.'

'Wait!' She was in a panic, not knowing what to do. She had heard horror stories of what had happened to people who had been arrested and become *zeks*. She had thought that that was all finished, but now she could see that it was not. *Perestroika* was still just a fantasy. They would not allow her to have an attorney, or talk to anyone. In the past, friends of hers had been raped and murdered by the GRU. She was trapped. If she went to jail they could keep her for weeks, beating her and raping her, maybe worse. With these two men, at least it would be over in a few minutes and then they would let her go. Olga made her decision.

'All right,' she said miserably. 'Do you wish to go back to my apartment?'

Gromkov said, 'I know a better place.' He turned the car around.

Zemsky whispered, 'I'm sorry about this, but he's in charge. I can't stop him.'

Olga said nothing.

They drove past the bright red Shevchenko Opera House, and headed for a large park bordered by trees. It was completely deserted at this hour. Gromkov drove the car under the trees and turned off the lights and engine.

'Let's get out,' he said.

The three of them got out of the car.

Gromkov looked at Olga. 'You're lucky. We're letting you off easy. I hope you appreciate it.'

Olga nodded, too frightened to speak.

Gromkov led them to a small cleared area. 'Get undressed.'

'It's cold,' Olga said, 'couldn't we . . . ?'

Gromkov slapped her hard across the face. 'Do as you're told before I change my mind.'

Olga hesitated an instant, and as his arm drew back to hit her again, she started unbuttoning her coat.

'Take it off.'

She let it drop to the ground.

'Now the nightgown.'

Slowly, Olga lifted the nightgown over her head

and pulled it off, shivering in the cold night air, standing naked in the moonlight.

'Nice body,' Gromkov said. He squeezed her nipples.

'Please . . .'

'You make one sound, and we take you to headquarters.' He pushed her to the ground.

I won't think about this. I'll pretend I'm in Switzerland on the bus tour, looking at all the beautiful scenery.

Gromkov had dropped his pants and was spreading Olga's legs apart.

I can see the Alps covered with snow. There is a sleigh going by with a young boy and girl in it.

She felt him place his hands under her hips, and he shoved his maleness into her, hurting her.

There are beautiful cars along the highway. More cars than I have ever seen in my life. In Switzerland everybody has a car.

He was plunging into her harder now, pinching her, making wild, animal noises.

I will have a little home in the mountains. What do the Swiss call them? Chalets. And I will have chocolates every day. Boxes of them.

Gromkov was withdrawing now, breathing heavily. He stood up and turned to Zemsky. 'Your turn.'

I will get married and have children, and we will all go skiing in the Alps in winter.

Zemsky had zipped open his pants and was climbing on top of her.

It will be such a wonderful life. I will never return to Russia. Never. Never. Never.

He was inside her now, hurting her more than the other man had, squeezing her buttocks, and pushing her body into the cold ground until the pain was almost unbearable.

We will live on a farm, where it's quiet and peaceful all the time, and we will have a garden with beautiful flowers.

Zemsky finished with her and looked up at his companion. 'I bet she enjoyed it,' he grinned.

He reached down for Olga's neck and broke it.

The following day there was an item in the local paper about a librarian who had been raped and strangled in the park. There was a stern warning from the authorities that it was dangerous for young women to go to the park alone at night.

FLASH MESSAGE
TOP SECRET ULTRA
DEPUTY DIRECTOR GRU TO DEPUTY
DIRECTOR NSA
EYES ONLY
COPY ONE OF (ONE) COPIES
SUBJECT: OPERATION DOOMSDAY
8. OLGA ROMANCHANKO – KIEV – TERMINATED
END OF MESSAGE

Chapter Thirty-Two

Willard Stone and Monte Banks were natural enemies. They were both ruthless predators, and the jungle they prowled was the stone canyons of Wall Street, with its high-powered takeovers, leveraged buy-outs and stock deals.

The first time the two men clashed was during the attempted takeover of a huge utility company. Willard Stone made the first bid, and anticipated no problem. He was so powerful, and his reputation so fearsome, that very few people dared challenge him. It was a great surprise then when he learned that a young upstart named Monte Banks was contesting his bid. Stone was forced to raise his own bid, and the ante kept going up. Willard Stone finally acquired control of the company, but at a much higher price than he had anticipated paying.

Six months later, in a takeover bid for a large electronics firm, Stone was confronted again by Monte Banks. The bidding kept escalating, and this time, Banks won.

When Willard Stone learned that Monte Banks intended to compete with him for control of a computer company, he decided it was time to meet with his competitor. The two men met on neutral ground in Paradise Island, in the Bahamas. Willard Stone had

had a thorough investigation made of his competitor and had learned that Monte Banks came from a wealthy oil family, and had brilliantly managed to parlay his inheritance into an international conglomerate.

The two men sat down to lunch. Willard Stone, old and wise, Monte Banks, young and eager.

Willard Stone opened the conversation. 'You're becoming a pain in the ass.'

Monte Banks grinned. 'Coming from you, that's a big compliment.'

'What is it you want?' Stone asked.

'The same as you. I want to own the world.'

Willard Stone said thoughtfully, 'Well, it's a big enough world.'

'Meaning?'

'There's room enough for both of us.'

That was the day they became partners. Each ran his own business separately but when it came to new projects – timber and oil and real estate – they went into deals together, instead of competing with each other. Several times the Anti-Trust Division of the Justice Department tried to stop their deals, but Willard Stone's connections always prevailed. Monte Banks owned chemical companies responsible for massive pollution of lakes and rivers, but when he was indicted, the indictment was mysteriously dropped.

The two men had a perfect symbiotic relationship.

Operation Doomsday was a natural for them, and they were heavily involved in it. They were on the verge of closing a deal to purchase ten million acres of lush, tree-rich land in the Amazon. It was going to be one of the most profitable deals they had ever gone into.

They could not afford to let anything stand in their way.

Chapter Thirty-Three

DAY THIRTEEN
Washington, DC

The Senate of the United States was in plenary session. The junior senator from Utah had the floor.

'... and what is happening to our ecology is a national disgrace. It is time that this great body realized that it is its sworn duty to preserve the precious heritage that our forefathers entrusted to us. It is not only our sworn duty but our privilege to protect the land, the air and the seas against those vested interests that are selfishly destroying it. And are we doing this? Are we in all conscience doing our best? Or are we allowing the voice of Mammon to influence us . . . ?'

Kevin Parker, seated in the visitors' gallery, glanced at his watch for the third time in the past five minutes. He wondered how much longer the speech was going to last. He was sitting through this only because he was having lunch with the senator, and he needed a favour from him. Kevin Parker enjoyed walking through the corridors of power, hobnobbing with congressmen and senators, dispensing largesse in return for political favours.

He had grown up poor in Eugene, Oregon. His father was an alcoholic who had owned a small lumber yard. An inept businessman, he had turned what should have been a thriving business into a disastrous failure. The young boy had to work from the age of fourteen, and because his mother had run away with another man years earlier, he had no home life at all. He could easily have become a drifter and ended up like his father, but his saving grace was that he was extraordinarily handsome and personable. He had wavy blond hair and fine aristocratic features that he must have inherited from some long-forgotten ancestor. A few affluent townspeople took pity on the boy, giving him jobs, encouragement, and going out of their way to assist him. The wealthiest man in town, Jeb Goodspell, was particularly eager to help Kevin, and gave him a part-time job with one of his companies. A bachelor, Goodspell often invited young Parker to join him for dinner at his home.

'You can *be* somebody in this life,' Goodspell told him, 'but you can't make it without friends.'

'I know that, sir. And I certainly appreciate your friendship. Working for you is a real life saver.'

'I could do a lot more for you,' Goodspell said. They were seated on the couch in the living room, after dinner. He put his arm around the young boy. 'A *lot* more.' He squeezed the boy's shoulder. 'You have a good body, do you know that?'

'Thank you, sir.'

'Do you ever get lonely?'

He was lonely all the time. 'Yes, sir.'

'Well, you don't have to be lonely anymore.' He stroked the boy's arm. 'I get lonely, too, you know.

You need someone to hold you close and comfort you.'

'Yes, sir.'

'Have you ever had any girls?'

'Well, I went with Sue Ellen for a while.'

'Did you sleep with her?'

The boy blushed. 'No, sir.'

'How old are you, Kevin?'

'Sixteen, sir.'

'It's a great age. It's an age when you should be beginning to start a career.' He studied the boy a moment. 'I'll bet you'd be darn good in politics.'

'Politics? I don't know anything about that, sir.'

'That's why you're going to school, to learn things. And I'm going to help you.'

'Thank you.'

'There are plenty of ways of thanking people,' Goodspell said. He rubbed his hand along the boy's thigh. 'Many ways.' He looked into Parker's eyes. 'You know what I mean?'

'Yes, Jeb.'

That was the beginning.

When Kevin Parker was graduated from Churchill High School, Goodspell sent him to the University of Oregon. The boy studied political science, and Goodspell saw to it that his protégé met everybody. They were all impressed with the attractive young man. With his connections, Parker found that he was able to do favours for important people, and to bring people together. Becoming a lobbyist in Washington was a natural step, and Parker was good at the job.

Goodspell had died two years earlier, but Parker had by then acquired a talent and a taste for what his mentor had taught him. He liked to pick up young boys and take them to out-of-the-way hotels where he would not be recognized.

The senator from Utah was finally finishing. '... and I say to you now that we must pass this bill if we want to save what is left of our ecology. At this time, I would like to ask for a roll call vote.'

Thank God, the endless session was almost over. Kevin Parker thought about the evening that lay ahead of him, and he began to get an erection. The night before, he had met a young man at Danny's 'P' Street Station, a well-known gay bar. Unfortunately, the young man had been with a companion. But they had eyed each other during the evening, and before he left, Parker had written a note and slipped it into the young man's hand. It said simply, 'Tomorrow night.' The young man had smiled and nodded.

Kevin Parker was hurriedly getting dressed to go out. He wanted to be at the bar when the boy arrived. The young man was much too attractive, and Parker did not want him picked up by someone else. The front doorbell rang. *Damn*. Parker opened the door.

A stranger stood there. 'Kevin Parker?'

'Yes...'

'My name is Bellamy. I'd like to talk to you for a minute.'

Parker said, impatiently, 'You'll have to make an

appointment with my secretary. I don't discuss business outside of office hours.'

'This isn't exactly business, Mr Parker. It concerns your trip to Switzerland a couple of weeks ago.'

'My trip to Switzerland? What about it?'

'My agency is interested in some of the people you might have met over there.' Robert flashed his false CIA identification.

Kevin Parker studied the man more carefully. What could the CIA want with him? They were so goddamn nosey. *Have I covered my ass?*

There was no point in antagonizing the man. He smiled. 'Come in. I'm late for an appointment, but you said this won't take more than a minute?'

'No, sir. I believe you took a bus tour out of Zürich?'

So that's what this is all about. That flying saucer business. It had been the goddamnedest thing he had ever seen. 'You want to know about the UFO, don't you? Well, I want to tell you, it was a weird experience.'

'It must have been, but, frankly, we at the Agency don't believe in flying saucers. I'm here to find out what you can tell me about your fellow passengers on the bus.'

Parker was taken aback. 'Oh. Well, I'm afraid I can't help you there. They were all strangers.'

'I understand that, Mr Parker,' Robert said patiently, 'but you must remember *something* about them.'

Parker shrugged. 'Well, a few things . . . I remember exchanging a few words with an Englishman who took our pictures.'

Leslie Mothershed. 'Who else?'

'Oh, yes. I talked a little to a Russian girl. She seemed very pleasant. I think she said she was a librarian somewhere.'

Olga Romanchanko. 'That's excellent. Can you think of anyone else, Mr Parker?'

'No, I guess that's about ... oh, there were two other men. One was an American, a Texan.'

Dan Wayne. 'And the other one?'

'He was a Hungarian. He owned a carnival or circus or something like that in Hungary.' He remembered. 'It was a carnival.'

'Are you sure about that, Mr Parker?'

'Oh, yes. He was telling me some stories about the carnival business. He was certainly excited seeing that UFO. I think if he could have, he would have put it in his carnival as a sideshow. I must admit, it was a pretty awesome sight. I would have reported it, but I can't afford to get mixed up with all the weirdos who claim they saw flying saucers.'

'Did he happen to mention his name?'

'Yes, but it was one of these unpronounceable foreign names. I'm afraid I don't remember it.'

'Do you remember anything else about him?'

'Only that he was in a hurry to get back to his carnival.' He glanced at his watch. 'Is there anything else I can do for you? I'm running a little late.'

'No, thank you, Mr Parker. You've been very helpful.'

'My pleasure.' He flashed Robert a beautiful smile.

'You must drop by my office and see me sometime. We'll have a nice chat.'

'I'll do that.'

So it's nearly over, Robert thought. *They can take my job and shove it. It's time to pick up the pieces of my life and start over.*

Robert placed a call to General Hilliard. 'I've just about wrapped it up, General. I found Kevin Parker. He's a lobbyist in Washington, DC. I'm on my way to check out the last passenger.'

'I'm very pleased,' General Hilliard said. 'You've done an excellent job, Commander. Get back to me as quickly as you can.'

'Yes, sir.'

**FLASH MESSAGE
TOP SECRET ULTRA
NSA TO DEPUTY DIRECTOR CIA
EYES ONLY
COPY ONE OF (ONE) COPIES
SUBJECT: OPERATION
DOOMSDAY
9. KEVIN PARKER –
WASHINGTON, DC
END OF MESSAGE**

When Kevin Parker arrived at Danny's 'P' Street Station, he found it even more crowded than it had been the evening before. The older men were dressed in conservative suits, while most of the younger men were in Levis, blazers and boots. There were a few who looked out of place, in black leather outfits, and Parker thought that this element was disgusting. Rough trade was dangerous, and he had never gone in for that sort of bizarre behaviour. *Discretion*, that had always been his motto. *Discretion*. The handsome young boy was not there yet, but Parker had not expected him to be. He would make his entrance later, beautiful and fresh, when the others in the bar would be tired and sweaty. Kevin Parker walked up to the bar, ordered a drink and looked around. Television sets on the walls were playing MTV stations. Danny's was an S and M – stand and model – bar. The younger men would assume poses that made them appear as attractive as possible, while the older men – the buyers – would look them over and make their selections. The S and M bars were the classiest. There were never any fights in them, for most of the customers had capped teeth, and they could not afford to chance having them knocked out.

Kevin Parker noticed that many of the patrons had already selected their partners. He listened to the familiar conversations going on around him. It fascinated him that the conversations were always the same, whether they took place in leather bars, dance bars, video bars or underground clubs that changed their locations every week. There was an indigenous argot.

'That queen is nobody. She thinks she's Miss Thing . . .'

'He went off on me for no reason. He gets so terribly upset. Talk about sensitive . . .'

'Are you a top or a bottom?'

'A top. I have to give the orders, girl.' Snapping his fingers.

'Good. I like taking them . . .'

'He read me for filth . . . Just stood there criticizing me . . . my weight, my complexion, my attitude. I said "Mary, it's over between us". But it hurt. That's why I'm here tonight . . . trying to forget him. Could I have another drink . . . ?'

At one a.m., the young boy walked in. He looked around, saw Parker and walked over to him. The boy was even more beautiful than Parker had remembered.

'Good evening.'

'Good evening. Sorry I'm late.'

'That's all right. I didn't mind waiting.'

The young man took out a cigarette and waited while the older man lit it for him.

'I've been thinking about you,' Parker said.

'Have you?'

The boy's eyelashes were incredible.

'Yes. Can I buy you a drink?'

'If it will make you happy.'

Parker smiled. 'Are you interested in making me happy?'

The boy looked him in the eyes and said softly, 'I think so.'

'I saw the man you were here with last night. He's wrong for you.'

'And you're right for me?'

'I could be. Why don't we find out? Would you like to go for a little walk?'

'Sounds good.'

Parker felt a tingle of excitement. 'I know a cosy place where we can be alone.'

'Fine. I'll skip the drink.'

As they started toward the front door, it suddenly opened and two large young men entered the bar. They stepped in front of the boy, blocking his way. 'There you are, you sonofabitch. Where's the money you owe me?'

The young man looked up at him, bewildered. 'I don't know what you're talking about. I've never seen you be . . .'

'Don't give me that shit.' The man grabbed him by the shoulder and started marching him out to the street.

Parker stood there, furious. He was tempted to interfere, but he could not afford to get involved in anything that might turn into a scandal. He stayed where he was, watching the boy disappear into the night.

The second man smiled at Kevin Parker sympathetically.

'You should choose your company more carefully. He's bad news.'

Parker took a closer look at the speaker. He was blond and attractive, with almost perfect features. Parker had a feeling that the evening might not be a total loss, after all. 'You could be right,' he said.

'We never know what fate has in store for us, do we?' He was looking into Parker's eyes.

'No, we don't. My name's Tom. What's your name?'

'Paul.'

'Why don't you let me buy you a drink, Paul?'

'Thank you.'

'Do you have any special plans for tonight?'

'That's up to you.'

'How would you like to spend the night with me?'

'That sounds like fun.'

'How much money are we talking about?'

'I like you. For you, two hundred.'

'That seems reasonable.'

'It is. You won't be sorry.'

Thirty minutes later Paul was leading Kevin Parker into an old apartment building on Jefferson Street. They walked upstairs to the third floor, and entered a small room. Parker looked around. 'It's not much, is it? A hotel would have been nicer.'

Paul grinned. 'It's more private here. Besides, all we need is the bed.'

'You're right. Why don't you get undressed? I want to see what I'm buying.'

'Sure.' Paul started stripping. He had a great body. Parker watched him and he felt the old familiar urge beginning to build.

'Now, you get undressed,' Paul whispered. 'Hurry, I want you.'

'I want you, too, Mary.' Parker began to take off his clothes.

'What do you like?' Paul asked. 'Lips or hips?'

'Let's make it a cocktail. Excuse the pun. We've got all night.'

'Sure. I'm going into the bathroom,' Paul said. 'I'll be right back.'

Parker lay on the bed naked, anticipating the exquisite pleasures that were about to happen. He heard his companion come out of the bathroom and approach the bed.

He held out his arms. 'Come to me, Paul,' he said.

'I'm coming.'

And Parker felt a burst of agony as a knife slashed into his chest. His eyes flew open. He looked up, gasping. 'My God, what . . . ?'

Paul was getting dressed. 'Don't worry about the money,' he said. 'It's on the house.'

**FLASH MESSAGE
TOP SECRET ULTRA
CIA TO DEPUTY DIRECTOR NSA
EYES ONLY
COPY ONE OF (ONE) COPIES
SUBJECT: OPERATION
DOOMSDAY
9. KEVIN PARKER –
WASHINGTON, DC –
TERMINATED
END OF MESSAGE**

Robert Bellamy missed the late news bulletin because he was on a plane to Hungary to find a man who owned a carnival.

Chapter Thirty-Four

DAY FOURTEEN
Budapest

The flight from Paris to Budapest on Malév Airlines took two hours and five minutes. Robert knew very little about Hungary except that during World War II it had been a partner in the Axis, and had later become a Russian satellite. Robert took the airport bus to the centre of Budapest, impressed by what he saw. The buildings were old and the architecture classic. The Parliament House on the Rudolph Quay was a huge, Neo-gothic structure that dominated the city, and high on Castle Hill above the city was the Royal Palace. The streets were crowded with automobiles and shoppers.

The bus stopped in front of the Hotel Duna Intercontinental. Robert walked into the lobby and approached the concierge.

'Excuse me,' Robert said. 'Do you speak English?'

'*Igan*. Yes. What may I do for you?'

'A friend of mine was in Budapest a few days ago, and he told me he saw a wonderful carnival. I thought as long as I was in town, I might take a look at it. Can you tell me where I might find it?'

The concierge frowned. 'Carnival?' He pulled out

a sheet of paper and scanned it. 'Let's see. In Budapest at the present time, we have an opera, several theatre productions, ballet, night and day tours of the city, excursions in the country...' He looked up. 'I'm sorry. There are no carnivals.'

'Are you sure?'

The concierge handed the list to Robert. 'See for yourself.' It was written in Hungarian.

Robert handed it back. 'Right. Is there anyone else I might talk to about this?'

The concierge said, 'The Ministry of Culture might be able to help you.'

Thirty minutes later, Robert was speaking to a clerk in the office of the Ministry of Culture.

'There is no carnival in Budapest. Are you sure your friend saw it in Hungary?'

'Yes.'

'But he did not say where?'

'No.'

'I am sorry. I cannot help you.' The clerk was impatient. 'If there is nothing else...'

'No.' Robert rose to his feet. 'Thank you.' He hesitated. 'I do have one more question. If I wanted to bring a circus or a carnival into Hungary, would I have to get a permit?'

'Certainly.'

'Where would I go for that?'

'To the Budapest Administration of Licences.'

The licences building was located in Buda near the medieval city wall. Robert waited for thirty minutes before he was ushered into the office of a formal, pompous official.

'Can I help you?'

Robert smiled. 'I hope so. I hate to take up your time with something as trivial as this, but I'm here with my young son, and he heard about a carnival playing somewhere in Hungary and I promised to take him to see it. You know how kids are when they get an idea in their heads.'

The official stared at Robert, puzzled. 'What is it you wanted to see me about?'

'Well, to tell you the truth, no one seems to know where the carnival is, and Hungary is such a big and beautiful country . . . Well, I was told that if anyone knew what was going on in Hungary, it would be you.'

The official nodded. 'Yes. Nothing like that is permitted to open without being issued a licence.' He pressed the buzzer and a secretary came in. There was a rapid exchange in Hungarian. The secretary left and came back two minutes later with some papers. She handed them to the official. He looked at them and said to Robert, 'In the past three months, we have issued two permits for carnivals. One closed a month ago.'

'And the other?'

'The other is currently playing in Sopron. A little town near the German frontier.'

'Do you have the owner's name?'

The official consulted the paper again. 'Bushfekete. Laslo Bushfekete.'

*

Laslo Bushfekete was having one of the best days of his life. Few people are lucky enough to spend their lives doing exactly what they want to do and Laslo Bushfekete was one of those fortunate few. Bushfekete was a big man, six foot four, weighing three hundred pounds. He sported a diamond wristwatch, diamond rings, and a large gold bracelet. His father had owned a small carnival, and when he died, the son had taken it over. It was the only life he had ever known.

Laslo Bushfekete had grandiose dreams. He intended to expand his little carnival into the biggest and best in Europe. He wanted to be known as the P. T. Barnum of carnivals. At the moment, however, he could only afford the usual sideshow attractions: the Fat Lady and the Tattooed Man, the Siamese Twins and the Thousand-Year-Old Mummy 'dug up from the bowels of the tombs of ancient Egypt'. Then there were the Sword Swallower and the Flame Eater, and the cute little Snake Charmer, Marika. But in the end, all they really added up to was just another travelling carnival.

Now, overnight, all that was going to change. Laslo Bushfekete's dream was about to come true.

He had gone to Switzerland to audition an escape artist he had heard about. The *pièce de résistance* of the act was a routine where the performer was blindfolded, handcuffed, locked in a small trunk, then locked in a larger trunk, and finally lowered into a tank of water. It had sounded fantastic over the telephone, but when Bushfekete flew to Switzerland to see it, he found that there was one insurmountable problem: it took the escape artist thirty minutes to escape. No audience in the world was going to stay around staring at a trunk in a tank of water for thirty minutes.

It had looked as though the trip had been a complete waste of time. Laslo Bushfekete had decided to take a tour to kill the day until it was time to catch his plane. As it turned out, that ride changed his life.

Like his fellow passengers, Bushfekete had seen the explosion and raced across the field to try to help any survivors in what they all thought was a plane crash. But the sight that had confronted him was incredible. There was no question but that it was a flying saucer, and in it were two strange-looking little bodies. The other passengers stood there, gaping at it. Laslo Bushfekete had walked around to see what the back of the UFO looked like, and then he had stopped, staring. About ten feet behind the wreck, lying on the ground out of sight of the others, was a tiny severed hand, with six fingers and two opposing thumbs. Without even thinking, Bushfekete had taken out his handkerchief, scooped up the hand and slipped it into his pocket. His heart was beating wildly. He had in his possession the hand of a genuine extraterrestrial! *From now on you can forget all your Fat Ladies, Tattooed Men, Sword Swallowers and Flame Eaters*, he thought. *Step right up, ladies and gentlemen, for the thrill of a lifetime. What you're about to see is a sight that no mortal has ever seen before. You are looking at one of the most incredible objects in the universe. It's not an animal. It's not a vegetable. It's not a mineral. What is it? It's part of the remains of an extraterrestrial ... A creature from outer space ... This is not science fiction, ladies and gentlemen, this is the real thing ... For 500 forints you can have your photograph taken with the ...*

And that reminded him. He hoped that the photographer who had been at the crash site would remember to send the photograph he had promised. He would have it blown up and put next to the exhibit. That would be a neat touch. *Showmanship. That's what life was all about. Showmanship.*

He could not wait to return to Hungary and start to fulfil his grandiose dream.

When he arrived home and unwrapped the handkerchief, he noticed that the hand had shrivelled. But when Bushfekete rinsed off the dirt, amazingly, it regained its original firmness.

Bushfekete had hidden the hand safely away and had ordered an impressive glass case with a special humidifier built for it. When he was through exhibiting it in his carnival, he planned to travel with it all over Europe. All over the world. He would set up exhibits in museums. He would have private showings for scientists, perhaps, even heads of state. And he would charge them all. There was no end to the fabulous fortune that lay ahead.

He had told no one about his good luck, not even his sweetheart, Marika, the sexy little dancer who worked with cobras and puff adders, two of the most dangerous of the species *Ophidia*. Of course, their poison sacs had been removed but the audience did not know that because Bushfekete also kept a cobra, its poison sac intact, which he displayed free of charge to the public, who watched it kill rats. It wasn't surprising that people got a thrill out of watching the beautiful Marika let her pet snakes slither across her sensuous, half-naked body. Two or three nights a week, Marika came into Laslo Bushfekete's tent and crawled across his body, her tongue flicking in and out, like her pets. They had made love the night before, and Bushfekete was still exhausted from Marika's incredible gymnastics. His reminiscences were interrupted by a visitor.

'Mr Bushfekete?'

'You're talking to him. What can I do for you?'

'I understand you were in Switzerland last week.'

Bushfekete was instantly wary. *Had someone seen him pick up the hand?* 'What ... what about it?'

'You went on a bus tour last Sunday?'

Bushfekete said cautiously, 'Yes.'

Robert Bellamy relaxed. It was finally over. This was the last witness. He had taken on an impossible assignment and he had done a good job. *A damned good job, if I say so myself. We have no idea where they are.* And he had found them all. He felt as though a tremendous burden had been lifted from his shoulders. He was free now. Free to return home and begin a new life.

'What about my trip, mister?'

'It's not important,' Robert Bellamy assured him. And it wasn't, not any longer. 'I was interested in your fellow passengers, Mr Bushfekete, but now I think I have all the information I need, so . . .'

'Oh, hell, I can tell you all about them,' Laslo Bushfekete said. 'There was an Italian priest from Orvieto, Italy, a German – I think he was a chemistry professor from Munich – some Russian girl who worked in the library in Kiev, a rancher from Waco, Texas, a Canadian banker from the territories and some lobbyist named Parker from Washington, DC.'

My God, Robert thought. *If I had gotten to him first, I could have saved a lot of time. The man is amazing. He recalled them all.* 'You have quite a memory,' Robert said.

'Yeah.' Bushfekete smiled. 'Oh, and there was that other woman.'

'The Russian woman.'

'No, no, the *other* woman. The tall, thin one, who was dressed in white.'

Robert thought for a moment. None of the others had mentioned a second woman. 'I think you must be mistaken.'

'No, I'm not.' Bushfekete was insistent. 'There were two women there.'

Robert made a mental count. It simply did not add up. 'There couldn't have been.'

Bushfekete was insulted. 'When that photographer fellow took the pictures of all of us in front of that UFO, she was standing right next to me. She was a real beauty.' He paused. 'The funny part is I don't recall seeing her on the bus. She was probably in the back somewhere. I remember she seemed kind of pale. I was a little worried about her.'

Robert frowned. 'When all of you returned to the bus, was she with you?'

'Come to think of it, I don't remember seeing her after that. But I was so excited by that UFO thing, I wasn't paying much attention.'

There was something here that did not fit. *Could there have been eleven witnesses instead of ten? I'll have to check that out*, Robert thought. 'Thank you, Mr Bushfekete,' he said.

'My pleasure.'

'Good luck.'

Bushfekete grinned. 'Thanks.' He didn't need luck. Not any more. Not with the hand of a real genuine alien in his possession.

That night Robert Bellamy made his final report to General Hilliard. 'I have his name. It's Laslo Bushfekete. He runs a carnival, outside of Sopron, Hungary.'

'That's the last of the witnesses?'

Robert hesitated an instant. 'Yes, sir.' He had started to mention the eighth passenger, but he decided to wait until he had verified it. It seemed too improbable.

'Thank you, Commander. Well done.'

FLASH MESSAGE
TOP SECRET ULTRA
NSA TO DEPUTY DIRECTOR HRQ
EYES ONLY
COPY ONE OF (ONE) COPIES
SUBJECT: OPERATION
DOOMSDAY
10. LASLO BUSHFEKETE – SOPRON
END OF MESSAGE

They arrived in the middle of the night when the carnival was shut down. They left fifteen minutes later, as silently as they had come.

Laslo Bushfekete dreamed he was standing at the entrance to the large white tent, watching the huge crowd lined up at the box office to buy their 500-forint tickets.

Come right this way, folks. See the genuine body part of an alien from outer space. Not a drawing, not a photograph, but an actual part of an actual ET. Only 500 forints for the thrill of a lifetime, a sight you will never forget.

And then he was in bed with Marika, and they were both naked, and he could feel her nipples pressing against his chest and her tongue slithering across his body and she was crawling all over him, and he got an erection, and he reached for her and his hands closed over something cold and slimy, and he woke up and opened his eyes and screamed, and that was when the cobra struck.

They found his body in the morning. The cage for the poisonous snake was empty.

**FLASH MESSAGE
TOP SECRET ULTRA
HRQ TO DEPUTY DIRECTOR NSA
EYES ONLY
COPY ONE OF (ONE) COPIES
SUBJECT: OPERATION
DOOMSDAY
10. LASLO BUSHFEKETE – SOPRON –
TERMINATED
END OF MESSAGE**

General Hilliard made a call on the red phone. 'Janus, I've received the final report from Commander Bellamy. He's found the last of the witnesses. They've all been taken care of.'

'Excellent. I'll inform the others. I want you to proceed at once with the rest of our plan.'

'Immediately.'

**FLASH MESSAGE
TOP SECRET ULTRA
NSA TO DEPUTY DIRECTORS:
SIFAR, MI6, GRU, CIA, COMSEC, DCI,
CGHQ, BFV EYES ONLY
COPY ONE OF (ONE) COPIES
SUBJECT: OPERATION DOOMSDAY
11. COMMANDER ROBERT
BELLAMY –
TERMINATE
END OF MESSAGE**

BOOK TWO
The Hunted

Chapter Thirty-Five

DAY FIFTEEN

Robert Bellamy was in a dilemma. *Could there have been an eleventh witness? And if there was, why hadn't any of the witnesses mentioned her before?* The clerk who sold the bus tickets had told him there were only seven passengers. Robert was convinced that the Hungarian carnival owner had made a mistake. It would have been easy to ignore it, to assume that it was untrue, but Robert's training would not permit it. He had been too well disciplined. Bushfekete's story had to be checked out. *How?* Robert thought about it. *Hans Beckerman. The bus driver will know.*

He placed a call to Sunshine Tours. The office was closed. There was no listing in Kappel for a Hans Beckerman. *I'm going to have to go back to Switzerland and settle this*, Robert thought. *I can't leave any loose ends.*

It was late at night when Robert arrived in Zürich. The air was cold and crisp and there was a full moon. Robert rented a car and took the now familiar drive to the little village of Kappel. He drove past the church and pulled up in front of Hans Beckerman's home, convinced that he was on a wild goose chase. The house was dark. Robert knocked on the door and waited. He knocked again, shivering in the cold night air.

Mrs Beckerman finally answered the door. She was wearing a faded flannel robe. '*Bitte?*'

'Mrs Beckerman, I wonder if you remember me? I'm the reporter who's writing an article on Hans. I'm sorry to bother you so late, but it's important that I speak to your husband.'

His words were greeted with silence. 'Mrs Beckerman?'

'Hans is dead.'

Robert felt a small shock go through him. 'What?'

'My husband is dead.'

'I . . . I'm sorry. How?'

'His car went over the side of the mountain.' Her voice was filled with bitterness. 'The *Dummkopf Polizei* said it was because he was full of drugs.'

'Drugs?' *I'm sorry I cannot offer you a drink. Ulcers. The doctors cannot even give me drugs to relieve the pain. I am allergic to all of them.*

'The police said it was an accident?'

'*Ja.*'

'Did they perform an autopsy?'

'They did, and they found drugs. It makes no sense.'

He had no answer. 'I'm terribly sorry, Mrs Beckerman. I . . .'

The door closed, and Robert stood there, alone in the cold night.

One witness was gone. No . . . two. Leslie Mothershed had died in a fire. Robert stood there for a long time. Two witnesses dead. He could hear the voice of his instructor at the Farm: *There's one more thing I want to discuss today. Coincidence. In our work, there is no such animal. It usually spells danger. If you keep running into the same person again and again, or if you keep spotting the same automobile when you're on the move, cover your ass. You're probably in trouble.*

Probably in trouble. Robert was caught up in a series of conflicting emotions. What had happened *had* to be coincidences, and yet . . . *I've got to check out the mystery passenger.*

His first call was to Fort Smith, Canada. A distraught woman's voice answered the telephone. 'Yes?'

'William Mann, please.'

The voice said, tearfully, 'I'm sorry. My husband is . . . is no longer with us.'

'I don't understand.'

'He committed suicide.'

Suicide? That hard-headed banker? What the hell is going on? Robert wondered. What he was thinking was inconceivable, and yet . . . He began making one phone call after another.

'Professor Schmidt, please.'

'*Ach*! The professor died in an explosion in his laboratory . . .'

'I'd like to speak to Dan Wayne.'
'Poor devil. His prize stallion kicked him to death last...'

'Laslo Bushfekete, please.'
'The carnival's closed. Laslo is dead...'

'Fritz Mandel, please.'
'Fritz was killed in a freak accident...'
The alarms were going full blast now.

'Olga Romanchanko.'
'The poor girl. And she was so young...'

'I'm calling to check on Father Patrini.'
'The poor soul passed away in his sleep.'

'I have to speak to Kevin Parker.'
'Kevin was murdered...'

Dead. Every one of the witnesses dead. And he was the one who had found them and identified them. Why had he not known what was going on? Because the bastards had waited until he was out of each country before executing their victims. The only one he had reported to was General Hilliard. *We must not involve anyone else in this mission ... I want you to report your progress to me every day.*

They had used him to finger the witnesses. *What was behind all this?* Otto Schmidt had been killed in Germany, Hans Beckerman and Fritz Mandel in Switzerland. Olga Romanchanko in Russia, Dan Wayne and Kevin Parker in America, William Mann in Canada, Leslie Mothershed in England, Father Patrini in Italy, and Laslo Bushfekete in Hungary. That meant that the security agencies in more than half a dozen countries were engaged in the biggest cover-up in history. Someone at a very high level had decided that all the witnesses to the UFO crash must die. *But who? And why?*

It was an international conspiracy and he was in the middle of it.

Priority: get under cover. It was hard for Robert to believe that they intended to kill him, too. He was one of them. But until he knew for certain, he could not take any chances. The first thing he had to do was to get a phony passport. That meant Ricco in Rome.

Robert caught the next plane out and found himself fighting to stay awake. He had not realized how exhausted he was. The pressure of the last fifteen days, in addition to all the jet lag, had left him drained.

He landed at the Leonardo da Vinci airport, and when he walked into the terminal, the first person he saw was Susan. He stopped, in shock. Her back was to him and for a moment he thought he might be mistaken. And then he heard her voice.

'Thank you. I have a car picking me up.'

Robert moved to her side. 'Susan...'

She turned, startled. 'Robert! What ... what a coincidence! But what a lovely surprise.'

'I thought you were in Gibraltar,' Robert said.

She smiled uneasily. 'Yes. We're on our way there. Monte had some business here to take care of first. We're leaving tonight. What are you doing in Rome?'

Running for my life. 'I'm finishing up on a job.' *It's my last. I've quit, darling. We can be together from now on, and nothing will ever separate us again. Leave Monte and come back to me.* But he could not bring himself to say the words. He had done enough to her. She was happy in her new life. *Leave it alone,* Robert thought.

She was watching him. 'You look tired.'

He smiled. 'I've been running around a little.'

They looked into each other's eyes, and the magic was still there. The burning desire, and the memories, and the laughter, and the yearning.

Susan took his hand in hers and said softly, 'Robert. Oh, Robert. I wish we...'

'Susan...'

And at that moment, a burly man in a chauffeur's uniform walked up to Susan. 'The car is ready, Mrs Banks.' And the spell was broken.

'Thank you.' She turned to Robert. 'I'm sorry. I have to go now. Please take care of yourself.'

'Sure.' He watched her leave. There were so many things he wanted to say to her. *Life has a lousy sense of timing.* It had been wonderful seeing Susan again but what was it that was troubling him? Of course! *Coincidence. Another coincidence.*

He took a taxi to the Hassler Hotel.

'Welcome back, Commander.'

'Thank you.'

'I'll have a bellman take up your bags.'

'Wait.' Robert looked at his watch. Ten p.m. He was tempted to go upstairs and get some sleep, but he had to arrange his passport first.

'I won't be going to my room right away,' Robert said. 'I would appreciate it if you would have my bags sent up.'

'Of course, Commander.'

As Robert turned to leave, the elevator door opened and half a dozen Shriner fraternity men came pouring out, laughing and chattering. They had obviously had a few drinks. One of them, a stout, red-faced man, waved to Robert.

'Hi there, buddy . . . having a good time?'

'Wonderful,' Robert said. 'Just wonderful.'

Robert walked through the lobby to the taxi stand outside. As he started to get into the taxi, he noticed an inconspicuous grey Opel parked across the street. It was too inconspicuous. It stood out among the large, luxurious automobiles around it.

'Via Monte Grappa,' Robert told the taxi driver. During the drive, Robert looked out of the rear window. No grey Opel. *I'm getting jumpy*, he thought. When they arrived at Via Monte Grappa,

Robert got out at the corner. As he started to pay the driver, he saw, out of the corner of his eye, the grey Opel half a block down the street, yet he could have sworn it had not followed him. He started walking, moving away from the car, strolling slowly, stopping to look in shop windows. In the reflection of a store window, he saw the Opel, moving slowly behind him. When Robert reached the next corner, he noticed that it was a one-way street. He turned into it, going against the heavy traffic. The Opel hesitated at the corner, then sped away to pick Robert up at the other end. Robert reversed direction and walked back to Via Monte Grappa. The Opel was nowhere in sight.

Robert hailed a taxi. 'Via Monticelli.'

The building was old and unprepossessing, a relic of better days. Robert had visited it many times before, on various missions. He walked down three basement steps and knocked on the door. An eye appeared at the peephole, and a moment later the door was flung open.

'Roberto!' a man exclaimed. He threw his arms around Robert. 'How are you, *mio amico*?'

The speaker was a fat man in his sixties with white, unshaven stubble, thick eyebrows, yellowed teeth and several chins. He closed the door behind him and locked it.

'I'm fine, Ricco.'

Ricco had no second name. *For a man like me*, he liked to boast, *one name is enough. Like Garbo.* 'What can I do for you today, my friend?'

'I'm working on a case,' Robert said, 'and I'm in a hurry. Can you fix me up with a passport?'

Ricco smiled. 'Is the Pope Catholic?' He waddled over to a cabinet in the corner and unlocked it. 'What country would you like to be from?' He pulled out a handful of passports with different-coloured covers, and sorted through them. 'We have a Greek passport, Turkish, Yugoslavian, English . . .'

'American,' Robert said.

Ricco pulled out a passport with a blue cover. 'Here we are. Does the name of Arthur Butterfield appeal to you?'

'Perfect,' Robert said.

'If you'll stand over by the wall, I will take your picture.'

Robert moved over to the wall. Ricco opened a drawer and took out a Polaroid camera. A minute later, Robert was looking at a picture of himself.

'I wasn't smiling,' Robert said.

Ricco looked at him, puzzled. 'What?'

'I wasn't smiling. Take another one.'

Ricco shrugged. 'Sure. Whatever you say.'

Robert smiled while the second passport picture was taken. He looked at it and said, 'That's better.' He casually slipped the first picture into his pocket.

'Now comes the high-tech part,' Ricco announced. Robert watched as Ricco walked over to a work bench where there was a laminating machine. He placed the picture on the inside of the passport.

Robert moved to a table covered with pens, ink and other paraphernalia, and slipped a razor blade and a small bottle of glue into his jacket pocket.

Ricco was studying his handiwork. 'Not bad,' he said. He handed the passport to Robert. 'That will be five thousand dollars.'

'And well worth it,' Robert assured him, as he peeled off ten five-hundred-dollar bills.

'It's always a pleasure doing business with you people. You know how I feel about you.'

Robert knew exactly how he felt. Ricco was an expert cobbler who worked for half a dozen different governments, and was loyal to none. He put the passport in his pocket.

'Good luck, Mr Butterfield.' Ricco smiled.

'Thanks.'

The moment the door closed behind Robert, Ricco reached for the telephone. Information was always worth money to someone.

Outside, twenty yards down the street, Robert took the new passport out of his pocket and buried it in a trash can. *Chaff.* The technique he had used as a pilot to lay false trails for enemy missiles. *Let them look for Arthur Butterfield.*

The grey Opel was parked half a block away. Waiting. *Impossible.* Robert was sure that the car was the only tail they had on him. He was certain the Opel had not followed him, and yet it kept finding him. They had to have some way of keeping track of him. There was only one answer: they were using some kind of homing device. And he had to be carrying it. Attached to his clothes? No. They had had no opportunity. Captain Dougherty had stayed with him while he packed, but he would not have known what clothes Robert would take. Robert made a mental inventory of what he was carrying ... cash, keys, a wallet, handkerchief, credit card. *The credit card! I doubt if I'll need that, General. Take it. And keep it with you at all times.*

The sneaky sonofabitch. No wonder they had been able to find him so easily.

The grey Opel was no longer in sight. Robert took out the card and examined it. It was slightly thicker than an ordinary credit card. By squeezing it, he could feel an inner layer. They would have a remote control to activate the card. *Good,* Robert thought. *Let's keep the bastards busy.*

There were several trucks parked along the street, loading and unloading goods. Robert examined the licence plates. When he came to a red truck with French plates, he looked around to make sure he was not observed, and tossed the card in the back of the truck.

He flagged down a taxi. 'Hassler, *per favore.*'

In the lobby, Robert approached the concierge. 'See if there's a flight out of here tonight to Paris, please.'

'Certainly, Commander. Do you prefer any particular airline?'

'It doesn't matter. The first flight out.'

'I will be happy to arrange it.'

'Thank you.' Robert walked over to the hotel clerk. 'My key, please. Room 314. And I'll be checking out in a few minutes.'

'Very good, Commander Bellamy.' The clerk reached in a pigeonhole and pulled out a key and an envelope. 'There's a letter here for you.'

Robert stiffened. The envelope was sealed, and

addressed simply: *Commander Robert Bellamy.* He fingered it, feeling for plastique or any metal inside. Carefully, he opened it. Inside was a printed card advertising an Italian restaurant. It was innocent enough. Except, of course, for his name on the envelope.

'Do you happen to remember who gave you this?'

'I'm sorry,' the clerk said apologetically, 'but we have been so busy this evening...'

It was not important. The man would have been faceless. He would have picked up the card somewhere, slipped it into the envelope and stood by the desk, watching to see the room number of the slot that the envelope was placed in. He would be upstairs now, in Robert's room, waiting. It was time to see the face of the enemy.

Robert became aware of raised voices and turned to watch the Shriners he had seen earlier, entering the lobby, laughing and singing. They had obviously had a few more drinks. The portly man said, 'Hi there, pal. You missed a great party.'

Robert's mind was racing. 'You like parties?'

'Hoo hoo!'

'There's a real live one going on upstairs,' Robert said. 'Booze, girls – anything you want. Just follow me, fellows.'

'That's the American spirit, pal.' The man clapped Robert on the back. 'You hear that, boys? Our friend here is throwing a party!'

They crowded into the elevator together and rode up to the third floor.

The Shriner said, 'These Italians sure know how to live it up. I guess they invented orgies, huh?'

'I'm going to show you a *real* orgy,' Robert promised.

They followed him down the hall to his room. Robert put the key in the lock and turned to the group. 'Are you all ready to have some fun?'

There was a chorus of 'yeses' . . .

Robert turned the key, pushed the door open, and stepped to one side. The room was dark. He snapped on the light. A tall, thin stranger was standing in the middle of the room with a Mauser, equipped with a silencer, half drawn. The man looked at the group with a startled expression, and quickly shoved the gun back in his jacket.

'Hey! Where's the booze?' one of the Shriners demanded.

Robert pointed to the stranger. 'He has it. Go get it.'

The group surged toward the man. 'Where's the liquor, buddy? . . . Where are the girls? . . . Let's get this party on the road . . .'

The thin man was trying to get through to Robert, but the crowd was blocking his way. He watched helplessly as Robert bolted out of the door. He took the stairs two at a time.

Downstairs in the lobby, Robert was moving toward the exit when the concierge called out, 'Oh, Commander Bellamy, I made your reservation for you. You are on Air France flight 312 to Paris. It leaves at one a.m.'

'Thanks,' Robert said hurriedly.

He was out of the door, into the small square overlooking the Spanish Steps. A taxi was discharging a passenger. Robert stepped into it. 'Via Monte Grappa.'

He had his answer now. They intended to kill him. *They're not going to find it easy.* He was the hunted now instead of the hunter, but he had one big advantage. They had trained him well. He knew all their techniques, their strengths, and their weaknesses, and he intended to use that knowledge to stop them. First, he had to find a way to throw them off his trail. The men after him would have been given a story of some kind. They would have been told he was wanted for smuggling drugs, or for murder, or espionage. They would have been warned: *He's dangerous. Take no chances. Shoot to kill.*

Robert said to the taxi driver, 'Roma Termini.' They were hunting for him, but they would not have had enough time to disseminate his photograph. So far, he was faceless.

The taxi pulled up at Via Giovanni Giolitti 36, and the driver announced, 'Stazione Termini, *signore.*'

'Let's just wait here a minute.' Robert sat in the taxi, studying the front of the railway station. There seemed to be only the usual activity. Everything appeared to be normal. Taxis and limousines were arriving and departing, discharging and picking up passengers. Porters were loading and unloading luggage. A policeman was busily ordering cars to move out of the restricted parking zone. But something was disturbing Robert. He suddenly realized what was wrong with the picture. Parked directly in front of the station, in a no-parking zone, were three unmarked sedans, with no one inside. The policeman ignored them.

'I've changed my mind,' Robert said to the driver. 'Via Veneto 110/A.' It was the last place anyone would look for him.

The American Embassy and consulate are located in a pink stucco building facing the Via Veneto, with a black wrought-iron fence in front of it. The embassy was closed at this hour, but the passport division of the consulate was open on a twenty-four-hour basis, to handle emergencies. In the foyer on the first floor, a marine sat behind a desk.

The marine looked up as Robert approached. 'May I help you, sir?'

'Yes,' Robert said. 'I want to inquire about getting a new passport. I lost mine.'

'Are you an American citizen?'

'Yes.'

The marine indicated an office at the far end. 'They'll take care of you in there, sir. Last door.'

'Thank you.'

There were half a dozen people in the room applying for passports, reporting lost passports, and getting renewals and visas.

'Do I need a visa to visit Albania? I have relatives there . . .'

'I need this passport renewed by tonight. I have a plane to catch . . .'

'I don't know what happened to it. I must have left it in Milan...'

'They grabbed my passport right out of my purse...'

Robert stood there, listening. Stealing passports was a thriving cottage industry in Italy. Someone here would be getting a new passport. At the head of the line was a well-dressed, middle-aged man being handed an American passport.

'Here is your new passport, Mr Cowan. I'm sorry you had such a bad experience. I'm afraid there are a lot of pickpockets in Rome.'

'I'll sure see to it that they don't get hold of this one,' Cowan said.

'You do that, sir.'

Robert watched Cowan put the passport in his jacket pocket and turn to leave. Robert stepped ahead of him. As a woman brushed by, Robert lunged into Cowan, as though he had been pushed, almost knocking him down.

'I'm terribly sorry,' Robert apologized. He leaned over and straightened the man's jacket for him.

'No problem,' Cowan said.

Robert turned and walked into the public men's room down the hall, the stranger's passport in his pocket. He looked around to make sure he was alone, then went into one of the booths. He took out the razor blade and bottle of glue he had stolen from Ricco. Very carefully, he slit the top of the plastic and removed Cowan's photograph. Next, he inserted the picture of himself that Ricco had taken. He glued the top of the plastic slot closed, and examined his handiwork. Perfect. He was now Henry Cowan. Five minutes later, he was out in the Via Veneto, getting into a taxi. 'Leonardo da Vinci.'

It was twelve thirty when Robert arrived at the airport. He stood outside, looking for anything unusual. On the surface, everything appeared to be normal. No police cars, no suspicious-looking men. Robert entered the terminal, and stopped just inside the door. There were various airline counters scattered around the large terminal. There seemed to be no one loitering or hiding behind posts. He stayed where he was, wary. He could not explain it, even to himself, but somehow, everything seemed *too* normal.

Across the room was an Air France counter. *You are on Air France flight 312 to Paris. It leaves at one a.m.* Robert walked past the counter and approached a woman in uniform behind the Alitalia counter. 'Good evening.'

'Good evening. Can I help you, *signore*?'

'Yes,' Robert said. 'Would you please page Commander Robert Bellamy to come to the courtesy telephone?'

'Certainly,' she said. She picked up a microphone.

A few feet away, a fat middle-aged woman was checking a number of suitcases, heatedly arguing with an airline attendant about overweight fees. 'In America, they never charged me for overweight.'

'I'm sorry, madam. But if you wish all these bags to go on, you must pay for excess baggage.'

Robert moved closer. He heard the attendant's voice over the loudspeaker. 'Will Commander Robert

Bellamy please come to the white courtesy telephone. Commander Robert Bellamy, please come to the white courtesy telephone.' The announcement echoed throughout the airport.

A man holding a carry-on bag was walking past Robert. 'Excuse me . . .' Robert said.

The man turned. 'Yes?'

'I hear my wife paging me but . . .' he indicated the woman's bags, 'I can't leave my luggage.' He pulled out a ten-dollar bill and handed it to the man. 'Would you please go over to that white telephone and tell her I'll pick her up at our hotel in an hour? I'd really appreciate it.'

The man looked at the ten-dollar bill in his hand. 'Sure.'

Robert watched him walk over to the courtesy telephone and pick it up. He held the receiver to his ear and said, 'Hello . . . hello . . . ?'

The next moment, four large men in black suits appeared from nowhere and closed in, pinning the hapless man to the wall.

'Hey! What is this?'

'Let's do this quietly,' one of the men said.

'What do you think you're doing? Get your hands off me!'

'Don't make a fuss, Commander. There's no point . . .'

'*Commander?* You've got the wrong man! My name is Melvyn Davis. I'm from Omaha!'

'Let's not play games.'

'Wait a minute! I've been set up. The man you want

is over there!' He pointed to where Robert had been standing.

There was no one there.

Outside the terminal, an airport bus was getting ready to depart. Robert boarded it, mingling with the other passengers. He sat at the back of the bus, concentrating on his next move.

He was desperate to talk to Admiral Whittaker, to try to get answers about what was going on, to learn who was responsible for killing innocent people because they had witnessed something they were not supposed to have seen. Was it General Hilliard? Dustin Thornton? Or Thornton's father-in-law, Willard Stone, the man of mystery? Could he be involved in this in some way? Was it Edward Sanders, the Director of NSA? Did it go as high as the President? Robert needed answers.

The bus trip into Rome took an hour. When the bus stopped in front of the Eden Hotel, Robert disembarked.

I've got to get out of the country, Robert thought. There was only one man in Rome he could trust. Colonel Francesco Cesar, head of SIFAR, the Italian Secret Service. He was going to be Robert's escape from Italy.

Colonel Cesar was working late. Messages had been flashing back and forth among foreign security agencies, and they all involved Commander Robert Bellamy. Colonel Cesar had worked with Robert in the past and he was very fond of him. Cesar sighed as he looked at the latest message in front of him. *Terminate*. And as he was reading it, his secretary came into the office.

'Commander Bellamy is on line one for you.'

Colonel Cesar stared at her. 'Bellamy? Himself? Never mind.' He waited until the secretary left the room, then snatched up the telephone.

'Robert?'

'*Ciao*, Francesco. What the hell is going on?'

'You tell me, *amico*. I've been getting all kinds of urgent communiqués about you. What have you done?'

'It's a long story,' Robert said. 'And I haven't time. What have you heard?'

'That you've gone private. That you've been turned, and are singing like a canary.'

'*What?*'

'I heard you've made a deal with the Chinese and . . .'

'*Jesus Christ*. That's ridiculous!'

'Is it? Why?'

'Because an hour later they'd be hungry for more information.'

'For God's sake, Robert, this is nothing to joke about.'

'Tell me about it, Francesco. I've just sent ten innocent people to their deaths. I'm scheduled to be number eleven.'

'Where are you?'

'I'm in Rome. I can't seem to get out of your fucking city.'

'*Cacatura!*' There was a thoughtful silence. 'What can I do to help?'

'Get me to a safe house where we can talk, and I can figure out how to get away. Can you arrange that?'

'Yes, but you must be careful. Very careful. I will pick you up myself.'

Robert breathed a deep sigh of relief. 'Thanks, Francesco. I really appreciate it.'

'As you Americans say, you owe me one. Where are you?'

'The Lido bar in Trastevere.'

'Wait right there. I'll see you in exactly one hour.'

'Thanks, *amico*.' Robert replaced the receiver. It was going to be a long hour.

Thirty minutes later, two unmarked cars coasted to a stop ten yards from the Lido bar. There were four men in each car and they were all carrying automatic weapons.

Colonel Cesar got out of the first car. 'Let's do this quickly. We don't want anyone else to get hurt. *Andate al dietro, subito.*'

Half the men silently went around to cover the back of the building.

Robert Bellamy watched from the rooftop of the building across the street as Cesar and his men raised their weapons and charged into the bar.

All right, you bastards, Robert thought grimly, *we'll play it your way.*

Chapter Thirty-Six

DAY SIXTEEN
Rome, Italy

Robert placed a call to Colonel Cesar from a phone booth in the Piazza del Duomo. 'Whatever happened to friendship?' Robert asked.

'Don't be naïve, my friend. I'm under orders, just as you are. I can assure you, there is no use in your running. You're at the head of every intelligence agency's most wanted list. Half the governments of the world are looking for you.'

'Do you believe I'm a traitor?'

Cesar sighed. 'It doesn't matter what I believe, Robert. This is nothing personal. I have my orders.'

'To take me out.'

'You can make it easier by turning yourself in.'

'Thanks, *paesano*. If I need more advice, I'll call Dear Abby.' He slammed down the receiver.

Robert was aware that the longer he was at large, the greater the danger he was in. There would be security agents closing in on him from half a dozen countries.

There has to be a tree, Robert thought. The line came from a legend about a hunter who was relating an experience he had on safari. 'This huge lion was racing toward me, and all my gun bearers had fled. I had no gun, and there was nowhere to hide. Not a bush or a tree in sight. And the beast was charging straight at me, coming closer and closer.' 'How did you escape?' a listener asked. 'I ran over to the nearest tree and climbed it.' 'But you said there were no trees.' 'You don't understand. There *has* to be a tree!' *And I have to find it*, Robert thought.

He looked around the piazza. It was almost deserted at this hour. He decided it was time to have a talk with the man who had started him on this nightmare, General Hilliard. But he would have to be careful. Modern electronic phone tracing was almost instantaneous. Robert observed that the two telephone booths next to the one he was in were both empty. *Perfect*. Ignoring the private number General Hilliard had given him, he dialled the switchboard of NSA. When an operator answered, Robert said, 'General Hilliard's office, please.'

A moment later, he heard a secretary's voice. 'General Hilliard's office.'

Robert said, 'Please hold for an overseas call.' He dropped the receiver and hurried into the next booth. He quickly redialled the number. A different secretary answered, 'General Hilliard's office.'

'Please hold for an overseas call,' Robert said. He let the receiver hang and walked into the third booth, and dialled. When another secretary answered, Robert said, 'This is Commander Bellamy. I want to speak to General Hilliard.'

There was a gasp of surprise. 'Just a moment, Commander.' The secretary buzzed the intercom. 'General, Commander Bellamy is on line three.'

General Hilliard turned to Harrison Keller. 'Bellamy is on line three. Start a trace, fast.'

Harrison Keller hurried over to a telephone on a side table, and dialled the Network Operations Centre, manned and monitored twenty-four hours a day. The senior officer on duty answered. 'NOC. Adams.'

'How long will it take to do an emergency trace on an incoming call?' Keller whispered.

'Between one and two minutes.'

'Start it. General Hilliard's office, line three. I'll hang on.' He looked over at the General and nodded.

General Hilliard picked up the telephone.

'Commander . . . is that you?'

In the Operations Centre, Adams punched a number into a computer. 'Here we go,' he said.

'I thought it was time you and I had a talk, General.'

'I'm glad you called, Commander. Why don't you come in and we can discuss the situation? I'll arrange a plane for you, and you can be here in . . .'

'No thanks. Too many accidents happen in airplanes, General.'

In the communications room, ESS, the electronic switching system, had been activated. The computer screen began lighting up. AX_{121}-B . . . AX_{122}-C . . . AX_{123}-C . . .

'What's happening?' Keller whispered into the phone.

'The Network Operations Centre in New Jersey is

searching the Washington, DC trunks, sir. Hold on.'

The screen went blank. Then the words: *OVERSEAS TRUNK LINE ONE* flashed onto the screen.

'The call is coming from somewhere in Europe. We're tracing the country . . .'

General Hilliard was saying, 'Commander Bellamy, I think there's been a misunderstanding. I have a suggestion . . .'

Robert replaced the receiver.

General Hilliard looked over at Keller. 'Did you get it?'

Harrison Keller talked into the phone to Adams. 'What happened?'

'We lost him.'

Robert moved into the second booth and picked up the telephone.

General Hilliard's secretary said, 'Commander Bellamy is calling on line two.'

The two men looked at each other. General Hilliard pressed the button for line two.

'Commander?'

'Let *me* make a suggestion,' Robert said.

General Hilliard put his hand over the mouthpiece. 'Get the trace working again.'

Harrison Keller picked up the telephone and said to Adams, 'He's on again. Line two. Move fast.'

'Right.'

'My suggestion, General, is that you call off all your men. And I mean *now*.'

'I think you misunderstand the situation, Commander. We can work this problem out if . . .'

'I'll tell you how we can work it out. There's a

termination order out on me. I want you to cancel it.'

In the Network Operations Centre, the computer screen was flashing a new message: *AX155-C Subtrunk A21 verified. Circuit 301 to Rome. Atlantic Trunk 1.*

'We've got it,' Adams said into the phone. 'We've traced the trunk to Rome.'

'Get me the number and location,' Keller told him.

In Rome, Robert was glancing at his watch. 'You gave me an assignment. I carried it out.'

'You did very well, Commander. Here is what I . . .'

The line went dead.

The General turned to Keller. 'He hung up, again.'

Keller spoke into the phone. 'Did you get it?'

'Too quick, sir.'

Robert moved into the next booth and picked up the tele phone.

General Hilliard's secretary's voice came over the intercom. 'Commander Bellamy is on line one, General.'

The General snapped, 'Find the bastard!' He picked up the telephone. 'Commander?'

'I want you to listen, General, and listen closely. You've murdered a lot of innocent people. If you don't call off your men, I'm going to the media to tell them what's going on.'

'I wouldn't advise you to do that, unless you want to start a worldwide panic. The aliens are real, and we're defenceless against them. They're getting ready to make their move. You have no idea what would happen if word of this leaked out.'

'Neither have you,' Bellamy retorted. 'I'm not giving you a choice. Call off the contract on me. If there's one more attempt made on my life, I'm going public.'

'All right,' General Hilliard said. 'You win. I'll call it off. Why don't we do this? We can . . .'

'Your trace should be working pretty good, now,' Robert said. 'Have a good day.'

The connection was broken.

'Did you get it?' Keller barked into the phone.

Adams said, 'Close, sir. He was calling from an area in Central Rome. He kept switching numbers on us.'

The General looked over at Keller. 'Well?'

'I'm sorry, General. All we know is that he's somewhere in Rome. Do you believe his threat? Are we going to call off the contract on him?'

'No. We're going to eliminate him.'

Robert went over his options again. They were pitifully few. They would be watching the airports, railroad stations, bus terminals and car rental agencies. He could not check into a hotel because SIFAR would be circulating red notices. Yet he had to get out of Rome. He needed a cover. A companion. They would not be looking for a man and a woman together. It was a beginning.

A taxi was standing at the corner. Robert mussed his hair, pulled down his tie, and staggered drunkenly toward the taxi. 'Hey, there,' he called. 'You!'

The driver looked at him, distastefully.

Robert pulled out a twenty-dollar bill and slapped it into the man's hand. 'Hey, buddy, I'm lookin' a'get laid. You know what tha' means? D'you speak any goddamn English?'

The driver looked at the bill. 'You wish a woman?'

'You got it, pal. I wish a woman.'

'*Andiamo*,' the driver said.

Robert lurched into the cab, and it took off. He looked back. He was not being followed. The adrenalin was pumping. *Half the governments in the world are looking for you*. And there would be no appeal. Their orders were to assassinate him.

Twenty minutes later they had reach Tor di Ounto, Rome's red light district, populated by whores and pimps. They drove down Passeggiata Archeologica, and the driver pulled to a stop at a corner.

'You will find a woman here,' he said.

'Thanks, buddy.' Robert paid the amount on the meter, and stumbled out of the taxi. It pulled away with a squeal of tyres.

Robert looked around, studying his surroundings. No police. A few cars and a handful of pedestrians. There were more than a dozen whores cruising the street. In the spirit of 'let's round up the usual suspects', the police had conducted their bi-monthly sweep to satisfy the voices of morality, and moved the city's prostitutes from the Via Veneto, with its high visibility, to this area where they would not offend the dowagers taking tea at Doney's. For that reason, most of the ladies were attractive and well dressed. There was one in particular who caught Robert's eye.

She appeared to be in her early twenties. She had long, dark hair and was dressed in a tasteful black skirt and white blouse, covered by a camelhair coat. Robert guessed that she was a part-time actress or model. She was watching Robert.

Robert staggered up to her. 'Hi, baby,' he mumbled. 'D'you speak English?'

'Yes.'

'Good. Le's you an' me have a party.'

She smiled uncertainly. *Drunks could be trouble.* 'Maybe you should go sober up first.' She had a soft Italian accent.

'Hey, I'm sober enough.'

'It will cost you a hundred dollars.'

'Tha's okay, honey.'

She made her decision. '*Va bene.* Come. There is a hotel just around the corner.'

'Great. What's your name, baby?'

'Pier.'

'Mine's Henry.' A police car appeared in the distance, headed their way. 'Let's get outta here.'

The other women cast envious glances as Pier and her American customer walked away.

The hotel was no Hassler, but the pimply-faced boy at the desk downstairs did not ask for a passport. In fact, he barely glanced up as he handed Pier a key. 'Fifty thousand lire.'

Pier looked at Robert. He took the money from his pocket and gave it to the boy.

The room they entered contained a large bed in the corner, a small table, two wooden chairs and a mirror over the basin. There was a clothes rack behind the door.

'You must pay me in advance.'

'Sure.' Robert counted out one hundred dollars.

'*Grazie.*'

Pier began to get undressed. Robert walked over to the window. He pushed aside a corner of the curtain and peered out. Everything appeared to be normal. He hoped that by now the police were following the red truck back to France. Robert dropped the curtain and turned around. Pier was naked. She had a surprisingly lovely body. Firm, young breasts, rounded hips, a small waist and long, shapely legs.

She was watching Robert. 'Aren't you going to get undressed, Henry?'

This was the tricky part. '. . . tell you the truth,' Robert said, 'I think I had a little too much to drink. I can't give you any action.'

She was regarding him with wary eyes. 'Then why did you . . . ?'

'If I stay here and sleep it off, we can make love in the morning.'

She shrugged. 'I have to work. It would cost me money to . . .'

'Don't worry. I'll take care of that.' He pulled out several hundred-dollar bills and handed them to her. 'Will that cover it?'

Pier looked at the money, making up her mind. It was tempting. It was cold outside, and business was slow. On the other hand, there was something strange about this man. First of all, he did not really seem to be drunk. He was nicely dressed and for this much money he could have checked them into a fine hotel. *Well*, Pier thought, *what the hell? Che cazzo me ne frega?* 'All right. There's only this bed for the two of us.'

'That's fine.'

Pier watched as Robert walked over to the window again and moved the edge of the curtain aside.

'You are looking for something?'

'Is there a back door out of the hotel?'

What am I getting myself into? Pier wondered. Her best friend had been murdered, hanging out with mobsters. Pier considered herself wise in the ways of men, but this one puzzled her. He did not seem like a criminal, but still . . . 'Yes, there is,' she said.

There was a sudden scream, and Robert whirled around.

'*Dio! Dio! Sono venuta tre volte!*' It was a woman's voice, coming from the next room through the paper-thin walls.

'What's that?' Robert's heart was pounding.

Pier grinned. 'She's having fun. She said she just came for the third time.'

Robert heard the creaking of bed springs.

'Are you going to bed?' Pier stood there naked, unembarrassed, watching him.

'Sure.' Robert sat down on the bed.

'Aren't you going to get undressed?'

'No.'

'Suit yourself.' Pier moved over to the bed and lay down beside Robert. 'I hope you don't snore,' Pier said.

'You can tell me in the morning.'

Robert had no intention of sleeping. He wanted to check the street during the night, to make sure they did not come to the hotel. They would get around to these small, third-class hotels eventually, but it would take them time. They had too many other places to cover first. He lay there, feeling bone-tired, and closed his eyes for a moment to rest. He slept. He was back home, in his own bed, and he felt Susan's warm body next to his. *She's back*, he thought, happily. *She's come back to me. Baby, I've missed you so much.*

DAY SEVENTEEN
Rome, Italy

Robert was awakened by the sun hitting his face. He sat up abruptly, looking around for an instant in alarm, disorientated. When he saw Pier, memory flooded back. He relaxed. Pier was at the mirror, brushing her hair.

'*Buon giorno*,' she said. 'You do not snore.'

Robert looked at his watch. Nine o'clock. He had wasted precious hours.

'Do you want to make love now? You have already paid for it.'

'That's all right,' Robert said.

Pier walked over to the bed, naked and provocative. 'Are you sure?'

I couldn't if I wanted to, lady. 'I'm sure.'

'*Va bene.*' She began to dress. She asked casually, 'Who is Susan?'

The question caught him off guard. 'Susan? What made you ask?'

'You talk in your sleep.'

He remembered his dream. Susan had come back to him. Maybe it was a sign. 'She's a friend.' *She's my wife. She's going to get tired of Moneybags and return to me some day. If I'm still alive, that is.*

Robert walked over to the window. He lifted the curtain and looked out. The street was crowded now with pedestrians and merchants opening up their shops. There were no signs of danger.

It was time to put his plan into motion. He turned to the girl. 'Pier, how would you like to go on a little trip with me?'

She looked at him with suspicion. 'A trip ... where?'

'I have to go to Venice on business, and I hate travelling alone. Do you like Venice?'

'Yes ...'

'Good. I'll pay you for your time, and we'll have a little holiday together.' He was staring out of the window again. 'I know a lovely hotel there. The Cipriani.' Years ago, he and Susan had stayed at the Royal Danieli, but he had been back since, and it had become sadly run-down, and the beds were impossible. The only thing that remained of the hotel's former elegance was Luciano, at the reception desk.

'It will cost you a thousand dollars a day.' She was ready to settle for five hundred.

'It's a deal.' Robert said. He counted out two thousand dollars. 'We'll start with this.'

Pier hesitated. She had a premonition that something was wrong. But the start of the movie she had been promised a bit part in had been delayed, and she needed the money. 'Very well,' she said.

'Let's go.'

Downstairs, Pier watched him scan the street carefully before stepping out to hail a taxi. *He's a target for somebody*, Pier thought. *I'm getting out of here.*

'Look,' Pier said, 'I'm not sure I should go to Venice with you. I . . .'

'We're going to have a great time,' Robert told her.

Directly across the street he saw a jewellery store. He took Pier's hand. 'Come on. I'm going to get you something pretty.'

'But . . .'

He led her across the street to the jewellery store.

The clerk behind the counter said, '*Buon giorno, signore*. Can I help you?'

'Yes,' Robert said. 'We're looking for something lovely for the lady.' He turned to Pier. 'Do you like emeralds?'

'I . . . yes.'

Robert said to the clerk, 'Do you have an emerald bracelet?'

'*Si, signore*. I have a beautiful emerald bracelet.' He walked over to a case and took out a bracelet. 'This is our finest. It is fifteen thousand dollars.'

Robert looked at Pier. 'Do you like it?'

She was speechless. She nodded.

'We'll take it,' Robert said. He handed the clerk his ONI credit card.

'One moment, please.' The clerk disappeared into the back room. When he returned, he said, 'Shall I wrap it for you, or . . . ?'

'No. My friend will wear it.' Robert put the bracelet on Pier's wrist. She was staring at it, stunned.

Robert said, 'That will look pretty in Venice, won't it?'

Pier smiled up at him. 'Very.'

When they were out on the street, Pier said, 'I . . . I don't know how to thank you.'

'I just want you to have a good time,' Robert told her. 'Do you have a car?'

'No. I used to have an old one, but it was stolen.'

'Do you still have your driver's licence?'

She was watching him, puzzled. 'Yes, but without a car, what good is a driver's licence?'

'You'll see. Let's get out of here.'

He hailed a taxi. 'Via Po, please.'

She sat in the taxi, studying him. Why was he so anxious for her company? He had not even touched her. *Could he be . . . ?*

'*Qui!*' Robert called to the driver. They were a hundred yards away from Maggiore's Car Rental Agency.

'We're getting out here,' Robert told Pier. He paid the driver and waited until the taxi was out of sight. He handed Pier a large bundle of bank notes. 'I want you to rent a car for us. Ask for a Fiat or an Alfa Romeo. Tell them we'll want it for four or five days. This money will cover the deposit. Rent it in your name. I'll wait for you in the bar across the street.'

Less than eight blocks away, two detectives were questioning the hapless driver of a red truck with French licence plates.

'*Vous me faites chier*. I have no idea how the fuck that card got in the back of my truck,' the driver screamed. 'Some crazy Italian probably put it in there.'

The two detectives looked at each other. One of them said, 'I'll phone it in.'

Francesco Cesar sat at his desk, thinking about the latest development. Earlier, the assignment had seemed so simple. '*You won't have any trouble finding him. When the time comes, we will activate the homing device, and it will lead you right to him.*' Someone had obviously underestimated Commander Bellamy.

Colonel Frank Johnson was seated in General Hilliard's office, his huge frame filling the chair.

'We have half the agents in Europe looking for him,' General Hilliard said. 'So far, they've had no luck.'

'It's going to take more than luck,' Colonel Johnson said. 'Bellamy's good.'

'We know he's in Rome. The sonofabitch just charged a bracelet for fifteen thousand dollars. We have him bottled up. There's no way he can get out of Italy. We know the name he's using on his passport – Arthur Butterfield.'

Colonel Johnson shook his head. 'If I know Bellamy, you haven't a clue about what name he's using. The only thing you can count on is that Bellamy won't do what you count on him to do. We're after a man who's as good as the best in the business. Maybe better. If there's any place to run, Bellamy will run there. If there's any place to hide, he'll hide there. I think our best bet is to bring him out in the open, smoke him out. Right now, he's controlling all the moves. We have to take the initiative away from him.'

'You mean, go public? Give it to the press?'

'Exactly.'

General Hilliard pursed his lips. 'That's going to be touchy. We can't afford to expose ourselves.'

'We won't have to. We'll put out a release that he's wanted on a drug-smuggling charge. That way we can get Interpol and all the police departments in Europe involved without tipping our hand.'

General Hilliard thought about it for a moment. 'I like it.'

'Good. I'm leaving for Rome,' Colonel Johnson said. 'I'm going to take charge of the hunt myself.'

When Colonel Frank Johnson returned to his office, he was in a thoughtful mood. He was playing a dangerous game. There was no question about it. He had to find Commander Bellamy.

Chapter Thirty-Seven

Robert listened to the phone ring again and again. It was six a.m. in Washington. *I'm always waking the old man up,* Robert thought.

The Admiral answered on the sixth ring. 'Hello . . .'

'Admiral, I . . .'

'Robert! What . . . ?'

'Don't say anything. Your phone is probably bugged. I'm going to make this fast. I just wanted to tell you not to believe anything they're saying about me. I'd like you to try to find out what's going on. I may need your help later.'

'Of course. Anything I can do, Robert.'

'I know.'

'I'll call you later.'

Robert replaced the receiver. No time for a trace. He saw a blue Fiat pull up outside the bar. Pier was at the wheel.

'Move over,' Robert said. 'I'll drive.'

Pier made room for him as he slid in behind the wheel.

'Are we on our way to Venice?' Pier asked.

'Uh huh. We have a couple of stops to make first.' It was time to spread some more chaff around. He turned onto Viale Rossini. Ahead was the Rossini

Travel Service. Robert pulled over to the kerb. 'I'll be back in a minute.'

Pier watched him walk into the travel agency. *I could just drive away*, she thought, *and keep the money, and he would never find me. But the damn car is rented in my name. Cacchio!*

Inside the agency, Robert walked up to the woman behind the counter.

'Good day. May I help you?'

'Yes. I'm Commander Robert Bellamy. I'm going to do a bit of travelling,' Robert told her. 'I'd like to make some reservations.'

She smiled. 'That's what we are here for, *signore*. Where are you planning to go?'

'I'd like a first-class airline ticket to Beijing, one way.'

She made a note. 'And when would you like to leave?'

'This Friday.'

'Very good.' She pressed some keys on the computer. 'There's an Air China flight leaving at seven forty p.m. Friday night.'

'That will do nicely.'

She pressed some more keys. 'There we are. Your reservation is confirmed. Will that be cash or . . . ?'

'Oh, I'm not through yet. I want to reserve a train ticket to Budapest.'

'And when would that be, Commander?'

'Next Monday.'

'And in what name?'

'The same.'

She looked at him strangely. 'You are flying to Beijing on Friday and . . .'

'I'm not finished,' Robert said pleasantly. 'I want a one-way airline ticket to Miami, Florida, on Sunday.'

Now she was openly staring at him. '*Signore*, if this is some kind of a . . .'

Robert pulled out his ONI credit card and handed it to her. 'Just charge the tickets to this card.'

She studied it a moment. 'Excuse me.' She went into the back office and came out a few minutes later. 'That will be perfectly all right. We will be happy to make the arrangements. Do you wish all the reservations under one name?'

'Yes. Commander Robert Bellamy.'

'Very good.'

Robert watched as she pressed more buttons on the computer. A minute later, three tickets appeared. She tore them off the printer.

'Please put the tickets in separate envelopes,' Robert said.

'Of course. Would you like me to send them to . . . ?'

'I'll take them with me.'

'*Si, signore*.'

Robert signed the credit card slip and she handed him his receipt.

'There you are. Have a nice trip . . . trips . . . er . . .'

Robert grinned. 'Thanks.' A minute later he was behind the wheel of the car.

'Are we going now?' Pier asked.

'We have just a few more stops to make,' Robert said.

Pier watched him carefully scan the street again before pulling out.

'I want you to do something for me,' Robert told her.

Now it's coming, Pier thought. *He's going to ask me to do something terrible.* 'What is it?' she asked.

They had stopped in front of the Hotel Victoria. Robert handed Pier one of the envelopes. 'I want you to go to the desk and reserve a suite in the name of Commander Robert Bellamy. Tell them you're his secretary and that he'll be arriving in an hour, but that you want to go up to the suite and approve it. When you get inside, leave this envelope on a table in the room.'

She looked at him, puzzled. 'That's all?'

'That's all.'

The man made no sense at all. '*Bene.*' She wished she knew what the crazy American was up to. *And who is Commander Robert Bellamy?* Pier got out of the car and walked into the lobby of the hotel. She was a bit nervous. In the course of practising her profession, she had been thrown out of a few first-class hotels. But the clerk behind the desk greeted her politely. 'May I help you, *signora*?'

'I am the secretary to Commander Robert Bellamy. I wish to reserve a suite for him. He will be here in an hour.'

The clerk consulted the room chart. 'We do happen to have one very nice suite available.'

'May I see it, please?' Pier asked.

'Certainly. I'll have someone show it to you.'

An assistant manager escorted Pier upstairs. They walked into the living room of the suite and Pier looked around. 'Will this be satisfactory, *signora*?'

Pier had not the faintest idea. 'Yes, this will be fine.' She removed the envelope from her purse and laid it on a coffee table. 'I will leave this here for the Commander,' she said.

'*Bene.*'

Curiosity got the better of Pier. She opened the envelope. Inside was a one-way plane ticket to Beijing in the name of Robert Bellamy. Pier put the ticket back in the envelope, left it on the table and went downstairs.

The blue Fiat was parked in front of the hotel.

'Any problem?' Robert asked.

'No.'

'We have just two more stops to make, and then we're on our way,' Robert said cheerfully.

The next stop was the Hotel Valadier. Robert handed Pier another envelope. 'I want you to reserve a suite here in the name of Commander Robert Bellamy. Tell them he'll be checking in within an hour. Then...'

'I leave the envelope upstairs.'

'Right.'

This time Pier walked into the hotel with more confidence. *Just act like a lady*, she thought. *You've got to have dignity. That's the fucking secret.*

There was a suite available in the hotel.

'I would like to look at it,' Pier said.

'Of course, *signora*.'

An assistant manager escorted Pier upstairs. 'This is one of our nicest suites.' It was beautiful.

Pier said haughtily, 'I suppose it might do. The Commander is very particular, you know.' She took the second envelope out of her purse, opened it, and glanced inside. It contained a train ticket to Budapest in the name of Commander Robert Bellamy. Pier stared at it, confused. *What kind of game is this?* She left the ticket by the bed stand.

When Pier returned to the car, Robert asked, 'How did it go?'

'Fine.'

'Last stop.'

This time it was the Hotel Leonardo da Vinci. Robert handed Pier the third envelope. 'I would like you to . . .'

'I know.'

Inside the hotel, a clerk said, 'Yes, indeed, *signora*, we have a lovely suite. When did you say the Commander will be arriving?'

'In an hour. I would like to examine the suite to see if it is satisfactory.'

'Of course, *signora*.'

The suite was more lavish than the other two Pier had looked at. The assistant manager showed her the huge bedroom with a large canopied bed in the centre. *What a waste*, Pier thought. *In one night, I could make a fortune here.* She took out the third envelope and looked inside. It contained an airplane ticket to Miami, Florida. Pier left the envelope on the bed.

The assistant manager escorted Pier back to the living room. 'We have colour TV,' he said. He walked over to the television set and turned it on. A picture of Robert leaped onto the screen. The anchorman's voice was saying: '... and Interpol believes that he is presently in Rome. He is wanted for questioning in an international drug-smuggling operation. This is Bernard Shaw for CNN News.' Pier was staring at the screen, transfixed.

The assistant manager turned off the television set. 'Is everything satisfactory?'

'Yes,' Pier said slowly. *A drug smuggler!*

'We'll be looking forward to seeing the Commander.'

When Pier joined Robert in the car downstairs, she looked at him with different eyes.

'Now we're ready,' Robert smiled.

At the Hotel Victoria, a man in a dark suit was studying the guest register. He looked up at the clerk. 'What time did Commander Bellamy check in?'

'He has not been here yet. His secretary reserved the suite. She said he would be here within the hour.'

The man turned to his companion. 'Have the hotel staked out. Get reinforcements. I'll wait upstairs.' He turned to the clerk. 'Open the suite for me.'

Three minutes later the clerk was opening the door to the suite. The man in the dark suit moved in cautiously, gun in hand. The suite was empty. He saw the envelope on the table and picked it up. The front of it read: 'Commander Robert Bellamy'. He opened the envelope and glanced inside. A moment later he was dialling the headquarters of SIFAR.

Francesco Cesar was in the middle of a meeting with Colonel Frank Johnson. Colonel Johnson had landed at Leonardo da Vinci airport two hours earlier, but he showed no signs of fatigue.

'As far as we know,' Cesar was saying, 'Bellamy is still in Rome. We've had more than thirty reports on his whereabouts.'

'Any of them check out?'

'No.'

The phone rang. 'It's Luigi, Colonel,' the voice on the telephone said. 'We've got him. I'm in his hotel suite at the Hotel Victoria. I have his airline ticket to Beijing. He is planning to leave Friday.'

Cesar's voice filled with excitement. 'Good! Stay there. We will be right over.' He hung up and turned to Colonel Johnson. 'I'm afraid your journey was for nothing, Colonel. We've got him. He's registered at the Hotel Victoria. They found an airline ticket in his name for Beijing on Friday.'

Colonel Johnson said mildly, 'Bellamy registered at the hotel in his own name?'

'Yes.'

'And the plane ticket is in his name?'

'Yes.' Colonel Cesar rose. 'Let's get on over there.'

Colonel Johnson shook his head. 'Don't waste your time.'

'What?'

'Bellamy would never . . .'

The telephone rang again. Cesar snatched it up. A voice said, 'Colonel? This is Mario. We've located Bellamy. He's at the Hotel Valadier. He's taking a train Monday to Budapest. What do you want us to do?'

'I'll get back to you,' Colonel Cesar said. He turned to look at Colonel Johnson. 'They found a train ticket to Budapest in Bellamy's name. I don't understand what . . .'

The telephone rang again.

'Yes?' His voice was pitched higher.

'It's Bruno. We've located Bellamy. He's registered at the Hotel Leonardo da Vinci. He's planning to leave Sunday for Miami. What shall I . . . ?'

'Come back here,' Cesar snapped. He slammed down the phone. 'What the hell is his game?'

Colonel Johnson said grimly. 'He's seeing to it that you're wasting a lot of manpower, isn't he?'

'What do we do now?'

'We trap the bastard.'

They were driving on the Via Cassia, near Olgiata, headed north toward Venice. The police would be covering all the major exits from Italy, but they would be expecting him to go west, to head for France or Switzerland. *From Venice*, Robert thought, *I can take the hydrofoil to Trieste and make my way up to Austria. After that . . .*

Pier's voice interrupted his thoughts. 'I'm hungry.'

'What?'

'We haven't had any breakfast or lunch.'

'I'm sorry,' Robert said. He had been too preoccupied to think about eating. 'We'll stop at the next restaurant.'

Pier watched him as he drove. She was more puzzled than ever. She lived in a world of pimps and thieves, and drug smugglers. This man was no criminal.

They stopped at the next town in front of a small trattoria. Robert pulled into the parking lot and he and Pier got out of the car.

The restaurant was crowded with patrons, and noisy with conversation and the clatter of dishes. Robert found a table against the wall, and took a seat facing the door. A waiter approached and handed them menus.

Robert was thinking: *Susan should be on the boat by now. This may be my last chance to talk to her.*

'Look over the menu.' Robert rose. 'I'll be right back.'

Pier watched him walk over to the public telephone near their table. He put a coin in the slot.

'I would like to talk to the marine operator in Gibraltar. Thank you.'

Who is he calling in Gibraltar? Pier wondered. *Is that his get-away?*

'Operator, I want to place a collect call to the American yacht, *Halcyon*, off Gibraltar. Whiskey Sugar 337. Thank you.'

A few minutes passed while the operators talked to each other and his call was accepted.

Robert heard Susan's voice on the telephone.

'Susan . . .'

'Robert! Are you all right?'

'I'm fine. I just wanted to tell you . . .'

'I know what you want to tell me. It's all over the radio and television. Why is Interpol hunting you?'

'It's a long story.'

'Take your time. I want to know.'

He hesitated. 'It's political, Susan. I have evidence that some governments are trying to suppress. That's why Interpol is after me.'

Pier was listening intently to Robert's end of the conversation.

'What can I do to help?' Susan asked.

'Nothing, honey. I just called to hear your voice once more in case . . . in case I don't get out of this.'

'Don't say that.' There was panic in her voice. 'Can you tell me what country you're in?'

'Italy.'

There was a brief silence. 'All right. We're not far from you. We're just off the coast of Gibraltar. We can pick you up at any place you say.'

'No, I . . .'

'Listen to me. It's probably your only chance of escape.'

'I can't let you do that, Susan. You'd be in jeopardy.'

Monte had walked into the saloon in time to hear part of the conversation. 'Let me talk to him.'

'Just a moment, Robert, Monte wants to speak to you.'

'Susan, I haven't . . .'

Monte's voice came over the line. 'Robert, I understand you're in serious trouble.'

The understatement of the year. 'You might say that.'

'We'd like to help you out. They won't be looking

for you on a yacht. Why don't you let us pick you up?'

'Thanks, Monte, I appreciate it. The answer is no.'

'I think you're making a mistake. You'll be safe here.'

Why was he so eager to help? 'Thanks, anyway. I'll take my chances. I'd like to speak to Susan again . . .'

'Of course.' Monte Banks handed the phone to Susan. 'Talk him into it,' he urged.

Susan spoke into the phone. 'Please let us help you.'

'You have helped me, Susan.' He had to stop for a moment. 'You're the best part of my life. I just want you to know that I'll always love you.' He gave a little laugh. 'Although *always* may not be such a big deal anymore.'

'Will you call me again?'

'If I can.'

'Promise me.'

'All right. I promise.'

He slowly replaced the receiver. *Why did I do that to her? Why did I do that to myself? You're a sentimental idiot, Bellamy.* He walked back to the table.

'Let's eat,' Robert said. They ordered.

'I heard your conversation. The police are looking for you, aren't they?'

Robert stiffened. *Careless. She was going to be trouble.* 'It's just a little misunderstanding. I . . .'

'Don't treat me like a fool. I want to help you.'

He was watching her warily. 'Why should you help me?'

Pier leaned forward. 'Because you've been generous to me. And I hate the police. You don't know what

333

it's like to be out on the streets, hounded by them, treated like dirt. They arrest me for prostitution, but they take me to their back rooms and pass me around. They are animals. I would do anything to get even with them. Anything. I can help you.'

'Pier, there's nothing you . . .'

'In Venice the police will catch you easily. If you stay at a hotel, they will find you. If you try to get on a ship, they will trap you. But I know a place where you will be safe from them. My mother and brother live in Naples. We can stay at their house. The police will never look for you there.'

Robert was silent for a moment, thinking about it. What Pier said made a good deal of sense. A private house would be much safer than any other place, and Naples was a big port. It would be easy to get a ship out of there. He hesitated before he answered. He did not want to put Pier in danger.

'Pier, if the police find me, they have orders to kill me. You would be considered an accomplice. You could be letting yourself in for trouble.'

'It's very simple.' Pier smiled. 'We won't let them find you.'

Robert returned her smile. He made up his mind. 'All right. Eat your lunch. We're going to Naples.'

Colonel Frank Johnson said, 'Your men have no idea where he is headed?'

Francesco Cesar sighed. 'Not at the moment. But it is only a matter of time before . . .'

'We don't have time. Have you checked the whereabouts of his ex-wife?'

'His ex-wife? No. I don't see what . . .'

'Then you haven't done your homework,' Colonel Johnson snapped. 'She's married to a man named Monte Banks. I would suggest that you locate them, and fast.'

Chapter Thirty-Eight

She wandered down the broad boulevard, barely conscious of where she was going. How many days had it been since the terrible crash? She had lost count. She was so tired that it was difficult for her to concentrate. She desperately needed water; not the polluted water that the Earthlings drank, but fresh, clear rain water. She needed the pure fluid to revive her life essence, to gain the strength to find the crystal. She was dying.

She staggered and bumped into a man.

'Hey! Watch where...' The American salesman took a closer look at her and smiled. 'Hi, there. Imagine bumping into you like this!' *What a doll.*

'Yes, I can imagine that.'

'Where are you from, honey?'

'The seventh sun of the Pleiades.'

He laughed. 'I like a gal with a sense of humour. Where you headed?'

She shook her head. 'I do not know. I am a stranger here.'

Jesus, I think I'm on to something. 'Have you had dinner?'

'No. I cannot eat your food.'

I've got a real weirdo here. But a beauty. 'Where are you staying?'

'I am not staying anywhere.'

'You don't have a hotel?'

'A hotel?' She remembered. *Boxes for travelling strangers.* 'No. I must find a place to sleep. I am very tired.'

His smile broadened. 'Well, Papa can take care of that. Why don't we go up to my hotel room? I've got a nice, big comfortable bed there. Would you like that?'

'Oh, yes, very much.'

He could not believe his good luck. 'Wonderful!' *I'll bet she's great in the hay.*

She looked at him, puzzled. 'Your bed is made of hay?'

He was staring at her. 'What? No, no. You like your little jokes, don't you?'

She could barely keep her eyes open. 'Could we go to bed now?'

He rubbed his hands together. 'You bet! My hotel is just around the corner.'

He picked up his key at the desk and they took the elevator to his floor. When they got to his room, the man asked, 'Would you like a little drink?' *Let's loosen you up.*

She wanted one desperately, but not the liquids the Earthlings had to offer. 'No,' she said. 'Where is the bed?'

My God, she's a hot little thing. 'In here, honey.' He led her into the bedroom. 'You're sure you wouldn't like a drink?'

'I am sure.'

He licked his lips. 'Then why don't you – er – get undressed?'

She nodded. It was an Earthling custom. She removed the dress she was wearing. She was wearing nothing underneath. Her body was exquisite.

The man stared at her and said, happily, 'This is my lucky night, honey. Yours, too.' *I'm going to fuck you like you've never been fucked before.* He tore off his clothes as fast as he could and jumped into bed beside her. 'Now!' he said. 'I'm going to show you some real action.' He glanced up. 'Damn! I left the light on.' He started to get up.

'Never mind,' she said sleepily. 'I will turn it off.'

And as he watched, her arm reached out, out, across the wide room, and her fingers became leafy green tendrils as they brushed against the light switch.

He was alone in the dark with her. He screamed.

Chapter Thirty-Nine

They were travelling at high speed on the Autostrada del Sole, the freeway to Naples. They had been driving in silence for the last half hour, each preoccupied with his own thoughts.

Pier broke the silence. 'How long would you like to stay at my mother's house?' she asked.

'Three or four days, if that's all right.'

'That will be fine.'

Robert had no intention of staying there for more than one night, two at the most. But he kept his plans to himself. As soon as he found a ship that was safe, he would be on his way out of Italy.

'I'm looking forward to seeing my family,' Pier said.

'You have just one brother?'

'Yes. Carlo. He is younger than me.'

'Tell me about your family, Pier.'

She shrugged. 'There is not much to tell. My father worked at the docks all his life. A crane fell on him and killed him when I was fifteen. My mother was ill, and I had to support her and Carlo. I had a friend at Cinecittà studios and he got me bit parts. They paid very little and I had to sleep with the assistant director. I decided I could make more money on the streets.

Now I do a little of both.' There was no self-pity in her voice.

'Pier . . . are you sure your mother won't object to your bringing a stranger home?'

'I am sure. We are very close. Mother will be happy to see me. Do you love her very much?'

Robert glanced over at her in surprise. 'Your mother?'

'The woman you were talking to on the telephone in the restaurant — Susan.'

'What makes you think I love her?'

'The tone of your voice. Who is she?'

'A friend.'

'She is very lucky. I wish I had someone who cared for me like that. Is Robert Bellamy your real name?'

'Yes.'

'And are you a commander?'

That was more difficult to answer. 'I'm not sure, Pier,' he said. 'I used to be.'

'Can you tell me why Interpol is after you?'

He said carefully, 'It's better if I don't tell you anything. You could be in enough trouble just being with me. The less you know the better.'

'All right, Robert.'

He thought about the strange circumstances that had brought the two of them together. 'Let me ask you something. If you knew that there were aliens coming down to earth in spaceships, would you panic?'

Pier studied him a moment. 'Are you serious?'

'Very.'

She shook her head. 'No. I think it would be exciting. Do you believe such things exist?'

'There's a possibility,' he said cautiously.

Pier's face lit up. 'Really? Do they have real . . . I mean . . . are they built like men?'

Robert laughed. 'I don't know.'

'Does this have anything to do with why the police are after you?'

'No,' Robert said quickly. 'Nothing.'

'If I tell you something, will you promise not to be angry with me.'

'I promise.'

When she spoke, her voice was so low he could hardly hear her. 'I think I am falling in love with you.'

'Pier . . .'

'I know. I am being foolish. But I have never said that to anyone before. I wanted you to know.'

'I'm flattered, Pier.'

'You're not making fun of me?'

'No. I'm not.' He looked at the gas gauge. 'We'd better find a filling station soon.'

They came to a service station fifteen minutes later. 'We'll fill the tank here,' Robert said.

'Fine,' Pier smiled. 'I can call my mother and let her know that I am bringing home a handsome stranger.'

Robert drove up to the gas pump and said to the attendant, '*Fate il pieno, per favore.*'

'*Si, signore.*'

Pier leaned over and gave Robert a kiss on the cheek. 'I will be right back.'

Robert watched her walk into the office and get change for the telephone. *She's really very pretty,*

Robert thought. *And intelligent. I must be careful not to hurt her.*

Inside the office, Pier was dialling. She turned to smile and wave at Robert. When the operator came on, Pier said, 'Get me Interpol. *Subito!*'

Chapter Forty

From the moment Pier had seen the news broadcast about Robert Bellamy, she had known she was going to be rich. If Interpol, the international criminal police force, was looking for Robert, there had to be a huge reward out for him. And she was the only one who knew where he was! The reward would be all hers. Persuading him to go to Naples, where she could keep an eye on him, had been a stroke of genius.

A man's voice on the telephone said, 'Interpol. May I help you?'

Pier's heart was pounding. She glanced out of the window to make sure Robert was still at the gas pump. 'Yes. You are looking for a man named Commander Robert Bellamy, yes?'

There was a moment of silence. 'Who is calling, please?'

'Never mind. Are you after him or not?'

'I'll have to transfer you to someone else. Will you hold the line, please?' He turned to his assistant. 'Put a trace on this. *Pronto!*'

Thirty seconds later, Pier was speaking with a senior official. 'Yes, *signora*. Can I help you?'

No, you fool. I'm trying to help you. 'I have Commander Robert Bellamy. Do you want him, or don't you?'

'But, yes, *signora*, we want him very much. And you say you have him?'

'That's right. He's with me now. How much is he worth to you?'

'Are you speaking of a reward?'

'Of course I'm speaking of a reward.' She glanced out of the window again. *What kind of idiots are these?*

The official signalled to his assistant to move faster.

'We have not yet set a price on him, *signora*, so . . .'

'Well, set one now. I'm in a hurry.'

'How much of a reward are you expecting?'

'I don't know.' Pier thought for a moment. 'Would fifty thousand dollars be all right?'

'Fifty thousand dollars is a lot of money. If you tell me where you are, we could come to you and negotiate a deal that . . .'

He must think I'm pazza. 'No. You either agree to pay me what I want now or . . .' Pier looked up and saw Robert approaching the office. 'Hurry! Yes or no?'

'Very well, *signora*. Yes. We will agree to pay you . . .'

Robert came through the door, moving toward her.

Pier said into the telephone, 'We should be there in time for dinner, Mama. You will like him. He is very nice. Good. We will see you later. *Ciao*.'

Pier replaced the receiver and turned to Robert. 'Mother is dying to meet you.'

*

At Interpol headquarters, the senior official said, 'Did you trace the call?'

'Yes. It came from a filling station on the Autostrada del Sole. It looks like they're on their way to Naples.'

Colonel Francesco Cesar and Colonel Frank Johnson were studying a map on the wall of Cesar's office.

'Naples is a big city,' Colonel Cesar was saying. 'There are a thousand places for him to hide there.'

'What about the woman?'

'We have no idea who she is.'

'Why don't we find out?' Johnson asked.

Cesar looked at him, puzzled. 'How?'

'If Bellamy needed a woman companion in a hurry, as a cover, what would he do?'

'He would probably pick up a whore.'

'Right. Where do we start?'

'Tor di Ounto.'

They drove down the Passeggiata Archeologica and watched the streetwalkers peddling their wares. In the car with Colonel Cesar and Colonel Johnson was Captain Bellini, the police supervisor of the district.

'This is not going to be easy,' Bellini said. 'They're all in competition with one another, but when it comes to the police, they're like blood sisters. They won't talk.'

'We'll see,' Colonel Johnson said.

Bellini ordered the driver to pull over to the kerb and the three men got out of the car. The prostitutes were eyeing them warily. Bellini walked up to one of the women. 'Good afternoon, Maria. How's business?'

'It will be better when you leave.'

'We're not planning to stay. I just want to ask you a question. We're looking for an American who picked up one of the girls last night. We think they are travelling together. We want to know who she is. Can you help us?' He showed her a photograph of Robert.

Several other prostitutes had gathered around to listen to the conversation.

'I can't help you,' Maria said, 'but I know someone who can.'

Bellini nodded approvingly. 'Good. Who?'

Maria pointed to a store-front across the street. A sign in the window read: 'Fortune Teller – Palm Reader'. 'Madam Lucia might help you.'

The girls laughed appreciatively.

Captain Bellini looked at them, and said, 'So you like jokes, do you? Well, we're going to play a little joke I think you're going to love. These two gentlemen are very anxious to have the name of the girl who went off with the American. If you don't know who she is, I suggest you talk to your friends, find someone who does know, and when you have the answer, give me a call.'

'Why should we?' one of them asked defiantly.

'You'll find out.'

One hour later the prostitutes of Rome found themselves under siege. Patrol wagons swept the city, picking up all the women working the streets, and their pimps. There were screaming protests.

'You can't do this . . . I pay police protection.'

'This has been my beat for five years . . .'

'I've been giving it to you and your friends for free. Where's your gratitude . . . ?'

'What do I pay you protection for . . . ?'

By the following day, the streets were virtually empty of prostitutes, and the jails were full.

Cesar and Colonel Johnson were sitting in Captain Bellini's office. 'It's going to be difficult to keep them in jail,' Captain Bellini warned. 'I might also add that this is very bad for tourism.'

'Don't worry,' Colonel Johnson said, 'someone will talk. Just keep the pressure on.'

Their break came late in the afternoon. Captain Bellini's secretary said, 'There's a Mr Lorenzo to see you.'

'Send him in.'

Mr Lorenzo was dressed in a very expensive suit, and wore diamond rings on three fingers. Mr Lorenzo was a pimp.

'What can I do for you?' Bellini asked.

Lorenzo smiled. 'It's what I can do for *you* gentlemen. Some of my associates inform me that you are looking for a particular working girl who left town with an American, and since we are always eager to cooperate with the authorities, I thought I would give you her name.'

Colonel Johnson said, 'Who is she?'

Lorenzo ignored the question. 'Naturally, I'm sure you would want to express your appreciation by releasing my associates and their friends.'

Colonel Cesar said, 'We are not interested in any

of your whores. All we want is the name of the girl.'

'That is very gratifying news, sir. It's always a pleasure to deal with reasonable men. I know that . . .'

'Her name, Lorenzo.'

'Yes, of course. Her name is Pier. Pier Valli. The American spent the night with her at the L'Incrocio Hotel, and the next morning they took off. She is not one of my girls. If I may say so . . .'

Bellini was already on the telephone. 'Bring up the records on a Pier Valli. *Subito!*'

'I hope you gentlemen are going to show your gratitude by . . .'

Bellini looked up, and then said into the phone, 'And cancel Operation Puttana.'

Lorenzo beamed. '*Grazie.*'

Pier Valli's records were on Bellini's desk five minutes later. 'She started streetwalking when she was fifteen. She has been arrested a dozen times since then. She . . .'

'Where does she come from?' Colonel Johnson interrupted.

'Naples.' The two men looked at each other. 'She has a mother and brother living there.'

'Can you find out where?'

'I can check it out.'

'Do that. *Now.*'

Chapter Forty-One

They were approaching the suburbs of Naples. Old apartment houses lined the narrow streets, with laundry hanging out of almost every window, making the buildings look like concrete mountains flying colourful flags.

Pier asked, 'Have you ever been to Naples?'

'Once.' Robert's voice was tight. *Susan was sitting beside him, giggling. I heard Naples is a wicked city. Can we do a lot of wicked things here, darling?*

We're going to invent some new things, Robert promised.

Pier was watching him. 'Are you all right?'

Robert brought his mind back to the present. 'I'm fine.'

They were driving along the bay of the Castel Dell' Ovo, the old abandoned castle near the water.

When they arrived at Via Toledo, Pier said, excitedly, 'Turn here.'

They were approaching Spaccanapoli, the old section of Naples.

Pier said, 'It's just up ahead. Turn left onto Via Benedetto Croce.'

Robert made the turn. The traffic here was heavier, and the noise of horns deafening. He had forgotten how noisy Naples could be. He slowed the car down to avoid hitting the pedestrians and dogs that ran in front of the car as though they were blessed with some kind of immortality.

'Turn right here,' Pier directed, 'into Piazza del Plebiscito.' The traffic was even worse here, and the neighbourhood more run down.

'Stop!' Pier cried out.

Robert pulled over to the kerb. They had stopped in front of a row of seedy shops.

Robert glanced around. 'This is where your mother lives?'

'No,' Pier said. 'Of course not.' She leaned over and pressed the horn. A moment later, a young woman came out of one of the shops. Pier got out of the car and raced to greet her. They hugged each other.

'You look wonderful!' the woman exclaimed. 'You must be doing very well.'

'I am.' Pier held out her wrist. 'Look at my new bracelet!'

'Are those real emeralds?'

'Of course they are real.'

The woman yelled at someone inside the store, 'Anna! Come on out. Look who is here!'

Robert was watching the scene, unbelievingly. 'Pier . . .'

'In a minute, darling,' she said. 'I have to say hello to my friends.'

Within minutes, half a dozen women were clustered around Pier, admiring her bracelet, while Robert sat there helplessly, gritting his teeth.

'He is crazy about me,' Pier announced. She turned to Robert, 'Aren't you, *caro*?'

Robert wanted to strangle her, but there was nothing he could do. 'Yes,' he said. 'Can we go now, Pier?'

'In a minute.'

'*Now!*' Robert said.

'Oh, very well.' Pier turned to the women. 'We must leave now. We have an important appointment. *Ciao!*'

'*Ciao!*'

Pier got into the car beside Robert, and the women stood there, watching them drive away.

Pier said happily. 'They are all old friends.'

'Wonderful. Where's your mother's house?'

'Oh, she doesn't live in the city.'

'*What?*'

'She lives outside, in a little farmhouse, half an hour from here.'

The farmhouse was on the southern outskirts of Naples, an old stone building set off from the road.

'There it is!' Pier exclaimed. 'Isn't it beautiful?'

'Yes.' Robert liked the fact that the house was away from the centre of town. There would be no reason for anyone to come looking for him here. *Pier was right. It's a perfect safe house.*

They walked up to the front door, and before they reached it the door flew open and Pier's mother stood there, smiling at them. She was an older version of her daughter, thin and grey-haired, with a lined, careworn face.

'Pier, *cara! Mi sei mancata!*'

'I've missed you, too, Mama. This is the friend I telephoned you about that I was bringing home.'

Mama did not miss a beat. 'Ah? *Si*, you are welcome Mr . . . ?'

'Jones,' Robert said.

'Come in, come in.'

They entered the living room. It was a large room, comfortable and homey, crammed with furniture.

A boy in his early twenties entered the room. He was short and dark, with a thin, sullen face and brooding brown eyes. He wore jeans and a jacket with the name *Diavoli Rossi* sewn on it. His face lit up when he saw his sister. 'Pier!'

'Hello, Carlo.' They hugged.

'What are you doing here?'

'We came to visit for a few days.' She turned to Robert. 'This is my brother, Carlo. Carlo, this is Mr Jones.'

'Hello, Carlo.'

Carlo was sizing Robert up. 'Hello.'

Mama said, 'I will fix a nice bedroom for you two lovebirds, in the back.'

Robert said, 'If you don't mind . . . that is, if you have an extra bedroom, I'd prefer a room to myself.'

There was an awkward pause. The three of them were staring at Robert.

Mama turned to Pier. '*Omosessuale?*'

Pier shrugged. *I don't know*. But she was sure he was not a homosexual.

Mama looked at Robert. 'As you wish.' She hugged

Pier again. 'I'm so happy to see you. Come into the kitchen. I will make some coffee for us.'

In the kitchen, Mama exclaimed, '*Benissimo!* How did you meet him? He looks very rich. And that bracelet you are wearing. It must have cost a fortune. My goodness! Tonight I will cook a big dinner. I will invite all the neighbours so they can meet your . . .'

'No, Mama. You must not do that.'

'But, *cara*, why should we not spread the news of your good luck? All our friends will be so pleased.'

'Mama, Mr Jones just wants to rest for a few days. No party. No neighbours.'

Mama sighed, 'All right. Whatever you wish.'

I'll arrange for him to be picked up away from the house, so that Mama will not be disturbed.

Carlo had noticed the bracelet, too. 'That bracelet. Those are real emeralds, huh? Did you buy that for my sister?'

There was an attitude about the boy that Robert did not like. 'Ask her.'

Pier and Mama came out of the kitchen. Mama looked at Robert. 'You are sure you do not want to sleep with Pier?'

Robert was embarrassed. 'Thank you. No.'

Pier said, 'I'll show you your bedroom.' She led him toward the back of the house, to a large, comfortable bedroom with a double bed in the middle of the room.

'Robert, are you afraid of what Mama might think if we slept together? She knows what I do.'

'It's not that,' Robert said. 'It's . . .' There was no way he could explain. 'I'm sorry, I . . .'

Pier's voice was cold. 'Never mind.'

She felt unreasonably offended. Twice now he had refused to sleep with her. *It serves him right that I am turning him over to the police*, she thought. And yet she felt a small, nagging sense of guilt. He was really very nice. But fifty thousand dollars was fifty thousand dollars.

At dinner, Mama was talkative, but Pier and Robert and Carlo were silent and preoccupied.

Robert was busily working out his plan of escape. *Tomorrow*, he thought, *I'll go down to the docks and find a ship out of here.*

Pier was thinking about the phone call she was planning to make. *I'll call from town, so the police cannot trace it here.*

Carlo was studying the stranger his sister had brought to the house. *He should be an easy mark.*

When dinner was over, the two women went into the kitchen. Robert was alone with Carlo.

'You're the first man my sister has ever brought here,' Carlo said. 'She must like you a lot.'

'I like her a lot.'

'Do you? Are you going to take care of her?'

'I think your sister can take care of herself.'

Carlo smirked. 'Yeah. I know.' The stranger seated across from him was well dressed and obviously rich. Why was he staying here when he could have stayed at some fancy hotel? The only reason Carlo could think of was that the man was in hiding. And that brought up an interesting point. When a rich man was in hiding, somehow, some way, there was money to be made from the situation.

'Where are you from?' Carlo asked.

'From no place in particular,' Robert said pleasantly. 'I travel a lot.'

Carlo nodded. 'I see.' *I'll find out from Pier who he is. Somebody will probably be willing to pay a lot of money for him, and Pier and I can split it.*

'Are you in business?' Carlo asked.

'Retired.'

It would not be hard to force this man to talk, Carlo decided. Lucca, the leader of the Diavoli Rossi, could crack him open in no time.

'How long will you be staying with us?'

'It's hard to say.' The boy's curiosity was beginning to get on Robert's nerves.

Pier and her mother came out of the kitchen.

'Would you like some more coffee?' Mama asked.

'No, thank you. That was a delicious dinner.'

Mama smiled. 'That was nothing. Tomorrow I will prepare a feast for you.'

'Good.' He would be gone by then. He stood up. 'If you don't mind, I'm rather tired. I'd like to turn in.'

'Of course,' Mama said. 'Good night.'

'Good night.'

They watched Robert as he walked toward the bedroom.

Carlo grinned. 'He doesn't think you're good enough to sleep with him, eh?'

The remark stung Pier, as it was meant to. She would not have minded it, if Robert were a homosexual, but she had heard him talk to Susan, and she knew better. *I'll show the* stronzo.

Robert lay in bed, thinking about his next move. Laying a false trail with the homing device that had been hidden in the credit card would give him a little time, but he was not depending too much on it. They probably would have caught up with the red truck by now. The men who were after him were ruthless and smart. Were heads of world governments involved in the massive cover-up? Robert wondered. Or was it an organization within an organization, a cabal in the intelligence community acting illegally on its own? The more Robert thought about it, the more feasible it seemed that the heads of state might be unaware of what was going on. And a thought struck him. It had always seemed odd to him that Admiral Whittaker had suddenly been retired from ONI and relegated to some Siberia. But if someone had *forced* him out because they knew he would never be part of the conspiracy, then it began to make sense. *I have to contact the Admiral*, Robert thought. He was the only one he could trust to get to the truth of what was happening. *Tomorrow*, he thought. *Tomorrow*. He closed his eyes, and slept.

The creaking of the bedroom door awakened him. He sat up in bed, instantly alert. Someone was moving toward the bed. Robert tensed, ready to spring. He smelled her perfume then, and felt her slide in bed beside him.

'Pier . . . What are you . . . ?'

'Ssh.' Her body pressed against his. She was naked. 'I got lonely,' she whispered. She snuggled closer to him.

'I'm sorry, Pier, I . . . I can't do anything for you.'

Pier said, 'No? Then let me do something for you.' Her voice was soft.

'It's no use. You can't.' Robert felt a deep frustration. He wanted to spare both of them the embarrassment of what was not going to happen.

'Don't you like me, Robert? Do you not think I have a beautiful body?'

'Yes.' And she did. He could feel the warmth of her body pressing closer.

She was stroking him gently, rippling her fingers up and down his chest, moving lightly toward his groin.

He had to stop her before the humiliating fiasco was repeated. 'Pier, I can't make love. I haven't been able to be with a woman since . . . for a long time.'

'You don't have to do anything, Robert,' she said. 'I just want to play. Do you like being played with?'

He felt nothing. *Goddamn Susan!* She had taken more than herself away from him, she had taken a part of his manhood.

Pier was sliding down his body now. 'Turn over,' she said.

'It's no use, Pier. I . . .'

She rolled him over and he lay there cursing Susan, cursing his impotence. He could feel Pier's tongue moving along his back, making tiny, delicate circles, moving lower and lower. Her fingers were gently flicking over his skin.

'Pier...'

'Ssh.'

He felt her tongue spiralling down deeper and deeper, and he began to feel aroused. He started to move.

'Ssh. Lie still.'

Her tongue was soft and warm, and he could feel her breasts trailing along his skin. His pulse began to quicken. *Yes*, he thought. *Yes! Oh, yes!* His tumescence grew until he became rock-hard, and when he could stand it no longer, he grabbed Pier and turned her over.

She felt him and gasped, 'My God, you're enormous. I want you inside me.'

And a moment later Robert plunged into her, again and again, and it was as if he had been reborn. Pier was skilful and wild, and Robert revelled in the dark cave of her velvety softness. They made love three times that night. Finally, they slept.

DAY EIGHTEEN

Naples, Italy

In the morning, as the pale light was coming through the window, Robert awakened. He held Pier close in his arms and whispered, 'Thank you.'

Pier smiled mischievously. 'How do you feel?'

'Wonderful,' Robert said. And he did.

Pier snuggled against him. 'You are an animal!'

Robert grinned. 'You're good for my ego,' he said.

Pier sat up and said seriously, 'You are not a drug smuggler, are you?'

It was a naïve question. 'No.'

'But Interpol is after you.'

That hit closer to home. 'Yes.'

Her face lit up. 'I know! You're a spy!' She was as excited as a child.

Robert had to laugh. 'Am I?' And he thought, *Out of the mouths of babes.*

'Admit it,' Pier insisted. 'You're a spy, aren't you?'

'Yes,' Robert said gravely. 'I'm a spy.'

'I knew it!' Pier's eyes were glowing. 'Can you tell me some secrets?'

'What kind of secrets?'

'You know, spy secrets ... codes and things like that. I love to read spy novels. I read them all the time.'

'Do you?'

'Oh, yes! But they're just made-up stories. You know all the real things, don't you? Like the signals that spies use. Are you allowed to tell me one?'

Robert said seriously, 'Well, I really shouldn't, but I suppose *one* would be all right.' *What can I tell her that she'll believe?* 'There's the old window shade trick.'

She was wide-eyed. 'The old window shade trick?'

'Yes.' Robert pointed to a window in the bedroom. 'If everything is under control, you leave the shades up. But if there's trouble, you pull one shade down. That's the signal to warn your fellow agent away.'

Pier said excitedly, 'That's wonderful! I've never read that in a book.'

'You won't,' Robert said. 'It's very secret.'

'I won't tell anyone,' Pier promised. 'What else?'

What else? Robert thought for a moment. 'Well, there's the telephone trick.'

Pier snuggled closer to him. 'Tell me about that.'

'Er . . . let's say a fellow spy telephones you to find out if everything is all right. He'll ask for Pier. If everything is fine, you say, "This is Pier." But if there is any problem, you say, "You have the wrong number."'

'That's wonderful!' Pier exclaimed.

My instructors at the Farm would have a heart attack if they heard me talking this nonsense.

'Can you tell me anything else?' Pier asked.

Robert laughed. 'I think those are enough secrets for one morning.'

'All right.' She rubbed her body along his body. 'Would you like to take a shower?' Pier asked.

'Love to.'

They soaped each other under the warm water, and as Pier spread Robert's legs and began to wash him, he became tumescent again.

They made love in the shower.

While Robert was getting dressed, Pier put on a robe and said, 'I'll see about breakfast.'

Carlo was waiting for her in the dining room.

'Tell me about your friend,' he said.

'What about him?'

'Where did you meet him?'

'In Rome.'

'He must be very rich to have brought you that emerald bracelet.'

She shrugged. 'He likes me.'

Carlo said, 'Do you know what I think? I think your friend is running away from something. If we told the right party, there could be a big reward in it.'

Pier moved over to her brother, her eyes blazing. 'Stay out of this, Carlo.'

'So, he *is* running away.'

'Listen, you little *piscialetto*, I'm warning you – mind your own business.' She had no intention of sharing the reward with anyone.

Carlo said reproachfully, 'Little sister, you want it all for yourself.'

'No. You don't understand, Carlo.'

'No?'

Pier said earnestly, 'I'll tell you the truth. Mr Jones is running away from his wife. She has hired a detective to find him. That's all there is to it.'

Carlo smiled. 'Why didn't you tell me this before? Then it's no big deal, I'll forget about it.'

'Good,' Pier said.

And Carlo thought, *I've got to find out who he really is.*

Janus was on the telephone. 'Have you any news yet?'

'We know that Commander Bellamy is in Naples.'

'Do you have any assets there?'

'Yes. They're looking for him now. We have a lead. He's travelling with a prostitute who has a family in Naples. We think they may have gone there. We're following through on it.'

'Keep me informed.'

In Naples, the Bureau of Municipal Housing was busily trying to track down the whereabouts of Pier Valli's mother.

A dozen security agents and the Naples police force were scouring the city for Robert.

Carlo was busily making his own plans for Robert.

Pier was getting ready to telephone Interpol again.

Chapter Forty-Two

The danger in the air was almost palpable and Robert felt he could reach out and touch it. The waterfront was a beehive of activity, with cargo ships busily loading and unloading. But another element had been added: there were police cars cruising up and down the quay, and uniformed policemen and obvious-looking detectives questioning dock workers and sailors. The concentrated manhunt took Robert by complete surprise. It was almost as though they had known he was in Naples, for it would have been impossible for them to be conducting this intense a search for him in every major city in Italy. He did not even bother to get out of the car. He turned around and headed away from the docks. What he had thought would be an easy plan – to board a cargo ship bound for France – had now become too dangerous. Somehow, they had managed to track him here. He went over his options again. Travelling any distance by car was too risky. There would be roadblocks around the city by now. The docks were guarded. That meant the railroad station and airport would be covered, as well. He was in a vice, and it was closing in on him.

Robert thought about Susan's offer. *We're just off the coast of Gibraltar. We can pick you up at any place you say. It's probably your only chance of escape.* He was reluctant to involve Susan in his danger, and yet he could think of no other alternative. It was the only way out of the trap he was in. They would not be looking for him on a private yacht. *If I can find a way to get to the* Halcyon, *he thought, they could drop me off near the coast near Marseilles, and I can get ashore by myself. That way, they won't be in danger.*

He parked the car in front of a small trattoria on a side street, and went inside to make the call. In five minutes, he was connected with the *Halcyon*.

'Mrs Banks, please.'

'Who shall I say is calling?'

Monte has a fucking butler to answer his phone on the yacht. 'Just tell her an old friend.'

A minute later he heard Susan's voice. 'Robert . . . is that you?'

'The bad penny.'

'They . . . they haven't arrested you, have they?'

'No. Susan.' It was difficult for him to ask the question. 'Is your offer still open?'

'Of course it is. When . . . ?'

'Can you reach Naples by tonight?'

Susan hesitated. 'I don't know. Hold on a moment.' Robert heard talking in the background. Susan came on the line again. 'Monte says we have an engine problem, but we can reach Naples in two days.'

Damn. Every day here increased the chances of his getting caught. 'All right. That will be fine.'

'How will we find you?'

'I'll contact you.'

'Robert, please take care of yourself.'

'I'm trying. I really am.'

'You won't let anything happen to you?'

'No, I won't let anything happen to me.' *Or to you.*

When Susan replaced the receiver, she turned to her husband and smiled. 'He's coming aboard.'

One hour later, in Rome, Francesco Cesar handed a cablegram to Colonel Frank Johnson. It was from the *Halcyon*. It read: 'Bellamy coming aboard *Halcyon*. Will keep you informed.' It was unsigned.

'I've made arrangements to monitor all communication to and from the *Halcyon*,' Cesar said. 'As soon as Bellamy steps aboard, we've got him.'

Chapter Forty-Three

The more Carlo Valli thought about it, the more certain he was that he was about to make a big score. Pier's fairy tale about the American running away from his wife was a joke. Mr Jones was on the run, all right, but he was running from the police. There was probably a reward out for the man. Maybe a big reward. This had to be handled very delicately. Carlo decided to discuss it with Mario Lucca, the leader of the Diavoli Rossi.

Early in the morning, Carlo got on his Vespa motor scooter and headed for Via Sorcella, behind the Piazza Garibaldi. He stopped in front of a run-down apartment building, and pressed the bell on a broken mailbox marked 'Lucca'.

A minute later a voice yelled out, 'Who the fuck is it?'

'Carlo. I have to talk to you, Mario.'

'It better be good at this hour of the morning. Come on up.'

The door buzzer sounded, and Carlo went upstairs. Mario Lucca was standing at an open door, naked. At the end of the room Carlo could see a girl in his bed.

'*Che cosa?* What the hell are you doing up so early?'

'I couldn't sleep, Mario. I'm too excited. I think I'm on to something big.'

'Yeah? Come in.'

Carlo entered the small, messy apartment. 'Last night my sister brought home a mark.'

'So what? Pier's a whore. She . . .'

'Yeah, but this one is rich. And he's in hiding.'

'Who is he hiding from?'

'I don't know. But I'm going to find out. I think there might be a reward out for him.'

'Why don't you ask your sister?'

Carlo frowned. 'Pier wants to keep it all for herself. You should see the bracelet he bought her – emeralds.'

'A bracelet? Yeah? How much is it worth?'

'I'll let you know. I'm going to sell it this morning.'

Lucca stood there, thoughtful. 'I'll tell you what, Carlo. Why don't we have a talk with your sister's friend? Let's pick him up and take him over to the club this morning.' The club was an empty warehouse in Pascalone Quartiere Sanita, with a room that was soundproof.

Carlo smiled. '*Bene*. I can get him down there easy enough.'

'We'll be waiting for him,' Lucca said. 'We'll have a little talk with him. I hope he has a nice voice, because he's going to sing for us.'

When Carlo returned to the house, Mr Jones was gone. Carlo panicked.

'Where did your friend go?' he asked Pier.

'He said he had to go into town for a little while. He'll be back. Why?'

He forced a smile. 'Just curious.'

Carlo waited until his mother and Pier were in the kitchen preparing lunch, then hurried into Pier's room. He found the bracelet hidden under some lingerie in a dresser drawer. He swiftly pocketed it and was on his way out when his mother came out of the kitchen.

'Carlo, aren't you staying for lunch?'

'No. I have an appointment, Mama. I'll be back later.'

He got on his Vespa and headed toward the Quartiere Spagnolo. *Maybe the bracelet is phony*, he thought. *It could be paste. I hope I don't make a fool of myself with Lucca.* He parked the motorbike in front of a small jewellery store that had a sign in front that read: '*Orologia*'. The owner, Gambino, was an elderly, wizened man, with an ill-fitting black wig and a mouthful of false teeth. He looked up as Carlo entered.

'Good morning, Carlo. You're out early.'

'Yeah.'

'What have you got for me today?'

Carlo took out the bracelet and laid it on the counter. 'This.'

Gambino picked it up. As he studied it, his eyes widened. 'Where did you get this?'

'A rich aunt died and left it to me. Is it worth anything?'

'It could be,' Gambino said cautiously.'

'Don't fuck around with me.'

Gambino looked hurt. 'Have I ever cheated you?'

'All the time.'

'You boys are always kidding around. I'll tell you what I will do, Carlo. I'm not sure I can handle this by myself. It's very valuable.'

Carlo's heart skipped a beat. 'Really?'

'I'll have to see if I can lay it off somewhere. I'll give you a call tonight.'

'Okay,' Carlo said. He snatched up the bracelet. 'I'll keep this until I hear from you.'

Carlo left the shop, walking on air. So, he had been right! The sucker was rich, and he was also crazy. *Why else would someone give an expensive bracelet to a whore?*

In the store, Gambino watched Carlo leave. He thought, *What the hell have those idiots got themselves into?* From under the counter, he picked up a circular that had been sent to all pawn shops. It had a description of the bracelet he had just seen, but at the bottom, instead of the usual police number to call, there was a special notice: 'Notify SIFAR immediately'. Gambino would have ignored an ordinary police circular, as he had hundreds of times in the past, but he knew enough about SIFAR to know that one never crossed them. He hated to lose the profit on the bracelet, but neither did he intend to put his neck in a noose. Reluctantly, he picked up the telephone and dialled the number on the circular.

Chapter Forty-Four

It was the season of fear, of swirling, deadly shadows. Years earlier, Robert had been sent on a mission to Borneo and had gone into the deep jungle after a traitor. It had been in October, during *musim takoot*, the traditional head-hunting season, when the jungle natives lived in terror of *Balli Salang*, the spirit that sought out humans for their blood. It was a season of murders, and now for Robert, Naples had suddenly become the jungles of Borneo. Death was in the air. *Do not go gentle into the fucking night*, Robert thought. *They'll have to catch me first*. How had they traced him here? *Pier*. They must have tracked him down through Pier. *I have to get back to the house and warn her*, Robert thought. *But first I have to find a way out of here.*

He drove toward the outskirts of the city, to where the autostrada began, hoping that by some miracle, it might be clear. Five hundred yards before he reached the entrance, he saw the police roadblock. He turned around and headed back toward the centre of the city.

Robert drove slowly, concentrating, putting himself into the minds of his pursuers. They would have all avenues of escape out of Italy blocked. Every ship leaving the country would be searched. And a plan suddenly came to him. They would have no reason to search ships *not* leaving Italy. *It's a chance*, Robert thought. He headed for the harbour again.

The little bell over the door of the jewellery shop rang, and Gambino looked up. Two men in dark suits walked in. They were not customers.

'Can I help you?'

'Mr Gambino?'

He exposed his false teeth. 'Yes.'

'You called about an emerald bracelet.'

SIFAR. He had been expecting them. But this time he was on the side of the angels. 'That's right. As a patriotic citizen, I felt it was my duty . . .'

'Cut the bullshit. Who brought it in?'

'A young boy named Carlo.'

'Did he leave the bracelet?'

'No, he took it with him.'

'What's Carlo's last name?'

Gambino lifted a shoulder. 'I don't know his last name. He's one of the boys in the Diavoli Rossi. That's one of our local gangs. It's run by a kid named Lucca.'

'Do you know where we can find this Lucca?'

Gambino hesitated. If Lucca found out that he had talked, he would have his tongue cut out. If he did *not* tell these men what they wanted to know, he would have his brains bashed in. 'He lives on Via Sorcella, behind the Piazza Garibaldi.'

'Thank you, Mr Gambino. You've been very helpful.'

'I'm always happy to cooperate with . . .'
The men were gone.

Lucca was in bed with his girlfriend when the two men shoved open the door to his apartment.

Lucca leaped out of bed. 'What the hell is this? Who are you?'

One of the men pulled out his identification.

SIFAR! Lucca swallowed. 'Hey, I haven't done anything wrong. I'm a law-abiding citizen who . . .'

'We know that, Lucca. We're not interested in you. We're interested in a boy named Carlo.'

Carlo. So that was what this was about. That fucking bracelet! What the hell had Carlo got himself into? SIFAR did not send men around looking for stolen jewellery.

'Well . . . do you know him or don't you?'

'I might.'

'If you aren't sure, we'll refresh your memory down at headquarters.'

'Wait! I do remember, now,' Lucca said. 'You must mean Carlo Valli. What about him?'

'We'd like to have a talk with him. Where does he live?'

Every member of the Diavoli Rossi had to swear a blood oath of loyalty, an oath that they would die before they would betray a fellow member. That was what made the Diavoli Rossi such a great club. They stuck together. One for all and all for one.

'Do you want to take that trip downtown?'

'What for?' Lucca shrugged. He gave them Carlo's address.

Thirty minutes later, Pier opened the door to find two strangers standing there.

'Signorina Valli?'

Trouble. 'Yes.'

'May we come in?'

She wanted to say no, but she did not dare. 'Who are you?'

One of the men pulled out a wallet and flashed an identification card. *SIFAR.* These were not the people she had made her deal with. Pier felt a sense of panic that they were going to try to cheat her out of her reward. 'What do you want with me?'

'We'd like to ask you a few questions.'

'Go ahead. I have nothing to hide.' *Thank God,* Pier thought, *Robert is out. I can still negotiate.*

'You drove down from Rome yesterday, didn't you.' It was a statement.

'Yes. Is that against the law . . . was I speeding?'

The man smiled. It did nothing to change the expression on his face. 'You had a companion with you?'

Pier answered carefully. 'Yes.'

'Who was he, *signorina*?'

She shrugged. 'Some man I picked up on the road. He wanted a ride to Naples.'

The second man asked, 'Is he here with you now?'

'I don't know where he is. I dropped him off when we got into town and he disappeared.'

'Was your passenger's name Robert Bellamy?'

She knitted her brow in concentration. 'Bellamy? I don't know. I don't think he told me his name.'

'Oh, we think he did. He picked you up on the Tor di Ounto, you spent the night with him at the L'Incrocio Hotel, and the next morning he bought you an emerald bracelet. He sent you to some hotels with airline and train tickets, and you rented a car and you came down to Naples, right?'

They know everything. Pier nodded, her eyes filled with fear.

'Is your friend coming back, or has he left Naples?'

She hesitated, deciding which was the best answer. If she told them that Robert had left town, they would not believe her, anyway. They would wait here at the house and when he turned up, they could accuse her of lying for him and hold her as an accomplice. She decided that the truth would serve her better. 'He's coming back,' Pier said.

'Soon?'

'I'm not sure.'

'Well, we'll just make ourselves comfortable. You don't mind if we look around, do you?' They opened their jackets, exposing their guns.

'N . . . no.'

They fanned out, moving through the house.

Mama walked in from the kitchen. 'Who are these men?'

'They are friends of Mr Jones,' Pier said. 'They have come to see him.'

Mama beamed. 'Such a nice man. Would you like some lunch?'

'Sure, Mama,' one of the men said. 'What are we having?'

Pier's mind was in a turmoil. *I have to call Interpol again*, she thought. *They said they would pay fifty thousand dollars.* Meanwhile, she had to keep Robert away from the house until she could make arrangements to turn him in. But how? She suddenly remembered their conversation that morning. *If there's trouble you pull one shade down.* The two men were seated at the dining-room table, eating a bowl of *capellini*.

'It's too bright in here,' Pier said. She rose and walked into the living room and pulled down the window shade. Then she went back to the table. *I hope Robert remembers about the warning.*

Robert was driving toward the house, reviewing his plan of escape. *It's not perfect*, he thought, *but at least it should get them off the trail long enough to buy me some time.* He was approaching the house. As he neared it, he slowed down and looked around. Everything appeared to be normal. He would warn Pier to get out, and then take off. As Robert started to park in front of the house, something struck him as odd. One of the front shades was down. The others were up. It was probably a coincidence, but still . . . an alarm bell sounded. Could Pier have taken his little game seriously? Was it meant to be a warning of some kind? Robert stepped on the accelerator and kept driving. He could not afford to take any chances, no matter how remote. He drove to a bar a mile away, and went inside to use the telephone.

They were seated at the dining-room table when the telephone rang. The men tensed. One of them started to rise.

'Would Bellamy be calling here?'

Pier gave him a scornful look. 'Of course not. Why should he?' She rose and walked over to the telephone. She picked up the receiver. 'Hello?'

'Pier? I saw the window shade and ...'

All she had to do was say that everything was all right, and he would come back to the house. The men would arrest him, and she could demand her reward. But would they merely arrest him? She could hear Robert's voice saying: *If the police find me, they have orders to kill me.*

The men at the table were watching her. There was so much she could do with fifty thousand dollars. There were beautiful clothes to buy, cruises to take, a pretty little apartment in Rome ... and Robert would be dead. Besides, she hated the goddamned police. Pier said into the telephone, 'You have the wrong number.'

Robert heard the click of the receiver and stood there, stunned. She had believed the tall tales he had told her and it had probably saved his life. *Bless her.*

Robert turned the car around and headed away from the house, toward the docks, but instead of going to the main part of the port that serviced the freighters and ocean liners leaving Italy, he drove to the other side, past Santa Lucia, to a small pier where the sign over a kiosk read: 'Capri and Ischia'. Robert parked the car where it could easily be spotted, and walked up to the ticket seller.

'When does the next hydrofoil leave for Ischia?'

'In thirty minutes.'

'And for Capri?'

'Five minutes.'

'Give me a one-way ticket to Capri.'

'*Si, signore.*'

'What's this *"si signore"* crap?' Robert said in a loud voice. 'Why don't you people speak English like everybody else?'

The man's eyes widened in shock.

'You goddamn guineas are all alike. Stupid! Or, as you people would say, *stupido*.' Robert shoved some money at the man, grabbed the ticket and walked toward the hydrofoil.

Three minutes later he was on his way to the island of Capri. The boat started out slowly, making its way cautiously through the channel. When it reached the outer limits, it surged forward, rising out of the water like a graceful porpoise. The ferry was full of tourists from a variety of countries, happily chattering away in different tongues. No one was paying any attention to Robert. He made his way to the small bar where they served drinks. He said to the bartender, 'Give me a vodka and tonic.'

'Yes, sir.'

He watched the bartender mix the drink. 'There you are, *signore*.'

Robert picked up the glass and took a swallow. He slammed the glass back down on the bar. 'You call this a drink for Christ's sakes?' he said. 'It tastes like horse piss. What's the matter with you goddamn Italians?'

People around him were turning to stare.

The bartender said, stiffly, 'I'm sorry, *signore*, we use the best . . .'

'Don't give me that shit!'

An Englishman nearby said stiffly, 'There are ladies present. Why don't you watch your language?'

'I don't have to watch my language,' Robert yelled. 'Do you know who I am? I'm Commander Robert Bellamy. And they call this a boat? It's a piece of junk!'

He made his way to the bow and sat down. He could feel the eyes of the other passengers on him. His heart was hammering, but the charade was not over yet.

When the hydrofoil docked at Capri, Robert walked over to the ticket booth at the entrance to the funicular. An elderly man was in the booth selling tickets.

'One ticket,' Robert yelled. 'And hurry up! I don't have all day. You're too old to be selling tickets, anyway. You should stay home. Your wife is probably screwing all your neighbours.'

The old man started to rise in anger. Passers-by were giving Robert furious glances. Robert grabbed the ticket and stepped into the crowded funicular. *They'll remember me*, he thought grimly. He was leaving a trail that no one could miss.

When the funicular came to a stop, Robert shoved his way through the crowd. He walked up the winding Via Vittorio Emanuele, to the Quisisana Hotel.

'I need a room,' Robert told the clerk behind the desk.

'I'm sorry,' the clerk apologized, 'but we are fully booked. There is . . .'

Robert handed him sixty thousand lire. 'Any room will do.'

'Well, in that case, I think we can accommodate you, *signore*. Would you register, please?'

Robert signed his name. Commander Robert Bellamy.

'How long will you be staying with us, Commander?'

'One week.'

'That will be fine. May I have your passport?'

'It's in my luggage. It'll be here in a few minutes.'

'I will have a bellboy show you to your room.'

'Not now. I have to go out for a few minutes. I'll be right back.'

Robert stepped out of the lobby, into the street. Memories hit him like a blast of cold air. He had walked here with Susan, exploring the little side streets, and strolled down Via Ignazio Cerio and Via di Campo. It had been a magic time. They visited the Grotta Azzurra, and had morning coffee at the Piazza Umberto. They took the funicular up to Anacapri, and rode donkeys to Villa Jovis, Tiberius's villa, and swam in the emerald green waters at the Marina Piccola. They shopped along Via Vittorio Emanuele and took the chair lift to the top of Monte Solaro, their feet skimming over the vine leaves and leafy trees. Off to the right they could see the houses sprinkled down the hillside toward the sea, yellow broom covering the ground, an eleven-minute ride through a colourful fairyland of green trees, white houses and, in the distance, the blue sea. At the top, they had coffee at the Barbarossa Ristorante, and then went into the little church in Anacapri to thank God for all their blessings, and for each other. Robert had thought then that the magic was Capri. He had been wrong. The magic was Susan, and the magician had left the stage.

Robert went back to the funicular station at the Piazza Umberto, and took the tram down, quietly mingling with the other passengers. When the funicular arrived at the bottom, he walked out, carefully avoiding the ticket seller. He went over to the kiosk at the boat landing. In a heavy Spanish accent, Robert asked, '*A que hora sale el barco a Ischia?*'

'*Sale en treinta minutos.*'

'*Gracias.*' Robert bought a ticket.

He walked into a bar at the waterfront, took a seat in the back and nursed a scotch. By now they would have undoubtedly found the car, and the hunt for him would narrow. He spread out the map of Europe in his mind. The logical thing for him to do would be to head for England, and find a way to get back to the States. It would make no sense for him to return to France. *So, France it is*, Robert thought. A busy seaport to leave Italy from. *Civitavecchia. I have to get to Civitavecchia. The* Halcyon.

He got change from the owner of the bar, and used the telephone. It took the marine operator ten minutes to put his call through. Susan was on the line almost immediately.

'We've been waiting to hear from you. *We*. He found that interesting. 'The engine is fixed. We can be in Naples early in the morning. Where shall we pick you up?'

It was too risky for the *Halcyon* to come here. Robert said, 'Do you remember the palindrome? We went there on our honeymoon.'

'The what?'

'I made a joke about it because I was so exhausted.'

There was a silence on the other end of the line. Then Susan said softly, 'I remember.'

'Can the *Halcyon* meet me there tomorrow?'

'Hold on a moment.'

He waited.

Susan returned to the telephone. 'Yes, we can be there.'

'Good.' Robert hesitated. He thought of all the innocent people who had already died. 'I'm asking a lot of you. If they ever found out you helped me, you could be in terrible danger.'

'Don't worry. We'll meet you there. Be careful.'

'Thanks.'

The connection was broken.

Susan turned to Monte Banks. 'He's coming.'

At SIFAR headquarters in Rome they were listening to the con versation. There were four men in the room. The radio operator said, 'We've recorded it, if you would like to hear it again, sir.'

Colonel Cesar looked at Frank Johnson questioningly.

'Yes. I'm interested in hearing the part about where they're going to meet. It sounded like he said Palindrome. Is that somewhere in Italy?'

Colonel Cesar shook his head. 'I never heard of it. We'll check it out.' He turned to his aide. 'Look it up on the map. And keep monitoring all transmissions to and from the *Halcyon*.'

'Yes, sir.'

At the farmhouse in Naples, the phone rang. Pier started to get up to answer it.

'Hold it,' one of the men said. He walked over to the phone and picked it up. 'Hello?' He listened for a moment, then threw the phone down and turned to his companion. 'Bellamy took the hydrofoil to Capri. Let's go!'

Pier watched the two men hurry out of the door, and thought: *God never meant me to have so much money, anyway. I hope he gets away.*

When the ferry boat to Ischia arrived, Robert mingled with the crowd boarding it. He kept to himself, avoiding eye contact. Thirty minutes later, when the boat docked at Ischia, Robert disembarked and walked over to the ticket booth on the pier. A sign announced that the ferry to Sorrento was due in ten minutes.

'A round trip ticket to Sorrento,' Robert said.

Ten minutes later he was on his way to Sorrento, back to the mainland. *With a little luck, the search will have shifted to Capri*, Robert thought. *With a little luck.*

The food market at Sorrento was crowded. Farmers had come in from the countryside bringing fresh fruit and vegetables and sides of beef that lined the meat stalls. The street was thronged with vendors and shoppers.

Robert approached a husky man in a stained apron, loading a truck. '*Pardon, monsieur . . .*' Robert spoke with a perfect French accent. 'I'm looking for transportation to Civitavecchia. Would you happen to be going that way?'

'No. Salerno.' He pointed to a man loading another truck nearby. 'Giuseppe might be able to help you.'

'*Merci.*'

Robert moved over to the next truck. '*Monsieur*, would you be going to Civitavecchia by any chance?'

The man said, noncommittally, 'I might be.'

'I would be glad to pay you for the ride.'

'How much?'

Robert handed the man a hundred thousand lire.

'You could buy yourself a plane ticket to Rome for that much money, couldn't you?'

Robert instantly realized his mistake. He looked around nervously. 'The truth is, I have some creditors watching the airport. I'd prefer to go by truck.'

The man nodded. 'Ah. I understand. All right, get in. We're ready to leave.'

Robert yawned. 'I am *très fatigué*. How do you say? – tired. Would you mind if I slept in the back?'

'It's going to be a bumpy ride, but suit yourself.'
'*Merci.*'

The back of the truck was filled with empty crates and boxes. Giuseppe watched Robert climb in, and he closed up the tailgate. Inside, Robert concealed himself behind some crates. He suddenly realized how exhausted he really was. The chase was beginning to wear him down. How long had it been since he had slept? He thought of Pier and how she had come to him in the night and had made him feel whole again, a man again. He hoped she was all right. Robert slept.

In the cab of the truck, Giuseppe was thinking about his passenger. The word was out about an American the authorities were looking for. His passenger had a French accent, but he looked like an American and he dressed like an American. It would be worth checking out. There might be a nice reward.

One hour later, at a truck stop along the highway, Giuseppe pulled up in front of a gas pump. 'Fill it up,' he said. He walked around to the back of the truck and peered inside. His passenger was asleep.

Giuseppe went inside the restaurant and made a telephone call to the local police.

Chapter Forty-Five

The call had been routed to Colonel Cesar. 'Yes,' he said to Giuseppe, 'that sounds very much like our man. Listen carefully. He is dangerous, so I want you to do exactly as I tell you. Do you understand?'

'Yes, sir.'

'Where are you now?'

'At the AGIP truck stop on the highway to Civitavecchia.'

'And he's in the back of your truck now?'

'Yes.' The conversation was making him nervous. *Maybe I should have minded my own business.*

'Don't do anything to make him suspicious. Get back in your truck and keep driving toward Civitavecchia. Give me your licence number and a description of your truck.'

Giuseppe gave it to him.

'Fine. We will take care of everything. Now get moving.'

Colonel Cesar turned to Colonel Johnson and nodded. 'We have him. I'll have a roadblock set up. We can be there by helicopter in thirty minutes.'

'Let's go.'

When Giuseppe replaced the receiver, he wiped his sweaty palms on his shirt, and headed for the truck. *I hope there won't be a shoot-out. Maria would kill me. On the other hand, if the reward is large enough* . . . He climbed into the cab of the truck and headed for Civitavecchia.

Thirty-five minutes later, Giuseppe heard the sound of a helicopter overhead. He looked up. It had the markings of the State Police. Ahead of him on the highway, he saw two police cars lined up next to each other, forming a roadblock. Behind the cars were policemen with automatic weapons. The helicopter landed at the side of the road, and Cesar and Colonel Frank Johnson stepped out.

As he neared the roadblock, Giuseppe slowed the truck down. He shut off the ignition and jumped out, running toward the officers. 'He's in the back!' he shouted.

The truck rolled to a stop. Cesar shouted, 'Close in.'

The policemen converged on the truck, weapons ready.

'Don't shoot,' Colonel Johnson yelled. 'I'll take him.' He moved toward the back of the truck. 'Come on out, Robert,' Colonel Johnson called, 'it's over.'

There was no response.

'Robert, you have five seconds.'

Silence. They waited.

Cesar turned to his men and nodded.

'No!' Colonel Johnson yelled. But it was too late.

The police began firing into the back of the truck. The noise of the automatic fire was deafening. Splinters of crates began flying into the air. After ten seconds, the firing ceased. Colonel Frank Johnson jumped into the back of the truck and moved the crates and boxes out of his way.

He turned to Cesar. 'He's not here.'

DAY NINETEEN
Civitavecchia, Italy

Civitavecchia is the ancient seaport for Rome, guarded by a massive fort completed by Michelangelo in 1537. The port is one of the busiest in Europe, servicing all sea-going traffic to and from Rome and Sardinia. It was early in the morning, but the port was already alive with noisy activity. Robert made his way past the railroad yards and stepped into a small trattoria filled with pungent cooking odours and ordered breakfast.

The *Halcyon* would be waiting for him at the appointed place, Elba. He was grateful that Susan had remembered it. On their honeymoon, they had stayed in their room there for three days and nights, making love. Susan had said, 'Would you like to go for a swim, darling?'

Robert had shaken his head. 'No. I can't move. "Able was I, ere I saw Elba."' And Susan had laughed and they had made love again. *And bless her, she had remembered the palindrome.*

Now all he had to do was to find a boat to take him to Elba. He walked down the streets leading to the harbour. It was bustling with maritime activity, crowded with freighters, small motor boats and private yachts. There was a landing for a ferry boat.

Robert's eyes lit up when he saw it. *That would be the safest way to get over to Elba*. He would be able to lose himself in the crowds.

As Robert started toward the ferry landing, he noticed a dark, unmarked sedan parked half a block away, and he stopped. It had official licence plates. There were two men seated inside the car watching the docks. Robert turned and walked in the other direction.

Scattered among the dockworkers and tourists, he spotted plainclothes detectives trying to look unobtrusive. They stood out like beacons. Robert's heart began to pound. How could they possibly have tracked him here? And then he realized what had happened. *My God, I told the truck driver where I was going! Stupid! I must be very tired.*

He had fallen asleep in the truck, and the absence of movement had awakened him. He had got up to look out, and had seen Giuseppe go into the gas station and make a phone call. Robert had slipped out of the truck and climbed into the back of another truck headed north toward Civitavecchia.

He had trapped himself. They were looking for him here. A few hundred yards away were dozens of boats that could have afforded him an escape. Not any longer.

Robert turned away from the harbour and walked toward town. He passed a building with a huge colourful poster on the wall. It read: 'Come to the Fairgrounds. Fun for All! Food! Games! Rides! See the Big Race!' He stopped and stared.

He had found his escape.

Chapter Forty-Six

At the fairgrounds, five miles outside of Civitavecchia, were a dozen large, colourful balloons spread across the field, looking like round rainbows. They were moored to trucks while ground crews were busily filling their envelopes with cold air. Half a dozen chase cars stood by, ready to track the balloons, two men in each car, the driver and the spotter.

Robert walked up to a man who seemed to be in charge. 'It looks like you're getting ready for the big race,' Robert said.

'That's right. Ever been in a balloon?'

'No.'

They were skimming over Lake Como and he dropped the balloon down until it touched the water. 'We're going to crash,' Susan screamed. He smiled. 'No, we're not.' The bottom of the balloon was dancing on the waves. He threw out a sandbag and the balloon began to lift again. Susan laughed and hugged him and said . . .

The man was speaking. 'You should try it sometime. It's a great sport.'

'Yeah. Where is the race heading?'

'Yugoslavia. We have a nice easterly wind. We'll be taking off in a few minutes. It's better to fly early in the morning when the wind is cool.'

'Really?' Robert said politely. He had a quick flash of a summer day in Yugoslavia. *We have four people to smuggle out of here, Commander. We must wait until the air is cooler. A balloon that can lift four people in the winter air can only lift two people in the summer air.*

Robert noticed that the crews were finishing filling the balloons with air and starting to light the large propane burners, pointing the flame into the envelope opening, to warm the air inside. The balloons, which were lying on their sides, began to rise until the baskets stood upright.

'Mind if I look around?' Robert asked.

'Go ahead. Just stay out of everyone's way.'

'Right.' Robert walked over to a yellow and red balloon that was filled with propane gas. The only thing holding it to the ground was a rope attached to one of the trucks.

The crewman who had been working on it had wandered off to talk to someone. There was no one else near.

Robert climbed into the basket of the balloon, and the huge envelope seemed to fill the sky above him. He checked the rigging and equipment, the altimeter, charts, a pyrometer to monitor the temperature of the envelope, a rate of climb indicator, and a tool kit. Everything was in order. Robert reached into the tool kit and pulled out a knife. He sliced into the mooring rope, and a moment later, the balloon started to ascend.

'Hey!' Robert yelled. 'What's going on here? Get me down!'

The man he had spoken to was gaping up at the runaway balloon. '*Figlio d'una mignotta!* Don't panic,' he shouted. 'There's an altimeter on board. Use your ballast and stay at one thousand feet. We'll meet you in Yugoslavia. Can you hear me?'

'I hear you.'

The balloon was rising higher and higher, carrying him east, away from Elba, which was to the west. But Robert was not concerned. The wind changed direction at varying altitudes. None of the other balloons had taken off yet. Robert spotted one of the chase cars start up, moving to track him. He dropped ballast and watched the altimeter climb. Six hundred feet . . . seven hundred feet . . . nine hundred feet . . . eleven hundred feet . . .

At fifteen hundred feet the wind began to weaken. The balloon was almost stationary now. Robert dropped more ballast. He used the stair step technique, stopping at different altitudes to check the wind direction.

At two thousand feet, Robert could feel the wind begin to shift. It swayed in the turbulent air for a moment, then slowly began to reverse direction and move west.

In the distance far below, Robert could see the other balloons rising and moving east toward Yugoslavia. There was no sound at all except for the soft whispering of the wind. *It's so quiet, Robert. It's like flying on a cloud. I wish we could stay up here forever.* She had held him close. *Have you ever made love in a balloon? she murmured. Let's try it.*

And later, I'll bet we're the only people in the world who have made love in a balloon, darling.

Robert was over the Tyrrhenian Sea now, heading northwest toward the coast of Tuscany. Below, a string of islands stretched in a circle off the coast, with Elba the largest.

Napoleon had been exiled here, and he had probably chosen it because on a clear day, Robert thought, *he could see his beloved island of Corsica. In exile, Napoleon's one thought was how to escape and get to France. Mine, too. Only Napoleon didn't have Susan and the* Halcyon *to rescue him.*

In the distance, Monte Capanne suddenly loomed up, rising three thousand feet into the sky. Robert pulled the safety line that opened the valve at the top of the balloon to allow the hot air to escape, and the balloon began to descend. Below him, Robert could see the lush pink and green of Elba, the pink that came from the granite outcrops and Tuscan houses, and the green of the heavy forests. Below, pristine white beaches were scattered around the edges of the island.

He landed the balloon at the base of the mountain, away from the city, to attract as little attention to himself as possible. There was a road not far from where he had landed and he walked over to it and waited until a car came by.

'Could you give me a lift into town?' Robert called.

'Certainly. Jump in.'

The driver appeared to be somewhere in his eighties, with an old, wrinkled face.

'I could have sworn I saw a balloon in the sky a little while ago. Did you see it, mister?'

'No,' Robert said.

'Visiting?'

'Just passing through. I'm on my way to Rome.'

The driver nodded. 'I was there once.'

The rest of the ride was made in silence.

When they reached Portoferraio, the capital and only city of Elba, Robert stepped down from the car.

'Have a nice day,' the driver said in English.

My God, Robert thought, *Californians have been here.*

Robert walked along Via Garibaldi, the main street, crowded with tourists, mostly families, and it was as though time had stood still. Nothing had changed; *except that I've lost Susan, and half the governments in the world are trying to assassinate me. Otherwise*, Robert thought wryly, *everything is exactly the same.*

He bought binoculars in a gift shop, and walked to the waterfront and sat at a table outside the Stella Mariner Restaurant, where he had a clear view of the harbour. There were no suspicious cars, no police boats, and no policemen in sight. They still thought they had him bottled up on the mainland. It would be safe for him to board the *Halcyon*. All he had to do now was wait for it to arrive.

He sat there sipping *procanico*, the delicate native white wine, watching for the *Halcyon*. He went over his plan again. The yacht would drop him off near the coast of Marseilles, and he would make his way to Paris where he had a friend, Li Po, who would help him. It was ironic. He heard Francesco Cesar's voice saying: *I've heard you've made a deal with the Chinese.*

He knew that Li Po would help him, because Li had once saved Robert's life, and according to ancient Chinese tradition, he had become responsible for Robert. It was a matter of *win yu* – honour.

Li Po was with the Guojia Anquanbu, the Chinese Ministry of State Security that dealt with espionage. Years earlier, Robert had been caught while trying to smuggle a dissident out of China. He had been sent to Qincheng, the top security prison in Beijing. Li Po was a double agent who had worked with Robert before. He managed to arrange for Robert to escape.

At the Chinese border, Robert had said, 'You should get out of this while you're still alive, Li. Your luck won't last forever.'

Li Po had smiled. 'I have *ren* – the ability to endure, to survive.'

One year later, Li Po had been transferred to the Chinese Embassy in Paris.

Robert decided that it was time to make his first move. He left the restaurant and wandered down to the waterfront. It was crowded with large and small boats leaving from Portoferraio.

Robert approached a man polishing the hull of a sleek motor boat. It was a Donzi, powered by a V-8 351 inboard engine.

'Nice boat,' Robert said.

The man nodded. '*Merci.*'

'I wonder if I could rent it to take a little cruise around the harbour?'

The man stopped what he was doing and studied Robert. 'That might be possible. Are you familiar with boats?'

'Yes. I have a Donzi back home.'

The man nodded approvingly. 'Where are you from?'

'Oregon,' Robert said.

'It will cost you four hundred francs an hour.'

Robert smiled. 'That's fine.'

'And a deposit, of course.'

'Of course.'

'She's ready to go. Would you like to take her out now?'

'No, I have some errands to run. I thought tomorrow morning.'

'What time?'

'I'll let you know,' Robert said.

He handed the man some money. 'Here's a partial deposit. I'll see you tomorrow.'

He had decided it would be dangerous to let the *Halcyon* come into port. There were formalities. The *capitano di porto* – the harbourmaster – issued each yacht an *autorizzazione* and recorded its stay. Robert intended for the *Halcyon* to be as little involved with him as possible. He would meet it at sea.

In the office of the French Marine Ministry, Colonel Cesar and Colonel Johnson were talking to the marine operator. 'Are you sure there has been no further communication with the *Halcyon*?'

'No, sir, not since the last conversation I reported to you.'

'Keep listening.' Colonel Cesar turned to Colonel Johnson and smiled. 'Don't worry. We'll know the moment Commander Bellamy boards the *Halcyon*.'

'But I want to get him before he's aboard.'

The marine operator said, 'Colonel Cesar, there is no Palindrome listed on the map of Italy. But I think we've pinned it down.'

'Where is it?'

'It's not a place, sir. It's a word.'

'*What?*'

'Yes, sir. A palindrome is a word or sentence that is spelled the same forward or backward. For example, 'Madam I'm Adam'. We've run some through our computers.' He handed him a long list of words.

Colonel Cesar and Colonel Johnson scanned the list. 'Kook ... deed ... bib ... bob ... boob ... dad ... dud ... eve ... gag ... mom ... non ... noon ... Otto ... pop ... sees ... tot ... toot ...' Cesar looked up. 'It's not much help, is it?'

'It might be, sir. They were obviously using some kind of code. And one of the most famous palindromes was supposedly said by Napoleon: "Able was I ere I saw Elba."'

Colonel Cesar and Colonel Johnson looked at each other. '*Elba*. Jesus Christ! That's where he is!'

DAY TWENTY
The Island of Elba

It first appeared as a faint speck on the horizon, rapidly looming larger in the early morning light. Through the binoculars, Robert watched it materialize into the *Halcyon*. There was no mistaking the ship. There were not many at sea like it.

Robert hurried down to the beach where he had arranged to rent the motor boat.

'Good morning.'

The owner of the boat looked up. '*Bonjour, monsieur*. Are you ready to take it out?'

Robert nodded. 'Yes.'

'How long will you want it for?'

'No more than an hour or two.'

Robert gave the man the rest of the deposit, and stepped down into the boat.

'Take good care of it,' the man said.

'Don't worry,' Robert assured him, 'I will.'

The owner untied the painter, and moments later the boat was headed out to sea, racing toward the *Halcyon*. It took Robert ten minutes to reach the yacht. As he approached it, he saw Susan and Monte Banks standing on the deck. Susan waved to him and he could see the anxiety in her face. Robert manoeuvred the small boat next to the yacht and tossed a line to a deckhand.

'Do you want to bring it aboard, sir?' the man called.

'No, let it go.' The owner would find it soon enough.

Robert walked up the ladder to the spotless teak deck. Susan had once described the *Halcyon* to Robert, and he had been impressed, but in actuality it was even more impressive. The *Halcyon* was two hundred and eighty feet long, with a luxurious owner's cabin, eight double suites for guests, and cabins for a crew of sixteen. It had a drawing room, a dining room, an office, a saloon and a swimming pool.

The ship was propelled by two 1250 horsepower sixteen-cylinder turbo-charged caterpillar D399 diesel engines, and carried six tenders. The interior design had been done in Italy by Luigi Sturchio. It was a floating palace.

'I'm glad you made it,' Susan said.

And Robert had the impression that she was ill at ease, that something was wrong. Or was it just his nerves?

She looked absolutely beautiful, and somehow, he was disappointed. *What the hell had I expected? That she would look pale and miserable?*

He turned to Monte. 'I want you to know how much I appreciate this.'

Monte shrugged. 'Glad to help you out.'

The man was a saint.

'What's your plan?'

'I'd like you to turn and head due west to Marseilles. You can drop me off the coast and . . .'

A man in a crisp white uniform approached. He

was in his fifties, heavyset, with a neatly trimmed beard.

'This is Captain Simpson. This is . . .' Monte Banks looked at Robert for help.

'Smith. Tom Smith.'

Monte said, 'We'll be heading for Marseilles, Captain.'

'We're not going into Elba?'

'No.'

Captain Simpson said, 'Very well.' He sounded surprised.

Robert scanned the horizon. All clear.

'I'd suggest we go below,' Monte Banks said.

When the three of them were seated in the saloon, Monte asked, 'Don't you think you owe us an explanation?'

'Yes, I do,' Robert said, 'but I'm not going to give you one. The less you know about this whole affair the better. I can only tell you that I'm innocent. I'm involved in a political situation. I know too much, and I'm being hunted. If they find me, they'll kill me.'

Susan and Monte exchanged a look.

'They have no reason to connect me with the *Halcyon*,' Robert went on. 'Believe me, Monte, if there were any other way for me to escape, I would have taken it.'

Robert thought of all the people who had been killed because he had tracked them down. He could not bear to have anything happen to Susan. He tried to keep his voice light. 'I would appreciate it for your own sakes, if you didn't mention that I was ever aboard this ship.'

'Of course not,' Monte said.

The yacht had slowly swung around and was heading west.

'If you'll excuse me, I have to have a word with the captain.'

Dinner was an awkward affair. There were strange undercurrents that Robert did not understand, a tension that was almost tangible. Was it because of his presence? Or was it something else? Something between the two of them? *The sooner I get away from here, the better,* Robert thought.

They were in the saloon having an after-dinner drink when Captain Simpson came into the room.

'When will we reach Marseilles?' Robert asked.

'If the weather holds, we should be there tomorrow afternoon, Mr Smith.'

There was something about Captain Simpson's manner that irritated Robert. The captain was gruff, almost to the point of being rude. *But he must be good,* Robert thought, *or Monte would not have hired him. Susan deserves this yacht. She deserves the best of everything.*

At eleven o'clock Monte looked at his watch and said to Susan, 'I think we had better turn in, darling.'

Susan glanced at Robert. 'Yes.'

The three of them rose.

Monte said, 'You'll find a change of clothes in your cabin. We're about the same size.'

'Thank you.'

'Good night, Robert.'

'Good night, Susan.'

Robert stood there, watching the woman he loved going off to bed with his rival. *Rival? Who the hell am I kidding? He's the winner. I'm the loser.*

Sleep was an elusive shadow, dancing just out of reach. Lying in his bed, Robert was thinking that on the other side of the wall, only a few feet away, was the woman he loved more than anyone in the world. He thought of Susan lying in her bed, naked . . . *she never wore a nightgown* . . . and he felt himself beginning to get an erection. *Was Monte making love to her at this moment or was she alone? . . . and was she thinking of him and remembering all the great times they had had together? Probably not. Well, he would be out of her life soon. He would probably never see her again.*

It was dawn before he closed his eyes.

In the communications room at SIFAR, radar was tracking the *Halcyon*. Colonel Cesar turned to Colonel Johnson, and said, 'Too bad we couldn't intercept him at Elba, but we've got him now! We have a cruiser standing by. We're just waiting word from the *Halcyon* to board her.'

DAY TWENTY-ONE

Early in the morning Robert was on deck, looking out over the calm sea. Captain Simpson approached him. 'Good morning. It looks like the weather is going to hold, Mr Smith.'

'Yes.'

'We'll be in Marseilles by three o'clock. Will we be staying there long?'

'I don't know,' Robert said pleasantly. 'We'll see.'

'Yes, sir.'

Robert watched Simpson stride off. *What was there about the man?*

Robert walked back to the stern of the yacht and scanned the horizon. He could see nothing, and yet ... In the past, his instincts had saved his life more than once. He had long ago learned to rely on them. Something was wrong.

Over the horizon out of sight, the Italian Navy cruiser *Stromboli* was stalking the *Halcyon*.

When Susan appeared for breakfast, she looked pale and drawn.

'Did you sleep well, darling?' Monte asked.

'Fine,' Susan said.

So they didn't share the same cabin! Robert felt an

unreasonable sense of pleasure from that knowledge. He and Susan had always slept in the same bed, her naked, nubile body spooning into his. *Jesus, I've got to stop thinking like this.*

Ahead of the *Halcyon*, on the starboard bow, was a fishing boat from the Marseilles fleet, bringing in a fresh catch.

'Would you like some fish for lunch?' Susan asked.

Both men nodded. 'Fine.'

They were almost abreast of the fishing boat.

As Captain Simpson walked by, Robert asked, 'What is our ETA to Marseilles?'

'We'll be there in two hours, Mr Smith. Marseilles is an interesting port. Have you ever been there?'

'It *is* an interesting port,' Robert said.

In the communications room, at SIFAR, the two colonels were reading the message that had just come in from the *Halcyon*. It read simply: '*Now.*'

'What's the *Halcyon*'s position?' barked Colonel Cesar.

'They're two hours out of Marseilles, heading for the port.'

'Order the *Stromboli* to overtake and board her immediately.'

Thirty minutes later, the Italian Navy cruiser *Stromboli* was closing in on the *Halcyon*. Susan and Monte were at the fantail of the yacht, watching the warship racing toward them.

A voice came over the cruiser's loudspeaker. 'Ahoy, *Halcyon*. Heave to. We're coming aboard.'

Susan and Monte exchanged a look. Captain Simpson came hurrying toward them.

'Mr Banks . . .'

'I heard it. Do as they say. Stop the engines.'

'Yes, sir.'

A minute later, the pulse of the engines stopped, and the yacht lay still in the water. Susan and her husband watched as armed sailors from the Navy cruiser were lowered into a dinghy.

Ten minutes later a dozen sailors were swarming up the ladder of the *Halcyon*.

The naval officer in charge, a lieutenant commander, said, 'I'm sorry to trouble you, Mr Banks. The Italian government has reason to believe that you are harbouring a fugitive. We have orders to search your ship.'

Susan stood there watching, as the sailors started spreading out, moving along the deck and going below to search the cabins.

'Don't say anything.'

'But . . .'

'Not a word.'

They stood on the deck in silence, watching the search go on.

Thirty minutes later they were assembled again on the main deck.

'There's no sign of him, Commander,' a sailor reported.

'You're certain of that?'

'Absolutely, sir. There are no passengers aboard, and we have identified each member of the crew.'

The Commander stood there a moment, frustrated. His superiors had made a serious mistake.

He turned to Monte and Susan and Captain Simpson. 'I owe you an apology,' he said. 'I'm terribly sorry to have inconvenienced you. We'll leave now.' He turned to go.

'Commander . . .'

'Yes?'

'The man you're looking for got away on a fishing boat half an hour ago. You should have no trouble picking him up.'

Five minutes later, the *Stromboli* was speeding toward Marseilles. The Lieutenant Commander had every reason to be pleased with himself. Half the governments of the world had been pursuing Commander Robert Bellamy, and he was the one who had found him. *There could be a nice promotion in this,* he thought.

From the bridge, the navigation officer called out, 'Commander, could you come up here, please?'

Had they spotted the fishing boat already? The Lieutenant Commander hurried up to the bridge.

'Look, sir!'

The Commander took one look and his heart sank. In the distance ahead, covering the horizon, was the entire Marseilles fishing fleet, a hundred identical boats returning to port. There was no way in the world to identify the one Commander Bellamy was on.

Chapter Forty-Seven

He stole a car in Marseilles. It was a Fiat 1800 Spider convertible, parked on a dimly lit side street. It was locked and there was no key in the ignition. No problem. Looking around to make sure he was not observed, Robert made a rip in the canvas top and shoved his hand inside to unlock the door. He slid inside the car, reached under the dashboard and pulled out all the wires of the ignition switch. He held the thick red wire in one hand while, one by one, he touched the other wires to it until the dashboard lit up. He hooked two wires together, and touched the remaining ones to the two wires hooked together until the engine began to turn over. He pulled out the choke and the engine roared into life. A moment later, Robert was on his way to Paris.

His first priority was to get hold of Li Po. When he reached the Paris suburbs, he stopped at a phone booth. He telephoned Li's apartment and heard the familiar voice on the answering machine: *Zao, mes amis . . . Je regrette que je ne sois pas chez moi mais il n'y a pas du danger que je ne réponde pas à votre coup de téléphone. Prenez garde que vous attendiez le signal de l'appareil.*

Good morning. I regret I am not home, but there is no danger of my not returning your call. Be careful to wait for the tone. Robert counted out the words in their private code. The key words were: Regret . . . danger . . . careful.

The phone was tapped, of course. Li had been expecting his call, and this was his way of warning Robert. He had to get to him as quickly as possible. He would use another code they had employed in the past.

Robert walked along the Rue St Honoré. He had walked this street with Susan. She had stopped in front of a shop window and posed like a mannequin. *Would you like to see me in that dress, Robert? No, I'd prefer to see you out of it.* And they had visited the Louvre, and Susan had stood transfixed in front of the Mona Lisa, her eyes brimming with tears . . .

Robert headed for *Le Matin.* Half a block from the newspaper office, he stopped a teenager on the street.

'Would you like to make fifty francs?'

The boy looked at him suspiciously. 'Doing what?'

Robert scribbled something on a piece of paper and handed it to the boy with a fifty-franc note.

'Just take this into *Le Matin* to the Want Ads desk.'

'*Bon, d'accord.*'

Robert watched the boy go into the building. The ad would get in in time to make next morning's edition. It read: 'Tilly. Dad very ill, needs you. Please meet with him soon. Mother.'

There was nothing to do now but wait. He dared not check into a hotel because they would all have been alerted. Paris was a ticking time bomb.

Robert boarded a crowded tour bus and sat at the back, keeping a low, silent profile. The tour group visited the Luxembourg Gardens, the Louvre, Napoleon's Tomb in Les Invalides, and a dozen other monuments. And always, Robert managed to lose himself in the middle of the crowd.

He bought a ticket for the midnight show at the Moulin Rouge as part of another tour group. The show started at two a.m. When it was over, he filled in the rest of the night moving around Montmartre, going from small bar to small bar.

DAY TWENTY-TWO
Paris, France

The morning papers would not be out on the streets until five a.m. A few minutes before five, Robert was standing near a newspaper stand, waiting. A red truck drove up and a boy threw a bundle of papers onto the pavement. Robert picked up the first one. He turned to the Want Ads. His ad was there. Again there was nothing to do but wait.

At noon, Robert wandered into a small tobacconist shop, where dozens of personal messages were tacked to a board. There were help-wanted ads . . . advertisements for apartments to let . . . students seeking roommates . . . bicycles for sale . . . In the middle of the board, Robert found the message he was looking for. 'Tilly eager to see you. Call her at 50 41 26 45.'

Li Po answered on the first ring. 'Robert?'

'*Zao*, Li.'

'My God, man, what is happening?'

'I was hoping you could tell me.'

'My friend, you're getting more attention than the President of France. The cables are burning up about you. What have you done? No, don't tell me. Whatever it is, you're in serious trouble. They've tapped the phone at the Chinese Embassy, my phone at home is tapped, and they're watching my flat. They've been asking me a lot of questions about you.'

'Li, do you have any idea what this is all . . . ?'

'Not over the phone. Do you remember where Sung's apartment is?'

Li's girlfriend. 'Yes.'

'I'll meet you there in half an hour.'

'Thanks.' Robert was keenly aware of what jeopardy Li Po was putting himself in. He remembered what had happened to Al Traynor, his friend at the FBI. *I'm a fucking Jonah. Everyone I come near dies.*

The apartment was on Rue Benouville in a quiet arrondissement of Paris. When Robert reached the building, the sky was heavy with rain clouds, and he could hear the distant rumble of thunder. He walked into the lobby and rang the doorbell of the apartment. Li Po opened the door at once.

'Come inside,' he said. 'Quickly.' He closed the door behind Robert and locked it. Li Po had not changed since the last time Robert had seen him. He was tall and thin, and ageless.

The two men clasped hands.

'Li, do you know what the hell is going on?'

'Sit down, Robert.'

Robert sat.

Li studied him for a moment. 'Have you ever heard of Operation Doomsday?'

Robert frowned. 'No. Does it have anything to do with UFOs?'

'It has everything to do with UFOs. The world is facing disaster, Robert.'

Li Po began to pace. 'Aliens are coming to earth to destroy us. Three years ago they landed here and met with government officials to demand that all the industrial powers close down their nuclear plants and stop burning fossil fuel.'

Robert was listening, puzzled.

'They demanded a stop to the manufacturing of petroleum, chemicals, rubber, plastics ... That would mean the closing down of thousands of factories all over the world. Automobile and steel plants would be forced to shut down. The world economy would be a shambles.'

'Why should they ... ?'

'They claim we're polluting the universe, destroying the earth and the seas ... they want us to stop making weapons, to stop waging war.'

'Li ...'

'A group of powerful men from a dozen countries got together – top industrialists from the United States, Japan, Russia, China ... A man with the code name of Janus organized intelligence agencies around the world to form Operation Doomsday, to stop the aliens.' He turned to Robert. 'You've heard of SDI?'

'Star Wars. The satellite system to shoot down Soviet intercontinental ballistic missiles.'

Li shook his head. 'No. That was a cover. SDI was not created to fight the Russians. It is being designed for the specific purpose of knocking down UFOs. It's the only chance there is of stopping them.'

Robert sat there in stunned silence, trying to absorb what Li Po was saying, while the rumble of thunder grew louder. 'You mean, the governments are behind . . . ?'

'Let's say, there are cabals within each government. Operation Doomsday is being run privately. Do you understand now?'

'My God! The governments aren't aware that . . .' He looked up at Li. 'Li – how did you learn all this?'

'It's very simple, Robert,' Li said quietly, 'I'm the Chinese connection.' There was a Beretta in his hand.

Robert stared at the gun. 'Li . . . !'

Li squeezed the trigger, and the sound of the shot mingled with a sudden deafening crack of thunder and a flash of lightning outside the window.

Chapter Forty-Eight

The first few drops of clean rain water awakened her. She was lying on a park bench, too exhausted to move. For the last two days, she had felt her life energy flowing out of her. *I am going to die here on this planet.* She drifted into what she thought would be her last sleep. And then, the rain came. The blessed rain. She could hardly believe it. She lifted her head to the sky and felt the cool drops running down her face. It began to rain harder, and harder. Fresh, pure liquid. She stood up then, and raised her hands high, letting the water pour over her, giving her new strength, bringing her back to life. She let the rain water fill her body, absorbing it into her very essence, until she began to feel her tiredness vanish. She felt herself growing stronger and stronger, until finally, she thought, *I am ready. I can think clearly. I know who can help me find my way back.* She took out the small transmitter, closed her eyes, and began to concentrate.

Chapter Forty-Nine

It was the lightning streak that saved Robert's life. At the instant that Li Po started to squeeze the trigger, the sudden flash of light outside the window distracted him for a moment. Robert moved, and the bullet hit him in his right shoulder instead of his chest.

As Li raised the gun to fire again, Robert gave a side-thrust kick, knocking the gun out of Li's hand. Li spun forward and punched Robert hard in his wounded shoulder. The pain was excruciating. Robert's jacket was covered with blood. He lashed out with a forward elbow smash. Li grunted with pain. He riposted with a deadly *shuto* chop to the neck, and Robert evaded it. The two men circled each other, both of them breathing hard, looking for an opening. They fought silently in a deadly ritual older than time, and each knew that only one of them would come out of this alive. Robert was weakening. The pain in his shoulder was increasing, and he could see his blood dripping to the floor.

Time was on Li Po's side. *I've got to end this quickly*, Robert thought. He moved in with a front snap kick. Instead of evading it, Li took the full force of it, and was close enough to Robert to drive his elbow into Robert's shoulder. Robert staggered. Li moved in with a spin and back kick, and Robert faltered. Li was on top of him in an instant, pummelling him, pounding his shoulder again and again, backing him across the room. Robert was too weak to stop the rain of punishing blows. His eyes began to dim. He fell against Li, grabbing him, and the two men went down, smashing a glass table, shattering it. Robert lay on the floor, powerless to move. *It's over*, he thought. *They've won*.

He lay there, half-conscious, waiting for Li to finish him off. Nothing happened. Slowly, painfully, Robert lifted his head. Li lay next to him on the floor, his eyes opened wide, staring at the ceiling. A large shard of glass, like a transparent dagger, protruded from his chest.

Robert struggled to sit up. He was weak from the loss of blood. His shoulder was an ocean of pain. *I have to get to a doctor*, he thought. *There was a name . . . someone that the Agency used in Paris . . . someone at the American Hospital. Hilsinger. That was it. Leon Hilsinger.*

Dr Hilsinger was ready to leave his office for the day when the telephone call came in. His nurse had already gone home, so he picked up the phone. The voice at the other end of the phone was slurred.

'Dr Hilsinger?'

'Yes.'

'This is Robert Bellamy . . . need your help. I've been badly hurt. Will you help me?'

'Of course. Where are you?'

'Never mind that. I'll meet you at the American Hospital in half an hour.'

'I'll be there. Go right to the Emergency Room.'

'Doctor – don't mention this call to anyone.'

'You have my word.' The line went dead.

Dr Hilsinger dialled a number. 'I just heard from Commander Bellamy. I'm meeting him at the American Hospital in half an hour . . .'

'Thank you, Doctor.'

Dr Hilsinger replaced the receiver. He heard the reception door open and looked up. Robert Bellamy was standing there with a gun in his hand.

'On second thoughts,' Robert said, 'it might be better if you treated me here.'

The doctor tried to conceal his surprise. 'You . . . you should be in a hospital.'

'Too close to the morgue. Patch me up and make it fast.' It was difficult to talk.

Dr Hilsinger started to protest, then thought better of it. 'Yes. Whatever you say. I'd better give you an anaesthetic. It will . . .'

'Don't even think about it,' Robert said. 'No tricks.' He was holding the gun in his left hand. 'If I don't get out of here alive, neither do you. Any questions?' He felt faint.

Dr Hilsinger swallowed. 'No.'

'Then get to work.'

Dr Hilsinger led Robert into the next room, an examining room filled with medical equipment. Slowly and carefully, Robert slipped out of his jacket. Holding the gun in his hand, he sat down on the table. Dr Hilsinger had a scalpel in his hand. Robert's fingers tightened on the trigger.

'Relax,' Dr Hilsinger said nervously. 'I'm just going to cut your shirt.'

The wound was raw and red, and seeping blood. 'The bullet is still in there,' Dr Hilsinger said. 'You won't be able to stand the pain unless I give you . . .'

'No!' He was not going to let himself be drugged. 'Just take it out.'

'Whatever you say.'

Robert watched the doctor walk over to a sterilizing unit and put in a pair of forceps. Robert sat on the edge of the table, fighting off the dizziness that threatened to engulf him. He closed his eyes for a moment, and Dr Hilsinger was standing in front of him, the forceps in his hand.

'Here we go.' He pushed the forceps into the raw wound and Robert screamed aloud with the pain. Bright lights flashed in front of his eyes. He started to lose consciousness.

'It's out,' Dr Hilsinger said.

Robert sat there for a moment, trembling, taking deep breaths, fighting to regain control of himself.

Dr Hilsinger was watching him closely. 'Are you all right?'

It took Robert a moment to find his voice. 'Yes . . . patch it up.'

The doctor poured peroxide into the wound, and Robert started to pass out again. He gritted his teeth. *Hang on. We're almost there.* And finally, blessedly, the worst was over. The doctor was strapping a heavy bandage across Robert's shoulder.

'Give me my jacket,' Robert said.

Dr Hilsinger stared at him. 'You can't go out now. You can't even walk.'

'Bring me my jacket.' His voice was so weak he could hardly talk. He watched the doctor walk across the room to get his jacket, and there seemed to be two of him.

'You've lost a lot of blood,' Dr Hilsinger cautioned. 'It would be dangerous for you to leave.'

And more dangerous for me to stay, Robert thought. Carefully, he slipped his jacket on and tried to stand. His legs began to buckle. He grabbed the side of the table.

'You'll never make it,' Dr Hilsinger warned.

Robert looked up at the blurry figure in front of him. 'I'll make it.'

But he knew that the moment he left, Dr Hilsinger would be on the phone again. Robert's eyes fell on the spool of heavy surgical tape Dr Hilsinger had used.

'Sit in the chair.' His words were slurred.

'Why? What are you . . . ?'

Robert raised the gun. 'Sit down.'

Dr Hilsinger sat. Robert picked up the roll of tape. It was awkward, because he only had the use of one hand. He pulled the end of the wide tape loose and began to unroll it. He moved over to Dr Hilsinger. 'Just sit quietly and you won't get hurt.'

He fastened the end of the tape to the arm of the chair, and then started winding it around the doctor's hands.

'This really isn't necessary,' Dr Hilsinger said. 'I won't...'

'Shut up.' Robert continued to bind the doctor to the chair. The effort had started the rivers of pain flowing again. He looked at the doctor and said quietly, 'I'm not going to faint.'

He fainted.

He was floating in space, drifting weightlessly through white clouds, at peace. *Wake up.* He did not want to wake up. He wanted this wonderful feeling to go on forever. *Wake up.* Something hard was pressing against his side. Something in his jacket pocket. With his eyes still closed, he reached in and held it in his hand. It was the crystal. He drifted back to sleep.

Robert. It was a woman's voice, soft and soothing. He was in a lovely green meadow, and the air was filled with music, and there were bright lights in the sky overhead. A woman was moving toward him. She was tall and beautiful, with a gentle, oval face and a soft, almost translucent complexion. She was dressed in a snow-white gown. Her voice was gentle and hushed.

No one's going to hurt you anymore, Robert. Come to me. I'm waiting here for you.

Slowly, Robert opened his eyes. He lay there for a long moment, then sat up, filled with a sudden sense of excitement. He knew now who the eleventh witness was, and he knew where he was to meet her.

Chapter Fifty

DAY TWENTY-THREE

Paris, France

He telephoned Admiral Whittaker from the doctor's office.

'Admiral. Robert.'

'Robert! What's going on? They told me...'

'Never mind that now. I need your help, Admiral. Have you ever heard of the name Janus?'

Admiral Whittaker said slowly, 'Janus? No. I never heard of him.'

Robert said, 'I've found out he's heading some kind of secret organization that's killing innocent people, and now he's trying to kill me. We have to stop him.'

'How can I help?'

'I need to get to the President. Can you arrange a meeting?'

There was a moment of silence. 'I'm certain I can.'

'There's more. General Hilliard is involved.'

'What? How...?'

'And there are others. Most of the intelligence agencies in Europe are in it, too. I can't explain any more now. I want you to call Hilliard. Tell him I've found an eleventh witness.'

'I don't understand. An eleventh witness to what?'

'I'm sorry, Admiral, but I can't tell you. Hilliard will know. I want him to meet me in Switzerland.'

'Switzerland?'

'Tell him I'm the only one who knows where the eleventh witness is. If he makes one wrong move, the deal is off. Tell him to go to the Dolder Grand in Zürich. There will be a note waiting for him at the desk. Tell him I also want Janus in Switzerland, in person.'

'Robert, are you certain you know what you're doing?'

'No, sir, I'm not. But this is the only chance I've got. I want you to tell him my conditions are not negotiable. Number one, I want safe passage to Switzerland. Number two, I want General Hilliard and Janus to meet me there. Number three, after that, I want a meeting with the President of the United States.'

'I will do everything I can, Robert. How will I get in touch with you?'

'I'll call you back. How much time will you need?'

'Give me one hour.'

'Right.'

'And Robert . . .'

He could hear the pain in the old man's voice. 'Yes, sir?'

'Be careful.'

'Don't worry, sir. I'm a survivor. Remember?'

One hour later Robert was speaking to Admiral Whittaker again.

'You have a deal. General Hilliard seemed shaken by the news of another witness. He's given me his word you will not be harmed. Your conditions will be met. He's flying to Zürich and will be there tomorrow morning.'

'And Janus?'

'Janus will be on the plane with him.'

Robert felt a surge of relief. 'Thank you, Admiral. And the President?'

'I spoke to him myself. His aides will arrange a meeting for you whenever you're ready.'

Thank God!

'General Hilliard has a plane to fly you to . . .'

'No way.' He was not going to let them get him into a plane. 'I'm in Paris. I want a car and I'll drive it myself. I want it left in front of the Hotel Littré in Montparnasse within half an hour.'

'I'll see to it.'

'Admiral?'

'Yes, Robert?'

It was difficult to keep his voice steady. 'Thank you.'

He walked down Rue Littré, moving slowly because of the pain. He approached the hotel cautiously. Parked directly in front of the building was a black Mercedes sedan. There was no one inside. Across the street was a blue and white police car, with a uniformed policeman behind the wheel. On the sidewalk, two men in civilian clothes stood watching Robert approach. *French Secret Service.*

Robert found that he was having trouble breathing. His heart was pounding. Was he stepping into a trap? The only insurance he had was the eleventh witness. Did Hilliard believe him? Was it enough?

He walked toward the sedan, waiting for the men to make a move. They stood there, silently watching him.

Robert moved toward the driver's side of the Mercedes and looked inside. The keys were in the ignition. He could feel the eyes of the men fastened on him as he opened the door and slid into the driver's seat. He sat there a moment, staring at the ignition. *If General Hilliard had double-crossed Admiral Whittaker, this was the moment when everything would end in a violent explosion.*

Here goes. Robert took a deep breath, reached down with his left hand and turned the key. The motor purred into life. The Secret Service men stood there, watching him drive away. As Robert approached the intersection, a police car pulled in front of his car, and for a moment, Robert thought he was going to be stopped. Instead, the police turned on their red flashing light, and the traffic seemed to melt away. *They're giving me a fucking escort!*

Overhead Robert heard the sound of a helicopter. He glanced up. The side of the helicopter was marked with the insignia of the French National Police. General Hilliard was doing everything possible to see that he arrived in Switzerland safely. *And after I show him the last witness*, Robert thought grimly, *he thinks he's going to kill me. But the General is in for a surprise.*

Robert reached the Swiss border at four o'clock in the afternoon. At the border, the French police car turned back, and a Swiss police car became his escort. For the first time since the affair had started, Robert began to relax. *Thank God Admiral Whittaker had friends in high places.* With the President expecting a meeting with Robert, General Hilliard would not dare to harm him. His mind turned to the woman in white, and at that instant, he heard her voice. The sound of it reverberated through the car.

Hurry, Robert. We are all waiting for you.

All? Was there more than one? I'll find out soon enough, Robert *All? Was there more than one? I'll find out soon enough,* Robert thought.

In Zürich, Robert stopped at the Dolder Grand Hotel and wrote a note at the desk for the General.

'General Hilliard will ask for me,' Robert told the clerk. 'Please give this to him.'

'Yes, sir.'

Outside, Robert walked over to the police car that had been escorting him. He leaned down to talk to the driver. 'From here on in, I want to be on my own.'

The driver hesitated. 'Very well, Commander.'

Robert got back in his car and started driving toward Uetendorf and the scene of the UFO crash. As he drove, he thought of all the tragedies that had occurred because of it and all the lives that had been taken. *Hans Beckerman and Father Patrini; Leslie Mothershed and William Mann; Daniel Wayne and Otto Schmidt; Laslo Bushfekete and Fritz Mandel; Olga Romanchanko and Kevin Parker. Dead. All of them dead.*

I want to see the face of Janus, Robert thought, *and look into his eyes.*

The villages seemed to race by, and the pristine beauty of the Alps belied all the bloodshed and terror that had started here. The car approached Thun, and Robert's adrenalin began to flow. Ahead was the field where he and Beckerman had found the weather balloon, where the nightmare had begun. Robert pulled the car over to the side of the road and switched off the engine. He said a silent prayer. Then he got out of the car, crossed the highway and went into the field.

A thousand memories flashed through Robert's mind. The phone call at four in the morning. *You are ordered to report to General Hilliard at National Security Agency Headquarters at Fort Meade at 0600 this morning. Is the message understood, Commander?*

How little he had understood it then. He recalled General Hilliard's words: *You must find those witnesses. All of them.* And the search had led from Zürich to Bern, London, Munich, Rome and Orvieto; from Waco to Fort Smith; from Kiev to Washington, and Budapest. Well, the bloody trail had finally come to an end, here, where it had all begun.

She was waiting for him, as Robert had known she would be, and she looked exactly as she had appeared in his dream. They moved toward each other, and she seemed to be floating toward him, a radiant smile on her face.

Thank you for coming, Robert.

Had he actually heard her speak, or was he hearing her thoughts? How did one talk to an alien being?

'I had to come,' he said simply. There was a totally unreal quality to the scene. *I'm standing here speaking with someone from another world! I should be terrified, but in my whole life, I've never felt more at peace.* 'I have to warn you,' Robert said. 'Some men are coming here who want to harm you. It would be better if you left before they arrive.'

I cannot leave.

And Robert understood. He reached in his pocket with his left hand and pulled out the small piece of metal containing the crystal.

Her face lit up. *Thank you, Robert.*

He handed it to her and watched her fit it into the piece she held in her hand.

'What happens now?' Robert asked.

Now I can communicate with my friends. They will be coming for me.

Was there something ominous in that sentence? Robert recalled General Hilliard's words: *They intend to take over this planet and make slaves of us.*

What if General Hilliard was right? What if the aliens did intend to take over the earth? Who was going to stop them? Robert looked at his watch. It was almost time for General Hilliard and Janus to arrive, and even as Robert thought it, he heard the sound of a giant Huey helicopter approaching from the north.

Your friends are here.

Friends. They were his mortal enemies, and he was determined to expose them as murderers, to destroy them.

The grass and flowers in the field began to flutter wildly as the helicopter came to a landing.

He was about to come face to face with Janus. The thought of it filled him with a murderous rage. The door of the helicopter opened.

Susan stepped out.

Chapter Fifty-One

In the mothership, floating high above earth, there was great joy. All the lights on the panels were flashing green.

We have found her!

We must hurry.

The huge ship started to hurl itself toward the planet far below.

Chapter Fifty-Two

For a single instant, time was frozen, and then it shattered into a thousand pieces. Robert watched, stunned, as Susan stepped out of the helicopter. She stood there for a second, and then started toward Robert, but Monte Banks who was right behind her, grabbed her and held her back.

'Run, Robert! Run! They're going to kill you!'

Robert took a step toward her, and at that moment, General Hilliard and Colonel Frank Johnson stepped out of the helicopter.

General Hilliard said, 'I'm here, Commander. I've kept my part of the bargain.' He walked over to Robert and the woman in white. 'I assume this is the eleventh witness. The missing alien. I'm sure we'll find her very interesting. So it's finally finished.'

'Not yet. You said you would bring Janus.'

'Oh, yes. Janus insisted on coming to see you.'

Robert turned toward the helicopter. Admiral Whittaker was standing in the doorway.

'You asked to see me, Robert?'

Robert stared at him, unbelievingly, and there was a red film before his eyes. It was as though his world had collapsed. 'No! Why . . . ? *Why* in God's name?'

The Admiral was moving toward him. 'You don't

understand, do you? You never did. You're worried about a few meaningless lives. We're worried about saving our world. This earth belongs to us, to do with as we please.'

He turned to stare at the woman in white. 'If you creatures want war, you're going to get war. And we'll beat you!' He turned back to Robert. 'You betrayed me. You were my son. I let you take Edward's place. I gave you a chance to serve your country. And how did you repay me? You came whining to me to let you stay home so you could be with your wife.' His voice was filled with contempt. 'No son of mine would ever do that. I should have seen then how distorted your values were.'

Robert stood there, immobile, too shocked to speak.

'I broke up your marriage because I still had faith in you, but . . .'

'You broke up my . . . ?'

'Remember when the CIA sent you after the Fox? I arranged that. I hoped it would bring you to your senses. You failed because there was no Fox. I thought I had straightened you out, that you were one of us. And then you told me you were going to quit the Agency. That's when I knew you were no patriot, that you had to be eliminated, destroyed. But first you had to help us with our mission.'

'Your *mission*? To kill all those innocent people? You're insane!'

'They had to be killed to stop them from spreading panic. We're ready now for the aliens. All we needed was a little more time, and you've given it to us.'

The woman in white had stood there listening, saying nothing, but now her thoughts floated into the minds of those standing in the field. *We have come here to prevent you from destroying your planet. We are all part of one universe. Look up.*

Their heads turned toward the sky. There was an enormous white cloud overhead, and as they stared up at it, it seemed to change before their eyes. They were looking at a vision of a polar ice cap, and as they watched, it began to melt, and the water came pouring through the rivers and oceans of the world, flooding London and Los Angeles, New York, and Tokyo, and coastal cities around the world in a dizzying montage. The vision changed to an enormous vista of desolate farmlands, with crops burnt to cinders under a broiling, merciless sun, and the corpses of dead animals strewn across the landscape. The scene before their eyes changed again, and they saw riots in China, and famines in India, and a devastating nuclear war, and finally, people living in caves. The vision slowly disappeared.

There was a moment of awed silence. *That is your future if you go on as you are.*

Admiral Whittaker was the first to recover. 'Mass hypnosis,' he snapped. 'I'm sure you can show us other interesting tricks.' He moved toward the alien. 'I'm taking you back to Washington with me. We have a lot of information to get from you.' The Admiral looked at Robert. 'You're finished.' He turned to Frank Johnson. 'Take care of him.'

Colonel Johnson removed his pistol from his holster.

Susan broke away from Monte, and ran to Robert's side. 'No!' she screamed.

'Kill him!' Admiral Whittaker said.

Colonel Johnson was pointing a gun at the Admiral. 'Admiral – you're under arrest.'

Admiral Whittaker was staring at him. 'What ... What are you saying? I told you to kill him. You're one of us.'

'You're wrong. I never have been. I infiltrated your organization a long time ago. I was looking for Commander Bellamy not to kill him, but to save him.' He turned to Robert. 'I'm sorry I couldn't get to you sooner.'

Admiral Whittaker's face had turned ashen. 'Then you'll be destroyed too. Nobody can stand in our way. Our organization...'

'You no longer have an organization. At this moment, all the members are being rounded up. It's finished, Admiral.'

Overhead, the sky seemed to be vibrating with light and sound. The huge mothership was floating down directly above them, bright green lights flashing from its interior. They stared in awe as they watched it land. A smaller spaceship appeared, and then another, and then two more and another two, until the sky seemed to be filled with them, and there was a great roar in the air that became a glorious music that echoed throughout the mountains. The door of the mothership opened and an alien appeared.

The woman in white turned to Robert. *I am leaving now.* She moved toward Admiral Whittaker, General

Hilliard, and Monte Banks. *You shall come with me.*

Admiral Whittaker drew back. 'No! I won't go!'

Yes. We will not hurt you. She held out her hand, and for an instant nothing happened. Then, as the others watched, the three men began slowly moving toward the spaceship in a hypnotic daze.

Admiral Whittaker screamed, 'No!'

He was still screaming when the three men disappeared inside the spaceship.

The woman in white turned to the others. *They will not be harmed. They have much to learn. When they have learned, they will be brought back here.*

Susan was holding Robert tightly.

Tell people they must stop killing this planet, Robert. Make them understand.

'I'm only one man.'

There are thousands of you. Every day your numbers grow. One day there will be millions, and you must all speak with one strong voice. Will you do it?

'I'll try. I'll try.'

We are leaving now. But we will be watching you. And we will be back.

The woman in white turned and entered the mothership. The lights inside began to glow brighter and brighter, until they seemed to light up the entire sky. Suddenly, without warning, the mothership took off, followed by the smaller ships, until finally they all vanished from sight.

Tell the people they must stop killing the planet.
Right, Robert thought. *I know now what I'm going to do with the rest of my life.*

He looked at Susan and smiled.

THE BEGINNING

Author's Note

In researching this novel, I have read numerous books, and magazine and newspaper articles citing astronauts who had reportedly had extraterrestrial experiences: Colonel Frank Borman on *Gemini* 7 supposedly took pictures of a UFO that followed his capsule. Neil Armstrong on *Apollo* 11 saw two unidentified spacecraft when he landed on the moon. Buzz Aldrin photographed unidentified spacecraft on the moon. Colonel L. Gordon Cooper, on a Project Mercury flight, encountered a large UFO over Perth, Australia, and recorded voices speaking languages later found to belong to no known earth language.

I talked to these men, as well as to other astronauts, and each one assured me that the stories were apocryphal, rather than apocalyptic, that they had had no experiences of any kind with UFOs. A few days after my telephone conversation with Colonel Gordon Cooper, he called me back. I returned his call, but he had suddenly become unavailable. One year later, I managed to acquire a letter written by him, dated November 9th, 1978, discussing UFOs.

I telephoned Colonel Cooper again to ask him if the letter was authentic. This time, he was more forthcoming. He informed me that it was, and that on his journeys into space he had personally witnessed several flights of UFOs. He also mentioned that other astronauts had had similar experiences that they were warned not to discuss.

I have read a dozen books that prove conclusively that flying saucers exist. I have read a dozen books that prove conclusively that flying saucers do *not* exist. I have run video tapes purporting to be photographs of flying saucers, and have met with therapists in the United States and abroad who specialize in hypnotizing people who claim to have been taken up into UFOs. The therapists say that they have handled hundreds of cases in which the details of the victims' experiences are startlingly similar, including identical, unexplainable marks on their bodies.

An Air Force general in charge of the Blue Book project – a US government group formed to investigate flying saucers – assured me that there has never been any hard evidence of flying saucers, or of aliens.

Yet, in the foreword to *Above Top Secret*, a remarkable book by Timothy Good, Lord Hill-Norton, Admiral of the Fleet and British Chief of Defence Staff from 1971 to 1973, writes:

> The evidence that there are objects which have been seen in our atmosphere, and even on terra firma, that cannot be accounted for either as man-made objects or as any physical force or effect known to our scientists seems to me to be overwhelming ... A very large number of sightings have been vouched for by persons whose credentials seem to me unimpeachable. It is striking that so many have been trained

observers, such as police officers and airline or military pilots . . .

In 1933, the 4th Swedish Flying Corps began an investigation of mysterious unmarked aircraft appearing over Scandinavia, and on April 30th, 1934, Major-General Erik Reuterswaerd issued the following statement to the press:

> Comparisons of these reports show that there can be no doubt about illegal air traffic over our secret military areas. There are many reports from reliable people which describe close observation of the enigmatic flier. And in every case, the same remark can be noted; no insignias or identifying marks are visible on the machines . . . the question is: Who or what are they, and why have they been invading our air territory?

In 1947, Professor Paul Santorini, a leading Greek scientist, was asked to investigate missiles flying over Greece. 'We soon established that they were not missiles. But, before we could do any more, the Army, after conferring with foreign officials, ordered the investigation stopped. *Foreign scientists flew to Greece for secret talks with me.*' [Emphasis added.] The professor confirmed that a 'world blanket of secrecy' surrounded the UFO question because, among other reasons, the authorities were unwilling to admit the existence of a force against which there was 'no possibility of defence'.

From 1947 to 1952, ATIC (Air Technical Intelligence Centre) received approximately 1,500 official reports of sightings. Of these the Air Force carries 20 per cent as unexplained.

Air Chief Marshal Lord Dowding, Commander-in-Chief of RAF Fighter Command during the Battle of Britain in 1940, wrote:

> More than 10,000 sightings have been reported, the majority of which cannot be accounted for by any 'scientific explanation'. They have been tracked on radar screens ... and the observed speeds have been as great as 9,000 miles an hour ... I am convinced that these objects do exist and that they are not manufactured by any nation on earth. I can therefore see no alternative to accepting the theory that they come from an extraterrestrial source ...

Recently, in Elmwood, Wisconsin, the entire town watched as flying saucers moved across their skies for several days.

General Lionel Max Chassin, who rose to the rank of Commanding General of the French Air Forces and served as General Air Defence Co-ordinator, Allied Air Forces, Central Europe (NATO), wrote:

> That strange things have been seen is now beyond question ... The number of thoughtful, intelligent, educated people in full possession of their faculties who have 'seen something' and described it grows every day.

Then there was the famous Roswell Incident, in 1947. According to eyewitness reports, on the evening of July 2nd, a bright disc-shaped object was seen over Roswell, New Mexico. The following day, widely scattered wreckage was discovered by a local ranch manager and his two children. The authorities were alerted and an official statement was released confirming that the wreckage of a flying disc had been recovered.

A second press statement was immediately issued stating that the wreckage was nothing more than the remains of a weather balloon, which was dutifully displayed at a press conference. Meanwhile the real wreckage was reported to have been sent to Wright Field. The bodies were described by one witness as 'like human but they were not humans. The heads were round, the eyes were small, and they had no hair. Their eyes were widely spaced. They were quite small by our standards and their heads were larger in proportion to their bodies. Their clothing seemed to be one-piece and grey in colour. They seemed to be all males and there were a number of them . . . Military personnel took over and we were told to leave the area and not to talk to anyone about what we had seen.'

According to a document acquired from an intelligence source in 1984, a highly secret panel, codenamed 'Majestic 12' or 'MJ-12', was formed by President Truman in 1947 to investigate UFOs and report its findings to the President. The document, dated November 18th, 1952 and classified TOP SECRET/MAJIC/EYES ONLY, was allegedly prepared by Admiral Hillenkoetter for President-elect Dwight Eisenhower, and includes the astonishing statement that the remains of four alien bodies were recovered two miles from the Roswell wreckage site.

Five years after the panel was formed, the committee wrote a memo to then President-elect Eisenhower about the UFO project and the need for secrecy:

> Implications for the National Security are of continuing importance, in that motives and ultimate intentions of these visitors remain completely unknown... It is for these reasons, as well as the obvious international technological considerations and the ultimate need to avoid a public panic at all costs, that the Majestic 12 Group remains of the unanimous opinion that imposition of the strictest security precautions should continue without interruption into the new administration.

The official explanation of denial is that the document's authenticity is questionable.

The National Security Agency is reported to be withholding more than one hundred documents relating to UFOs, the CIA approximately fifty documents, and the DIA six.

Major Donald Keyhoe, a former aide to Charles Lindbergh, publicly accused the US government of denying the existence of UFOs, in order to prevent public panic.

In August 1948, when a top secret 'Estimate of the Situation' by the Air Technical Intelligence Centre offered its opinion that UFOs were interplanetary visitors, General Vandenberg, Air Force Chief of Staff at the time, ordered the document burned.

Is there a worldwide government conspiracy to conceal the truth from the public?

In the short space of six years, twenty-three English scientists who worked on Star-Wars-type projects have died under questionable circumstances. All of them had worked on different facets of electronic warfare, which includes UFO research.

A list of the deceased and the dates and circumstances of their deaths follows.

1982. Professor Keith Bowden, killed in auto crash.

July 1982. Jack Wolfenden, died in a glider accident.

November 1982. Ernest Brockway, suicide.

1983. Stephen Drinkwater, suicide by strangulation.

April 1983. Lieutenant Colonel Anthony Godley, missing, declared dead.

April 1984. George Franks, suicide by hanging.

1985. Stephen Oke, suicide by hanging.

November 1985. Jonathan Wash, suicide by jumping from a building.

1986. Dr John Brittan, suicide by carbon monoxide poisoning.

October 1986. Arshad Sharif, suicide by placing a rope around his neck, tying it to a tree and then driving away at high speed. Took place in Bristol, one hundred miles away from his home in London.

October 1986. Vimal Dajibhai, suicide by jumping

from a bridge in Bristol, one hundred miles away from his home in London.

January 1987. Avtar Singh-Gida, missing, declared dead.

February 1987. Peter Peapell, suicide after crawling under car in garage.

March 1987. David Sands, suicide by driving car into café at high speed.

April 1987. Mark Wisner, death by self-strangulation.

April 10th, 1987. Stuart Gooding, killed in Cyprus.

April 1987. Shani Warren, suicide by drowning.

May 1987. Michael Baker, killed in auto crash.

May 1988. Trevor Knight, suicide.

August 1988. Alistair Beckham, suicide by self-electrocution.

August 1988. Brigadier Peter Ferry, suicide by self-electrocution.

Date unknown. Victor Moore, suicide.

Coincidences?

In the past three decades, there have been at least 70,000 reports of mysterious objects in the sky and countless more sightings, perhaps ten times as many, that have gone unreported.

Reports of UFOs have come from hundreds of countries all over the globe. In Spain, UFOs are known as *Objetos Foladores No Identificados* . . . in Germany, they are *Fliegende Untertassen* . . . in France, *Soucoupes Volantes* . . . in Czechoslovakia, *Letajici Talire*.

The eminent astronomer Carl Sagan has estimated that our Milky Way galaxy alone may contain some 250 billion stars. About a million of these, he believes, may have planets capable of supporting some form of civilization.

Our government denies the existence of extraterrestrial intelligence, yet on Columbus Day, in 1992, in California and Puerto Rica, NASA will activate radio telescopes equipped with special receivers and computers capable of analysing tens of millions of radio channels at once, to search for signs of intelligent life in the universe.

NASA has nicknamed the mission 'MOP' for Microwave Observing Project, but astronomers refer to it as 'SETI', for Search for Extraterrestrial Intelligence.

I have asked two former presidents of the United States whether they have any knowledge of UFOs or aliens, and their responses were negative. Would they have told me if they had had any information? Given the blanket of secrecy that seems to surround the subject, I think not.

Do flying saucers really exist? Are we being visited by aliens from another planet? With new technology probing deeper and deeper into the universe, looking for signs of intelligent life in space, perhaps we will have the answer much sooner than we expect.

There are many working in space exploration, astronomy and cosmology who, not content to wait for that answer, put themselves out on a limb and make a prediction of their own. Jill Tartar, an astrophysicist and SETI project scientist at NASA's Ames Research Centre, in Ames, Iowa, is among them.

> There are 400 billion stars in the galaxy. We're made of stardust, really common stuff. In a universe filled with stardust, it's hard to believe that we are the only creatures who could be.

Text of a letter from Colonel L. Gordon Cooper to Ambassador Griffith

Ambassador Griffith
Mission of Grenada to the United Nations
866 Second Avenue
Suite 502
New York, New York 10017

Dear Ambassador Griffith:

I wanted to convey to you my views on our extraterrestrial visitors popularly referred to as 'UFOs', and suggest what might be done to properly deal with them.

I believe that these extraterrestrial vehicles and their crews are visiting this planet from other planets, which obviously are a little more technically advanced than we are here on earth. I feel that we need to have a top level, coordinated program to scientifically collect and analyze data from all over the earth concerning any type of encounter, and to determine how best to interface with these visitors in a friendly fashion. We may first have to show them that we have learned to resolve our problems by peaceful means, rather than warfare, before we are accepted as fully qualified universal team members. This acceptance would have tremendous possibilities of advancing our world in all areas. Certainly then it would seem that the UN has a vested interest in handling this subject properly and expeditiously.

I should point out that I am not an experienced UFO professional researcher. I have not yet had the privilege of flying a UFO, nor of meeting the crew of one. I do feel that I am somewhat qualified to discuss them since I have been into the fringes of the vast areas in which they travel. Also I did have occasion in 1951 to have two days of observation of many flights of them, of different sizes, flying in fighter formation, generally from east to west over Europe. They were at a higher altitude than we could reach with our jet fighters of that time.

I would also like to point out that most astronauts are very reluctant to even discuss UFOs due to the great numbers of people who have indiscriminately sold fake stories and forged documents abusing their names and reputations without hesitation. Those few astronauts who have continued to have a participation in the UFO field have to do so very cautiously. There are several of us who do believe in UFOs and who have had occasion to see a UFO on the ground, or from an airplane.

If the UN agrees to pursue this project, and to lend their credibility to it, perhaps many more well qualified people will agree to step forth and provide help and information.

I am looking forward to seeing you soon.
Sincerely,
L. Gordon Cooper
Col. USAF (kct)
Astronaut

The Stars Shine Down

**The stars shine down
And watch us live
Our little lives
And weep for us.**

    MONET NODLEHS

Acknowledgements

I owe a debt of gratitude to those who were so generous with their time and expertise:

Larry Russo who led me through the arcane maze of the biggest gamblers of all – the real estate developers.

The musical mavens who invited me inside their private world – Mona Gollabeck, John Lill, Zubin Mehta, Dudley Moore, André Previn, and the Trustees of The Leonard Bernstein Estate.

I wish also to express my appreciation to the citizens of Glace Bay for their warm hospitality. I hope they will forgive me for the few dramatic licences I felt it necessary to take.

The expertise in the book belongs to those listed above. Any errors are mine.

THE AUTHOR

*This one is for Morton Janklow,
A Man for All Seasons*

Book One

1

Thursday, September 10, 1992
8:00 p.m.

The 727 was lost in a sea of cumulus clouds that tossed the plane around like a giant silver feather. The pilot's worried voice came over the speaker.

'Is your seat belt fastened, Miss Cameron?'

There was no response.

'Miss Cameron . . . Miss Cameron . . .'

She was shaken out of a deep reverie. 'Yes.' Her thoughts had been drifting to happier times, happier places.

'Are you all right? We should be out of this storm soon.'

'I'm fine, Roger.'

Maybe we'll get lucky and crash, Lara Cameron thought. It would be a fitting end. Somewhere, somehow, it had all gone wrong. *It's the Fates*, Lara thought. *You can't fight the Fates*. In the past year her life had spun wildly out of control. She was in danger of losing everything. *At least nothing else can go wrong*, she thought wryly. *There is nothing else*.

The door of the cockpit opened and the pilot came into the cabin. He paused for a moment to admire his passenger. The woman was beautiful, with shiny black hair swept up in a crown, a flawless complexion, intelligent eyes, cat-grey. She had changed clothes after they had taken off from Reno, and she was wearing a white, off-the-shoulder Scaasi evening gown that accented a slender, seductive figure. Around her throat was a diamond and ruby necklace. *How can she look so damn calm with her world collapsing around her?* he wondered. The newspapers had been mercilessly attacking her for the past month.

'Is the phone working yet, Roger?'

'I'm afraid not, Miss Cameron. There's a lot of interference because of the storm. We're going to be about an hour late getting into La Guardia. I'm sorry.'

I'm going to be late for my birthday party, Lara thought. *Everyone is going to be there. Two hundred guests, including the Vice President of the United States, the Governor of New York, the Mayor, Hollywood celebrities, famous athletes, and financiers from half a dozen countries*. She had approved the guest list herself.

She could visualize the Grand Ballroom of the Cameron Plaza, where the party was being held. Baccarat crystal chandeliers would hang from the ceiling, prisms of light reflecting a dazzling diamond-like brilliance. There would be place settings for two hundred guests, at twenty tables. The finest linens, china, silver and stemware would adorn each place setting, and in the centre of each table would be a floral display of white orchids mixed with white freesias.

Bar service would have been set up at both ends of the large reception hall outside. In the middle of the hall would be a long buffet with an ice carving of a swan, and surrounding it, Beluga caviar, gravlax, shrimps, lobster and crab, while buckets of champagne were being iced. A ten-tier birthday cake would be in the kitchen waiting. Waiters, maître d's and security guards would all be in position by now.

In the ballroom, a society orchestra would be on the bandstand, ready to tempt the guests to dance the night away in celebration of her fortieth birthday. Everything would be in readiness.

The dinner was going to be delicious. She had chosen the menu herself. Foie gras to begin with, followed by a cream of mushroom soup under a delicate crust, fillets of John Dory, and then the main course: Lamb with rosemary and pommes soufflées with French beans and a mesclun salad with hazelnut oil. Cheese and grapes would be next, followed by the birthday cake and coffee.

It was going to be a spectacular party. She would hold her head high, and face her guests as though nothing were wrong. She was Lara Cameron.

When the private jet finally landed at La Guardia, it was an hour and a half late.

Lara turned to the pilot. 'We'll be flying back to Reno later tonight, Roger.'

'I'll be here, Miss Cameron.'

Her limousine and driver were waiting for her at the ramp.

'I was getting worried about you, Miss Cameron.'

'We ran into some weather, Max. Let's get to the Plaza as fast as possible.'

'Yes, ma'am.'

Lara reached for the car phone and dialled Jerry Townsend's number. He had made all the arrangements for the party. Lara wanted to make sure that her guests were being looked after. There was no answer. *He's probably in the ballroom*, Lara thought.

'Hurry, Max.'

'Yes, Miss Cameron.'

The sight of the huge Cameron Plaza Hotel never failed to give Lara a glow of satisfaction at what she had created, but on this evening, she was in too much of a hurry to think about it. Everyone would be waiting for her in the Grand Ballroom.

She pushed through the revolving door and hurried across the large spectacular lobby. Carlos, the assistant manager, saw her and came running to her side.

'Miss Cameron . . .'

'Later,' Lara said. She kept walking. She reached the closed door of the Grand Ballroom and stopped to take a deep breath. *I'm ready to face them*, Lara thought. She flung open the door, a smile on her face, and stopped in shock. The room was in total darkness. Were they planning some kind of surprise? She reached for the switch behind the door and flicked it up. The huge room was flooded with incandescent light. There was no one there. Not one single person. Lara stood there, stunned.

What in the world could have happened to two hundred guests? The invitations had read eight o'clock. It was now almost ten o'clock. How could that many people disappear into thin air? It was eerie. She looked around the enormous empty ballroom and shivered. Last year, at her birthday party, this same room had been filled with her friends, filled with music and laughter. She remembered that day so well . . .

2

One year earlier, Lara Cameron's appointment schedule for the day had been routine.

September 10, 1991

5:00 a.m.	Workout with trainer
7:00 a.m.	Appearance on 'Good Morning America'
7:45 a.m.	Meeting with Japanese bankers
9:30 a.m.	Jerry Townsend
10:30 a.m.	Executive Planning Committee
11:00 a.m.	Faxes, overseas calls, mail
11:30 a.m.	Construction meeting
12:30 p.m.	S & L meeting
1:00 p.m.	Lunch – *Fortune* Magazine Interview – Hugh Thompson
2:30 p.m.	Metropolitan Union bankers
4:00 p.m.	Zoning Commission

5:00 p.m.	Meeting with Mayor – Gracie Mansion
6:15 p.m.	Architects meeting
6:30 p.m.	Housing Commission
7:30 p.m.	Cocktails with Dallas Investment Group
8:00 p.m.	Birthday party at Grand Ballroom – Cameron Plaza

She had been in her workout clothes impatiently waiting when Ken, her trainer, arrived.

'You're late.'

'Sorry, Miss Cameron. My alarm didn't go off and . . .'

'I have a busy day. Let's get started.'

'Right.'

They did stretches for half an hour and then switched to energetic aerobics.

She's got the body of a twenty-one year old, Ken thought. *I'd sure love to get that into my bed.* He enjoyed coming here every morning just to look at her, to be near her. People constantly asked him what Lara Cameron was like. He would answer, 'The lady's a ten.'

Lara went through the strenuous routine easily, but her mind was not on it this morning.

When the session was finally over, Ken said, 'I'm going to watch you on "Good Morning America".'

'What?' For a moment Lara had forgotten about it. She had been thinking about the meeting with the Japanese bankers.

'See you tomorrow, Miss Cameron.'

'Don't be late again, Ken.'

Lara showered and changed and had breakfast alone on the terrace of the penthouse, a breakfast of grapefruit, cereal, and green tea. When she had finished, she went into her study.

Lara buzzed her secretary. 'I'll do the overseas calls from the office,' Lara said. 'I have to be at ABC at seven. Have Max bring the car around.'

The segment on 'Good Morning America' went well. Joan Lunden did the interview and was gracious, as always.

'The last time you were on this programme,' Joan Lunden said, 'you had just broken ground for the tallest skyscraper in the world. That was almost four years ago.'

Lara nodded. 'That's right. Cameron Towers will be finished next year.'

'How does it feel to be in your position – to have accomplished all the incredible things you've done, and to still be so young and beautiful? You're a role model for so many women.'

'You're very flattering,' Lara laughed. 'I don't have time to think about myself as a role model. I'm much too busy.'

'You're one of the most successful real estate developers in a business that's usually considered a man's domain. How do you operate? How do you decide, for instance, where to put up a building?'

'I don't choose the site,' Lara said. 'The site chooses me. I'll be driving along and I'll pass a vacant field – but that's not what I see. I see a beautiful office building or a lovely apartment building filled with people living comfortably in a nice atmosphere. I dream.'

'And you make those dreams come true. We'll be right back after this commercial.'

The Japanese bankers were due at 7:45. They had arrived from Tokyo the evening before and Lara had arranged the meeting at that early morning hour so that they would still be jetlagged after their twelve hour and ten minute flight. When they had protested, Lara had said, 'I'm so sorry, gentlemen, but I'm afraid it's the only time I have. I'm leaving for South America immediately after our meeting.'

And they had reluctantly agreed. There were four of them, diminutive and polite, with minds as sharp as the edges of Samurai swords. In an earlier decade, the financial community had wildly underestimated the Japanese. It no longer made that mistake.

The meeting was held at Cameron Center on Sixth Avenue. The men were there to invest a hundred million dollars in a new hotel complex Lara was developing. They were ushered into the large conference room. Each of the men carried a gift. Lara thanked them and in turn gave each of them a gift. She had instructed her secretary to make certain the presents were wrapped in plain brown or grey paper. White, to the Japanese, represented death, and gaudy wrapping paper was unacceptable.

Lara's assistant, Tricia, brought in tea for the Japanese and coffee for Lara. The Japanese would have preferred coffee, but they were too polite to say so.

When they had finished their tea, Lara made sure their cups were replenished.

Howard Keller, Lara's associate, came into the room. He was in his fifties, pale and thin, with sandy hair, wearing a rumpled suit, and managing to look as though he had just got out of bed. Lara made the introductions. Keller passed around copies of the investment proposal.

'As you can see, gentlemen,' Lara said, 'we already have a first mortgage commitment. The complex will contain seven hundred and twenty guest units, approximately thirty thousand square feet of meeting space, and a one-thousand car parking garage . . .'

Lara's voice was charged with energy. The Japanese bankers were studying the investment proposal, fighting to stay awake.

The meeting was over in less than two hours and it was a complete success. Lara had learned long ago that it was easier to make a hundred-million-dollar deal than it was to try to borrow fifty thousand dollars.

As soon as the Japanese delegation left, Lara had her meeting with Jerry Townsend. The tall, hyper, ex-Hollywood publicity man was in charge of public relations for Cameron Enterprises.

'That was a great interview on "Good Morning America" this morning. I've been getting a lot of calls.'

'What about *Forbes*?'

'All set. *People* has you on the cover next week. Did you see the *New Yorker* article on you? Wasn't it great?'

Lara walked over to her desk. 'Not bad.'

'The *Fortune* interview is set for this afternoon.'

'I changed it.'

He looked surprised. 'Why?'

'I'm having their reporter here for lunch.'

'Soften him up a little?'

Lara pressed down the intercom button. 'Come in, Kathy.'

A disembodied voice said, 'Yes, Miss Cameron.'

Lara Cameron looked up. 'That's all, Jerry. I want you and your staff to concentrate on Cameron Towers.'

'We're already doing . . .'

'Let's do more. I want it written about in every newspaper and magazine there is. For God's sake, it's going to be the tallest building in the world. *In the world!* I want people talking about it. By the time we open, I want people to be *begging* to get into those apartments and shops.'

Jerry Townsend got to his feet. 'Right.'

Kathy, Lara's executive assistant, came into the office. She was an attractive, neatly dressed black woman in her early thirties.

'Did you find out what he likes to eat?'

'The man's a gourmet. He likes French food. I called Le Cirque and asked Sirio to cater a lunch here for two.'

'Good. We'll eat in my private dining room.'

'Do you know how long the interview will take? You have a two thirty with the Metropolitan bankers downtown.'

'Push it to three o'clock, and have them come here.'

Kathy made a note. 'Do you want me to read you your messages?'

'Go ahead.'

'The Children's Foundation wants you to be their guest of honour on the twenty-eighth.'

'No. Tell them I'm flattered. Send them a cheque.'

'Your meeting has been arranged in Tulsa for Tuesday at . . .'

'Cancel it.'

'You're invited to a luncheon next Friday for a Manhattan Women's Group.'

'No. If they're asking for money, send them a cheque.'

'The Coalition for Literacy would like you to speak at a luncheon on the fourth.'

'See if we can work it out.'

'There's an invitation to be guest of honour at a fund-raiser for muscular dystrophy, but there's a conflict in dates. You'll be in San Francisco.'

'Send them a cheque.'

'The Srbs are giving a dinner party next Saturday.'

'I'll try to make that,' Lara said. Kristian and Deborah Srb were amusing, and good friends, and she enjoyed being with them.

'Kathy, how many of me do you see?'

'What?'

'Take a good look.'

Kathy looked at her. 'One of you, Miss Cameron.'

'That's right. There's only one of me. How did you expect me to meet with the bankers from Metropolitan at two thirty today, the Zoning Commission at four, then meet with the mayor at five, the architects at six fifteen, the housing commission at six thirty, have a cocktail party at seven thirty and my birthday dinner at eight? The next time you make up a schedule, try using your brain.'

'I'm sorry. You wanted me to . . .'

'I wanted you to *think*. I don't need stupid people

around me. Reschedule the appointments with the architects and the housing commission.'

'Right,' Kathy said stiffly.

'How's the baby?'

The question caught the secretary by surprise. 'David? He's . . . he's fine.'

'He must be getting big by now.'

'He's almost two.'

'Have you thought about a school for him?'

'Not yet. It's too early to . . .'

'You're wrong. If you want to get him into a decent school in New York, you start before he's born.'

Lara made a note on a desk pad. 'I know the principal at Dalton. I'll arrange to have David registered there.'

'I . . . thank you.'

Lara did not bother to look up. 'That's all.'

'Yes, ma'am.' Kathy walked out of the office not knowing whether to love her boss or hate her. When Kathy had first come to work at Cameron Enterprises, she had been warned about Lara Cameron. 'The Iron Butterfly is a bitch on wheels,' she had been told. 'Her secretaries don't figure their employment there by the calendar – they use stopwatches. She'll eat you alive.'

Kathy remembered her first interview with her. She had seen pictures of Lara Cameron in half a dozen magazines, but none of them had done her justice. In person, the woman was breathtakingly beautiful.

Lara Cameron had been reading Kathy's résumé. She looked up and said, 'Sit down, Kathy.' Her voice was husky and vibrant. There was an energy about her that was almost overpowering.

'This is quite a résumé.'

'Thank you.'

'How much of it is real?'

'I'm sorry?'

'Most of the ones that come across my desk are fiction. Are you good at what you do?'

'I'm very good at what I do, Miss Cameron.'

'Two of my secretaries just quit. Everything's snowballing around here. Can you handle pressure?'

'I think so.'

'This isn't a guessing contest. Can you handle pressure or can't you?'

At that moment Kathy was not sure she wanted the job. 'Yes, I can.'

'Good. You're on a one-week trial. You'll have to sign a form saying that at no time will you discuss me or your work here at Cameron Enterprises. That means no interviews, no books, nothing. Everything that happens here is confidential.'

'I understand.'

'Fine.'

That was how it had begun five years earlier. During that time Kathy had learned to love, hate, admire and despise her boss. In the beginning Kathy's husband had asked, 'What is the legend like?'

It was a difficult question. 'She's larger than life,' Kathy had said. 'She's drop-dead beautiful. She works harder than anyone I've ever known. God only knows when she sleeps. She's a perfectionist, so she makes everyone around her miserable. In her own way, she's a genius. She can be petty and vengeful and incredibly generous.'

Her husband had smiled. 'In other words, she's a woman.'

Kathy had looked at him and said, unsmiling, 'I don't know what she is. Sometimes she scares me.'

'Come on, honey, you're exaggerating.'

'No. I honestly believe that if someone stood in Lara Cameron's way . . . she would kill.'

When Lara finished with the faxes and overseas calls, she buzzed Charlie Hunter, the ambitious young man in charge of accounting. 'Come in, Charlie.'

'Yes, Miss Cameron.'

A minute later, he entered her office.

'Yes, Miss Cameron?'

'I read the interview you gave in the *New York Times* this morning,' Lara said.

He brightened. 'I haven't seen it yet. How was it?'

'You talked about Cameron Enterprises and about some of the problems we're having.'

He frowned. 'Well, you know, that reporter fellow probably misquoted some of my . . .'

'You're fired.'

'What? Why? I . . .'

'When you were hired, you signed a paper agreeing not to give any interviews. I'll expect you out of here this morning.'

'I . . . you can't do that. Who would take my place?'

'I've already arranged that,' Lara told him.

The luncheon was almost over. The *Fortune* reporter, Hugh Thompson, was an intense, intellectual-looking man with sharp brown eyes behind black horn-rimmed glasses.

'It was a great lunch,' he said. 'All my favourite dishes. Thanks.'

'I'm glad you enjoyed it.'

'You really didn't have to go to all that trouble for me.'

'No trouble at all,' Lara smiled. 'My father always told me that the way to a man's heart was through his stomach.'

'And you wanted to get to my heart before we started the interview?'

Lara smiled. 'Exactly.'

'How much trouble is your company really in?'

Lara's smile faded. 'I beg your pardon?'

'Come on. You can't keep a thing like that quiet. The word on the street is that some of your properties are on the verge of collapse because of the principal payments due on your junk bonds. You've done a lot of leveraging, and with the market down, Cameron Enterprises has to be pretty overextended.'

Lara laughed. 'Is that what the street says? Believe me, Mr Thompson, you'd be wise not to listen to silly rumours. I'll tell you what I'll do. I'll send you a copy of my financials to set the record straight. Fair enough?'

'Fair enough. By the way, I didn't see your husband at the opening of the new hotel.'

Lara sighed. 'Philip wanted so much to be there, but unfortunately he had to be away on a concert tour.'

'I went to one of his recitals once about three years ago. He's brilliant. You have been married a year now, haven't you?'

'Yes – the happiest year of my life. I'm a very

lucky woman. I travel a lot, and so does Philip, but when I'm away from him, I can listen to his recordings wherever I am.'

Thompson smiled. 'And he can see your buildings wherever he is.'

Lara laughed. 'You flatter me.'

'It's pretty true, isn't it? You've put up buildings all over this fair country of ours. You own apartment buildings, office buildings, a hotel chain . . . How do you do it?'

She smiled. 'With mirrors.'

'You're a puzzle.'

'Am I? Why?'

'At this moment, you're arguably the most successful builder in New York. Your name is plastered on half the real estate in this town. You're putting up the world's tallest skyscraper. Your competitors call you the Iron Butterfly. You've made it big in a business traditionally dominated by men.'

'Does that bother you, Mr Thompson?'

'No. What bothers me, Miss Cameron, is that I can't figure out who you are. When I ask two people about you, I get three opinions. Everyone grants that you're a brilliant businesswoman. I mean . . . you didn't fall off a hay wagon and become a success. I know a lot about construction crews – they're a rough, tough bunch of men. How does a woman like you keep them in line?'

She smiled. 'There *are* no women like me. Seriously, I simply hire the best people for the job, and I pay them well.'

Too simplistic, Thompson thought. *Much too simplistic. The real story is what she's not telling me.* He decided to change the direction of the interview.

'Every magazine on the stands has written about how successful you are. I'd like to do a more personal story. There's been very little printed about your background.'

'I'm very proud of my background.'

'Good. Let's talk about that. How did you get started in the real estate business?'

Lara smiled and he could see that her smile was genuine. She suddenly looked like a little girl.

'Genes.'

'Your genes?'

'My father's.' She pointed to a portrait on a wall behind her. It showed a handsome-looking man with a leonine head of silver hair. 'That's my father – James Hugh Cameron.' Her voice was soft. 'He's responsible for my success. I'm an only child. My mother died when I was very young, and my father brought me up. My family left Scotland a long time ago, Mr Thompson, and emigrated to Nova Scotia – New Scotland, Glace Bay.'

'Glace Bay?'

'It's a fishing village in the north-east part of Cape Breton, on the Atlantic shore. It was named by early French explorers. It means ice bay. More coffee?'

'No, thanks.'

'My grandfather owned a great deal of land in Scotland and my father acquired more. He was a very wealthy man. We still have our castle there near Loch Morlich. When I was eight years old, I had my own horse, my dresses were bought in London, we lived in an enormous house with a lot of servants. It was a fairytale life for a little girl.' Her voice was alive with echoes of long-ago memories.

'We would go ice skating in the winter, and watch

hockey games, and go swimming at Big Glace Bay Lake in the summer. And there were dances at the Forum and the Venetian Gardens.'

The reporter was busily making notes.

'My father put up buildings in Edmonton, and Calgary, and Ontario. Real estate was like a game to him, and he loved it. When I was very young, he taught me the game, and I learned to love it, too.'

Her voice was filled with passion. 'You must understand something, Mr Thompson. What I do has nothing to do with the money or the bricks and steel that make a building. It's the people who matter. I'm able to give them a comfortable place to work or to live, a place where they can raise families and have decent lives. That's what was important to my father, and it became important to me.'

Hugh Thompson looked up. 'Do you remember your first real estate venture?'

Lara leaned forward. 'Of course. On my eighteenth birthday, my father asked me what I would like as a gift. A lot of newcomers were arriving in Glace Bay and it was getting crowded. I felt the town needed more places for them to live. I told my father I wanted to build a small apartment house. He gave me the money as a present, but two years later, I was able to pay him back. Then I borrowed money from a bank to put up a second building. By the time I was twenty-one, I owned three buildings, and they were all successful.'

'Your father must have been very proud of you.'

There was that warm smile again. 'He was. He named me Lara. It's an old Scottish name that comes from the Latin. It means "well known" or "famous". From the time I was a little girl, my father always told me I would be famous one day.' Her smile faded. 'He died of a heart attack, much too young.' She paused. 'I go to Scotland to visit his grave every year. I . . . I found it very difficult to stay on in the house without him. I decided to move to Chicago. I had an idea for small boutique hotels, and I persuaded a banker there to finance me. The hotels were a success.' She shrugged. 'And the rest, as the cliché goes, is history. I suppose that a psychiatrist would say that I haven't created this empire just for myself. In a way, it's a tribute to my father. James Cameron was the most wonderful man I've ever known.'

'You must have loved him a lot.'

'I did. And he loved me a lot.' A smile touched her lips. 'I've heard that on the day I was born, my father bought every man in Glace Bay a drink.'

'So, really,' Thompson said, 'everything started in Glace Bay.'

'That's right,' Lara said softly, 'everything started in Glace Bay. That's where it all began, almost forty years ago . . .'

3

*Glace Bay, Nova Scotia
September 10, 1952*

James Cameron was in a whorehouse, drunk, the night his daughter and son were born. He was in bed, sandwiched between the Scandinavian twins, when Kirstie, the madam of the brothel, pounded on the door.

'James!' she called out. She pushed open the door and walked in.

'*Och, ye auld hen!*' James yelled out indignantly. 'Can't a mon have any privacy even here?'

'Sorry to interrupt your pleasure, James. It's about your wife.'

'Fuck my wife,' Cameron roared.

'You did,' Kirstie retorted, 'and she's having your baby.'

'So? Let her have it. That's what you women are guid for, nae?'

'The doctor just called. He's been trying desperately to find you. Your wife is bad off. You'd better hurry.'

James Cameron sat up and slid to the edge of the bed, bleary-eyed, trying to clear his head. 'Damned woman. She niver leaves me in peace.' He looked up at the madam. 'All right, I'll go.' He glanced at the naked girls in the bed. 'But I'll nae pay for these two.'

'Never mind that now. You'd just better get back to the boarding house.' She turned to the girls. 'You two come along with me.'

James Cameron was a once-handsome man whose face reflected fulfilled sins. He appeared to be in his early fifties. He was thirty years old and the manager of one of the boarding houses owned by Sean MacAllister, the town banker. For the past five years, James Cameron and his wife Peggy had divided the chores: Peggy did the cleaning and cooking for the two dozen boarders, and James did the drinking. Every Friday it was his responsibility to collect the rents from the four other boarding houses in Glace Bay owned by MacAllister. It was another reason, if he needed one, to go out and get drunk.

James Cameron was a bitter man, who revelled in his bitterness. He was a failure, and he was convinced that everyone else was to blame. Over the years he had come to enjoy his failure. It made him feel like a martyr. When James was a year old, his family had emigrated to Glace Bay from Scotland with nothing but the few possessions they could carry, and they had struggled to survive. His father had put James to work in the coal mines when the boy was fourteen. James had suffered a slight back injury in a mining accident when he was sixteen, and had promptly quit the mine. One year later his parents were killed in a train disaster. So it was that James Cameron had decided that he was not responsible for his adversity – it was the Fates that were against him. But he had two great assets: He was extraordinarily handsome and, when he wished to, he could be charming. One weekend in Sydney, a town near Glace Bay, he met an impressionable young American girl named Peggy Maxwell, who was there on vacation with her family. She was not attractive, but the Maxwells were very wealthy, and James Cameron was very poor. He swept Peggy Maxwell off her feet, and against the advice of her father, she married him.

'I'm giving Peggy a dowry of five thousand dollars,' her father told James. 'The money will give you a chance to make something of yourself. You can invest it in real estate, and in five years it will double. I'll help you.'

But James was not interested in waiting five years. Without consulting anyone, he invested the money in a wildcat oil venture with a friend, and sixty days later, he was broke. His father-in-law, furious, refused to help him any further. 'You're a fool, James, and I will not throw good money after bad.'

The marriage that was going to be James Cameron's salvation turned out to be a disaster, for he now had a wife to support, and no job.

It was Sean MacAllister who had come to his rescue. The town banker was a man in his mid fifties, a stumpy, pompous man, a pound short of being obese, given to wearing vests adorned with a heavy gold watch chain. He had come to Glace Bay twenty years earlier, and had immediately seen the possibilities there. Miners and lumbermen were pouring into the town, and were unable to find adequate housing. MacAllister could have financed homes for them, but he had a better plan. He decided it would be cheaper to herd the men together in boarding houses. Within two years, he had built a hotel and five boarding houses, and they were always full.

Finding managers was a difficult task because the work was exhausting. The manager's job was to keep all the rooms rented, supervise the cooking, handle the meals, and see that the premises were kept reasonably clean. As far as salaries were concerned, Sean MacAllister was not a man to throw away his money.

The manager of one of his boarding houses had just quit, and MacAllister decided that James Cameron was a likely candidate. Cameron had borrowed small amounts of money from the bank from time to time, and payment on a loan was overdue. MacAllister sent for the young man.

'I have a job for you,' MacAllister said.

'You have?'

'You're in luck. I have a splendid position that's just opened up.'

'Working at the bank, is it?' James Cameron asked. The idea of working in a bank appealed to him. Where there was a lot of money, there was always a possibility of having some stick to one's fingers.

'Not at the bank,' MacAllister told him. 'You're a very personable young man, James, and I think you would be very good at dealing with people. I'd like you to run my boarding house on Cablehead Avenue.'

'A *boarding* house, you say?' There was contempt in the young man's voice.

'You need a roof over your head,' MacAllister pointed out. 'You and your wife will have free room and board, and a small salary.'

'How sma'?'

'I'll be generous with you. James. Twenty-five dollars a week.'

'Twenty-fi . . . ?'

'Take it or leave it. I have others waiting.'

In the end, James Cameron had no choice. 'I'll tak' it.'

'Good. By the way, every Friday I'll also expect you to collect the rents from my other boarding houses, and deliver the money to me on Saturday.'

When James Cameron broke the news to Peggy, she was dismayed. 'We don't know anything about running a boarding house, James.'

'We'll learn. We'll share the work.'

And she had believed him. 'All right. We'll manage,' she said.

And, in their own fashion, they had managed.

Over the years, several opportunities had come along for James Cameron to get better jobs, employment that would give him dignity and more money, but he was enjoying his failure too much to leave it.

'Why bother?' he would grumble. 'When Fate's agin you, naething guid can happen.'

And on this September night, he thought to himself, *they won't even let me enjoy my whores in peace. Goddamn my wife.*

When he stepped out of Madame Kirstie's establishment, a chilly September wind was blowing.

I'd best fortify myself for the troubles aheid, James Cameron decided. He stopped in at the Ancient Mariner.

One hour later, he wandered toward the boarding house in New Aberdeen, the poorest section of Glace Bay.

When he finally arrived, half a dozen boarders were anxiously waiting for him.

'The doctor is in wi' Peggy,' one of the men said. 'You'd better hurry, mon.'

James staggered into the tiny, dreary back bedroom he and his wife shared. From another room, he could hear the whimpering of a newborn baby. Peggy lay on the bed, motionless. Dr Patrick Duncan was leaning over her. He turned as he heard James enter.

'Wa's goin' on here?' James asked.

The doctor straightened up and looked at James with distaste. 'You should have had your wife come to see me,' he said.

'And throw guid money away? She's only havin' a baby. Wa's the big . . . ?'

'Peggy's dead. I did everything I could. She had twins. I couldn't save the boy.'

'Oh, Jesus,' James Cameron whimpered. 'It's the Fates agin.'

'What?'

'The Fates. They've always been agin me. Now they've taine my bairn frae me. I dinna . . .'

A nurse walked in, carrying a tiny baby wrapped in a blanket. 'This is your daughter, Mr Cameron.'

'A *daughter*? Wha' the hell will I dae wi' a daughter?' His speech was becoming more slurred.

'You disgust me, mon,' Dr Duncan said.

The nurse turned to James. 'I'll stay until tomorrow, and show you how to take care of her.'

James Cameron looked at the tiny wrinkled bundle

in the blanket and thought, hopefully: *Maybe she'll die, too.*

For the first three weeks, no one was sure whether the baby would live or not. A wetnurse came in to tend to her. And finally, the day came when the doctor was able to say, 'Your daughter is going to live.'

And he looked at James Cameron and said under his breath, 'God have mercy on the poor child.'

The wetnurse said, 'Mr Cameron, you must give the child a name.'

'I dinna care wha' the hell ye call it. *Ye* gie her a name.'

'Why don't we name her Lara? That's such a pretty . . .'

'Suit your bloody self.'

And so she was christened Lara.

There was no one in Lara's life to care for her or nurture her. The boarding house was filled with men too busy with their own lives to pay attention to the baby. The only woman around was Bertha, the huge Swede who was hired to do the cooking and handle the chores.

James Cameron was determined to have nothing to do with his daughter. The damned Fates had betrayed him once again by letting her live. At night he would sit in the living room with his bottle of whiskey and complain. 'The bairn murdered my wife and my son.'

'You shouldn't say that, James.'

'Weel, it's sae. My son would hae grown up to be a big strapping mon. He would hae been smart and rich, and taine good care of his father in his auld age.'

And the boarders let him ramble on.

James Cameron tried several times to get in touch with Maxwell, his father-in-law, hoping he would take the child off his hands, but the old man had disappeared. *It would be just my luck the auld fool's daid*, he thought.

Glace Bay was a town of transients who moved in and out of the boarding houses. They came from France and China and the Ukraine. They were Italian and Irish and Greek, carpenters and tailors and plumbers and shoemakers. They swarmed into lower Main Street, Bell Street, North Street and Water Street, near the waterfront area. They came to work the mines and cut timber and fish the seas. Glace Bay was a frontier town, primitive and rugged. The weather was an abomination. The winters were harsh with heavy snowfalls that lasted until April, and because of the heavy ice in the harbour, even April and May were cold and windy, and from July to October it rained.

There were eighteen boarding houses in town, some of them accommodating as many as seventy-two guests. At the boarding house managed by James Cameron, there were twenty-four boarders, most of them Scotsmen.

Lara was hungry for affection, without knowing what the hunger was. She had no toys or dolls to cherish nor any playmates. She had no one except her father. She made childish little gifts for him, desperate to please him, but he either ignored or ridiculed them.

When Lara was five years old, she overheard her father say to one of the boarders, 'The wrong child died, ye ken. My son is the one who should hae lived.'

That night Lara cried herself to sleep. She loved her father so much. And she hated him so much.

When Lara was six, she resembled a Keane painting, enormous eyes in a pale, thin face. That year, a new boarder moved in. His name was Mungo McSween, and he was a huge bear of a man. He felt an instant affection for the little girl.

'What's your name, wee lassie?'

'Lara.'

'Ah. 'Tis a braw name for a braw bairn. Dae ye gan to school, then?'

'School? No.'

'And why not?'

'I don't know.'

'Weel, we maun find out.'

And he went to find James Cameron. 'I'm tauld your bairn does nae gae to school.'

'And why should she? She's only a girl. She dinna need nae school.'

'You're wrong, mon. She maun have an education. She maun be gien a chance in life.'

'Forget it,' James said. 'It wad be a waste.'

But McSween was insistent, and finally, to shut

him up, James Cameron agreed. It would keep the brat out of his sight for a few hours.

Lara was terrified by the idea of going to school. She had lived in a world of adults all her short life, and had had almost no contact with other children.

The following Monday, Big Bertha dropped her off at St Anne's Grammar School, and Lara was taken to the principal's office.

'This is Lara Cameron.'

The principal, Mrs Cummings, was a middle-aged grey-haired widow with three children of her own. She studied the shabbily dressed little girl standing before her. 'Lara. What a pretty name,' she said smiling. 'How old are you, dear?'

'Six.' She was fighting back tears.

The child is terrified, Mrs Cummings thought. 'Well, we're very glad to have you here, Lara. You'll have a good time, and you're going to learn a lot.'

'I can't stay,' Lara blurted out.

'Oh? Why not?'

'My papa misses me too much.' She was fiercely determined not to cry.

'Well, we'll only keep you here for a few hours a day.'

Lara allowed herself to be taken into a classroom filled with children, and she was shown to a seat near the back of the room.

Miss Terkel, the teacher, was busily writing letters on a blackboard.

'*A* is for apple,' she said. '*B* is for boy. Does anyone know what *C* is for?'

A tiny hand was raised. 'Candy.'

'Very good! And *D*?'
'Dog.'
'And *E*?'
'Eat.'
'Excellent. Can anyone think of a word beginning with *F*?'
Lara spoke up. 'Fuck.'

Lara was the youngest one in her class, but it seemed to Miss Terkel that in many ways she was the oldest. There was a disquieting maturity about her.
'She's a small adult, waiting to grow taller,' her teacher told Mrs Cummings.
The first day at lunch, the other children took out their colourful little lunch pails and pulled out apples and cookies, and sandwiches wrapped in wax paper.
No one had thought to pack a lunch for Lara.
'Where is your lunch, Lara?' Miss Terkel asked.
'I'm not hungry,' Lara said stubbornly. 'I had a big breakfast.'
Most of the girls at school were nicely dressed in clean skirts and blouses. Lara had outgrown her few faded plaid dresses and threadbare blouses. She had gone to her father.
'I need some clothes for school,' Lara said.
'Dae ye now? Weel, I'm nae made of money. Get yourself something frae the Salvation Army Citadel.'
'That's charity, Papa.'
And her father had slapped her hard across the face.

*

The children at school were familiar with games Lara had never even heard of. The girls had dolls and toys, and some of them were willing to share them with Lara, but she was painfully aware that nothing belonged to her. And there was something more. Over the next few years, Lara got a glimpse of a different world, a world where children had mothers and fathers who gave them presents and birthday parties and loved them and held them and kissed them. And for the first time, Lara began to realize how much was missing in her life. It only made her feel lonelier.

The boarding house was a different kind of school. It was an international microcosm. Lara learned to tell where the boarders came from by their names. Mac was from Scotland . . . Hodder and Pyke were from Newfoundland . . . Chiasson and Aucoin were from France . . . Dudash and Kosick from Poland. The boarders were lumbermen, fishermen, miners and tradesmen. They would gather in the large dining room in the morning for breakfast and in the evening for supper, and their talk was fascinating to Lara. Each group seemed to have its own mysterious language.

There were thousands of lumbermen in Nova Scotia, scattered around the peninsula. The lumbermen at the boarding house smelled of sawdust and burnt bark, and they spoke of arcane things like chippers and edging and trim.

'We should get out almost two hundred million board feet this year,' one of them announced at supper.

'How can feet be bored?' Lara asked.

There was a roar of laughter. 'Child, board foot is a piece of lumber a foot square by an inch thick. When you grow up and get married, if you want to build a five-room, all wood house, it will take twelve thousand board feet.'

'I'm not going to get married,' Lara swore.

The fishermen were another breed. They returned to the boarding house stinking of the sea, and they talked about the new experiment of growing oysters on the Bras d'Or lake, and bragged to one another of their catches of cod and herring and mackerel and haddock.

But the boarders who fascinated Lara the most were the miners. There were 3,500 miners in Cape Breton, working the collieries at Lingan and Prince and Phalen. Lara loved the names of the mines. There was the Jubilee and the Last Chance and the Black Diamond and the Lucky Lady.

She was fascinated by their discussion of the day's work.

'What's this I hear about Mike?'

'It's true. The poor bastard was travelling inbye in a man-rake, and a box jumped the track and crushed his leg. The sonofabitch of a foreman said it was Mike's fault for not gettin' out of the way fast enough, and he's having his lamp stopped.'

Lara was baffled. 'What does that mean?'

One of the miners explained. 'It means Mike was on his way to work – going inbye – in a man-rake – that's a car that takes you down to your working level. A box – that's a coal train – jumped the track and hit him.'

'And stopped his lamp?' Lara asked.

The miner laughed. 'When you've had your lamp stopped, it means you've been suspended.'

When Lara was fifteen, she entered St Michael's High School. She was gangly and awkward, with long legs, stringy black hair, and intelligent grey eyes still too large for her pale, thin face. No one quite knew how she was going to turn out. She was on the verge of womanhood, and her looks were in a stage of metamorphosis. She could have become ugly or beautiful.

To James Cameron, his daughter was ugly. 'Ye hae best marry the first mon fool enough to ask ye,' he told her. 'Ye'll nae hae the looks to make a guid bargain.'

Lara stood there, saying nothing.

'And tell the poor mon nae to expect a dowry frae me.'

Mungo McSween had walked into the room. He stood there listening, furious.

'That's all, girl,' James Cameron said. 'Gae back to the kitchen.'

Lara fled.

'Why dae ye dae that to yeer daughter?' McSween demanded.

James Cameron looked up, his eyes bleary. 'Nane of your business.'

'You're drunk.'

'Aye. And what else is there? If it isn't women, it's the whiskey, isn't it?'

McSween went into the kitchen where Lara was washing dishes at the sink. Her eyes were hot with tears. McSween put his arms around her. 'Niver ye mind, lassie,' he said. 'He dinna mean it.'

'He hates me.'

'Nae, he doesna.'

'He's never given me one kind word. Never once. Never!'

There was nothing McSween could say.

In the summer, the tourists would arrive at Glace Bay. They came in their expensive cars, wearing beautiful clothes, and shopped along Castle Street and dined at the Cedar House and at Jasper's, and they visited Ingonish Beach and Cape Smoky and the Bird Islands. They were superior beings from another world, and Lara envied them and longed to escape with them when they left at the end of summer. But how?

Lara had heard stories about Grandfather Maxwell.

'The auld bastard tried to keep me frae marryin' his precious daughter,' James Cameron would complain to any of the boarders who would listen. 'He was filthy rich, but do ye think he wad gie me aught? Nae. But I took guid care of his Peggy, anyway . . .'

And Lara would fantasize that one day her grandfather would come to take her away to glamorous cities she had read about: London and Rome and Paris. *And I'll have beautiful clothes to wear. Hundreds of dresses and new shoes.*

But as the months and the years went by, and there was no word, Lara finally came to realize that she would never see her grandfather. She was doomed to spend the rest of her life in Glace Bay.

4

There were myriad activities for a teenager growing up in Glace Bay: There were football games and hockey games, skating rinks and bowling, and in the summer, swimming and fishing. Carl's Drug Store was the popular after-school hangout. There were two movie theatres, and for dancing, the Venetian Gardens.

Lara had no chance to enjoy any of those things. She rose at five every morning to help Bertha prepare breakfast for the boarders, and make up the beds before she left for school. In the afternoon, she would hurry home to begin preparing supper. She helped Bertha serve, and after supper, Lara cleared the table and washed and dried the dishes.

The boarding house served some favourite Scottish dishes: *Howtowdie* and *hairst bree*, *cabbieclaw* and *skirlie*. Black Bun was a favourite, a spicy mixture encased in a shortpaste jacket made from half a pound of flour.

The conversation of the Scotsmen at supper made the Highlands of Scotland come alive for Lara. Her ancestors had come from the Highlands, and the stories about them gave Lara the only sense of belonging that she had. The boarders talked of the Great Glen containing Lochs Ness, Lochy, and Linnhe, and of the rugged islands off the coast.

There was a battered piano in the sitting room, and sometimes at night, after supper, half a dozen boarders would gather around and sing the songs of home: 'Annie Laurie', and 'Comin' Through the Rye', and 'The Hills of Home', and 'The Bonnie Banks o' Loch Lomon''.

Once a year there was a parade in town, and all the Scotsmen in Glace Bay would proudly put on their kilts or tartans and march through the streets to the loud, raucous accompaniment of bagpipes.

'Why do the men wear skirts?' Lara asked Mungo McSween.

He frowned. 'It's *nae* a skirt, lass. It's a kilt. Our ancestors invented it long ago. I' the Highlands, a plaid covered a mon's body agin the bitter cold, but kept his legs free sae he could race across the heather and peat and escape his enemies. And at night, if he was in the open, the great length of the cloth was both bed and tent for him.'

The names of the Scottish places were poetry to Lara. There was Breadalbane, Glenfinnan and Kilbride, Kilninver and Kilmichael. Lara learned that 'kil' referred to a monk's cell of medieval times. If a name began with 'inver' or 'aber', it meant the village was at the mouth of a stream. If it began with 'strath', it was in a valley. 'Bad' meant the village was in a grove.

There were fierce arguments every night at the

supper table. The Scotsmen argued about everything. Their ancestors had belonged to proud clans and they were still fiercely protective of their history.

'The House of Bruce produced cowards. They lay down for the English like grovelling dogs.'

'You dinna ken wha' you're talking aboot, as usual, Ian. It was the great Bruce himself who stood up to the English. It was the House of Stuart that grovelled.'

'Och, you're a fool, and your clan comes from a long line of fools.'

The argument would grow more heated.

'You ken wha' Scotland needed? Mair leaders like Robert the Second. Now, there was a great mon. He sired twenty-one bairns.'

'Aye, and half of them were bastards!'

And another argument would start.

Lara could not believe that they were fighting over events that had happened more than six hundred years earlier.

Mungo McSween said to Lara, 'Dinna let it bother ye, lassie. A Scotsman wi' start a fight in an empty house.'

It was a poem by Sir Walter Scott that set Lara's imagination on fire.

> *Oh, young Lochinvar is come out of the west,*
> *Through all the wide Border his steed was the best;*
> *And save his good broadsword he weapons had none,*
> *He rode all unarmed, and he rode all alone.*

*So faithful in love, and so dauntless in war.
There never was knight like the young
   Lochinvar.*

And the glorious poem went on to tell how Lochinvar risked his life to rescue his beloved, who was being forced to marry another man.

*So daring in love, and so dauntless in war,
Have ye e'er heard of gallant like young
   Lochinvar?*

Some day, Lara thought, *a handsome Lochinvar will come and rescue me.*

One day Lara was working in the kitchen, when she came across an advertisement in a magazine, and her breath caught in her throat. It showed a tall, handsome man, blond, elegantly dressed in tails and white tie. He had blue eyes and a warm smile, and he looked every inch a prince. *That's what my Lochinvar will look like*, Lara thought. *He's out there somewhere, looking for me. He'll come and rescue me from here. I'll be at the sink washing dishes and he'll come up behind me, put his arms around me, and whisper, 'Can I help you?' And I'll turn and look into his eyes. And I'll say, 'Do you dry dishes?'*

Bertha's voice said, 'Do I *what*?'

Lara whirled around. Bertha was standing behind her. Lara had not realized she had spoken aloud.

'Nothing,' Lara blushed.

To Lara, the most fascinating dinner conversations revolved around the stories of the notorious

Highland Clearances. She had heard them told over and over but could never get enough of it.

'Tell me again,' she would ask. And Mungo McSween was eager to oblige . . .

'Weel, it began in the year 1792 and it went on for more than sixty years. At first they called it *Bliadhna nan Caorach* – The Year of the Sheep. The landowners in the Highlands had decided that their land would be more profitable with sheep than with tenant farmers, so they brought flocks of sheep into the Highlands, and found that they could survive the cold winters. That was when the clearances began.

'The cry became, "*Mo thruaighe ort a thir, tha'n caoraich mhor a' teachd!*" Woe to thee, oh land, the Great Sheep is coming. First there were a hundred sheep, then a thousand, then ten thousand. It was a bloody invasion.

'The lairds saw riches beyond their dreams, but they maun get rid of the tenants first, who worked their wee patches of land. They had little enough to begin with, God knows. They lived in sma' stone houses with na chimneys and na windows. But the lairds forced them out.'

The young girl was wide-eyed. 'How?'

'The government regiments were ordered to attack the villages and evict the tenants. The soldiers wad come to a little village and gie the tenants six hours to remove their cattle and furniture and get oot. They maun leave their crops behind. Then the soldiers burned their huts to the ground. More than a quarter of a million men, women and children were forced frae their holdings and driven to the shores of the sea.'

'But how could they drive them from their own land?'

'Ah, they niver owned the land, you see. They had the use of an acre or two frae a laird, but it was niver theirs. They paid a fee in goods or labour in order to till the land and grow some tatties and raise a few cattle.'

'What happened if the people wouldn't move?' Lara asked breathlessly.

'The old folk that didn't get out in time were burned in their huts. The government was ruthless. Och, it was a terrible time. The people had naething to eat. Cholera struck, and diseases spread like wildfire.'

'How awful,' Lara said.

'Aye, lassie. Our people lived on tatties and bread and porridge, when they could git it. But there's one thing the government could nae take away frae the Highlanders – their pride. They fought back as best they could. For days after the burning was over, the homeless people remained in the glen, trying to salvage what they could from the ruins. They put canvas over their heids for protection agin the night rain. My great-great-grandfather and my great-great-grandmother were there and suffered through it all. It's part of our history, and it's been burned into our very souls.'

Lara could visualize the thousands of desperate, forlorn people robbed of everything they possessed, stunned by what had happened to them. She could hear the crying of the mourners, and the screams of the terrified children.

'What finally happened to the people?' Lara asked.

'They left for other lands on ships that were death traps. The crowded passengers died of fever or frae dysentery. Sometimes, the ships would hit storms that delayed them for weeks, so they ran out of food. Only the strong were still alive when the ships landed in Canada. But once they landed here, they were able to hae somethin' they niver had before.'

'Their own land,' Lara said.

'That's right, lass.'

Some day, Lara thought fiercely, *I will have my own land, and no one – no one – will ever take it away from me.*

On an evening in early July, James Cameron was in bed with one of the whores at Kirstie's Bawdy House, when he suffered a heart attack. He was quite drunk, and when he suddenly toppled over, his playmate assumed he had simply fallen asleep.

'Oh, no, you don't! I have other customers waitin' for me. Wake up, James! Wake up!'

He was gasping for breath and clutching his chest.

'For Gude's sake,' he moaned, 'git me a doctor.'

An ambulance took him to the little hospital on Quarry Street. Dr Duncan sent for Lara. She walked into the hospital, her heart pounding. Duncan was waiting for her.

'What happened?' Lara asked urgently. 'Is my father dead?'

'No, Lara, but I'm afraid he's had a heart attack.'

She stood there, frozen. 'Is he . . . is he going to live?'

'I don't know. We're doing everything we can for him.'

'Can I see him?'

'It would be better if you came back in the morning, lass.'

She walked home, numb with fear. *Please don't let him die, God. He's all I have.*

When Lara reached the boarding house, Bertha was waiting for her. 'What happened?'

Lara told her.

'Oh, God!' Bertha said. 'And today is Friday.'

'What?'

'Friday. The day the rents have to be collected. If I know Sean MacAllister, he'll use this as an excuse to throw us all out into the streets.'

At least a dozen times in the past when James Cameron had been too drunk to handle it himself, he had sent Lara around to collect the rents from the other boarding houses that Sean MacAllister owned. Lara had given the money to her father, and the next day he had taken it to the banker.

'What are we going to do?' Bertha moaned.

And suddenly Lara knew what had to be done.

'Don't worry,' she said. 'I'll take care of it.'

In the middle of supper that evening Lara said, 'Gentlemen, would you listen to me, please?' The conversations stopped. They were all watching her. 'My father has had a . . . a little dizzy spell. He's in the hospital. They want to keep him under observation for a bit. So, until he comes back, I'll be collecting the rents. After supper, I'll wait for you in the parlour.'

'Is he going to be all right?' one of the boarders asked.

'Oh, yes,' Lara said with a forced smile. 'It's nothing serious.'

After supper the men came into the parlour and handed Lara their week's rent.

'I hope your father recovers soon, child . . .'

'If there's anything I can do, let me know . . .'

'You're a braw lassie to do this for your father . . .'

'What about the other boarding houses?' Bertha asked Lara. 'He has to collect from four more.'

'I know,' Lara said. 'If you'll take care of the dishes, I'll go collect the rents.'

Bertha looked at her dubiously. 'I wish you luck.'

It was easier than Lara had expected. Most of the boarders were sympathetic, and happy to help out the young girl.

Early the following morning, Lara took the rent envelopes and went to see Sean MacAllister. The banker was seated in his office when Lara walked in.

'My secretary said you wanted to see me.'

'Yes, sir.'

MacAllister studied the scrawny, unkempt girl standing before him. 'You're James Cameron's daughter, aren't you?'

'Yes, sir.'

'Sarah.'

'Lara.'

'Sorry to hear about your father,' MacAllister said. There was no sympathy in his voice. 'I'll have to make other arrangements, of course, now that your father's too ill to carry out his job. I . . .'

'Oh, no, sir!' Lara said quickly. 'He asked me to handle it for him.'

'You?'

'Yes, sir.'

'I'm afraid that won't . . .'

Lara put the envelopes on his desk. 'Here are this week's rents.'

MacAllister looked at her, surprised. 'All of them?'

She nodded.

'And you collected them?'

'Yes, sir. And I'll do it every week until Papa gets better.'

'I see.' He opened the envelopes and carefully counted the money. Lara watched him enter the amount in a large green ledger.

For some time now, MacAllister had intended to replace James Cameron because of his drunkenness and erratic performance, and now he saw his opportunity to get rid of the family.

He was sure that the young girl in front of him would not be able to carry out her father's duties, but at the same time, he realized what the town's reaction would be if he threw James Cameron and his daughter out of the boarding house into the street. He made his decision.

'I'll try you for one month,' he said. 'At the end of that time, we'll see where we stand.'

'Thank you, Mr MacAllister. Thank you very much.'

'Wait.' He handed Lara twenty-five dollars. 'This is yours.'

Lara held the money in her hand, and it was like a taste of freedom. It was the first time she had ever been paid for what she had done.

From the bank, Lara went to the hospital. Dr Duncan was just coming out of her father's room.

Lara felt a sudden sense of panic. 'He isn't . . . ?'

'No . . . no . . . he's going to be all right, Lara.' He hesitated. 'When I say "all right", I mean he is not going to die . . . not yet, at least . . . but he is going to have to stay in bed for a few weeks. He'll need someone to take care of him.'

'I'll take care of him,' Lara said.

He looked at her and said, softly, 'Your father doesn't know it, my dear, but he's a very lucky man.'

'May I go in and see him now?'

'Yes.'

Lara walked into her father's room and stood there staring at him. James Cameron lay in bed, looking pale and helpless, and he suddenly seemed very old. Lara was engulfed by a wave of tenderness. She was finally going to be able to do something for her father, something that would make him appreciate her and love her. She approached the bed.

'Papa . . .'

He looked up and muttered, 'What the bluidy hell are you doin' here? You've work to dae at the boardin' house.'

Lara froze. 'I . . . I know, Papa. I just wanted to tell you that I saw Mr MacAllister. I told him I would collect the rents until you got better and . . .'

'*Ye* collect the rents? Dinna make me laugh.' He was shaken with a sudden spasm. When he spoke again, his voice was weak. 'It's the Fates,' he moaned. 'I'm gang to be thrown oot into the streets.'

He was not even thinking about what would happen to her. Lara stood there looking at him for a long time. Then she turned and walked out.

*

James Cameron was brought home three days later, and put to bed.

'You're not to get out of bed for the next couple of weeks,' Dr Duncan told him. 'I'll come back and check on you in a day or two.'

'I canna stay in bed,' James Cameron protested. 'I'm a busy mon. I have a lot to dae.'

The doctor looked at him and said, quietly, 'You have a choice. You can either stay in bed and live, or get up and die.'

MacAllister's boarders were, at first, delighted to see the innocent young girl come around to collect their rents. But when the novelty wore off, they had a myriad of excuses:

'I was sick this week, and I had medical bills . . .'

'My son sends me money every week, but the mail's been delayed . . .'

'I had to buy some equipment . . .'

'I'll have the money for you next week for sure . . .'

But the young girl was fighting for her life. She listened politely and said, 'I'm so sorry, but Mr MacAllister says that the money is due today, and if you don't have it, you'll have to vacate immediately.'

And somehow, they all managed to come up with the money.

Lara was inflexible.

'It was easier dealing with your father,' one of the boarders grumbled. 'He was always willing to wait a few days.'

But, in the end, they had to admire the young girl's spunk.

If Lara had thought that her father's illness would bring him closer to her, she was sadly mistaken. Lara tried to anticipate his every need, but the more solicitous she was, the more badly he behaved.

She brought him fresh flowers every day, and little treats.

'For Gude's sakes!' he cried. 'Stop hoverin' aboote. Hae ye nae work to dae?'

'I just thought you'd like . . .'

'*Oot!*' He turned his face to the wall.

I hate him, Lara thought. *I hate him*.

At the end of the month, when Lara walked into Sean MacAllister's office with the envelopes filled with rent money, and he had finished counting it, he said, 'I don't mind admitting, young lady, that you've been quite a surprise to me. You've done better than your father.'

The words were thrilling. 'Thank you.'

'As a matter of fact, this is the first month that everybody has paid on time in full.'

'Then my father and I can stay on at the boarding house?' Lara asked eagerly.

MacAllister studied her a moment. 'I suppose so. You must love your father very much.'

'I'll see you next Saturday, Mr MacAllister.'

5

At seventeen, the spindly, gaunt little girl had grown into a woman. Her face bore the imprint of her Scottish forebears. The gleaming skin, the arched, fine eyebrows, the thundercloud grey eyes, the stormy black hair. And in addition, there was a strain of melancholy that seemed to hover around her, the bleed-through of a people's tragic history. It was hard to look away from Lara Cameron's face.

Most of the boarders were without women, except for the companions they paid for at Madame Kirstie's and some of the other houses of prostitution, and the beautiful young girl was a natural target for them. One of the men would corner her in the kitchen or in his bedroom when she was cleaning it and say, 'Why don't you be nice to me, Lara? I could do a lot for you.'

Or, 'You don't have a boy friend, do you? Let me show you what a man is like.'

Or, 'How would you like to go to Kansas City? I'm leaving next week and I'd be glad to take you with me.'

After one or another of the boarders had tried to persuade Lara to go to bed with him, she would walk into the small room where her father lay helpless, and say, 'You were wrong, Father. All the men want me.' And she would walk out, leaving him staring after her.

James Cameron died on an early morning in spring, and Lara buried him at the Greenwood Cemetery in the Passiondale area. The only other person at the funeral was Bertha. There were no tears.

A new boarder moved in, an American named Bill Rogers. He was in his seventies, bald and fat, an affable man who liked to talk. After supper, he would sit and chat with Lara. 'You're too damned pretty to be stuck in a hick town like this,' he advised her. 'You should go to Chicago or New York. Big time.'

'I will one day,' Lara said.

'You've got your whole life ahead of you. Do you know what you want to do with it?'

'I want to own things.'

'Ah, pretty clothes and . . .'

'No. Land. I want to own land. My father never owned anything. He had to live off other people's favours all his life.'

Bill Rogers' face lit up. 'Real estate was the business I was in.'

'Really?'

'I had buildings all over the Midwest. I even had a chain of hotels once.' His tone was wistful.

'What happened?'

He shrugged. 'I got greedy. Lost it all. But it was sure fun while it lasted.'

After that they talked about real estate almost every night.

'The first rule in real estate,' Rogers told her, 'is OPM. Never forget that.'

'What's OPM?'

'Other people's money. What makes real estate a great business is that the government lets you take deductions on interest and depreciation while your assets keep growing. The three most important things in real estate are location, location and location. A beautiful building up on a hill is a waste of time. An ugly building downtown will make you rich.'

Rogers taught Lara about mortgages and refinancing and the use of bank loans. Lara listened and learned and remembered. She was like a sponge, eagerly soaking up every bit of information.

The most meaningful thing Rogers said to her was, 'You know, Glace Bay has a big housing shortage. It's a great opportunity for someone. If I were twenty years younger . . .'

From that moment on, Lara looked at Glace Bay with different eyes, visualizing office buildings and homes on vacant lots. It was exciting and it was frustrating. Her dreams were there, but she had no money to carry them out.

The day Bill Rogers left town he said, 'Remember – other people's money. Good luck, kid.'

A week later, Charles Cohn moved into the boarding house. He was a small man in his sixties, neat and trim, and well dressed. He sat at the supper table with the other boarders, but said very little. He seemed cocooned in his own private world.

He watched Lara as she worked around the boarding house, smiling, never complaining.

'How long do you plan to stay with us?' Lara asked Cohn.

'I'm not sure. It could be a week or a month or two . . .'

Charles Cohn was a puzzle to Lara. He did not fit in with the other boarders at all. She tried to imagine what he did. He was certainly not a miner or a fisherman, and he did not look like a merchant. He seemed superior to the other boarders, better educated. He told Lara that he had tried to get into the one hotel in town, but that it was full. Lara noticed that at meal times he ate almost nothing.

'If you have a little fruit,' he would say, apologetically, 'or some vegetables . . .'

'Are you on some special kind of diet?' Lara asked.

'In a way. I eat only kosher food, and I'm afraid Glace Bay doesn't have any.'

The next evening, when Charles Cohn sat down to supper, a plate of lamb chops was placed in front of him. He looked up at Lara in surprise. 'I'm sorry. I can't eat this,' he said. 'I thought I explained . . .'

Lara smiled, 'You did. This is kosher.'

'*What*?'

'I found a kosher meat market in Sydney. The *shochet* there sold me this. Enjoy it. Your rent includes two meals a day. Tomorrow you're having a steak.'

From that time on, whenever Lara had a free moment, Cohn made it a point to talk to her, to draw her out. He was impressed by her quick intelligence and her independent spirit.

One day Charles Cohn confided to Lara what he was doing in Glace Bay. 'I'm an executive with Continental Supplies.' It was a famous national chain. 'I'm here to find a location for our new store.'

'That's exciting,' Lara said. *I knew he was in Glace Bay for some important reason.* 'You're going to put up a building?'

'No. We'll find someone else to do that. We just lease our buildings.'

At three o'clock in the morning, Lara awakened out of a sound sleep and sat up in bed, her heart pounding wildly. Had it been a dream? No. Her mind was racing. She was too excited to go back to sleep.

When Charles Cohn came out of his room for breakfast, Lara was waiting for him.

'Mr Cohn . . . I know a great place,' she blurted out.

He stared at her, puzzled. 'What?'

'For the location you're looking for.'

'Oh? Where?'

Lara evaded the question. 'Let me ask you something. If I owned a location that you liked, and if I put up a building on it, would you agree to lease it from me for five years?'

He shook his head. 'That's a rather hypothetical question, isn't it?'

'Would you?' Lara persisted.

'Lara, what do you know about putting up a building?'

'I wouldn't be putting it up,' she said. 'I'd hire an architect and a good construction firm to do that.'

Charles Cohn was watching her closely. 'I see. And where is this wonderful piece of land?'

'I'll show it to you,' Lara said. 'Believe me, you're going to love it. It's perfect.'

After breakfast, Lara took Charles Cohn downtown. At the corner of Main and Commercial Streets in the centre of Glace Bay was a vacant square block. It was a site Cohn had examined two days earlier.

'This is the location I had in mind,' Lara said.

Cohn stood there, pretending to study it. 'You have an *ahf* – a nose. It's a very good location.'

He had already made discreet inquiries and learned that the property was owned by a banker, Sean MacAllister. Cohn's assignment was to locate a site, arrange for someone to construct the building, and then lease it from them. It would not matter to the company who put up the building so long as its specifications were met.

Cohn was studying Lara. *She's too young*, he thought. *It's a foolish idea. And yet* . . . *'I found a kosher meat market in Sydney* . . . *Tomorrow you're having a steak.'* She had such compassion.

Lara was saying, excitedly, 'If I could acquire this land and put up a building to meet your specifications, would you give me a five-year lease?'

He paused, and then said slowly, 'No, Lara. It would have to be a ten-year lease.'

That afternoon, Lara went to see Sean MacAllister. He looked up in surprise as she walked into his office.

'You're a few days early, Lara. Today's only Wednesday.'

'I know. I want to ask a favour, Mr MacAllister.'

Sean MacAllister sat there, watching her. *She has really turned into a beautiful-looking girl. Not a girl, a woman.* He could see the swell of her breasts against the cotton blouse she was wearing.

'Sit down, my dear. What can I do for you?'

Lara was too excited to sit. 'I want to take a loan.'

It took him by surprise. 'What?'

'I'd like to borrow some money.'

He smiled indulgently. 'I don't see why not. If you need a new dress or something, I'll be happy to advance . . .'

'I want to borrow two hundred thousand dollars.'

MacAllister's smile died. 'Is this some kind of joke?'

'No, sir.' Lara leaned forward and said earnestly, 'There's a piece of land I want to buy to put up a building. I have an important tenant who's willing to give me a ten-year lease. That will guarantee the cost of the land and the building.'

MacAllister was studying her, frowning. 'Have you discussed this with the owner of the land?'

'I'm discussing it with him now,' Lara said.

It took a moment for it to sink in. 'Wait a minute. Are you telling me that this is land that *I* own?'

'Yes. It's the lot on the corner of Main and Commercial Streets.'

'You came here to borrow money from *me* to buy *my* land?'

'That lot is worth no more than twenty thousand dollars. I checked. I'm offering you thirty. You'll make a profit of ten thousand dollars on the land plus interest on the two hundred thousand dollars you're going to loan me to put up the building.'

MacAllister shook his head. 'You're asking me

to loan you two hundred thousand dollars with no security. It's out of the question.'

Lara leaned forward. 'There *is* security. You'll hold the mortgage on the building and the land, and I've already got the tenant. You can't lose.'

MacAllister sat there studying her, turning her proposal over in his mind. He smiled, 'You know,' he said, 'you have a lot of nerve. But I could never explain a loan like that to my board of directors.'

'You have no board of directors,' Lara told him.

The smile turned to a grin. 'True.'

Lara leaned forward and he could see her breasts touching the edge of his desk.

'If you say yes, Mr MacAllister, you'll never regret it. I promise.'

He could not take his eyes off her breasts. 'You're not a bit like your father, are you?'

'No, sir.' *Nothing, like him*, Lara thought fiercely.

'Supposing, for the sake of argument,' MacAllister said carefully, 'that I was interested. Who is this tenant of yours?'

'His name is Charles Cohn. He's an executive with Continental Supplies.'

'The chain store?'

'Yes.'

MacAllister was suddenly very interested.

Lara went on. 'They want to have a big store built here to supply the miners and lumbermen with equipment.'

To MacAllister, it had the smell of instant success.

'Where did you meet this man?' he asked casually.

'He's staying at the boarding house.'

'I see. Let me think about it, Lara. We'll discuss it again tomorrow.'

Lara was almost trembling with excitement. 'Thank you, Mr MacAllister. You won't be sorry.'

He smiled. 'No, I don't think I will be.'

That afternoon, Sean MacAllister went to the boarding house to meet Charles Cohn.

'I just dropped by to welcome you to Glace Bay,' MacAllister said. 'I'm Sean MacAllister. I own the bank here. I heard you were in town. But you shouldn't be staying at my boarding house, you should be staying at my hotel. It's much more comfortable.'

'It was full,' Mr Cohn explained.

'That's because we didn't know who you were.'

Mr Cohn said pleasantly, 'Who am I?'

Sean MacAllister smiled. 'We don't have to play games, Mr Cohn. Word gets around. I understand that you're interested in leasing a building to be put up on a property I own.'

'What property would that be?'

'The lot at Main and Commercial. It's a great location, isn't it? I don't think we'll have any problem making a deal.'

'I already have a deal with someone.'

Sean MacAllister laughed. 'Lara? She's a pretty little thing, isn't she? Why don't you come down to the bank with me and we'll draw up a contract?'

'I don't think you understand, Mr MacAllister. I said I already have a deal.'

'I don't think *you* understand, Mr Cohn. Lara doesn't own that land. I do.'

'She's trying to buy it from you, isn't she?'

'Yes. I don't have to sell it to her.'

'And I don't have to use that lot. I've seen three other lots that will do just as nicely. Thanks for dropping by.'

Sean MacAllister looked at him for a long moment. 'You mean . . . you're serious?'

'Very. I never go into a deal that's not kosher, and I never break my word.'

'But Lara doesn't know anything about building. She . . .'

'She plans to find people who do. Naturally, we'll have final approval.'

The banker was thoughtful. 'Do I understand that Continental Supplies is willing to sign a ten-year lease?'

'That's correct.'

'I see. Well, under the circumstances, I . . . let me think about it.'

When Lara arrived at the boarding house, Charles Cohn told her about his conversation with the banker.

Lara was upset. 'You mean Mr MacAllister went behind my back and . . . ?'

'Don't worry,' Cohn assured her, 'he'll make the deal with you.'

'Do you really think so?'

'He's a banker. He's in business to make a profit.'

'What about you? Why are you doing this for me?' Lara asked.

He had asked himself the same question. *Because you're achingly young*, he thought. *Because you don't belong in this town. Because I wish I had a daughter like you.*

But he said none of those things.

'I have nothing to lose, Lara. I found some other locations that would serve just as well. If you can acquire this land, I'd like to do this for you. It doesn't matter to my company who I deal with. If you get your loan, and I approve your builder, we're in business.'

A feeling of elation swept over Lara. 'I . . . I don't know how to thank you. I'll go to see Mr MacAllister and . . .'

'I wouldn't if I were you,' Cohn advised her. 'Let him come to you.'

She looked worried. 'But what if he doesn't . . . ?'

Cohn smiled, 'He will.'

He handed her a printed lease. 'Here's the ten-year lease we discussed. It's contingent, you understand, on your meeting all our requirements for the building.' He handed her a set of blueprints. 'These are our specifications.'

Lara spent the night studying the pages of drawings and instructions.

The following morning, Sean MacAllister telephoned Lara.

'Can you come down to see me, Lara?'

Her heart was pounding. 'I'll be there in fifteen minutes.'

He was waiting for her.

'I've been thinking about our conversation,' MacAllister said. 'I would need a written agreement for a ten-year lease from Mr Cohn.'

'I already have it,' Lara said. She opened her bag and took out the contract.

Sean MacAllister examined it carefully. 'It seems to be in order.'

'Then we have a deal?' Lara asked. She was holding her breath.

MacAllister shook his head. 'No.'

'But I thought . . .'

His fingers were drumming restlessly on his desk. 'To tell you the truth, I'm really in no hurry to sell that lot, Lara. The longer I hold on to it, the more valuable it will become.'

She looked at him blankly. 'But you . . .'

'Your request is completely unorthodox. You've had no experience. I would need a very special reason to make this loan to you.'

'I don't under . . . what kind of reason?'

'Let's say . . . a little bonus. Tell me, Lara, have you ever had a lover?'

The question caught her completely off-guard.

'I . . . no.' She could feel the deal slipping away from her. 'What does that have . . . ?'

MacAllister leaned forward. 'I'm going to be frank with you, Lara. I find you very attractive. I'd like to go to bed with you. *Quid pro quo*. That means . . .'

'I know what it means.' Her face had turned to stone.

'Look at it this way. This is your chance to make something of yourself, isn't it? To own something, to be somebody. To prove to yourself that you're not like your father.'

Lara's mind was spinning.

'You'll probably never have another chance like this again, Lara. Perhaps you'd like some time to think it over, and . . .'

'No.' Her voice sounded hollow in her own ears. 'I can give you my answer now.' She pressed her arms tightly against her sides to stop her body from trembling. Her whole future, her very life, hung on her next words.

'I'll go to bed with you.'

Grinning, MacAllister rose and moved toward her, his fat arms outstretched.

'Not now,' Lara said. 'After I see the contract.'

The following day, Sean MacAllister handed Lara a contract for the bank loan.

'It's a very simple contract, my dear. It's a ten-year, two-hundred-thousand-dollar loan at eight per cent.' He gave her a pen. 'You can just sign here on the last page.'

'If you don't mind, I'd like to read it first,' Lara said. She looked at her watch, 'But I don't have time now. May I take it with me? I'll bring it back tomorrow.'

Sean MacAllister shrugged. 'Very well.' He lowered his voice. 'About our little date. Next Saturday I have to go into Halifax. I thought we might go there together.'

Lara looked at his leering smile and felt sick to her stomach. 'All right.' It was a whisper.

'Good. You sign the contract and bring it back and we're in business.' He was thoughtful for a moment. 'You're going to need a good builder. Are you familiar with the Nova Scotia Construction Company?'

Lara's face lit up. 'Yes. I know their foreman, Buzz Steele.'

He had put up some of the biggest buildings in Glace Bay.

'Good. It's a fine outfit. I would recommend them.'

'I'll talk to Buzz tomorrow.'

That evening Lara showed the contract to Charles Cohn. She did not dare tell him about the private deal she had made with MacAllister. She was too ashamed. Cohn read the contract carefully, and when he finished, he handed it back to Lara. 'I would advise you not to sign this.'

She was dismayed. 'Why?'

'There's a clause in there that stipulates that the building must be completed by December 31st, or title reverts to the bank. In other words, the building will belong to MacAllister, and my company will become *his* tenant. You forfeit the deal and are still obligated to repay the loan with interest. Ask him to change that.'

MacAllister's words rang in Lara's ears. *I'm really in no hurry to sell that lot. The longer I hold on to it the more valuable it will become.*

Lara shook her head. 'He won't.'

'Then you're taking a big gamble, Lara. You could wind up with nothing, and a debt of two hundred thousand dollars plus interest.'

'But if I bring the building in on time . . .'

'That's a big "if". When you put up a building, you're at the mercy of a lot of other people. You'd be surprised at the number of things that can go wrong.'

'There's a very good construction company in Sydney. They've put up a lot of buildings around here. I know the foreman. I'll talk to him. If he says he can have the building up in time, I want to go ahead.'

It was the desperate eagerness in Lara's voice that made him put aside his doubts. 'All right,' he finally said, 'talk to him.'

Lara found Buzz Steele walking the girders of a five-storey building he was erecting in Sydney. Steele was a grizzled, weather-beaten man in his forties. He greeted Lara warmly. 'This is a nice surprise,' he said. 'How did they let a pretty girl like you get out of Glace Bay?'

'I sneaked out,' Lara told him. 'I have a job for you, Mr Steele.'

He smiled. 'You do? What are we building – a doll's house?'

'No.' She pulled out the blueprints Charles Cohn had given her. 'This is the building.'

Buzz Steele studied it a moment. He looked up, surprised. 'This is a pretty big job. What does it have to do with you?'

'I put the deal together,' Lara said proudly. 'I'm going to own the building.'

Steele whistled softly. 'Well, good for you, honey.'

'There are two catches.'

'Oh?'

'The building has to be finished by December 31st or it reverts to the bank, and it can't cost more than $170,000.'

'December 31st is just ten months away.'

'I know. Can it be done?'

Steele looked at the blueprints again. Lara watched him silently calculating.

Finally he spoke. 'It can be finished by December 31st if you give us the green light now.'

'Then you've got a deal.'

It was all Lara could do not to shout out loud. *I've done it*, she thought. *I've done it!*

They shook hands. 'You're the prettiest boss I've ever had,' Buzz Steele said.

'Thank you. How soon can you get started?'

'Tell you what. I'll go into Glace Bay tomorrow to look over the lot. I'm going to give you a building you'll be proud of.'

When Lara left, she felt that she had wings.

Lara returned to Glace Bay and told Charles Cohn the news.

'Are you sure this company is reliable, Lara?'

'I know it is,' Lara assured him. 'They've put up buildings here and in Sydney, and Halifax and . . .'

Her enthusiasm was contagious.

Cohn smiled. 'Well, then, it looks like we're in business.'

'It does, doesn't it?' Lara beamed. And then she remembered the deal she had made with Sean MacAllister, and her smile faded. *Next Saturday I have to go into Halifax. I thought we might go there together*. Saturday was only two days away.

Lara signed the contracts the following morning. As Sean MacAllister watched her leave the office, he was very pleased with himself. He had no intention of letting her have the new building. And he almost laughed aloud at her naïveté. He would loan her the money, but he would really be loaning it to himself. He thought about making love to that wonderful young body, and he began to get an erection.

Lara had been to Halifax only twice. Compared to Glace Bay, it was a bustling town, full of pedestrians and automobiles, and shops crammed with merchandise. Sean MacAllister drove Lara to a motel on the outskirts of town. He pulled into the parking lot and patted her on the knee. 'You wait here while I register for us, honey.'

Lara sat in the car, waiting, panicky. *I'm selling myself*, she thought. *Like a whore. But it's all I've got to sell, and at least he thinks I'm worth two hundred thousand dollars. My father never saw two hundred thousand dollars in his life. He was always too* . . .

The car door opened and MacAllister was standing there, grinning. 'All set. Let's go.'

Lara suddenly found it hard to breathe. Her heart was pounding so hard she thought it was going to fly out of her chest. *I'm having a heart attack*, she thought.

'Lara . . .' He was looking at her strangely. 'Are you all right?'

No. I'm dying. They'll take me to the hospital and I'll die there. A virgin. 'I'm fine,' she said.

Slowly she got out of the car and followed MacAllister into a drab cabin with a bed, two chairs, a battered dressing table, and a tiny bathroom.

She was caught up in a nightmare.

'So this is your first time, eh?' MacAllister said.

She thought of the boys at school who had fondled

her and kissed her breasts and tried to put their hands between her legs. 'Yes,' she said.

'Well, you mustn't be nervous. Sex is the most natural thing in the world.'

Lara watched as MacAllister began to strip off his clothes. His body was pudgy.

'Get undressed,' MacAllister ordered.

Slowly, Lara took off her blouse and skirt and shoes. She was wearing a brassière and panties.

MacAllister looked at her figure and walked over to her. 'You're beautiful, you know that, baby?'

She could feel his male hardness pressing against her body. MacAllister kissed her on the lips and she felt disgust.

'Get the rest of your clothes off,' he said urgently. He walked over to the bed and stripped off his shorts. His penis was hard and red.

That will never fit inside me, Lara thought. *It will kill me*.

'Hurry up.'

Slowly Lara took off her brassière and stepped out of her panties.

'My God,' he said, 'you're fantastic. Come over here.'

Lara walked over to the bed and sat down. MacAllister squeezed her breasts hard and she cried aloud with the pain.

'That felt good, didn't it? It's time you had yourself a man.' MacAllister pushed her down on her back and spread her legs.

Lara was suddenly panicky. 'I'm not wearing anything,' she said. 'I mean . . . I could get pregnant.'

'Don't worry,' MacAllister promised her, 'I won't come inside you.'

An instant later, Lara felt him pushing inside her, hurting her.

'Wait!' she cried, 'I . . .'

MacAllister was past the waiting. He rammed himself into her and the pain was excruciating. He was pounding into her body now, harder and harder, and Lara put her hand to her mouth to keep from screaming. *It will be over in a minute*, she thought, *and I'll own a building. And I can put up a second building. And another . . .*

The pain was becoming unbearable.

'Move your ass,' MacAllister cried. 'Don't just lay there. Move it!'

She tried to move, but it was impossible. She was in too much pain.

Suddenly, MacAllister gave a gasp and Lara felt his body jerk. He let out a satisfied sigh and lay limp against her.

She was horrified. 'You said you wouldn't . . .'

He lifted himself up on his elbows and said earnestly, 'Darling, I couldn't help it, you're just so beautiful. But don't worry. If you get pregnant, I know a doctor who'll take care of you.'

Lara turned her face away so he could not see her revulsion. She limped into the bathroom, sore and bleeding. She stood in the shower, letting the warm water wash over her body, and she thought, *It's over with. I've done it. I own the land. I'm going to be rich.*

Now all she had to do was get dressed and go back to Glace Bay and get her building started.

She walked out of the bathroom and Sean MacAllister said, 'That was so good, we're going to do it again.'

6

Charles Cohn had inspected five buildings erected by the Nova Scotia Construction Company.

'They're a first rate outfit,' he had told Lara. 'You shouldn't have any problem with them.'

Now, Lara, Charles Cohn, and Buzz Steele were inspecting the new site.

'It's perfect,' Buzz Steele said. 'The measurements come to 43,560 square feet. That will give you the twenty-thousand-square-foot building you want.'

Charles Cohn asked, 'Can you have the building finished by December 31st?' He was determined to protect Lara.

'Sooner,' Steele said. 'I can promise it to you by Christmas Eve.'

Lara was beaming. 'How soon can you get started?'

'I'll have my crew here by the middle of next week. Do I have the go-ahead?'

Cohn looked at Lara and nodded.

'You have the go-ahead,' Lara said happily.

Watching the new building going up was the most exciting thing Lara had ever experienced. She was there every day. 'I want to learn,' she told Charles Cohn. 'This is just the beginning for me. Before I'm through, I'm going to put up a hundred buildings.'

Cohn wondered whether Lara really knew what she was getting into.

The first men to set foot on the project site were members of the survey team. They established the legal geometric borders of the property and drove hubs into the ground at each corner, every hub painted with a fluorescent colour for easy identification. The survey work was finished in two days, and early the following morning, heavy earth-moving equipment – a truck-mounted Caterpillar front-end loader – arrived at the site.

Lara was there, waiting. 'What happens now?' she asked Buzz Steele.

'We clear and grub.'

Lara looked at him. 'What does that mean?'

'The Caterpillar is gonna dig up tree stumps and do some rough grading.'

The next piece of equipment that came in was a backhoe to dig the trenches for foundations, utility conduits, and drainage piping.

By now, the boarders at the house had all heard what was happening, and it became the main topic of conversation at breakfast and supper. They were all cheering for Lara.

'What happens next?' they would ask.

She was becoming an expert. 'This morning, they put the underground piping in place. Tomorrow they start to put in the wood and concrete formwork, so they can wire-tie the steel bars into the skeletal gridiron.' She grinned. 'Do you understand what I'm saying?'

Pouring the concrete was the next step, and when the concrete foundation was cured, large truckloads of lumber rolled in, and crews of carpenters began to assemble the wooden frames. The noise was horrendous, but to Lara it was music. The place was filled with the sounds of rhythmic hammers and whining power saws. After two weeks, the wall panels, punctuated with window and door openings, were stood upright as if the building had suddenly been inflated.

To passers-by, the building was a maze of wood and steel, but to Lara it was something else. It was her dream come to life. Every morning and every evening, she went downtown and stared at what was being built. *I own this*, Lara thought. *This belongs to me*.

After the episode with MacAllister, Lara had been terrified that she might become pregnant. The thought of it made her sick to her stomach. When her period came, she was weak with relief. *Now all I have to worry about is my building*.

She continued to collect the rents for Sean MacAllister because she needed a place to live, but she had to steel herself to go into his office and face him.

'We had a good time in Halifax, didn't we, honey? Why don't we do it again?'

'I'm busy with my building,' Lara said firmly.

The level of activity began to heighten as the sheet metal crews, roofers and carpenters worked simultaneously, the number of men, materials, and trucks tripling.

Charles Cohn had left Glace Bay, but he telephoned Lara once a week.

'How is the building going?' he had asked the last time he called.

'Great!' Lara said enthusiastically.

'Is it on schedule?'

'It's ahead of schedule.'

'That's wonderful. I can tell you now that I wasn't really sure you could do it.'

'But you gave me a chance, anyway. Thank you, Charles.'

'One good turn deserves another. Remember, if it hadn't been for you, I might have starved to death.'

From time to time, Sean MacAllister would join Lara at the building site.

'It's coming along just fine, isn't it?'

'Yes,' Lara said.

MacAllister seemed genuinely pleased. Lara thought: *Mr Cohn was wrong about him. He's not trying to take advantage of me.*

By the end of November, the building was progressing rapidly. The windows and doors were in place, and the exterior walls were set. The structure was ready to accept the network of nerves and arteries.

On Monday, the first week of December, work on the building began to slow down. Lara went to the site one morning and there were only two men there, and they seemed to be doing very little.

'Where's the rest of the crew today?' Lara asked.

'They're on another job,' one of the men explained. 'They'll be here tomorrow.'

The following day no one was there.

Lara took a bus into Halifax to see Buzz Steele. 'What's happening?' Lara asked. 'The work has stopped.'

'Nothing to worry about,' Steele assured her. 'We ran into a little snag on another job and I had to pull my men off temporarily.'

'When will they be coming back to work?'

'Next week. We'll be on schedule.'

'Buzz, you know how much this means to me.'

'Sure, Lara.'

'If the building's not completed on time, I lose it. I lose everything.'

'Don't worry, kid. I won't let that happen.'

When Lara left, she had a feeling of unease.

The following week, the workmen still had not appeared. She went into Halifax again to see Steele.

'I'm sorry,' the secretary said, 'Mr Steele is not in.'

'I must talk to him. When will he be back?'

'He's out of town on a job. I don't know when he'll be back.'

Lara felt the first stirrings of panic. 'This is very important,' Lara insisted. 'He's putting up a building for me. It has to be finished in three weeks.'

'I wouldn't worry, Miss Cameron. If Mr Steele said it will be finished, it will be finished.'

'But nothing's happening,' Lara cried. 'No one's working on it.'

'Would you like to talk to Mr Ericksen, his assistant?'

'Yes, please.'

Ericksen was a giant of a man, broad shouldered and amiable. He radiated reassurance.

'I know why you're here,' he said, 'but Buzz told me to assure you that you have nothing to worry about. We've been held back a little on your project because of some problems on a couple of big construction jobs we're handling, but your building is only three weeks away from completion.'

'There's still so much to do . . .'

'Not to worry. We'll have a crew out there first thing Monday morning.'

'Thank you,' Lara said, relieved. 'I'm sorry to have bothered you, but I'm a little nervous. This means a great deal to me.'

'No problem,' Ericksen smiled. 'You just go home and relax. You're in good hands.'

On Monday morning there was not a single workman at the site. Lara was frantic. She telephoned Charles Cohn.

'The men have stopped working,' she told him, 'and I can't find out why. They keep making promises and breaking them.'

'What's the name of the company – Nova Scotia Construction?'

'That's right.'

'I'll call you back,' Cohn said.

Two hours later, Charles Cohn telephoned. 'Who recommended the Nova Scotia Construction Company to you?'

She thought back. 'Sean MacAllister.'

'I'm not surprised. He owns the company, Lara.'

Lara felt suddenly faint. 'And he's stopping the men from finishing it on time . . . ?'

'I'm afraid it looks that way.'

'Oh, my God.'

'He's a *nahash tzefa* – a poisonous snake.'

He was too kind to say that he had warned her. All he managed was, 'Maybe . . . maybe something will turn up.'

He admired the young girl's spirit and ambition, and he despised Sean MacAllister. But he was helpless. There was nothing he could do.

Lara lay awake all night thinking about her folly. The building she had put up would belong now to Sean MacAllister, and she would be left with a staggering debt which she would spend the rest of her life working to repay. The thought of how MacAllister might exact payment made her shudder. Finally, at dawn, exhausted from crying, she fell asleep.

When Lara awakened, she went to see Sean MacAllister.

'Good morning, my dear. You're looking lovely today.'

Lara came right to the point. 'I need an extension. The building won't be ready by the thirty-first.'

MacAllister sat back in his chair and frowned. 'Really? That's bad news, Lara.'

'I need another month.'

MacAllister sighed. 'I'm afraid that's not possible. Oh dear, no. You signed a contract. A deal is a deal.'

'But . . .'

'I'm sorry, Lara. On the thirty-first, the property reverts to the bank.'

*

When the boarders at the house heard what was happening, they were furious.

'That sonofabitch!' one of them cried. 'He can't do this to you.'

'He's done it,' Lara said, despairingly. 'It's over.'

'Are we going to let him get away with this?'

'Hell, no. What have you got left – three weeks?'

Lara shook her head, 'Less. Two and a half weeks.'

The man turned to the others. 'Let's go down and take a look at that building.'

'What good will . . . ?'

'We'll see.'

Soon, half a dozen boarders were standing at the building site, carefully inspecting it.

'The plumbing hasn't been put in,' one of the men said.

'Nor the electricity.'

They stood there, shivering in the freezing December wind, discussing what still remained to be done.

One of the men turned to Lara. 'Your banker's a tricky fellow. He's had the building almost finished so that he wouldn't have much to do when your contract was up.' He turned to the others. 'I would say that this could be finished in two and a half weeks.'

There was a chorus of agreement.

Lara was bewildered. 'You don't understand. The workmen won't come.'

'Look, lassie, in your boarding house you've got plumbers and carpenters and electricians, and we've got lots of friends in town who can handle the rest.'

'I don't have any money to pay you,' Lara said. 'Mr MacAllister won't give me . . .'

'It will be our Christmas gift to you.'

What happened after that was incredible. Word quickly spread around Glace Bay of what was happening. Construction workers on other buildings came to take a look at Lara's property. Half of them were there because they liked Lara, and the other half because they had had dealings with Sean MacAllister and hated him.

'Let's fix the bastard,' they said.

They dropped by to lend a hand after work, working past midnight and on Saturdays and Sundays, and the sound of construction began again, filling the air with a joyful noise. Beating the deadline became a challenge, and the building was soon swarming with carpenters and electricians and plumbers, all eager to pitch in. When Sean MacAllister heard what was happening, he rushed over to the site.

He stood there, stunned. 'What's going on?' he demanded. 'Those aren't my workmen.'

'They're mine,' Lara said defiantly. 'There's nothing in the contract that says I can't use my own men.'

'Well, I . . .' MacAllister sputtered. 'That building had better be up to specifications.'

'It will be,' Lara assured him.

The day before New Year's Eve, the building was completed. It stood proud against the sky, solid and strong, and it was the most beautiful thing Lara had ever seen. She stood there staring at it, dazed.

'It's all yours,' one of the workmen said proudly. 'Are we going to have a party or what?'

That night, it seemed that the whole town of Glace Bay celebrated Lara Cameron's first building.

It was the beginning.

*

There was no stopping Lara after that. Her mind was brimming with ideas.

'Your new employees are going to need places to live in Glace Bay,' she told Charles Cohn. 'I'd like to build houses for them. Are you interested?'

He nodded. 'I'm very interested.'

Lara went to see a banker in Sydney and borrowed enough money on her building to finance the new project.

When the houses were finished, Lara said to Charles Cohn, 'Do you know what else this town needs, Charles? Cabins to accommodate the summer tourists who come here to fish. I know a wonderful place near the Bay where I could build . . .'

Charles Cohn became Lara's unofficial financial advisor, and during the next three years, Lara built an office building, half a dozen sea-shore cottages, and a shopping mall. The banks in Sydney and Halifax were happy to loan her money.

Two years later, when Lara sold out her real estate holdings, she had a certified cheque for three million dollars. She was twenty-one years old.

The following day, she said goodbye to Glace Bay and left for Chicago.

7

Chicago was a revelation. Halifax had been the largest city Lara had ever seen, but it was like a hamlet compared to the giant of the Midwest. Chicago was a loud and noisy city, bustling and energetic, and everyone seemed to be hurrying to some important destination.

Lara checked into Stevens Hotel. She took one look at the smartly dressed women walking through the lobby and became self-conscious about the clothes she was wearing. *Glace Bay, yes*, Lara thought. *Chicago, no.* The following morning, Lara went into action. She visited Kane's and Ultimo for designer dresses, Joseph's for shoes, Saks Fifth Avenue and Marshall Field's for lingerie, Trabert and Hoeffer for jewellery, and Ware for a mink coat. And every time she bought something, she heard her father's voice saying, *'I'm nae made of money. Get yourself something frae the Salvation Army Citadel.'* Before her shopping spree was over, the closets in her hotel suite were filled with beautiful clothes.

Lara's next move was to look in the yellow pages of the telephone book under real estate brokers. She selected the one that had the largest advertisement,

Parker & Associates. Lara telephoned and asked to speak to Mr Parker.

'May I tell him who's calling?'

'Lara Cameron.'

A moment later, a voice said, 'Bruce Parker speaking. How can I help you?'

'I'm looking for a location where I can put up a beautiful new hotel,' Lara said.

The voice at the other end of the phone grew warmer. 'Well, we're experts at that, Mrs Cameron.'

'*Miss* Cameron.'

'Right. Did you have any particular area in mind?'

'No. To tell you the truth, I'm not really familiar with Chicago.'

'That's no problem. I'm sure we can line up some very interesting properties for you. Just to give me an idea of what we're looking for, how much equity do you have?'

Lara said proudly, 'Three million dollars.'

There was a long silence. 'Three million dollars?'

'Yes.'

'And you want to build a beautiful new hotel?'

'Yes.'

Another silence.

'Were you interested in building or acquiring something in the inner city area, Miss Cameron?'

'Of course not,' Lara said. 'What I have in mind is exactly the opposite. I want to build an exclusive boutique hotel in a nice area that . . .'

'With an equity of three million dollars?' Parker chuckled. 'I'm afraid we're not going to be able to help you.'

'Thank you,' Lara said. She replaced the receiver. She had obviously called the wrong broker.

She went back to the yellow pages again and made half a dozen more calls. By the end of the afternoon, Lara was forced to face reality. None of the brokers was interested in trying to find a prime location where she could build a hotel with a down payment of three million dollars. They had offered Lara a variety of suggestions, and they had all come down to the same thing: A cheap hotel in an inner city area.

Never, Lara thought. *I'll go back to Glace Bay first.*

She had dreamed for months about the hotel she wanted to build and in her mind it was already a reality – beautiful, vivid, three-dimensional. Her plan was to turn a hotel into a real home away from home. It would have mostly suites, and each suite would have a living room and a library with a fireplace in each room, and be furnished with comfortable couches, easy chairs and a grand piano. There would be two large bedrooms and an outside terrace running the length of the apartment. There would be a jacuzzi and a mini-bar. Lara knew exactly what she wanted. The question was how she was going to get it.

Lara walked into a print shop on Lake Street. 'I would like to have a hundred business cards printed up, please.'

'Certainly. And how will the cards read?'

'*Miss Lara Cameron*, and at the bottom, *Real Estate Developer*.'

'Yes, Miss Cameron. I can have them for you in two days.'

'No. I would like them this afternoon, please.'

*

The next step was to get acquainted with the city.

Lara walked along Michigan Avenue and State Street and La Salle, strolled along Lake Shore Drive and wandered through Lincoln Park with its zoo and golf course and lagoon. She visited the Merchandise Mart, and went to Kroch-Brentano's and bought books about Chicago. She read about the famous who had made Chicago their home: Carl Sandburg, Frank Lloyd Wright, Louis Sullivan, Saul Bellow. She read about the pioneer families of Chicago; the John Bairds and Gaylord Donnelleys, the Marshall Fields and Potter Palmers and Walgreens, and she passed by their homes on Lake Shore Drive and their huge estates in suburban Lake Forest. Lara visited the southside and she felt at home there because of all the ethnic groups: Swedes, Poles, Irish, Lithuanians. It reminded her of Glace Bay.

She took to the streets again, looking at buildings with 'For Sale' signs, and she went to see the listed brokers. 'What's the price of that building?'

'Eighty million dollars . . .'

'Sixty million dollars . . .'

'A hundred million dollars . . .'

Her three million dollars was becoming more and more insignificant. Lara sat in her hotel room considering her options. She could either go to one of the slum sections of the city and put up a little hotel there, or she could return home. Neither choice appealed to her.

I've too much at stake to give up now, Lara thought.

*

The following morning, Lara stopped in at a bank on La Salle Street. She walked up to a clerk behind the counter. 'I would like to speak to your vice president, please.'

She handed the clerk her card.

Five minutes later, she was in the office of Tom Peterson, a flaccid, middle-aged man, with a nervous tic. He was studying her card.

'What can I do for you, Miss Cameron?'

'I'm planning to put up a hotel in Chicago. I'll need to borrow some money.'

He gave her a genial smile. 'That's what we're here for. What kind of hotel were you planning to build?'

'A beautiful boutique hotel in a nice area.'

'Sounds interesting.'

'I have to tell you,' Lara said, 'that I only have three million dollars to put down, and . . .'

He smiled. 'No problem.'

She felt a thrill of excitement. 'Really?'

'Three million can go a long way if you know what to do with it.' He looked at his watch. 'I have another appointment now. I wonder if we could get together for dinner tonight and talk about this.'

'Certainly,' Lara said. 'That would be fine.'

'Where are you staying?'

'At the Palmer House.'

'Why don't I pick you up at eight?'

Lara got to her feet. 'Thank you so much. I can't tell you how good you make me feel. Frankly, I was beginning to get discouraged.'

'No need,' he said. 'I'm going to take good care of you.'

At eight o'clock, Tom Peterson picked up Lara and took her to Henrici's for dinner. When they were seated, he said, 'You know, I'm glad that you came to me. We can do a lot for each other.'

'We can?'

'Yes. There's a lot of ass around this town, but none of it as beautiful as yours, honey. You can open a luxury whorehouse and cater to an exclusive . . .'

Lara froze. 'I beg your pardon?'

'If you can get half a dozen girls together we . . .'

Lara was gone.

The following day, Lara visited three more banks. When she explained her plans to the manager of the first, he said, 'I'm going to give you the best advice you'll ever get: Forget it. Real estate development is a man's game. There's no place for women in it.'

'And why is that?' Lara asked tonelessly.

'Because you'd be dealing with a bunch of macho roughnecks. They'd eat you alive.'

'They didn't eat me alive in Glace Bay,' Lara said.

He leaned forward. 'I'm going to let you in on a little secret. Chicago is not Glace Bay.'

At the next bank, the manager said to her, 'We'll be glad to help you out, Miss Cameron. Of course, what you have in mind is out of the question. What I would suggest is to let us handle your money and invest it . . .'

Lara was out of his office before he finished his sentence.

*

At the third bank, Lara was ushered into the office of Bob Vance, a pleasant-looking, grey-haired man who looked exactly as the president of a bank should look. In the office with him was a pale, thin, sandy-haired man in his early thirties, wearing a rumpled suit, and looking completely out of place.

'This is Howard Keller, Miss Cameron, one of our vice presidents.'

'How do you do?'

'What can I do for you this morning?' Bob Vance asked.

'I'm interested in building a hotel in Chicago,' Lara said, 'and I'm looking for finance.'

Bob Vance smiled. 'You've come to the right place. Do you have a location in mind?'

'I know the general area I want. Near the loop, not too far from Michigan Avenue . . .'

'Excellent.'

Lara told him about her boutique hotel idea.

'That sounds interesting,' Vance said. 'And how much equity do you have?'

'Three million dollars. I want to borrow the rest.'

There was a thoughtful pause. 'I'm afraid I can't help you. Your problem is that you have big ideas and a small purse. Now, if you would like us to invest your money for you . . .'

'No, thank you,' Lara said. 'Thanks for your time. Good afternoon, gentlemen.' She turned and left the office, fuming. In Glace Bay three million dollars was a fortune. Here, people seemed to think it was nothing.

As Lara reached the street, a voice said, 'Miss Cameron!'

Lara turned. It was the man she had been introduced to – Howard Keller. 'Yes?'

'I'd like to talk to you,' he said. 'Perhaps we could have a cup of coffee.'

Lara stiffened. *Was everyone in Chicago a sex maniac?*

'There's a good coffee shop just around the corner.'

Lara shrugged. 'All right.'

When they had ordered, Howard Keller said, 'If you don't mind my butting in, I'd like to give you some advice.'

Lara was watching him, wary. 'Go ahead.'

'In the first place, you're going about this all wrong.'

'You don't think my idea will work?' she asked stiffly.

'On the contrary. I think a boutique hotel is a really great idea.'

She was surprised. 'Then why . . . ?'

'Chicago could use a hotel like that, but I don't think you should build it.'

'What do you mean?'

'I would suggest that, instead, you find an old hotel in a good location and remodel it. There are a lot of rundown hotels that can be bought at a low figure. Your three million dollars would be enough equity for a down payment. Then you could borrow enough from a bank to refurbish it and turn it into your boutique hotel.'

Lara sat there thinking. He was right. It was a better approach.

'Another thing, no bank is going to be interested in financing you unless you come in with a solid architect and builder. They'll want to see a complete package.'

Lara thought about Buzz Steele. 'I understand. Do you know a good architect and builder?'

Howard Keller smiled. 'Quite a few.'

'Thanks for your advice,' Lara said. 'If I find the right site, could I come back and talk to you about it?'

'Any time. Good luck.'

Lara was waiting for him to say something like, 'Why don't we talk it over at my apartment?' Instead, all Howard Keller said was, 'Would you care for more coffee, Miss Cameron?'

Lara roamed the downtown streets again, but this time she was looking for something different. A few blocks from Michigan Avenue, on Delaware, Lara passed a pre-war, rundown transient hotel. A sign outside said, 'Cong essi nal Hotel.' Lara started to pass it, then suddenly stopped. She took a closer look. The brick façade was so dirty that it was difficult to tell what its original colour had been. It was eight storeys high. Lara turned and entered the hotel lobby. The interior was even worse than the exterior. A clerk dressed in jeans and a torn sweater was pushing a derelict out of the door. The front desk looked more like a ticket window than a reception area. At one end of the lobby was a staircase leading to what once were meeting rooms, now turned into rented offices. On the mezzanine, Lara could see a travel agency, a theatre ticket service, and an employment agency.

The clerk returned to the front desk. 'You wanna room?'

'No. I wanted to know . . .' She was interrupted by a heavily made-up young woman in a tight-fitting skirt. 'Give me a key, Mike.' There was an elderly man at her side.

The clerk handed her a key.

Lara watched the two of them head for the elevator.

'What can I do for you?' the clerk asked.

'I'm interested in this hotel,' Lara said. 'Is it for sale?'

'I guess everything's for sale. Is your father in the real estate business?'

'No,' Lara said, 'I am.'

He looked at her in surprise. 'Oh. Well, the one you want to talk to is one of the Diamond brothers. They own a chain of these dumps.'

'Where would I find them?' Lara asked.

The clerk gave her an address on State Street.

'Would you mind if I looked around?'

He shrugged. 'Help yourself.' He grinned. 'Who knows, you might wind up being my boss.'

Not if I can help it, Lara thought.

She walked around the lobby, examining it closely. There were old marble columns lining the entrance. On a hunch, Lara pulled up an edge of the dirty, worn carpet. Underneath was a dull marble floor. She walked up to the mezzanine. The mustard-coloured wallpaper was peeling. She pulled away an edge of it and underneath was the same marble. Lara was becoming more and more excited. The handrail of the staircase was painted black. Lara turned to make sure that the room clerk was not watching and took out her key from Stevens Hotel and scratched away some of the paint. She found what she was hoping for, a solid brass railing. She approached the elevators that were painted with the same black paint, scratched a bit away and found more brass.

Lara walked back to the clerk, trying to conceal her excitement. 'I wonder if I might look at one of the rooms.'

He shrugged. 'No skin off my nose.' He handed her a key. 'Four-ten.'

'Thank you.'

Lara got in the elevator. It was slow and antiquated. *I'll have it redone*, Lara thought. *And I'll put a mural inside*.

In her mind, she was already beginning to decorate the hotel.

Room four-ten looked a disaster, but the possibilities were immediately evident. It was a surprisingly large room with antiquated facilities and tasteless furniture. Lara's heart began to beat faster. *It's perfect*, she thought.

She walked downstairs. The stairway was old and had a musty smell. The carpets were worn, but underneath she found the same marble.

Lara returned the key to the desk clerk.

'Did you see what you wanted?'

'Yes,' Lara said. 'Thank you.'

He grinned at her. 'You really going to buy this joint?'

'Yes,' Lara said. 'I'm really going to buy this joint.'

'Cool,' he said.

The elevator door opened and the young hooker and her elderly john emerged. She handed the key and some money to the clerk. 'Thanks, Mike.'

'Have a nice day,' Mike called. He turned to Lara. 'Are you coming back?'

'Oh, yes,' Lara assured him, 'I'm coming back.'

Lara's next stop was at the City Hall of Records. She asked to see the records on the property that she was interested in. For a fee of ten dollars, she was handed a file on the Congressional Hotel. It had been sold to the Diamond brothers five years earlier for six million dollars.

The office of the Diamond brothers was in an old building on a corner in State Street. An oriental receptionist in a tight red skirt greeted Lara as she walked in.

'Can I help you?'

'I'd like to see Mr Diamond.'

'Which one?'

'Either of them.'

'I'll give you John.'

She picked up the phone and spoke into it. 'There's a lady here to see you, John.' She listened a moment then looked up at Lara. 'What's it about?'

'I want to buy one of his hotels.'

She spoke into the mouthpiece again. 'She says she wants to buy one of your hotels. Right.' She replaced the receiver. 'Go right in.'

John Diamond was a huge man, middle-aged and hairy, and he had the pushed-in face of a man who had once played a lot of football. He was wearing a short-sleeved shirt and smoking a large cigar. He looked up as Lara entered his office.

'My secretary said you wanted to buy one of my buildings.' He studied her a moment. 'You don't look old enough to vote.'

'Oh, I'm old enough to vote,' Lara assured him. 'I'm also old enough to buy one of your buildings.'

'Yeah? Which one?'

'The Cong essi nal Hotel.'

'The *what*?'

'That's what the sign says. I assume it means "Congressional".'

'Oh. Yeah.'

'Is it for sale?'

He shook his head. 'Gee, I don't know. That's one of our big money-makers. I'm not sure we could let it go.'

'You *have* let it go,' Lara said.

'Huh?'

'It's in terrible shape. The place is falling apart.'

'Yeah? Then what the hell do *you* want with it?'

'I'd like to buy it and fix it up a little. Of course, it would have to be delivered to me vacant.'

'That's no problem. Our tenants are on a week-to-week basis.'

'How many rooms does the hotel have?'

'A hundred and twenty-five. The gross building area is a hundred thousand square feet.'

Too many rooms, Lara thought. *But if I combine them to create suites, I would end up with sixty to seventy-five keys. It could work.*

It was time to discuss price.

'*If* I decided to buy the building, how much would you want for it?'

Diamond said, '*If* I decided to sell the building,

I'd want ten million dollars, a six million cash down payment . . .'

Lara shook her head, 'I'll offer . . .'

'. . . period. No negotiating.'

Lara sat there, mentally figuring the cost of renovation. It would be approximately eighty dollars per square foot, or eight million dollars, plus furniture, fixtures and equipment.

Lara's mind was furiously calculating. She was sure she could get a bank to finance the loan. The problem was that she needed six million dollars in equity, and she only had three million. Diamond was asking too much for the hotel, but she wanted it. She wanted it more than anything she had ever wanted in her life.

'I'll make you a deal,' Lara said.

He was listening. 'Yeah?'

'I'll give you your asking price . . .'

He smiled. 'So far so good.'

'And I'll give you a down payment of three million in cash.'

He shook his head. 'Can't do it. I've got to have six million in cash up front.'

'You'll have it.'

'Yeah? Where's the other three coming from?'

'From you.'

'What?'

'You're going to give me a second mortgage for three million.'

'You want to borrow money from *me* to buy my building?'

It was the same thing Sean MacAllister had asked her in Glace Bay.

'Look at it this way,' Lara said. 'You're really

borrowing the money from yourself. You'll own the building until I pay it off. There's no way you can lose.'

He thought about it and grinned. 'Lady, you just bought yourself a hotel.'

Howard Keller's office in the bank was a cubicle with his name on the door. When Lara walked in, he looked more rumpled than ever.

'Back so soon?'

'You told me to come and see you when I found a hotel. I found one.'

Keller leaned back in his chair. 'Tell me about it.'

'I found an old hotel called the Congressional. It's on Delaware. It's a few blocks from Michigan Avenue. It's rundown and seedy, and I want to buy it and turn it into the best hotel in Chicago.'

'Tell me the deal.'

Lara told him.

Keller sat there, thinking. 'Let's run it past Bob Vance.'

Bob Vance listened and made some notes. 'It might be possible,' he said, 'but . . .' He looked at Lara. 'Have you ever run a hotel before, Miss Cameron?'

Lara thought about all the years of running the boarding house in Glace Bay, making the beds, scrubbing the floors and doing the laundry and the dishes, trying to please the different personalities, and keep the peace.

'I ran a boarding house full of miners and lumbermen. A hotel will be a cinch.'

Howard Keller said, 'I'd like to take a look at the property, Bob.'

Lara's enthusiasm was irresistible. Howard Keller watched Lara's face as they walked through the seedy hotel rooms, and he saw them through her eyes.

'This will be a beautiful suite with a sauna,' Lara said excitedly. 'The fireplace will be here, and the grand piano in that corner.' She began to pace back and forth. 'When affluent travellers come to Chicago, they stay at the best hotels, but they're all the same – cold rooms without any character. If we can offer them something like this, even though it may cost a little more, there's no doubt about which they'll choose. This will *really* be a home away from home.'

'I'm impressed,' Howard Keller said.

Lara turned to him eagerly. 'Do you think the bank will loan me the money?'

'Let's find out.'

Thirty minutes later, Howard Keller was in conference with Vance.

'What do you think about it?' Vance asked.

'I think the lady's on to something. I like her idea about a boutique hotel.'

'So do I. The only problem is that she's so young and inexperienced. It's a gamble.' They spent the next half hour discussing costs and projected earnings.

'I think we should go ahead with it,' Keller finally

said. 'We can't lose.' He grinned. 'If worse comes to worst, you and I can move into the hotel.'

Howard Keller telephoned Lara at the Stevens Hotel. 'The bank has just approved your loan.'

Lara let out a shriek. 'Do you mean it? That's wonderful! Oh, thank you, thank you!'

'We have a few things to talk about,' Howard Keller said. 'Are you free for dinner this evening?'

'Yes.'

'Fine. I'll pick you up at seven thirty.'

They had dinner at the Imperial House. Lara was so excited that she barely touched her food.

'I can't tell you how thrilled I am,' she said. 'It's going to be the most beautiful hotel in Chicago.'

'Easy,' Keller warned, 'there's a long way to go.' He hesitated. 'May I be frank with you, Miss Cameron?'

'Lara.'

'Lara. You're a dark horse. You have no track record.'

'In Glace Bay . . .'

'This isn't Glace Bay. To mix metaphors, it's a different ballpark.'

'Then why is the bank doing this?' Lara asked.

'Don't get me wrong. We're not a charitable organization. The worst thing that can happen is that the bank will break even. But I have a feeling about you. I believe you're going to make it. I think there could be a big upside. You don't intend to stop with this one hotel, do you?'

'Of course not,' Lara said.

'I didn't think so. What I want to say is that when we make a loan, we don't usually get personally involved in the project. But in this case, I'd like to give you whatever help you might need.'

And Howard Keller intended to get personally involved with her. He had been attracted to Lara from the moment he had seen her. He was captivated by her enthusiasm and determination. She was a beautiful woman-child. He wanted desperately to impress her. *Maybe*, Keller thought, *one day I'll tell her how close I came to being famous . . .*

8

It was the final game of the World Series and Wrigley Field was packed with 38,710 screaming fans. 'It's the top of the ninth, with the score Cubs – 1, Yankees – 0. The Yankees are up at bat, with two outs. The bases are loaded with Tony Kubek on first, Whitey Ford on second, and Yogi Berra on third.'

As Mickey Mantle stepped up to the plate, the crowd roared. 'The Mick' had hit .304 for the season and had 42 homeruns under his belt for the year.

Jack Brickhouse, the Wrigley Field announcer said, excitedly, 'Oh, oh . . . it looks like they're going to change pitchers. They're taking out Moe Drabowsky . . . Cub Manager, Bob Scheffing is talking to the umpire . . . let's see who's coming in . . . it's Howard Keller! Keller is walking up to the pitcher's mound, and the crowd is screaming! The whole burden of the World Series rests on this youngster's shoulders. Can he strike out the great Mickey Mantle? We'll know in a moment! Keller is on the mound now . . . he looks around the loaded bases . . . takes a deep breath, and winds up. Here's the pitch . . . Mantle hauls back the bat . . . takes a swing, and misses! Strike one!'

The crowd had become hushed. Mantle moved forward a little, his face grim, his bat cocked, ready to swing. Howard Keller checked the runners. The pressure was enormous, but he seemed to be cool and composed. He turned to the catcher, looked in for the sign, and wound up for another pitch.

'There's the wind up and the pitch!' the announcer yelled. 'It's Keller's famous curve ball . . . Mantle swings on and misses! Strike Two! If young Keller can strike out "The Mick", the Chicago Cubs will win the World Series! We're watching David and Goliath, ladies and gentlemen! Young Keller has only played in the big leagues for one year, but during that time, he has made an enviable reputation for himself. Mickey Mantle is Goliath . . . can the rookie Keller beat him? Everything is riding on this next pitch.

'Keller checks the runners again . . . here's the wind up . . . and here we go! It's the curve . . . Mantle bails out as it curves right over the heart of the plate . . . Strike Three called!' The announcer was screaming now. 'Mantle is caught looking! The mighty Mick has struck out, ladies and gentlemen! Young Howard Keller struck out the great Mickey Mantle! The game is over – the World Series belongs to the Chicago Cubs! The fans are on their feet going crazy!'

On the field, Howard Keller's teammates raced up to him and picked him up on their shoulders and started to cross the . . .

'Howard, what in the world are you doing?'

'My homework, Mom.' Guiltily the fifteen-year-old Howard Keller turned off the television set. The ball game was almost over anyway.

Baseball was Howard's passion and his life. He knew that one day he would play in the Major leagues. At the age of six he was competing against kids twice his age in Stickball, and when he was twelve, he began pitching for an American Legion team. At fifteen, a scout for the Chicago Cubs was told about the young boy. 'I've never seen anything like him,' his informant said. 'The kid has an outstanding curve, and a mean slider, and a change-up you wouldn't believe!'

The scout was sceptical. Grudgingly, he said, 'All right. I'll take a look at the kid.' He went to the next American Legion game that Howard Keller played in and he became an instant convert. He sought out the young boy after the game. 'What do you want to do with your life, son?'

'Play baseball,' said Keller promptly.

'I'm glad to hear that. We're going to sign you to a contract with our minor league team.'

Howard couldn't wait to tell his parents the exciting news.

The Kellers were a close-knit, Catholic family. They went to Mass every Sunday and they saw to it that their son attended church. Howard Keller, Sr was a typewriter salesman, and he was on the road a great deal. When he was at home, he spent as much time as possible with his son. Howard was close to both his parents. His mother made it a point to attend all the ball games when her son was playing, and cheer him on. Howard got his first glove and uniform when he was six years old. He was a fanatic about baseball. He had an encyclopaedic memory for the statistics of games that were played before he was even born. He knew all the stats of the winning pitchers – the strikes, the outs, the number of saves and shut-outs. He won money betting with his schoolmates that he could name the starting pitchers in any team line-up.

'Nineteen forty-nine.'

'That's easy,' Howard said. 'Newcombe, Roe,

Hatten and Branca for the Dodgers. Reynolds, Raschi, Byrne and Lopat for the Yankees.'

'All right,' one of his teammates challenged. 'Who played the most consecutive games in major league history?' The challenger was holding the *Guinness Book of Records* in front of him.

Howard Keller didn't even pause. 'Lou Gehrig – 2,130.'

'Who had the record for the most shut-outs?'

'Walter Johnson – one hundred and thirteen.'

'Who hit the most homeruns in his career?'

'Babe Ruth – seven hundred and fourteen.'

Word of the young player's ability began to circulate, and professional scouts came to take a look at the young phenomenon who was playing on the Chicago Cubs minor league team. They were stunned. By the time Keller was seventeen, he had been approached by scouts from the St Louis Cardinals and the Baltimore Orioles and the New York Yankees.

Howard's father was proud of him. 'He takes after me,' he would boast. 'I used to play baseball when I was a youngster.'

During the summer of his senior year in high school, Howard Keller worked as a junior clerk in a bank owned by one of the sponsors of his American Legion team.

Howard was going steady with a pretty schoolmate named Betty Quinlan. It was understood that when they finished college they would get married. Howard would talk baseball by the hour with her, and because she cared for him, she listened patiently. Howard loved the anecdotes about his favourite ballplayers and every time he heard a new one, he would rush to tell it to Betty.

'Casey Stengel said, "The secret of managing is to keep the five guys who hate you away from the five who are undecided."'

'Someone asked Yogi Berra what time it was, and he said, "You mean right now?"'

And when a player was hit in the shoulder by a pitched ball, his teammate said, 'There's nothing wrong with his shoulder except some pain – and pain doesn't hurt you.'

Young Keller knew that he was soon going to join the pantheon of the great players. But the gods had other plans for him.

Howard came home from school one day with his best friend, Jesse, who played shortstop on the team. There were two letters waiting for Keller. One offered him a baseball scholarship at Princeton, and the other a baseball scholarship at Harvard.

'Gee, that's great!' Jesse said. 'Congratulations!' And he meant it. Howard Keller was his idol.

'Which one do you think you're going to take?' Howard's father asked.

'Why do I have to go to college at all?' Howard wondered. 'I could get on one of the big league teams now.'

His mother said firmly, 'There's plenty of time for that, son. You're going to get a good education first, then when you're through playing baseball, you'll be fit to do anything you like.'

'All right,' Howard said. 'Harvard. Betty is going to Wellesley and I can be near her.'

Betty Quinlan was delighted when Howard told her what he had decided.

'We'll get to see each other over the weekends!' she said.

His buddy, Jesse, said, 'I'm sure going to miss you.'

The day before Howard Keller was to leave for the university, his father ran off with the secretary of one of his customers.

The young boy was stunned. 'How could he do that?'

His mother was in shock. 'He . . . he must be going through a change of life,' she stammered. 'Your . . . your father loves me very much. He'll . . . he'll come back. You'll see . . .'

The following day, Howard's mother received a letter from an attorney, formally stating that his client, Howard Keller, Sr, wanted a divorce, and since he had no money to pay for alimony, was willing to let his wife have their small house.

Howard held his mother in his arms. 'Don't worry, Mom, I'm going to stay here and take care of you.'

'No. I don't want you to give up college for me. From the day you were born, your father and I planned for you to go to college.' Then quietly, after a moment, 'Let's talk about it in the morning. I'm very tired.'

Howard stayed up all night, thinking about his choices. He could go to Harvard on a baseball scholarship or take one of the offers in the major leagues. Either way he would be leaving his mother alone. It was a difficult decision.

When his mother didn't appear at breakfast the next morning, Howard went into her bedroom. She was sitting up in bed, unable to move, her face pulled up on one side. She had suffered a stroke.

With no money to pay for the hospital or doctors, Howard went back to work at the bank, full-time. He was finished at four o'clock, and each afternoon he hurried home to take care of his mother.

It was a mild stroke, and the doctor assured Howard that in time his mother would be fine. 'She's had a terrible shock, but she's going to recover.'

Howard still got calls from scouts from the major leagues, but he knew that he could not leave his mother. *I'll go when she's better*, he told himself.

The medical bills kept piling up.

In the beginning, he talked to Betty Quinlan once a week, but after a few months the calls became less and less frequent.

Howard's mother did not seem to be improving. Howard talked to the doctor. 'When is she going to be all right?'

'In a case like this, it's hard to tell, son. She could go on for months like this, or even years. Sorry I can't be more specific.'

The year ended and another began, and Howard was still living with his mother and working at the bank. One day he received a letter from Betty Quinlan, telling him that she had fallen in love with someone else, and that she hoped his mother was feeling better. The calls from scouts became less frequent and finally stopped altogether. Howard's life centred on taking care of his mother. He did the shopping and the cooking, and carried on with his job. He no longer thought about baseball. It was difficult enough just getting through each day.

When his mother died four years later, Howard Keller was no longer interested in baseball. He was now a banker.

His chance of fame had vanished.

9

Howard Keller and Lara were having dinner.

'How do we get started?' Lara asked.

'First of all, we're going to get you the best team money can buy. We'll start out with a real estate lawyer to work out the contract with the Diamond brothers. Then we want to get you a top architect. I have someone in mind. After that, we want to hire a top construction company. I've done a little arithmetic of my own. The soft costs for the project will come to about three hundred thousand dollars a room. The cost of the hotel will be about seven million dollars. If we plan it right, it can work.'

The architect's name was Ted Tuttle, and when he heard Lara's plans, he grinned and said, 'Bless you. I've been waiting for someone to come along with an idea like this.'

Ten working days later, he had rendered his drawings. They were everything Lara had dreamed.

'Originally, the hotel had a hundred and twenty-five rooms,' the architect said. 'As you can see, I've cut it down to seventy-five keys, as you've asked.'

In the drawing there were fifty suites and twenty-five deluxe rooms.

'It's perfect,' Lara said.

Lara showed the plans to Howard Keller. He was equally enthusiastic.

'Let's go to work. I've set up a meeting with a contractor. His name is Steve Rice.'

Steve Rice was one of the top contractors in Chicago. Lara liked him immediately. He was a rugged, no-nonsense, down-to-earth type.

Lara said, 'Howard Keller tells me that you're the best.'

'He's right,' Rice said. 'Our motto is "We build for posterity."'

'That's a good motto.'

Rice grinned. 'I just made it up.'

The first step was to break down each element into a series of drawings. The drawings were sent to potential subcontractors; steel manufacturers, bricklayers, window companies, electrical contractors. All in all, more than sixty subcontractors were involved.

The day escrow closed, Howard Keller took the afternoon off to celebrate with Lara.

'Does the bank mind your taking this time off?' Lara asked.

'No,' Keller lied. 'It's part of my job.' The truth was that he was enjoying this more than he had enjoyed anything in years. He loved being with Lara, he loved talking to her, looking at her. He wondered how she felt about marriage.

Lara said, 'I read this morning that they've almost completed the Sears Tower. It's a hundred and ten storeys – the tallest building in the world.'

'That's right,' Keller said.

Lara said gravely, 'Some day I'm going to build a higher one, Howard.'

He believed her.

They were having lunch with Steve Rice at the Whitehall. 'Tell me what happens next,' Lara asked.

'Well,' Rice said, 'first we're going to clean up the interior of the building. We'll keep the marble. We'll remove all the windows and gut the bathrooms. We'll take out the electrical risers for the installation of the new electrical wiring, and update the plumbing. When the demolition company is through, we'll be ready to begin building your hotel.'

'How many people will be working on it?'

Rice laughed. 'A mob, Miss Cameron. There'll be a window team, a bathroom team, a corridor team. These teams work floor by floor, usually from the top floor down. The hotel is scheduled to have two restaurants, and you'll have room service.'

'How long is all this going to take?'

'I would say – equipped and furnished – eighteen months.'

'I'll give you a bonus if you finish it in a year,' Lara told him.

'Great. The Congressional should . . .'

'I'm changing the name. It's going to be called the Cameron Palace.' Lara felt a thrill just saying the words. It was almost a sexual feeling. Her name was going to be on a building for all the world to see.

At six o'clock on a rainy September morning, the reconstruction of the hotel began. Lara was at the site eagerly watching as the workmen trooped into the lobby and began to tear it apart.

To Lara's surprise, Howard Keller appeared.

'You're up early,' Lara said.

'I couldn't sleep,' Keller grinned. 'I have a feeling this is the beginning of something big.'

Twelve months later, the Cameron Palace opened to rave reviews and land office business.

The architectural critic for the *Chicago Tribune* wrote, 'Chicago finally has a hotel that lives up to the motto: "Your home away from home!" Lara Cameron is someone to keep an eye on . . .'

By the end of the first month, the hotel was full and had a long waiting list.

Howard Keller was enthusiastic. 'At this rate,' he said, 'the hotel will be paid off in twelve years. That's wonderful. We . . .'

'Not good enough,' Lara said. 'I'm raising the rates.' She saw the expression on Keller's face. 'Don't worry. They'll pay it. Where else can they get two fireplaces, a sauna, and a grand piano?'

Two weeks after the Cameron Palace opened, Lara had a meeting with Bob Vance and Howard Keller.

'I found another great site for a hotel,' Lara said. 'It's going to be like the Cameron Palace, only bigger and better.'

Howard Keller grinned. 'I'll take a look at it.'

*

The site was perfect, but there was a problem.

'You're too late,' the broker told Lara. 'A developer named Steve Murchison was here this morning, and he made me an offer. He's going to buy it.'

'How much did he offer?'

'Three million.'

'I'll give you four. Draw up the papers.'

The broker only blinked once. 'Right.'

Lara received a telephone call the following afternoon.

'Lara Cameron?'

'Yes.'

'This is Steve Murchison. I'm going to let it go this time, bitch, because I don't think you know what the hell you're doing. But in the future, stay out of my way – you could get hurt.'

And the line went dead.

It was 1974 and momentous events were occurring around the world. President Nixon resigned to avoid impeachment, and Gerald Ford stepped into the White House. OPEC ended its oil embargo, and Isabel Perón became the President of Argentina. And in Chicago, Lara started construction on her second hotel, the Chicago Cameron Plaza. It was completed eighteen months later, and it was an even bigger success than the Cameron Palace. There was no stopping Lara after that. As *Forbes* magazine was to write later, 'Lara Cameron is a phenomenon. Her innovations are changing the concept of hotels. Miss Cameron has invaded the traditionally male turf of real estate developers and has proved that a woman can outshine all of them.'

Lara received a telephone call from Charles Cohn.

'Congratulations,' he said. 'I'm proud of you. I've never had a protégée before.'

'I've never had a mentor before. Without you, none of this would have happened.'

'You would have found a way,' Cohn said.

In 1975, the movie *Jaws* swept the country, and people stopped going into the ocean. The world population passed four billion, reduced by one when Teamster President James Hoffa disappeared. When Lara heard the four billion population figure, she said to Keller, 'Do you have any idea how much housing that would require?'

He was not sure whether she was joking.

Over the next three years, two apartment buildings and a condominium were completed. 'I want to put up an office building next,' Lara told Keller, 'right in the heart of the loop.'

'There's an interesting piece of property coming on the market,' Keller told her. 'If you like it, we'll finance you.'

That afternoon, they went to look at it. It was on the waterfront, in a choice location.

'What's it going to cost?' Lara asked.

'I've done the numbers. It will come to a hundred and twenty million dollars.'

Lara swallowed. 'That scares me.'

'Lara, in real estate the name of the game is to borrow.'

Other people's money, Lara thought. That's what

Bill Rogers had told her at the boarding house. All that seemed so long ago, and so much had happened since then. *And it's only the beginning*, Lara thought. *It's only the beginning*.

'Some developers put up buildings with almost no cash of their own.'

'I'm listening.'

'The idea is to rent or resell the building for enough money to pay off the debt on it, and still have money left over to buy some more property with that cash, and then borrow more money for another property. It's an inverted pyramid – a real estate pyramid – that you can build on a very small initial cash investment.'

'I understand,' Lara said.

'Of course, you have to be careful. The pyramid is built on paper – the mortgages. If anything goes wrong, if the profit from one investment fails to cover the debt on the next one, the pyramid can topple and bury you.'

'Right. How can I acquire the waterfront property?'

'We'll set up a joint venture for you. I'll talk to Vance about it. If it's too big for our bank to handle, we'll go to an insurance company or a savings and loan. You'll take out a fifty-million-dollar mortgage loan. You'll get their mortgage coupon rate – that would be five million and a ten per cent rate, plus amortization on the mortgage – and they'll be your partners. They'll take the first ten per cent of the earnings, but you'll get your property, fully financed. You can get your cash repaid and keep one hundred per cent of the depreciation, because financial institutions have no use for losses.'

Lara was listening, absorbing every word.

'Are you with me so far?'

'I'm with you.'

'In five or six years, after the building is leased, you sell it. If the property sells for seventy-five million, after you pay off the mortgage, you'll net twelve and a half million dollars. Besides that, you'll have a tax sheltered earning stream of eight million in depreciation that you can use to reduce taxes on other income. All of this for a cash investment of ten million.'

'That's fantastic!' Lara said.

Keller grinned. 'The government wants you to make money.'

'How would *you* like to make some money, Howard? Some real money?'

'I beg your pardon?'

'I want you to come to work for me.'

Keller was suddenly quiet. He knew he was facing one of the most important decisions of his life, and it had nothing to do with money. It was Lara. He had fallen in love with her. There had been one painful episode when he had tried to tell her. He had practised his marriage proposal all night, and the following morning, he had gone to her and stammered, 'Lara, I love you,' and before he could say more, she had kissed him on the cheek and said, 'I love you, too, Howard. Take a look at this new production schedule.' And he had not had the nerve to try again.

Now she was asking him to be her partner. He would be working near her every day, unable to touch her, unable to . . .

'Do you believe in me, Howard?'

'I'd be crazy not to, wouldn't I?'

'I'll pay you twice whatever you're making now, and give you five per cent of the company.'

'Can I . . . can I think about it?'

'There's really nothing to think about, is there?'

He made his decision. 'I guess not . . . partner.'

Lara gave him a hug. 'That's wonderful! You and I are going to build beautiful things. There are so many ugly buildings around. There's no excuse for them. Every building should be a tribute to this city.'

He put his hand on her arm. 'Don't ever change, Lara.'

She looked at him hard.

'I won't.'

10

The late 1970s were years of growth and change and excitement. In 1976 there was a successful Israeli raid on Entebbe, and Mao Tse-tung died, and James Earl Carter, Jr was elected President of the United States.

Lara erected another office building.

In 1977, Charlie Chaplin died, and Elvis Presley temporarily died.

Lara built the largest shopping mall in Chicago.

In 1978 Reverend Jim Jones and nine hundred and eleven followers committed mass suicide in Guyana. The United States recognized Communist China, and the Panama Canal Treaties were ratified.

Lara built a series of high-rise condominiums in Rogers Park.

In 1979, Israel and Egypt signed a peace treaty at Camp David; there was a nuclear accident at Three Mile Island, and Muslim fundamentalists seized the United States Embassy in Iran.

Lara built a skyscraper and a glamorous resort and country club in Deerfield, north of Chicago.

Lara seldom went out socially, and when she did, she usually went to a club where jazz was played. She liked Andy's, a club where the top jazz artists performed. She listened to Von Freeman, the great saxophonist, and Eric Schneider, and reed man Anthony Braxton, and Art Hodes at the piano.

Lara had no time to feel lonely. She spent every day with her family: The architects and the construction crew, the carpenters, the electricians and surveyors and plumbers. She was obsessed with the buildings she was putting up. Her stage was Chicago and she was the star.

Her professional life was proceeding beyond her wildest dreams, but she had no personal life. Her experience with Sean MacAllister had soured her on sexual relationships, and she never met anyone she was interested in seeing for more than an evening or two. In the back of Lara's mind was an elusive image, someone she had once met and wanted to meet again. But she could never seem to capture it. For a fleeting moment she would recall it, and then it was gone.

There were plenty of suitors. They ranged from business executives to oil men to poets, and even included some of her employees. Lara was pleasant to all of the men, but she never permitted any relationship to go further than a goodnight handshake at the door.

But then Lara found herself attracted to Pete Ryan, the head foreman on one of Lara's building jobs, a handsome strapping young man with an Irish brogue and a quick smile, and Lara started visiting the project Ryan was working on, more and more often. They would talk about construction problems, but underneath they were both aware that they were speaking about other things.

'Are you going to have dinner with me?' Ryan asked. The word 'dinner' was stretched out slowly.

Lara felt her heart give a little jump. 'Yes.'

Ryan picked Lara up at her apartment, but they never got to dinner. 'My God, you're a lovely thing,' he said. And his strong arms went around her.

She was ready for him. Their foreplay had been going on for months. Ryan picked her up and carried her into the bedroom. They undressed together, quickly, urgently. He had a lean, hard build, and Lara had a quick mental picture of Sean MacAllister's heavy, pudgy body. The next moment she was in bed and Ryan was on top of her, his hands and tongue all over her, and she cried aloud with the joy of what was happening to her.

When they were both spent, they lay in each other's arms. 'My God,' Ryan said softly, 'you're a bloody miracle.'

'So are you,' Lara whispered.

She could not remember when she had been so happy. Ryan was everything she wanted. He was intelligent and warm, and they understood each other, they spoke the same language.

Ryan squeezed her hand. 'I'm starved.'

'So am I. I'll make us some sandwiches.'

'Tomorrow night,' Ryan promised, 'I'll take you out for a proper dinner.'

Lara held him close. 'It's a date.'

The following morning, Lara went to visit Ryan at the building site. She could see him high up on one of the steel girders, giving orders to his men. As Lara walked toward the work elevator, one of the workmen grinned at her. 'Mornin', Miss Cameron.' There was an odd note in his voice.

Another workman passed her and grinned. 'Mornin', Miss Cameron.'

Two other workmen were leering at her. 'Morning, boss.'

Lara looked around. Other workmen were watching her, all smirking. Lara's face turned red. She stepped into the work elevator and rode up to the level where Ryan was. As she stepped out, Ryan saw her and smiled.

'Morning, sweetheart,' Ryan said. 'What time is dinner tonight?'

'You'll starve first,' Lara said fiercely. 'You're fired.'

Every building Lara put up was a challenge. She erected small office buildings with floor spaces of five thousand square feet, and large office buildings and hotels. But no matter what type of building it was, the most important thing to her was the location.

Bill Rogers had been right. *Location, location, location.*

Lara's empire kept expanding. She was beginning to get recognition from the City Fathers and from the press and the public. She was a glamorous figure, and when she went to charity events or to the opera or a museum, photographers were always eager to take her picture. She began to appear in the media more and more often. All her buildings were successes, and still she was not satisfied. It was as though she were waiting for something wonderful to happen to her, waiting for a door to open, waiting to be touched by some unknown magic.

Keller was puzzled. 'What do you want, Lara?'

'More.'
And it was all he could get out of her.

One day Lara said to Keller, 'Howard, do you know how much we're paying every month for janitors and linen service and window washers?'

'It goes with the territory,' Keller said.

'Then let's buy the territory.'

'What are you talking about?'

'We're going to start a subsidiary. We'll supply those services to ourselves and to other builders.'

The idea was a success from the beginning. The profits kept pouring in.

It seemed to Keller that Lara had built an emotional wall around herself. He was closer to her than anyone else, and yet Lara never spoke to him about her family or her background. It was as though she had emerged full blown out of the mists of nowhere. In the beginning, Keller had been Lara's mentor, teaching her and guiding her, but now Lara made all the decisions alone. The pupil had out-grown the teacher.

Lara let nothing stand in her way. She was becoming an irresistible force, and there was no stopping her. She was a perfectionist. She knew what she wanted and insisted on getting it.

At first, some of the workmen tried to take advantage of her. They had never worked for a woman before, and the idea amused them. They were in for a shock. When Lara caught one of the foremen pencil-whipping – signing off for work that had not been done – she called him in front of the crew and fired him. She was at the building site every morning. The crew would arrive at six o'clock and find Lara already there, waiting for them. There was rampant sexism. The men would wait until Lara was in earshot and exchange lewd jokes.

'Did you hear about the talking pussy at the farm? It fell in love with a cock and . . .'

'So the little girl said, "Can you get pregnant swallowing a man's seed?" And her mama said, "No. From that, darling, you get jewellery . . ."'

There were some overt gestures. Occasionally, one of the workmen passing Lara would 'accidentally' brush his arm across her breasts or press against her bottom.

'Oops, sorry.'

'No problem,' Lara said. 'Pick up your cheque and get out of here.'

Their amusement eventually began to change to respect.

One day, when Lara was driving along Kedzie Avenue with Howard Keller, she came to a block filled with small shops. She stopped the car.

'This block is being wasted,' Lara said. 'There should be a high-rise here. These little shops can't bring much of an income.'

'Yeah, but the problem is, you'd have to persuade every one of these tenants to sell out,' Keller said. 'Some of them may not want to.'

'We can buy them out,' Lara declared.

'Lara, if even one tenant refuses to sell, you could be stuck for a bundle. You'll have bought a lot of little shops you don't want and you won't be able to put up your building. And if the tenants get wind that a big high-rise is going up here, they'll hold you up.'

'We won't let them know what we're doing,' Lara said. She was beginning to get excited. 'We'll have different people approach the owners of the shops.'

'I've been through this before,' Keller warned. 'If word leaks out, they're going to gouge you for every penny they can get.'

'Then we'll have to be careful. Let's get an option on the property.'

The block on Kedzie Avenue consisted of more than a dozen small stores and shops. There was a bakery, a hardware store, a barber shop, a clothing store, a butcher, a tailor, a drug store, a stationery store, a coffee shop, and a variety of other businesses.

'Don't forget the risk,' Keller warned Lara. 'If there's one hold-out, you've lost all the money you've put in to buy those businesses.'

'Don't worry,' Lara said. 'I'll handle it.'

A week later, a stranger walked into the two-chair barber shop. The barber was reading a magazine. As the door opened, he looked up and nodded. 'Can I help you, sir? Hair cut?'

The stranger smiled. 'No,' he said. 'I just arrived in town. I had a barber shop in New Jersey, but my wife wanted to move here to be near her mother. I'm looking for a shop I can buy.'

'This is the only barber shop in the neighbourhood,' the barber said. 'It's not for sale.'

The stranger smiled. 'When you come right down

to it, everything's for sale, isn't it? At the right price, of course. What's this shop worth – about fifty, sixty thousand dollars?'

'Something like that,' the barber admitted.

'I really am anxious to have my own shop again. I'll tell you what. I'll give you seventy-five thousand dollars for this place.'

'No, I couldn't think of selling it.'

'A hundred.'

'Really, mister, I don't . . .'

'And you can take all the equipment with you.'

The barber was staring at him. 'You'll give me a hundred thousand and let me take the barber chairs and the rest of the equipment?'

'That's right. I have my own equipment.'

'Can I think about it? I'll have to talk to my wife.'

'Sure. I'll drop back tomorrow.'

Two days later, the barber shop was acquired.

'That's one down,' Lara said.

The bakery was next. It was a small family bakery owned by a husband and wife. The ovens in the back room permeated the store with the smell of fresh bread. A woman was talking to one of the owners.

'My husband died and left me his insurance money. We had a bakery in Florida. I've been looking for a place just like this. I'd like to buy it.'

'It's a comfortable living,' the owner said. 'My wife and I have never thought about selling.'

'If you *were* interested in selling, how much would you want?'

The owner shrugged. 'I don't know.'

'Would you say the bakery's worth sixty thousand dollars?'

'Oh, at least seventy-five,' the owner said.

'I'll tell you what,' the woman said. 'I'll give you a hundred thousand dollars for it.'

The owner stared at her. 'Are you serious?'

'I've never been more serious in my life.'

The next morning, Lara said, 'That's two down.'

The rest of the deals went just as smoothly. They had a dozen men and women going around impersonating tailors, bakers, pharmacists and butchers. Over the period of the next six months, Lara bought out the stores, then hired people to come in and run the different operations. The architects had already started to draw up plans for the high-rise.

Lara was studying the latest reports. 'It looks like we've done it,' she told Keller.

'I'm afraid we have a problem.'

'Why? The only one left is the coffee shop.'

'That's our problem. He's there on a five-year lease, but he won't give up the lease.'

'Offer him more money . . .'

'He says he won't give it up at any price.'

Lara was staring at him. 'Does he know about the high-rise going up?'

'No.'

'All right. I'll go talk to him. Don't worry, he'll get out. Find out who owns the building he's in.'

The following morning, Lara paid a visit to the site. Haley's Coffee Shop was at the far end of the southwest corner of the block. The shop was small, with half a dozen stools along the counter and four booths. A man Lara presumed to be the proprietor was behind the counter. He appeared to be in his late sixties.

Lara sat down at a booth.

'Morning,' the man said pleasantly. 'What can I bring you?'

'Orange juice and coffee, please.'

'Coming up.'

She watched him squeeze some fresh orange juice.

'My waitress didn't show up today. Good help's hard to get these days.' He poured the coffee and came from behind the counter. He was in a wheelchair. He had no legs. Lara watched silently as he brought the coffee and orange juice to the table.

'Thank you,' Lara said. She looked around. 'Nice place you have here.'

'Yep. I like it.'

'How long have you been here?'

'Ten years.'

'Did you ever think of retiring?'

He shook his head. 'You're the second person who asked me that this week. No, I'll never retire.'

'Maybe they didn't offer you enough money,' Lara suggested.

'It has nothing to do with money, Miss. Before I came here, I spent two years in a veterans' hospital. No friends. Not much point to life. And then someone talked me into leasing this place.' He smiled. 'It changed my whole life. All the people in the neighbourhood drop in here. They've become my friends, almost like my family. It's given me a reason for living.' He shook his head. 'No. Money has nothing to do with it. Can I bring you more coffee?'

Lara was in a meeting with Howard Keller and the architect. 'We don't even have to buy out his lease,'

Keller was saying. 'I just talked to the landlord. There's a forfeiture clause if the coffee shop doesn't gross a certain amount each month. For the last few months he's been under that gross, so we can close him out.'

Lara turned to the architect. 'I have a question for you.' She looked down at the plans spread out on the table, and pointed to the south-west corner of the drawing. 'What if we built a set-back here, eliminated this little area and let the coffee shop stay? Could the building still be put up?'

The architect studied the plan. 'I suppose so. I could slope that side of the building and counterbalance it on the other side. Of course it would look better if we didn't have to do that . . .'

'But it *could* work,' Lara pressed.

'Yes.'

Keller said, 'Lara, I told you we can force him out of there.'

Lara shook her head. 'We've bought up the rest of the block, haven't we?'

Keller nodded. 'You bet. You're the proud owner of a clothing store, a tailor shop, a stationery store, a drug store, a bakery, a . . .'

'All right,' Lara said. 'The tenants of the new highrise are going to have a coffee shop to drop in on. And so do we. Haley stays.'

On her father's birthday, Lara said to Keller, 'Howard, I want you to do me a favour.'

'Sure.'

'I want you to go to Scotland for me.'

'Are we going to build something in Scotland?'

'We're going to buy a castle.'

He stood there, listening.

'There's a place in the Highlands called Loch Morlich. It's on the road to Glenmore near Aviemore. There are castles all around there. Buy one.'

'Kind of a summer home?'

'I don't plan to live in it. I want to bury my father in the grounds.'

Keller said, slowly, 'You want me to buy a castle in Scotland to bury your father in?'

'That's right. I haven't time to go over myself. You're the only one I can trust to do it. My father is in the Greenwood Cemetery at Glace Bay.'

It was the first real insight Keller ever had into Lara's feelings about her family.

'You must have loved your father very much.'

'Will you do it for me?'

'Certainly.'

'After he's buried, arrange for a caretaker to tend the grave.'

Three weeks later, Keller returned from Scotland and said, 'It's all taken care of. You own a castle. Your father's resting in the grounds. It's a beautiful place in the hills and with a small lochan close by. You'll love it. When are you going over?'

Lara looked up in surprise. 'Me? I'm not,' she said.

Book Two

11

In 1984, Lara Cameron decided that the time had come to conquer New York. When she told Keller her plan, he was appalled.

'I don't like the idea,' he said flatly. 'You don't know New York. Neither do I. It's a different city, Lara. We . . .'

'That's what they told me when I came from Glace Bay to Chicago,' Lara pointed out. 'Buildings are the same whether you put them up in Glace Bay, Chicago, New York or Tokyo. We all play by the same rules.'

'But you're doing so great here,' Keller protested. 'What is it you want?'

'I told you. *More*. I want my name up on the New York skyline. I'm going to build a Cameron Plaza there, and a Cameron Center. And one day, Howard, I'm going to build the tallest skyscraper in the world. *That's* what I want. Cameron Enterprises is moving to New York.'

New York was in the middle of a building boom, and it was peopled by real estate giants – the Zeckendorfs, Harry Helmsley, Donald Trump, the Urises and the Rudins.

'We're going to join the club,' Lara told Keller.

They checked into the Regency and began to explore the city. Lara could not get over the size and dynamics of the bustling metropolis. It was a canyon of skyscrapers, with rivers of cars running through it.

'It makes Chicago look like Glace Bay!' Lara said. She could not wait to get started.

'The first thing we're going to do is assemble a team. We'll find the best real estate lawyer in New York. Then a great management team. Find out who Rudin uses. See if you can lure them away.'

'Right.'

Lara said, 'Here's a list of buildings I like the look of. Find out who the architects are. I want to meet with them.'

Keller was beginning to feel Lara's excitement. 'I'll open up a line of credit with the banks. With the assets we have in Chicago, that won't be any problem. I'll make contacts with some savings and loan companies, and some real estate brokers.'

'Fine.'

'Lara, before we start to get involved in all this, don't you think you should decide what your next project is going to be?'

Lara looked up and asked innocently, 'Didn't I tell you? We're going to buy Manhattan Central Hospital.'

Several days earlier, Lara had gone to a hairdresser on Madison Avenue. While she was having her hair done, she had overheard a conversation in the next booth.

'. . . We're going to miss you, Mrs Walker.'

'Same here, Darlene. How long have I been coming here?'

'Almost fifteen years.'

'Time certainly flies, doesn't it? I'm going to miss New York.'

'When will you be leaving?'

'Right away. We just got the closing notice this morning. Imagine – a hospital like Manhattan Central closing down because they've run out of cash. I've been supervisor there for almost twenty years, and they send me a memo telling me I'm through! You'd think they'd have the decency to do it in person, wouldn't you? What's the world coming to?'

Lara was now listening intently.

'I haven't seen anything about the closing in the papers.'

'No. They're keeping it quiet. They want to break the news to the employees first.'

Her beautician was in the middle of blow drying Lara's hair. Lara started to get up.

'I'm not through yet, Miss Cameron.'

'Never mind,' Lara said, 'I'm in a hurry.'

Manhattan Central Hospital was a dilapidated, ugly-looking building located on the East Side between 68th and 69th Streets, and it took up an entire block. Lara stared at it for a long time, and what she was seeing in her mind was a majestic new skyscraper with chic retail stores on the ground floor and luxury condominiums on the upper floors.

Lara walked into the hospital and asked the name

of the corporation that owned it. She was sent to the offices of a Roger Burnham on Wall Street.

'What can I do for you, Miss Cameron?'

'I hear that Manhattan Central Hospital is for sale.'

He looked at her in surprise. 'Where did you hear that?'

'Is it true?'

He hedged. 'It might be.'

'I might be interested in buying it,' Lara said. 'What's your price?'

'Look, lady . . . I don't know you from Adam. You can't walk in off the street and expect me to discuss a ninety-million-dollar deal with you. I . . .'

'Ninety million?' Lara had a feeling it was high, but she wanted that site. It would be an exciting beginning. 'Is that what we're talking about?'

'We're not talking about anything.'

Lara handed Roger Burnham a hundred-dollar bill.

'What's this for?'

'That's for a forty-eight hour option. All I'm asking is forty-eight hours. You weren't ready to announce that it was for sale, anyway. What can you lose? If I meet your asking price, you've got what you wanted.'

'I don't know anything about you.'

'Call the Mercantile Bank in Chicago. Ask for Bob Vance. He's the president.'

He stared at her for a long moment, shook his head and muttered something with the word 'crazies' in it.

He looked up the telephone number himself. Lara sat there while his secretary got Bob Vance for him.

'Mr Vance? This is Roger Burnham in New York. I have a Miss . . .' He looked up at her.

'Lara Cameron.'

'Lara Cameron here. She's interested in buying a property of ours here, and she says that you know her.'

He sat there listening.

'She is . . . ? I see . . . Really . . . ? No, I wasn't aware of that . . . Right . . . Right.' After a long time, he said, 'Thank you very much.'

He replaced the receiver and stared at Lara. 'You seem to have made quite an impression in Chicago.'

'I intend to make quite an impression in New York.'

Burnham looked at the hundred dollar bill. 'What am I supposed to do with this?'

'Buy yourself some Cuban cigars. Do I have the option if I meet your price?'

He sat there, studying her. 'It's a little unorthodox . . . but, yes. I'll give you forty-eight hours.'

'We have to move fast on this,' Lara had told Keller. 'We have forty-eight hours to line up our financing.'

'Do you have any figures on it?'

'Ballpark. Ninety million for the property, and I estimate another two hundred million to demolish the hospital and put up the building.'

Keller was staring at her. 'That's two hundred and ninety million dollars.'

'You were always quick with figures,' Lara said.

He ignored it. 'Lara, where's that kind of money coming from?'

'We'll borrow it,' Lara said. 'Between my collateral in Chicago and the new property, it shouldn't be any problem.'

'It's a big risk. A hundred things could go wrong. You'll be gambling everything you have on . . .'

'That's what makes it exciting,' Lara said, 'the gamble. And winning.'

Getting finance for a building in New York was even simpler than in Chicago. Mayor Koch had instituted a tax programme called the 421-A, and under it, a developer replacing a functionally obsolete building could claim tax exemptions, with the first two years tax free.

When the banks and savings and loan companies checked on Lara Cameron's credit, they were more than eager to do business with her.

Before forty-eight hours had passed, Lara walked into Burnham's office and handed him a cheque for three million dollars.

'This is a down payment on the deal,' Lara said. 'I'm meeting your asking price. By the way, you can keep the hundred dollars.'

During the next six months, Keller worked with banks on financing, and Lara worked with architects on planning.

Everything was proceeding smoothly. The architects and builders and marketing people were on schedule. Work was to begin on the demolition of the hospital and the construction of the new building in April.

Lara was restless. At six o'clock every morning, she was at the construction site watching the new building going up. She felt frustrated because at this stage the building belonged to the workmen. There was nothing for her to do. She was used to more action. She liked to have a half a dozen projects going at once.

'Why don't we look around for another deal?' Lara asked Keller.

'Because you're up to your ears in this one. If you even breathe hard this whole thing is going to collapse. Do you know you've leveraged every penny you have to put this building up? If anything goes wrong . . .'

'Nothing is going to go wrong.' She was watching his expression. 'What's bothering you?'

'The deal you made with the savings and loan company . . .'

'What about it? We got our financing, didn't we?'

'I don't like the completion date clause. If the building's not finished by March 15th, they'll take it over, and you stand to lose everything you have.'

Lara thought of the building she had put up in Glace Bay, and how her friends had pitched in and finished it for her. But this was different.

'Don't worry,' she told Keller. 'The building will be finished. Are you sure we can't look around for another project?'

Lara was talking to the marketing people.

'The downstairs retail stores are already signed

up,' the marketing manager told Lara. 'And more than half the condominiums have been taken. We estimate we'll have sold three-fourths of them before the building is finished, and the rest of them shortly after.'

'I want them *all* sold before the building is completed,' Lara said. 'Step up the advertising.'

'Very well.'

Keller came into the office. 'I have to hand it to you, Lara. You were right. The building's on schedule.'

'This is going to be a money machine.'

On January 15th, sixty days before the date of completion, the huge girders and walls were finished, and the workers were already installing the electrical wiring and plumbing lines.

Lara stood there watching the men working on the girders high above. One of the workmen stopped to pull out a pack of cigarettes, and as he did so, a wrench slipped from his hand and fell to the ground far below. Lara watched in disbelief as the wrench came hurtling down toward her. She leaped out of the way, her heart pounding. The workman was looking down. He waved a 'sorry'.

Grim-faced, Lara got into the construction elevator and took it to the level where the workman was. Ignoring the dizzying empty space below, she walked across the scaffolding to the man.

'Did you drop that wrench?'

'Yeah, sorry.'

She slapped him hard across the face. 'You're fired. Now get off my building.'

'Hey,' he said, 'it was an accident. I . . .'

'Get out of here.'

The man glared at her for a moment then walked away and took the elevator down.

Lara took a deep breath to control herself. The other workers were watching her.

'Get back to work,' she ordered.

Lara was having lunch with Sam Gosden, the New York attorney who handled her contracts for her.

'I hear everything's going very well,' Gosden said.

Lara smiled. 'Better than very well. We're only a few weeks away from completion.'

'Can I make an admission?'

'Yes, but be careful not to incriminate yourself.'

He laughed. 'I was betting that you couldn't do it.'

'Really? Why?'

'Real estate development on the level where you're operating is a man's game. The only women who should be in real estate are the little old blue-haired ladies who sell co-ops.'

'So you were betting against me,' Lara said.

Sam Gosden smiled. 'Yeah.'

Lara leaned forward. 'Sam . . .'

'Yes?'

'No one on my team bets against me. You're fired.'

He sat there open-mouthed as Lara got up and walked out of the restaurant.

On the following Monday morning, as Lara drove toward the building site, she sensed that something was wrong. And suddenly she realized what it was. It was the silence. There were no sounds of hammers or drills. When Lara arrived at the construction site, she stared in disbelief. The workmen were collecting their equipment and leaving. The foreman was packing up his things. Lara hurried up to him.

'What's going on?' Lara demanded. 'It's only seven o'clock.'

'I'm pulling the men.'

'What are you talking about?'

'There's been a complaint, Miss Cameron.'

'What kind of complaint?'

'Did you slap one of the workmen?'

'What?' She had forgotten. 'Yes. He deserved it. I fired him.'

'Did the City give you a licence to go around slapping the people who work for you?'

'Wait a minute,' Lara said. 'It wasn't like that. He dropped a wrench. It almost killed me. I suppose I lost my temper. I'm sorry, but I don't want him back here.'

'He won't be coming back here,' the foreman said. 'None of us will.'

Lara stared at him. 'Is this some kind of joke?'

'My union doesn't think it's a joke,' the foreman told her. 'They gave us orders to walk. We're walking.'

'You have a contract.'

'You broke it,' the foreman told her. 'If you have any complaints, take it up with the union.'

He started to walk away.

'Wait a minute. I said I'm sorry. I'll tell you what. I . . . I'm willing to apologize to the man, and he can have his job back.'

'Miss Cameron, I don't think you get the picture. He doesn't want his job back. We've all got other jobs waiting for us. This is a busy city. And I'll tell you something else, lady. We're too goddamn busy to let our bosses slap us around.'

Lara stood there watching him walk away. It was her worst nightmare.

Lara hurried back to the office to tell the news to Keller.

Before she could speak, he said, 'I heard. I've been on the phone talking to the union.'

'What did they say?' Lara asked eagerly.

'They're going to hold a hearing next month.'

Lara's face filled with dismay. 'Next month! We've less than two months left to finish the building.'

'I told them that.'

'And what did they say?'

'That it's not their problem.'

Lara sank onto the couch. 'Oh, my God. What are we going to do?'

'I don't know.'

'Maybe we could persuade the bank to . . .' She saw the look on his face. 'I guess not.' Lara suddenly brightened. 'I know. We'll hire another construction crew and . . .'

'Lara, there isn't a union worker who will touch that building.'

'I should have killed that bastard.'

'Right. That would have helped a lot,' Keller said dryly.

Lara got up and began pacing. 'I could ask Sam Gosden to . . .' she suddenly remembered. 'No, I fired him.'

'Why?'

'Never mind.'

Keller was thinking aloud. 'Maybe if we got hold of a good labour lawyer . . . someone with clout.'

'That's a good idea. Someone who can move fast. Do you know anybody?'

'No. But Sam Gosden mentioned someone in one of our meetings. A man named Martin. Paul Martin.'

'Who is he?'

'I'm not sure, but we were talking about union problems and his name came up.'

'Do you know what firm he's with?'

'No.'

Lara buzzed her secretary. 'Kathy, there's a lawyer in Manhattan named Paul Martin. Get me his address.'

Keller said, 'Don't you want his phone number so you can make an appointment?'

'There's no time. I can't afford to sit around waiting for an appointment. I'm going to see him today. If he can help us, fine. If he can't, we'll have to come up with something else.'

But Lara was thinking to herself, *There is nothing else.*

12

Paul Martin's office was on the twenty-fifth floor in an office building on Wall Street. The frosted sign on the door read, 'Paul Martin, Attorney at Law.'

Lara took a deep breath and stepped inside. The reception office was smaller than she had expected. It contained one scarred desk with a bottle-blonde secretary behind it.

'Good morning. Can I help you?'

'I'm here to see Mr Martin,' Lara said.

'Is he expecting you?'

'Yes, he is.' There was no time for explanations.

'And your name?'

'Cameron. Lara Cameron.'

The secretary looked at her quizzically. 'Just a moment. I'll see whether Mr Martin can see you.'

The secretary got up from behind the desk and disappeared into the inner office.

He's got to see me, Lara thought.

A moment later, the secretary emerged. 'Yes, Mr Martin will see you.'

Lara concealed a sigh of relief. 'Thank you.'

She walked into the inner office. It was small and simply furnished. A desk, two couches, a coffee table and a few chairs. *Not exactly a citadel of power*, Lara thought. The man behind the desk appeared to be in his early sixties. He had a deeply-lined face, a hawk nose, and a mane of white hair. There was a feral, animal-like vitality about him. He was wearing an old-fashioned pin-stripe double-breasted grey suit and a white shirt with a narrow collar. When he spoke, his voice was raspy, low, somehow compelling.

'My secretary said that I was expecting you.'

'I'm sorry,' Lara said. 'I had to see you. It's an emergency.'

'Sit down, Miss . . .'

'Cameron. Lara Cameron.' She took a chair.

'What can I do for you?'

Lara took a deep breath. 'I have a little problem.' *A skeleton twenty-four storeys of uncompleted steel and concrete standing idle.* 'It's about a building.'

'What about it?'

'I'm a real estate developer, Mr Martin. I'm in the middle of putting up an office building on the East Side, and I'm having a problem with the union.'

He was listening, saying nothing.

Lara hurried on. 'I lost my temper and slapped one of the workmen, and the union called a strike.'

He was studying her, puzzled. 'Miss Cameron . . . what does all this have to do with me?'

'I heard you might be able to help me.'

'I'm afraid you heard wrong. I'm a corporate attorney. I'm not involved with buildings and I don't deal with unions.'

Lara's heart sank. 'Oh, I thought . . . isn't there anything you can do?'

He placed the palms of his hands on the desk, as though he were about to rise. 'I can give you a couple of pieces of advice. Get hold of a labour lawyer. Have him take the union to court and . . .'

'There's no time. I'm up against a deadline. I . . . what's the second piece of advice?'

'Get out of the building business.' His eyes were fixed on her breasts. 'You don't have the right equipment for it.'

'*What?*'

'It's no place for a woman.'

'And what *is* the place for a woman?' Lara asked angrily. 'Barefoot, pregnant and in the kitchen?'

'Something like that. Yeah.'

Lara rose to her feet. It was all she could do to control herself. 'You must come from a long line of dinosaurs. Maybe you haven't heard the news. Women are free now.'

Paul Martin shook his head. 'No. Just noisier.'

'Goodbye, Mr Martin. I'm sorry I took up your valuable time.'

Lara turned and strode out of the office, slamming the door behind her. She stopped in the corridor, and took a deep breath. *This was a mistake*, she thought. She had finally reached a dead end. She had risked everything it had taken her years to build up, and she had lost it in one swift instant. There was no one to turn to. Nowhere to go.

It was over.

Lara walked the cold, rainy streets. She was completely unaware of the icy wind and her surroundings. Her mind was filled with the terrible disaster that had befallen her. Howard Keller's warning was ringing in her ears. *You put up buildings and borrow on them. It's like a pyramid, only if you're not careful, that pyramid can fall down.* And it had. The banks in Chicago would foreclose on her properties there, and she would lose all the money she had invested in the new building. She would have to start all over, from the beginning. *Poor Howard,* she thought. *He believed in my dreams and I've let him down.*

The rain had stopped and the sky was beginning to clear. A pale sun was fighting its way through the clouds. She suddenly realized it was dawn. She had walked all night. Lara looked around and saw where she was for the first time. She was only two blocks from the doomed property. *I'll take a last look at it,* Lara thought, resignedly.

She was a full block away when she first heard it. It was the sound of pneumatic drills and hammers, and the roar of cement mixers filling the air. Lara stood there, listening for an instant, then started running toward the building site. When she reached it, she stood there, staring, unbelievingly.

The full crew was there, hard at work.

The foreman came up to her, smiling. 'Morning, Miss Cameron.'

Lara finally found her voice. 'What . . . What's happening? I . . . I thought you were pulling your men off the job.'

He said sheepishly. 'That was a little misunderstanding, Miss Cameron. Bruno could have killed you when he dropped that wrench.'

Lara swallowed. 'But he . . .'

'Don't worry. He's gone. Nothing like that will

happen again. You don't have a thing to worry about. We're right back on schedule.'

Lara felt as though she were in a dream. She stood there watching the men swarming over the skeleton of the building and she thought, *I got it all back again. Everything. Paul Martin.*

Lara telephoned him as soon as she returned to her office. His secretary said, 'I'm sorry, Mr Martin is not available.'

'Would you ask him to call me, please?' Lara left her number.

At three o'clock in the afternoon, she still had not heard from him. She called him again.

'I'm sorry. Mr Martin is not available.'

He did not return her call.

At five o'clock, Lara went to Paul Martin's office.

She said to the blonde secretary, 'Would you please tell Mr Martin that Lara Cameron is here to see him.'

The secretary looked uncertain. 'Well, I'll . . . Just a moment.' She disappeared into the inner office and returned a minute later. 'Go right in, please.'

Paul Martin looked up as Lara walked in.

'Yes, Miss Cameron?' His voice was cool, neither friendly nor unfriendly. 'What can I do for you?'

'I came to thank you.'

'Thank me for what?'

'For . . . for straightening things out with the union.'

He frowned. 'I don't know what you're talking about.'

'All the workmen came back this morning, and

everything's wonderful. The building is back on schedule.'

'Well, congratulations.'

'If you'll send me a bill for your fee . . .'

'Miss Cameron, I think you're a little confused. If your problem is solved, I'm glad. But I had nothing to do with it.'

Lara looked at him for a long time. 'All right. I'm . . . I'm sorry I bothered you.'

'No probiem.' He watched her leave the office.

A moment later his secretary came in. 'Miss Cameron left a package for you, Mr Martin.'

It was a small package, tied with bright ribbon. Curious, he opened it. Inside was a silver knight in full armour, ready to do battle. An apology. *What did she call me? A dinosaur.* He could still hear his grandfather's voice. *Those were dangerous times, Paul. The young men decided to take control of the mafia, to get rid of the old-timers, the moustache Petes, the dinosaurs. It was bloody, but they did it.*

But all that was a long, long time ago, in the old country. Sicily.

13

Gibellina, Sicily, 1879

The Martinis were *stranieri* – outsiders, in the little Sicilian village of Gibellina. The countryside was desolate, a barren land of death, bathed in blazing, pitiless sunlight, a landscape painted by a sadistic artist. In a land where the large estates belonged to the *gabelloti*, the wealthy landowners, the Martinis had bought a small farm and tried to run it themselves.

The *soprintendente* had come calling on Giuseppe Martini one day.

'This little farm of yours,' he said, 'the land is too rocky. You will not be able to make a decent living on it, growing olives and grapes.'

'Don't worry about me,' Martini said. 'I've been farming all my life.'

'We're all worried about you,' the *soprintendente* insisted. 'Don Vito has some good farmland that he is willing to lease to you.'

'I know about Don Vito and his land,' Giuseppe Martini snorted. 'If I sign a *mezzadria* with him to farm his land, he will take three-fourths of my crops and charge me a hundred per cent interest on the seed. I will end up with nothing, like the other fools who deal with him. Tell him I said "no, thank you."'

'You are making a big mistake, *signore*. This is dangerous country. Serious accidents can happen here.'

'Are you threatening me?'

'Certainly not, *signore*. I was merely pointing out . . .'

'Get off my land,' Giuseppe Martini said.

The overseer looked at him for a long time then shook his head sadly. 'You are a stubborn man.'

Giuseppe Martini's young son Ivo said, 'Who was that, Papa?'

'He's the overseer for one of the large landowners.'

'I don't like him,' the young boy said.

'I don't like him either, Ivo.'

The following night, Giuseppe Martini's crops were set on fire and the few cattle he had disappeared.

That was when Giuseppe Martini made his second mistake. He went to the Guardia in the village.

'I demand protection,' he said.

The chief of police studied him noncommittally. 'That's what we are here for,' he said. 'What is your problem, *signore*?'

'Last night Don Vito's men burned my crops and stole my cattle.'

'That is a serious charge. Can you prove it?'

'His *soprintendente* came to me and threatened me.'

'Did he tell you they were going to burn your crops and steal your cattle?'

'Of course not,' Giuseppe Martini said.

'What *did* he say to you?'

'He said that I should give up my farm and lease land from Don Vito.'

'And you refused?'

'Naturally.'

'*Signore*, Don Vito is a very important man. Do you wish me to arrest him simply because he offered to share his rich farmland with you?'

'I want you to protect me,' Giuseppe Martini demanded. 'I'm not going to let them drive me off my land.'

'*Signore*, I am most sympathetic. I will certainly see what I can do.'

'I would appreciate that.'

'Consider it done.'

The following afternoon, as young Ivo was returning from town, he saw half a dozen men ride up to his father's farm. They dismounted and went into the house.

A few minutes later, Ivo saw his father dragged out to the field.

One of the men took out a gun. 'We are going to give you a chance to escape. Run for it.'

'No! This is my land! I . . .'

Ivo watched, terrified, as the man shot at the ground near his father's feet.

'Run!'

Giuseppe Martini started to run.

The *campagni* got on their horses and began circling Martini, yelling all the while.

Ivo hid, watching in horror at the terrible scene that was unfolding before his eyes.

*

The mounted men watched the farmer run across the field, trying to escape. Each time he reached the edge of the dirt road, one of them raced to cut him off and knock him to the ground. The man was bleeding and exhausted. He was slowing down.

The *campagni* decided they had had enough sport. One of them put a rope around the man's neck and dragged him toward the well.

'Why?' he gasped. 'What have I done?'

'You went to the Guardia. You should not have done that.'

They pulled down the victim's trousers and one of the men took out a knife, while the others held him down.

'Let this be a lesson to you.'

The man screamed, 'No, please! I'm sorry.'

The *campagni* smiled. 'Tell that to your wife.'

He reached down, grabbed the man's member, and slashed through it with the knife.

His screams filled the air.

'You won't need this any more,' the captain assured him.

He took the member and stuffed it in the man's mouth. He gagged and spat it out.

The captain looked at the other *campagni*. 'He doesn't like the taste of it.'

'*Uccidi quel figlio di puttana!*'

One of the *campagni* dismounted from his horse and picked up some heavy stones from the field. He pulled up the victim's bloodied trousers and filled his pockets with the stones.

'Up you go.' They lifted the man and carried him to the top of the well. 'Have a nice trip.'

They dumped him in the well.

'That water's going to taste like piss,' one of them said.

Another one laughed, 'The villagers won't know the difference.'

They stayed for a moment, listening to the diminishing sounds and finally the silence, then mounted their horses and rode toward the house.

Ivo Martini stayed in the distance, watching in horror, hidden by the brush. The ten-year-old boy hurried to the well.

He looked down and whispered, 'Papa . . .'

But the well was deep, and he heard nothing.

When the *campagni* had finished with Giuseppe Martini, they went to find his wife Maria. She was in the kitchen when they entered.

'Where's my husband?' she demanded.

A grin. 'Getting a drink of water.'

Two of the men were closing in on her. One of them said, 'You're too pretty to be married to an ugly man like that.'

'Get out of my house,' Maria ordered.

'Is that a way to treat guests?' One of the men reached out and tore her dress. 'You're going to be wearing widow's clothes, so you won't need that any more.'

'Animal!'

There was a boiling pot of water on the stove. Maria reached for it and threw it in the man's face.

He screamed in pain. '*Fica*!' He pulled out his gun and fired at her.

She was dead before she hit the floor.

The captain shouted, '*Idiot! First* you fuck them, *then* you shoot them. Come on, let's report back to Don Vito.'

Half an hour later, they were back at Don Vito's *azienda*.

'We took good care of the husband and wife,' the captain reported.

'What about the son?'

The captain looked at Don Vito in surprise. 'You didn't say anything about a son.'

'*Cretino!* I said to take care of the family.'

'But he's only a boy, Don Vito.'

'Boys grow up to be men. Men want their vengeance. Kill him.'

'As you say.'

Two of the men rode back to the Martini farm.

Ivo was in a state of shock. He had watched both his parents murdered. He was alone in the world with no place to go and no one to turn to. *Wait!* There *was* one person to turn to: His father's brother, Nuncio Martini, in Palermo. Ivo knew that he had to move quickly. Don Vito's men would be coming back to kill him. He wondered why they had not done so already. The young boy threw some food into a knapsack, slung it over his shoulder and hurriedly left the farm.

Ivo made his way to the little dirt road that led away from the village, and started walking. Whenever he heard a cart coming, he moved off the road and hid in the trees.

An hour after he had started his journey, he saw

a group of *campagni* riding along the road searching for him. Ivo stayed hidden, motionless until long after they were gone. Then he began walking again. At night, he slept in the orchards and he lived off the fruit from the trees and the vegetables in the fields. He walked for three days.

When he felt he was safe from Don Vito, he approached a small village, where there was a market. An hour later, he was in the back of a farm cart headed for Palermo.

Ivo reached the house of his uncle in the middle of the night. Nuncio Martini lived in a large, prosperous-looking house on the outskirts of the city. It had a spacious balcony, terraces, and a courtyard. Ivo pounded on the front door. There was a long silence, and then a deep voice called out, 'Who the hell is it?'

'It's Ivo, Uncle Nuncio.'

Moments later, Nuncio Martini opened the door. Ivo's uncle was a large, middle-aged man with a generous Roman nose and flowing white hair. He was wearing a nightshirt. He looked at the boy in surprise. 'Ivo! What are you doing here in the middle of the night? Where are your mother and father?'

'They're dead,' Ivo sobbed.

'Dead? Come in, come in.'

Ivo stumbled into the house.

'That's terrible news. Was there some kind of an accident?'

Ivo shook his head. 'Don Vito had them murdered.'

'Murdered? But why?'

'My father refused to lease land from him.'

'Ah.'

'Why would he have them killed? They never did anything to him.'

'It was nothing personal,' Nuncio Martini said.

Ivo stared at him. '*Nothing personal?* I don't understand.'

'Everyone knows of Don Vito. He has a reputation. He is an *uomo rispettato* – a man of respect and power. If he let your father defy him, then others would try to defy him and he would lose his power. There is nothing that can be done.'

The boy was watching him, aghast. 'Nothing?'

'Not now, Ivo. Not now. Meanwhile, you look as though you could use a good night's sleep.'

In the morning, at breakfast, they talked.

'How would you like to live in this fine house and work for me?' Nuncio Martini was a widower.

'I think I would like that,' Ivo said.

'I can use a smart boy like you. And you look strong.'

'I am strong,' Ivo told him.

'Good.'

'What business are you in, Uncle?' Ivo asked.

Nuncio Martini smiled. 'I protect people.'

The Mafia, originally known as 'The Black Hand', had sprung up throughout Sicily and other poverty-stricken parts of Italy to protect the people from a ruthless, autocratic government. The Mafia corrected injustices and avenged wrongs, and finally became so powerful that the government itself feared it, and merchants and farmers paid tribute to it.

Legend had it that the word Mafia was coined after an incident where a young girl was raped and murdered, and her anguished mother ran into the night screaming for her daughter, '*Ma fia! Ma fia!*'

Nuncio Martini was the Mafia *capo* in Palermo. He saw to it that proper tribute was collected and that those who did not pay were punished. Punishment could range from a broken arm or leg to a slow and painful death.

Ivo went to work for his uncle.

For the next fifteen years, Palermo was Ivo's school, and his Uncle Nuncio was his teacher. Ivo started out as an errand boy, then moved up to collector, and finally became his uncle's trusted lieutenant.

When Ivo was twenty-five years old, he married Carmela, a buxom Sicilian girl, and a year later, they had a son, Gian Carlo. Ivo moved his family into their own house. When his uncle died, Ivo took his position and became even more successful and prosperous. But he had some unfinished business to attend to.

One day, he said to Carmela, 'Start packing, We're moving to America.'

She looked at him in surprise. 'Why are we going to America?'

Ivo was not accustomed to being questioned. 'Just do as I say. I'm leaving now. I'll be back in two or three days.'

'Ivo . . .'

'Pack.'

*

Three black carriages pulled up in front of the Guardia headquarters in Gibellina. The captain, now heavier by thirty pounds, was seated at his desk when the door opened and half a dozen men walked in. They were well dressed and prosperous looking.

'Good morning, gentlemen. Can I help you?'

'We have come to help *you*,' Ivo said. 'Do you remember me? I'm the son of Giuseppe Martini.'

The police captain's eyes widened. '*You*,' he said. 'What are you doing here? It is dangerous for you.'

'I came because of your teeth.'

'My teeth?'

'Yes.' Two of Ivo's men closed in on the captain and pinned his arms to his side. 'You need dental work. Let me fix them.'

Ivo shoved the gun into the chief's mouth and pulled the trigger.

Ivo turned to his companions. 'Let's go.'

Fifteen minutes later, the three carriages drove up to Don Vito's house. There were two guards outside. They watched the procession curiously. When the cars came to a stop, Ivo got out.

'Good morning. Don Vito's expecting us,' he said.

One of the guards frowned. 'He didn't say anything about . . .'

In the next instant, the guards were gunned down. The guns were loaded with *lupare*, cartridges with large leaden balls, a hunter's trick to spread the pellets. The guards were cut to pieces.

Inside the house, Don Vito heard the shooting. When he looked out of the window and saw what was happening, he quickly crossed to a drawer and pulled out a gun. 'Franco!' he called, 'Antonio! Quickly!'

There were more sounds of shots from outside.

A voice said, 'Don Vito . . .'

He spun around.

Ivo stood there, a gun in his hand. 'Drop your gun.'

'I . . .'

'Drop it.'

Don Vito let his gun fall to the floor. 'Take whatever you want and get out.'

'I don't want anything,' Ivo said. 'As a matter of fact, I came here because I owe you something.'

Don Vito said, 'Whatever it is, I'm prepared to forget it.'

'I'm not. Do you know who I am?'

'No.'

'Ivo Martini.'

The old man frowned, trying to remember. He shrugged. 'It means nothing to me.'

'More than fifteen years ago. Your men killed my mother and father.'

'That's terrible,' Don Vito exclaimed. 'I will have them punished, I'll . . .'

Ivo reached out and smashed him across his nose with his gun. Blood started pouring out. 'This isn't necessary,' Don Vito gasped. 'I . . .'

Ivo pulled out a knife. 'Take down your trousers.'

'Why? You can't . . .'

Ivo raised the gun. 'Take down your trousers.'

'No!' It was a scream. 'Think about what you're doing. I have sons and brothers. If you harm me, they will track you down and kill you like a dog.'

'If they can find me,' Ivo said. 'Your trousers.'

'No.'

Ivo shot one of his kneecaps. The old man screamed out in pain.

'Let me help you,' Ivo said. He reached out and pulled the old man's trousers down, and then his underwear. 'There's not much there, is there? Well, we'll have to do the best we can.' He grabbed Don Vito's member and slashed it off with a knife.

Don Vito fainted.

Ivo took the penis and shoved it into the man's mouth. 'Sorry I don't have a well to drop you into,' Ivo said. As a parting gesture, he shot the old man in the head then turned and walked out of the house to the car.

His friends were waiting for him.

'Let's go.'

'He has a large family, Ivo. They'll come after you.'

'Let them.'

Two days later, Ivo, his wife and son Gian Carlo were on a boat to New York.

At the end of the last century, the new world was a land of opportunity. New York had a large population of Italians. Many of Ivo's friends had already emigrated to the big city and decided to use their expertise in what they knew best: The protection racket. The Mafia began spreading its tentacles. Ivo anglicized his family name from Martini to Martin, and enjoyed uninterrupted prosperity.

Gian Carlo was a big disappointment to his father. He had no interest in working. When he was twenty-seven, he got an Italian girl pregnant, married her in a quiet and hurried ceremony, and three months later they had a son, Paul.

Ivo had big plans for his grandson. Lawyers were very important in America, and Ivo decided that his grandson should be an attorney. The young boy was ambitious and intelligent, and when he was twenty-two, he was admitted to Harvard Law School. When Paul was graduated, Ivo arranged for him to join a prestigious law firm and he soon became a partner. Five years later, Paul opened his own law firm. By this time, Ivo had invested heavily in legitimate businesses, but he still kept his contacts with the Mafia, and his grandson handled his business affairs for him. In 1967, the year Ivo died, Paul married an Italian girl, Nina, and a year later his wife gave birth to twins.

In the '70s Paul was kept busy. His main clients were the unions, and because of that, he was in a position of power. Heads of businesses and industries deferred to him.

One day, Paul was having lunch with a client, Bill Rohan, a respected banker who knew nothing of Paul's family background.

'You should join Sunnyvale, my golf club,' Bill Rohan said. 'You play golf, don't you?'

'Occasionally,' Paul said. 'When I have time.'

'Fine. I'm on the admissions board. Would you like me to put you up for membership?'

'That would be nice.'

The following week the board met to discuss new members. Paul Martin's name was brought up.

'I can recommend him,' Bill Rohan said. 'He's a good man.'

John Hammond, another member of the board, said, 'He's Italian, isn't he? We don't need any dagos in this club, Bill.'

The banker looked at him. 'Are you going to blackball him?'

'You're damn right I am.'

'Okay, then we'll pass on him. Next . . .'

The meeting continued.

Two weeks later, Paul Martin was having lunch with the banker again. 'I've been practising my golf,' Paul joked.

Bill Rohan was embarrassed. 'There's been a slight hitch, Paul.'

'A hitch?'

'I did propose you for membership. But I'm afraid one of the members of the board blackballed you.'

'Oh? Why?'

'Don't take this personally. He's a bigot. He doesn't like Italians.'

Paul smiled. 'That doesn't bother me, Bill. A lot of people don't like Italians. This Mr . . .'

'Hammond. John Hammond.'

'The meat packer?'

'Yes. He'll change his mind. I'll talk to him again.'

Paul shook his head. 'Don't bother. To tell you the truth, I'm really not that crazy about golf anyway.'

Six months later, in the middle of July, four Hammond Meat Packing Company refrigerated trucks loaded with pork and steaks and headed from the packing house in Minnesota to supermarkets in

Buffalo and New Jersey pulled off the road. The drivers opened the back doors of the trucks and walked away.

When John Hammond heard the news, he was furious. He called in his manager.

'What the hell is going on?' he demanded. 'A million and a half dollars' worth of meat spoiled in the sun. How could that happen?'

'The union called a strike,' the supervisor said.

'Without telling us? What are they striking about? More money?'

The supervisor shrugged. 'I don't know. They didn't say anything to me. They just walked.'

'Tell the local union guy to come in and see me. I'll settle it,' Hammond said.

That afternoon, the union representative was ushered into Hammond's office.

'Why wasn't I told there was going to be a strike?' Hammond demanded.

The representative said, apologetically, 'I didn't know it myself, Mr Hammond. The men just got mad and walked out. It happened very suddenly.'

'You know I've always been a reasonable man to deal with. What is it they want? A raise?'

'No, sir. It's soap.'

Hammond stared at him. 'Did you say *soap*?'

'That's right. They don't like the soap you're using in their bathrooms. It's too strong.'

Hammond could not believe what he was hearing. '*The soap was too strong?* And that's why I lost a million and a half dollars?'

'Don't blame me,' the foreman said. 'It's the men.'

'Jesus,' Hammond said. 'I can't believe this. What

kind of soap would they like – fairy soap?' He slammed his fist on the desk. 'The next time the men have any problem, you come to me first. You hear me?'

'Yes, Mr Hammond.'

'You tell them to get back to work. There will be the best soap money can buy in those washrooms by six o'clock tonight. Is that clear?'

'I'll tell them, Mr Hammond.'

John Hammond sat there for a long time fuming. *No wonder this country is going to hell*, he thought. *Soap*!

Two weeks later, at noon on a hot day in August, five Hammond Meat Packing trucks on their way to deliver meat to Syracuse and Boston pulled off the road. The drivers opened the back doors of the refrigerated trucks and left.

John Hammond got the news at six o'clock that evening.

'What the hell are you talking about?' he screamed. 'Didn't you put in the new soap?'

'I did,' his manager said, 'the same day you told me to.'

'Then what the hell is it this time?'

The manager said helplessly, 'I don't know. There haven't been any complaints. No one said a word to me.'

'Get the goddamned union representative in here.'

At seven o'clock that evening, Hammond was talking to the union representative.

'Two million dollars' worth of meat was ruined

this afternoon because of your men,' Hammond screamed. 'Have they gone crazy?'

'Do you want me to tell the president of the union you asked that, Mr Hammond?'

'No, no,' Hammond said quickly. 'Look, I've never had any problem with you fellows before. If the men want more money, just come to me and we'll discuss it like reasonable people. How much are they asking for?'

'Nothing.'

'What do you mean?'

'It isn't the money, Mr Hammond.'

'Oh? What is it?'

'Lights.'

'Lights?' Hammond thought he had misunderstood him.

'Yes. The men are complaining that the lights in the washrooms are too dim.'

John Hammond sat back in his chair, suddenly quiet. 'What's going on here?' he asked softly.

'I told you, the men think that . . .'

'Never mind that crap. What's going on?'

The union representative said, 'If I knew, I would tell you.'

'Is someone trying to put me out of business? Is that it?'

The union representative was silent.

'All right,' John Hammond said. 'Give me a name. Who can I talk to?'

'There's a lawyer who might be able to help you. The union uses him a lot. His name is Paul Martin.'

'Paul . . . ?' And John Hammond suddenly remembered. 'Why that blackmailing guinea bastard. Get out of here,' he yelled. '*Out!*'

Hammond sat there seething. *No one blackmails me. No one.*

One week later, six more of his refrigerated trucks were abandoned on side roads.

John Hammond arranged a luncheon with Bill Rohan. 'I've been thinking about your friend, Paul Martin,' Hammond said. 'I may have been a bit hasty in blackballing him.'

'Why, it's very generous of you to say that, John.'

'I'll tell you what. You propose him for membership next week and I'll give him my vote.'

The following week, when Paul Martin's name came up, he was accepted unanimously by the membership committee.

John Hammond personally put in a call to Paul Martin. 'Congratulations, Mr Martin,' he said. 'You've just been accepted as a member of Sunnyvale. We're delighted to have you aboard.'

'Thank you,' Paul said. 'I appreciate the call.'

John Hammond's next call was to the district attorney's office. He made an appointment to meet him the following week.

On Sunday, John Hammond and Bill Rohan were part of a foursome at the club.

'You haven't met Paul Martin yet, have you?' Bill Rohan asked.

John Hammond shook his head. 'No. I don't think he's going to be playing a lot of golf. The Grand Jury is going to be keeping your friend too busy.'

'What are you talking about?'

'I'm going to give information about him to the district attorney that will certainly interest a Grand Jury.'

Bill Rohan was shocked. 'Do you know what you're doing?'

'You bet I do. He's a cockroach, John. I'm going to step on him.'

The following Monday, on his way to the district attorney's office, John Hammond was killed in a hit and run accident. There were no witnesses. The police never found the driver.

Every Sunday after that, Paul Martin took his wife and the twins to the Sunnyvale club for lunch. The buffet there was delicious.

Paul Martin took his marriage vows seriously. For instance, he would never have dreamed of dishonouring his wife by taking her and his mistress to the same restaurant. His marriage was one part of his life, his affairs were another. All of Paul Martin's friends had mistresses. It was part of their accepted lifestyle. What bothered Martin was to see old men taking out young girls. It was undignified, and Paul Martin placed great value on dignity. He resolved that when he reached the age of sixty he would stop having mistresses. And on his sixtieth birthday, two years earlier, he had stopped. His wife, Nina, was a good companion to him. That was enough. *Dignity*.

It was this man to whom Lara Cameron had come to ask for help. Martin had been aware of Lara Cameron by name, but he was stunned by how young and beautiful she was. She was ambitious and angrily independent, and yet she was very feminine. He found himself strongly attracted to her. *No*, he thought, *she's a young girl. I'm an old man. Too old*.

When Lara had stormed out of his office on her first visit, Paul Martin sat there for a long time, thinking about her. And then he had picked up the telephone and made a call.

14

The new building was progressing on schedule. Lara visited the site every morning and every afternoon, and there was a new respect in the attitude of the men toward her. She sensed it in the way they looked at her, talked to her and worked for her. She knew it was because of Paul Martin, and, disturbingly, she found herself thinking more and more about the ugly-attractive man with the strangely compelling voice.

Lara telephoned him again.

'I wondered if we might have lunch, Mr Martin?'

'Are you having another problem of some kind?'

'No. I just thought it would be nice if we got to know each other better.'

'I'm sorry, Miss Cameron. I never have lunch.'

'What about dinner one evening?'

'I'm a married man, Miss Cameron. I have dinner with my wife and children.'

'I see. If . . .' The line went dead. *What's the matter with him?* Lara wondered. *I'm not trying to go to bed with the man, I just want to find some way to thank him.* She tried to put him out of her mind.

Paul Martin was disturbed by how pleased he was to hear Lara Cameron's voice. He told his secretary,

'If Miss Cameron calls again, tell her I'm not in.' He did not need temptation, and Lara Cameron was temptation.

Howard Keller was delighted with the way things were progressing.

'I must admit, you had me a little worried there for a while,' he said. 'It looked as though we were going right down the tube. You pulled off a miracle.'

It wasn't my miracle, Lara thought. *It was Paul Martin's.* Perhaps he was angry with her because she had not paid him for his services.

On an impulse, Lara sent Paul a cheque for fifty thousand dollars.

The following day, the cheque was returned with no note.

Lara telephoned him again. His secretary said, 'I'm sorry, Mr Martin is not available.'

Another snub. It was as though he could not be bothered with her. *And if he can't be bothered with me*, Lara wondered, *why did he go out of his way to help me?*

She dreamed about him that night.

Howard Keller walked into Lara's office.

'I've got two tickets for the new Andrew Lloyd Webber musical, *Song and Dance*. I have to go to Chicago. Can you use the tickets?'

'No, I . . . wait.' She was quiet for a moment. 'Yes, I think I can use them. Thank you, Howard.'

That afternoon Lara put one of the tickets in an

envelope and addressed it to Paul Martin at his office.

When he received the ticket the next day, he looked at it, puzzled. Who would send him a single ticket to the theatre? *The Cameron girl. I'll have to put a stop to this*, he thought.

'Am I free Friday evening?' he asked his secretary.

'You're having dinner with your brother-in-law, Mr Martin.'

'Cancel it.'

Lara sat through the first act, and the seat next to her remained empty. *So he's not coming*, Lara thought. *Well, to hell with him. I've done everything I can.*

As the first act curtain came down, Lara debated whether she should stay for the second act or leave. A figure appeared at the seat next to hers.

'Let's get out of here,' Paul Martin commanded.

They had dinner at a bistro on the east side. He sat across the table from her, studying her, quiet and wary. The waiter came to take their drink order.

'I'll have a Scotch and soda,' Lara said.

'Nothing for me.'

Lara looked at him in surprise.

'I don't drink.'

After they had ordered dinner, Paul Martin said, 'Miss Cameron, what do you want from me?'

'I don't like owing anyone anything,' Lara said. 'I

owe you something, and you won't let me pay you. That bothers me.'

'I told you before . . . you don't owe me anything.'

'But I . . .'

'I hear your building is coming along well.'

'Yes.' She started to say 'thanks to you,' then thought better of it.

'You're good at what you do, aren't you?'

Lara nodded. 'I want to be. It's the most exciting thing in the world to have an idea and watch it grow into concrete and steel, and become a building that people work in and live in. In a way, it becomes a monument, doesn't it?' Her face was vibrant and alive.

'I suppose it does. And is one monument going to lead to another?'

'You bet it is,' Lara said enthusiastically. 'I intend to become the most important real estate developer in this city.'

There was a sexuality about her that was mesmerizing.

Paul Martin smiled. 'I wouldn't be surprised.'

'Why did you decide to come to the theatre tonight?' Lara asked.

He had come to tell her to leave him alone, but being with her now, being this close to her, he could not bring himself to say it. 'I heard good things about the show.'

Lara smiled. 'Maybe we'll go again and see it together, Paul.'

He shook his head. 'Miss Cameron, I'm not only married, I'm very much married. I happen to love my wife.'

'I admire that,' Lara said. 'The building will be

finished on the fifteenth of March. We're having a party to celebrate. Will you come?'

He hesitated a long time trying to word his refusal as gently as possible. When he finally spoke, he said, 'Yes. I'll come.'

The celebration for the opening of the new building was a moderate success. Lara Cameron's name was not big enough to attract many members of the press nor any of the city's important dignitaries. But the mayor's assistant was there and a reporter from the *Post*.

'The building is almost fully leased out,' Keller told Lara. 'And we have a flood of inquiries.'

'Good,' Lara said absently. Her mind was on something else. She was thinking about Paul Martin and wondering whether he would appear. For some reason it was important to her. He was an intriguing mystery. He denied that he had helped her, and yet . . . She was pursuing a man old enough to be her father. Lara put the connection out of her mind.

Lara attended to her guests. Hors d'oeuvres and drinks were being served, and everyone seemed to be having a good time. In the midst of the festivities, Paul Martin arrived, and the tone of the party immediately changed. The workmen greeted him as though he were royalty. They were obviously in awe of him.

I'm a corporate attorney. I don't deal with unions.

Martin shook hands with the mayor's assistant and some of the union officials there, then went up to Lara.

'I'm glad you could come,' Lara said.

Paul Martin looked around at the huge building and said, 'Congratulations. You've done a good job.'

'Thank you.' She lowered her voice. 'And I do mean thank you.'

He was staring at her, bemused by how ravishing Lara looked, and the way he felt, looking at her.

'The party's almost over,' Lara said. 'I was hoping you would take me to dinner.'

'I told you, I have dinner with my wife and children.' He was looking into her eyes. 'I'll buy you a drink.'

Lara smiled. 'That will do nicely.'

They stopped at a small bar on Third Avenue. They talked, but afterward neither of them would remember what they talked about. The words were camouflage for the sexual tension between them.

'Tell me about yourself,' Paul Martin said. 'Who are you? Where are you from? How did you get started in this business?'

Lara thought of Sean McAllister and his repulsive body on top of hers. *'Come back to bed, honey. That was so good we're going to do it again.'*

'I come from a little town in Nova Scotia,' Lara said. 'Glace Bay. My father collected rents from some boarding houses there. When he died, I took over. One of the boarders helped me buy a lot, and I put up a building on it. That was the beginning.'

He was listening closely.

'After that, I went to Chicago and developed some buildings there. I did well and came to New York.' She smiled. 'That's really the whole story.' *Except for the agony of growing up with a father who hated her, the shame of poverty, of never owning anything, of giving her body to Sean McAllister . . .*

As though reading her mind, Paul Martin said, 'I'll bet it wasn't really all that easy, was it?'

'I'm not complaining.'

'What's your next project?'

Lara shrugged. 'I'm not sure. I've looked at a lot of possibilities, but there's nothing I'm really wild about.'

He could not take his eyes off her.

'What are you thinking?' Lara asked.

He took a deep breath. 'The truth? I was thinking that if I weren't married, I would tell you that you're one of the most exciting women I've ever met. But I am married, so you and I are going to be just friends. Do I make myself clear?'

'Very clear.'

He looked at his watch. 'Time to go.' He turned to the waiter. 'Check, please.' He rose to his feet.

'Can we have lunch next week?' Lara asked.

'No. Maybe I'll see you again when your next building is finished.'

And he was gone.

That night, Lara dreamed they were making love. Paul Martin was on top of her, stroking her body with his hands and whispering in her ear.

'Ye ken, I maun hae ye, and onie ye . . . Gude forgie me, my bonnie darlin', for I've niver tauld you how meikle I love ye, love ye, love ye . . .'

And then he was inside her and her body was suddenly molten. She moaned and her moans awakened her. She sat up in bed, trembling.

*

Two days later, Paul Martin telephoned. 'I think I have a location you might be interested in,' he said crisply. 'It's over on the West Side, on 69th Street. It's not on the market yet. It belongs to a client of mine who wants to sell.'

Lara and Howard Keller went to look at it that morning. It was a prime piece of property.

'How did you hear about this?' Keller asked.

'Paul Martin.'

'Oh. I see.' There was disapproval in his voice.

'What is that supposed to mean?'

'Lara . . . I checked on Martin. He's Mafia. Stay away from him.'

She said indignantly, 'He has nothing to do with the Mafia. He's a good friend. Anyway, what does that have to do with this site? Do you like it?'

'I think it's great.'

'Then let's buy it.'

Ten days later, they closed the deal.

Lara sent Paul Martin a large bouquet of flowers. There was a note attached: 'Paul – please don't send these back. They're very sensitive.'

She received a call from him that afternoon.

'Thanks for the flowers. I'm not used to getting flowers from beautiful women.' His voice sounded gruffer than usual.

'Do you know your problem?' Lara said. 'No one has ever spoiled you enough.'

'Is that what you want to do, spoil me?'

'Rotten.'

Paul laughed.

'I mean it.'

'I know you do.'

'Why don't we talk about it at lunch?' Lara asked.

Paul Martin had not been able to get Lara out of his mind. He knew that he could easily fall in love with her. There was a vulnerability about her, an innocence, and at the same time, something wildly sensual. He knew that he would be smart never to see her again, but he was unable to control himself. He was drawn to her by something more powerful than his will.

They had lunch at the Twenty-One Club.

'When you're trying to hide something,' Paul Martin advised, 'always do it out in the open. Then no one will believe you're doing anything wrong.'

'Are we trying to hide something?' Lara asked softly.

He looked at her and made his decision. *She's beautiful and smart, but so are a thousand other women. It will be easy to get her out of my system. I'll go to bed with her once and that will be the end of it.*

As it turned out, he was wrong.

When they arrived at Lara's apartment, Paul was unaccountably nervous.

'I feel like a fuckin' schoolboy,' Paul said. 'I'm out of practice.'

'It's like riding a bicycle,' Lara murmured. 'It will come back to you. Let me undress you.'

She took off his jacket and tie and started unbuttoning his shirt.

'You know that this could never become serious, Lara.'

'I know that.'

'I'm sixty-two years old. I could be your father.'

She went still for an instant, remembering her dream. 'I know.' She finished undressing him. 'You have a beautiful body.'

'Thanks.' His wife never told him that.

Lara slid her arms along his thighs. 'You're very strong, aren't you?'

He found himself standing straighter. 'I played basketball when I was in . . .'

Her lips were on his and they were in bed, and he experienced something that had never happened to him before in his life. He felt as though his body were on fire. They were making love and it was without a beginning or an ending, a river that swept him along faster and faster, and the tide began to pull at him, sucking him down and down, deeper and deeper, into a velvet darkness that exploded into a thousand stars. And the miracle was that it happened again, and once again, until he lay there panting and exhausted.

'I can't believe this,' he said.

His love-making with his wife had always been conventional, routine. But with Lara it was an incredibly sensual experience. Paul Martin had had many women before, but Lara was like no one he had ever known. She had given him a gift no woman had ever given him: She made him feel young.

When Paul was getting dressed, Lara asked, 'Will I see you again?'

'Yes.' *God help me*. 'Yes.'

*

The 1980s were a time of changes. Ronald Reagan was elected President of the United States and Wall Street had the busiest day in its history. The Shah of Iran died in exile, and Anwar Sadat was assassinated. The public debt hit one trillion dollars, and the American hostages in Iran were freed. Sandra Day O'Connor became the first woman to serve on the Supreme Court.

Lara was in the right place at the right time. Real estate development was booming. Money was abundant and banks were willing to finance projects that were both speculative and highly leveraged.

Savings and loan companies were a big source of equity. High yield and high risk bonds – nicknamed junk bonds – had been popularized by a young financial genius named Mike Milken, and they were manna to the real estate industry. The financing was there for the asking.

'I'm going to put up a hotel on the 69th Street property, instead of an office building.'

'Why?' Howard Keller asked. 'It's a perfect location for an office building. With a hotel, you have to run it twenty-four hours a day. Tenants come and go like ants. With an office building, you only have to worry about a lease every five or ten years.'

'I know, but in a hotel you have drop-dead power, Howard. You can give important people suites and entertain them in your own restaurant. I like that idea. It's going to be a hotel. I want you to set up meetings with the top architects in New York: Skidmore, Owings and Merrill, Peter Eisenman and Philip Johnson.'

The meetings took place over the next two weeks. Some of the architects were patronizing. They had never worked for a female developer before.

One of them said, 'If you'd like us to copy . . .'

'No. We're going to build a hotel that *other* builders will copy. If you want a buzzword, try "elegance". I see an entry way flanked by twin fountains, a lobby with Italian marble. Off the lobby we'll have a comfortable conference room where . . .'

By the end of the meeting, they were impressed.

Lara put together a team. She hired a lawyer named Terry Hill, an assistant named Jim Belon, a project manager named Tom Chriton, and an advertising agency headed by Tom Scott. She hired the architectural firm of Higgins, Almont & Clark, and the project was under way.

'We'll meet once a week,' Lara told the group, 'but I'll want daily reports from each of you. I want this hotel to go up on schedule and on budget. I selected all of you because you're the best at what you do. Don't let me down. Are there any questions?'

The next two hours were spent in answering them.

Later Lara said to Keller, 'How do you think the meeting went?'

'Fine, boss.'

It was the first time he had called her that. She liked it.

Charles Cohn telephoned.

'I'm in New York. Can we have lunch?'

'You bet we can!' Lara said.

They had lunch at Sardi's.

'You look wonderful,' Cohn said. 'Success agrees with you, Lara.'

'It's only the beginning,' Lara said. 'Charles . . . how would you like to join Cameron Enterprises? I'll give you a piece of the company and . . .'

He shook his head. 'Thanks, but no. You've just started the journey. I'm near the end of the road. I'll be retiring next summer.'

'Let's stay in touch,' Lara said. 'I don't want to lose you.'

The next time Paul Martin came to Lara's apartment, she said, 'I have a surprise for you, darling.'

She handed him half a dozen packages.

'Hey! It's not my birthday.'

'Open them.'

Inside were a dozen Bergdorf Goodman shirts and a dozen Pucci ties.

'I have shirts and ties,' he laughed.

'Not like these,' Lara told him. 'They'll make you feel younger. I got the name of a good tailor for you, too.'

The following week Lara had a new barber style Paul's hair.

Paul Martin looked at himself in the mirror and thought, *I do look younger*. Life had become exciting. *And all because of Lara*, he thought.

Paul's wife tried not to notice the change in her husband.

They were all there for the meeting: Keller, Tom Chriton, Jim Belon and Terry Hill.

'We're going to fast track the hotel,' Lara announced.

The men looked at one another. 'That's dangerous,' Keller said.

'Not if you do it right.'

Tom Chriton spoke up. 'Miss Cameron, the safe way to do this is to complete one phase at a time. You do your grading, and when that's done, you begin digging the trenches for foundations. When that's done, you put in the utility conduits and drainage piping. Then . . .'

Lara interrupted. '. . . You put in the wooden concrete formwork and the skeletal gridiron. I know all that.'

'Then why . . . ?'

'Because that will take two years. I don't want to wait two years.'

Jim Belon said, 'If we fast track it, that means starting all the different steps at once. If anything goes wrong, nothing will fit together. You could have a lopsided building with electric circuits in the wrong place and . . .'

'Then we have to see to it that nothing goes wrong, don't we?' Lara said. 'If we do it this way, we'll get the building up in a year instead of two, and we'll save close to twenty million dollars.'

'True, but it's taking a big chance.'

'I like taking chances.'

15

Lara told Paul Martin about her decision to fast track the hotel, and the discussion she had had with the committee.

'They may have been right,' Paul said. 'What you're doing could be dangerous.'

'Trump does it. Uris does it.'

Paul said gently, 'Baby, you're not Trump or Uris.'

'I'm going to be bigger than they are, Paul. I'm going to put up more buildings in New York than anyone ever has before. It's going to be my city.'

He looked at her for a long moment. 'I believe you.'

Lara had an unlisted telephone installed in her office. Only Paul Martin had the number. He installed a telephone in his office for Lara's calls. They spoke to each other several times a day.

Whenever they could get away in the afternoon, they went to Lara's apartment. Paul Martin looked forward to those trysts more than he had ever believed possible. Lara had become an obsession with him.

When Keller became aware of what was happening, he was concerned.

'Lara,' he said, 'I think you're making a mistake. He's dangerous.'

'You don't know him. He's wonderful.'

'Are you in love with him?'

Lara thought about it. Paul Martin fulfilled a need in her life. But was she in love with him?

'No.'

'Is he in love with you?'

'I think so.'

'Be careful. Be very careful.'

Lara smiled. Impulsively, she kissed Keller's cheek. 'I love the way you take care of me, Howard.'

Lara was at the construction site, studying a report.

'I notice we're paying for an awful lot of lumber,' Lara said. She was talking to Pete Reese, the new project manager.

'I didn't want to mention it before, Miss Cameron, because I wasn't sure – but you're right. A lot of our lumber's missing. We've had to double order it.'

She looked up at him. 'You mean someone is stealing it?'

'It looks that way.'

'Do you have any idea who?'

'No.'

'We have night watchmen here, don't we?'

'One watchman.'

'And he hasn't seen anything?'

'No. But with all this activity going on, it could be happening during the day. It could be anybody.'

Lara was thoughtful. 'I see. Thanks for letting me know, Pete. I'll take care of it.'

That afternoon, Lara hired a private detective, Steve Kane.

'How does anyone walk away in broad daylight with a load of lumber?' Kane asked.

'You tell me.'

'You say there's a night watchman at the site?'

'Yes.'

'Maybe he's in on it.'

'I'm not interested in maybes,' Lara said. 'Find out who's behind it and get back to me.'

'Can you get me hired as a member of the construction crew?'

'I'll take care of it.'

Steve Kane went to work at the site the next day.

When Lara told Keller what was happening, he said, 'You didn't have to get involved in this. I could have handled it for you.'

'I like handling things myself,' Lara said.

That was the end of the conversation.

Five days later, Kane appeared at Lara's office.

'Have you found out anything?'

'Everything,' he said.

'Was it the watchman?'

'No. The lumber wasn't stolen from the building site.'

'What do you mean?'

'I mean it never reached there. It was sent to another construction site in Jersey and double billed. The invoices were doctored.'

'Who's behind it?' Lara asked.

Kane told her.

The following afternoon, there was a meeting of the committee. Terry Hill, Lara's lawyer, was there,

Howard Keller, Jim Belon, the project manager, and Pete Reese. There was also a stranger at the conference table. Lara introduced him as Mr Conroy.

'Let's have a report,' Lara said.

Pete Reese said, 'We're right on schedule. We estimate four more months. You were right about going fast track. It's all going smooth as silk. We've already started on the electrical and plumbing.'

'Good,' Lara said.

'What about the stolen lumber?' Keller asked.

'Nothing new on it yet,' Pete Reese said. 'We're keeping an eye open.'

'I don't think we have to worry about that any more,' Lara announced. 'We found out who's stealing it.' She nodded toward the stranger. 'Mr Conroy is with the Special Fraud Squad. It's actually *Detective* Conroy.'

'What's he doing here?' Pete Reese asked.

'He's come to take you away.'

Reese looked up, startled. 'What?'

Lara turned to the group. 'Mr Reese has been selling our lumber to another construction job. When he found out that I was checking the reports, he decided to tell me there was a problem.'

'Wait a minute,' Pete Reese said. 'I . . . I . . . You have it wrong.'

She turned to Conroy. 'Would you please get him out of here?'

She turned to the others. 'Now, let's discuss the opening of the hotel.'

As the hotel grew nearer completion, the pressure became more intense. Lara was becoming impossible. She badgered everyone constantly. She made phone calls in the middle of the night.

'Howard, did you know the shipment of wallpaper hasn't arrived yet?'

'For God's sakes, Lara, it's four o'clock in the morning.'

'It's ninety days to the opening of the hotel. We can't open a hotel without wallpaper.'

'I'll check it out in the morning.'

'This *is* morning. Check it out now.'

Lara's nervousness increased as the deadline grew closer. She met with Tom Scott, head of the advertising agency.

'Do you have small children, Mr Scott?'

He looked at her in surprise. 'No. Why?'

'Because I just went over the new advertising campaign and it seems to have been devised by a small retarded child. I can't believe that grown men sat down and thought up this junk.'

Scott frowned. 'If there's something about it that displeases you . . .'

'Everything about it displeases me,' Lara said. 'It lacks excitement. It's bland. It could be about any hotel anywhere. This isn't *any* hotel, Mr Scott. This is the most beautiful, most modern hotel in New York. You make it sound like a cold, faceless building. It's a warm, exciting home. Let's spread the word. Do you think you can handle that?'

'I assure you we can handle it. We'll revise the campaign and in two weeks . . .'

'Monday,' Lara said flatly. 'I want to see the new campaign Monday.'

*

The new ads went out in newspapers and magazines and billboards all over the country.

'I think the campaign turned out great,' Tom Scott said. 'You were right.'

Lara looked at him and said quietly, 'I don't want to be right. I want *you* to be right. That's what I pay you for.'

She turned to Jerry Townsend, in charge of publicity.

'Have the invitations all been sent out?'

'Yes. We've got most of our replies already. Everybody's coming to the opening. It's going to be quite a party.'

'It should be,' Keller grumbled, 'it's costing enough.'

Lara grinned. 'Stop being a banker. We'll get a million dollars' worth of publicity. We're going to have dozens of celebrities there and . . .'

He held up his hand. 'All right, all right.'

Two weeks before the opening, everything seemed to be happening at once. The wallpaper had arrived and carpets were being installed, halls were being painted and pictures were being hung. Lara inspected every suite, accompanied by a staff of five.

She walked into one suite and said, 'The drapes are wrong. Switch them with the suite next door.'

In another suite, she tried the piano. 'It's out of tune. Take care of it.'

In a third suite the electric fireplace didn't work. 'Fix it.'

It seemed to the harried staff that Lara was trying to do everything herself. She was in the kitchen and in the laundry room and in the utility closets. She was everywhere, demanding, complaining, fixing.

The man whom she had hired to manage the hotel said, 'Don't get so excited, Miss Cameron. At the opening of any hotel, little things always go wrong.'

'Not in my hotels,' Lara said. 'Not in my hotels.'

The day of the opening, Lara was up at four a.m., too nervous to sleep. She wanted desperately to talk to Paul Martin, but there was no way she could call him at that hour. She dressed and went for a walk.

Everything is going to be fine, she told herself. *The reservation computer is going to be fixed. They'll get the third oven working. The lock on suite seven will be repaired. We'll find a replacement for the maids who quit yesterday. The air conditioning unit in the penthouse will work* . . .

At six o'clock that evening, the invited guests began to arrive. A uniformed guard at each entrance to the hotel examined their invitations before admitting them. There was a mix of celebrities, famous athletes and corporation executives. Lara had gone over the list carefully, eliminating the names of the freeloaders and the hangers-on.

She stood in the spacious lobby greeting the newcomers as they arrived. 'I'm Lara Cameron. So nice of you to come . . . Please feel free to look around.'

Lara took Keller aside. 'Why isn't the mayor coming?'

'He's pretty busy, you know, and . . .'

'You mean he thinks I'm not important enough.'

'One day he'll change his mind.'

One of the mayor's assistants arrived.

'Thank you for coming,' Lara said. 'This is an honour for the hotel.'

Lara kept looking nervously for Todd Grayson, the architectural critic for the *New York Times*, who had been invited. *If he likes it*, Lara thought, *we have a winner*.

Paul Martin arrived with his wife. It was the first time Lara had seen Mrs Martin. She was an attractive, elegant looking woman. Lara felt an unexpected pang of guilt.

Paul walked up to Lara. 'Miss Cameron, I'm Paul Martin. This is my wife, Nina. Thank you for inviting us.'

Lara gripped his hand a second longer than necessary. 'I'm delighted that you're here. Please make yourself at home.'

Paul looked around the lobby. He had seen it half a dozen times before. 'It's beautiful,' he exclaimed. 'I think you're going to be very successful.'

Nina Martin was staring at Lara. 'I'm sure she will be.'

And Lara wondered if she knew.

The guests began to stream in.

An hour later, Lara was standing in the lobby when Keller rushed up to her. 'For God's sakes,' he said, 'everyone's looking for you. They're all in the ballroom, eating. Why aren't you in there?'

'Todd Grayson hasn't arrived. I'm waiting for him.'

'*The Times*' architectural critic? I saw him an hour ago.'

'*What?*'

'Yes. He went on a tour of the hotel with the others.'

'Why didn't you tell me?'

'I thought you knew.'

'What did he say?' Lara asked eagerly. 'How did he look? Did he seem impressed?'

'He didn't say anything. He looked fine. And I don't know whether he was impressed or not.'

'Didn't he say *anything*?'

'No.'

Lara frowned. 'He would have said something if he had liked it. It's a bad sign, Howard.'

The party was a huge success. The guests ate and drank and toasted the hotel. When the evening was over, Lara was showered with compliments.

'It's such a lovely hotel, Miss Cameron . . .'

'I'll certainly stay here when I come back to New York . . .'

'What a great idea, having a piano in every living room . . .'

'I love the fireplaces . . .'

'I'll certainly recommend this to all my friends . . .'

Well, Lara thought, *even if the New York Times hates it, it's going to be a success.*

Lara saw Paul Martin and his wife as they were leaving.

'I think you really have a winner here, Miss Cameron. It's going to be the talk of New York.'

'You're very kind, Mr Martin,' Lara said. 'Thank you for coming.'

Nina Martin said quietly, 'Goodnight, Miss Cameron.'

'Goodnight.'

As they were walking out of the lobby door, Lara heard her say, "She's very beautiful, isn't she, Paul?"

The following Thursday, when the first edition of the *New York Times* came out, Lara was at the newsstand at 42nd Street and Broadway at four o'clock in the morning to pick up a copy. She hurriedly turned to the Home Section. Todd Grayson's article began:

> Manhattan has long needed a hotel that does not remind travellers that they're staying in a hotel. The suites at the Cameron Plaza are large and gracious, and done in beautiful taste. Lara Cameron has finally given New York . . .

She yelled aloud with joy. She telephoned Keller and woke him up.

'We're in!' she said. '*The Times* loves us.'

He sat up in bed, groggy. 'That's great. What did they say?'

Lara read the article to him. 'All right,' Keller said, 'now you can get some sleep.'

'Sleep? Are you joking? I have a new site picked out. As soon as the banks open, I want you to start negotiating a loan . . .'

The New York Cameron Plaza was a triumph. It was completely booked, and there was a waiting list.

'It's only the beginning,' Lara told Keller. 'There are ten thousand builders in the metropolitan area but only a handful of the big boys – the Tisches, the Rudins, the Rockefellers, the Sterns. Well, whether they like it or not, we're going to play in their sandbox. We're going to change the skyline. We're going to invent the future.'

Lara began to get calls from banks offering her loans. She cultivated the important real estate brokers, taking them to dinner and the theatre. She had power breakfasts at the Regency, and was told about properties that were about to come on the market. She acquired two more downtown sites and began construction.

Paul Martin telephoned Lara at the office. 'Have you seen *Business Week*? You're a hot ticket,' he said. 'The word's out that you're a shaker. You get things done.'

'I try.'

'Are you free for dinner?'

'I'll make myself free.'

Lara was in a meeting with the partner of a top architectural firm. She was examining the blueprints and drawings they had brought.

'You're going to like this,' the chief architect said. 'It has grace and symmetry, and the scope that you asked for. Let me explain some of the details . . .'

'That won't be necessary,' Lara said. 'I understand them.' She looked up. 'I want you to turn these plans over to an artist.'

'What?'

'I want large colour drawings of the building. I

want drawings of the lobby, the corridors and the offices. Bankers have no imagination. I'm going to *show* them what the building is going to look like.'

'That's a great idea.'

Lara's secretary appeared. 'I'm sorry I'm late.'

'This meeting was called for nine o'clock, Kathy. It's nine fifteen.'

'I'm sorry, Miss Cameron, my alarm didn't go off and . . .'

'We'll discuss it later.'

She turned to the architects. 'I want a few changes made . . .'

Two hours later, Lara had finished discussing the changes she wanted. When the meeting was over, she said to Kathy, 'Don't leave. Sit down.'

Kathy sat.

'Do you like your job?'

'Yes, Miss Cameron.'

'This is the third time you've been late this week. I won't put up with that again.'

'I'm terribly sorry, I . . . I haven't been feeling well.'

'What's your problem?'

'It's nothing, really.'

'It's obviously enough to keep you from coming in on time. What is it?'

'I haven't been sleeping very well lately. To tell you the truth, I . . . I'm scared.'

'Scared of what?' Lara asked impatiently.

'I . . . I have a lump.'

'Oh.' Lara was silent for a moment. 'Well, what did the doctor say?'

Kathy swallowed. 'I haven't seen a doctor.'

'Not seen one!' Lara exploded. 'For God's sakes, do you come from a family of ostriches? Of course you've got to see a doctor.'

Lara picked up the phone. 'Get me Dr Peters.'

She replaced the receiver. 'It's probably nothing, but you can't let it go.'

'I have a mother and brother who died of cancer,' Kathy said miserably. 'I don't want a doctor to tell me I have it.'

The telephone rang. Lara picked it up. 'Hello? He what? I don't care if he is. You tell him I want to talk to him *now*.'

She replaced the receiver.

A few moments later the phone rang again. Lara picked it up. 'Hello, Alan . . . no, I'm fine. I'm sending my secretary over to see you. Her name is Kathy Turner. She'll be there in half an hour. I want her examined this morning, and I want you to stay on top of it . . . I know you are . . . I appreciate it . . . thanks.'

She replaced the receiver. 'Get over to Sloan-Kettering Hospital. Dr Peters will be waiting for you.'

'I don't know what to say, Miss Cameron.'

'Say that you'll be on time tomorrow.'

Howard Keller came into the office. 'We have a problem, boss.'

'Go.'

'It's the property on Fourteenth Street. We've cleared the tenants out of the whole block except for one apartment house. The Dorchester Apartments.

Six of the tenants refuse to leave, and the City won't let us force them out.'

'Offer them more money.'

'It's not a question of money. Those people have lived there a long time. They don't want to leave. They're comfortable there.'

'Then let's make them *un*comfortable.'

'What do you mean?'

Lara got up. 'Let's go take a look at the building.'

On the drive down, they passed bag ladies and homeless people roaming the streets, asking for handouts.

'In a country as wealthy as this,' Lara said, 'that's a disgrace.'

The Dorchester Apartments was a six-storey brick building in the middle of a block filled with old structures waiting for the bulldozers.

Lara stood in front of it, examining it. 'How many tenants are in there?'

'We got sixteen out of the apartments. Six are still hanging on.'

'That means we have sixteen apartments available.'

He looked at her, puzzled. 'That's right. Why?'

'Let's fill those apartments.'

'You mean lease them? What's the point . . . ?'

'We're not going to lease them. We're going to donate them to the homeless. There are thousands of homeless people in New York. We're going to take care of some of them. Crowd in as many as you can. See that they're given some food.'

Keller frowned. 'What makes me think this isn't one of your better ideas?'

'Howard, we're going to become benefactors. We're going to do something the City can't do – shelter the homeless.'

Lara was studying the building more closely, looking at the windows. 'And I want those windows boarded up.'

'What?'

'We're going to make the building look like an old derelict. Is the top floor apartment still occupied, the one with the roof garden?'

'Yes.'

'Put up a big billboard on the roof to block the view.'

'But . . .'

'Get to work on it.'

When Lara returned to the office, there was a message for her. 'Dr Peters would like you to call him,' Tricia said.

'Get him for me.'

He came on the phone almost immediately.

'Lara, I examined your secretary.'

'Yes?'

'She has a tumour. I'm afraid it's malignant. I recommend an immediate mastectomy.'

'I want a second opinion,' Lara said.

'Of course, if you wish, but I *am* head of the department and . . .'

'I still want a second opinion. Have someone else examine her. Get back to me as soon as possible. Where is Kathy now?'

'She's on her way back to your office.'

'Thanks, Alan.'

Lara replaced the receiver. She pressed down the intercom button. 'When Kathy returns, send her in to me.'

Lara studied the calendar on her desk. She had only thirty days left to clear out the Dorchester Apartments before construction was scheduled to start.

Six stubborn tenants. All right, Lara thought, *let's see how long they can hold out.*

Kathy walked into Lara's office. Her face was puffy and her eyes were red.

'I heard the news,' Lara told her. 'I'm so sorry, Kathy.'

'I'm going to die,' Kathy said.

Lara rose and put her arms around her, holding her close. 'You're not going to do anything of the kind. They've made a lot of progress with cancer. You're going to have the operation and you're going to be all right.'

'Miss Cameron, I can't afford . . .'

'Everything will be taken care of. Dr Peters is going to see that you have one more examination. If it verifies his diagnosis, you should have the operation right away. Now go home and get some rest.'

Kathy's eyes filled with tears again. 'I . . . thank you.'

As Kathy walked out of the office she thought, *No one really knows that lady.*

16

The following Monday, Lara had a visitor.

'There's a Mr O'Brian here to see you from the city Housing Commissioner's office, Miss Cameron.'

'What about?'

'He didn't say.'

Lara buzzed Keller on the intercom. 'Will you come in here, Howard?' She said to the secretary, 'Send Mr O'Brian in.'

Andy O'Brian was a burly red-faced Irishman with a slight brogue. 'Miss Cameron?'

Lara remained seated behind her desk. 'Yes. What can I do for you, Mr O'Brian?'

'I'm afraid you're in violation of the law, Miss Cameron.'

'Really? What is this all about?'

'You own the Dorchester Apartments on East Fourteenth Street?'

'Yes.'

'We have a report that about a hundred homeless people have crowded into those apartments.'

'Oh, that.' Lara smiled. 'Yes, I thought that since the City wasn't doing anything about the homeless, I would help out. I'm giving them shelter.'

Howard Keller walked into the room.

'This is Mr Keller. Mr O'Brian.'

The two men shook hands.

Lara turned to Keller. 'I was just explaining how

we're helping the City out by providing housing.'

'You invited them in, Miss Cameron?'

'That's right.'

'Do you have a licence from the City?'

'A licence for what?'

'If you're setting up a shelter, it has to be approved by the City. There are certain strict conditions that are enforced.'

'I'm sorry. I wasn't aware of that. I'll arrange for the licence immediately.'

'I don't think so.'

'What does that mean?'

'We've had complaints from the tenants in that building. They say you're trying to force them out.'

'Nonsense.'

'Miss Cameron, the City is giving you forty-eight hours to move those homeless people out of there. And when they leave, we have an order for you to take down the boards that you put up to cover the windows.'

Lara was furious. 'Is that all?'

'No, ma'am. The tenant who has the roof garden says you put up a sign blocking his view. You'll have to take that down, too.'

'What if I won't?'

'I think you will. All this comes under harassment. You'll save yourself a lot of trouble and unpleasant publicity by not forcing us to take you to court.' He nodded and said, 'Have a nice day.'

They watched him walk out of the office.

Keller turned to Lara. 'We'll have to get all those people out of there.'

'No.' She sat there, thinking.

'What do you mean "no"? The man said . . .'

'I know what he said. I want you to bring in *more* homeless. I want that building packed with street people. We're going to stall. Call Terry Hill. Tell him the problem. Have him get a stay or something. We've got to get those six tenants out by the end of the month or it's going to cost us three million dollars.'

The intercom buzzed. 'Dr Peters is on the phone.'

Lara picked up the telephone. 'Hello, Alan.'

'I just wanted to tell you that we finished the operation. It looks like we got it all. Kathy's going to be fine.'

'That's wonderful news. When can I visit her?'

'You can come by this afternoon.'

'I'll do that. Thanks, Alan. See that I get all the bills, will you?'

'Will do.'

'And you can tell the hospital to expect a donation. Fifty thousand dollars.'

Lara said to Tricia, 'Fill her room with flowers.' She looked at her schedule. 'I'll go down to see her at four o'clock.'

Terry Hill arrived at the office. 'There's a warrant for your arrest coming in.'

'What?'

'Weren't you warned to get those homeless people out of the building?'

'Yes, but . . .'

'You can't get away with this, Lara. There's an old adage: "Don't fight City Hall, you can't win."'

'Are they really going to arrest me?'

'You're damn right they are. You were given

notice by the City to get those people out of there.'

'All right,' Lara said. 'Let's get them out.' She turned to Keller. 'Remove them. But don't put them out on the street. That's not right. We have those empty rooming houses that we're waiting to convert in the West 20s. Let's put them there. Take all the help you need. I want them gone in an hour.'

She turned to Terry Hill. 'I'll be out of here, so they can't serve me. By the time they do, the problem will be solved.'

The intercom buzzed. 'There are two gentlemen here from the district attorney's office.'

Lara motioned to Howard Keller. He walked over to the intercom and said, 'Miss Cameron isn't here.'

There was a silence. 'When do you expect her?'

Keller looked at Lara. Lara shook her head. Keller said into the intercom, 'We don't know.' He flicked the key up.

'I'll go out the back way,' Lara said.

Lara hated hospitals. A hospital was her father lying in bed, pale and suddenly old. *'What the bluidy hell are you doin' here? You've work to dae at the boardin' house.'*

Lara walked into Kathy's room. It was filled with flowers. Kathy was sitting up in bed.

'How do you feel?' Lara asked.

Kathy smiled. 'The doctor said I'm going to be fine.'

'You'd better be. Your work is piling up. I need you.'

'I . . . I don't know how to thank you for all this.'

'Don't.'

Lara picked up the bedside phone and put a call through to her office. She spoke to Terry Hill.

'Are they still there?'

'They're still here. They intend to stay until you return.'

'Check with Howard. As soon as he clears the street people out of the building, I'll come back.'

Lara replaced the receiver.

'If you need anything, let me know,' Lara said. 'I'll be back to see you tomorrow.'

Lara's next stop was at the architectural offices of Higgins, Almont & Clark. She was ushered in to see Mr Clark. He rose as she walked into his office.

'What a nice surprise. What can I do for you, Miss Cameron?'

'Do you have the plans here for the project on Fourteenth Street?'

'Yes, indeed.'

He went over to his drawing board. 'Here we are.'

There was a sketch of a beautiful high-rise complex with apartment buildings and shops around it.

'I want you to redraw it,' Lara said.

'What?'

Lara pointed to a space in the middle of the block. 'There's a building still standing in this area. I want you to draw the same concept, but construct it *around* that building.'

'You mean you want to put up the project with one of the old buildings still standing? It would never work. First of all, it would look terrible and . . .'

'Just do it, please. Send it over to my office this afternoon.'

211

And Lara was gone.

From the car, she telephoned Terry Hill. 'Have you heard from Howard yet?'

'Yes. The squatters have all been cleared out.'

'Good. Get the district attorney on the phone. Tell him that I had ordered those squatters out two days ago, and that there was a lack of communication. The minute I heard about it, today, I had them evicted. I'm on my way back to the office now. See if he still wants to arrest me.'

She said to the driver, 'Drive through the park. Take your time.'

Thirty minutes later, when Lara reached her office, the men with the warrant were gone.

Lara was in a meeting with Howard Keller and Terry Hill.

'The tenants still won't budge,' Keller said. 'I even went back and offered them more money. They're not leaving. We've only got five days left before we have to begin bulldozing.'

Lara said, 'I asked Mr Clark to draw up a new blueprint for the project.'

'I saw it,' Keller said. 'It doesn't make any sense. We can't leave that old building standing in the middle of a new giant construction. We're going to have to go to the bank and ask them if they'll move back the start date.'

'No,' Lara said. 'I want to move it *up*.'

'*What?*'

'Get hold of the contractor. Tell him we want to start bulldozing tomorrow.'

'*Tomorrow?* Lara . . .'

'First thing in the morning. And take that blueprint and give it to the foreman of the construction crew.'

'What good will that do?' Keller asked.

'We'll see.'

The following morning, the remaining tenants of the Dorchester Apartments were awakened by the roar of a bulldozer. They looked out of their windows. Halfway down the block, as they watched, a mechanical behemoth was moving toward them, levelling everything in its path. The tenants were stunned.

Mr Hershey, who lived on the top floor, rushed outside and hurried over to the foreman. 'What do you think you're doing?' he screamed. 'You can't go ahead with this.'

'Who says so?'

'The City does.' Hershey pointed to the building he lived in. 'You're not permitted to touch that building.'

The foreman looked at the blueprint in front of him. 'That's right,' he said. 'We have orders to leave that building standing.'

Hershey frowned. 'What? Let me see that.' He looked at the plan and gasped. 'They're going to put up the plaza and leave this building *standing*?'

'That's right, mister.'

'But they can't do that! The noise and dirt!'

'That's not my problem. Now, if you'll get out of my way, I'd like to get back to work.'

*

Thirty minutes later, Lara's secretary said, 'There's a Mr Hershey on line two, Miss Cameron.'

'Tell him I'm not available.'

When Hershey called for the third time that afternoon, Lara finally picked up the phone and spoke with him.

'Yes, Mr Hershey. What can I do for you?'

'I'd like to come in and see you, Miss Cameron.'

'I'm afraid I'm rather busy. Whatever it is you have to say you can say on the phone.'

'Well, you'll be glad to know that I've talked to the other tenants in our building and we've agreed that it might be best after all to take your offer and vacate our apartments.'

'That offer is no longer good, Mr Hershey. You can all stay where you are.'

'If you build around us, we're never going to get any sleep!'

'Who told you we were going to build around you?' Lara demanded. 'Where did you get that information?'

'The foreman on the job showed me a blueprint and . . .'

'Well, he's going to be fired.' There was fury in Lara's voice. 'That was confidential information.'

'Wait a minute. Let's talk like two reasonable people, okay? Your project would be better off if we got out of here, and I think we'd be better off leaving. I don't want to live in the middle of a damned high-rise.'

Lara said, 'It doesn't matter to me whether you go or stay, Mr Hershey.' Her voice softened. 'I'll tell you what I'll do. If that building is vacated by next month, I'm willing to go with our first offer.'

She could hear him thinking it over.

Finally he said reluctantly, 'Okay. I'll talk to the others, but I'm sure it will be all right. I really appreciate this, Miss Cameron.'

Lara said, 'It's been my pleasure, Mr Hershey.'

The following month, work on the new project began in earnest.

Lara's reputation was growing. Cameron Enterprises was putting up a high-rise in Brooklyn, a shopping centre in Westchester, a mall in Washington, DC. There was a low-cost housing project being constructed in Dallas and a block of condominiums in Los Angeles. Capital flowed in from banks, savings and loan companies and eager private investors. Lara had become a Name.

Kathy had returned to work.

'I'm back.'

Lara studied her a moment. 'How do you feel?'

Kathy smiled. 'Great. Thanks to . . .'

'Do you have a lot of energy?'

She was surprised at the question. 'Yes, I . . .'

'Good. You're going to need it. I'm making you my executive assistant. There will be a nice raise for you.'

'I don't know what to say. I . . .'

'You've earned it.'

Lara saw the memo in Kathy's hand. 'What's that?'

'*Gourmet* magazine would like to publish your favourite recipe. Are you interested?'

'No. Tell them I'm too . . . wait a minute.' She sat there a moment, lost in thought. Then she said softly, 'Yes. I'll give them a recipe.'

The recipe appeared in the magazine three months later. It began:

> Black Bun – A classic Scottish dish. A mixture encased in a shortpaste jacket made from half a pound of flour, a quarter pound of butter, a touch of cold water, and a half a teaspoon of baking powder. Inside are two pounds of raisins, half a pound of chopped almonds, three-quarters of a pound of flour, half a pound of sugar, two teaspoons of allspice, a teaspoon each of ground ginger and ground cinnamon, a half teaspoon of baking powder, and a dash of brandy . . .

Lara looked at the article for a long time, and it brought back the taste of it, the smell of the boarding house kitchen, the noise of the boarders at supper. Her father helpless in his bed. She put the magazine away.

People recognized Lara on the street, and when she walked into a restaurant, there were always excited whispers. She was escorted around town by half a dozen eligible suitors and had flattering proposals, but she was not interested. In a strange, almost eerie way, she was still looking for someone. Someone familiar. Someone she had never met.

Lara would wake up at five o'clock every morning and have her driver, Max, take her to one of the buildings under construction. She would stand there, staring at what she was creating, and she thought, *You were wrong, Father. I can collect the rents.*

For Lara, the sounds of the day began with the

rat-a-tat-tat of the jackhammers, the roar of the bulldozers, the clanging of heavy metal. She would ride the rickety construction elevator to the top, and stand on the steel girders with the wind blowing in her face, and she thought, *I own this city.*

Paul Martin and Lara were in bed.

'I hear you chewed out a couple of your construction workers pretty good today.'

'They deserved it,' Lara said. 'They were doing sloppy work.'

Paul grinned. 'At least you've learned not to slap them.'

'Look what happened when I *did* slap one.' She snuggled up to him. 'I met you.'

'I have to take a trip to LA,' Paul said. 'I'd like you to come with me. Can you get away for a few days?'

'I'd love to, Paul, but it's impossible. I schedule my days with a stopwatch.'

He sat up and looked down at her. 'Maybe you're doing too much, baby. Don't ever get too busy for me.'

Lara smiled and began to stroke him. 'Don't worry about that. It will never happen.'

It had been there in front of her all the time, and she had not seen it. It was a huge waterfront property in the Wall Street area, near the World Trade Center. And it was for sale. Lara had passed it a dozen times, but she looked at it now and saw what should have been there all along: In her mind, she could see the world's tallest building. She knew what Howard was going to say: *You're getting in over your head, Lara. You can't get involved with this.* But she knew that nothing was going to stop her.

When she got to the office, she called a meeting of her staff.

'The Wall Street property on the waterfront,' Lara said. 'We're going to buy it. We're going to put up the tallest skyscraper in the world.'

'Lara . . .'

'Before you say anything, Howard, let me point out a few things. The location is perfect. It's in the heart of the business district. Tenants will be fighting to get office space there. And remember, it's going to be the tallest skyscraper in the world. That's a big sizzle. It's going to be our flagship. We'll call it Cameron Towers.'

'Where's the money coming from?'

Lara handed him a piece of paper.

Keller was examining the figures. 'You're being optimistic.'

'I'm being realistic. We're not talking about just any building. We're talking about a jewel, Howard.'

He was thinking hard. 'You'll be stretching yourself thin.'

Lara smiled. 'We've done that before, haven't we?'

Keller said, thoughtfully, 'The tallest skyscraper in the world . . .'

'That's right. And the banks call us every day, throwing money at us. They'll jump at this.'

'They probably will,' Keller said. He looked at Lara. 'You really want this, don't you?'

'Yes.'

Keller sighed. He looked around at the group. 'All right. The first step is to take an option on the property.'

Lara smiled. 'I've already done that. And I have some other news for you. Steve Murchison was negotiating for that property.'

'I remember him. We took that hotel site away from him in Chicago.'

I'm going to let it go this time, bitch, because I don't think you know what the hell you're doing. But in the future, stay out of my way – you could get hurt.

'Right.' Murchison had become one of the most ruthless and successful real estate developers in New York.

Keller said, 'Lara, he's bad news. He enjoys destroying people.'

'You worry too much.'

The financing for Cameron Towers went smoothly. Lara had been right. The bankers felt that there was a sizzle to the tallest skyscraper in the world. And the name of Cameron was an added cachet. They were eager to be associated with her.

Lara was more than a glamorous figure. She was a symbol to the women of the world, an icon. *If she can accomplish this, why not me?* A perfume was named after her. She was invited to all the important social events, and hostesses were eager to have her at their dinner parties. Her name on a building seemed to ensure success.

*

'We're going to start our own construction company,' Lara decided one day. 'We have the crews. We'll rent them out to other builders.'

'That's not a bad idea,' Keller said.

'Let's go for it. How soon are we going to break ground for Cameron Towers?'

'The deal's in place. I would say three months from now.'

Lara sat back in her chair. 'Can you imagine it, Howard? The tallest skyscraper in the world.'

He wondered what Freud would have made of that.

The ground-breaking ceremony for Cameron Towers had the atmosphere of a three-ring circus. America's Princess, Lara Cameron, was the main attraction. The event had been heavily publicized in the newspapers and on television, and a crowd of more than two hundred people had gathered, waiting for Lara to arrive. When her white limousine pulled up to the building site, there was a roar from the crowd.

'There she is!'

As Lara stepped out of the car and moved toward the building site to greet the mayor, police and security guards held the crowd back. The people pushed forward, screaming and calling her name, and the photographers' flashbulbs began popping.

In a special roped-off section were the bankers, heads of advertising agencies, company directors, contractors, project managers, community representatives, and architects. One hundred feet away, large bulldozers and backhoes were standing by, ready to go to work. Fifty trucks were lined up to cart the rubble away.

Lara was standing next to the mayor and the Manhattan borough president. It had started to drizzle. Jerry Townsend, head of public relations for Cameron Enterprises, hurried toward Lara with an umbrella. She smiled and waved him away.

The mayor spoke into the cameras. 'Today is a great day for Manhattan. This ground-breaking ceremony at Cameron Towers marks the beginning of one of the largest real estate projects in Manhattan's history. Six blocks of Manhattan real estate will be converted into a modern community that will include apartment buildings, two shopping centres, a convention centre, and the tallest skyscraper in the world.'

There was applause from the crowd.

'Wherever you look,' the mayor continued, 'you can see Lara Cameron's contribution written in concrete.' He pointed. 'Uptown is the Cameron Center. And near it, Cameron Plaza and half a dozen housing projects. And across the country is the great Cameron Hotel chain.'

The mayor turned to Lara and smiled. 'And she's not only brainy, she's beautiful.'

There was laughter and more applause.

'Lara Cameron, ladies and gentlemen.'

Lara looked into the television cameras and smiled. 'Thank you, Mr Mayor. I'm very pleased to have made some small contribution to this fabulous city of ours. My father always told me that the reason we were put on this earth was . . .' she hesitated. Out of the corner of her eye, she had seen a familiar face in the crowd. Steve Murchison. She had seen his photograph in the newspapers. What was he doing here? Lara went on, '. . . was to leave it a better place than when we came into it. Well, I hope that in my own small way, I've been able to do that.'

There was more applause. Lara was handed a ceremonial hard hat and a chrome-plated shovel.

'Time to go to work, Miss Cameron.'

The flashbulbs began to pop again.

Lara pushed the shovel into the dirt and dug up the first bit of earth.

At the conclusion of the ceremony, refreshments were served, while the television cameras kept recording the event. When Lara looked around again, Murchison was nowhere in sight.

Thirty minutes later, Lara Cameron was back in the limousine headed for the office. Jerry Townsend was seated next to her.

'I thought it went great,' he said. 'Just great.'

'Not bad,' Lara grinned. 'Thanks, Jerry.'

The executive suites of Cameron Enterprises occupied the entire fiftieth floor of Cameron Center.

Lara got off at the fiftieth floor, and by then word had got around that she was arriving. The secretaries and staff were busily at work.

Lara turned to Jerry Townsend. 'Come into my office.'

The office was an enormous corner suite overlooking the city.

Lara glanced at some papers on her desk and looked up at Jerry.

'How's your father? Is he any better?'

What did she know about his father?

'He's . . . he's not well.'

'I know. He has Huntington's Chorea, hasn't he, Jerry?'

'Yes.'

It was a terrible disease. It was progressive and degenerative, characterized by spasmodic involuntary movements of the face and extremities, accompanied by the loss of mental faculties.

'How do you know about my father?'

'I'm on the board at the hospital where he's being treated. I heard some doctors discussing his case.'

Jerry said tightly, 'It's incurable.'

'Everything is incurable until they find the cure,' Lara said. 'I did some checking. There's a doctor in Switzerland who's doing some advanced research on the disease. He's willing to take on your father's case. I'll handle the expenses.'

Jerry stood there, stunned.

'Okay?'

He found it difficult to speak. 'Okay.' *I don't know her*, Jerry Townsend thought. *Nobody knows her.*

History was being made, but Lara was too busy to notice. Ronald Reagan had been re-elected, and a man named Mikhail Gorbachev had succeeded Chernenko as leader of the USSR.

Lara built a low-income housing development in Detroit.

In 1986, Ivan Boesky had been fined a hundred million dollars in an insider trading scandal and sentenced to three years in prison.

Lara started development on condominiums in Queens. Investors were eager to be a part of the magic of her name. A group of German investment bankers flew to New York to meet with Lara. She arranged for the meeting immediately after their plane landed. They had protested, but Lara said, 'I'm so sorry, gentlemen. It's the only time I have. I'm leaving for Hong Kong.'

The Germans were served coffee. Lara had tea. One of the Germans complained about the taste of the coffee. 'It's a special brand made for me,' Lara explained. 'The flavour will grow on you. Have another cup.'

By the end of the negotiations, Lara had won all her points.

Life was a series of serendipities, except for one disturbing incident. Lara had had several run-ins with Steve Murchison over various properties and she had always managed to outwit him.

'I think we should back off,' Keller warned.

'Let him back off.'

And one morning a beautiful package wrapped in rose paper arrived from Bendels. Kathy laid it on Lara's desk.

'It's awfully heavy,' Kathy said. 'If it's a hat, you're in trouble.'

Curious, Lara unwrapped it and opened the lid. The box was packed with dirt. A printed card inside read: *The Frank E. Campbell Funeral Chapel.*

The building projects were all going well. When Lara read about a proposed inner-city playground that was stymied because of bureaucratic redtape, she stepped in, had her company build it and donated it to the City. The publicity she received on it was enormous. One headline read: *Lara Cameron stands for 'CAN DO.'*

She was seeing Paul once or twice a week, and she talked to him every day.

Lara bought a house in Southampton and lived in a fantasy world of expensive jewels and furs and limousines. Her closets were filled with beautiful designer clothes. *'I need some clothes for school.' 'Weel, I'm nae made of money. Get yourself somethin' frae the Salvation Army Citadel.'*

And Lara would order another outfit.

Her employees were her family. She worried about them, and was generous with them. They were all she had. She remembered their birthdays and anniversaries. She helped get their children into good schools, and set up scholarship funds for them. When they tried to thank her, Lara was embarrassed. It was difficult for her to express her emotions. Her father had ridiculed her when she had tried. Lara had built a protective wall around herself. *No one is ever going to hurt me again*, she vowed. *No one*.

Book Three

17

'I'm leaving for London in the morning, Howard.'

'What's up?' Keller asked.

'Lord MacIntosh has invited me to come over and take a look at a property he's interested in. He wants to go into partnership.'

Brian MacIntosh was one of the wealthiest real estate developers in England.

'What time do we leave?' Keller asked.

'I've decided to go alone.'

'Oh?'

'I want you to keep an eye on things here.'

He nodded. 'Right. I'll do that.'

'I know you will. I can always count on you.'

The trip to London was uneventful. The private 727 she had purchased took off in the morning and landed at the Magec Terminal at Luton Airport outside London. She had no idea her life was about to change.

When Lara arrived at the lobby of Claridge's, Ronald Jones, the manager, was there to greet her. 'It's a pleasure to have you back, Miss Cameron. I'll show you to your suite. By the way, we have some messages for you.' There were more than two dozen.

The suite was lovely. There were flowers from Brian MacIntosh and from Paul Martin, and champagne and hors d'oeuvres from the management. The phone began to ring the minute Lara walked in. The calls were from all over the United States.

'The architect wants to make some changes in the plans. It will cost a fortune . . .'

'There's a hold-up on the cement delivery . . .'

'The First National Savings and Loan wants in on our next deal . . .'

'The mayor wants to know if you can be in LA for the opening. He'd like to plan a big ceremony . . .'

'The toilets haven't arrived . . .'

'Bad weather is holding us up. We're falling behind schedule . . .'

Each problem required a decision, and when Lara finally finished with her calls, she was exhausted. She had dinner in her room alone and sat looking out of the window, at the Rolls-Royces and Bentleys pulling up to the Brook Street entrance, and a feeling of elation swept over her. *The little girl from Glace Bay has come a long way, Daddy.*

The following morning Lara went with Brian MacIntosh to look at the proposed site. It was enormous – two miles of riverside frontage filled with old rundown buildings and storage sheds.

'The British Government will give us a lot of tax relief on this,' Brian MacIntosh explained, 'because we're going to rehabilitate this whole section of the city.'

'I'd like to think about it,' Lara said. She had already made up her mind.

'By the way, I have tickets to a concert tonight,' Brian MacIntosh told her. 'My wife has a club meeting. Do you like classical music?'

Lara had no interest in classical music. 'Yes.'

'Philip Adler is playing Rachmaninoff.' He looked at Lara as though expecting her to say something. She had never heard of Philip Adler.

'It sounds wonderful,' Lara said.

'Good. We'll have supper afterward at Scott's. I'll pick you up at seven.'

Why did I say I liked classical music? Lara wondered. It was going to be a boring evening. She would have preferred to take a hot bath and go to sleep. *Oh, well, one more evening won't hurt me. I'll fly back to New York in the morning.*

The Festival Hall was crowded with music aficionados. The men wore dinner jackets and the women were dressed in beautiful evening gowns. It was a gala evening and there was a feeling of excited expectation in the large hall.

Brian MacIntosh purchased two programmes from the usher, and they were seated. He handed Lara a programme. She barely glanced at it. The London Philharmonic Orchestra . . . Philip Adler playing Rachmaninoff's piano concerto no. 3 in D minor, Opus 30.

I've got to call Howard and remind him about the revised estimates on the Fifth Avenue site.

The conductor appeared on stage and the audience applauded. Lara paid no attention. *The contractor in Boston is moving too slowly. He needs a carrot. I'll tell Howard to offer him a bonus.*

There was another loud round of applause from the audience. A man was taking his place at the piano at centre stage. The conductor gave a down-beat and the music began.

Philip Adler's fingers flashed across the keys.

A woman seated behind Lara said with a loud Texas accent, 'Isn't he fantastic? I *told* you, Agnes!'

Lara tried to concentrate again. *The London deal is out. It's the wrong neighbourhood*, Lara thought. *People aren't going to want to live there. Location. Location. Location.* She thought about a project that had been brought to her, near Columbus Circle. *Now that one could work*.

The woman behind Lara said, loudly, 'His *expression* . . . he's fabulous! He's one of the most . . .'

Lara tried to tune her out.

The cost of an office building there would be approximately four hundred dollars per rentable square foot. If I can bring in the construction cost at one hundred and fifty million, the land costs at one hundred twenty-five million, the soft costs . . .

'My God!' the woman behind Lara exclaimed.

Lara was startled out of her reverie.

'He's so brilliant!'

There was a drum roll from the orchestra and Philip Adler played four bars alone, and the orchestra began to play faster and faster. The drums began to beat . . .

The woman could not contain herself. 'Listen to that! The music is going from *più vivo* to *più mosso*. Have you ever heard anything so exciting?'

Lara gritted her teeth.

The minimum break-even should work out all

right, she thought. *The cost of the rentable square feet would be three hundred and fifty million, the interest at ten per cent would be thirty-five million, plus ten million in operating expenses . . .*

The tempo of the music was increasing, reverberating through the hall. The music came to a sudden climax and stopped, and the audience was on its feet, cheering. There were calls of *bravo!* The pianist had risen and was taking bows.

Lara did not even bother to look up. *Taxes would be about six, free rent concessions would come to two. We're talking about fifty-eight million.*

'He's incredible, isn't he?' Brian MacIntosh said.

'Yes.' Lara was annoyed at having her thoughts interrupted again.

'Let's go backstage. Philip is a friend of mine.'

'I really don't . . .'

He took Lara's hand and they were moving toward an exit.

'I'm glad I'll have a chance to introduce you to him,' Brian MacIntosh said.

It's six o'clock in New York, Lara thought. *I'll be able to call Howard and tell him to start negotiations.*

'He's a once in a lifetime experience, isn't he?'

Once is enough for me, Lara thought. 'Yes.'

They had reached the outside artists' entrance. There was a large crowd waiting. Brian MacIntosh knocked on the door. A doorman opened it.

'Yes, sir?'

'Lord MacIntosh to see Mr Adler.'

'Right, My Lord. Come in, please.' He opened the door wide enough to let Brian MacIntosh and Lara enter, then closed it against the crowd.

'What do all these people want?' Lara asked.

He looked at her in surprise. 'They're here to see Philip.'

She wondered why.

The doorman said, 'Go right into the green room, My Lord.'

'Thank you.'

Five minutes, Lara thought, *and I'll say I have to leave*.

The green room was noisy and already full. People were crowded around a figure Lara could not see. The crowd shifted and for an instant he was clearly visible. Lara froze, and for a moment she felt her heart stop. The vague, evanescent image that had been at the back of her mind all those years had suddenly materialized out of nowhere. Lochinvar, the vision in her fantasies, had come to life! The man at the centre of the crowd was tall and blond, with delicate, sensitive features. He was wearing white tie and tails, and a feeling of *déjà vu* swept over Lara: *She was standing at the kitchen sink in the boarding house, and the handsome young man in white tie and tails came up behind her and whispered, 'Can I help you?'*

Brian MacIntosh was watching Lara, concerned. 'Are you all right?'

'I . . . I'm fine.' She was finding it difficult to breathe.

Philip Adler was moving toward them, smiling, and it was the same warm smile Lara had imagined. He held out his hand. 'Brian, how good of you to come.'

'I wouldn't have missed it,' MacIntosh said. 'You were simply marvellous.'

'Thank you.'

'Oh, Philip, I would like you to meet Lara Cameron.'

Lara was looking into his eyes and the words came out unbidden. 'Do you dry?'

'I beg your pardon?'

Lara turned red. 'Nothing. I . . .' She was suddenly tongue-tied.

People were crowding around Philip Adler, heaping praise on him.

'You've never played better . . .'

'I think Rachmaninoff was with you tonight . . .'

The praise went on and on. The women in the room were crowding around him, touching and pulling at him. Lara stood there watching, mesmerized. Her childhood dream had come true. Her fantasy had become flesh and blood.

'Are you ready to go?' Brian MacIntosh asked Lara.

No. She wanted nothing more than to stay. She wanted to talk to the vision again, to touch him, to make sure he was real. 'I'm ready,' Lara said reluctantly.

The following morning, Lara was on her way back to New York. She wondered whether she would ever see Philip Adler again.

She was unable to get him out of her mind. She tried to tell herself that it was ridiculous, that she was trying to relive a childhood dream, but it was no use. She kept seeing his face, hearing his voice. *I must see him again*, Lara thought.

Early the next morning, Paul Martin telephoned.

'Hi, baby. I missed you. How was London?'

'Fine,' Lara said carefully. 'Just fine.'

When they had finished talking, Lara sat at her desk thinking about Philip Adler.

'They're waiting for you in the conference room, Miss Cameron.'

'I'm coming.'

'We lost the Queens deal,' Keller said.

'Why? I thought it was all set.'

'So did I, but the Community Board refuses to change the zoning.'

Lara looked around at the Executive Committee assembled in the room. There were architects, lawyers, publicity men, and construction engineers.

Lara said, 'I don't understand. Those tenants have an average income of nine thousand dollars a year, and they're paying less than two hundred dollars a month in rent. We're going to rehabilitate the apartments for them, at no increase in rent, and we're going to provide new apartments for some of the other residents in the neighbourhood. We're giving them Christmas in July and they turned you down? What's the problem?'

'It's not the board so much. It's their chairman. A lady named Edith Benson.'

'Set up another meeting with her. I'll go there myself.'

Lara took her chief construction supervisor, Bill Whitman, to the meeting.

Lara said, 'Frankly, I was stunned when I heard that your Board turned us down. We're going to put up over a hundred million dollars to improve this neighbourhood and yet you refuse to . . .'

Edith Benson cut her short. 'Let's be honest, Miss Cameron. You're not putting up the money to improve the neighbourhood. You're putting up the money so Cameron Enterprises can make more money.'

'Of course we expect to make money,' Lara said. 'But the only way we can do that is to help you people. We're going to make the living conditions in your area better, and . . .'

'Sorry. I don't agree. Right now, we're a quiet little neighbourhood. If we let you in, we're going to become a higher density area – more traffic, more automobiles, more pollution. We don't want any of that.'

'Neither do I,' Lara said. 'We don't intend to put up Dingbats that . . .'

'Dingbats?'

'Yes, those ugly, stripped-down, three-storey stucco boxes. We're interested in designs that won't increase the noise level or reduce the light or change the feel of the neighbourhood. We're not interested in hot-dog, show-off architecture. I've already hired Stanton Fielding, the top architect in the country, to design this project, and Andrew Burton from Washington to do the landscaping.'

Edith Benson shrugged. 'I'm sorry. It's no use. I don't think there's anything more to discuss.' She started to rise.

I can't lose this, Lara thought desperately. *Can't they see it's for the good of their neighbourhood? I'm trying to do something for them and they won't let me.* And suddenly she had a wild idea.

'Wait a minute,' Lara said. 'I understand that the other members of the Board are willing to make the deal but you are the one blocking it.'

'That's correct.'

Lara took a deep breath. 'There *is* something to discuss.' She hesitated. 'It's very personal.' She was fidgeting now. 'You say I'm not worried about pollution and what happens to the environment in this neighbourhood if we move in? I'm going to tell you something that I hope you will keep in confidence. I have a ten-year-old daughter that I'm crazy about, and she's going to live in the new building with her father. He has custody of her.'

Edith Benson was looking at her in surprise. 'I . . . I didn't know you had a daughter.'

'No one does,' Lara said quietly. 'I've never been married. That's why I'm asking you to keep this confidential. If it gets out, it could be very damaging to me. I'm sure you understand that.'

'I do understand.'

'I love my daughter very much, and I assure you that I would never do anything in the world that would hurt her. I intend to do everything I can to make this project wonderful for all the people who live here. And she'll be one of them.'

There was a sympathetic silence. 'I must say, this . . . this puts quite a different complexion on things, Miss Cameron. I'd like to have some time to think about it.'

'Thank you. I appreciate that.' *If I did have a*

daughter, Lara thought, *it would be safe for her to live here.*

Three weeks later, Lara got the approval from the Community Board to go ahead with the project.

'Great,' Lara said. 'Now we'd better get hold of Stanton Fielding and Andrew Burton and see if they're interested in working on the project.'

Howard Keller could not believe the news. 'I heard what happened,' he said. 'You conned her! That's incredible. You don't *have* a daughter!'

'They need this project,' Lara said. 'This was the only way I could think of to change their minds.'

Bill Whitman was listening. 'There'll be hell to pay if they ever find out.'

In January, construction was completed on a new building on East 63rd Street. It was a forty-five storey apartment building, and Lara reserved the duplex penthouse for herself. The rooms were large, and the apartment had terraces that covered a full block. She brought in a top decorator to do the apartment. There was a housewarming for a hundred people.

'All it lacks is a man,' one of the lady guests said cattily.

And Lara thought of Philip Adler and wondered where he was and what he was doing.

Lara and Howard Keller were in the middle of a discussion when Bill Whitman came into the office.

'Hi, boss. Got a minute?'

Lara looked up from her desk. 'Just about, Bill. What's the problem?'

'My wife.'

'If you're having marital difficulties . . .'

'It's not that. She thinks we ought to go away for a while on vacation. Maybe go to Paris for a few weeks.'

Lara frowned. 'Paris? We're in the middle of half a dozen jobs.'

'I know, but I've been working long hours lately, and I don't get to see much of my wife. You know what she said to me this morning? She said, "Bill, if you got a promotion and a nice raise, you wouldn't have to work so hard."' He smiled.

Lara sat back in her chair, studying him. 'You aren't due for a raise until next year.'

Whitman shrugged. 'Who knows what can happen in a year? We might run into problems with that Queens deal, for instance. You know, old Edith Benson might hear something that would make her change her mind. Right?'

Lara sat very still. 'I see.'

Bill Whitman got to his feet. 'Think about it, and let me know.'

Lara forced a smile. 'Yes.'

She watched him walk out of her office, her face grim.

'Jesus,' Keller said. 'What was that all about?'

'It's called blackmail.'

The following day, Lara had lunch with Paul Martin.

Lara said, 'Paul, I have a problem. I'm not sure

how to handle it.' She told him about her conversation with Bill Whitman.

'Do you think he'll really go back to the old lady?' Paul Martin asked.

'I don't know. But if he does, I could get in a lot of trouble with the Building Commission.'

Paul shrugged. 'I wouldn't worry about him. He's probably bluffing.'

Lara sighed. 'I hope so.'

'How would you like to go to Reno?' Paul asked.

'I'd love to, but I can't get away.'

'I'm not asking you to get away. I'm asking if you'd like to buy a hotel and casino there.'

Lara studied him. 'Are you serious?'

'I got word that one of the hotels is going to lose its licence. The place is a gold mine. When the news gets out, everyone is going to be after it. The hotel's going on auction, but I think I can fix it for you to get it.'

Lara hesitated. 'I don't know. I'm pretty heavily committed. Howard Keller says the banks won't lend me any more until I can pay off some loans.'

'You don't have to go to a bank.'

'Then where . . . ?'

'Junk bonds. A lot of Wall Street firms offer them. There are savings and loan companies. You put up five per cent equity, and a savings and loan company will put up sixty-five per cent in high-yield notes. That leaves thirty per cent uncovered. You can get that from a foreign bank that invests in casinos. You've got choices – Switzerland, Germany, Japan. There are half a dozen banks that will put up the thirty per cent in commercial notes.'

Lara was beginning to get excited. 'It sounds great.

Do you really think you can get the hotel for me?'

Paul grinned. 'It will be your Christmas present.'

'You're wonderful. Why are you so good to me?'

'I haven't the vaguest idea,' he teased. But he knew the answer. He was obsessed with her. Lara made him feel young again, and she made everything exciting for him. *I never want to lose you*, he thought.

Keller was waiting for Lara when she walked into the office.

'Where have you been?' he asked. 'There was a two o'clock meeting that . . .'

'Tell me about junk bonds, Howard. We've never dealt with them. How are bonds rated?'

'Well, at the top you have Triple A. That would be a company like AT&T. Down the ladder you have Double A, Single A, BAA, and at the bottom of the ladder, Double B – those are the junk bonds. An investment bond will pay nine per cent. A junk bond will pay fourteen per cent. Why do you ask?'

Lara told him.

'A *casino*, Lara? Jesus! Paul Martin is behind this, isn't he?'

'No, Howard. If I go ahead with this, *I'm* behind it. Did we get an answer on our offer on the Battery Park property?'

'Yes. She won't sell to us.'

'The property is up for sale, isn't it?'

'In a way.'

'Stop talking in circles.'

'It's owned by a doctor's widow, Eleanor Royce. Every real estate developer in town has been bidding on that property.'

'Have we been out-bid?'

'It isn't that. The old lady isn't interested in money. She's loaded.'

'What *is* she interested in?'

'She wants some kind of monument to her husband. Apparently she thinks she was married to Albert Schweitzer. She wants to keep his flame burning. She doesn't want her property turned into anything crass or commercial. I hear Steve Murchison has been trying to talk her into selling.'

'Oh?'

Lara sat there quietly for a full minute. When she spoke, she said, 'Who's your doctor, Howard?'

'What?'

'Who's your doctor?'

'Seymour Bennett. He's Chief of Staff at Midtown Hospital.'

The following morning Lara's attorney, Terry Hill, was sitting in the office of Dr Seymour Bennett.

'My secretary told me that you wanted to see me urgently, and that it has nothing to do with a medical problem.'

'In a sense,' Terry Hill said, 'it does concern a medical problem, Dr Bennett. I represent an investment group that wants to put up a non-profit clinic. We want to be able to take care of those unfortunate people who can't afford regular medical care.'

'That's a splendid idea,' Dr Bennett said. 'What can I do to help you?'

Terry Hill told him.

*

The following day, Dr Bennett was having tea in the home of Eleanor Royce.

'They've asked me to approach you on behalf of this group, Mrs Royce. They want to build a beautiful clinic, and they want to name it after your late husband. They visualize it as sort of a shrine to him.'

Mrs Royce's face lit up. 'They do?'

They discussed the group's plans for an hour, and at the end of that time, Mrs Royce said, 'George would have loved this. You tell them that they have a deal.'

Construction began six months later. When it was completed, it was gigantic. The entire square block was filled with huge apartment buildings, an enormous shopping mall, and a theatre complex. In a remote corner of the property was a small one-storey brick building. A simple sign over the door read:

GEORGE ROYCE
MEDICAL CLINIC.

18

On Christmas Day, Lara stayed at home. She had been invited to a dozen parties, but Paul Martin was going to drop by. 'I have to be with Nina and the kids today,' he had explained, 'but I want to come by and see you.'

She wondered what Philip Adler was doing on this Christmas Day.

It was a Currier and Ives postcard kind of day. New York was blanketed in a beautiful white snowfall, wrapped in silence. When Paul Martin arrived, he had a shopping bag full of gifts for Lara.

'I had to stop at the office to pick these up,' he said. *So his wife wouldn't know*.

'You give me so much, Paul. You don't have to bring anything.'

'I wanted to. Open them up now.'

Lara was touched by his eagerness to see her reaction.

The gifts were thoughtful and expensive. A necklace from Cartier's, scarves from Hermes, books from Rizzoli, an antique carriage clock, and a small white envelope. Lara opened it. It read: *Cameron Reno Hotel & Casino* in large block letters. She looked up at him in surprise. 'I have the hotel?'

He nodded confidently. 'You will have. The

bidding starts next week. You're going to have fun with it,' Paul Martin predicted.

'I don't know anything about running a casino.'

'Don't worry. I'll put some professionals in to manage it for you. The hotel, you can handle yourself.'

'I don't know how to thank you. You do so much for me.'

He took her hands in his. 'There isn't anything in the world that I wouldn't do for you. Remember that.'

'I will,' she said solemnly.

He was looking at his watch. 'I have to get back home. I wish . . .' He hesitated.

'Yes?'

'Never mind. Merry Christmas, Lara.'

'Merry Christmas, Paul.'

She went to the window and looked out. The sky had become a delicate curtain of dancing snowflakes. Restless, Lara walked to the radio and turned it on. An announcer was saying, '. . . and now, for its holiday programme, the Boston Symphony Orchestra presents Beethoven's Piano Concerto No. 5 in E flat, with Philip Adler, soloist.'

Lara listened with her eyes, seeing him at the piano, handsome and elegant. When the music ended, she thought, *I've got to see him again*.

Bill Whitman was one of the best construction supervisors in the business. He had risen through the ranks and was in great demand. He worked steadily and earned good money, but he was dissatisfied. For years he had watched builders reaping enormous fortunes while he got nothing but a salary. *In a way*, he thought, *they're making their money off of me. The owner gets the cake; I get the crumbs.* But the day Lara Cameron had gone before the Zoning Commission, everything changed. She had lied to get the Board's permission, and that lie could destroy her. *If I went to the Board and told them the truth, she'd be out of business.*

But Bill Whitman had no intention of doing that. He had a better plan. He intended to use what had happened as leverage. The boss lady was going to give him anything he asked for. He could sense from their meeting at which he had asked for promotion and a raise that she was going to give in. She had no choice. *I'll start small*, Bill Whitman thought happily, *and then I'll really begin squeezing.*

Two days after Christmas, work began again on the Eastside Plaza project. Whitman looked around at the huge site and thought, *This one's going to be a real money-maker. Only this time, I'm going to cash in on it, too.*

The site was crowded with heavy equipment. Cranes were digging into the earth and lifting tons of it into waiting trucks. A crane wielding a giant saw-toothed scoop bucket seemed to be stuck. The huge arm hung suspended high in mid air. Whitman strode toward the cab, under the huge metal bucket.

'Hey, Jesse,' he called. 'What's the matter up there?'

The man in the cab mumbled something that Whitman could not hear.

Whitman moved closer. 'What?'

Everything happened in a split second. A chain slipped and the huge metal bucket came crashing down on Whitman, smashing him to the ground. Men came running toward the body, but there was nothing to be done.

'The safety brake slipped,' the operator explained later. 'Gee, I feel really awful. I liked Bill a lot.'

When she heard the news, Lara immediately telephoned Paul Martin. 'Did you hear about Bill Whitman?'

'Yes. It was on television.'

'Paul, you didn't . . . ?'

He laughed. 'Don't go getting any crazy ideas. You've been seeing too many movies. Remember, the good guys always win in the end.'

And Lara wondered, *Am I one of the good guys?*

There were more than a dozen bidders for the Reno hotel.

'When do I bid?' Lara asked Paul.

'You don't. Not until I tell you. Let the others jump in first.'

The bidding was secret and the bids were sealed, to be opened on the following Friday. By Wednesday, Lara still had not made a bid. She telephoned Paul Martin.

'Sit tight,' he said. 'I'll tell you when.'

They stayed in touch by phone several times a day.

At 5 p.m., one hour before the bidding was to close, Lara received a phone call.

'Now! The high bid is a hundred and twenty million. I want you to go five million over it.'

Lara gasped. 'But if I do that, I'll lose money on the deal.'

'Trust me,' Paul said. 'After you get the hotel and start redoing it, you can cut corners on the changes. They'll all be endorsed by the supervising engineer. You'll make up the five million and then some.'

The following day, Lara was notified that hers was the winning bid.

Now Lara and Keller were on their way to Reno.

The hotel was called the Reno Palace. It was large and sumptuous, with 1,500 rooms, and a huge, glittering casino that was empty. Lara and Howard Keller were being escorted through the casino by a man named Tony Wilkie.

'The people who owned this got a bum deal,' Wilkie said.

'What kind of bum deal?' Keller asked.

'Well, it seems that a couple of the boys were pocketing a little money from the cash cage . . .'

'Skimming,' Keller interjected.

'Yeah. Of course, the owners didn't know anything about it.'

'Of course not.'

'But someone blew the whistle and the Gaming Commission pulled out the rug. It's too bad. It was a very profitable operation.'

'I know.' Keller had already studied the books.

When the tour of inspection was completed, and Lara and Howard were alone, she said, 'Paul was right. This is a gold mine.' She saw the expression on Howard's face. 'What's the matter?'

He shrugged. 'I don't know. I just don't like us getting involved in anything like this.'

'What's "anything like this"? It's a cash cow, Howard.'

'Who's going to run the casino?'

'We'll find people,' Lara said evasively.

'Where from? The Girl Scouts? It takes gamblers to run an operation like this. I don't know any, do you?'

Lara was silent.

'I'll bet Paul Martin does.'

'Leave him out of this,' Lara said.

'I'd like to, and I'd like to leave you out of it. I don't think this is such a great idea.'

'You didn't think the Queens project was a great idea either, did you? Or the shopping centre on Houston Street. But they're making money, aren't they?'

'Lara, I never said they weren't good deals. All I said was that I think we're moving too fast. You're swallowing up everything in sight, but you haven't digested anything yet.'

Lara patted his cheek. 'Relax.'

The members of the Gaming Commission received Lara with elaborate courtesy.

'We don't often meet a beautiful young woman in here,' the Chairman said. 'It brightens up our day.'

Lara did look beautiful. She was wearing a Donna Karan beige wool suit, with a cream-coloured silk blouse, and, for good luck, one of the scarves Paul had given her for Christmas. She smiled. 'Thank you.'

'What can we do for you?' one of the Gaming Commissioners asked. They all knew perfectly well what they could do for her.

'I'm here because I would like to do something for Reno,' Lara said earnestly. 'I would like to give it the biggest, most beautiful hotel in Nevada. I'd like to add five storeys to the Reno Palace, and put up a large convention centre to attract more tourists here to gamble.'

The members of the board glanced at one another. The Chairman said, 'I think something like that would have a very beneficial effect on the city. Of course, our job is to make sure that an operation like this would be run completely above board.'

'I'm not exactly an escaped convict,' Lara smiled.

They chuckled at her little joke. 'We know your record, Miss Cameron, and it is admirable. However, you've had no experience in running a casino.'

'That's true,' Lara admitted. 'On the other hand, I'm sure it will be easy to find fine, qualified employees who will meet the approval of this board. I would certainly welcome your guidance.'

One of the members of the board spoke up. 'As far as the financing is concerned, can you guarantee . . . ?'

The Chairman interrupted. 'That's all right, Tom, Miss Cameron has submitted the financials on it. I'll see that you each get a copy.'

Lara sat there, waiting.

The Chairman said, 'I can't promise anything at this moment, Miss Cameron, but I think I'm safe in saying that I don't see any obstacles to your being granted a licence.'

Lara beamed. 'That's wonderful. I'd like to get moving as quickly as possible.'

'I'm afraid things don't move quite that fast here. There will be a one month waiting period before we can give you a definite answer.'

Lara was dismayed. 'A month?'

'Yes. We have a bit of checking to do.'

'I understand,' Lara said. 'That will be fine.'

There was a music store in the hotel's shopping complex. In the window was a large poster of Philip Adler, advertising his new compact disc.

Lara was not interested in the music. She bought the CD for Philip's photograph on the back of the case.

On their way back to New York, Lara said, 'Howard, what do you know about Philip Adler?'

'Just what everybody else knows. He's probably the top concert pianist in the world today. He plays with the finest symphony orchestras. I read somewhere that he just set up a foundation for scholarships for minority musicians in inner cities.'

'What's it called?'

'The Philip Adler Foundation, I think.'

'I'd like to make a contribution,' Lara said. 'Send them a cheque for ten thousand dollars in my name.'

Keller looked at her in surprise. 'I thought you didn't care for classical music.'

'I'm starting to get interested in it,' Lara said.

*

The headline read:

> DISTRICT ATTORNEY PROBE OF PAUL MARTIN –
> ATTORNEY REPUTED TO HAVE MAFIA TIES

Lara read the story with dismay, and telephoned Paul immediately.

'What's going on?' Lara asked.

He chuckled. 'The DA is on another fishing expedition. They've been trying to tie me in with the boys for years, and they haven't had any luck. Every time an election comes up, they try to use me as their whipping boy. Don't worry about it. What about dinner tonight?'

'Fine,' Lara said.

'I know a little place on Mulberry Street where no one will bother us.'

Over dinner, Paul Martin said, 'I hear that the meeting with the Gaming Commission went well.'

'I think it did. They seemed friendly, but I've never done anything like this before.'

'I don't think you'll have any problem. I'll get you some good boys for the casino. The man who owned the licence got greedy.' He changed the subject. 'How are all the construction jobs going?'

'Fine. I have three projects in the works, Paul.'

'You're not getting in over your head, are you, Lara?'

He sounded like Howard Keller. 'No. Every job is on budget and on schedule.'

'That's good, baby. I wouldn't want anything to ever go wrong for you.'

'Nothing will.' She put her hand on his. 'You're my safety net.'

'I'll always be there.' He squeezed her hand.

Two weeks went by and Lara had not heard from Philip Adler. She sent for Keller. 'Did you make that $10,000 contribution to the Adler Foundation?'

'Yes, the day you mentioned it.'

'Strange. I would have thought he would have called me.'

Keller shrugged. 'He's probably travelling somewhere.'

'Probably.' She tried to conceal her disappointment. 'Let's talk about the building in Queens.'

'That's going to take a big financial bite out of us,' Keller said.

'I know how to protect us. I'd like to lock the deal in with one tenant.'

'Do you have anyone in mind?'

'Yes. Mutual Security Insurance. The president is a man named Horace Guttman. I've heard they're looking for a new location. I'd like it to be our building.'

'I'll check it out,' Keller said.

Lara noticed that he made no notes. 'You constantly amaze me. You remember everything, don't you?'

Keller grinned. 'I have a photographic memory. It used to be for baseball statistics.' *It all seems so long ago*, Howard thought. *The kid with the magic arm, the star of the Chicago Cubs minor league. Someone else and another time*. 'Sometimes it's a curse. There are a few things in my life I'd like to forget.'

'Howard, have the architect go ahead and draw up the plans for the Queens building. Find out how many floors Mutual Security will need, and how much floor space.'

Two days later, Keller walked into Lara's office. 'I'm afraid I have some bad news.'

'What's the problem?'

'I did a little snooping around. You were right about Mutual Security Insurance. They *are* looking for a new headquarters, but Guttman is thinking about a building in Union Square. It's your old friend, Steve Murchison's building.'

Murchison again! She was sure that the box of dirt had been sent by him. *I'm not going to let him bluff me*.

'Has Guttman committed to it?' Lara asked.

'Not yet.'

'All right. I'll handle it.'

That afternoon, Lara made a dozen phone calls. She hit the jackpot on the last call. Barbara Roswell.

'Horace Guttman? Sure, I know him, Lara. What's your interest in him?'

'I'd like to meet him. I'm a big fan of his. I want you to do me a favour. Could you please invite him to dinner next Saturday night, Barbara?'

'You've got it.'

The dinner party was simple but elegant. There were fourteen people at the Roswell residence. Alice Guttman wasn't feeling well that evening, so Horace Guttman had come to the party alone. Lara had been seated next to him. He was in his sixties, but he seemed much older. He had a stern, worn face and a stubborn chin. Lara looked enchanting, provocative. She was wearing a low-cut, black Halston gown and simple but stunning jewellery. They had had their cocktails and were seated at the dining table.

'I've been wanting to meet you,' Lara confessed. 'I've heard so much about you.'

'I've heard a lot about you, young lady. You've made quite a splash in this town.'

'I hope I'm making a contribution,' Lara said modestly. 'It's such a wonderful town.'

'Where are you from?'

'Gary, Indiana.'

'Really?' He looked at her in surprise. 'That's where I was born. So, you're a Hoosier, eh?'

Lara smiled. 'That's right. I have such fond memories of Gary. My father worked for the *Post Tribune*. I went to Roosevelt High. On weekends, we'd go to Gleason Park for picnics and outdoor concerts, or we'd go bowling at the Twelve and Twenty. I hated having to leave.'

'You've done well for yourself, Miss Cameron.'

'Lara.'

'Lara. What are you up to these days?'

'The project I'm most excited about,' Lara told him, 'is a new building I'm putting up in Queens. It's going to have thirty storeys, and 200,000 square feet of floor space.'

'That's interesting,' Guttman said, thoughtfully.

'Oh,' Lara said innocently. 'Why?'

'It happens that we're looking for a building just about that size for our new headquarters.'

'Really? Have you chosen one yet?'

'Not exactly, but . . .'

'If you'd like, I can show you the plans for our new building. They've already been drawn up.'

He studied her a moment. 'Yes, I'd like to see them.'

'I can bring them to your office Monday morning.'

'I'll look forward to it.'

The rest of the evening went well.

When Horace Guttman reached home that night, he walked into his wife's bedroom.

'How are you feeling?' he asked.

'Better, darling. How was the party?'

He sat down on the bed. 'Well, they all missed you, but I had an interesting time. Have you ever heard of Lara Cameron?'

'Certainly. Everyone has heard of Lara Cameron.'

'She's quite a woman. A little strange. Says she was born in Gary, Indiana, same as me. Knew all about Gary – Gleason Park and the Twelve and Twenty.'

'What's strange about that?'

Guttman looked at his wife and grinned. 'The little lady comes from Nova Scotia.'

Early Monday morning, Lara appeared at Horace Guttman's office, carrying the blueprints for the Queens project. She was ushered in immediately.

'Nice to see you, Lara. Sit down.'

She laid the blueprints on his desk and sat across from him.

'Before you look at these,' Lara said, 'I have something to confess, Horace.'

Guttman leaned back in his chair. 'Yes?'

'That story I told on Saturday about Gary, Indiana...'

'What about it?'

'I've never even been to Gary, Indiana. I was trying to impress you.'

He laughed. 'Now you've succeeded in confusing me. I'm not sure I'm going to be able to keep up with you, young lady. Let's look at these blueprints.'

Half an hour later, he was through examining them.

'You know,' he said reflectively, 'I was pretty well set on another location.'

'Were you?'

'Why should I change my mind and move into your building?'

'Because you're going to be happier there. I'll see that you have everything you need.' She smiled. 'Besides, it's going to cost your company ten per cent less.'

'Really? You don't know what my deal is for the other building.'

'It doesn't matter. I'll take your word for it.'

'You *could* have come from Gary, Indiana,' Guttman said. 'You've got a deal.'

When Lara returned to her office there was a message that Philip Adler had telephoned.

19

The ballroom at the Waldorf Astoria was crowded with patrons of Carnegie Hall. Lara moved through the crowd, looking for Philip. She recalled the telephone conversation they had had a few days earlier.

'Miss Cameron, this is Philip Adler.'

Her throat went suddenly dry.

'I'm sorry I wasn't able to thank you earlier for the donation you made to the Foundation. I've just returned from Europe and learned about it.'

'It was my pleasure,' Lara said. She had to keep him talking. 'As . . . as a matter of fact, I'm interested in knowing more about the Foundation. Perhaps we could get together and discuss it.'

There was a pause. 'There's going to be a charity dinner at the Waldorf on Saturday evening. We could meet there. Are you free?'

Lara quickly glanced at her schedule. She had a dinner meeting that evening with a banker from Texas.

She made a quick decision. 'Yes. I'd be delighted to go.'

'Wonderful. There will be a ticket at the door for you.'

When Lara replaced the receiver, she was beaming.

Philip Adler was nowhere in sight. Lara moved through the huge ballroom, listening to the conversations around her.

'. . . So the leading tenor said, "Dr Klemperer, I have only two high Cs left. Do you want to hear them now, or tonight at the performance?" . . .'

'. . . Oh, I admit that he has a good stick. His dynamics and tonal shadings are excellent . . . but the *tempi! Tempi!* Spare me! . . .'

'. . . you're insane! Stravinsky is too structured. His music could have been written by a robot. He holds back his feelings. Bartok, on the other hand, lets loose the floodgates, and we're bathed in emotions . . .'

'I simply can't stand her playing. Her Chopin is an exercise in tortured *rubato*, butchered textures, and purple passion . . .'

It was an arcane language that was beyond Lara's comprehension. And then she saw Philip, surrounded by an admiring coterie. Lara pushed her way through the crowd. An attractive young woman was saying, 'When you played the B-flat minor sonata, I felt that Rachmaninoff was smiling. Your tone and voicing, and the soft-grained readings . . . Wonderful!'

Philip smiled. 'Thank you.'

A middle-aged dowager was gushing, 'I keep listening to your recording of the *Hammerklavier* over and over. My God! The vitality is irresistible! I think you must be the only pianist left in this world who really understands that Beethoven sonata . . .'

Philip saw Lara. 'Ah. Excuse me,' he said.

He made his way over to where she was standing, and took her hand. His touch aroused her. 'Hello. I'm glad you could come, Miss Cameron.'

'Thank you.' She looked around. 'This is quite a crowd.'

He nodded. 'Yes. I assume that you're a lover of classical music?'

Lara thought of the music she had grown up with. *'Annie Laurie', 'Comin' Through the Rye', 'The Hills of Home'* . . .

'Oh, yes,' Lara said. 'My father brought me up on classical music.'

'I want to thank you again for your contribution. That was really very generous.'

'Your foundation sounds so interesting. I would love to hear more about it. If . . .'

'Philip, darling! There are no words! Magnificent!' He was surrounded again.

Lara managed to make herself heard. 'If you're free one evening next week . . .'

Philip shook his head. 'I'm sorry, I leave for Rome tomorrow.'

Lara felt a sudden sense of loss. 'Oh.'

'But I'll be back in three weeks. Perhaps then we could . . .'

'Wonderful!' Lara said.

'. . . spend an evening discussing music.'

Lara smiled. 'Yes. I'll look forward to that.'

At that moment, they were interrupted by two middle-aged men. One wore his hair in a ponytail, the other had on a single earring.

'Philip! You must settle an argument for us. When you're playing Liszt, which do you think is more important – a piano with heavy action that gives you a colourful sound, or light action where you can do a colourful manipulation?'

Lara had no idea what they were talking about. They went off into a discussion about neutral sonority and long sounds and transparency. Lara watched the animation in Philip's face as he talked, and she thought, *This is his world. I've got to find a way to get into it.*

The following morning, Lara appeared at the Manhattan School of Music. She said to the woman at the reception desk, 'I'd like to see one of the music professors, please.'

'Anyone in particular?'

'No.'

'Just a moment, please.' She disappeared into another room.

A few minutes later, a small, grey-haired man appeared at Lara's side.

'Good morning. I'm Leonard Meyers. How may I help you?'

'I'm interested in classical music.'

'Ah, you wish to enroll here. What instrument do you play?'

'I don't play any instrument. I just want to learn about classical music.'

'I'm afraid you've come to the wrong place. This school is not for beginners.'

'I'll pay you five thousand dollars for two weeks of your time.'

Professor Meyers blinked. 'I'm sorry, Miss . . . I didn't get your name.'

'Cameron. Lara Cameron.'

'You wish to pay me five thousand dollars for a two-week *discussion* of classical music?' He had trouble getting the words out.

'That's right. You can use the money for a scholarship fund if you wish.'

Professor Meyers lowered his voice. 'That will not be necessary. This can just be between you and me.'

'That's fine.'

'When . . . er . . . would you like to begin?'

'Now.'

'I have a class at the moment, but give me five minutes . . .'

Lara and Professor Meyers were seated in a classroom alone.

'Let us start at the beginning. Do you know anything about classical music?'

'Very little.'

'I see. Well, there are two ways to understand music,' the professor began. 'Intellectually and emotionally. Someone once said that music reveals to man his hidden soul. Every great composer was able to accomplish that.'

Lara was listening intently.

'Are you familiar with *any* composers, Miss Cameron?'

She smiled. 'Not too many.'

The professor frowned. 'I don't really understand your interest in . . .'

'I want to get enough of a background so that I can talk intelligently to a professional musician about the classics. I'm . . . I'm particularly interested in piano music.'

'I see.' Meyers thought for a moment. 'I'll tell you how we're going to begin. I'm going to give you some CDs to play.'

Lara watched him walk over to a shelf and pull down some compact discs.

'We'll start with these. I want you to listen carefully to the *allegro* in Mozart's Piano Concerto No. 21 in C, K.467, and the *adagio* in Brahms' Piano Concerto No. 1, and the *moderato* in Rachmaninoff's Piano Concerto No. 2 in C minor, Op. 18, and finally, the *romanze* in Chopin's Piano Concerto No. 1. They're all marked.'

'Right.'

'If you would like to play these and come back in a few days . . .'

'I'll be back tomorrow.'

The following day, when Lara came in, she was carrying half a dozen CDs of Philip Adler's concerts and recitals.

'Ah, splendid!' Professor Meyers said. 'Maestro Adler is the best. You are particularly interested in his playing?'

'Yes.'

'The maestro has recorded many beautiful sonatas.'

'Sonatas?'

He sighed. 'You don't know what a sonata is?'

'I'm afraid I don't.'

'A sonata is a piece, usually in several movements, that has a certain basic musical form. And when that form is used in a piece for a solo instrument, like a piano or violin, the piece is called a sonata. A symphony is a sonata for orchestra.'

'I understand.' *That shouldn't be difficult to work into a conversation.*

'The piano was originally known as the *pianoforte*. That is Italian for "soft-loud" . . .'

They spent the next few days discussing tapes that Philip had recorded – Beethoven, Liszt, Bartok, Mozart, Chopin.

Lara listened, and absorbed, and remembered.

'He likes Liszt. Tell me about him.'

'Franz Liszt was a boy genius. Everyone admired him. He was brilliant. He was treated like a pet by the aristocracy, and he finally complained that he had become on par with a juggler or a performing dog . . .'

'Tell me about Beethoven.'

'A difficult man. He was such an unhappy person that in the middle of his great success he decided he didn't like the work that he had done, and he changed to longer and more emotional compositions, like the *Eroica* and the *Pastoral* . . .'

'Chopin?'

'Chopin was criticized for writing music only for the piano; the critics of his day called him limited . . .'

Later: 'Liszt could play Chopin better than Chopin could . . .'

Another day: 'There's a difference between French pianists and American pianists. The French like clarity and elegance. Traditionally, their technical schooling is grounded in *jeu perlé* – perfectly pearly evenness of articulation with a steady wrist . . .'

Each day they played one of Philip's recordings and discussed it.

At the end of the two weeks, Professor Meyers said, 'I must confess that I'm impressed, Miss Cameron. You are a truly dedicated pupil. Perhaps you should take up an instrument.'

Lara laughed. 'Let's not get carried away.' She handed him a cheque. 'Here you are.'

She could not wait for Philip to return to New York.

20

The day started with good news. Terry Hill called.

'Lara?'

'Yes?'

'We just heard from the Gaming Commission. You've got your licence.'

'That's wonderful, Terry!'

'I'll go over the details when I see you, but it's a green light. Apparently you impressed the hell out of them.'

'I'll get everything started right away,' Lara said. 'Thanks.'

Lara told Keller what had happened.

'That's great. We can sure use the cash flow. That will take care of a lot of our problems . . .'

Lara looked at her calendar. 'We can fly down there on Tuesday and get things moving.'

Kathy buzzed her. 'There's a Mr Adler on line two. Shall I tell him . . . ?'

Lara was suddenly nervous. 'I'll take it.' She picked up the telephone. 'Philip?'

'Hello. I'm back.'

'I'm glad.' *I missed you.*

'I know it's short notice, but I wondered whether you might be free for dinner this evening.'

She had a dinner engagement with Paul Martin. 'Yes. I'm free.'

'Wonderful. Where would you like to dine?'
'It doesn't matter.'
'Le Côte Basque?'
'Fine.'
'Why don't we meet there? Eight o'clock?'
'Yes.'
'See you tonight.'

When Lara hung up, she was smiling.

'Was that *Philip* Adler?' Keller asked.

'Uh huh. I'm going to marry him.'

Keller was looking at her, stunned. 'Are you serious?'

'Yes.'

It was a jolt. *I'm going to lose her*, Keller thought. And then: *Who am I kidding? I could never have her*.

'Lara . . . you hardly know him!'

I've known him all my life.

'I don't want you to make a mistake.'

'I'm not. I . . .' Her private telephone rang. The one she had had installed for Paul Martin. Lara picked it up. 'Hello, Paul.'

'Hi, Lara. What time would you like to make dinner tonight? Eight?'

She felt a sudden sense of guilt. 'Paul . . . I'm afraid I can't make it tonight. Something came up. I was going to call you.'

'Oh? Is everything all right?'

'Yes. Some people just flew in from Rome' – that part at least was true – 'and I have to meet with them.'

'My bad luck. Another night, then.'

'Of course.'

'I hear the licence came through for the Reno hotel.'

'Yes.'

'We're going to have fun with that place.'

'I'm looking forward to it. I'm sorry about tonight. I'll talk to you tomorrow.'

The line went dead.

Lara replaced the receiver slowly.

Keller was watching her. She could see the disapproval on his face.

'Is something bothering you?'

'Yeah. It's all this modern equipment.'

'What are you talking about?'

'I think you have too many phones in your office. He's bad news, Lara.'

Lara stiffened. 'Mr Bad News has saved our hides a few times, Howard. Anything else?'

Keller shook his head. 'No.'

'Right. Let's get back to work.'

Philip was waiting for her when she arrived at Le Côte Basque. People turned to stare at Lara as she walked into the restaurant. Philip stood up to greet her, and Lara's heart skipped a beat.

'I hope I'm not late,' she said.

'Not at all.' He was looking at her admiringly. His eyes were warm. 'You look lovely.'

She had changed clothes half a dozen times. *Should I wear something simple or elegant or sexy?* Finally, she had decided on a simple Dior. 'Thank you.'

When they were seated, Philip said, 'I feel like an idiot.'

'Oh? Why?'

'I never connected the name. You're *that* Cameron.'

She laughed. 'Guilty.'

'My God! You're a hotel chain, you're apartment buildings, office buildings. When I travel, I see your name all over the country.'

'Good,' Lara smiled. 'It will remind you of me.'

He was studying her. 'I don't think I need any reminding. Do you get tired of people telling you that you're very beautiful?'

She started to say, 'I'm glad you think I'm beautiful.' What came out was, 'Are you married?' She wanted to bite her tongue.

He smiled. 'No. It would be impossible for me to get married.'

'Why?' For an instant she held her breath. *Surely he's not* . . .

'Because I'm on tour most of the year. One night I'm in Budapest, the next night in London or Paris or Tokyo.'

There was a sweeping sense of relief. 'Ah. Philip, tell me about yourself.'

'What do you want to know?'

'Everything.'

Philip laughed. 'That would take at least five minutes.'

'No, I'm serious. I really want to know about you.'

He took a deep breath. 'Well, my parents were Viennese. My father was a musical conductor and my mother was a piano teacher. They left Vienna to escape Hitler and settled in Boston. I was born there.'

'Did you always know you wanted to be a pianist?'

'Yes.'

He was six years old. He was practising the piano and his father came storming into the room. 'No, no, no! Don't you know a major chord from a minor?' *His hairy finger slashed at the sheet music.* 'That's a minor chord. Minor. Do you understand?'

'Father, please, can I go? My friends are waiting for me outside.'

'No. You will sit here until you get it right.'

He was eight years old. He had practised for four hours that morning, and had had a terrible fight with his parents. 'I hate the piano,' *he cried.* 'I never want to touch it again.'

His mother said, 'Fine. Now, let me hear the Andante once more.'

He was ten years old. The apartment was filled with guests, most of them old friends of his parents from Vienna. All of them were musicians.

'Philip is going to play something for us now,' *his mother announced.*

'We'd love to hear little Philip play,' *they said in patronizing voices.*

'Play the Mozart, Philip.'

Philip looked into their bored faces and sat down at the piano, angry. They went on chatting among themselves.

He began to play, his fingers flashing across the keyboard. The talking suddenly stopped. He played a Mozart sonata, and the music was alive. And at that moment he was Mozart, filling the room with the magic of the master.

As Philip's fingers struck the last chord, there was an awed silence. His parents' friends rushed over to the piano, talking excitedly, effusive with their praise. He listened to their applause and adulation, and that was the moment of his epiphany, when he knew who he was and what he wanted to do with his life.

'Yes, I always knew I wanted to be a pianist,' Philip told Lara.

'Where did you study piano?'

'My mother taught me until I was fourteen, and then they sent me to study at the Curtis Institute in Philadelphia.'

'Did you enjoy that?'

'Very much.'

He was fourteen years old, alone in the city with no friends. The Curtis Institute of Music was located in four turn-of-the-century mansions near Philadelphia's Rittenhouse Square. It was the closest American equivalent to the Moscow Conservatory of Viardo, Egorov and Toradze. Its graduates included Samuel Barber, Leonard Bernstein, Gian Carlo Menotti, Peter Serkin, and dozens of other brilliant musicians.

'Weren't you lonely there?'

'No.'

He was miserable. He had never been away from home before. He had auditioned for the Curtis Institute, and when they accepted him, the realization struck him that he was about to begin a new life, that he would never go home again. The teachers recognized the young boy's talent immediately. His piano teachers were Isabelle Vengerova and Rudolf Serkin, and Philip studied piano, theory, harmony, orchestration and flute. When he was not in class, he played chamber music with the other students. The piano, which he had been forced to practise from the time he was three years old, was now the focus of his life. To him, it had become a magical instrument out of which his fingers could draw romance and passion and thunder. It spoke a universal language.

'I gave my first concert when I was eighteen with the Detroit Symphony.'

'Were you frightened?'

He was terrified. He found that it was one thing to play before a group of friends. It was another to face a huge auditorium filled with people who had paid money to hear him. He was nervously pacing backstage when the stage manager grabbed his arm and said, 'Go. You're on.' He had never forgotten the feeling he had when he walked out onto the stage and the audience began to applaud him. He sat down at the piano and his nervousness vanished in an instant. After that, his life became a marathon of concerts. He toured all over Europe and Asia, and after each tour his reputation grew. William Ellerbee, an important artists' manager, agreed to represent him. Within two years, Philip Adler was in demand everywhere.

Philip looked at Lara and smiled. 'Yes. I still get frightened before a concert.'

'What's it like to go on tour?'

'It's never dull. Once I was on a tour with the Philadelphia Symphony. We were in Brussels, on our way to give a concert in London. The airport was closed because of fog, so they took us by bus to Schiphol Airport in Amsterdam. The man in charge explained that the plane they had chartered for us was small, and that the musicians could take either their instruments or their luggage. Naturally, they chose their instruments. We arrived in London just in time to begin the concert. We played it in jeans, sneakers, and unshaven.'

Lara laughed. 'And I'll bet the audience loved it.'

'They did. Another time I was giving a concert in Indiana, and the piano was locked away in a closet and no one had a key. We had to break the door down.'

Lara giggled.

'Last year I was scheduled to do a Beethoven concerto in Rome, and one of the music critics wrote: "Adler gave a ponderous performance, with his phrasing in the finale completely missing the point. The tempo was too broad, rupturing the pulse of the piece."'

'That's awful!' Lara said sympathetically.

'The awful part was that I never even gave that concert. I had missed my plane!'

Lara leaned forward, eagerly. 'Tell me more.'

'Well, one time in São Paulo the pedals fell off the piano in the middle of a Chopin concert.'

'What did you do?'

'I finished the sonata without pedals. Another time, the piano slid clear across the stage.'

When Philip talked about his work, his voice was filled with enthusiasm.

'I'm very lucky. It's wonderful to be able to touch people and transport them into another world. The music gives each of them a dream. Sometimes I think music is the only sanity left in an insane world.' He laughed self-consciously. 'I didn't mean to sound pompous.'

'No. You make millions of people so happy. I love to hear you play.' She took a deep breath. 'When I hear you play Debussy's *Voiles*, I'm on a lonely beach, and I see the mast of a ship sailing in the distance . . .'

He smiled. 'Yes, so do I.'

'And when I listen to your Scarlatti, I'm in Naples, and I can hear the horses and the carriages, and see the people walking through the streets . . .' She could see the pleasure in his face as he listened to her.

She was dredging up every memory of her sessions with Professor Meyers.

'With Bartok, you take me to the villages of Central Europe, to the peasants of Hungary. You're painting pictures, and I lose myself in them.'

'You're very flattering,' Philip said.

'No. I mean every word of it.'

Dinner arrived. It consisted of a Chateaubriand with pommes frites, a Waldorf salad, fresh asparagus, and a fruit torte for dessert. There was a wine for each course. Over dinner, Philip said, 'Lara, we keep talking about me. Tell me about you. What is it like to put up enormous buildings all over the country?'

Lara was silent for a moment. 'It's difficult to describe. *You* create with your hands. *I* create with my mind. I don't physically put up a building, but I make it possible. I dream a dream of bricks and concrete and steel, and make it come true. I create jobs for hundreds of people; architects and bricklayers and designers and carpenters and plumbers. Because of me, they're able to support their families. I give people beautiful surroundings to live in and make them comfortable. I build attractive stores where people can shop and buy things they need. I build monuments to the future.' She smiled, sheepishly. 'I didn't mean to make a speech.'

'You're quite remarkable, do you know that?'
'I want you to think so.'

It was an enchanted evening, and by the time it was over, Lara knew that for the first time in her life she was in love. She had been so afraid that she might be disappointed, that no man could live up to the image in her imagination. But here was Lochinvar in the flesh, and she was stirred.

When Lara got home, she was so excited she was unable to go to sleep. She went over the evening in her mind, replaying the conversation again and again and again. Philip Adler was the most fascinating man she had ever met. The telephone rang. Lara smiled and picked it up. She started to say, 'Philip . . .' when Paul Martin said, 'Just checking to make sure you got home safely.'

'Yes,' Lara said.

'How did your meeting go?'

'Fine.'

'Good. Let's have dinner tomorrow night.'

Lara hesitated. 'All right.' *I wonder if there's going to be a problem.*

21

The following morning, a dozen red roses were delivered to Lara's apartment. *So, he enjoyed the evening, too*, Lara thought happily. She hurriedly tore open the card attached to the flowers. It read:

'Baby, looking forward to our dinner tonight. Paul.'

Lara felt a sharp sense of disappointment. She waited all morning for a call from Philip. She had a busy schedule, but she was unable to keep her mind on her work.

At ten o'clock Kathy said, 'The new secretaries are here for you to interview.'

'Start sending them in.'

There were half a dozen of them, all highly qualified. Gertrude Meeks was the choice of the day. She was in her thirties, bright and up-beat, and obviously in awe of Lara.

Lara looked over her résumé. It was impressive. 'You've worked in the real estate development field before.'

'Yes, ma'am. But I've never worked for anyone like you. To tell you the truth, I'd take this job for no salary!'

Lara smiled. 'That won't be necessary. These are good references. All right, we'll give you a try.'

'Thank you so much.' She was almost blushing.

'You'll have to sign a form agreeing not to give any interviews or ever to discuss anything that happens at this firm. Is that agreeable?'

'Of course.'

'Kathy will show you to your desk.'

There was an eleven o'clock publicity meeting with Jerry Townsend.

'How's your father?' Lara asked.

'He's in Switzerland. The doctor says he may have a chance.' His voice grew husky. 'If he has, it's because of you.'

'Everyone deserves a chance, Jerry. I hope he gets well.'

'Thanks.' He cleared his throat. 'I . . . I don't know how to tell you how grateful I . . .'

Lara stood up. 'I'm late for a meeting.'

And she walked out, leaving him standing there, looking after her.

The meeting was with the architects on a New Jersey development. 'You've done a good job,' Lara said, 'but I'd like some changes. I want an elliptical arcade with lobbies on three sides and marble walls. Change the roof to the shape of a copper pyramid, with a beacon to light up at night. Any problem with that?'

'I don't see any, Miss Cameron.'

When the meeting was over, the intercom buzzed.

'Miss Cameron, Raymond Duffy, one of the construction foremen, is on the line for you. He says it's urgent.'

Lara picked up the telephone. 'Hello, Raymond.'

'We have a problem, Miss Cameron.'

'Go on.'

'They just delivered a load of cement blocks. They won't pass inspection. There are cracks in them. I'm going to send them back, but I wanted to tell you first.'

Lara was thoughtful for a moment. 'How bad is it?'

'Bad enough. The point is, they don't meet our specifications, and . . .'

'Can they be fixed?'

'I guess they could, but it would be expensive.'

'Fix them,' Lara said.

There was a silence at the other end of the line.

'Right. You're the boss.'

Lara replaced the receiver. There were only two cement suppliers in the city, and it would be suicide to antagonize them.

By five o'clock, Philip still had not called. Lara dialled the number at his foundation. 'Philip Adler, please.'

'Mr Adler is out of town on tour. Can I help you?'

He hadn't mentioned that he was leaving town. 'No, thank you.'

That's that, Lara thought. *For now*.

The day ended with a visit from Steve Murchison. He was a huge man, built like a stack of bricks. He stormed into Lara's office.

'What can I do for you, Mr Murchison?' Lara asked.

'You can keep your nose out of my fucking business,' Murchison said.

Lara looked at him calmly. 'What's your problem?'

'You. I don't like people horning in on my deals.'

'If you're talking about Mr Guttman . . .'

'You're damn right I am.'

'. . . he preferred my building to yours.'

'You suckered him into it, lady. You've been getting in my hair long enough. I warned you once. I'm not going to warn you again. There's not room enough for both of us in this town. I don't know where you keep your balls, but hide 'em, because if you ever do that to me again, I'm going to cut them off.'

And he stormed out.

The dinner at her apartment that evening with Paul was strained.

'You seem preoccupied, baby,' Paul said. 'Any problems?'

Lara managed a smile. 'No. Everything's fine.' *Why didn't Philip tell me he was going away?*

'When does the Reno project start?'

'Howard and I are going to fly down again next week. We should be able to open in about nine months.'

'You could have a baby in nine months.'

Lara looked at him in surprise. 'What?'

Paul Martin took her hand in his. 'You know I'm crazy about you, Lara. You've changed my whole life. I wish things could have turned out differently. I would have loved for us to have had kids together.'

There was nothing Lara could say to that.

'I have a little surprise for you.' He reached into his pocket and pulled out a jewellery box. 'Open it.'

'Paul, you've already given me so much . . .'

'Open it.'

Inside the box was an exquisite diamond necklace. 'It's lovely.'

He stood up and she felt his hands on her as he put the necklace around her neck. His hands slid down, caressing her breasts, and he said huskily, 'Let's check it out.'

Paul was leading her into the bedroom. Lara's mind was spinning. She had never been in love with him, and going to bed with him had been easy – the payment for all he had done for her – but now there was a difference. She was in love. *I'm a fool*, Lara thought. *I'll probably never see Philip again.*

She undressed slowly, reluctantly, and then they were in bed, and Paul Martin was on top of her, inside her, moaning, 'Baby, I'm nuts about you.' And she looked up and it was Philip's face she saw.

Everything was progressing smoothly. The renovations on the Reno hotel were proceeding rapidly, Cameron Towers was going to be finished on schedule, and Lara's reputation kept growing. She had called Philip Adler several times over the past few months, but he was always away on tour.

'Mr Adler is in Beijing . . .'

'Mr Adler is in Paris . . .'

'Mr Adler is in Sydney . . .'

To hell with him, Lara thought.

*

During the next six months, Lara managed to outbid Steve Murchison on three properties he was after.

Keller came to Lara, worried. 'The word around town is that Murchison is making threats against you. Maybe we should cool it with him. He's a dangerous enemy, Lara.'

'So am I,' Lara said. 'Maybe he should get into another business.'

'It's not a joking matter, Lara. He . . .'

'Forget about him, Howard. I just got a tip about a property in Los Angeles. It's not on the market yet. If we move fast, I think we can get it. We'll fly out in the morning.'

The property was on the site of the old Biltmore Hotel and consisted of five acres. A real estate agent was showing Lara and Howard around the grounds.

'Prime property,' he was saying. 'Yes, sir. You can't go wrong with this. You can build a beautiful little city in this area . . . apartment buildings, shopping centres, theatres, malls . . .'

'No.'

He looked at Lara in surprise. 'I beg your pardon?'

'I'm not interested.'

'You're not? Why?'

'The neighbourhood,' Lara said. 'I don't think people are going to move into this area. Los Angeles is moving west. People are like lemmings. You aren't going to get them to reverse direction.'

'But . . .'

'I'll tell you what I *am* interested in. Condos. Find me a good location.'

Lara turned to Howard, 'I'm sorry I wasted our time. We'll fly back this afternoon.'

When they returned to their hotel, Keller bought a newspaper at the newsstand. 'Let's see what the market is doing today.'

They looked through the paper. In the entertainment section was a large advertisement that read: TONIGHT AT THE HOLLYWOOD BOWL – PHILIP ADLER. Lara's heart gave a little jump.

'Let's go back tomorrow,' Lara said.

Keller studied her a moment. 'Are you interested in the music or the musician?'

'Get us two tickets.'

Lara had never been to the Hollywood Bowl before. The largest natural amphitheatre in the world, it is surrounded by the hills of Hollywood, the grounds a park, open year round for visitors to enjoy. The Bowl itself seats 18,000 people. It was filled to capacity, and Lara could sense the anticipation of the crowd. The musicians began to come onto the stage, and they were greeted with expectant applause. André Previn appeared and the applause grew more enthusiastic. There was a hush, then loud applause from the audience as Philip Adler walked out on the stage, elegant in white tie and tails.

Lara squeezed Keller's arm. 'Isn't he handsome?' she whispered.

Keller did not answer.

Philip sat down at the piano, and the programme began. His magic took over instantly, enveloping the audience. There was a mysticism about the night.

The stars were shining down, lighting the dark hills surrounding the Bowl. Thousands of people sat there silently, moved by the majesty of the music. When the last notes of the concerto died away, there was a roar from the audience, as the people leaped to their feet, applauding and cheering. Philip stood there, taking bow after bow.

'Let's go backstage,' Lara said.

Keller turned to look at her. Her voice was trembling with excitement.

The backstage entrance was at the side of the orchestra shell. A guard stood at the door, keeping the crowd out. Keller said, 'Miss Cameron is here to see Mr Adler.'

'Is he expecting you?' the guard asked.

'Yes,' Lara said.

'Wait here, please.' A moment later the guard returned. 'You can go in, Miss Cameron.'

Lara and Keller walked into the green room. Philip was in the centre of a crowd that was congratulating him.

'Darling, I've never heard Beethoven played so exquisitely. You were unbelievable . . .'

Philip was saying, 'Thank you . . .'

'. . . thank you . . . with music like that, it's easy to be inspired . . .'

'. . . thank you . . . André is such a brilliant conductor . . .'

'. . . thank you . . . I always enjoy playing at the Bowl . . .'

He looked up and saw Lara and again there was that smile. 'Excuse me,' he said. He made his way through the crowd, toward her. 'I had no idea you were in town.'

'We just flew in this morning. This is Howard Keller, my associate.'

'Hello,' Keller said curtly.

Philip turned to a short, heavy-set man, standing behind him. 'This is my manager, William Ellerbee.' They exchanged hellos.

Philip was looking at Lara. 'There's a party tonight at the Beverly Hilton. I was wondering . . .'

'We'd love to,' Lara said.

When Lara and Keller arrived at the Beverly Hilton's International Ballroom, it was filled with musicians and music lovers, talking music.

'. . . Have you ever noticed that the closer you get to the equator, the more demonstrative and hot-blooded the fans are . . . ?'

'. . . When Franz Liszt played, his piano became an orchestra . . .'

'. . . I disagree with you. DeGroote's talent is not for Liszt or Paganini études, but more for Beethoven . . .'

'. . . You have to dominate the concerto's emotional landscape . . .'

Musicians speaking in tongues, Lara thought.

Philip was surrounded, as usual, by adoring fans. Just watching him gave Lara a warm glow.

When Philip saw her arrive, he greeted her with a broad smile. 'You made it. I'm so glad.'

'I wouldn't have missed it.'

Howard Keller watched the two of them talking, and he thought, *Maybe I should have learned to play the piano. Or maybe I should just wake up to reality.* It seemed so long ago when he had first met the bright, eager, ambitious, young girl. Time had been good to her, and it had stood still for him.

Lara was saying, 'I have to go back to New York tomorrow, but perhaps we could have breakfast.'

'I wish I could. I'm leaving for Tokyo early in the morning.'

She felt a sharp pang of disappointment. 'Why?'

He laughed. 'That's what I do, Lara. I give a hundred and fifty concerts a year. Sometimes two hundred.'

'How long will you be gone this time?'

'Eight weeks.'

'I'll miss you,' Lara said quietly. *You have no idea how much.*

22

During the next few weeks Lara and Keller flew to Atlanta to investigate two sites at Ansley Park and one at Dunwoody.

'Get me some prices on Dunwoody,' Lara said. 'We might put up some condos there.'

From Atlanta, they flew to New Orleans. They spent two days exploring the Central Business District, and a day at Lake Pontchartrain. Lara found two sites she liked.

A day after they returned, Keller walked into Lara's office. 'We had some bad luck on the Atlanta project,' he said.

'What do you mean?'

'Someone beat us to it.'

Lara looked at him, surprised. 'How could they? Those properties weren't even on the market.'

'I know. Word must have leaked out.'

Lara shrugged. 'I guess you can't win them all.'

That afternoon Keller had more bad news. 'We lost the Lake Pontchartrain deal.'

The following week they flew to Seattle and explored Mercer Island and Kirkland. There was one site that interested Lara, and when they returned to New York, she said to Keller, 'Let's go after it. I think it could be a money-maker.'

'Right.'

At a meeting the next day, Lara asked, 'Did you put in the bid on Kirkland?'

Keller shook his head. 'Someone got there ahead of us.'

Lara was thoughtful. 'Oh. Howard, see if you can find out who's jumping the gun on us.'

It took him less than twenty-four hours. 'Steve Murchison.'

'Did he get all those deals?'

'Yes.'

'So someone in this office has a big mouth.'

'It looks that way.'

Her face was grim. The next morning she hired a detective agency to find the culprit. They had no success.

'As far as we can tell, all your employees are clean, Miss Cameron. None of the offices is bugged, and your phones haven't been tapped.'

They had reached a dead end.

Maybe they were just coincidences, Lara thought. She did not believe it.

The 68-storey residential tower in Queens was half completed, and Lara had invited the bankers to come and inspect its progress. The higher the number of floors, the more expensive the unit. Lara's 68 storeys had only 57 actual floors. It was a trick she had learned from Paul Martin.

'Everybody does it,' Paul had laughed. 'All you do is change the floor numbers.'

'How do you do that?'

'It's very simple. Your first bank of elevators is from the lobby to the 24th floor. The second bank of elevators is from the 35th floor to the 68th. It's done all the time.'

Because of the unions, the construction jobs had half a dozen phantoms on salary – people who did not exist. There was a Director of Safety Practices, the Coordinator of Construction, the Supervisor of Materials, and others with impressive-sounding titles. In the beginning, Lara had questioned it.

'Don't worry about it,' Paul had told her. 'It's all part of the CDB – the cost of doing business.'

Howard Keller had been living in a small apartment in Washington Square, and when Lara had visited him one evening, she had looked around the tiny apartment and said, 'This is a rat trap. You've got to move out of here.' At Lara's urging, he had moved into a condominium uptown.

One night, Lara and Keller were working late, and when they finally finished, Lara said, 'You look exhausted. Why don't you go home and get some sleep, Howard?'

'Good idea,' Keller yawned. 'See you in the morning.'

'Come in late,' Lara told him.

Keller got into his car and started driving home. He was thinking about a deal they had just closed and how well Lara had handled it. It was exciting working with her. Exciting and frustrating. Somehow, in the back of his mind, he kept hoping that a miracle would happen. *I was blind not to have seen it before,*

Howard darling. I'm not interested in Paul Martin or Philip Adler. It's you I've loved all along.
Fat chance.

When Keller reached his apartment, he took out his key and put it in the lock. It did not fit. Puzzled, he tried again. Suddenly the door flew open from the inside, and a stranger was standing there. 'What the hell do you think you're doing?' the man asked.

Keller looked at him, bewildered. 'I live here.'

'The hell you do.'

'But I . . .' Realization suddenly hit him. 'I . . . I'm sorry,' he stammered, red-faced. 'I *used* to live here. I . . .'

The door was slammed in his face. Keller stood there, disconcerted. *How could I have forgotten that I moved? I've been working too hard.*

Lara was in the middle of a conference when her private phone rang. 'You've been pretty busy lately, baby. I've missed you.'

'I've been travelling a lot, Paul.' She couldn't bring herself to say that she had missed him.

'Let's have lunch today.'

Lara thought about all he had done for her.

'I'd like that,' she said. The last thing in the world she wanted to do was to hurt him.

They had lunch at Mr Chow's.

'You're looking great,' Paul said. 'Whatever

you've been doing agrees with you. How's the Reno hotel coming?'

'It's coming along beautifully,' Lara said enthusiastically. She spent the next fifteen minutes describing how the work was progressing. 'We should be ready to open in two months.'

A man and woman across the room were just leaving. The man's back was to Lara, but he looked familiar. When he turned for an instant, she caught a glimpse of his face. Steve Murchison. The woman with him looked familiar, also. She stooped to pick up her purse and Lara's heart skipped a beat. *Gertrude Meeks, my secretary.* 'Bingo,' Lara said softly.

'Is anything wrong?' Paul asked.

'No. Everything's fine.'

Lara went on describing the hotel.

When Lara returned from lunch, she sent for Keller.

'Do you remember the property in Phoenix we looked at a few months ago?'

'Yeah, we turned it down. You said it was a dog.'

'I've changed my mind.' She pressed down the intercom. 'Gertrude, would you come in here, please?'

'Yes, Miss Cameron.'

Gertrude Meeks came into the office.

'I want to dictate a memo,' Lara said. 'To the Baron Brothers in Phoenix.'

Gertrude started writing.

'Gentlemen, I have reconsidered the Scottsdale property and have decided to go ahead with it immediately. I think in time it is going to be my most valuable asset.' Keller was staring at her. 'I'll be in touch with you regarding price in the next few days. Best regards. I'll sign it.'

'Yes, Miss Cameron. Is that all?'

'That's all.'

Keller watched Gertrude leave the room. He turned to Lara. 'Lara, what are you doing? We had that property analysed. It's worthless! If you . . .'

'Calm down. We're not making a deal for it.'

'Then why . . . ?'

'Unless I miss my guess, Steve Murchison will. I saw Gertrude having lunch with him today.'

Keller was staring at Lara. 'I'll be damned.'

'I want you to wait a couple of days and then call Baron and ask about the property.'

Two days later, Keller came into Lara's office, grinning. 'You were right,' he said. 'Murchison took the bait – hook, line and sinker. He's now the proud owner of fifty acres of worthless land.'

Lara sent for Gertrude Meeks.

'Yes, Miss Cameron?'

'You're fired,' Lara said.

Gertrude looked at her in surprise. 'Fired? Why?'

'I don't like the company you keep. Go back to Steve Murchison and tell him I said so.'

Gertrude's face lost its colour. 'But I . . .'

'That's all. I'll have you escorted out of here.'

At midnight, Lara buzzed Max, her chauffeur. 'Bring the car around to the front,' Lara said.

'Yes, Miss Cameron.'

The car was there waiting for her.

'Where would you like to go, Miss Cameron?' Max asked.

'Drive around Manhattan. I want to see what I've done.'

He was staring at her. 'I beg your pardon?'

'I want to look at my buildings.'

They drove around the city, and stopped at the shopping mall, the housing centre, and the skyscraper. There was Cameron Square, Cameron Plaza, Cameron Center and the skeleton of Cameron Towers. Lara sat in the car, staring at each building, thinking about the people living there and working there. She had touched all their lives. *I've made this city better*, Lara thought. *I've done everything I wanted to do. Then why am I restless? What is missing?* But she knew.

The following morning, Lara telephoned William Ellerbee, Philip's concert manager.

'Good morning, Mr Ellerbee.'

'Good morning, Miss Cameron. What can I do for you?'

'I was wondering where Philip Adler is playing this week.'

'Philip has a pretty heavy schedule. Tomorrow night he'll be in Amsterdam, then he goes on to Milan, Venice and . . . do you want to know the rest of his . . . ?'

'No, no. That's fine. I was just curious. Thank you.'

'No problem.'

Lara walked into Keller's office. 'Howard, I have to go to Amsterdam.'

He looked at her in surprise. 'What do we have going on there?'

'It's just an idea,' Lara said evasively. 'I'll let you know if it checks out. Have them get the jet ready for me, will you?'

'You sent Bert to London on it, remember? I'll tell them to have it back here tomorrow, and . . .'

'I want to leave today.' There was an urgency in her that took her completely by surprise. 'I'll fly commercial.' She returned to her office and said to Kathy, 'Get me a seat on the first flight to Amsterdam on KLM.'

'Yes, Miss Cameron.'

'Are you going to be gone long?' Keller asked. 'We have some meetings coming up that . . .'

'I'll be back in a day or two.'

'Do you want me to come with you?'

'Thanks, Howard. Not this time.'

'I talked to a senator friend of mine in Washington. He thinks there's a chance they're going to pass a bill that will remove most of the tax incentives for building. If it passes, it's going to kill capital gains taxes and stop accelerated depreciation.'

'That would be stupid,' Lara said. 'It would cripple the real estate industry.'

'I know. He's against the bill.'

'A lot of people will be against it. It will never pass,' Lara predicted. 'In the first place . . .'

The private phone on the desk rang. Lara stared at it. It rang again.

'Aren't you going to answer it?' Keller asked.

Lara's mouth was dry. 'No.'

Paul Martin listened to the hollow ring a dozen times before he replaced the receiver. He sat there a long time thinking about Lara. It seemed to him that lately she had been less accessible, a little cooler. *Could there be someone else? No*, Paul Martin thought. *She belongs to me. She'll always belong to me.*

The flight on KLM was pleasant. The first class seats in the wide-bodied 747 were spacious and comfortable, and the cabin attendants were attentive.

Lara was too nervous to eat or drink anything. *What am I doing?* she wondered. *I'm going to Amsterdam uninvited, and he'll probably be too busy to even see me. Running after him is going to ruin whatever chance I might have had. Too late.*

She checked in at the Grand Hotel on Oudezijds Voorburgwal 197, one of the most beautiful hotels in Amsterdam.

'We have a lovely suite for you, Miss Cameron,' the clerk said.

'Thank you. I understand that Philip Adler is giving a recital this evening. Do you know where he would be playing?'

'Of course, Miss Cameron. At the *Concertgebouw*.'

'Could you arrange a ticket for me?'

'It will be my pleasure.'

As Lara entered her suite, the telephone was ringing. It was Howard Keller.

'Did you have a nice flight?'

'Yes, thanks.'

'I thought you'd like to know that I've spoken to the two banks about the Seventh Avenue deal.'

'And?'

His voice was vibrant. 'They're jumping at it.'

Lara was elated. 'I told you! This is going to be a big one. I want you to start assembling a team of architects, builders – our construction group – the works.'

'Right. I'll talk to you tomorrow.' She replaced the receiver and thought about Howard Keller. He was so dear. *I'm so lucky. He's always there for me. I have to find someone wonderful for him.*

Philip Adler was always nervous before playing. He had rehearsed with the orchestra in the morning, and had a light lunch, and then, to take his mind off the concert, had gone to see an English movie. As he watched the picture, his mind was filled with the music he was going to play that evening. He was unaware that he was drumming his fingers on the arm of his seat until the person next to him said, 'Would you mind stopping that awful sound?'

'I beg your pardon,' Philip said politely.

He got up and left the cinema, and roamed the streets of Amsterdam. He visited the Rijksmuseum, and he strolled through the Botanical Gardens of the Free University, and window shopped along P.C. Hooftstraat. At four o'clock he went back to his hotel to take a nap. He was unaware that Lara Cameron was in the suite directly above him.

At 7 p.m., Philip arrived at the Artists' Entrance of the *Concertgebouw*, the lovely old hall in the heart of Amsterdam. The lobby was already crowded with early arrivals.

Backstage, Philip was in his dressing room, changing into tails. The director of the *Concertgebouw* bustled into the room.

'We're completely sold out, Mr Adler! And we had to turn away so many people. If it were possible for you to stay another day or two, I would . . . I know you are fully booked . . . I will talk to Mr Ellerbee about your return here next year and perhaps . . .'

Philip was not listening. His mind was focused on the recital that lay ahead. The director finally shrugged apologetically and bowed his way out. Philip played the music over and over in his mind. A page knocked at the dressing room door.

'They're ready for you on stage, Mr Adler.'

'Thank you.'

It was time. Philip rose to his feet. He held out his hands. They were trembling slightly. The nervousness before playing never went away. It was true of all the great pianists – Horowitz, Rubenstein, Serkin. Philip's stomach was churning and his heart was pounding. *Why do I put myself through this agony?* he asked himself. But he knew the answer. He took one last look in the mirror, then stepped out of the dressing room, and walked through the long corridor, and started to descend the thirty-three steps that led onto the stage. There was a spotlight on him as he moved toward the piano. The applause grew thunderous. He sat down at the piano and, as if by magic, his nervousness disappeared. It was as though another person were taking his place, someone calm, and poised, and completely in charge. He began to play.

Lara, seated in the audience, felt a thrill as she watched Philip walk out on the stage. There was a presence about him that was mesmerizing. *I am going to marry him*, Lara thought. *I know it*. She sat back in her seat, and let his playing wash over her.

The recital was a triumph, and afterward, the green room was packed. Philip had long ago learned to divide the crowd invited to the green room into two groups: the fans and other musicians. The fans were always enthusiastic. If the performance was a success, the congratulations of the other musicians were cordial. If it was a failure, their congratulations were *very* cordial.

Philip had many avid fans in Amsterdam, and on this particular evening, the green room was crowded with them. He stood in the centre of the room, smiling, signing autographs, and being patiently polite to a hundred strangers. Invariably someone would say, 'Do you remember me?' And Philip would pretend to. 'Your face looks so familiar . . .'

He remembered the story of Sir Thomas Beecham, who had hit upon a device to conceal his bad memory. When someone asked, 'Do you remember me?', the great conductor would reply, 'Of course, I do! How are you, and how is your father, and what is he doing?' The device worked well until a concert in London when a young woman in the green room said, 'Your performance was wonderful, Maestro. Do you remember me?' and Beecham gallantly replied, 'Of course, I do, my dear. How is your father, and what is he doing?' The young woman said, 'Father is fine, thank you. And he's still King of England.'

Philip was busily signing autographs, listening to the familiar phrases: 'You made Brahms come alive for me!' . . . 'I can't tell you how moved I was!' . . . 'I have all your albums' . . . 'Would you sign an autograph for my mother, too? She's your biggest fan . . .' – when something made him look up. Lara was standing in the doorway, watching. His eyes widened in surprise. 'Excuse me.'

He made his way over to her and took her hand. 'What a wonderful surprise! What are you doing in Amsterdam?'

Careful, Lara. 'I had some business to attend to here, and when I heard you were playing, I had to come.' *That was innocent enough.* 'You were wonderful, Philip.'

'Thank you . . . I . . .' He stopped to sign another autograph. 'Look, if you're free for supper . . .'

'I'm free,' Lara said quickly.

They had supper at the Bali restaurant on Leidsestraat. As they entered the restaurant, the patrons rose and applauded. *In the United States*, Lara thought, *the excitement would have been for me*. But she felt a warm glow, simply being at Philip's side.

'It's a great honour to have you with us, Mr Adler,' the maître d' said as he led them to their table.

'Thank you.'

As they were being seated, Lara looked around at all the people staring admiringly at Philip. 'They really love you, don't they?'

He shook his head. 'It's the music they love. I'm just the messenger. I learned that a long time ago. When I was very young and perhaps a little arrogant, I gave a concert, and when I had finished my solo, there was tremendous applause, and I was bowing to the audience and smugly smiling at them, and the conductor turned to the audience and held up the score over his head to remind everyone that they were really applauding Mozart. It's a lesson I've never forgotten.'

'Don't you ever get tired of playing the same music over and over, night after night?'

'No, because no two recitals are the same. The music may be the same, but the conductor is different, and the orchestra is different.'

They ordered a *rijsttafel* dinner, and Philip said, 'We try to make each recital perfect, but there's no such thing as a completely successful one because we're dealing with music that is always better than we are. We have to re-think the music each time in order to recreate the sound of the composer.'

'You're never satisfied?'

'Never. Each composer has his own distinctive sound. Whether it's Debussy, Brahms, Haydn, Beethoven . . . Our goal is to capture that particular sound.'

Supper arrived. The *rijsttafel* was an Indonesian feast, consisting of twenty-one courses, including a variety of meats, fish, chicken, noodles and two desserts.

'How can anyone eat all this?' Lara laughed.

'The Dutch have hearty appetites.'

Philip found it difficult to take his eyes off Lara. He found himself ridiculously pleased that she was there. He had been involved with more than his share of beautiful women, but Lara was like no one he had ever known. She was strong and yet very feminine, and totally unselfconscious about her beauty. He liked her throaty, sexy voice. *In fact, I like everything about her*, Philip admitted to himself.

'Where do you go from here?' Lara was asking.

'Tomorrow I'll be in Milan. Then Venice and Vienna, Paris and London, and finally New York.'

'It sounds so romantic.'

Philip laughed. 'I'm not sure romantic is the word I would choose. We're talking about iffy airline schedules, strange hotels, and eating out in restaurants every night. I don't really mind because the act of playing is so wonderful. It's the "say cheese" syndrome that I hate.'

'What's that?'

'Being put on exhibit all the time, smiling at people you care nothing about, living your life in a world of strangers.'

'I know what that's like,' Lara said slowly.

As they were finishing supper, Philip said, 'Look, I'm always keyed up after a concert. Would you care to take a ride on the canal?'

'I'd love to.'

They boarded a canal bus that cruised the Amstel. There was no moon, but the city was alive with thousands of sparkling lights. The canal trip was an enchantment. A loudspeaker poured out information in four languages:

'We are now passing centuries-old merchants'

houses with their richly decorated gables. Ahead are ancient church towers. There are 1,200 bridges on the canals, all in the shade of magnificent avenues of elm trees . . .'

They passed the Smalste Huis – the narrowest house in Amsterdam – which was only as wide as the front door, and the 'Westerkerk' with the Crown of the Hapsburg Emperor Maximilian, and they went under the wooden lift bridge over the Amstel, and the Magere Brug – the skinny bridge – and passed scores of houseboats that served as home for hundreds of families.

'This is such a beautiful city,' Lara said.

'You've never been here before?'

'No.'

'And you're here on business.'

Lara took a deep breath. 'No.'

He looked at her, puzzled. 'I thought you said . . .'

'I came to Amsterdam to see you.'

He felt a sudden frisson of pleasure. 'I . . . I'm very flattered.'

'And I have another confession to make. I told you I was interested in classical music. That's not true.'

A smile touched the corner of Philip's lips. 'I know.'

Lara looked at him in surprise. 'You know?'

'Professor Meyers is an old friend of mine,' he said gently. 'He called to tell me that he was giving you a crash course on Philip Adler. He was concerned that you might have designs on me.'

Lara said softly, 'He was right. Are you involved with anyone?'

'You mean seriously?'

Lara was suddenly embarrassed. 'If you're not interested I'll leave and . . .'

He took her hand in his. 'Let's get off at the next stop.'

When they arrived back at the hotel, there were a dozen messages from Howard Keller. Lara put them in her purse, unread. At this moment, nothing else in her life seemed important.

'Your room or mine?' Philip asked lightly.

'Yours.'

There was a burning urgency in her.

It seemed to Lara that she had waited all her life for this moment. This was what she had been missing. She had found the stranger she was in love with. They reached Philip's room and there was an urgency in both of them. Philip took her in his arms and kissed her softly and tenderly, exploring, and Lara murmured, 'Oh, my God,' and they began to undress each other.

The silence of the room was broken by a sudden clap of thunder outside. Slowly, grey clouds in the sky spread their skirts open, wider and wider, and soft rain began to fall. It started quietly and gently, caressing the warm air erotically, licking at the sides of buildings, sucking at the soft grass, kissing all the dark corners of the night. It was a hot rain, wanton and sensuous, sliding down slowly, slowly, until the tempo began to increase and it changed to a driving, pounding storm, fierce and demanding, an orgiastic beat in a steady, savage rhythm, plunging down harder and harder, moving faster and faster until it finally exploded in a burst of thunder. Suddenly, as quickly as it had started, it was over.

Lara and Philip lay in each other's arms, spent. Philip held Lara close, and he could feel the beating of her heart. He thought of a line he had once heard in a movie. *Did the earth move for you? By God, it did*, Philip thought. *If she were music, she would be Chopin's Barcarolle or Schumann's Fantasy*.

He could feel the soft contours of her body pressed against him, and he began to get aroused again.

'Philip . . .' Her voice was husky.

'Yes?'

'Would you like me to go with you to Milan?'

He found himself grinning. 'Oh, my God, yes!'

'Good,' Lara murmured. She leaned over him and her soft hair started to trail down his lean, hard body.

It began to rain again.

When Lara finally returned to her room, she telephoned Keller. 'Did I wake you up, Howard?'

'No.' His voice was groggy. 'I'm always up at four in the morning. What's going on there?'

Lara was bursting to tell him, but she said. 'Nothing. I'm leaving tomorrow for Milan.'

'What? We aren't doing anything in Milan.'

Oh yes we are, Lara thought happily.

'Did you see my messages?'

She had forgotten to look at them. Guiltily, she said, 'Not yet.'

'I've been hearing rumours about the casino.'

'What's the problem?'

'There have been some complaints about the bidding.'

'Don't worry about it. If there's any problem, Paul Martin will take care of it.'

'You're the boss.'

'I want you to send the plane to Milan. Have the pilots wait for me there. I'll get in touch with them at the airport.'

'All right, but . . .'

'Go back to sleep.'

At four o'clock in the morning, Paul Martin was wide awake. He had left several messages on Lara's private answering machine at her apartment, but none of his calls had been returned. In the past, she had always let him know when she was going to be away. Something was happening. What was she up to? *Be careful, my darling*, he whispered. *Be very careful.*

23

In Milan, Lara and Philip Adler checked into the Antica Locanda Solferino, a charming hotel with only twelve rooms, and they spent the morning making passionate love. Afterward, they took the drive to Cernobia and had lunch at Lake Como, at the beautiful Villa d'Este.

The concert that night was a triumph, and the green room at La Scala Opera House was packed with well-wishers.

Lara stood to one side, watching as Philip's fans surrounded him, touching him, adoring him, asking for autographs, handing him little gifts. Lara felt a sharp pang of jealousy. Some of the women were young and beautiful, and it seemed to Lara that all of them were obvious. An American woman in an elegant Fendi gown was saying, coyly, 'If you're free tomorrow, Mr Adler, I'm having an intimate little dinner at my villa. *Very* intimate.'

Lara wanted to strangle the bitch.

Philip smiled. 'Er . . . thank you, but I'm afraid I'm not free.'

Another woman tried to slip Philip her hotel key. He shook his head.

Philip looked over at Lara and grinned. Women kept crowding around him.

'*Lei era magnifico, Maestro!*'

'*Moito gentile da parte sua,*' Philip replied.

'*L'ho sentita suonare il anno scorso. Bravo!*'

'*Grazie,*' Philip smiled.

A woman was clutching his arm, '*Sarebbe possibile cenare insieme?*'

Philip shook his head. '*Ma non credo che sarai impossibile.*'

To Lara, it seemed to go on for ever. Finally, Philip made his way over to Lara and whispered, 'Let's get out of here.'

'Si!' Lara grinned.

They went to Biffy, the restaurant in the opera house, and the moment they walked in, the patrons, dressed in black-tie for the concert, rose to their feet and began applauding. The maître d' led Philip and Lara toward a table in the centre of the room. 'It's such an honour to have you with us, Mr Adler.'

A complimentary bottle of champagne arrived and they drank a toast.

'To us,' Philip said warmly.

'To us.'

Philip ordered two of the specialities of the house, *Osso Buco* and *Penne all' Arrabbiata*. All during supper they talked, and it was as though they had known each other for ever.

They were constantly interrupted by people coming up to the table to compliment Philip, and to ask for autographs.

It's always like this, isn't it?' Lara asked.

Philip shrugged. 'It goes with the territory. For every two hours you spend on stage, you spend countless more signing autographs or giving interviews.'

As if to punctuate what he was saying, he stopped to sign another autograph.

'You've made this tour wonderful for me.' Philip sighed. 'The bad news is that I have to leave for Venice tomorrow. I'm going to miss you a lot.'

'I've never been to Venice,' Lara said.

Lara's jet was waiting for them at Linate Airport. When they arrived there, Philip looked at the huge jet in astonishment.

'This is *your* plane?'

'Yes. It's going to take us to Venice.'

'You're going to spoil me, lady.'

Lara said softly, 'I intend to.'

They landed at Marco Polo Airport in Venice thirty-five minutes later, where a limousine waited to drive them the short distance to the dock. From the dock they would take a motorboat to the island of Giudecca, where the Cipriani Hotel was located.

'I arranged for two suites for us,' Lara said. 'I thought it would be more discreet that way.'

In the motorboat on the way to the hotel, Lara asked, 'How long will we be here?'

'Only one night, I'm afraid. I'm giving a recital at La Fenice, and then we head for Vienna.'

The 'we' gave Lara a little thrill. They had discussed it the night before. 'I'd like you to stay with me as long as you can,' Philip had said, 'but are you sure I'm not keeping you from something more important?'

'There *is* nothing more important.'

'Are you going to be all right by yourself this afternoon? I'm going to be busy rehearsing.'

'I'll be fine,' Lara assured him.

After they had checked into their suites, Philip took Lara in his arms. 'I have to go to the theatre now, but there's a lot to see here. Enjoy Venice. I'll see you later this afternoon.' They kissed. It was meant to be a brief one, but it turned into a long, lingering kiss. 'I'd better get out of here while I can,' Philip murmured, 'or I'll never be able to make it through the lobby.'

'Happy rehearsal,' Lara grinned.

And Philip was gone.

Lara telephoned Howard Keller.

'Where are you?' Keller demanded. 'I've been trying to reach you.'

'I'm in Venice.'

There was a pause. 'Are we buying a canal?'

'I'm checking it out,' Lara laughed.

'You really should be back here,' Keller said. 'There's a lot going on. Young Frank Rose brought in some new plans. I like them, but I need your approval so we can get . . .'

'If you like them,' Lara interrupted, 'go ahead.'

'You don't want to see them?' Keller's voice was filled with surprise.

'Not now, Howard.'

'All right. And on the negotiations for the West Side property, I need your okay to . . .'

'You have it.'

'Lara . . . are you feeling all right?'

'I've never felt better in my life.'
'When are you coming home?'
'I don't know. I'll stay in touch. Goodbye, Howard.'

Venice was the kind of magical city that Prospero might have created. Lara spent the rest of the morning and all afternoon exploring. She roamed through San Marco Square, and visited the Doges' Palace and the Bell Tower, and wandered along the crowded Riva degli Schiavoni, and everywhere she went she thought of Philip. She walked through the winding little side streets, crammed with jewellery shops and leather goods and restaurants, and stopped to buy expensive sweaters and scarves and lingerie for the secretaries at the office, and wallets and ties for Keller and some of the other men. She stopped in at a jeweller's to buy Philip a Piaget watch with a gold band.

'Would you please inscribe it "To Philip with Love from Lara"?' Just saying his name made her miss him.

When Philip returned to the hotel, they had coffee in the verdant garden of the Cipriani.

Lara looked across at Philip and thought, *What a perfect place this would be for a honeymoon*.

'I have a present for you,' Lara said. She handed him the box with the watch in it.

He opened it, and stared. 'My God! This must have cost a fortune. You shouldn't have, Lara.'

'Don't you like it?'

'Of course I do. It's beautiful, but . . .'

'Ssh! Wear it and think of me.'

'I don't need this to think of you, but thank you.'

'What time do we have to leave for the theatre?' Lara asked.

'Seven o'clock.'

Lara glanced at Philip's new watch, and said innocently, 'That gives us two hours.'

The theatre was packed. The audience was volatile, applauding and cheering each number.

When the concert was over, Lara went back to the green room to join Philip. It was London and Amsterdam and Milan all over again, and the women seemed even more nubile and eager. There were at least half a dozen beautiful women in the room, and Lara wondered which one Philip would have spent the night with if she were not there.

They had supper at the storied Harry's Bar and were warmly greeted by the affable owner, Arrigo Cipriano.

'What a pleasure to see you, *signore*. And *signorina*. Please!'

He led them to a corner table. They ordered *Bellinis*, the speciality of the house. Philip said to Lara, 'I recommend starting with the *Pasta Fagiole*. It's the best in the world.'

Later, Philip had no memory of what he had eaten for dinner. He was mesmerized by Lara. He knew he was falling in love with her and it terrified him. *I can't make a commitment*, he thought. *It's impossible. I'm a nomad*. He hated to think about the moment when she would leave him to go back to New York. He wanted to prolong their evening as long as possible.

When they had finished supper, Philip said, 'There's a casino out on the Lido. Do you gamble?'

Lara laughed aloud.

'What's so funny?'

Lara thought about the hundreds of millions of dollars she gambled on her buildings. 'Nothing,' she said. 'I'd love to go.'

They took a motorboat to Lido Island. They walked past the Excelsior Hotel and went over to the huge white building that housed the casino. It was filled with eager gamblers.

'Dreamers,' Philip said.

Philip played roulette, and within half an hour, had won two thousand dollars. He turned to Lara. 'I've never won before. You're my good luck charm.'

They played until 3 a.m., and by that time they were hungry again.

A motorboat took them back to San Marco Square, and they wandered through the side streets until they came to the Cantina Do Mori.

'This is one of the best *Bacaros* in Venice,' Philip said.

Lara said, 'I believe you. What's a *Bacaro*?'

'It's a wine bar where they serve *Cicchetti Tapas* – little nibbles of local delicacies.'

Bottle-glass doors led to a dark, narrow space where copper pots hung from the ceiling and dishes gleamed on a long banquette.

It was dawn before they got back to their hotel. They got undressed and Lara said, 'Speaking of nibbles . . .'

*

Early the following morning, Lara and Philip flew to Vienna.

'Going to Vienna is like going into another century,' Philip explained. 'There's a legend that airline pilots say, "Ladies and gentlemen, we're on our final approach to Vienna Airport. Please make sure your seatbacks and table trays are in the upright position, refrain from smoking until inside the terminal, and set your watches back one hundred years."'

Lara laughed.

'My parents were born here. They used to talk about the old days, and it made me envious.'

They were driving along the Ringstrasse and Philip was filled with excitement, like a small boy eager to share his treasures with her.

'Vienna is the city of Mozart, Haydn, Beethoven, Brahms.' He looked at Lara and grinned. 'Oh, I forgot – you're an expert on classical music.'

They checked into the Imperial Hotel.

'I have to go to the concert hall,' Philip told Lara, 'but I've decided that tomorrow we're going to take the whole day off. I'm going to show you Vienna.'

'I'd like that, Philip.'

He held Lara in his arms. 'I wish we had more time now,' he said ruefully.

'So do I.'

He kissed her lightly on the forehead. 'We'll make up for it tonight.'

She held him close. 'Promises, promises.'

The concert that evening took place at the *Musikverein*. The recital consisted of compositions by Chopin,

Schumann and Prokofiev, and it was another triumph for Philip.

The green room was packed again, but this time the language was German.

'*Sie waren wunderbar, Herr Adler!*'

Philip smiled. '*Das ist sehr nett von ihnen. Danke.*'

'*Ich bin ein grosser Anhänger von ihner.*'

Philip smiled again. '*Sie sind sehr freundlich.*'

He was talking to them, but he could not take his eyes off Lara.

After the recital, Lara and Philip had a late supper in the hotel. They were greeted by the maître.

'What an honour!' he exclaimed. 'I was at the concert tonight. You were magnificent! Magnificent!'

'You're very kind,' Philip said modestly.

The dinner was delicious, but they were both too excited by each other to eat. When the waiter asked, 'Would you like some dessert?' Philip said quickly, 'Yes.' And he was looking at Lara.

His instincts told him that something was wrong. She had never been gone this long without telling him where she was. Was she deliberately avoiding him? If she was, there could be only one reason. *And I can't allow that*, Paul Martin thought.

A beam of pale moonlight streamed through the window, making soft shadows on the ceiling. Lara and Philip lay in bed, naked, watching their shadows move above their heads. The ripple of the curtains made the shadows dance, in a soft swaying motion. The shadows came slowly together and separated and came together again, until the two became entwined, became one, and the movement of the dance became faster, and faster, a wild, savage pounding, and suddenly it stopped, and there was only the gentle ripple of the curtains.

Early the following morning, Philip said, 'We have a whole day and an evening here. I have a lot to show you.'

They had breakfast downstairs in the hotel dining room, then walked over to the Kärtner Strasse, where no cars were permitted. The shops there were filled with beautiful clothes and jewellery and antiques.

Philip hired a horse-drawn *Fiaker*, and they rode through the wide streets of the city along the Ring Road. They visited Schönbrunn Palace, and looked at the colourful Imperial Coach collection. In the afternoon they got tickets for the Spanish Riding School, and saw the Lipizzaner stallions. They rode the huge ferris wheel at the Prater, and afterward Philip said, 'Now we're going to sin!'

'Ooh!'

'No,' Philip laughed. 'I had something else in mind.'

He took Lara to Demel's for their incomparable pastry and coffee.

Lara was fascinated by the mix of architecture in Vienna: Beautiful Baroque buildings centuries old, that faced neo-modern buildings.

Philip was interested in the composers. 'Did you

know that Franz Schubert started as a singer here, Lara? He was in the Imperial Chapel choir, and when his voice changed at seventeen, he was thrown out. That's when he decided to compose music.'

They had a leisurely dinner at a small bistro, and stopped at a wine tavern in Grinzing. Afterward, Philip said, 'Would you like to go for a cruise on the Danube?'

'I'd love to.'

It was a perfect night, with a bright full moon and a soft summer breeze. The stars were shining down.

They're shining down on us, Lara thought, *because we're so happy*. Lara and Philip boarded one of the cruise ships, and from the ship's loudspeaker system came the soft strains of 'The Blue Danube'. In the distance, they saw a falling star.

'Quick! Make a wish,' Philip said.

Lara closed her eyes and was silent for a moment.

'Did you make your wish?'

'Yes.'

'What did you wish for?'

Lara looked up at him and said seriously. 'I can't tell you, or it won't come true.' *I'm going to make it come true*, Lara thought.

Philip leaned back and smiled at Lara. 'This is perfect, isn't it?'

'It can always be this way, Philip.'

'What do you mean?'

'We could get married.'

And there it was, out in the open. He had been thinking of nothing else for the past few days. He was deeply in love with Lara, but he knew he could not make a commitment to her.

'Lara, that's impossible.'

'Is it? Why?'

'I've explained it to you, darling. I'm almost always on tour like this. You couldn't travel with me all the time, could you?'

'No,' Lara said, 'but . . .'

'There you are. It would never work. Tomorrow in Paris, I'll show you . . .'

'I'm not going to Paris with you, Philip.'

He thought he had misunderstood her. 'What?'

Lara took a deep breath. 'I'm not going to see you again.'

It was like a blow to the stomach. 'Why? I love you, Lara. I . . .'

'And I love you. But I'm not a groupie. I don't want to be just another one of your fans, chasing you around. You can have all of those you want.'

'Lara, I don't want anyone but you. But don't you see, darling, our marriage could never work. We have separate lives that are important to both of us. I would want us to be together all the time, and we couldn't be.'

'That's it then, isn't it?' Lara said tightly. 'I won't see you again, Philip.'

'Wait. Please! Let's talk about this. Let's go to your room, and . . .'

'No, Philip. I love you very much, but I won't go on like this. It's over.'

'I don't want it to be over,' Philip insisted. 'Change your mind.'

'I can't. I'm sorry. It's all or nothing.'

They were silent the rest of the way back to their hotel. When they reached the lobby, Philip said,

'Why don't I come up to your room? We can talk about this and . . .'

'No, my darling. There's nothing more to talk about.'

He watched Lara get into the elevator and disappear.

When Lara reached her suite, the telephone was ringing. She hurried to pick it up. 'Philip . . .'

'It's Howard. I've been trying to reach you all day.'

She managed to hide her disappointment. 'Is anything wrong?'

'No. Just checking in. There's a lot going on around here. When do you think you'll be coming back?'

'Tomorrow,' Lara said. 'I'll be back in New York tomorrow.' Slowly, Lara replaced the receiver.

She sat there, staring at the telephone, willing it to ring. Two hours later, it was still silent. *I made a mistake*, Lara thought miserably. *I gave him an ultimatum, and I lost him. If I had only waited . . . If only I had gone to Paris with him . . . if . . . if . . .* She tried to visualize her life without Philip. It was too painful to think about. *But we can't go on this way*, Lara thought. *I want us to belong to each other.* Tomorrow she would have to return to New York.

Lara lay down on the couch, fully dressed, the telephone by her side. She felt drained. She knew it would be impossible to get any sleep.

She slept.

In his room, Philip was pacing back and forth like a caged animal. He was furious with Lara, furious with himself. He could not bear the thought of not seeing her again, not holding her in his arms. *Damn all women!* he thought. His parents had warned him. *Your life is music. If you want to be the best, there's no room for anything else.* And until he met Lara, he had believed it. But now, everything had changed. *Damn it! What we had was wonderful. Why did she have to destroy it?* He loved her, but he knew he could never marry her.

Lara was awakened by the ringing of the telephone. She sat up on the couch, groggy, and looked at the clock on the wall. It was five o'clock in the morning. Sleepily, Lara picked up the telephone.

'Howard?'

It was Philip's voice. 'How would you like to get married in Paris?'

24

The marriage of Lara Cameron to Philip Adler made headlines around the world. When Howard Keller heard the news, he went out and got drunk for the first time in his life. He had kept telling himself that Lara's infatuation with Philip Adler would pass. *Lara and I are a team. We belong together. No one can come between us.* He stayed drunk for two days and when he sobered up, he telephoned Lara in Paris.

'If it's true,' he said, 'tell Philip I said he's the luckiest man who ever lived.'

'It's true,' Lara assured him brightly.

'You sound happy.'

'I've never been happier in my life!'

'I . . . I'm pleased for you, Lara. When are you coming home?'

'Philip is giving a concert in London tomorrow, and then we'll be back in New York.'

'Did you talk to Paul Martin before the wedding?'

She hesitated. 'No.'

'Don't you think you should do it now?'

'Yes, of course.' She had been more concerned about that than she wanted to admit to herself. She was not sure how he was going to take the news of her marriage. 'I'll talk to him when I get back.'

'I'll sure be glad to see you. I miss you.'

'I miss you, too, Howard.' And it was true. He was very dear. He had always been a good and loyal friend. *I don't know what I would have done without him*, Lara thought.

When the 727 taxied up to the Butler Aviation terminal at New York's La Guardia airport, the press was there in full force. There were newspaper reporters and television cameras.

The airport manager led Lara and Philip into the reception office. 'I can sneak you out of here,' he said, 'or . . .'

Lara turned to Philip. 'Let's get this over with, darling. Otherwise, they'll never let us have any peace.'

'You're probably right.'

The press conference lasted for two hours. 'Where did you two meet . . . ?'

'Have you always been interested in classical music, Mrs Adler . . . ?'

'How long have you known each other . . . ?'

'Are you going to live in New York . . . ?'

'Will you give up your touring, Mr Adler . . . ?'

Finally, it was over.

There were two limousines waiting for them. The second one was for luggage.

'I'm not used to travelling in this kind of style,' Philip said.

Lara laughed. 'You'll get used to it.'

When they were in the limousine, Philip asked, 'Where are we going? I have an apartment on Fifty-Seventh Street . . .'

'I think you might be more comfortable at my

321

place, darling. Look it over, and if you like it, we'll have your things moved in.'

They arrived at the Cameron Plaza. Philip looked up at the huge building.

'You *own* this?'

'A few banks and I.'

'I'm impressed.'

Lara squeezed his arm. 'Good. I want you to be.'

The lobby had been freshly decorated with flowers. Half a dozen employees were waiting to greet them.

'Welcome home, Mrs Adler, Mr Adler.'

Philip looked around, and said, 'My God! All this is yours?'

'*Ours*, sweetheart.'

The elevator took them up to the penthouse. It covered the whole forty-fifth floor. The door was opened by the butler.

'Welcome home, Mrs Adler.'

'Thank you, Simms.'

Lara introduced Philip to the rest of the staff and showed him through the duplex penthouse. There was a large white drawing room, filled with antiques, a large enclosed terrace, a dining room, four master bedrooms and three staff bedrooms, six bathrooms, a kitchen, a library, and an office.

'Do you think you could be comfortable here, darling?' Lara asked.

Philip grinned. 'It's a little small – but I'll manage.'

In the middle of the drawing room was a beautiful new Bechstein piano. Philip walked over to it and ran his fingers over the keys.

'It's wonderful!' he said.

Lara moved to his side. 'It's your wedding present.'

'Really?' He was touched. He sat down at the piano, and began to play.

'I just had it tuned for you.' Lara listened as the cascade of notes filled the room. 'Do you like it?'

'I love it! Thank you, Lara.'

'You can play here to your heart's content.'

Philip rose from the piano bench. 'I'd better give Ellerbee a call,' Philip said. 'He's been trying to reach me.'

'There's a telephone in the library, darling.'

Lara went into her office and turned on the answering machine. There were half a dozen messages from Paul Martin. 'Lara, where are you? I miss you, darling' . . . 'Lara, I assume you're out of the country, or I would have heard from you' . . . 'I'm worried about you, Lara. Call me . . .' Then the tone changed. 'I just heard about your marriage. Is it true? Let's talk.'

Philip had walked into the room. 'Who's the mysterious caller?' he asked.

Lara turned. 'An . . . an old friend of mine.'

Philip walked up to her, and put his arms around her. 'Is he someone I should be jealous of?'

Lara said, softly, 'You don't have to be jealous of anyone in the world. You're the only man I've ever loved.' *And it's true*.

Philip held her closely. 'You're the only woman I've ever loved.'

Later that afternoon, while Philip sat at the piano, Lara went back into her office and returned Paul Martin's telephone calls.

He came on the line almost immediately. 'You're back.' His voice was tight.

'Yes.' She had been dreading this conversation.

'I don't mind telling you that the news was quite a shock, Lara.'

'I'm sorry, Paul . . . I . . . it happened rather suddenly.'

'It must have.'

'Yes.' She tried to read his mood.

'I thought we had something pretty good going for us. I thought it was something special.'

'It was, Paul, but . . .'

'We'd better talk about it.'

'Well, I . . .'

'Let's make it lunch tomorrow. Vitello's. One o'clock.' It was an order.

Lara hesitated. It would be foolish to antagonize him any further. 'All right, Paul. I'll be there.'

The line went dead. Lara sat there worried. How angry was Paul, and was he going to do anything about it?

25

The following morning when Lara arrived at Cameron Center, the entire staff was waiting to congratulate her.

'It's wonderful news!'

'It was such a big surprise to all of us!'

'I'm sure you'll be very happy . . .'

And on it went.

Howard Keller was waiting in Lara's office for her. He gave her a big hug. 'For a lady who doesn't like classical music, you sure went and did it!'

Lara smiled. 'I did, didn't I?'

'I'll have to get used to calling you Mrs Adler.'

Lara's smile faded. 'I think it might be better, for business reasons, if I keep using Cameron, don't you?'

'Whatever you say. I'm sure glad you're back. Everything is piling up here.'

Lara settled in a chair opposite Howard. 'Okay, tell me what's been happening.'

'Well, the West Side hotel is going to be a money losing proposition. We have a buyer lined up from Texas who's interested in it, but I went over to the hotel yesterday. It's in terrible shape. It needs a complete refurbishing, and that's going to run into five or six million dollars.'

'Has the buyer seen it yet?'

'No. I told him I'd show it to him tomorrow.'

'Show it to him next week. Get some painters in there. Make it look squeaky clean. Arrange for a crowd to be in the lobby when he's there.'

He grinned. 'Right. Frank Rose is here with some new sketches. He's waiting in my office.'

'I'll take a look at them.'

'The Midland Insurance Company that was going into the new building?'

'Yes.'

'They haven't signed the deal yet. They're a little shaky.'

Lara made a note. 'I'll talk to them about it. Next?'

'Gotham Bank's seventy-five million loan on the new project?'

'Yes?'

'They're pulling back. They think you're getting over-extended.'

'How much interest were they going to charge us?'

'Seventeen per cent.'

'Set up a meeting with them. We're going to offer to pay twenty per cent.'

He was looking at her, aghast. 'Twenty per cent? My God, Lara! No one pays twenty per cent.'

'I would rather be alive at twenty per cent than dead at seventeen per cent. Do it, Howard.'

'All right.'

The morning went by swiftly. At twelve thirty, Lara said, 'I'm going to meet Paul Martin for lunch.'

Howard looked worried. 'Make sure you aren't lunch.'

'What do you mean?'

'I mean he's Sicilian. They don't forgive and they don't forget.'

'You're being melodramatic. Paul would never do anything to harm me.'

'I hope you're right.'

Paul Martin was waiting for Lara at the restaurant when she arrived. He looked thin and haggard, and there were circles under his eyes, as though he had not been sleeping well.

'Hello, Lara.' He did not get up.

'Paul.' She sat down across from him.

'I left some stupid messages on your answering machine. I'm sorry. I had no idea . . .' He shrugged.

'I should have let you know, Paul, but it all happened so fast.'

'Yeah.' He was studying her face. 'You're looking great.'

'Thank you.'

'Where did you meet Adler?'

'In London.'

'And you fell in love with him just like that?' There was a bitter undertone to his words.

'Paul, what you and I had was wonderful, but it wasn't enough for me. I needed something more than that. I needed someone to come home to every night.'

He was listening, watching her.

'I would never do anything in the world to hurt you, but this just . . . just happened.'

More silence.

'Please understand.'

'Yeah.' A wintry smile crossed his face. 'I guess I have no choice, have I? What's done is done. It was just kind of a shock to read about it in the newspapers and see it on television. I thought we were closer than that.'

'You're right,' Lara said again. 'I should have told you.'

His hand reached out and caressed her chin. 'I was crazy about you, Lara. I guess I still am. You were my *miracolo*. I could have given you anything in the world you wanted except what he could give you – a wedding ring. I love you enough to want you to be happy.'

Lara felt a wave of relief sweep through her. 'Thank you, Paul.'

'When am I going to meet your husband?'

'We're giving a party next week for our friends. Will you come?'

'I'll be there. You tell him that he had better treat you right, or he'll have to answer to me.'

Lara smiled. 'I'll tell him.'

When Lara returned to her office, Howard Keller was waiting for her. 'How did the luncheon go?' he asked nervously.

'Fine. You were wrong about Paul. He behaved beautifully.'

'Good. I'm glad I was wrong. Tomorrow morning I've set up some meetings for you with . . .'

'Cancel them,' Lara said. 'I'm staying home with my husband tomorrow. We're honeymooning for the next few days.'

'I'm glad you're so happy,' Howard said.

'Howard, I'm so happy it scares me. I'm afraid that I'll wake up and find this is all a dream. I never knew anyone could be this happy.'

He smiled. 'All right, I'll handle the meetings.'

'Thank you.' She kissed him on the cheek. 'Philip and I are giving a party next week. We expect you there.'

The party took place the following Saturday at the penthouse. There was a lavish buffet, and more than a hundred guests. Lara had invited the men and women she worked with: Bankers, builders, architects, construction chiefs, city officials, the zoning commissioner, and the heads of unions. Philip had invited his musician friends and music patrons and benefactors. The combination proved to be disastrous.

It wasn't that the two groups did not *try* to mix. The problem was that most of them had nothing in common. The builders were interested in construction and architecture, and the musicians were interested in music and composers.

Lara introduced the zoning commissioner to a group of musicians. The commissioner stood there, trying to follow the discussion.

'Do you know what Rossini felt about Wagner's music? One day, he sat his ass on the piano keys and said, "That's what Wagner sounds like to me."'

'Wagner deserved it. When a fire broke out at the Ring Theatre in Vienna during a performance of *The Tales of Hoffmann*, four hundred people burned to death. When Wagner heard about it he said, "That's what they get for listening to an Offenbach operetta."'

The commissioner hastily moved on.

Lara introduced some of Philip's friends to a group of real estate men.

'The problem,' one of the men said, 'is that you need thirty-five per cent of the tenants signed up before you can go co-op.'

'If you want my opinion, that's a pretty stupid rule.'

'I agree. I'm switching to hotels. Do you know the hotels in Manhattan now are averaging two hundred dollars a room per night? Next year . . .'

The musicians moved on.

Conversations seemed to be going on in two different languages.

'The trouble with the Viennese is that they love dead composers . . .'

'There's a new hotel going up on two parcels, between Forty-Seventh and Forty-Eighth Streets. Chase Manhattan is financing it . . .'

'He might not be the greatest conductor in the world, but his stick technique is *genau* . . .'

'. . . I remember a lot of the mavens said that the 1929 stock market crash wasn't a bad thing. It would teach people to put their money in real estate . . .'

'. . . and Horowitz wouldn't play for years because he thought his fingers were made of glass . . .'

'. . . I've seen the plans. There's going to be a classic base rising from three floors from Eighth Avenue, and inside an elliptical arcade with lobbies on three sides . . .'

'. . . Einstein loved the piano. He used to play with Rubenstein, but Einstein kept playing off beat. Finally, Rubenstein couldn't stand it any more and he yelled, "Albert, can't you count?"'

'. . . Congress must have been drunk to pass the Tax Reform Act. It's going to cripple the building industry . . .'

'. . . And at the end of the evening when Brahms left the party he said, "If there's anyone here I've forgotten to insult, I apologize."'

The Tower of Babel.

Paul Martin arrived alone and Lara hurried over to the door to greet him. 'I'm so glad you could come, Paul.'

'I wouldn't have missed it.' He looked around the room. 'I want to meet Philip.'

Lara took him over to where Philip was standing with a group. 'Philip, this is an old friend of mine, Paul Martin.'

Philip held out his hand. 'I'm pleased to meet you.'

The two men shook hands.

'You're a lucky man, Mr Adler. Lara's a remarkable woman.'

'That's what I keep telling him,' Lara smiled.

'She doesn't have to tell me,' Philip said. 'I know how lucky I am.'

Paul was studying him. 'Do you?'

Lara could feel the sudden tension in the air. 'Let me get you a cocktail,' she said to Paul.

'No, thanks. Remember? I don't drink.'

Lara bit her lip. 'Of course. Let me introduce you to some people.' She escorted him around the room, introducing him to some of the guests.

One of the musicians was saying, 'Leon Fleisher is giving a recital tomorrow night. I wouldn't miss it for the world.' He turned to Paul Martin, who was standing next to Howard Keller. 'Have you heard him play?'

'No.'

'He's remarkable. He plays only with his left hand, of course.'

Paul Martin was puzzled. 'Why would he do that?'

'Fleisher developed carpal-tunnel syndrome in his right hand about ten years ago.'

'But how can he give a recital with one hand?'

'Half a dozen composers wrote concertos for the left hand. There's one by Demuth, Franz Schmidt, Korngold, and a beautiful concerto by Ravel.'

Some of the guests were asking Philip to play for them.

'All right. This is for my bride.' He sat down at the piano and began to play a theme from a Rachmaninoff piano concerto. The room was hushed. Everyone seemed mesmerized by the lovely strains that filled the penthouse. When Philip rose, there was loud applause.

An hour later, the party began to break up. When they had seen the last guest to the door, Philip said, 'That was quite a party.'

'You hate big parties, don't you?' Lara said.

Philip took her in his arms and grinned. 'Did it show?'

'We'll only do this every ten years,' Lara promised. 'Philip, did you have a feeling that our guests were from two different planets?'

He put his lips to her cheek. 'It doesn't matter. We have our own planet. Let's make it spin . . .'

26

In order to spend more time with Philip, Lara decided to work at home in the mornings.

'I want us to be together as much as possible,' she told Philip.

Lara asked Kathy to arrange for some secretaries to be interviewed at the penthouse. Lara talked to half a dozen before Marian Bell appeared. She was in her middle twenties with soft, blonde hair, attractive features, and a warm personality.

'Sit down,' Lara said.

'Thank you.'

Lara was looking over her résumé. 'You were graduated from Wellesley College?'

'Yes.'

'And you have a BA. Why do you want a job as a secretary?'

'I think I can learn a lot working for you. Whether I get this job or not, I'm a big fan of yours, Miss Cameron.'

'Really? Why?'

'You're my role model. You've accomplished a lot, and you've done it on your own.'

Lara was studying the girl. 'This job would mean long hours. I get up early. You'd be working at my apartment. You'd start at six in the morning.'

'That wouldn't be a problem. I'm a hard worker.'

Lara smiled. She liked the girl. 'I'll give you a one-week trial,' she said.

By the end of the week, Lara knew that she had found a jewel. Marian was capable and intelligent and pleasant. Gradually, a routine was established. Unless there was an emergency, Lara spent the mornings working at the apartment. In the afternoon, she would go to the office.

Each morning, Lara and Philip had breakfast together and afterward Philip would go to the piano and sit in a sleeveless athletic shirt and jeans and practise for two or three hours while Lara went into her office and dictated to Marian. Sometimes Philip would play old Scottish tunes for Lara: 'Annie Laurie', and 'Comin' through the Rye'. She was touched. They would have lunch together.

'Tell me what your life was like in Glace Bay,' Philip said.

'It would take at least five minutes,' Lara smiled.

'No, I'm serious. I really want to know.'

She talked about the boarding house, but she could not bring herself to talk about her father. She told Philip the story of Charles Cohn, and Philip said, 'Good for him. I'd like to meet him one day.'

'I'm sure you will.'

Lara told him about her experience with Sean MacAllister, and Philip said, 'That bastard! I'd like to kill him!' He held Lara close and said, 'No one is ever going to hurt you again.'

*

Philip was working on a concerto. She would hear him play three notes at a time, over and over and then move on, practising slowly and picking up the tempo until the different phrases finally flowed into one.

In the beginning, Lara would walk into the drawing room while Philip was playing and interrupt him.

'Darling, we're invited to Long Island for the weekend. Would you like to go?'

Or, 'I have theatre tickets for the new Neil Simon play.'

Or, 'Howard Keller would like to take us out to dinner Saturday night.'

Philip had tried to be patient. Finally he said, 'Lara, please don't interrupt me while I'm at the piano. It breaks my concentration.'

'I'm sorry,' Lara said. 'But I don't understand why you practise every day. You're not giving a concert now.'

'I practise every day so I *can* give a concert. You see, my darling, when you put up a building and a mistake is made, it can be corrected. You can change the plans or you can redo the plumbing or the lighting or whatever. But at a recital, there is no second chance. You're live in front of an audience and every note has to be perfect.'

'I'm sorry,' Lara apologized. 'I understand.'

Philip took her in his arms. 'There's the old joke about a man in New York carrying a violin case. He was lost. He stopped a stranger and said, "How do you get to Carnegie Hall?" "Practise," the stranger said, "practise."'

Lara laughed. 'Go back to your piano. I'll leave you alone.'

She sat in her office listening to the faint strains of Philip playing and she thought, *I'm so lucky. Thousands of women would envy me sitting here listening to Philip Adler play*.

She just wished he did not have to practise so often.

They both enjoyed playing backgammon, and in the evening, after dinner, they would sit in front of the fireplace and have mock-fierce contests. Lara treasured those moments of being alone with him.

The Reno casino was getting ready to open. Six months earlier, Lara had had a meeting with Jerry Townsend. 'I want them to read about this opening in Timbuktu,' Lara said. 'I'm flying in the chef from Maxim's for the opening. I want you to get me the hottest talent available. Start with Frank Sinatra and work your way down. I want the invitation list to include the top names in Hollywood, New York and Washington. I want people fighting to get on that list.'

Now, as Lara looked it over, she said, 'You've done a good job. How many turn-downs have we had?'

'A couple dozen,' Townsend said. 'That's not bad from a list of six hundred.'

'Not bad at all,' Lara agreed.

*

Keller telephoned Lara in the morning. 'Good news,' he said. 'I got a call from the Swiss bankers. They're flying in to meet with you tomorrow to discuss the joint venture.'

'Great,' Lara said. 'Nine o'clock, my office.'

'I'll set it up.'

At dinner that evening, Philip said, 'Lara, I'm doing a recording session tomorrow. You've never been to one, have you?'

'No.'

'Would you like to come and watch?'

Lara hesitated, thinking about the meeting with the Swiss. 'Of course,' she said.

Lara telephoned Keller. 'Start the meeting without me. I'll get there as soon as I can.'

The recording studio was located on West 34th Street, in a large warehouse filled with electronic equipment. There were a hundred and thirty musicians seated in the room and a glass-enclosed control booth where the sound engineers worked. It seemed to Lara that the recording was going very slowly. They kept stopping and starting again. During one of the breaks she telephoned Keller.

'Where are you?' he demanded. 'I'm stalling, but they want to talk to you.'

'I'll be there in an hour or two,' she said. 'Keep them talking.'

Two hours later, the recording session was still going on.

Lara telephoned Keller again.

'I'm sorry, Howard, I can't leave. Have them come back tomorrow.'

'What's so important?' Keller demanded.

'My husband,' Lara said. And she replaced the receiver.

When they returned to the apartment, Lara said, 'We're going to Reno next week.'

'What's in Reno?'

'It's the opening of the hotel and casino. We'll fly down on Wednesday.'

Philip's voice was filled with distress. 'Damn!'

'What's the matter?'

'I'm sorry, darling, I can't.'

She was staring at him. 'What do you mean?'

'I thought I had mentioned it. I'm leaving on a tour on Monday.'

'What are you talking about?'

'Ellerbee has booked me on a six-week tour. I'm going to Australia and . . .'

'*Australia?*'

'Yes. Then Japan and Hong Kong.'

'You can't, Philip. I mean . . . why are you doing this? You don't have to. I want to be with you.'

'Well, come with me, Lara. I'd love that.'

'You know I can't. Not now. There's too much happening here,' Lara said miserably, 'I don't want you to leave me.'

'I don't want to. But darling, I warned you before we were married that this is what my life is about.'

'I know,' Lara said, 'but that was before. Now it's different. Everything has changed.'

'Nothing has changed,' Philip said gently, 'except

that I'm absolutely crazy about you and when I go away I'll miss you like the devil.'

There was nothing Lara could say to that.

Philip was gone, and Lara had never known such loneliness. In the middle of a meeting, she would suddenly think about Philip and her heart would melt.

She wanted him to go on with his career, but she needed him with her. She thought of the wonderful times they had had together, and of his arms around her, and his warmth and gentleness. She had never known she could love anyone so much. Philip telephoned her every day, but somehow it made the loneliness worse.

'Where are you, darling?'

'I'm still in Tokyo.'

'How's the tour going?'

'Beautifully. I miss you.'

'I miss you, too.' Lara could not tell him how much she missed him.

'I leave for Hong Kong tomorrow and then . . .'

'I wish you'd come home.' She regretted it the moment she said it.

'You know I can't.'

There was a silence. 'Of course not.'

They talked for half an hour and when Lara put the receiver down she was lonelier than ever. The time differences were maddening. Sometimes her Tuesday would be his Wednesday, and he would call in the middle of the night or in the early hours of the morning.

*

'How's Philip?' Keller asked.

'Fine. Why does he do it, Howard?'

'Why does he do what?'

'This tour of his. He doesn't have to do it. I mean, he certainly doesn't need the money.'

'Whoa. I'm sure he's not doing it for the money. It's what he *does*, Lara.'

The same words that Philip had used. She understood it intellectually, but not emotionally.

'Lara,' Keller said, 'you only married the man – you don't own him.'

'I don't want to own him. I was just hoping that I was more important to him than . . .' She stopped herself in mid-sentence. 'Never mind. I know I'm being silly.'

Lara telephoned William Ellerbee.

'Are you free for lunch today?' Lara asked.

'I can make myself free,' Ellerbee said. 'Is anything wrong?'

'No, no. I just thought we should have a talk.'

They met at Le Cirque.

'Have you talked to Philip lately?' Ellerbee asked.

'I talk to him every day.'

'He's having a successful tour.'

'Yes.'

Ellerbee said, 'Frankly, I never thought Philip would get married. He's like a priest – dedicated to what he does.'

'I know . . .' Lara hesitated, '. . . but don't you think he's travelling too much?'

'I don't understand.'

'Philip has a home now. There's no reason for

him to be running all over the world.' She saw the expression on Ellerbee's face. 'Oh, I don't mean he should just stay in New York. I'm sure you could arrange concerts for him in Boston, Chicago, Los Angeles. You know . . . where he wouldn't have to travel so far from home.'

Ellerbee said carefully, 'Have you discussed this with Philip?'

'No. I wanted to talk to you first. It *would* be possible, wouldn't it? I mean, Philip doesn't need the money, not any more.'

'Mrs Adler, Philip makes thirty-five thousand dollars a performance. Last year he was on tour for forty weeks.'

'I understand, but . . .'

'Do you have any idea how few pianists make it to the top, or how hard they have to struggle to get there? There are thousands of pianists out there, playing their fingers to the bone, and there are only about four or five superstars. Your husband is one of them. You don't know much about the concert world. The competition is murderous. You can go to a recital and see a soloist on the stage dressed in tails, looking prosperous and glamorous, but when he gets off that stage, he can barely afford to pay his rent or buy a decent meal. It took Philip a long time to become a world class pianist. Now you're asking me to take that away from him.'

'No, I'm not. I'm merely suggesting . . .'

'What you're suggesting would destroy his career. You don't really want to do that, do you?'

'Of course not,' Lara said. She hesitated. 'I understand that you get fifteen per cent of what Philip earns.'

'That's right.'

'I wouldn't want you to lose anything if Philip gave fewer concerts,' Lara said carefully. 'I'd be glad to make up the difference and . . .'

'Mrs Adler, I think this is something you should discuss with Philip. Shall we order?'

27

Liz Smith's column read:

> ### IRON BUTTERFLY ABOUT TO GET HER WINGS CLIPPED
>
> What beautiful real estate tycoon is about to hit her penthouse roof when she learns that a book about her, written by a former employee, is going to be published by Candlelight Press? The word is that it's going to be hot! Hot! Hot!

Lara slammed the newspaper down. It had to be Gertrude Meeks, the secretary she had fired! Lara sent for Jerry Townsend. 'Have you seen Liz Smith's column this morning?'

'Yes, I just read it. There isn't much we can do about it, boss. If you . . .'

'There's a lot we can do. All my employees sign an agreement that they will not write anything about me during or after their employment here. Gertrude Meeks has no right to do this. I'm going to sue the publisher for all he's worth.'

Jerry Townsend shook his head. 'I wouldn't do that.'

'Why not?'

'Because it will create a lot of unfavourable

publicity. If you let it ride, it becomes a small wind that will blow over. If you try to stop it, it will become a hurricane.'

She listened, unimpressed. 'Find out who owns the company,' Lara ordered.

One hour later, Lara was speaking on the phone to Lawrence Seinfeld, the owner and publisher of Candlelight Press.

'This is Lara Cameron. I understand you intend to publish a book about me.'

'You read the Liz Smith item, huh? Yes, it's true, Miss Cameron.'

'I want to warn you that if you publish the book, I'm going to sue you for invasion of privacy.'

The voice at the other end of the phone said, 'I think perhaps you should check with your attorney. You're a public figure, Miss Cameron. You have no right of privacy. And according to Gertrude Meeks' manuscript, you're quite a colourful character.'

'Gertrude Meeks signed a paper forbidding her to write anything about me.'

'Well, that's between you and Gertrude. You can sue her . . .'

But by then, of course, the book would be out.

'I don't want it published. If I can make it worth your while not to publish it . . .'

'Hold on. I think you're treading on dangerous ground. I would suggest that we terminate this conversation. Goodbye.' The line went dead.

Damn him! Lara sat there thinking. She sent for Howard Keller.

'What do you know about Candlelight Press?'

He shrugged. 'They're a small outfit. They do

exploitation books. They did a hatchet job on Cher, Madonna . . .'

'Thanks. That's all.'

Howard Keller had a headache. It seemed to him that he was getting a lot of headaches lately. Not enough sleep. He was under pressure and he felt that things were moving too rapidly. He had to find a way to slow Lara down. *Maybe this was a hunger headache.* He buzzed his secretary.

'Bess, order some lunch in for me, would you?'

There was a silence.

'Bess?'

'Are you joking, Mr Keller?'

'Joking? No, why?'

'You just had your lunch.'

Keller felt a chill go through him.

'But if you're still hungry . . .'

'No, no.' He remembered now. He had had a salad and a roast beef sandwich and . . . *My God*, he thought, *what's happening to me?*

'Just kidding, Bess,' he said. *Who am I kidding?*

The opening of the Cameron Palace in Reno was a smash. The hotel was fully booked, and the casino was crowded with players. Lara had spared no expense to see that the invited celebrities were well taken care of. Everyone was there. *There's only one person missing*, Lara thought. Philip. He had sent an enormous bouquet of flowers with a note: 'You're the music in my life. I adore you and miss you. Hub.'

Paul Martin arrived. He came up to Lara. 'Congratulations. You've outdone yourself.'

'Thanks to you, Paul. I couldn't have done it without you.'

He was looking around. 'Where's Philip?'

'He couldn't be here. He's on tour.'

'He's out playing piano somewhere? This is a big night for you, Lara. He should be at your side.'

Lara smiled. 'He really wanted to be.'

The manager of the hotel came up to Lara. 'This is quite a night, isn't it? The hotel is fully booked for the next three months.'

'Let's keep it that way, Donald.'

Lara had hired a Japanese and a Brazilian agent to bring in big players from abroad. She had spent a million dollars on each of the luxury suites, but it was going to pay off.

'You've got a gold mine here, Miss Cameron,' the manager said. He looked around. 'By the way, where's your husband? I've been looking forward to meeting him.'

'He couldn't be here,' Lara said. *He's out playing the piano somewhere*.

The entertainment was brilliant, but Lara was the star of the evening. Sammy Cahn had written special lyrics for *My Kind of Town*. It went, 'My Kind of Gal, Lara is . . .' She got up to make a speech, and there was enthusiastic applause. Everyone wanted to meet her, to touch her. The press was there in full force, and Lara gave interviews for television, radio and the press. It all went well until the interviewers asked, 'Where's your husband tonight?' And Lara found herself getting more and more upset. *He should have been at my side. The concert could have waited*. But she smiled sweetly and said, 'Philip was so disappointed he couldn't be here.'

When the entertainment was over, there was dancing. Paul Martin walked up to Lara's table. 'Shall we?'

Lara rose and stepped into his arms.

'How does it feel owning all this?' Paul asked.

'It feels wonderful. Thanks for all your help.'

'What are friends for? I notice that you have some heavyweight gamblers here. Be careful with them, Lara. Some of them are going to lose big, and you have to make them feel like they're winners. Get them a new car or girls or anything that will make them feel important.'

'I'll remember,' Lara said.

'It's good to hold you again,' Paul said.

'Paul . . .'

'I know. Do you remember what I said about your husband taking good care of you?'

'Yes.'

'He doesn't seem to be doing a very good job.'

'Philip wanted to be here,' Lara said defensively. And even as she said it she thought, *Did he really?*

He telephoned her late that night, and the sound of his voice made her twice as lonely.

'Lara, I've been thinking about you all day, darling. How did the opening go?'

'Wonderfully. I wish you could have been here, Philip.'

'So do I. I miss you like crazy.'

Then why aren't you here with me? 'I miss you, too. Hurry home.'

*

347

Howard Keller walked into Lara's office carrying a thick manila envelope.

'You're not going to like this,' Keller said.

'What's up?'

Keller laid the envelope on Lara's desk. 'This is a copy of Gertrude Meeks' manuscript. Don't ask me how I got hold of it. We could both go to jail.'

'Have you read it?'

He nodded. 'Yes.'

'And?'

'I think you'd better read it yourself. She wasn't even working here when some of these things happened. She must have done a lot of digging.'

'Thanks, Howard.'

Lara waited until he left the office, then she pressed down the key on the intercom. 'No calls.'

She opened the manuscript and began to read.

It was devastating. It was a portrait of a scheming, domineering woman who had clawed her way to the top. It depicted her temper tantrums and her imperious manner with her employees. It was mean spirited, filled with nasty little anecdotes. What the manuscript left out was Lara's independence and courage, her talent and vision and generosity. She went on reading.

'. . . One of the Iron Butterfly's tricks was to schedule her business meetings early on the first morning of negotiations so that the others were jet-lagged and Cameron was fresh.

'. . . At a meeting with the Japanese, they were served tea with Valium in it, while Lara Cameron drank coffee with Ritalin, a stimulant that speeds up the thought process.

'. . . At a meeting with some German bankers,

they were served coffee with Valium, while she drank tea with Ritalin.

'. . . When Lara Cameron was negotiating for the Queens property and the zoning commission turned her down, she got them to change their mind by making up a story that she had a young daughter who was going to live in one of the buildings . . .

'. . . When tenants refused to leave the building at the Dorchester Apartments, Lara Cameron filled it with homeless people . . .'

Nothing had been left out. When Lara finished reading it, she sat at her desk for a long time, motionless. She sent for Howard Keller.

'I want you to run a Dun and Bradstreet on Henry Seinfeld. He owns Candlelight Press.'

'Right.'

He was back fifteen minutes later. 'Seinfeld has a D-C rating.'

'Which means?'

'That's the lowest rating there is. A fourth line credit rating is poor, and he's four notches below that. A good stiff wind would blow him over. He lives from book to book. One flop and he's out of business.'

'Thanks, Howard.' She telephoned Terry Hill, her attorney.

'Terry, how would you like to be a book publisher?'

'What did you have in mind?'

'I want you to buy Candlelight Press in your name. It's owned by Henry Seinfeld.'

'That should be no problem. How much do you want to pay?'

'Try to buy him out for five hundred thousand. If

you have to, go to a million. Make sure that the deal includes all the literary properties he owns. Keep my name out of it.'

The offices of Candlelight Press were downtown in an old building on 34th Street. Henry Seinfeld's quarters consisted of a small secretarial office and a slightly larger office for himself.

Seinfeld's secretary said, 'There's a Mr Hill to see you, Mr Seinfeld.'

'Send him in.'

Terry Hill had called earlier that morning.

He walked into the shabby little office. Seinfeld was sitting behind the desk.

'What can I do for you, Mr Hill?'

'I'm representing a German publishing company that might be interested in buying your company.'

Seinfeld took his time lighting a cigar. 'My company's not for sale,' he said.

'Oh, that's too bad. We're trying to break into the American market, and we like your operation.'

'I've built this company up from scratch,' Seinfeld said. 'It's like my baby. I'd hate to part with it.'

'I understand how you feel,' the lawyer said sympathetically. 'We'd be willing to give you five hundred thousand dollars for it.'

Seinfeld almost choked on his cigar. 'Five hundred? Hell, I've got one book coming out that's going to be worth a million dollars alone. No, sir. Your offer's an insult.'

'My offer's a gift. You have no assets and you're over a hundred thousand dollars in debt. I checked.

Tell you what I'll do. I'll go up to six hundred thousand. That's my final offer.'

'I'd never forgive myself. Now, if you could see your way clear to going to seven . . .'

Terry Hill rose to his feet. 'Goodbye, Mr Seinfeld. I'll find another company.'

He started toward the door.

'Wait a minute,' Seinfeld said. 'Let's not be hasty. The fact is, my wife's been after me to retire. Maybe this would be a good time.'

Terry Hill walked over to the desk and pulled a contract out of his pocket. 'I have a cheque here for six hundred thousand dollars. Just sign where the "x" is.'

Lara sent for Keller.

'We just bought Candlelight Press.'

'Great. What do you want to do with it?'

'First of all, kill Gertrude Meeks' book. See that it doesn't get published. There are plenty of ways to keep stalling. If she sues to get her rights back, we can tie her up in court for a year.'

'Do you want to fold the company?'

'Of course not. Put someone in to run it. We'll keep it as a tax loss.'

When Keller returned to his office, he said to his secretary, 'I want to give you a letter. Jack Hellman, Hellman Realty. Dear Jack, I discussed your offer with Miss Cameron and we feel that it would be unwise to go into your venture at this time. However, we want you to know that we would be interested in any future . . .'

His secretary had stopped taking notes.

Keller looked up. 'Do you have that?'

She was staring at him. 'Mr Keller?'

'Yes.'

'You dictated this letter yesterday.'

Keller swallowed. 'What?'

'It's already gone out in the mail.'

Howard Keller tried to smile. 'I guess I'm on overload.'

At four o'clock that afternoon, Keller was being examined by Dr Seymour Bennett.

'You seem to be in excellent shape,' Dr Bennett said. 'Physically, there's nothing wrong with you at all.'

'What about these lapses of memory?'

'How long since you've had a vacation, Howard?'

Keller tried to think. 'I guess it's been quite a few years,' he said. 'We've been pretty busy.'

Dr Bennett smiled. 'There you are. You're on overload.' *That word again*. 'This is more common than you think. Go somewhere where you can relax for a week or two. Get business off your mind. When you come back, you'll feel like a new man.'

Keller stood up, relieved.

Keller went to see Lara in her office. 'Could you spare me for a week?'

'About as easily as I can spare my right arm. What did you have in mind?'

'The doctor thinks I should take a little vacation, Lara. To tell you the truth, I've been having some problems with my memory.'

She was watching him, concerned. 'Anything serious?'

'No, not really. It's just annoying. I thought I might go to Hawaii for a few days.'

'Take the jet.'

'No, no, you'll be using it. I'll fly commercial.'

'Charge everything to the company.'

'Thanks. I'll check in every . . .'

'No, you won't. I want you to forget about the office. Just take care of yourself. I don't want anything to happen to you.'

I hope he's all right, Lara thought. *He's got to be all right.*

Philip telephoned the next day. When Marian Bell said, 'Mr Adler is calling from Taipei,' Lara hurriedly picked up the telephone.

'Philip . . . ?'

'Hello, darling. There's been a phone strike. I've been trying to reach you for hours. How do you feel?'

Lonely. 'Wonderful. How is the tour going?'

'It's the usual. I miss you.'

In the background, Lara could hear music and voices.

'Where are you?'

'Oh, they're giving a little party for me. You know how it is.'

Lara could hear the sound of a woman laughing.

'Yes, I know how it is.'

'I'll be home Wednesday.'
'Philip?'
'Yes?'
'Nothing, darling. Hurry home.'
'I will. Goodbye.'

She replaced the receiver. What was he going to do after the party? Who was the woman? She was filled with a sense of jealousy so strong that it almost smothered her. She had never been jealous of anyone in her life.

Everything is so perfect, Lara thought. *I don't want to lose it. I can't lose it.*

She lay awake thinking about Philip and what he was doing.

Howard Keller was stretched out on Kona Beach at a small hotel on the big island of Hawaii. The weather had been ideal. He had gone swimming every day. He had gotten a tan, played some golf, and had daily massages. He was completely relaxed, and had never felt better. *Dr Bennett was right*, he thought. *Overload. I'm going to have to slow down a little when I get back.* The truth was that the episodes of memory loss had frightened him more than he wanted to admit.

Finally, it was time to return to New York. He took a midnight flight back, and was in Manhattan at four o'clock in the afternoon. He went directly to the office. His secretary was there, smiling. 'Welcome back, Mr Keller. You look great.'

'Thank you . . .' He stood there, and his face drained of colour.

He could not remember her name.

28

Philip arrived home on Wednesday afternoon, and Lara took the limousine to the airport to meet him. Philip stepped off the plane and the image of Lochinvar instantly sprang to Lara's mind.

My God, but he's handsome! She ran into his arms.

'I've missed you,' she said, hugging him.

'I've missed you too, darling.'

'How much?'

He held his thumb and forefinger half an inch apart. 'This much.'

'You beast,' she said. 'Where's your luggage?'

'It's coming.'

One hour later, they were back at the apartment. Marian Bell opened the door for them. 'Welcome back, Mr Adler.'

'Thanks, Marian.' He looked around. 'I feel as though I've been away for a year.'

'Two years,' Lara said. She started to add, 'Don't ever leave me again' and bit her lip.

'Can I do anything for you, Mrs Adler?' Marian asked.

'No. We're fine. You can run along now. I'll dictate some letters in the morning. I won't be going into the office today.'

'Very well. Goodbye.' Marian left.

'Sweet girl,' Philip said.

'Yes, isn't she?' Lara moved into Philip's arms. 'Now show me how much you missed me.'

Lara stayed away from the office for the next three days. She wanted to be with Philip, to talk to him, touch him, assure herself that he was real. They had breakfast in the morning and while Lara dictated to Marian, Philip was at the piano practising.

At lunch on the third day, Lara told Philip about the casino opening. 'I wish you could have been there, darling. It was fantastic.'

'I'm so sorry I missed it.'

He's out playing the piano somewhere. 'Well, you'll have your chance next month. The mayor is giving me the keys to the city.'

Philip said unhappily, 'Darling, I'm afraid I'm going to have to miss that, too.'

Lara froze. 'What do you mean?'

'Ellerbee's booked me for another tour. I leave for Germany in three weeks.'

'You can't!' Lara said.

'The contracts have already been signed. There's nothing I can do about it.'

'You just got back. How can you go away again so soon?'

'It's an important tour, darling.'

'And our marriage isn't important?'

'Lara . . .'

'You don't have to go,' Lara said angrily. 'I want a husband, not a part-time . . .'

Marian Bell came into the room carrying some letters. 'Oh, I'm sorry. I didn't mean to interrupt. I have these letters ready for you to sign.'

'Thank you,' Lara said stiffly. 'I'll call you when I need you.'

'Yes, Miss Cameron.'

They watched Marian retreat to her office.

'I know you have to give concerts,' Lara said, 'but you don't have to give them this often. It's not as though you were some kind of travelling salesman.'

'No, it isn't, is it?' His tone was cool.

'Why don't you stay here for the ceremony and then go on your tour?'

'Lara, I know that it's important to you, but you must understand that my concert tours are important to me. I'm very proud of you and what you're doing, but I want you to be proud of me.'

'I am,' Lara said. 'Forgive me, Philip, I just . . .' She was trying hard not to cry.

'I know, darling.' He took her in his arms. 'We'll work it out. When I come back we'll take a long vacation together.'

A vacation's impossible, Lara thought. *There are too many projects in the works.*

'Where are you going this time, Philip?'

'I'll be going to Germany, Norway, Denmark, England, and then back here.'

Lara took a deep breath. 'I see.'

'I wish you could come with me, Lara. It's very lonely out there without you.'

She thought of the laughing lady. 'Is it?' She shook herself out of her mood and managed to smile. 'I'll tell you what. Why don't you take the jet? It will make it more comfortable for you.'

'Are you sure you're . . . ?'

'Absolutely. I'll manage without it until you're back.'

'There's no one in the world like you,' Philip said.

Lara rubbed a finger slowly along his cheek. 'Remember that.'

Philip's tour was a huge success. In Berlin the audiences went wild and the reviews were ecstatic.

Afterward, the green rooms were always crowded with eager fans, most of them female:

'I've travelled three hundred miles to hear you play . . .'

'I have a little castle not far from here, and I was wondering . . .'

'I've prepared a midnight supper just for the two of us . . .'

Some of them were rich and beautiful, and most of them were very willing. But Philip was in love. He called Lara after the concert in Denmark. 'I miss you.'

'I miss you, too, Philip. How did the concert go?'

'Well, no one walked out while I was playing.'

Lara laughed. 'That's a good sign. I'm right in the middle of a meeting now, darling. I'll call you at your hotel in an hour.'

Philip said, 'I won't be going right to the hotel, Lara. The manager of the concert hall is giving a dinner party for me and . . .'

'Oh? Really? Does he have a beautiful daughter?' She regretted it the moment the words were out.

'What?'

'Nothing. I have to go now. I'll talk to you later.'

She hung up and turned to the men in the office. Keller was watching her. 'Is everything all right?'

'Fine,' Lara said lightly. She found it difficult to

concentrate on the meeting. She visualized Philip at the party, beautiful women handing him their hotel keys. She was consumed with jealousy, and she hated herself for it.

The mayor's ceremony honouring Lara was standing-room only. The press was out in force.

'Could we get a shot of you and your husband together?'

And Lara was forced to say, 'He wanted so much to be here . . .'

Paul Martin was there.

'He's gone again, huh?'

'He really wanted to be here, Paul.'

'Bullshit! This is a big honour for you. He should be at your side. What the hell kind of husband is he? Someone should have a talk with him!'

That night she lay in bed alone, unable to sleep. Philip was 10,000 miles away. The conversation with Paul Martin ran through Lara's mind. *What the hell kind of husband is he? Someone should have a talk with him!*

When Philip returned from Europe, he seemed happy to be home. He brought Lara an armload of gifts. There was an exquisite porcelain figurine from Denmark, lovely dolls from Germany, silk blouses and a gold purse from England. In the purse was a diamond bracelet.

'It's lovely,' Lara said. 'Thank you, darling.'

The next morning Lara said to Marian Bell, 'I'm going to work at home all day.'

Lara sat in her office dictating to Marian, and from the drawing room she could hear the sounds of Philip at the piano. *Our life is so perfect like this*, Lara thought. *Why does Philip want to spoil it?*

William Ellerbee telephoned Philip. 'Congratulations,' he said. 'I hear the tour went wonderfully.'

'It did. The Europeans are great audiences.'

'I got a call from the management at Carnegie Hall. They have an unexpected opening a week from Friday, on the seventeenth. They would like to book you for a recital. Are you interested?'

'Very much.'

'Good. I'll work out the arrangements. By the way,' Ellerbee said, 'are you thinking of cutting back on your concerts?'

Philip was taken aback. 'Cutting back? No. Why?'

'I had a talk with Lara and she indicated that you might want to just tour the United States. Perhaps it would be best if you talked to her and . . .'

Philip said, 'I will. Thank you.'

Philip replaced the receiver and walked into Lara's office. She was dictating to Marian.

'Would you excuse us?' Philip asked.

Marian smiled. 'Certainly.' She left the room.

Philip turned to Lara. 'I just had a call from William Ellerbee. Did you talk to him about my cutting down on foreign tours?'

'I might have mentioned something like that, Philip. I thought it might be better for both of us if . . .'

'Please, don't do that again.' Philip said. 'You know how much I love you. But apart from our lives together, you have a career and I have a career. Let's make a rule. I won't interfere in yours, and you won't interfere in mine. Is that fair enough?'

'Of course it is,' Lara said. 'I'm sorry, Philip. It's just that I miss you so much when you're away.' She went into his arms. 'Forgive me?'

'It's forgiven and forgotten.'

Howard Keller came to the penthouse to bring Lara contracts to sign. 'How's everything going?'

'Beautifully,' Lara said.

'The wandering minstrel is home?'

'Yes.'

'So music is your life now, huh?'

'The musician is my life. You have no idea how wonderful he is, Howard.'

'When are you coming into the office? We need you.'

'I'll come in a few days.'

Keller nodded. 'Okay.'

They began to examine the papers he had brought.

The following morning, Terry Hill telephoned. 'Lara, I just received a call from the Gaming Commission in Reno,' the attorney said. 'There's going to be a hearing on your casino licence.'

'Why?' Lara asked.

'There have been some allegations that the bidding was rigged. They want you to go there and testify on the seventeenth.'

'How serious is this?' Lara asked.

The lawyer hesitated. 'Are you aware of any irregularities in the bidding?'

'No, of course not.'

'Then you have nothing to worry about. I'll fly down to Reno with you.'

'What happens if I don't go?'

'They'll subpoena you. It would look better if you went on your own.'

'All right.'

Lara telephoned Paul Martin's private number at the office. He picked up the phone immediately.

'Lara?'

'Yes, Paul.'

'You haven't used this number in a long time.'

'I know. I'm calling about Reno . . .'

'I heard.'

'Is there a real problem?'

He laughed. 'No. The losers are upset that you beat them to it.'

'Are you sure it's all right, Paul?' She hesitated. 'We did discuss the other bids.'

'Believe me, it's done all the time. Anyway, they have no way of proving that. Don't worry about a thing.'

'All right. I won't.'

She replaced the receiver and sat there, worried.

At lunch Philip said, 'By the way, they offered me a concert at Carnegie Hall. I'm going to do it.'

'Wonderful,' Lara smiled. 'I'll buy a new dress. When is it?'

'The seventeenth.'

Lara's smile faded. 'Oh.'

'What's the matter?'

'I'm afraid I won't be able to be there, darling. I have to be in Reno. I'm so sorry.'

Philip put his hands over hers. 'Our timing seems to be off, doesn't it? Oh, well. Don't worry. There will be plenty more recitals.'

Lara was in her office at Cameron Center. Howard Keller had called her at home that morning.

'I think you'd better get down here,' he had said. 'We have a few problems.'

'I'll be there in an hour.'

They were in the middle of a meeting. 'A couple of deals have gone sour,' Keller told her. 'The insurance company that was moving into our building in Houston has gone bankrupt. They were our only tenant.'

'We'll find someone else,' Lara said.

'It's not going to be that simple. The Tax Reform Act is hurting us. Hell, it's hurting everybody. Congress has wiped out corporate tax shelters, and eliminated most deductions. I think we're heading for a goddamned recession. The savings and loan companies we're dealing with are in trouble. Drexel, Burnham, Lambert may go out of business. Junk bonds are turning into land mines. We're having problems with half a dozen of our buildings. Two of them are only half finished. Without financing, those costs will eat us up.'

Lara sat there, thinking. 'We can handle it. Sell whatever properties we have to to keep up our mortgage payments.'

'The bright side of it,' Keller said, 'is that we have

a cash flow from Reno that's bringing us in close to fifty million a year.'

Lara said nothing.

On Friday the seventeenth, Lara left for Reno. Philip rode with her to the airport. Terry Hill was waiting at the plane.

'When will you be back?' Philip asked.

'Probably tomorrow. This shouldn't take long.'

'I'll miss you,' Philip said.

'I'll miss you, too, darling.'

He stood there watching the plane taking off. *I am going to miss her*, Philip thought. *She's the most fantastic woman in the world.*

In the offices of the Nevada Gaming Commission, Lara was facing the same group of men she had met during the application for a casino licence. This time, however, they were not as friendly.

Lara was sworn in, and a court reporter took down her testimony.

The chairman said, 'Miss Cameron, some rather disturbing allegations have been made concerning the licensing of your casino.'

'What kind of allegations?' Terry Hill demanded.

'We'll come to those in due course.' The chairman turned his attention back to Lara. 'We understood that this was your first experience in acquiring a gambling casino.'

'That's right. I told you that at the first hearing.'

'How did you arrive at the bid you put in? I mean . . . how did you come to that precise figure?'

Terry Hill interrupted. 'I'd like to know the reason for the question.'

'In a moment, Mr Hill. Will you permit your client to answer the question?'

Terry Hill looked at Lara and nodded.

Lara said, 'I had my comptroller and accountants give me an estimate on how much we could afford to bid, and we figured in a small profit we could add to that, and that became my bid.'

The chairman scanned the paper in front of him. 'Your bid was five million dollars more than the next highest bid.'

'Was it?'

'You weren't aware of that at the time you made your bid?'

'No. Of course not.'

'Miss Cameron, are you acquainted with Paul Martin?'

Terry Hill interrupted. 'I don't see the relevance of this line of questioning.'

'We'll come to that in a moment. Meanwhile, I'd like Miss Cameron to answer the question.'

'I have no objection,' Lara said. 'Yes. I know Paul Martin.'

'Have you ever had any business dealings with him?'

Lara hesitated. 'No. He's just a friend.'

'Miss Cameron, are you aware that Paul Martin is reputed to be involved with the Mafia, that . . .'

'Objection. It's hearsay and it has no place in this record.'

'Very well, Mr Hill. I'll withdraw that. Miss Cameron, when was the last time you saw or talked to Paul Martin?'

Lara hesitated. 'I'm not sure, exactly. To be perfectly candid, since I got married, I've seen very little of Mr Martin. We run into each other at parties occasionally, that's all.'

'But it wasn't your habit to speak regularly with him on the telephone?'

'Not after my marriage, no.'

'Did you ever have any discussions with Paul Martin regarding this casino?'

Lara looked over at Terry Hill. He nodded. 'Yes, I believe that after I won the bid for it, he called to congratulate me. And then once again after I got the licence to operate the casino.'

'But you did not talk to him at any other time?'

'No.'

'I'll remind you that you're under oath, Miss Cameron.'

'Yes.'

'You're aware of the penalty for perjury?'

'Yes.'

He held up a sheet of paper. 'I have here a list of fifteen telephone calls between you and Paul Martin, made during the time sealed bids were being submitted for the casino.'

29

Most soloists are dwarfed by the huge twenty-eight hundred seat space at Carnegie Hall. There are not many musicians who can fill the prestigious hall, but on Friday night, it was packed. Philip Adler walked out onto the vast stage to the thunderous applause of the audience. He sat down at the piano, paused a moment, then began to play. The programme consisted of Beethoven sonatas. Over the years he had disciplined himself to concentrate only on the music. But on this night, Philip's thoughts drifted away to Lara and their problems, and for a split second, his fingers started to fumble, and he broke out in a cold sweat. It happened so swiftly that the audience did not notice.

There was loud applause at the end of the first part of the recital. At the intermission Philip went to his dressing room.

The concert manager said, 'Wonderful, Philip. You held them spellbound. Can I get anything for you?'

'No, thanks.' Philip closed the door. He wished the recital were over. He was deeply disturbed by the situation with Lara. He loved her a great deal, and he knew she loved him, but they seemed to have come to an impasse. There had been a lot of tension between them before Lara had left for Reno. *I've got to do something about it*, Philip thought. *But what? How do we compromise?* He was still thinking about it when there was a knock at the door, and the stage manager's voice said, 'Five minutes, Mr Adler.'

'Thank you.'

The second half of the programme consisted of the *Hammerklavier* sonata. It was a stirring, emotional piece, and when the last notes had thundered out through the vast hall, the audience rose to its feet with wild applause. Philip stood on the stage bowing, but his mind was elsewhere. *I've got to go home and talk to Lara.* And then he remembered that she was away. *We'll have to settle this now*, Philip thought. *We can't go on like this*.

The applause continued. The audience was shouting 'bravo' and 'encore'. Ordinarily, Philip would have played another selection, but on this evening he was too upset. He returned to his dressing room and changed into his street clothes. From outside, he could hear the distant rumble of thunder. The papers had said rain, but that had not kept the crowd away. The green room was filled with well-wishers waiting for him. It was always exciting to feel and hear the approval of his fans, but tonight he was in no mood for them. He stayed in his dressing room until he was sure the crowd had gone. When he came out, it was almost midnight. He walked through the empty back-stage corridors and went out the stage door. The limousine was not there. *I'll find a taxi*, Philip decided.

He stepped outside into a pouring rain. There was a cold wind blowing, and Fifty-Seventh street was dark. As Philip moved toward Sixth Avenue, a large man in a raincoat approached from the shadows.

'Excuse me,' he said, 'how do you get to Carnegie Hall?'

Philip thought of the old joke he had told Lara, and was tempted to say 'practise', but he pointed to the building behind him. 'It's right there.'

As Philip turned, the man shoved him hard against the building. In his hand was a deadly-looking switchblade knife. 'Give me your wallet.'

Philip's heart was pounding. He looked around for help. The rain-swept street was deserted. 'All right,' Philip said. 'Don't get excited. You can have it.'

The knife was pressing against his throat.

'Look, there's no need to . . .'

'Shut up! Just give it to me.'

Philip reached into his pocket and pulled out his wallet. The man grabbed it with his free hand and put it in his pocket. He was looking at Philip's watch. He reached down and tore it from Philip's wrist. As he took the watch, he grabbed Philip's left hand, held it tightly, and slashed the razor-sharp knife across Philip's wrist, slicing it to the bone. Philip screamed aloud with pain. Blood began to gush out. The man fled.

Philip stood there in shock, watching his blood mingling with the rain, dripping onto the street.

He fainted.

Book Four

Book Four

30

Lara received the news about Philip in Reno.
 Marian Bell was on the phone, near hysteria.
 'Is he badly hurt?' Lara demanded.
 'We don't have any details yet. He's at New York Hospital in the emergency room.'
 'I'll come back immediately.'

When Lara arrived at the hospital six hours later, Howard Keller was waiting there for her. He looked shaken.
 'What happened?' Lara asked.
 'Apparently, Philip was mugged after he left Carnegie Hall. They found him in the street, unconscious.'
 'How bad is it?'
 'His wrist was slashed. He's heavily sedated, but he's conscious.'
 They went into the hospital room. Philip was lying on a bed with IV tubes feeding liquid into his body.
 'Philip . . . Philip.' It was Lara's voice calling to him from a long way off. He opened his eyes. Lara and Howard Keller were there. There seemed to be two of each. His mouth was dry, and he felt groggy.
 'What happened?' Philip mumbled.
 'You were hurt,' Lara said. 'But you're going to be all right.'

Philip looked down and saw that his left wrist was heavily bandaged. Memory came flooding back. 'I was . . . I was held up. A man took my wallet and watch . . . and then he . . . cut my hand.' It was an effort to talk.

Keller said, 'The stage doorman found you lying in the street. You lost a lot of blood.'

Clarity was beginning to return. Philip looked at his hand again. 'My wrist . . . he slashed my wrist . . . how bad is it?'

'I don't know, darling,' Lara said. 'I'm sure it will be fine. The doctor is coming in to see you.'

Keller said reassuringly, 'Doctors can do anything these days.'

Philip was drifting back to sleep. 'I told him to take what he wanted. He shouldn't have hurt my wrist,' he mumbled. 'He shouldn't have hurt my wrist . . .'

Two hours later, Dr Dennis Stanton walked into Philip's room and the moment Philip saw the expression on his face he knew what he was going to say.

Philip took a deep breath. 'Tell me.'

Dr Stanton sighed. 'I'm afraid I don't have very good news for you, Mr Adler.'

'How bad is it?'

'The flexor tendons have been severed, so you'll have no motion in your hand, and there will be a permanent numbness. In addition to that, there's median and ulnar nerve damage.' He illustrated on his hand. 'The median nerve affects the thumb and first three fingers. The ulnar nerve goes to all the fingers.'

Philip closed his eyes tightly against the wave of sudden despair that engulfed him. After a moment, he spoke. 'Are you saying that I'll . . . I'll never have the use of my left hand again?'

'That's right. The fact is that you're lucky to be alive. Whoever did this, cut the artery. It's a wonder you didn't bleed to death. It took sixty stitches to sew your wrist together again.'

Philip said in desperation, 'My God, isn't there *anything* you can do?'

'Yes. We could put in an implant in your left hand so you would have some motion, but it would be very limited.'

He might as well have killed me, Philip thought despairingly.

'As your hand starts to heal, there's going to be a great deal of pain. We'll give you medication to control it, but I can assure you that in time the pain will go away.'

Not the real pain, Philip thought. *Not the real pain*. He was caught up in a nightmare. And there was no escape.

A detective came to see Philip at the hospital. He stood by the side of Philip's bed. He was one of the old breed, in his late fifties and tired, with eyes that had already seen it all twice.

'I'm Lieutenant Mancini. I'm sorry about what happened, Mr Adler,' he said. 'It's too bad they couldn't have broken your leg instead. I mean . . . if it had to happen . . .'

'I know what you mean,' Philip said curtly.

Howard Keller came into the room. 'I was looking for Lara.' He saw the stranger. 'Oh, sorry.'

'She's around here somewhere,' Philip said. 'This is Lieutenant Mancini. Howard Keller.'

Mancini was staring at him. 'You look familiar. Have we met before?'

'I don't think so.'

Mancini's face lit up. 'Keller! My God, you used to play baseball in Chicago.'

'That's right. How do you . . . ?'

'I was a scout for the White Sox one summer. I still remember your sliders and your change-ups. You could have had a big career.'

'Yeah. Well, if you'll excuse me . . .' He looked at Philip. 'I'll wait for Lara outside.' He left.

Mancini turned to Philip. 'Did you get a look at the man who attacked you?'

'He was a male Caucasian. A large man. About six foot two. Maybe fifty or so.'

'Could you identify him if you saw him again?'

'Yes.' It was a face he would never forget.

'Mr Adler, I could ask you to look through a lot of mug shots, but frankly, I think it would be a waste of your time. I mean, this isn't exactly a high-tech crime. There are hundreds of muggers all over the city. Unless someone nabs them on the spot, they usually get away with it.' He took out his notebook. 'What was taken from you?'

'My wallet and my wristwatch.'

'What kind of watch was it?'

'A Piaget.'

'Was there anything distinctive about it? Did it have an inscription, for example?'

It was the watch Lara had given him. 'Yes. On the

back of the case, it read "To Philip with Love from Lara."'

He made a note. 'Mr Adler . . . I have to ask you this. Had you ever seen this man before?'

Philip looked up at him in surprise. 'Seen him before? No. Why?'

'I just wondered.' Mancini put the notebook away. 'Well, we'll see what we can do. You're a lucky man, Mr Adler.'

'Really?' Philip's voice was filled with bitterness.

'Yeah. We have thousands of muggings a year in this city and we can't afford to spend much time on them, but our Captain happens to be a fan of yours. He collects all your records. He's going to do everything he can to catch the SOB who did this to you. We'll send out a description of your watch to pawn shops around the country.'

'If you catch him, do you think he can give me my hand back?' Philip asked bitterly.

'What?'

'Nothing.'

'You'll be hearing from us. Have a nice day.'

Lara and Keller were waiting in the corridor for the detective.

'You said you wanted to see me?' Lara asked.

'Yes. I'd like to ask you a couple of questions,' Lieutenant Mancini said. 'Mrs Adler, does your husband have any enemies that you know of?'

Lara frowned. 'Enemies? No. Why?'

'No one who might be jealous of him? Another musician maybe? Someone who wants to hurt him?'

'What are you getting at? It was a simple street mugging, wasn't it?'

'To be perfectly frank, this doesn't fit the pattern of an ordinary mugging. He slashed your husband's wrist *after* he took his wallet and watch.'

'I don't see what difference . . .'

'That was a pretty senseless thing to do, unless it was deliberate. Your husband didn't put up any resistance. Now, a kid on dope might do a thing like that, but . . .' He shrugged. 'I'll be in touch.'

They watched him walk away.

'Jesus!' Keller said. 'He thinks it was a set-up.'

Lara had turned pale.

Keller looked at her and said slowly, 'My God! One of Paul Martin's hoods! But why would he do this?'

Lara found it difficult to speak. 'He . . . he might have thought he was doing it for me. Philip has . . . has been away a lot, and Paul kept saying that it . . . it wasn't right, that someone should have a talk with him. Oh, Howard!' She buried her head in his shoulder, fighting back the tears.

'That sonofabitch! I warned you to stay away from that man.'

Lara took a deep breath. 'Philip is going to be all right. He *has* to be.'

Three days later, Lara brought Philip home from the hospital. He looked pale and shaken. Marian Bell was at the door, waiting for them. She had gone to the hospital every day to see Philip, and to bring him his messages. There had been an outpouring of sympathy from all around the world – cards and letters, and telephone calls from distraught fans. The newspapers had played the story up, condemning the violence on the streets of New York.

Lara was in the library when the telephone rang.

'It's for you,' Marian Bell said. 'A Mr Paul Martin.'

'I . . . I can't talk to him,' Lara told her. And she stood there, fighting to keep her body from trembling.

31

Overnight their lives together changed.

Lara said to Keller, 'I'm going to be working at home from now on. Philip needs me.'

'Sure. I understand.'

The calls and get well cards kept pouring in, and Marian Bell proved to be a blessing. She was self-effacing and never got in the way. 'Don't worry about them, Mrs Adler. I'll handle them, if you like.'

'Thank you, Marian.'

William Ellerbee called several times, but Philip refused to take his calls. 'I don't want to talk to anyone,' he told Lara.

Dr Stanton had been right about the pain. It was excruciating. Philip tried to avoid taking pain pills until he could no longer stand it.

Lara was always at his side. 'We're going to get you the best doctors in the world, darling. There must be *someone* who can fix your hand. I heard about a doctor in Switzerland . . .'

Philip shook his head. 'It's no use.' He looked at his bandaged hand. 'I'm a cripple.'

'Don't talk like that,' Lara said fiercely. 'There are a thousand things you can still do. I blame myself. If I hadn't gone to Reno that day, if I had been with you at the concert, this never would have happened. If . . .'

Philip smiled wryly. 'You wanted me to stay home more. Well, now I have nowhere else to go.'

Lara said huskily, 'Someone said, "Be careful what you wish for, because you might get it." I did want you to stay home, but not like this. I can't stand to see you in pain.'

'Don't worry about me,' Philip said. 'I just have to work a few things out in my mind. It's all happened so suddenly. I . . . I don't think I've quite realized it, yet.'

Howard Keller came to the penthouse with some contracts. 'Hello Philip. How do you feel?'

'Wonderful,' Philip snapped. 'I feel just wonderful.'

'It was a stupid question. I'm sorry.'

'Don't mind me,' Philip apologized. 'I haven't been myself lately.' He pounded his right hand against the chair. 'If the bastards had only cut my *right* hand. There are a dozen left-handed concertos I could have played.'

And Keller remembered the conversation at the party. *Oh, there are a lot of concertos written for the left hand. Half a dozen composers wrote concertos for the left hand. There's one by Demuth, Franz Schmidt. Korngold, and a beautiful concerto by Ravel.*

And Paul Martin had been there and heard it.

Dr Stanton came to the penthouse to see Philip. Carefully, he removed the bandage, exposing a long angry scar.

'Can you flex your hand at all?'

Philip tried.

It was impossible.

'How's the pain?' Dr Stanton asked.

'It's bad, but I don't want to take any more of those damned pain pills.'

'I'll leave another prescription anyway. You can take them when you have to. Believe me, the pain will stop in the next few weeks.' He rose to leave. 'I really am sorry. I happen to be a big fan of yours.'

'Buy my records,' Philip said curtly.

Marian Bell made a suggestion to Lara. 'Do you think it might help Mr Adler if a therapist came to work on his hand?'

Lara thought about it. 'We can try. Let's see what happens.'

When Lara suggested it to Philip, he shook his head. 'No. What's the point? The doctor said . . .'

'Doctor can be wrong,' Lara said firmly. 'We're going to try everything.'

The next day a young therapist appeared at the apartment. Lara brought him in to Philip. 'This is Mr Rossman. He works at Columbia Hospital. He's going to try to help you, Philip.'

'Good luck,' Philip said bitterly.

'Let's take a look at that hand, Mr Adler.'

Philip held out his hand. Rossman examined it carefully. 'Looks as though there's been quite a bit of muscle damage, but we'll see what we can do. Can you move your fingers?'

Philip tried.

'There's not much motion, is there? Let's try to exercise it.'

It was unbelievably painful.

They worked for half an hour and at the end of that time, Rossman said, 'I'll come back tomorrow.'

'No,' Philip said. 'Don't bother.'

Lara had come into the room. 'Philip, won't you try?'

'I tried,' he snarled. 'Don't you understand? My hand is dead. Nothing's going to bring it back to life.'

'Philip . . .' Her eyes filled with tears.

'I'm sorry,' Philip said. 'I just . . . give me time.'

That night, Lara was awakened by the sound of the piano. She got out of bed and quietly walked over to the entrance of the drawing room. Philip was in his robe, seated at the piano, his right hand softly playing. He looked up when he saw Lara.

'Sorry if I woke you up.'

Lara moved toward him. 'Darling . . .'

'It's a big joke, isn't it? You married a concert pianist and you wound up with a cripple.'

She put her arms around him and held him close. 'You're not a cripple. There are so many things you can do.'

'Stop being a goddamn Pollyanna!'

'I'm sorry. I just meant . . .'

'I know. Forgive me, I . . .' He held up his mutilated hand. '. . . I just can't get used to this.'

'Come back to bed.'

'No. You go ahead. I'll be all right.'

He sat up all night, thinking about his future, and he wondered angrily, *What future?*

*

Lara and Philip had dinner together every evening, and after dinner they read or watched television, and then went to sleep.

Philip said apologetically, 'I know I'm not being much of a husband, Lara. I just . . . I just don't feel like sex. Believe me, it has nothing to do with you.'

Lara sat up in bed, her voice trembling. 'I didn't marry you for your body. I married you because I was wildly head over heels in love with you. I still am. If we never make love again, it will be fine with me. All I want is for you to hold me and love me.'

'I do love you,' Philip said.

Invitations to dinner parties and charity events came in constantly, but Philip refused them all. He did not want to leave the apartment. 'You go,' he would tell Lara. 'It's important to your business.'

'Nothing is more important to me than you. We'll have a nice quiet dinner at home.'

Lara saw to it that their chef prepared all of Philip's favourite dishes. He had no appetite. Lara arranged to hold her meetings at the penthouse. When it was necessary for her to go out during the day, she would say to Marian, 'I'll be gone for a few hours. Keep an eye on Mr Adler.'

'I will,' Marian promised.

One morning Lara said, 'Darling, I hate to leave you, but I have to go to Cleveland for a day. Will you be all right?'

'Of course,' Philip said. 'I'm not helpless. Please go. Don't worry about me.'

Marian brought in some letters she had finished answering for Philip. 'Would you like to sign these, Mr Adler?'

Philip said, 'Sure. It's a good thing I'm right-handed, isn't it?' There was a bitter edge to his voice. He looked at Marian and said, 'I'm sorry. I didn't mean to take it out on you.'

Marian said quietly, 'I know that, Mr Adler. Don't you think it would be a good idea for you to go outside and see some friends?'

'My friends are all working,' Philip snapped. 'They're musicians. They're busy playing concerts. How can you be so stupid?'

He stormed out of the room.

Marian stood there looking after him.

An hour later, Philip walked back into the office. Marian was at the typewriter. 'Marian?'

She looked up. 'Yes, Mr Adler?'

'Please forgive me. I'm not myself. I didn't mean to be rude.'

'I understand,' she said quietly.

He sat down opposite her. 'The reason I'm not going out,' Philip said, 'is because I feel like a freak. I'm sure that everybody's going to be staring at my hand. I don't want anyone's pity.'

She was watching him, saying nothing.

'You've been very kind, and I appreciate it, I really do. But there's nothing anyone can do. You know the expression, "the bigger they are, the harder they fall"? Well, I was big, Marian – really big. Everybody came to hear me play . . . kings and queens and . . .' he broke off. 'People all over the world heard my music. I've given recitals in China and Russia and India and Germany.' His voice choked up and tears began rolling down his cheeks. 'Have you noticed I cry a lot lately?' he said. He was fighting to control himself.

Marian said softly, 'Please don't. Everything's going to be all right.'

'No! Nothing's going to be all right. Nothing! I'm a goddamn cripple.'

'Don't say that. Mrs Adler is right, you know. There are a hundred things you can do. When you get over this pain, you'll begin to do them.'

Philip took out a handkerchief and wiped his eyes. 'Jesus Christ, I'm becoming a damn cry baby.'

'If it helps you,' Marian said, 'do it.'

He looked up at her and smiled. 'How old are you?'

'Twenty-six.'

'You're a pretty wise twenty-six, aren't you?'

'No. I just know what you're going through, and I'd give anything if it hadn't happened. But it has happened, and I know that you're going to figure out the best way to deal with it.'

'You're wasting your time here,' Philip said. 'You should have been a shrink.'

'Would you like me to make a drink for you?'

'No, thanks. Are you interested in a game of backgammon?' Philip asked.

'I'd love it, Mr Adler.'

'If you're going to be my backgammon partner, you'd better start calling me Philip.'

'Philip.'

From that time on, they played backgammon every day.

*

Lara received a telephone call from Terry Hill.

'Lara, I'm afraid I have some bad news for you.'

Lara readied herself. 'Yes?'

'The Nevada Gaming Commission has voted to suspend your gambling licence until further investigation. You may be facing criminal charges.'

It was a shock. She thought of Paul Martin's words, *Don't worry. They can't prove anything*. 'Isn't there something we can do about it, Terry?'

'Not for the present. Just sit tight. I'm working on it.'

When Lara told Keller the news, he said, 'My God! We're counting on the cash flow from the casino to pay off the mortgages on three buildings. Are they going to reinstate your licence?'

'I don't know.'

Keller was thoughtful. 'All right. We'll sell the Chicago hotel and use the equity to pay the mortgage on the Houston property. The real estate market has gone to hell. A lot of banks and savings and loans are in deep trouble. Drexel, Burnham Lambert has folded. It's the end of Milken honey.'

'It will turn around,' Lara said.

'It had better turn around *fast*. I've been getting calls from the banks about our loans.'

'Don't worry,' Lara said confidently. 'If you owe a bank a million dollars, they own you. If you owe a bank a hundred million dollars, you own them. They can't afford to let anything happen to me.'

The following day, an article appeared in *Businessweek*. It was headlined: 'Cameron Empire Shaky – Lara Cameron Facing Possible Criminal Indictment In Reno. Can The Iron Butterfly Keep Her Empire Together?'

Lara slammed her fist against the magazine. 'How dare they print that. I'm going to sue them.'

Keller said, 'Not a great idea.'

Lara said earnestly, 'Howard, Cameron Towers is almost fully rented, right?'

'Seventy per cent, so far, and climbing. Southern Insurance has taken twenty floors and International Investment Banking has taken ten floors.'

'When the building is finished it will throw off enough money to take care of all our problems. How far away are we from completion?'

'Six months.'

Lara's voice was filled with excitement. 'Look what we'll have then. The biggest skyscraper in the world! It's going to be beautiful.'

She turned to the framed sketch of it behind her desk. It showed a towering glass-sheathed monolith, whose facets reflected the other buildings around it. On the lower floors were a promenade and atrium, with expensive shops. Above were apartments and Lara's offices.

'We'll have a big publicity promotion,' Lara said.

'Good idea.' He frowned.

'What's the matter?'

'Nothing. I was just thinking about Steve Murchison. He wanted that site pretty bad.'

'Well, we beat him to it, didn't we?'

'Yes,' Keller said slowly. 'We beat him to it.'

Lara sent for Jerry Townsend.

'Jerry, I want to do something special for the opening of Cameron Towers. Any ideas?'

'I have a great idea. The opening is September 10th?'

'Yes.'

'Doesn't that ring a bell?'

'Well, it's my birthday . . .'

'Right.' A smile lit up Jerry Townsend's face. 'Why don't we give you a big birthday party to celebrate the completion of the skyscraper?'

Lara was thoughtful for a moment. 'I like it. It's a wonderful idea. We'll invite everybody! We'll make a noise that will be heard around the world. Jerry, I want you to make up a guest list. Two hundred people. I want you to handle it personally.'

Townsend grinned. 'You've got it. I'll give you the guest list to approve.'

Lara slammed her fist down on the magazine again. 'We're going to show them!'

'Excuse me, Mrs Adler,' Marian said. 'I have the secretary of the National Builders Association on line three. You haven't responded to their invitation for the dinner Friday night.'

'Tell them I can't make it,' Lara said. 'Give them my apologies.'

'Yes, ma'am.' Marian left the room.

Philip said, 'Lara, you can't turn yourself into a hermit because of me. It's important for you to go to those things.'

'Nothing is more important than my being here with you. That funny little man who married us in Paris said, "For better or for worse."' She frowned. 'At least I *think* that's what he said. I don't speak French.'

Philip smiled. 'I want you to know how much I appreciate you. I feel like I'm putting you through hell.'

Lara moved closer to him. 'Wrong word,' she said. 'Heaven.'

Philip was getting dressed. Lara was helping him with the buttons on his shirt. Philip looked in the mirror. 'I look like a damned hippie,' Philip said. 'I need a haircut.'

'Do you want me to have Marian make an appointment with your barber?'

He shook his head. 'No. I'm sorry, Lara. I'm just not ready to go out.'

The following morning, Philip's barber and a manicurist appeared at the apartment. Philip was taken aback. 'What's all this?'

'If Mohammed won't go to the mountain, the mountain comes to Mohammed. They'll be here every week for you.'

'You're a wonder,' Philip said.

'You ain't seen nothin' yet,' Lara grinned.

The following day, a tailor arrived with some sample swatches for suits and shirts.

'What's going on?' Philip asked.

Lara said, 'You're the only man I know who has six pairs of tails, four dinner jackets, and two suits. I think it's time we got you a proper wardrobe.'

'Why?' Philip protested. 'I'm not going anywhere.'

But he allowed himself to be fitted for the suits and shirts.

A few days later, a custom shoe maker arrived.

'Now what?' Philip asked.

'It's time you had some new shoes.'

'I told you, I'm not going out.'

'I know, baby. But when you do, your shoes will be ready.'

Philip held her close. 'I don't deserve you.'

'That's what I keep telling you.'

They were in a meeting at the office. Howard Keller was saying, 'We're losing the shopping mall in Los Angeles. The banks have decided to call in the loans.'

'They can't do that.'

'They're doing it,' Keller said. 'We're over-leveraged.'

'We can pay the loans off by borrowing on one of the other buildings.'

Keller said, patiently, 'Lara, you're already leveraged to the hilt. You have a sixty-million-dollar payment coming up on the skyscraper.'

'I know that, but completion is only four months away now. We can roll the loan over. The building's on schedule, isn't it?'

'Yes.' Keller was studying her thoughtfully. It was a question she never would have asked one year ago. Then she would have known exactly where everything stood. 'I think it might be better if you spent more time here in the office,' Keller told her. 'Too many things are becoming unravelled. There are some decisions that only you can make.'

Lara nodded. 'All right,' she said reluctantly. 'I'll be in tomorrow morning.'

'William Ellerbee is on the telephone for you,' Marian announced.

'Tell him I can't talk to him.' Philip watched her as she returned to the phone.

'I'm sorry, Mr Ellerbee. Mr Adler is not available just now. Can I take a message?' She listened a moment. 'I'll tell him. Thank you.' She replaced the receiver and looked up at Philip. 'He's really anxious to have lunch with you.'

'He probably wants to talk about the commissions he's not getting any more.'

'You're probably right,' Marian said mildly. 'I'm sure he must hate you because you were attacked.'

Philip said quietly, 'Sorry. Is that the way I sounded?'

'Yes.'

'How do you put up with me?'

Marian smiled. 'It's not that difficult.'

The following day, William Ellerbee called again. Philip was out of the room. Marian spoke to Ellerbee for a few minutes then went to find Philip.

'That was Mr Ellerbee,' Marian said.

'Next time, tell him to stop calling.'

'Maybe you should tell him yourself,' Marian said. 'You're having lunch with him Thursday at one o'clock.'

'*I'm what?*'

'He suggested Le Cirque, but I thought a smaller restaurant might be better.' She looked at the pad in her hand. 'He's going to meet you at Fu's at one o'clock. I'll arrange for Max to drive you there.'

Philip was staring at her, furious. 'You made a lunch date for me without asking me?'

She said calmly, 'If I had asked you, you wouldn't have gone. You can fire me if you want to.'

He glared at her for a long moment and then he broke into a slow smile. 'You know something? I haven't had Chinese food in a long time.'

When Lara arrived home from the office, Philip said, 'I'm going out for lunch on Thursday with Ellerbee.'

'That's wonderful, darling! When did you decide that?'

'Marian decided it for me. She thought it would be a good idea for me to get out.'

'Oh, really?' *But you wouldn't go out when I suggested it.* 'That was very thoughtful of her.'

'Yes. She's quite a woman.'

I've been stupid, Lara thought. *I shouldn't have thrown them together like this. And Philip is so vulnerable right now.*

That was the moment when Lara knew she had to get rid of Marian.

When Lara arrived home the following day, Philip and Marian were playing backgammon in the game room.

Our game, Lara thought.

'How can I beat you if you keep rolling doubles?' Philip was saying, laughing.

Lara stood in the doorway watching. She had not heard Philip laugh in a long time.

Marian looked up and saw her. 'Good evening, Mrs Adler.'

Philip sprang to his feet. 'Hello, darling.' He kissed her. 'She's beating the pants off me.'

Not if I can help it, Lara thought.

'Will you need me tonight, Mrs Adler?'

'No, Marian. You can run along. I'll see you in the morning.'

'Thank you. Goodnight.'

'Good night, Marian.'

They watched her leave.

'She's good company,' Philip said.

Lara stroked his cheek. 'I'm glad, darling.'

'How's everything at the office?'

'Fine.' She had no intention of burdening Philip with her problems. She would have to fly to Reno and talk to the gaming commission again. If she was forced to, she would find a way to survive their cutting off the gambling at the hotel, but it would make it a lot easier if she could dissuade them.

'Philip, I'm afraid I'm going to have to start spending more time at the office. Howard can't make all the decisions himself.'

'No problem. I'll be fine.'

'I'm going to Reno in the next day or two,' Lara said. 'Why don't you come with me?'

Philip shook his head. 'I'm not ready yet.' He looked at his crippled left hand. 'Not yet.'

'All right, darling. I shouldn't be gone more than two or three days.'

Early the following morning when Marian Bell arrived for work, Lara was waiting for her. Philip was still asleep.

'Marian . . . you know the diamond bracelet that Mr Adler gave me for my birthday?'

'Yes, Mrs Adler?'

'When did you see it last?'

She stopped to think. 'It was on the dressing table in your bedroom.'

'So you did see it?'

'Why, yes. Is something wrong?'

'I'm afraid there is. The bracelet is missing.'

Marian was staring at her. 'Missing? Who could have . . . ?'

'I've questioned the staff here. They don't know anything about it.'

'Shall I call the police and . . . ?'

'That won't be necessary. I don't want to do anything that might embarrass you.'

'I don't understand.'

'Don't you? For your sake, I think it would be best if we dropped the whole matter.'

Marian was staring at Lara in shock. 'You know I didn't take that bracelet, Mrs Adler.'

'I don't know anything of the kind. You'll have to leave.' And she hated herself for what she was doing.

But no one is going to take Philip away from me. No one.

When Philip came down to breakfast, Lara said, 'By the way, I'm getting a new secretary to work here at the apartment.'

Philip looked at her in surprise. 'What happened to Marian?'

'She quit. She was offered a . . . a job in San Francisco.'

He looked at Lara in surprise. 'Oh. That's too bad. I thought she liked it here.'

'I'm sure she did, but we wouldn't want to stand in her way, would we?' *Forgive me*, Lara thought.

'No, of course not,' Philip said. 'I'd like to wish her luck. Is she . . . ?'

'She's gone.'

Philip said, 'I guess I'll have to find a new backgammon partner.'

'When things settle down a bit, I'll be here for you.'

Philip and William Ellerbee were seated in a corner table at Fu's restaurant.

Ellerbee said, 'It's so good to see you, Philip. I've been calling you, but . . .'

'I know, I'm sorry. I haven't felt like talking to anyone, Bill.'

'I hope they catch the bastard who did this to you.'

'The police have been good enough to explain to me that muggings are not a high priority in their lives. They equate them just below lost cats. They'll never catch him.'

Ellerbee said hesitantly, 'I understand that you're not going to be able to play again.'

'You understand right.' Philip held up his crippled hand. 'It's dead.'

Ellerbee leaned forward and said earnestly, 'But *you're* not, Philip. You still have your whole life ahead of you.'

'Doing what?'

'Teaching.'

There was a wry smile on Philip's lips. 'It's ironic,

isn't it? I had thought about doing that one day when I was through giving concerts.'

Ellerbee said quietly, 'Well, that day is here, isn't it? I took the liberty of talking to the head of the Eastman School of Music in Rochester. They would give anything to have you teach there.'

Philip frowned. 'That would mean my moving up there. Lara's headquarters are in New York.' He shook his head. 'I couldn't do that to her. You don't know how wonderful she's been to me, Bill.'

'I'm sure she has.'

'She's practically given up her business to take care of me. She's the most thoughtful, considerate woman I've ever known. I'm crazy about her.'

'Philip, would you at least think about the offer from Eastman?'

'Tell them I appreciate it, but I'm afraid the answer is no.'

'If you change your mind, will you let me know?'

Philip nodded. 'You'll be the first.'

When Philip returned to the penthouse, Lara had gone to the office. He wandered around the apartment, restless. He thought about his conversation with Ellerbee. *I would love to teach*, Philip thought, *but I can't ask Lara to move to Rochester, and I can't go there without her*.

He heard the front door open. 'Lara?'

It was Marian. 'Oh, I'm sorry, Philip. I didn't know anyone was here. I came to return my key.'

'I thought you'd be in San Francisco by now.'

She looked at him, puzzled. 'San Francisco? Why?'

'Isn't that where your new job is?'

'I have no new job.'

'But Lara said . . .'

Marian suddenly understood. 'I see. She didn't tell you why she fired me?'

'Fired you? She told me that you quit . . . that you had a better offer.'

'That's not true.'

Philip said slowly, 'I think you'd better sit down.'

They sat across from each other. 'What's going on here?' Philip asked.

Marian took a deep breath. 'I think your wife believes that I . . . that I had designs on you.'

'What are you talking about?'

'She accused me of stealing the diamond bracelet you gave her, as an excuse to fire me. I'm sure she has it put away somewhere.'

'I can't believe this,' Philip protested. 'Lara would never do anything like that.'

'She would do anything to hold on to you.'

He was studying her, bewildered. 'I . . . I don't know what to say. Let me talk to Lara and . . .'

'No. Please don't. It might be better if you didn't let her know I was here.' She rose.

'What are you going to do now?'

'Don't worry. I'll find another job.'

'Marian, if there's anything I can do . . .'

'There is nothing.'

'Are you sure?'

'I'm sure. Take care of yourself, Philip.' And she was gone.

Philip watched her leave, disturbed. He couldn't believe that Lara could be guilty of such a deception, and he wondered why she hadn't told him about it. Perhaps, he thought, Marian *did* steal the bracelet, and Lara had not wanted to upset him. Marian was lying.

32

The pawnshop was on South State Street in the heart of the Loop. When Jesse Shaw walked through the door, the old man behind the counter looked up.

'Good morning. Can I help you?'

Shaw laid a wristwatch on the counter. 'How much will you give me for this?'

The pawnbroker picked up the watch and studied it. 'A Piaget. Nice watch.'

'Yeah. I hate like hell to part with it, but I've run into a little bad luck. You understand what I mean?'

The pawnbroker shrugged. 'It's my business to understand. You wouldn't believe the hard luck stories I hear.'

'I'll redeem it in a few days. I'm starting a new job Monday. Meanwhile, I need to get as much cash as I can for it.'

The pawnbroker was looking at the watch more closely. On the back of the case, some writing had been scratched off. He looked up at the customer. 'If you'll excuse me a minute, I'll take a look at the movement. Sometimes these watches are made in Bangkok, and they forget to put anything inside.'

He took the watch into the back room. He put a loupe to his eye and studied the scratch marks. He could faintly make out the letters 'T   Phi p wi h   L v fro   L ra.'

The old man opened a drawer and took out a police flyer. It had a description of the watch and the engraving on the back, 'To Philip with Love from Lara.' He started to pick up the telephone, when the customer yelled, 'Hey, I'm in a hurry. Do you want the watch or don't you?'

'I'm coming,' the pawnbroker said. He walked back into the next room, 'I can loan you five hundred dollars on it.'

'Five hundred? This watch is worth . . .'

'Take it or leave it.'

'All right,' Shaw said grudgingly. 'I'll take it.'

'You'll have to fill out this form,' the pawnbroker said.

'Sure.' He wrote down *John Jones, 21 Hunt Street*. As far as he knew, there was no Hunt Street in Chicago, and he sure as hell was not John Jones. He pocketed the cash. 'Much obliged. I'll be back in a few days for it.'

'Right.'

The pawnbroker picked up the telephone and made a call.

A detective arrived at the pawnshop twenty minutes later.

'Why didn't you call while he was here?' he demanded.

'I tried. He was in a hurry, and he was jumpy.'

The detective studied the form the customer had filled out.

'That won't do you no good,' the pawnbroker said. 'It's probably a false name and address.'

The detective grunted. 'No kidding. Did he fill this out himself?'

'Yes.'

'Then we'll nail him.'

At police headquarters, it took the computer less than three minutes to identify the thumbprint on the form. *Jesse Shaw.*

The butler came into the drawing room. 'Excuse me, Mr Adler, there's a gentleman on the telephone for you. A Lieutenant Mancini. Shall I . . . ?'

'I'll take it.' Philip picked up the telephone. 'Hello?'

'Philip Adler?'

'Yes . . . ?'

'This is Lieutenant Mancini. I came to see you in the hospital.'

'I remember.'

'I wanted to bring you up to date on what's happening. We had a bit of luck. I told you that our Chief was going to send out flyers to pawnshops with a description of your watch?'

'Yes.'

'They found it. The watch was pawned in Chicago. They're tracking down the person who pawned it. You did say that you could identify your assailant, didn't you?'

'That's right.'

'Good. We'll be in touch.'

*

Jerry Townsend came into Lara's office. He was excited. 'I've worked out the party list we talked about. The more I think about the idea, the better I like it. We'll celebrate your fortieth birthday on the day the tallest skyscraper in the world opens.' He handed Lara the list. 'I've included the Vice President. He's a big admirer of yours.'

Lara scanned it. It read like a *Who's Who* from Washington, Hollywood, New York and London. There were government officials, motion picture celebrities, rock stars . . . it was impressive.

'I like it,' Lara said. 'Let's go with it.'

Townsend put the list in his pocket. 'Right. I'll have the invitations printed up and sent out. I've already called Carlos and told him to reserve the Grand Ballroom and arrange your favourite menu. We're setting up for two hundred people. We can always add or subtract a few if we have to. By the way, is there any more news on the Reno situation?'

Lara had talked to Terry Hill that morning. *'A Grand Jury is investigating, Lara. There's a possibility that they'll hand down a criminal indictment.'*

'How can they? The fact that I had some conversations with Paul Martin doesn't prove anything. We could have been talking about the state of the world, or his ulcers, or a dozen other damned things.'

'Lara, don't get angry with me. I'm on your side.'

Then do something. You're my lawyer. Get me the hell out of this.'

'No. Everything's fine,' Lara told Townsend.

'Good. I understand that you and Philip are going to the Mayor's dinner Saturday night.'

'Yes.' She had wanted to turn down the invitation at first, but Philip had insisted.

'You need these people. You can't afford to offend them. I want you to go.'

'Not without you, darling.'

He had taken a deep breath. 'All right. I'll go with you. I guess it's time I stopped being a hermit.'

On Saturday evening Lara helped Philip get dressed. She put his studs and cufflinks in his shirt, and tied his tie for him. He stood there, silently, cursing his helplessness.

'It's like Ken and Barbie, isn't it?'

'What?'

'Nothing.'

'There you are, darling. You'll be the most handsome man there.'

'Thanks.'

'I'd better get dressed,' Lara said. 'The Mayor doesn't like to be kept waiting.'

'I'll be in the library,' Philip told her.

Thirty minutes later, Lara walked into the library. She looked ravishing. She was dressed in a beautiful white Oscar de la Renta gown. On her wrist was the diamond bracelet Philip had given her.

Philip had difficulty sleeping on Saturday night. He looked across the bed at Lara, and wondered how she could have falsely accused Marian of stealing the bracelet. He knew he had to confront her with it, but he wanted to speak with Marian first.

Early on Sunday morning, while Lara was still asleep, Philip quietly got dressed and left the penthouse. He took a taxi to Marian's apartment. He rang the bell and waited.

A sleepy voice said, 'Who is it?'

'It's Philip. I have to talk to you.'

The door opened and Marian stood there.

'Philip? Is something wrong?'

'We have to talk.'

'Come in.'

He entered the apartment. 'I'm sorry if I woke you up,' Philip said, 'but this is important.'

'What's happened?'

He took a deep breath. 'You were right about the bracelet. Lara wore it last night. I owe you an apology, I thought . . . perhaps that you . . . I just wanted to say I'm sorry.'

Marian said quietly, 'Of course you would have believed her. She's your wife.'

'I'm going to confront Lara with it this morning, but I wanted to talk to you first.'

Marian turned to him. 'I'm glad you did. I don't want you to discuss it with her.'

'Why not?' Philip demanded. 'And why would she do such a thing?'

'You don't know, do you?'

'Frankly, no. It makes no sense.'

'I think I understand her better than you do. Lara is madly in love with you. She would do anything to hold on to you. You're probably the only person she has ever really loved in her life. She needs you. And I think you need her. You love her very much, don't you, Philip?'

'Yes.'

'Then let's forget all this. If you bring it up with her, it won't do any good, and it will only make things worse between the two of you. I can easily find another job.'

'But it's unfair to you, Marian.'

She smiled wryly. 'Life isn't always fair, is it?' *If it were, I would be Mrs Philip Adler*. 'Don't worry. I'll be fine.'

'At least let me do something for you. Let me give you some money to make up for . . .'

'Thank you, but no.'

There was so much she wanted to say, but she knew that it was hopeless. He was a man in love. What she said was, 'Go back to her, Philip.'

The construction site was on Chicago's Wabash Avenue, south of the Loop. It was a twenty-five-storey office building, and it was half finished. An unmarked police car pulled up to the corner, and two detectives got out. They walked over to the site, and stopped one of the workers passing by. 'Where's the foreman?'

He pointed to a huge, burly man cursing out a workman. 'Over there.'

The detectives went over to him. 'Are you in charge here?'

He turned and said impatiently, 'I'm not only in charge, I'm very busy. What do you want?'

'Do you have a man in your crew named Jesse Shaw?'

'Shaw? Sure. He's up there.' The foreman pointed to a man working on a steel girder a dozen storeys up.

'Would you ask him to come down, please?'

'Hell, no. He has work to . . .'

One of the detectives pulled out a badge. 'Get him down here.'

'What's the problem? Is Jesse in some kind of trouble?'

'No, we just want to talk to him.'

'Okay.' The foreman turned to one of the men working nearby, 'Go up top and tell Jesse to come down here.'

'Right.'

A few minutes later, Jesse Shaw was approaching the two detectives.

'These men want to talk to you,' the foreman said, and walked away.

Jesse grinned at the two men. 'Thanks. I can use a break. What can I do for you?'

One of the detectives pulled out a wristwatch. 'Is this your watch?'

Shaw's grin faded. 'No.'

'Are you sure?'

'Yeah.' He pointed to his wrist. 'I wear a Seiko.'

'But you pawned this watch.'

Shaw hesitated. 'Oh, yeah. I did. The bastard only gave me five hundred for it. It's worth at least . . .'

'You said it wasn't your watch.'

'That's right. It's not.'

'Where did you get it?'

'I found it.'

'Really? Where?'

'On the sidewalk near my apartment building.' He was warming up to his story. 'It was in the grass, and I got out of my car, and there it was. The sun hit the band and made it sparkle. That's how I happened to see it.'

'Lucky it wasn't a cloudy day.'

407

'Yeah.'

'Mr Shaw, do you like to travel?'

'No.'

'That's too bad. You're going to take a little trip to New York. We'll help you pack.'

When they got to Shaw's apartment, the two detectives began looking around.

'Hold it!' Shaw said. 'You guys got a search warrant?'

'We don't need one. We're just helping you pack your things.'

One of the men was looking in a clothes closet. There was a shoe box high up on a shelf. He took it down and opened it. 'Jesus!' he said. 'Look what Santa Claus left.'

Lara was in her office when Kathy's voice came over the intercom. 'Mr Tilly is on line four, Miss Cameron.'

Tilly was the project manager on Cameron Towers.

Lara picked up the phone. 'Hello?'

'We had a little problem this morning, Miss Cameron.'

'Yes?'

'We had a fire. It's out now.'

'What happened?'

'There was an explosion in the air conditioning unit. A transformer blew. There was a short circuit. It looks like someone wired it up wrong.'

'How bad is it?'

'Well, it looks like we'll lose a day or two. We

should be able to clean everything up and rewire it by then.'

'Stay on it. Keep me informed.'

Lara came home late each evening, worried and exhausted.

'I'm concerned about you,' Philip told her. 'Is there anything I can do?'

'Nothing, darling. Thank you.' She managed a smile. 'Just a few problems at the office.'

He took her in his arms. 'Did I ever tell you that I'm mad about you?'

She looked up at him and smiled. 'Tell me again.'

'I'm mad about you.'

She held him close and thought. *This is what I want. This is what I need.* 'Darling, when my little problems are over, let's go away somewhere. Just the two of us.'

'It's a deal.'

Someday, Lara thought, *I must tell him what I did to Marian. I know it was wrong. But I would die if I lost him.*

The following day, Tilly called again. 'Did you cancel the order for the marble for the lobby floors?'

Lara said slowly, 'Why would I do that?'

'I don't know. Somebody did. The marble was supposed to have been delivered today. When I called, they said it was cancelled two months ago by your order.'

Lara sat there fuming. 'I see. How badly are we delayed?'

'I'm not sure yet.'

'Tell them to put a rush on it.'

Keller came into Lara's office.

'I'm afraid the banks are getting nervous, Lara. I don't know how much longer I can hold them off.'

'Just until Cameron Towers is finished. We're almost there, Howard. We're only three months away from completion.'

'I told them that,' he sighed. 'All right. I'll talk to them again.'

Kathy's voice came over the intercom. 'Mr Tilly's on line one.'

Lara looked at Keller. 'Don't go.' She picked up the phone. 'Yes?' Lara said.

'We're having another problem here, Miss Cameron.'

'I'm listening,' Lara said.

'The elevators are malfunctioning. The programmes are out of sync, and the signals are all screwed up. You press the button for down and it goes up. Press the eighteenth floor and it will take you to the basement. I've never seen anything like this before.'

'Do you think it was done deliberately?'

'It's hard to say. Could have been carelessness.'

'How long will it take to straighten it out?'

'I have some people on the way over now.'

'Get back to me.' She replaced the receiver.

'Is everything all right?' Keller asked.

Lara evaded the question. 'Howard, have you heard anything about Steve Murchison lately?'

He looked at her, surprised. 'No. Why?'
'I just wondered.'

The consortium of bankers financing Cameron Enterprises had good reason to be concerned. It was not only Cameron Enterprises that was in trouble – a majority of their corporate clients had serious problems. The decline in junk bonds had become a full-fledged disaster, and it was a crippling blow to the corporations that had depended on them.

There were six bankers in the room with Howard Keller, and the atmosphere was grim.

'We're holding overdue notes for almost a hundred million dollars,' their spokesman said. 'I'm afraid we can't accommodate Cameron Enterprises any longer.'

'You're forgetting a couple of things,' Keller reminded them. 'Number one, we expect the casino gambling licence in Reno to be renewed any day now. That cash flow will more than take care of any deficit. Number two, Cameron Towers is right on schedule. It's going to be finished in ninety days. We already have a seventy per cent tenancy, and you can be assured that the day it's finished everybody is going to be clamouring to get in. Gentlemen, your money couldn't be more secure. You're dealing with the Lara Cameron magic.'

The men looked at one another.

The spokesman said. 'Why don't we discuss this among ourselves and we'll get back to you.'

'Fine. I'll tell Miss Cameron.'

*

Keller reported back to Lara.

'I think they'll go along with us,' he told her. 'But in the meantime, we're going to have to sell off a few more assets to stay afloat.'

'Do it.'

Lara was getting to the office early in the morning and leaving late at night, fighting desperately to save her empire. She and Philip saw very little of each other. Lara did not want him to know how much trouble she was facing. *He has enough problems*, Lara thought. *I can't burden him with any more.*

At six o'clock on Monday morning, Tilly was on the phone. 'I think you'd better get over here, Miss Cameron.'

Lara felt a sharp sense of apprehension. 'What's wrong?'

'I'd rather you saw it for yourself.'

'I'm on my way.'

Lara telephoned Keller. 'Howard, there's another problem at Cameron Towers. I'll pick you up.'

Half an hour later they were on their way to the construction site.

'Did Tilly say what the trouble was?' Keller asked.

'No, but I don't believe in accidents any more. I've been thinking about what you said. Steve Murchison wanted that property badly. I took it away from him.'

When they arrived at the site, they saw large sheets of crated tinted glass lying on the ground, and more glass being delivered by trucks. Tilly hurried over to Lara and Keller.

'I'm glad you're here.'

'What's the problem?'

'This isn't the glass we ordered. It's the wrong tint and the wrong cut. There's no way it will fit the sides of our building.'

Lara and Keller looked at each other. 'Can we re-cut it here?' Keller asked.

Tilly shook his head. 'Not a chance. You'd wind up with a mountain of silicate.'

Lara said, 'Who did we order this from?'

'The New Jersey Panel and Glass Company.'

'I'll call them,' Lara said. 'What's our deadline on this?'

Tilly stood there calculating. 'If it got here in two weeks, we could be back on schedule. It would be a push, but we'd be okay.'

Lara turned to Keller, 'Let's go.'

Otto Karp was the manager of the New Jersey Panel and Glass Company. He came on the phone almost immediately. 'Yes, Miss Cameron? I understand you have a problem.'

'No,' Lara snapped. '*You* have a problem. You shipped us the wrong glass. If I don't get the right order in the next two weeks, I'm going to sue your company out of business. You're holding up a three-hundred-million-dollar project.'

'I don't understand. Will you hold on, please?'

He was gone almost five minutes. When he came back on the line, he said, 'I'm terribly sorry, Miss Cameron, the order was written up wrong. What happened is . . .'

'I don't care what happened,' Lara interrupted. 'All I want you to do is to get our order filled and ship it out.'

'I'll be happy to do that.'

Lara felt a sharp sense of relief. 'How soon can we have it?'

'In two to three months.'

'Two to three months! That's impossible! We need it *now*.'

'I'd be happy to accommodate you,' Karp said, 'but unfortunately we're way behind in our orders.'

'You don't understand,' Lara said. 'This is an emergency and . . .'

'I certainly appreciate that. And we'll do the best we can. You'll have the order in two to three months. I'm sorry we can't do better . . .'

Lara slammed down the receiver. 'I don't believe this,' Lara said. She looked over at Tilly. 'Is there another company we can deal with?'

Tilly rubbed his hand across his forehead. 'Not at this late date. If we went to anyone else, they'd be starting from scratch, and their other customers would be ahead of us.'

Keller said, 'Lara, could I talk to you for a minute?' He took her aside. 'I hate to suggest this, but . . .'

'Go ahead.'

'. . . your friend Paul Martin might have some connections over there. Or he might know someone who knows someone.'

Lara nodded. 'Good idea, Howard. I'll find out.'

Two hours later, Lara was seated in Paul Martin's office.

'You don't know how happy I am that you called,'

the lawyer said. 'It's been too long. God, you look beautiful, Lara.'

'Thank you, Paul.'

'What can I do for you?'

Lara said hesitantly, 'I seem to come to you whenever I'm in trouble.'

'I've always been there for you, haven't I?'

'Yes. You're a good friend.' She sighed. 'Right now I need a good friend.'

'What's the problem? Another strike?'

'No. It's about Cameron Towers.'

He frowned. 'I heard that was on schedule.'

'It is. Or it was. I think Steve Murchison is out to sabotage the project. He has a vendetta against me. Things have suddenly started to go wrong at the building. Up to now, we've been able to handle them. Now . . . We have a big problem. It could put us past our completion date. Our two biggest tenants would pull out. I can't afford to let that happen.'

She took a deep breath, trying to control her anger.

'Six months ago we ordered tinted glass from the New Jersey Panel and Glass Company. We received our delivery this morning. It wasn't our glass.'

'Did you call them?'

'Yes, but they're talking about two or three months. I need that glass in two weeks. Until it's in, there's nothing for the men to do. They've stopped working. If that building isn't completed on schedule, I'll lose everything I have.'

Paul Martin looked at her and said quietly, 'No, you won't. Let me see what I can do.'

Lara felt an overwhelming sense of relief. 'Paul, I . . .' It was difficult to put into words. 'Thank you.'

He took her hand in his and smiled. 'The dinosaur isn't dead yet,' he said. 'I should have some word for you by tomorrow.'

The following morning, Lara's private phone rang for the first time in months. She picked it up eagerly. 'Paul?'

'Hello, Lara. I had a little talk with some of my friends. It's not going to be easy, but it can be done. They promised a delivery a week from Monday.'

On the day the glass shipment was scheduled to arrive, Lara telephoned Paul Martin again.

'The glass hasn't come yet, Paul,' Lara said.

'Oh?' There was a silence. 'I'll look into it.' His voice softened. 'You know, the only good thing about this, baby, is that I get to talk to you again.'

'Yes. I . . . Paul . . . if I don't get that glass on time . . .'

'You'll have it. Don't give up.'

By the end of the week, there was still no word.

Keller came into Lara's office. 'I just talked to Tilly. Our deadline is Friday. If the glass arrives by then, we'll be okay. Otherwise, we're dead.'

By Thursday, nothing had changed.

Lara went to visit Cameron Towers. There were no workmen there. The skyscraper rose majestically into the sky, overshadowing everything around it. It was going to be a beautiful building. Her monument. *I'm not going to let it fail*, Lara thought fiercely.

Lara telephoned Paul Martin again.

'I'm sorry,' his secretary said. 'Mr Martin is out of the office. Is there any message?'

'Please ask him to call me,' Lara said. She turned to Keller, 'I have a hunch I'd like you to check out. See if the owner of that glass factory happens to be Steve Murchison.'

Thirty minutes later, Keller returned to Lara's office. His face was pale.

'Well? Did you find out who owns the glass company?'

'Yes,' he said slowly. 'It's registered in Delaware. It's owned by Etna Enterprises.'

'Etna Enterprises?'

'Right. They bought it a year ago. Etna Enterprises is Paul Martin.'

33

The bad publicity about Cameron Enterprises continued. The reporters who had been so eager to praise Lara before now turned on her.

Jerry Townsend went in to see Howard Keller.

'I'm worried,' Townsend said.

'What's the problem?'

'Have you been reading the press?'

'Yeah. They're having a field day.'

'I'm worried about the birthday party, Howard. I've sent out the invitations. Since all this bad publicity, I've been getting nothing but turn-downs. The bastards are afraid they might be contaminated. It's a fiasco.'

'What do you suggest?'

'That we cancel the party. I'll make up some excuse.'

'I think you're right. I don't want anything to embarrass her.'

'Good. I'll go ahead and cancel it. Will you tell Lara?'

'Yes.'

Terry Hill called.

'I just received notice that you're being subpoenaed to testify before the Grand Jury in Reno, day after tomorrow. I'll go with you.'

Transcript of Interrogation of Jesse Shaw by Detective Lieutenant Sal Mancini.

> M: Good morning, Mr Shaw. I'm Lieutenant Mancini. You're aware that a stenographer is taking down our conversation?
> S: Sure.
> M: And you've waived the right to an attorney?
> S: I don't need no attorney. All I did was find a watch, for Christ's sake, and they drag me all the way up here like I'm some kind of animal.
> M: Mr Shaw, do you know who Philip Adler is?
> S: No. Should I?
> M: No one paid you to attack him?
> S: I told you – I never heard of him.
> M: The police in Chicago found fifty thousand dollars in cash in your apartment. Where did that money come from?
> S: [No response]
> M: Mr Shaw . . . ?
> S: I won it gambling.
> M: Where?
> S: At the track . . . football bets . . . you know.
> M: You're a lucky man, aren't you?
> S: Yeah. I guess so.

M: At present, you have a job in Chicago. Is that right?

S: Yes.

M: Did you ever work in New York?

S: Well, one time, yeah.

M: I have a police report here that says you were operating a crane at a development in Queens that killed a construction foreman named Bill Whitman. Is that correct?

S: Yeah. It was an accident.

M: How long had you been on that job?

S: I don't remember.

M: Let me refresh your memory. You were on that job seventy-two hours. You flew in from Chicago the day before the accident with the crane, and flew back to Chicago two days later. Is that correct?

S: I guess so.

M: According to American Airlines' records, you flew from Chicago to New York again two days before Philip Adler was attacked, and you returned to Chicago the following day. What was the purpose of such a short trip?

S: I wanted to see some plays.

M: Do you remember the names of the plays you saw?

S: No. That was a while ago.

M: At the time of the accident with the crane, who was your employer?

S: Cameron Enterprises.

M: And who is your employer on the

    construction job you're working on in Chicago?
S: Cameron Enterprises.

Howard Keller was in a meeting with Lara. For the past hour, they had been talking about damage control to offset the bad publicity the company was receiving. As the meeting was about to break up, Lara said, 'Anything else?'

Howard frowned. Someone had told him to tell Lara something, but he could not remember what it was. *Oh, well, it's probably not important.*

Simms, the butler, said, 'There's a telephone call for you, Mr Adler. A Lieutenant Mancini.'

Philip picked up the telephone. 'Lieutenant. What can I do for you?'

'I have some news for you, Mr Adler.'

'What is it? Did you find the man?'

'I'd prefer to come up and discuss it with you in person. Would that be all right?'

'Of course.'

'I'll be there in half an hour.'

Philip replaced the receiver, wondering what it was that the detective did not want to talk about on the telephone.

When Mancini arrived, Simms showed him into the library.

'Afternoon, Mr Adler.'

'Good afternoon. What's going on?'

'We caught the man who attacked you.'

'You did? I'm surprised,' Philip said. 'I thought you said it was impossible to catch muggers.'

'He's not an ordinary mugger.'

Philip frowned. 'I don't understand.'

'He's a construction worker. He works out of Chicago and New York. He has a police record – assault, breaking and entering. He pawned your watch and we got his prints.' Mancini held up a wristwatch. 'This is your watch, isn't it?'

Philip stared at it, not wanting to touch it. The sight of it brought back the horrible moment when the man had grabbed his wrist and slashed it. Reluctantly, he reached out and took the watch. He looked at the back of the case where some of the letters had been scratched off. 'Yes. It's mine.'

Lieutenant Mancini took the watch back. 'We'll keep this for the moment, as evidence. I'd like you to come downtown tomorrow morning to identify the man in a police line-up.'

The thought of seeing his attacker again, face to face, filled Philip with a sudden fury. 'I'll be there.'

'The address is One Police Plaza, Room 212. Ten o'clock?'

'Fine.' He frowned. 'What did you mean when you said he wasn't an ordinary mugger?'

Lieutenant Mancini hesitated. 'He was paid to attack you.'

Philip was staring at him, bewildered. *'What?'*

'What happened to you wasn't an accident. He got paid fifty thousand dollars to cut you up.'

'I don't believe it,' Philip said slowly. 'Who would pay anyone fifty thousand dollars to cripple me?'

'He was hired by your wife.'

34

He was hired by your wife!

Philip was stunned. *Lara?* Could Lara have done such a terrible thing? What reason would she have?

I don't understand why you practise every day. You're not giving a concert now . . .

You don't have to go. I want a husband. Not a part-time . . . It's not as though you were some kind of travelling salesman . . .

She accused me of stealing the diamond bracelet you gave her. She would do anything to hold on to you . . .

And Ellerbee: I had a talk with Lara. *Are you thinking of cutting back on your concerts? . . .*

Lara.

At One Police Plaza, a meeting was in progress with the District Attorney, the Police Commissioner, and Lieutenant Mancini.

The District Attorney was saying, 'We're not dealing here with Jane Doe. The lady has a lot of clout. How much solid evidence do you have, Lieutenant?'

Mancini said, 'I checked with personnel at Cameron Enterprises. Jesse Shaw was hired at the request of Lara Cameron. I asked them if she had ever personally hired anyone on the construction crew before. The answer was "no".'

'What else?'

'There was a rumour that a construction boss named Bill Whitman was bragging to his buddies that he had something on Lara Cameron that was going to make him a rich man. Shortly after that, he was killed by a crane operated by Jesse Shaw. Shaw had been pulled off his job in Chicago to go to New York. After the accident he went right back to Chicago. There's no question but that it was a hit. Incidentally, his airline ticket was paid for by Cameron Enterprises.'

'What about the attack on Adler?'

'Same MO. Shaw flew in from Chicago two days before the attack, and left the next day. If he hadn't got greedy and decided to pick up a little extra money by pawning the watch, instead of throwing it away, we would never have caught him.'

The Police Commissioner asked, 'What about motive? Why would she do that to her husband?'

'I talked to some of the servants. Lara Cameron was crazy about her husband. The only thing they ever quarrelled about was his going away on concert tours. She wanted him to stay home.'

'And now he's staying home.'

'Exactly.'

The District Attorney asked, 'What's her story? Does she deny it?'

'We haven't confronted her yet. We wanted to talk to you first to see if we have a case.'

'You say that Philip Adler can identify Shaw?'

'Yes.'

'Good.'

'Why don't you send one of your men over to question Lara Cameron? See what she has to say.'

Lara was in a meeting with Howard Keller when the intercom buzzed. 'There's a Lieutenant Mancini here to see you.'

Lara frowned. 'What about?'

'He didn't say.'

'Send him in.'

Lieutenant Mancini was treading on delicate ground. Without hard evidence, it was going to be difficult to get anything out of Lara Cameron. *But I've got to give it a try*, he thought. He had not expected to see Howard Keller there.

'Good afternoon, Lieutenant.'

'Afternoon.'

'You've met Howard Keller.'

'I certainly have. Best pitching arm in Chicago.'

'What can I do for you?' Lara asked.

This was the tricky part. *First establish that she knew Jesse Shaw and then lead her on from there.*

'We've arrested the man who attacked your husband.' He was watching her face.

'You have? What . . . ?'

Howard Keller interrupted. 'How did you catch him?'

'He pawned a watch that Miss Cameron gave her husband.' Mancini looked at Lara again. 'The man's name is Jesse Shaw.'

There was not the faintest change of expression. *She's good*, Mancini thought. *The lady is really good.*

'Do you know him?'

Lara frowned. 'No. Should I?'

That's her first slip, Mancini thought. *I've got her.*

'He worked on the construction crew of one of your buildings in Chicago. He also worked for you on a project in Queens. He was operating a crane that killed a man.' He pretended to consult his notebook. 'A Bill Whitman. The Coroner's inquest put it down as an accident.'

Lara swallowed. 'Yes . . .'

Before she could go on, Keller spoke up. 'Look, Lieutenant, we have hundreds of people working for this company. You can't expect us to know them all.'

'You don't know Jesse Shaw?'

'No. And I'm sure Miss Cameron . . .'

'I'd rather hear it from her, if you don't mind.'

Lara said, 'I've never heard of the man.'

'He was paid fifty thousand dollars to attack your husband.'

'I . . . I can't believe it!' Her face was suddenly drained of colour.

Now I'm getting to her, Mancini thought. 'You don't know anything about it?'

Lara was staring at him, her eyes suddenly blazing. 'Are you suggesting . . . ? How dare you! If someone put him up to that, I want to know who it was!'

'So does your husband, Miss Cameron.'

'You discussed this with Philip?'

'Yes. I . . .'

A moment later, Lara was flying out of the office.

*

When Lara reached the penthouse, Philip was in the bedroom packing, clumsily because of his crippled hand.

'Philip . . . what are you doing?'

He turned to face her, and it was as though he was seeing her for the first time. 'I'm leaving.'

'Why? You can't believe that . . . that terrible story?'

'No more lies, Lara.'

'But I'm *not* lying. You've got to listen to me. I had nothing to do with what happened to you. I wouldn't hurt you for anything in the world. I love you, Philip.'

He turned to face her. 'The police say that the man worked for you. That he was paid fifty thousand dollars to . . . to do what he did.'

She shook her head. 'I don't know anything about it. I only know that I had nothing to do with it. Do you believe me?'

He stared at her, silent.

Lara stood there for a long moment, then turned and blindly walked out of the room.

Philip spent a sleepless night at a downtown hotel. Visions of Lara kept coming to his mind. *I'm interested in knowing more about the foundation. Perhaps we could get together and discuss it . . .*

Are you married? Tell me about yourself . . .

When I listen to your Scarlatti, I'm in Naples . . .

I dream a dream of bricks and concrete and steel, and make it come true . . .

I came to Amsterdam to see you . . .

Would you like me to go with you to Milan . . . ?

You're going to spoil me, lady . . . I intend to . . .

And Lara's warmth, compassion, and caring. Could I have been that wrong about her?

When Philip arrived at police headquarters, Lieutenant Mancini was waiting for him. He led Philip into a small auditorium with a raised platform at the far end.

'All we need is for you to identify him in the line-up.'

So they can tie him in with Lara, Philip thought.

There were six men in the line-up, all roughly the same build and age. Jesse Shaw was in the middle. When Philip saw him, his head began to pound suddenly. He could hear his voice saying, '*Give me your wallet.*' He could feel the terrible pain of the knife slashing across his wrist. *Could Lara have done that to me?* '*You're the only man I've ever loved.*'

Lieutenant Mancini was speaking. 'Take a good look, Mr Adler.'

'*I'm going to be working at home from now on. Philip needs me . . .*'

'Mr Adler . . .'

'*We're going to get you the best doctors in the world.*' She had been there for him every moment, nurturing him, caring for him. '*If Mohammed won't go to the mountain . . .*'

'Would you point him out to me?'

'*I married you because I was wildly head over heels in love with you. I still am. If we never make love again it will be fine with me. All I want is for you to hold me and love me . . .*' And she had meant it.

And then the last scene in the apartment. '*I had

nothing to do with what happened to you. I wouldn't hurt you for anything in the world . . ,.'

'Mr Adler . . .'

The police must have made a mistake, Philip thought. *By God, I believe her. She couldn't have done it!*

Mancini was speaking again. 'Which one is he?'

And Philip turned to him and said, 'I don't know.'

'*What?*'

'I don't see him.'

'You told us you got a good look at him.'

'That's right.'

'Then tell me which one he is.'

'I can't,' Philip said. 'He's not up there.'

Lieutenant Mancini's face was grim. 'You're sure about that?'

Philip stood up. 'I'm positive.'

'Then I guess that's all, Mr Adler. Thanks a lot for your cooperation.'

I've got to find Lara, Philip thought. *I've got to find Lara.*

She was seated at her desk, staring out of the window. Philip had not believed her. That was what hurt so terribly. And Paul Martin. *Of course he was behind it. But why did he do it?* 'Do you remember what I said about your husband taking care of you? He doesn't seem to be doing a very good job. Someone should have a talk with him!' Was it because he loved her? Or was it an act of vengeance because he hated her?

Howard Keller walked in. His face looked white and drawn. 'I just got off the phone. We lost

Cameron Towers, Lara. Both Southern Insurance and International Investment Banking are pulling out because we can't meet our completion date. There's no way we can handle our mortgage payments. We almost made it, didn't we? The biggest skyscraper in the world. I'm . . . I'm sorry. I know how much it meant to you.'

Lara turned to face him, and Keller was shocked by her appearance. Her face was pale, and there were black circles under her eyes. She seemed dazed, as though the energy had been drained from her.

'Lara . . . did you hear what I said? We've lost Cameron Towers.'

When she spoke, her voice was unnaturally calm. 'I heard you. Don't worry, Howard. We'll borrow on some of the other buildings and pay everything off.'

She was frightening him. 'Lara, there's nothing more to borrow on. You're going to have to file for bankruptcy and . . .'

'Howard . . . ?'

'Yes?'

'Can a woman love a man too much?'

'What?'

Her voice was dead. 'Philip has left me.'

It suddenly explained a lot. 'I . . . I'm sorry, Lara.'

She had a strange smile on her face. 'It's funny, isn't it? I'm losing everything at once. First Philip, now my buildings. Do you know what it is, Howard? It's the Fates. They're against me. You can't fight the Fates, can you?'

He had never seen her in such pain. It tore at him. 'Lara . . .'

'They're not through with me yet. I have to fly to

Reno this afternoon. There's a Grand Jury hearing. If . . .'

The intercom buzzed. 'There's a Lieutenant Mancini here.'

'Send him in.'

Howard Keller looked at Lara quizzically. 'Mancini? What does he want?'

Lara took a deep breath. 'He's here to arrest me, Howard.'

'*Arrest* you? What are you talking about?'

Her voice was very quiet. 'They think I arranged the attack on Philip.'

'That's ridiculous! They can't . . .'

The door opened and Lieutenant Mancini walked in. He stood there, looking at the two of them for a moment, then moved forward.

'I have a warrant here for your arrest.'

Howard Keller's face was pale. He said hoarsely, 'You can't arrest her. She hasn't done anything.'

'You're right, Mr Keller. I'm not arresting her. The warrant is for you.'

35

Transcript of Interrogation of Howard Keller by Detective Lieutenant Sal Mancini.

M: You have been read your rights, Mr Keller?
K: Yes.
M: And you have waived the right to have an attorney present?
K: I don't need an attorney. I was going to come in anyway. I couldn't let anything happen to Lara.
M: You paid Jesse Shaw $50,000 to attack Philip Adler?
K: Yes.
M: Why?
K: He was making her miserable. She begged him to stay home with her, but he kept leaving her.
M: So you arranged to have him crippled.
K: It wasn't like that. I never meant for Jesse to go so far. He got carried away.
M: Tell me about Bill Whitman.
K: He was a bastard. He was trying to blackmail Lara. I couldn't let him do that. He could have ruined her.
M: So you had him killed?

K: For Lara's sake, yes.
M: Was she aware of what you were doing?
K: Of course not. She never would have allowed it. No. I was there to protect her, you see. Anything I did, I did for her. I would die for her.
Can I ask you a question? How did you know I was involved in this?
End of Interrogation.

At One Police Plaza, Captain Bronson said to Mancini, 'How *did* you know he was behind it?'

'He left a loose thread and I unravelled it. I almost missed it. In Jesse Shaw's rap sheet, it mentioned that he took a fall when he was seventeen for stealing some baseball equipment from a Chicago Cubs American Legion League team. I remembered that Howard Keller had played for that team. I checked it out and sure enough, they were team-mates. That's where Keller slipped up. When I asked him, he told me he had never heard of Jesse Shaw. I called a friend of mine who used to be a sports editor for the *Chicago Sun Times*. He remembered them both. They were buddies. I figured it was Keller who got Shaw the job with Cameron Enterprises. Lara Cameron hired Jesse Shaw because Howard Keller asked her to. She probably never even saw Shaw.'

'Nice work, Sal.'

Mancini shook his head. 'You know something? In the end, it really didn't matter. If I hadn't caught him, and if we had gone after Lara Cameron, Howard Keller would have come in and confessed.'

*

Her world was collapsing. It was unbelievable to Lara that Howard Keller, of all people, could have been responsible for the terrible things that had happened. *He did it for me*, Lara thought. *I have to try to help him.*

Kathy buzzed her. 'The car is here, Miss Cameron. Are you ready?'

'Yes.' She was on her way to Reno to testify before the Grand Jury.

Five minutes after Lara left, Philip telephoned the office.

'I'm sorry, Mr Adler. You just missed her. She's on her way to Reno.'

He felt a sharp pang of disappointment. He was desperately eager to see her, to ask her forgiveness. 'When you speak to her, tell her I'll be waiting for her.'

'I'll tell her.'

He made a second phone call, spoke for ten minutes, and then telephoned William Ellerbee.

'Bill . . . I'm going to stay in New York. I'm going to teach at Juilliard.'

'What can they do to me?' Lara asked.

Terry Hill said, 'That depends. They'll listen to your testimony. They can either decide that you're innocent, in which case you'll get your casino back, or they can recommend that there's enough evidence against you to indict you. If that's their verdict, you'll be tried on criminal charges and face prison.'

Lara mumbled something.

'I'm sorry?'

'I said Papa was right. It's the Fates.'

The Grand Jury hearing lasted for four hours. Lara was questioned about the acquisition of the Cameron Palace Hotel and Casino. When they came out of the hearing room, Terry Hill squeezed Lara's hand. 'You did very well, Lara. I think you really impressed them. They have no hard evidence against you, so there's a good chance that . . .' He broke off, stunned. Lara turned. Paul Martin had come into the anteroom. He was dressed in an old fashioned double breasted suit and his white hair was combed in the same style as when Lara had first met him.

Terry Hill said, 'Oh, God! He's here to testify.' He turned to Lara. 'How much does he hate you?'

'What do you mean?'

'Lara, if they've offered him leniency to testify against you, you're finished. You'll go to prison.'

Lara was looking across the room at Paul Martin. 'But . . . then he would destroy himself, too.'

'That's why I asked you how much he hates you. Would he do that to himself to destroy you?'

Lara said numbly, 'I don't know.'

Paul Martin was walking toward them. 'Hello, Lara. I hear things have been going badly for you.' His eyes revealed nothing. 'I'm so sorry.'

Lara remembered Howard Keller's words. *'He's Sicilian. They never forgive and they never forget.'* He had been carrying this burning thirst for vengeance inside him and she had had no idea.

Paul Martin started to move away.

'Paul...'

He stopped. 'Yes?'

'I need to talk to you.'

He hesitated a moment. 'All right.'

He nodded toward an empty office down the corridor. 'We can talk in there.'

Terry Hill watched as the two of them went into the office. The door closed behind them. He would have given anything to have heard their conversation.

She did not know how to begin.

'What is it you want, Lara?'

It was much more difficult than she had anticipated. When she spoke, her voice was hoarse. 'I want you to let me go.'

His eyebrows were raised. 'How can I? I don't have you.' He was mocking her.

She was finding it hard to breathe.

'Don't you think you've punished me enough?'

Paul Martin stood there, stone, his expression unreadable.

'The time we had together was wonderful, Paul. Outside of Philip, you've meant more to me than anyone in my life. I owe you more than I could ever repay. I never meant to hurt you. You must believe that.'

It was difficult to go on.

'You have the power to destroy me. Is that really what you want? Will sending me to prison make you happy?' She was fighting to hold back her tears. 'I'm begging you, Paul. Give me back my life. Please, stop treating me like an enemy...'

Paul Martin stood there, his black eyes giving away nothing.

'I'm asking for your forgiveness. I . . . I'm too tired to fight any more, Paul. You've won . . .' Her voice broke.

There was a knock on the door, and the bailiff peered into the room. 'The Grand Jury is ready for you, Mr Martin.'

He stood there, looking at Lara for a long time, then he turned and left without a word.

It's all over, Lara thought. *It's finished.*

Terry Hill came hurrying into the office. 'I wish to God I knew how he was going to testify in there. There's nothing to do now but wait.'

They waited. It seemed an eternity. When Paul Martin finally emerged from the Hearing Room, he looked tired and drawn. *He's become old*, Lara thought. *He blames me for that.* He was watching her. He hesitated a moment, then walked over to her.

'I can never forgive you. You made a fool of me. But you were the best thing that ever happened to me. I guess I owe you something for that. I didn't tell them anything in there, Lara.'

Her eyes filled with tears. 'Oh, Paul. I don't know how to . . .'

'Call it my birthday present to you. Happy Birthday, baby.'

She watched him walk away and his words suddenly hit her. *It was her birthday!* So many events had been piling on top of one another that she had completely forgotten about it. And the party. Two hundred guests were going to be waiting for her at the Manhattan Cameron Plaza!

Lara turned to Terry Hill. 'I've got to get back to New York tonight. There's a big party for me. Will they let me go?'

'Just a minute,' Terry Hill said. He disappeared inside the hearing room, and when he came out five minutes later, he said, 'You can go to New York. The Grand Jury will give its verdict in the morning, but it's just a formality now. You can return here tonight. By the way, your friend told you the truth. He didn't talk in there.'

Thirty minutes later, Lara was headed for New York.

'Are you going to be all right?' Terry Hill asked.

She looked at him and said, 'Of course I am.' There would be hundreds of important people at the party to honour her that night. She would hold her head high. She was Lara Cameron . . .

She stood in the centre of the deserted Grand Ballroom and looked around. *I created this. I created monuments that towered into the sky, that changed the lives of thousands of people all over America. And now it's all going to belong to the faceless bankers.* She could hear her father's voice so clearly. '*It's the Fates. They've always been agin' me.*' She thought of Glace Bay and the little boarding house where she had grown up. She remembered how terrified she had been on her first day at school: '*Can anyone think of a word beginning with F?*' She remembered the boarders. Bill Rogers . . . '*The first rule in real estate is other people's money. Never forget that.'* And Charles Cohn: *'I eat only kosher food, and I'm afraid Glace Bay doesn't have any.'* . . .

'If I could acquire this land, would you give me a five-year lease?' . . .

'No, Lara, it would have to be a ten-year lease.' . . .

And Sean MacAllister . . . *'I would need a very special reason to make this loan to you. Have you ever had a lover?'* . . .

And Howard Keller: *'You're going about this all wrong.'* . . .

'I want you to come and work for me.' . . .

And then the successes. The wonderful, brilliant successes. And Philip. Her Lochinvar. The man she adored. That was the greatest loss of all.

A voice called, 'Lara . . .'

She turned.

It was Jerry Townsend. 'Carlos told me you were here.' He walked up to her. 'I'm sorry about the birthday party.'

She looked at him. 'What . . . what happened?'

He was staring at her. 'Didn't Howard tell you?'

'Tell me what?'

'There were so many cancellations because of the bad publicity that we decided it would be best to call it off. I asked Howard to tell you.'

To tell you the truth, I've been having some problems with my memory.

Lara said softly, 'It doesn't matter.' She took one last look at the beautiful room. 'I had my fifteen minutes, didn't I?'

'What?'

'Nothing.' She started to walk toward the door.

'Lara, let's go up to the office. There are some things that have to be wound up.'

'All right.' *I'll probably never be in this building again*, Lara thought.

In the elevator on the way up to the Executive Offices, Jerry said, 'I heard about Keller. It's hard to believe he was responsible for what happened.'

Lara shook her head. 'I was responsible, Jerry. I'll never forgive myself.'

'It's not your fault.'

She felt a sudden wave of loneliness. 'Jerry, if you haven't had your dinner yet . . .'

'I'm sorry, Lara. I'm busy tonight.'

'Oh. That's all right.'

The elevator door opened and the two of them stepped out.

'The papers that you have to sign are on the Conference Room table,' Jerry said.

'Fine.'

The door to the Conference Room was closed. He let Lara open the door and as she did, forty voices started to sing out, 'Happy Birthday to you, Happy Birthday to you . . .'

Lara stood there, stunned. The room was filled with people she had worked with over the years – the architects, contractors and construction managers. Charles Cohn was there and Professor Meyers. Horace Guttman and Kathy and Jerry Townsend's father. But the only one that Lara saw was Philip. He was moving toward her, his arms outstretched, and she suddenly found it difficult to breathe.

'Lara . . .' It was a caress.

And she was in his arms, fighting to hold back the tears, and she thought, *I'm home. This is where I belong* and it was a healing, a blessed feeling of peace. Lara felt a warm glow as she held him. *This is all that matters*, Lara thought.

People were crowding around her and everyone seemed to be talking at once.

'Happy birthday, Lara . . .'

'You look wonderful . . .'

'Were you surprised . . . ?'

Lara turned to Jerry Townsend. 'Jerry, how did you . . . ?'

He shook his head. 'Philip arranged it.'

'Oh, darling!'

Waiters were coming in now with hors d'oeuvres and drinks.

Charles Cohn said, 'No matter what happens, I'm proud of you, Lara. You said you wanted to make a difference, and you did.'

Jerry Townsend's father was saying, 'I owe my life to this woman.'

'So do I,' Kathy smiled.

'Let's drink a toast,' Jerry Townsend said, 'to the best boss I ever had, or ever will have!'

Charles Cohn raised his glass. 'To a wonderful little girl who became a wonderful woman!'

The toasts went on, and finally it was Philip's turn. There was too much to say, and he put it in five words: 'To the woman I love.'

Lara's eyes were brimming with tears. She found it difficult to speak. 'I . . . I owe so much to all of you,' Lara said. 'There's no way I can ever repay you. I just want to say . . .' She choked up, unable to go on. '. . . thank you.'

Lara turned to Philip. 'Thank you for this, darling. It's the nicest birthday I've ever had.' She suddenly remembered. 'I have to fly back to Reno tonight!'

Philip looked at her and grinned. 'I've never been to Reno . . .'

Half an hour later they were in the limousine on their way to the airport. Lara was holding Philip's hand and thinking, *I haven't lost everything after all. I'll spend the rest of my life making it up to him. Nothing else matters. The only important thing is being with him and taking care of him. I don't need anything else.*

'Lara . . . ?'

She was looking out of the window. 'Stop, Max!'

The limousine braked to a quick stop.

Philip looked at her, puzzled. They had stopped in front of a huge empty lot, covered with weeds. Lara was staring at it.

'Lara . . .'

'Look, Philip!'

He turned to look. 'What?'

'Don't you see it?'

'See what?'

'Oh, it's beautiful! A shopping mall over there, in the far corner! In the middle we'll put up luxury apartment houses. There's room enough for four buildings. You see it now, don't you?'

He was staring at Lara, mesmerized.

She turned to him, her voice charged with excitement. 'Now, here's my plan . . .'